By the same author;

Life of Stone

Available in paperback and for Kindle download through Amazon.

This book, its content and cover are all subject to Copyright.

© Steven Rick 2016.

Published by Acidhorse books 2017.

Steven Rick has asserted himself as the author of this work;
'I wrote this,' Steve asserted.

Please don't copy, produce, distribute, or otherwise try to make a quid or two out of this work without letting the author in on the action... He's broke too.

The name "Firestone Copse" is taken from a small area of woodland situated just outside of Ryde on the Isle of Wight, an island off the south coast of England. It bears no similarity to the place described in this work.
Likewise "Beaper Shute" is a road name taken from the Isle of Wight.
"Arbor Low" is a set of fallen standing stones in the British East Midlands.
There was once a pub in Upper Hale near Farnham named "The Black Prince", it has since been demolished. It was by far the strangest public house the author has frequented.
Names of various family members, celebrities and acquaintances have been stolen, dissected and inserted throughout the work. Otherwise all names places and situations herein are fictitious and any similarity to people or events occurring in reality (whatever your perception of that might be) is purely coincidental.

Cover photograph taken and edited by the author. Original image captured in Firestone Copse on the Isle of Wight.

Facebook; 'Steven Rick Writings'
Twitter; @stevenrickwrit1
Web; stevenrickwritings.co.uk
Email; stevenrickwritings@gmail.com

Acknowledgements

Laura Hooper – Thank you for your valuable time and lending me your ninja like gramma and editing skills. IOU a never ending supply of tea and flapjack. And Dolly Mixtures.

Andrew Rick – For coping with an indecisive brother, but mostly for drawing all those amazing illustrations that I didn't end up using.

Johnny "Bill" Hull – Thank you for all your encouragement, and for sharing adventures with me into uncharted woods and beyond.

For my wife,

Amanda

Part One

Sunday 2nd November 1969

1.

The storm had risen angrily during the evening and now, in the early hours of the morning, it had taken a firm grip of Firestone Copse. The wind battered its Tudor buildings, rushing relentlessly through its deserted streets. The rain soaked every inch of the town as it was torn between the indecisive winds. It lashed down from the angry sky, throwing itself heavily upon the soaked ground to form puddles with ambitions of lakes. The eighty or so occupants slept uneasily, tortured by the howling winds, afeared of the condition they would find their town in come daybreak. Up a low hill at the northernmost point of the hamlet stood an ancient church, hunkered down into the land as if it might disappear into it at any moment. Its leaking roof sagged with age but it held out against the onslaught. The church was still in weekly use but only on the Sabbath and to a dwindling congregation. Under the shadow of the low steeple was set a small cottage, home to the Vicar Aldous Squires, who slept peacefully despite the weather. If you stood at the back door of the Vicarage and looked out toward the graveyard you would see a barrier of angry trees fighting against the wind. They form an encroaching wood that surrounds the buildings of the town in a ring of trunks and unkempt undergrowth. The wood around the town is only broken by the few roads that sweep through it, allowing people to dash through without needing to stop, without needing to pay any mind to the old buildings or the people that make them their homes. The trees trap the town of Firestone Copse, but they also protect the outside world from its secrets.

In the darkest hours of night a car struggled along the main road toward Firestone, the driver battling to control it against the storm. He pushed his spectacles a little further up his nose and squinted out at the abysmal weather. The rain splattered deafeningly against his windscreen, turning the view ahead into a patch of bleary grey in the weak headlights. He hoped the car would make it home; he did not want to find himself marooned in the copse on a night like this. He glanced sideways for a moment into the trees, watching as his headlight beam filtered through the trunks, sending shadows rising and falling all about him. A shape in the road suddenly loomed into his view, and he quickly stamped on the brake. The car screeched to a shuddering and sliding halt, leaving him breathless. He pried his fingernails out of the steering wheel and peered through the murky night at the obstacle that stood between him and his bed. A small tree lay across the road rather sadly, a victim of the storm. With infinite care he edged his car carefully around it, trying to avoid scratching the paint work on the upmost branches that had, until a few minutes ago, been reaching toward the dark cloud above. He nervously braved the wrong side of the carriage way for a minute as he navigated past, and once safely around he sped away into the night again toward the beleaguered buildings.

Moments later the peace of the Vicarage was disturbed by a dull thump at the front door. The sound thudded lazily through the tidy rooms, unsettling the regularity of silence that had lain upon the house for generations. It was not a loud sound, and the first was not the one that disturbed the lone occupant of the cottage. When Aldous finally woke from his slumber he sat up in bed in alarm. He squinted thoughtfully into the dark as he took a moment to try and determine what the noise might be, and where it was coming from. His bleary mind realised with a little panic that there was someone at his door, and that they wanted to come in. He leant over to his bedside table and fumbled in the dark for the switch to his lamp. With the light on he stopped squinting into the dark, and instead began squinting against the light to see his clock.

'Half passed one?' He raised an eyebrow in surprise at the lateness of the hour and wondered what he should do. Another bang at the door made him jump suddenly. They came irregularly, echoing unhindered through the peace of the cottage. It dawned on him that he was going to have to do something, so he regretfully crept out of bed, nervously slipping his feet into slippers that sat at his bed side waiting. Slowly he inched toward the door and pulled on his big warm dressing gown. The knocking thudded again, echoing up to his ears. He walked painfully out on to the landing, his old figure stood bent at the top of the stairs. He listened, hoping the noise had stopped. What was left of his grey hair had tussled together messily on his head, his leant his fragile figure on the bannister for support. The thud thumped through the door again, making the locks rattle. Disheartened he bravely crept downstairs. Every creak of wood under his foot seemed to echo noisily about the house. Every footstep betrayed his presence to the visitor at his door. He reached the threshold in a nervous sweat, almost too afraid to open it, unable to stop himself. He pulled back the heavy curtain, a barrier against the winter chill, and slid the bolt across but left the chain latch securely fastened. With a deep nervous breath he slowly eased the door open the slightest crack and peered fearfully outside. To his horror, no one was there.

A sudden gust of wind blew against the door and forced it open to the chain's limit, and Aldous was suddenly confronted with the intensity of the storm outside. Rain blustered into his face, and a cold wind rushed past him into the house, ridding it of heat. Soaked and freezing, the Vicar tried to slam the door shut but found it blocked. Checking the foot of the door Aldous could just see through the rain and the dark a man he had failed to notice. His coat was muddied and torn and he was soaked through. He slouched with his back leant against the door, head down, chin to chest. Aldous watched him for a moment, stunned, unable to believe his eyes. Then suddenly the man lurched his head back and cracked it against the door. The noise shattered through the cold to the Vicar's ears. The man suddenly realised the Vicar's presence and looked up gingerly to face him.

'Ahh, you're in,' he said gratefully, his voice croaking almost inaudibly against the storm. He then lost consciousness and slumped on to the porch. The Vicar studied him for a moment, trying to decide what to do. The man wasn't young, he guessed perhaps in his fifties but looking old for it. He had a prominent moustache and a fresh beard sprouting from his cheeks. He was pale, almost grey, and looked very ill. The Vicar looked out at the freezing night, at the trees fighting against the wind, and realised that there was only one thing he could do. He unlatched the door, picked up the man's sodden feet, and pulled him awkwardly into the house. He slammed the door shut on the awful storm. The unexpected guest was heavy, and the Vicar lacked the strength of his youth making it a considerable toil for him to drag him into the small living room of the humble cottage. Aldous wrestled his limp ragdoll body on to a makeshift bed quickly fashioned from sofa cushions in front of the fire, and placed his coat and shoes next to him to dry. He covered his sleeping body with musty blankets hurriedly collected from the spare room, then stopped to look at him. The man had not woken nor seemed distressed throughout it all, and now lay perfectly still save for the shallow rise and fall of his chest. Aldous quickly set about getting a fire lit, using newspaper and wood from a conveniently placed basket. After a few minutes the kindling was relenting to the heat and flames were lapping hungrily at logs. Next to the log basket sat an elegant brass bucket full of coal and a dirty short handled old spade. Aldous shovelled a spade full of coal on to the fire then changed into dry warm pyjamas and took the blanket from his bed. He hurried back to the living room where he hunkered down comfortably into in his armchair to begin his vigil over the man. Once settled he sat studying him, trying to calculate who he might be and where he might have come from. The suit jacket drying by the warming fire was well-tailored. The steaming brown leather shoes were drenched and covered in mud, but this did not distract from the fact that they were obviously expensive. The Vicar realised that this was no vagrant, and that he must be in some kind of trouble.

He hoped it was nothing more serious than his car breaking down, and having become lost in the copse the poor chap had stumbled upon his front door. The heat from the burning logs gently warmed the room, and the night crept in on the Vicar and the bedraggled man. He did his best to stay awake in case his guest roused, but with the heaviness of his eyelids and the lateness of the hour he eventually drifted off, sitting upright in his chair, back into his deep sleep.

There was of course no way Aldous could have known how serious the business involving this man was, or how deeply it would affect his life over the next seven days and beyond. If he had, he might not have slept so soundly.

2.

At almost the exact moment that the Vicar's mind settled comfortably back into unconsciousness, a green telephone began to ring. It sat in a dark hallway on a small circular table next to a closed book of telephone numbers and a pile of keys. It had two unseen bells that filled the air with two short rings between a second's pause. This it repeated over and over as it attempted to alert the house's lone occupant that someone wanted his attention. The sound searched the rooms on the ground floor, circling the simple front room with its two accent chairs and wireless before moving on to the simpler dining room, and kitchen. All empty of life. Boxes sat piled against walls or stacked in corners collecting dust, their contents awaiting a more permanent home. The ringing echoed upstairs, through the bathroom, undaunted by the lack of attention it was receiving. It drifted solemnly into the bedroom and found its way to the sleeping Constable Drew Gates.

He slowly woke, unwillingly at first, but as his mind recognised the sound and differentiated it from dream he forced himself awake from his disturbed sleep. He hurried out of bed, forgoing the slippers and dressing gown to rush downstairs to the telephone. On lifting the receiver the bell stopped ringing, leaving a 'ping' sustained in the air as he caught his breath.

'Yes?' he asked the mouthpiece, surprised at how asleep he sounded.

'What took you so long?' came the angry reply. Drew didn't recognise the voice at first, his mind was not fully awake. He slowly put a face to the gravelled tone and his heart sank a little. It was Sergeant Banks, his superior. He took a moment to think of the right question to ask.

'Sarge? Is everything alright?' He knew something must be up, else he wouldn't be receiving a call at this hour. It was not the question he really wanted to ask this man, but circumstances made communicating with Sergeant Banks a delicate game. Drew followed orders and didn't ask questions, hoping to merge unnoticed into the small force he had recently joined.

'I have just taken a call from the Major; he says he nearly landed his Rolls into a fallen tree.' Banks' accent denied the fact he hadn't set foot in a farmyard since he was a boy.

'It's on Beaper Chute, just passed the sharp left out of the copse. Reckon you could get up there and clear it before the morning?' The question was not phrased as a request but as a command, there was a clear air of superiority in the Sergeant's voice. He spoke of the matter slowly, as if he were discussing the milk yield of cows, or a bad crop of wheat. His anger at Drew's delay to answer his call had passed as quickly as it had arrived and Drew's mind raced despite the hour. Clearing trees was not the work of a policeman, and should rightly be given to Nettlestone's Highways department, even if it couldn't wait until morning.

'If I don't clear it now there'll be a bigger mess to clear up by nine, once the traffic starts coming through.' He replied complying unwillingly. He swallowed his defiance at Banks choosing him, as he did whenever he was handed a job that no one else wanted to do.

'I would do it myself of course, but I've been at the Mayor's for dinner, had a few too many ports I fear.'

'Well,' Drew thought on his cold naked feet. 'Not exactly the task of a superior officer anyway, is it Sarge?' *Nor a Constable's* he thought bitterly, keeping his true thoughts safely locked away.

'Indeed young Drew indeed. Don't call when you're done, I'll no doubt be back in bed and sound asleep by the time you're finished.' Drew winced at the jibe. Banks constantly suggested his work was slow and a burden to the force. He gritted his teeth and swallowed his resentment.

'Course Sarge, you get off, see you in the morning.' Drew told him kindly despite himself. Banks hung up his receiver before Drew had finished talking, and the words tasted bitterer for the dialling tone cutting him off. Drew recognised the slur in his voice. Banks' words had trickled drunkenly down the line to him. He returned the receiver to the telephone and waited for a moment in contemplation before picking it up again and dialling four numbers. He waited nervously, listening to the dull buzz of the dialling tone. Finally it stopped, and after a slight pause a man's voice said;

'Drew?'

'Yes, sorry for the hour,' he replied, relieved the man had guessed who would be calling him at this time of day.

'That's alright, what is it?' came the gruffled voice. The man on the other end was whispering with the mouth piece close to his whispering lips.

'Probably nothing, but there's a tree down on Beaper Chute, Banks wants me to go and clear it.' The man on the telephone considered for a moment.

'That's really a matter for the roads department at Nettlewood, but it's too late to call them out now. It should wait until morning

really,' he hissed back. 'Even so, you'd better get over and sort it, don't want to rock the boat do we? If it's not sorted by morning Banks might never forgive you.' The voice was reproachful, he wished that wasn't the answer. He was understanding, accepting and not in the slightest way troubled by the intrusion to his sleep.
'That's what I thought, but you said to let you know if he did anything, you know, that wasn't strictly police business.'
'Absolutely, you were right to call.' The voiced yawned. 'I'll wait up for you, call me when you're back. Take it easy out there Drew it's a horrible night.'
'Yes Frank, talk to you later.' The two men hung up their receivers. Drew's shoulders fell at the thought of going out into the storm, but he returned to his room nonetheless to get dressed. He found a clean shirt and a stiff starchy uniform from the wardrobe and began pulling them on in trepidation. Drew stood tall at six foot, broad of shoulder but not overbearing. He was healthy, athletically built, with a keen eye and a quick mind. He dressed quickly, pulling an extra jumper over his neat black hair. He pulled a pair of waterproof trousers on over his thick socks to protect against the rain then made his way back downstairs. At the door he put his Wellington boots and waxed jacket on, pulling the hood tightly around his head. He picked up his keys from the telephone table and walked through the kitchen to the back door which he unlocked to enter the ugly night. The wind did everything it could to keep him indoors, pushing at him and blasting cold rain into his face. He struggled out to his shed, un-padlocking the door quickly. Once inside he took a saw, some rope, a tarpaulin and a first aid kit which he placed in a large holdall from the back of the door. He then struggled back to the house, the weather battering and pummelled him, the wind picking him up off his feet several times. Already exhausted he struggled back through the house, picking up a bottle of water and on a whim he put his camera in his bag too. He then trudged back to the front door. Preparing himself with a resigned sigh, he opened the front door and stepped out into the dark night.
His car sat on the drive waiting for him and he struggled toward the boot. The cold rain blowing into his face made it almost impossible to see. Despite wearing gloves his hands were already soaked, so removing the keys from his pocket had become impossible. He placed the bag down carefully and struggled with the keys in his pocket. It took two frozen hands to pull them out. He could barely see in the dim light, but with some effort he managed to guide the

15

key home, his numb hands fumbling painfully at the cold metal. With the boot open he lifted the heavy bag into the back, then dragged himself along the car. He struggled once again with the key in the driver's door, enduring more of the weather than he'd like before the key nestled into the lock.

The weather did all it could to keep him from leaving, but he continued despite its attempts to stop him, and despite his sense of foreboding. With the car door open he leapt thankfully into the driver's seat, slamming the door shut and throwing back his coat hood. He took a deep breath and assessed his situation. The journey was going to be hard. The drive was not far, nothing was in Firestone, but the conditions were beyond anything he had ever witnessed. His hands were already frozen beyond feeling, so he got the engine started, turning the heating up to full to try and warm himself up. The motor chugged painfully into life, it too struggled against the wet and cold, so he turned the heating down again to give the engine a chance against the freezing night. He gently pressed the accelerator, revving the engine to prevent it from stalling. When he was convinced the car was ready to do battle, he turned the heat up and allowed himself to thaw out. The car's interior slowly warmed, and Drew watched as the condensation that blanketed him from the darkness outside slowly dispersed, revealing a black impenetrable exterior. When the feeling had returned to his hands and feet he decided to brave the drive out into the angry night. The car already faced the road, it was always reversed it into the drive on his return home of an evening to allow for a speedy exit should one be required. The town of Firestone was the unlikeliest of places to need such diligence, but living there made Drew feel uneasy. He always felt the need to have an escape route, should he feel the need to be liberated from the confines of the trees. He flicked a switch and the windscreen wipers leapt into life. They struggled back and forth against the wet but all was dark. He flicked another switch to turn the lights on, and was rewarded with the view of a dull patch of rain splattered drive. He could just make out individual drops of rain, smashing themselves on to the windscreen and the bonnet so quickly it was a blur. His headlights stubbornly tried to illuminate the world outside, but still the dark defeated the light. He turned the lights to full beams, the increased light allowing him to see slightly further ahead. He eased the car forward, creeping toward the road. With weather horrid and the hour unsociable, the roads were empty of any other vehicles but

Drew still crawled slowly out of his drive, checking each direction of his quiet street carefully. Once away the wind battered the chassis and Drew feared it might turn the car on to its side if there were a powerful enough gust. The engine occasionally gave a coughing splutter of unwillingness, and he hoped it would hold out long enough for him to get home.

'Please don't let it take long,' he muttered to himself hopefully as the houses gave way to trees. With the appearance of the trunks around him the darkness changed dramatically. It edged in closer, chasing him through the night. Drew found nothing he could recognise in what little the light illuminated to allow him to place his position along the road. He just drove doggedly onwards and hoped he would be able to see the fallen tree before he hit it. As he drove deeper into the Copse, the surrounding trees encroached and thickened around him. They grew as close to the road as they could get, their branches lay on the road side where their advance was halted by passing cars. With bricks and mortar gone his headlights now shone on trees, picking out the individual trunks as they flashed by his car. He kept himself from staring into them and concentrated on the view of the road in his lights. He focused on the road, avoiding the ever changing view of trunks that surrounded him. He proceeded with as much speed as his caution in the conditions would allow, waiting for a block in the road to stop him, or a tree to come crashing down on his roof. The road was littered with smaller branches that the wind had shaken free and he was surprised and thankful that only one tree had relented under the pressure of the storm. Above his head the branches swung around in the gale, their bare sticks dancing like many fingered hands on arms sprouting from the Earth.

He finally turned on to Beaper Chute, and slowed for the tight bend in the road which gave him some scope of his proximity along the otherwise straight drive. He turned closely around the corner and had just started to gain some speed again when suddenly the tree emerged through the night and appeared in his headlights. He quickly applied the brakes bringing the car to a controlled halt. He peered over the bonnet to assess the tree and how much work awaited him. Luckily the trunk was still young, bigger than a sapling but only just. He was relieved to find it so small, he had imagined something much bigger and more difficult to remove. He switched on the blue flashing light and it began revolving around the trees, slicing through the dark. He didn't waste a second; he took a deep breath, pulled his hood tightly over his head, and opened the door. Immediately the onslaught was upon him, and he had to battle it to force the door open. Once out the storm battered his waterproofs with an icy wind laced with balls of freezing water. A rumble of thunder in the distance shook his bones. He struggled through the wind to the boot and opened it up, taking the saw from his bag. He laid the tarpaulin out in the back, and then turned to face the tree. He felt a surge of adrenalin as he headed into the road with saw in hand. He ignored the wind and the rain, building a tolerance to it. The flashing blue light bounced amongst the trunks, unhindered by the conditions it sped around them, illuminating every corner of the scene for an instant as it rotated around and around. The trees rushed and soared in the gale, the roar of their branches and of the rain pummelling their trunks was deafeningly loud, and assaulted his ear drums from all directions.

He very quickly robbed the trunk of its branches, most of which were still thin and spindly from immaturity. Once free from the main body of the tree he deposited them in a ditch by the side of the road. The roots were still partially in the ground, and with some effort he sawed through the main bulk of the trunk close to the base. He then moved on to the rest of the trunk, which he resolutely sawed into three parts, pleased with his assumption that they would make excellent firewood when dried out. With some struggle he managed to get the pieces back to his car and into the boot. He took the water and the towel from the bag and climbed back into the driver's seat and breathed a deep sigh of relief, checking his watch; Two Thirty. The operation had taken him a little over an hour and left him hot and tired. He took a long grateful swig of the water and opened up his water proofs to try and cool down a little. The car began to steam up so he opened a window with a deft turn of the handle, letting in the cold air and rain. He actually relished the coolness of the air after working up such a sweat battling against the tree and the elements. Now that the road was clear he just wanted to be back in bed again. The blue light rolled around and around the scene, highlighting shapeless nothings in the darkness, picking out trees that seemed to have moved since its last fleeting visit. Drew shuddered under the intensity of the night. The woods looked and felt like they were crawling, moving toward him, always trying to reach him. He had managed not to think about them when he was outside, but now he was back in the relative safety of his squad car he felt brave enough to try and peer between the trunks. He expected at any moment to see something horrible appear from them, though he knew not what. Finally the fear became too great and he decided to leave them behind in favour of home. Despite having seen no other traffic since he began his journey into the night, he did not want to risk turning the car around so close to the bend. He drove the car along the road a little to move a safe distance away from the corner, and he was glad he did, as after just a few seconds two lights appeared suddenly in his mirror. He glanced up to see what the lights were, and what he saw caused him to slam on the break and stare at what his in mirror. The lights were stationery and not at headlight height as he had expected, but closer to head height. They had appeared in the spot he had just driven past, which was now about ten yards behind him. Drew did not take his eyes off of his mirror, trying to make out what the lights were attached to. He turned to look through the rear window, but the lights vanished. He physically jumped with surprise. He turned in his seat to face the front again, and the lights were once again visible in the mirror. This was disturbing enough, but he couldn't shake the feeling of being watched. The lights floated in the air, and were shaped like eyes. He approximated them to be the size of Rugby balls, but it was hard to tell with no scale for comparison. He slowly and unwillingly put his car into reverse. He was no longer in control of his actions. Fear had flown from him, and now his mind became ruled by its investigative nature.

He told himself there was a rational explanation, and that he was going to have to find out what that explanation was. He lifted the clutch and the car slowly trundled backwards towards the lights. He remained focused on the mirror, trying to work out what they were, hoping it would become clear before he reached them. As he approached they began to move sideways, into the trees. They retained their forward facing position; facing him. They stared continually as they disappeared into the undergrowth. Drew let out a sigh of confusion as to what the lights could be and fear began creeping into his mind again. Despite this fear he knew he had to follow them, no matter how great the ominous foreboding that filled him. When the car reached the spot where he guessed the lights had entered the trees he brought it to a halt. The dark and the wind and the rain all continued unabated outside, lashing at the window as if nothing untoward was happening. It was hard to tell if this was the position, but as Drew peered into the darkness he was just able to discern a thin break between the trunks that lead deeper into the canopy. This he decided had to be the path the lights had taken. To his relief the gap was large, almost the width of a bridleway, and not wanting to venture into the woods on foot he pulled his car off of the road and peered into meagre view afforded him by his head lights. Ahead an overgrown track made its way into the gloom of the trees. Though he could no longer see the lights he pressed the car on, leaving the road behind. The wheels skidded and slid as they tried to find a path across the grass and mud into the trees. The gap was just big enough to squeeze the car through it. He entered the trunks, and was swallowed by the trees. As he descended deeper into the gloom, branches from the undergrowth scraped noisily along the sides of the car. They reached at it like fingers, trying to stop him from going any further, trying to hold him back, but never finding a grip. Low hanging branches, leaves, and the occasional squalor of heavy rain was all he could see in his path. Brambles reached across his windscreen and he worried they might become caught in the toing and froing of his windscreen wipers, but suddenly the trees and brambles were gone, and the view ahead cleared. Illuminated in his headlights he found a clearing in the woods. The trees gathered, jostling for space around the edge as if frightful to step out from their crowded safety. The clouds raced overhead, being dragged across the sky in a torrent of bulbous unfathomable shapes, just visible in the dark. The car began to go downhill, slipping and sliding as it did. Drew pressed on the brakes but there was no grip for the wheels, and the car skidded through the mud. He tapped on the pedal quickly to try and stop it from skidding any further but in the thick mud it made no odds. He was unable to regain control, and the car slid sickeningly downward. The centre of the opening descended on a shallow angle to a dip in the ground. When the car reached the centre it slid to a sickening halt. Drew put it into reverse, but the wheels simply spun in the gloopy brown mess. He was stuck. He cursed himself for being so foolhardy as to take the car into the woods. His actions suddenly seemed ridiculous now that he was stuck. He prepared himself for the storm and once more opened his door to face the elements. However as he exited he was surprised to find the air outside to be calm, and still. Though the tops of the trees shook and swayed in the ruckus he found himself in a bed of tranquillity. Their swishing and swaying filled the air with noise, and he likened it to an angry sea beating ceaselessly against a stony shore. He marvelled at the cloud, spinning about the sky above him, making an almost perfect circle around the clearing he had discovered. His mind turned to the lights that had bought him down into the squalor, and despite himself he took to searching for them. He swallowed his fear and trepidation, ignoring the voice in his head that told him to stay in the car and fight his way out of the mire. The eeriness of the clearing, the sensation of the trees creeping around the edge did little to settle his mind. There was not a drop of rain falling here, not a sound other than the bare trees battling the wind. He scanned the area in the headlights, but all was mud and puddle. As he waded through the ankle deep mud his torch light flashed around the area his mind turned the shapes in the mud into hidden assailants waiting for him to step close enough for ambush. He apprehensively braved the slippery walk to the perimeter of the trees, and shone his torch to light up the inside of the wood. All there was to see was bark; his torch light could not penetrate further than a few yards due to the density of the trees. He tried to think of what the lights might have been, telling himself they were a slither of moonlight peeking through the clouds and reflected in his mirror, his tired eyes doubling the image. He shook his head, trying to rid himself of fear. Every atom in his body willed him to get back into the car, as if the marooned vehicle would offer some sanctuary from the unseen danger that an ethereal voice was telling him was there, but undetectable. He was unsettled by his lack of findings, but with no energy and realising the search was beyond his means, he gave in to his inner voice and traipsed back through the sticky mud to his car. The lights that led him here were nowhere to be seen, and even if he had found them he did not know what to do about them. He put their existence down to his lack of sleep, and cursed the air for allowing himself to become stuck. The going through the mud was hard, and he lost count of how often he lifted his foot and left his boot behind. He finally returned to the car exhausted, collapsing into the driver's seat with a resigned sigh. His head fell back and rested on the driver's headrest, and his eyes unwittingly started to close as sleep encroached upon him. He realised he was destined to spend the night here, but before allowing his body to slip into unconsciousness he remembered the car's headlights were still on, and that he should turn them off to prevent the battery going flat. He also realised that he should let someone know what had happened to him. He tilted his head forward again and drearily reopened his eyes, and in doing so a shape formed in the mud illuminated by the headlights. This shape was real, and not drawn by fear. He leant forward to get a better look, and when he realised what he was seeing, his eyes widened in shock.

Lying face down in a gradually deepening pool of its own blood, the body could not have been there for very long. Drew opened his door and fell out of the car on to the mud in a daze. He hoped to wake up, but this was not a dream. He carefully stalked around to the front of the car, subconsciously trying to keep out of view of the body, trying to hide from it. Steam rose into the moonlight from the quickly cooling corpse. He eventually found himself stood between it and the headlights, torch in hand but its light unrequired in the glare of the car's beams. His hands shook in fear, and despite the cold a nervous sweat dripped from every pore of his exhausted frame. Shaking his head at the impossibility of the body's appearance, he struggled to find an explanation as to how it could have appeared without him noticing. Dazed and in shock he climbed back into the car, and continued to stare through the windscreen at it for a few minutes. It obstinately refused to vanish, refusing to become part of his imagination or turn into a grotesquely formed pile of mud. Without taking his eyes from the corpse he picked up the receiver to his radio, and awaited the police operator to answer his call.

Monday 3rd November 1969

3.

The first train to arrive at Nettlewood Station from London on a Monday morning arrives at ten passed seven. On this particular Monday it arrived on time, a rare occurrence. Two men wearing smart suits under long coats stood on the northbound platform in well-polished shoes waiting to board it. Once the carriages came to a complete stop one of the men opened the closest door and they climbed into the same carriage together. They sat opposite each other, opened their newspapers, and began to read. These same events took place every Monday, indeed they happened almost every week day. The two men had seen each other every morning for years, and went through the familiar motions without needing to pass a single word to one another. They would make small talk on their journey regarding any items of interest they found in the news, and ask of each other's family occasionally. Today there was a slight change to their routine, as for once someone was alighting the train from their carriage. The man facing down the platform lowered a corner of his newspaper to watch, then gave his companion a tap with his foot so he didn't miss out. The guard helped the man to lift his three cases down from the caged luggage rack above his seat. One of the items of luggage was a briefcase, which the man picked up and carried off. The other cases were large and heavy and the porter had some trouble removing them from the train. Once the guard had deposited the final case on to the platform next to the man he tipped his hat politely to him before climbing back into the carriage, slamming the door closed. The station master waved a green flag, blew his whistle, and the train heaved itself out of the station and back on its journey to Birmingham in a flurry of smoke.

The man is short, not much over five feet tall. He is stocky, with a portly belly. He wears a black bowler hat and a long beige coat. Under this is a well cut black suit with a grey pinstripe, a white shirt and a red tie. On his face grows a bristly grey moustache interspersed with flicks of red. He stood alone on the platform for a moment, before the waiting room door opened and he was approached by a policeman.

'Good morning,' the policeman greeted him kindly. 'I'm Sergeant Frank Gates, Nettlewood constabulary.' He held out his right hand for the man to shake. 'As you are the only guest visiting our town this morning may I presume you to be the Inspector from Scotland Yard?' The Inspector accepted Sergeant Gates' hand and shook it.

'Indeed you may Sergeant.' Frank immediately felt relaxed in his presence. He was expecting an officious man, but the Inspector greeted him with a smile, and the handshake was firm but warm. The Inspector carried with him an air of confidence that only those from the capital can attain.

'It was you that put through the call to us in the early hours, yes?' The Inspector already knew this to be true, but asked as a matter of formality.

'Yes sir, I contacted you as soon as I received the call from the Constable at Firestone.'

'Very good.' There are a lot of questions circling the Inspector's mind regarding the report and why it was this man that made it, but he held back on asking any of them until he had a firmer understanding of the situation, and the relationship between the two towns and their police forces.

'Shall we go to my car? The poor lad who discovered the body has been there all night and I am eager to see him,' Sergeant Frank Gates said.

'Indeed, as am I. Poor chap must be out of his mind with worry, being out there by himself all night. We should get out to him without any more delay. Could I trouble you to assist me with my luggage?' the Inspector asked.

'Of course sir, here...' Sergeant Frank Gates picked up the two larger cases, leaving the small briefcase for the Inspector. They were unfathomably heavy, but Frank struggled silently with their weight. They exited the small station and found the squad car parked close to the door.

As they loaded the cases into the police car's boot, another pulled up. The driver parked in the bus stop that served the station and walked across the car park to where the Inspector and Frank stood.

'Nice parking Banks.' Frank pointed behind him as a bus arrived and was forced to stop on the road, causing traffic to build up behind it.

'Police business, Gates, there has been a murder you know,' he replied bluntly in his slow country accent. 'What are you doing here anyway?' Banks asked Frank.

'I arranged for him to be here.' The Inspector interjected. 'As the body was discovered in Nettlestone's jurisdiction I thought it best to telephone him, and have him drive me to the scene.' Neither man paid the Inspector any attention, they were locked together in a focus of hatred. Banks broke it, cautious of the man from London.

'You must be the Inspector, down from London.' Banks regarded him warily before shaking the Inspector's hand.

'Yes, Sergeant Banks is it?' the Inspector asked. 'I believe you spoke to my assistant.'

'That's right. Well now I'm here Frank you might as well be off, I can drive the Inspector down.'

'Fine, you can move the luggage into your car then.' Frank nodded at the cases in the boot.

'Well, Sergeant Banks, as I was saying, Nettlestone is on Frank's beat, and the body was technically discovered in Nettlestone.' Suddenly they both realised that the tables were turned. It took a moment for the surprise to sink in and for their minds to realign their responsibilities, and what was expected of them.

'Actually I arranged to meet you both here. I thought it best, as the body has appeared so close to both your towns.' The Inspector interrupted their thought processes and the two men shifted uneasily away from each other. Their mutual hatred was tangible, but the Inspector continued briefing them as if he hadn't noticed.

'I'll need two cars, one at the entrance to the woods so that the ambulance will know where to come, and one to take me to Constable Drew in the clearing, and perhaps attempt a rescue of his vehicle.' Both men were rather surprised at how well organised the Inspector was.

'You've already booked the ambulance?' Banks asked, incredulous. Unable to believe the Inspector had taken such liberty.

'Yes, it will be there at eight thirty, so time is short.' The Inspector paused for a moment, to make it clear that he was changing the subject.

'Gentlemen, the three of us will be working very closely together as this thing pans out, but I want to make it clear that Scotland Yard are now dealing with the case. I'll need you to let me have free reign over your supplies, vehicles, staff, offices, everything. I won't be intrusive, and will ensure anything used is replaced. I just need to know that you're both going to accept that, so we can wrap this all up as quickly and painlessly as possible.'

The two men regarded the Inspector carefully. Frank hadn't needed to be told this, he had presumed that would be the case when he received the telephone call at 4am to tell him the Inspector was on his way and where to meet him. He wondered if perhaps he gave the speech to every rural village he came to, thus ensuring the local constabulary were aware how things were going to operate. He then wondered if perhaps he made them aware of this to ensure Banks realised that he was off his turf and would have to fall in line.

'Now, I will travel with you Frank. Banks if you follow, hopefully we can find the scene between us.' The three men returned to their cars without another word. The traffic had dissipated now that the bus had continued along its journey. The cars pulled away and as they trundled along the quiet main road their wheels splashed through the deep puddles that remained from the previous night's downpour. The Inspector opened his briefcase and pulled out an ordinance survey map, folded open on the two towns of Firestone and Nettlewood, and the road in-between them.

'How was your journey?' Frank asked as they trundled along out of the town.

'Oh fine, nothing much to report,' the Inspector replied. 'My train was on time, that's the best one can hope for.'

The road was long, thin, and winding. As they left Nettlewood the countryside opened up around them, revealing a patchwork of greys and browns as the farmland slept through the winter.

'So the chap we are off to see, Constable Drew Gates,' the Inspector checked his notes. 'Any relation?' he asked.

'As a matter of fact yes, he's my nephew.' Frank replied.

'I see. Does he match up to your expectations as a police officer?' the Inspector asked friendlily.

'And more so besides,' Frank replied proudly. They gradually made their way up a shallow hill, and on reaching its peak they were confronted with a shallow valley, at its centre a broad expanse of trees stuck obtrusively out through the surrounding fields. The road ahead led directly into the trees.

'And this must be Firestone Copse,' the Inspector announced.

'Yes, sir that's right.' Frank replied simply.

The wind and rain had calmed from the previous evening, revealing in the thin morning light a dazed town rubbing its bruises. They descended into the valley, and soon the car was entering the trees. Their branches hung over the road, making a tunnel that did all it could to block out the dim early morning sun. On his map the Inspector had marked on his best guess as to where body was. He had based this on his conversation with Frank the previous night. Frank, the Inspector noticed, did not require a map, he drove confidently along the road, his eyes searching the under growth for evidence of the story that had been relayed to him by Drew.

'He should be along here somewhere then?' the Inspector asked Frank as they turned the corner on to Beaper Chute.

'Yes.' Frank replied. He slowed for a second. 'Look, there's the stump of the fallen tree.' Both men surveyed the damage. The tree had obviously been cut recently, the wood was still fresh from the saw, and a few flakes of sawdust remained, drenched and stuck to the tar mac.

'Must have been a hell of job to clear it in the weather we had last night,' Frank exclaimed.

'Was the weather truly bad?' The Inspector asked.

'Aye, one of the worst storms I've ever seen,' he replied. Banks' car suddenly came up behind them and slowed as it approached. The Inspector angled his head to watch him in the rear view mirror, and noticed that he paid no attention to the tree, or what they were doing. He sat in his car swearing, waiting for them to start moving again.

Frank took the car slowly forwards, looking for the same thing the Inspector was; tyre tracks into the trees. After an agonisingly slow cruise along the road, Frank finally saw them.

'The rain last night has made it so muddy, look, you can see his tracks right through the grass.' Sure enough two tyre tracks disappeared into the trees where wheels had bent the grass over a few hours earlier. A few hours more and the grass would regain its height, and the trail would be lost. Frank reversed up a little and turned in the direction of the tracks, following the tyre paths through the grass. His tyres slipped a little on the muddy verge but once he was on the vegetation the car found it easier going. The track was not a track at all, just a wide path through the trees where nothing grew. Their car was submerged in the brambles and branches as they tore their way through. Then, quite abruptly, the scraping stopped. They were in a wide open space dominated by huge bare oaks stretching around them. The opening dipped down at the centre, where a police car sat facing a tarpaulin laid out on the ground. At the top of the crater stood a policeman with his right hand up, indicating for them to stop.

4.

Drew woke shortly before sunrise from a thin sleep. His dreams had been riddled with glowing eyes following him through confusing mirrored corridors. It took him a moment to remember where he was, and the memory made his heart sink. A few stubborn crows sat in the surrounding trees cawing, determined to bear out the English winter. Their calls began a quiet chorus to signal the arrival of the new day. He hugged the blanket around his shoulders for warmth and looked out of the window the sun struggled into a drizzle lined grey sky. With a few sips of water he began rousing his tired body into action and pulled his boots on. He left the relative comfort of the car's back seat to examine the scene in the first meagre rays of the new day.

His boots squelched through the mud, which had dried a little since the rain ceased and so was slightly easier to navigate through. He made his way to the front of the car, where the sheet of tarpaulin he had placed there still sat, covering the corpse. It was pinned down along its edges with some heavy stones he had carried down from around the lip of the crater. In the centre the dead man's shape loomed conspicuously. Drew was tired, and still in a degree of shock from the events of the last few hours. He could still not quite place the body into his perspective of the world. It still did not seem real. The trees now stood perfectly still around him, his silent protectors against the hidden depths of forest that lurked behind them.

The storm had passed. The morning was cold but with the dulling of the gale came a sun determined to warm the wet land. As its heat penetrated the cold floor a mist rose unwillingly and lurked low around the trunks. The crows became a little more determined in their song, as if trying to sing away the feeling of menace between the trees.

Drew heard the cars before he saw them, the sound of their engines and of brambles scratching across metal came echoing through the trees. He made his way haphazardly out of the crater, and reached the summit just as they exited on to the mud. At this level the ground was drier, the mud wasn't as thick, and the cars were less likely to become stuck. He held up his hand for them to stop and Sergeant Gates wound down his window.

'Morning Drew, how are you?' he asked in a tone of concern.
'Fine Sarge, tired, and in a little shock I think, but otherwise alright.'

Banks drove into the clearing behind them, leapt out of his car and immediately made his way towards Drew, who did his best to hide his disappointment.

'Good.' Frank replied, unable to hide his relief. The passenger door of his car opened and the Inspector climbed out.

'This is the Inspector, down from Scotland Yard, he's here to investigate the body.' Frank informed him. The Inspector climbed out of the car and around to Drew before Banks could reach him. Frank noticed what he was trying to do, and climbed out to cut Banks off.

'Good to meet you Drew.' The Inspector shook his hand while Frank grabbed Banks and began educating him in the Highways Agency's responsibilities. He led him inconspicuously away from the two men.

'Did you mean what you said about feeling fine, or were you just being brave?' the Inspector asked him.

'No I meant it.' He replied with conviction, though his haggard face said otherwise.

'Good, because I need to ask you some questions, now, before the memories of last night begin to fade, or your mind alters them. No one would blame you if you weren't feeling up to these questions.'

'No, I understand the importance of asking them straight away. Would you like to go to the body?' The Inspector took a long look at the wide space in the trees.

'I do indeed, but I think it might be better traversed in Wellingtons. I see you stopped us up here to prevent us becoming trapped in the mud.'

'Yes, hopefully it will be dry enough soon to drag my car out.'

'We also have an ambulance arriving in an hour or so, leaving me eager to get on with the job before they arrive to take him away.' He made his way to the arguing Sergeants.

'Excuse me gentlemen, I am so sorry to interrupt.' The men turned to face the Inspector. Banks was pink in the cheeks with rising anger, while Frank smirked at his success of annoying his contemporary.

'Sergeant Gates, would you be so kind as to open your car boot and allow me access to my luggage?'

'Of course, Inspector.' He left the fuming Banks and went to open the boot.

'Sergeant Banks, could you drive back to the road and wait for the ambulance to arrive please?' Banks stood staring after Frank for a moment, then turned and left without a word. As there was no space to turn around without becoming stranded in the mud, he was forced to reverse back down the narrow space between the tress. The Inspector and Drew then joined Frank at his car boot. The Inspector manoeuvred the cases in the generous boot space and opened the larger of the two revealing a plethora of outdoor survival equipment such as a small tent, wet weather overalls, thermal coat, compass, rations, and a pair of green Wellingtons.

The Inspector perched himself on the edge of the boot space and changed his shoes. He did so with such casualness that both police officers were a little surprised. He placed his brown leather shoes in the space that the boots had occupied in the case and then closed its lid again. He opened a compartment in its lid and took out a camera, some spare rolls of film, and a large circular tape measure. These vanished into his briefcase. He then pulled out of a plastic bag from a compartment at the bottom of the case and took from it an unopened tin of white paint and a thick brush.

'Now, I am ready to see the body.' He removed the camera from his case, put it to his eye and took a picture of the scene from where he stood; the abandoned car, the blue tarpaulin, the big muddy hole.

'Sergeant Gates, would you please remain here and await the arrival of the ambulance?'

'Of course Inspector.' Frank watched as he dished out instructions, impressed by the finesse and character with which he did it all.

'Drew, if you would accompany me.' The Inspector led the way, following the path that Drew's footprints made in the mud that led down to the centre of the crater.

'So tell me what happened last night. How did you come to be in here, and find the body?' the Inspector asked.

'How much do you already know?'

'I want to hear your side of events.' They had arrived at the car. 'Start at the beginning.' Drew took a breath.

'I removed the tree from the road, then drove down a little away from the bend to turn the car around. Then...' he paused for a moment as he remembered the eyes. He was cautious about how much he wanted to share with this man. He was aware how the circumstances leading up to his arrival in the opening sounded, and he didn't want to seem foolish to an important Inspector from London. '... I noticed this opening, so I drove down here to have a look.'

'Impressive, it can't have been easy to see in the rain and dark. What was it that made you notice it?' The Inspector asked, gently probing.

Drew wondered if the Inspector already knew what he had seen, and was trying to convince him that he could confide it. Drew remained silent, thoughtful. The Inspector let him think, gauging the young man, reading his thoughts, allowing him time to trust him.

'As time is short, perhaps we should learn about how you got here later. For now tell me what you found when you arrived.' Drew was grateful for the change in subject.

'I drove through the trees, and when I arrived here in the opening I did not see the dip until it was too late. The car slid down the slope and I was unable to stop it, and it got stuck.' The Inspector studied the Constable's car. Each wheel sat in a deep trench, carved out in the rain and dark of the previous night. He turned his attention to the door, and the tracks that started there, following them as Drew told his story.

'So I got out, and checked the back tyres to see how stuck I was, then I went to the front.' Drew paused, thinking. He had looked about for the eyes, but he couldn't tell the Inspector that.

'And was the body there?' The Inspector asked.

'If it was, I didn't notice it.' Drew consciously edited the eyes from the story. 'When I realised I was stuck I sat back down in the front seat. I was still knackered from moving the tree, and when I began to drop off I woke myself up to turn the lights off and call in my position, and that's when I saw it. He paused as the memory of the body in the night played back across his mind. 'The shock was doubled by the surprise,' he admitted. 'It wasn't there before. I would have seen it. I'm sure I would have seen it.' The Inspector had been following the trail of footprints up to this point, and had noticed a second trail leading to the front.

'So then you got out again, and walked around to the front to get a better view.'

'Yes. Just to make absolutely sure it was actually there.'

'Did It look fresh?' the Inspector had to ask direct questions, but Drew wasn't sure if he liked it.

'Sorry, perhaps I shouldn't be so callous. You have been through a lot tonight after all.'

'No it's fine, it's funny because I know what you mean. It looked as though it had been placed there the moment I looked up. Like I happened to be looking at the right place at the right time, and suddenly it was there. It took me a few seconds, but I was out of the car quite quickly. It was still steaming when I got to the front. It just kept bleeding and bleeding, there was a lot of blood.' Drew fought back the impulse to vomit at the thought.

'And then you searched the area, looking for footprints, clues, trying to see if there was any trace of a culprit?' The Inspector had noticed the prints leading up to the edge of the trees. There were a few trails leading off to the back of the car, as he had prepared the site, covered the body, and a trail leading off when he had retrieved the stones.

'Yes, there was nothing that I could see, though I couldn't see an awful lot in the dark.'

'Then you covered he body.'

'Yes, I thought it might be a good idea.'

'Indeed.' The Inspector agreed. 'We don't want the poor chap exposed to the elements.'

Drew had been too immersed in the replaying of the night to notice that the Inspector was taking photographs of the ground, the car, the footprints, each piece of the scene committed to celluloid. He turned to face Drew.

'Shall we have a look at him?' the Inspector asked. Drew led him along the side of his car, retracing his path. They came to the blue tarpaulin, in its centre rose the ominous bulk of the corpse. The Inspector removed the rocks from one edge and gently rolled the plastic sheet back. When the body was fully revealed he put the rocks back on the sheet to hold it in place.

A dark red patch in the surrounding earth was now all that remained of the pool of blood that had immersed the body. The clothes were filthy and drenched in blood and mud. The Inspector began taking pictures of it all.

'Was there any blood at all when you found it?' he asked as the camera clicked.

'Only a little. More came out as I watched.' The Inspector knelt down to study it closely.

'Did you notice this when you saw it?' Drew studied the back of the body where the Inspector was indicating. A large hole descended down through the chest, blood pooled dull and crimson at the base.

'No I didn't. I didn't look too closely, if I'm honest.'

The Inspector took a photograph of the hole and the film ran out. He took a film from his case and reloaded the camera, then removed the tape measure and with Drew's help he measured the body. The length and angle of every limb was scribbled carefully into a little notebook. When he was satisfied he carefully painted around the corpse to leave a white line in the shape of the body on the mud. Not a drop went out of place, the dead man's clothes remained untarnished. While the paint dried he took more photographs of the wound.

'What was the weather like last night when you drove up here?' the Inspector asked between photographs. Drew took a moment to answer through the haze of sleep deprivation.

'Atrocious. I'm amazed I managed to shift that tree in it. Driving conditions were horrendous, the entire night was a nightmare,' he admitted candidly.

'What about when you reached this spot, what was it like here?' Hidden behind the camera, Drew was unable to tell if the Inspector asked this because he knew the conditions were different. Drew took a moment to answer again, trying to decide if he should tell the Inspector the truth, whatever it might be. As if sensing this turmoil, the Inspector lowered the camera and spoke to Drew quite directly, and confidentially.

'Perhaps I should explain. There is no ramification for telling the truth. I want to hear what you saw, everything you witnessed, there is no need for you to be worried about what it might sound like to me.' Drew felt reassured, as he had already decided to tell the truth. He nodded in understanding.

'It was very still here. The trees on the outer edge,' he pointed round the perimeter of the circular opening, 'were swaying in the wind, but down here there was no wind at all.'

'Was it raining?' Drew thought for a moment.

'No, it was wet on the ground, obviously, as the car was stuck in the wet mud. But it was dry otherwise. The clouds were all around the edge, but they didn't stray over the clearing.' He thought for a moment. 'Was the tarp dry when you rolled it up?' he asked. The Inspector was beginning to like the way Drew's mind worked.

'No it was dry, but it is a dry morning.'

'Yes, the clouds must have parted about the same time I arrived here, I remember seeing the moon.'

The Inspector checked the paint with his finger. It had dried quickly.

'Ok, I'm going to turn him over, could you manage the feet?' Between them they rolled the body on to its back. Its posture hardly moved, cold and rigamortis settling into the blood and muscles. The two men took a few steps back and studied the front of the body. With the corpse lying face up, so exposing the face, it looked less like a dead thing and more like a person. The Inspector's camera clicked again.

The face was locked into an awkward unnatural expression caused, by being faced down all night, but it was clear to see that the poor man's last moments had been incredibly painful. The mouth was open in a grimace, the eyes clenched shut. He wore a long brown coat, under which was a silver-grey suit with a tie to match, and a white shirt.

'Who do you think he was?' Drew asked, finding himself trying to imagine the pain he must have been through in his dying moments.

'No idea.' The Inspector answered honestly. He stopped taking photographs. 'Perhaps we can find out.' He knelt down next to the body and started riffling through the man's pockets. Firstly he searched his coat, inside of which he found some keys, which he dropped into an evidence bag from his ever present briefcase. He searched every pocket, and continued removing objects which he hurriedly placed into evidence bags and secured in his case, keeping his finds out of the sight of Drew. The Inspector checked the coats inside pockets and removed a wallet, which he opened and began looking through for something that might identify the victim. Inside he found a piece of plastic slightly smaller and slightly thicker than a playing card which had printed on it a photograph, a name and an address. The Inspector read it to himself, Drew was too far away to be able to see it.

'Matthew Berrow. From Swindon.' The Inspector announced to him. He calculated the distance between Firestone and Swindon, estimating it to be approximately ninety miles away. His eyes were drawn to the date of birth; March 25th, 2017.

He studied the date and the man carefully, his mind racing. The card was an odd item in itself, it proclaimed to be a driving licence, issued by the Driver and Vehicle Licensing Agency, however the Inspector had never seen anything like it. It certainly looked nothing like his own driving licence, it had unrecognisable insignias that reflected the light in strange ways. He also considered the other items he had removed from the body and concealed in his case and wondered to himself if, somehow, the date could be true. If it was then the man, who looked about thirty, had found his way here from approximately ninety years in the future.

The Inspector replaced the licence in the wallet then put the wallet in a bag, and put this in his briefcase. He decided to make sense of it later when time wasn't so sparse. He took a few more pictures of the body before turning the camera's attention to the surrounding trees. He decided to probe an earlier line of enquiry.

'So how did you find your way in here? We nearly missed it in the day, I imagine it would have been next to impossible during the night.' He continued to point and click the camera at the trees, and as he did the distant sound of branches snapping and scrapping on metal announced somebody's imminent arrival.

'Perhaps ask me again later.' Drew suggested, as the ambulance crept precariously through the trees and on to the mud, pulling up next to Frank's car. The mud was dry on the surface but still sticky underneath, and the driver carefully manoeuvred the ambulance around and reversed it across the mud toward the stricken police car. Its thicker tyres were better equipped to travel across the brown goop, but the driver wisely stopped half way to prevent coming stuck himself. The two ambulance men then climbed out with Sergeant Banks.

'Morning gentlemen.' The older of the two ambulance men carefully approached Drew and the Inspector, while Banks made his way back up to Frank.

'I'm looking for an Inspector, down from London.' The ambulance man called to them. The other much younger lad from the ambulance opened the back of the vehicle and started removing the stretcher.

'Yes good morning, that would be me.' The Inspector held out his hand and the man shook it.

'Hello there, I'm Andy. Do you know where we're taking the body?'

'I hope you're taking it to the hospital in Nettlewood,' the Inspector replied.

'Yes, that's it. The doctor there is very nice, Alan his name is, Doctor Collins. He can help you out when you get down there.'

'Thanks for the tip,' the Inspector replied. The young assistant arrived with the trolley, which he forced awkwardly across the mud. The Inspector could tell immediately that he had never seen a body before. He was ashen white, moved stiffly, and avoided all eye contact.

'This is Jim, Jim this is the Inspector down from London.'

'Hello Jim. A body is nothing to be afraid of, and you won't have to be around it for very long.' The Inspector reassured him.

'No sir.' Jim tried to swallow but his mouth was as dry as his throat.

'This is Jim's first body you see. Seen a fair few meself in thirty year of working in the hospital, but don't get many going like this.

Usually they just goes from their beds where they died straight to the funeral home. Don't worry Jim.' He put a friendly arm around his young assistant. 'Come on mate, best we get it over with.' He turned suddenly to the policemen. 'Presuming you're finished with it Inspector?'

'Yes thank you, all finished. Do you mind if I take a few photographs as you pick him up?'

'Course not we don't mind do we Jim?' Jim didn't look up but shook his head.

'No need to be nervous,' The Inspector addressed the nervous Jim. 'It'll all be over before you know it, and you'll have a great story to show off with to your mates later down the pub.' A smile crept into the corners of Jim's mouth, either it was from the unexpected frankness from the Inspector or the truth in his words the Inspector couldn't tell, but a little colour came back in his cheeks as he headed for the corpse. The Inspector began taking pictures again. Drew simply stood and watched as the trolley was collapsed to ground level and Andy arranged a black body bag on it for the body. The two men readied themselves to move the corpse toward the stretcher; Jim held the feet, Andy took the shoulders. As they eased it from the ground the torso lost contact with the earth, and partially clotted blood disturbed in the wound escaped and oozed out on to the mud like partially set jelly.

'Urgh!' Jim exclaimed involuntarily, though he wasn't disheartened.

'Come on lad, stay focused.' Andy reminded him professionally.

The body was lain carefully down in the bag which was quickly zipped up. The stretcher was then deftly converted back into a trolley again, and the two men dragged and lifted it as best they could over the crusting mud.

'We'll be on our way then. Like I said Inspector, Doctor Collins at the morgue when you want to see it.'

'Actually a colleague of mine may get there before I do to perform the autopsy. Could you ask Doctor Collins to offer every hospitality? I should get there sometime tomorrow afternoon, to allow them time to work.'

'I'll warn Doctor Collins, no problem. Nice meeting you.' He nodded at the Inspector. 'Constable.' He nodded at Drew. They secured the body inside the ambulance, climbed back in and carefully drove back through the trees. The wheels staggered and struggled through the mud, leaving four deep trenches in their wake, but the weight of the ambulance and the stoutness of its wheels saw it out safely. The Inspector took some photographs of the trenches before putting the camera away in the case and removing the tape measure again.

'Would you mind holding this?' The Inspector handed Drew the end of the tape. 'And standing here?' He took him by the shoulders and positioned him next to the body shape painted on to the bloodied mud.

'I'm going to take a few measurements, back in a minute. Please follow me as I move around, but try to stay in the same place as best you can.' The Inspector then took the metal disc containing the tape and began carefully walking over the mud, trying not to slip. As he did the tape unwound with a whirr that filled the area as the three policemen watched the Inspector from London begin his inspecting. After a trying walk the Inspector reached the edge of the trees and checked the distance between the body and the outside edge; thirty three feet. He wrote this down in his note book, then reached into his briefcase and removed a small compass. He angled it and found north, then began drawing a map of the clearing, the position of the body in it, and the angle it had lain in. He walked around the edge of the trees, checking the tape and the compass reading in between keeping his balance on the uneven slippery surface. He made his way cautiously around the full circumference, noting any deviance in the circle's edge.

The body lay facing east to west, head to the east, toward Nettlewood. The clearing was roughly circular, approximately two hundred feet in circumference, the fatal wound appearing to be at the approximate centre. There was no growth inside of the crater. He added a northerly pointing arrow to his map for reference, and also estimated the position on the map of the car, the opening, and the paths of all the vehicles across the mud. He then placed the compass in the bag, and removed a small battery powered machine, which he switched on using a button on the side. A dim green light bean to glow to show that it was on, and working. He pulled from its top a long aerial, and as he did so the green light shone a little brighter. As he moved around the muddy area he angled the aerial in different directions, and as he did so it emitted clicking noises, which rose and fell in frequency depending on what angle he aimed the aerial. With each change in the noises from the machine, the Inspector filled his note book with scribbles, and marked numbers on his hand drawn map. He constantly referred to the tape measure to give a distance on the map in relation to the centre. Once he had navigated around the area he switched the machine off again, then bought out a box with a metal rod attached by a curled wire, like one might find on a telephone. This machine did not emit any noises nor did it have a green light but it did have a small dial on the front which he studied. The dial ranged from green on the left to red on the right, with a needle to give a reading. For now the needle pointed toward the green on the left. The Inspector once again began walking around the area, following unseen paths that the instrument guided him along. All readings where the dial deviated from its position were scribbled down and marked on the map. He traipsed this way and that, from the crater's edge to the body and back again. He stopped at the edge of the crater and looked at trees. Anything that lurked between them was hidden by the darkness of the trunks. Their numbers blocked any chance of a view inside further than a few yards. They were silent, as if standing guard, hiding an inner world. As the breeze tossed the high branches around, shadows danced in contorted shapes on the trunks, giving the trees movement, bringing them to life. He wondered what Drew had seen in them that could have had led him here. He put the machine away and retrieved his camera. He took pictures as best he could of the inner copse as he wandered round the edge one last time. He then traipsed across the mud toward Drew. He checked the ground constantly, as he had on his way around the area. He was not only searching the ground for a safe path, his eyes examined every inch for a sign of entry, a clue as to how the body managed to appear here. He saw none. The only prints were his and Drew's, there was not even a bird's foot print to suggest any other living thing had been here.

'All done? Drew asked hopefully. He didn't mention the search he had just witnessed, the bizarre instruments or the noises they made.

'Yes, sorry for keeping you.' The Inspector could see how weary he must be feeling, and regretted having to delay Drew from getting to his bed. He took the end of the tape from Drew and placed it back in his briefcase. He knew that every detail could be vital and had to be recorded as soon after the event as possible.

'You are very thorough Inspector.' Drew pointed out. 'Though I am a little unsure what you are being thorough about.'

'One must be thorough to remain close to the facts,' the Inspector replied. 'The first few hours are the most important in collecting evidence. We can go now, Drew. If you try to get the car started, I'll fetch Sergeant Gates and ask him to try and pull you out.' The Inspector began the walk up to where Frank leant against his car waiting. Banks stood a few feet away. Both had been watching the two men closely the whole time.

Drew turned, still not entirely clear about what kind of evidence the Inspector had been searching for. He obediently walked back to the car, climbed in to the driver's seat, and pessimistically turned the key. The engine had been sat in cold mud all night, so Drew was not surprised but a little disheartened to hear the slow chug that the engine made as it tried to start. He put his foot on the accelerator and tried again, keeping the key fully turned. The engine turned over several times but refused to start, then suddenly it spluttered, the chug became a rapid series of barks, and with a blast of revs the car came to life, breathing out a thick cloud of acrid smoke in the process. Drew kept the revs high, allowing the engine time to become used the idea of being awake before trying to get it to move.

'Everything alright down there?' Frank asked as the Inspector approached.

'Yes, all fine thank you.'

'How long does the paint last?' Frank asked as it started to spit with rain. A blackening sky raced over head.

'Long enough.' the Inspector replied. 'We're all done now, so I thought I'd best come and ask you to pull his car out.'

'Certainly, sounds like Drew's managed to start it, I thought it was dead.' He checked himself. 'If you'll pardon the expression.' He nodded down the hill to the where the body had been. All that remained now was a thin line of paint on the red earth where the blood had soaked into the ground. He turned away in embarrassment and went to fetch the tow rope from the boot of his car. He returned, walking a few feet past the Inspector and called to Drew;

'Give it a go now, lad!' Drew put the car in reverse, and Banks, Frank and the Inspector all watched with interest to see what luck he would have getting it out of the mud. The car's engine strained, the chassis tried to move but the wheels stayed firmly glued to the spot like the hooves of a stubborn goat. Drew tried again, with more revs, forcing the tyres round as carefully as he could. Slowly they forced him out of the mud, and on to the surface. The car managed to creep backwards for a few feet before the tyres suddenly broke through the thin crust, and the front wheels began to spin in the mud. The three men watched in awkward anticipation, it was obvious he would become stuck at some point, and they wondered if this was it. Drew put the car into first and rocked it forwards and backwards a little to clear some space. He then attempted to pull forward to release the rear wheels, but was unsuccessful. The engine gave out under the strain, spluttered and died, and a resigned Drew climbed out of the car again.

'Good effort young man,' the Inspector surprised all of the local force by calling out.

'Thank you Inspector. I don't think it's going any further without a little help though.' Drew called back. Frank began carefully testing the ground between his cars and Drew's with his foot.

'I reckon I could get my car up to here.' He stood about four feet away from Drew's car's bumper. 'Tow rope's pretty long. We might get you out before breakfast.' He passed the rope to the Inspector, and then climbed into his car. With the Inspector's direction he moved his car as close as he thought possible, guided by the burly man's cautious waving and careful examination of the ground.

Frank stopped his car when he was as close as he could get and the Inspector bent down to examine the rear of Drew's car. The loop of metal for the tow rope was covered in mud and difficult to reach, but with a little effort he deftly tied two half hitches, and when he had safely attached the other end to Frank's car he signalled that the line was secure. Both policemen then started their engines, and the Inspector took a retreat back from the cars as quickly as he could. As Frank pulled forward the tow rope lost its slack, became taut, then was stretched and thinned as if to snap before the wheels on Drew's car gave against the gloopy brown sea. The wheels on Frank's car span, spraying mud a considerable distance into the air. It did not spray quite far enough to reach the Inspector, who watched with a bemused smile. Slowly the two cars made it clear of the worst, and Drew's wheels gained a grip on the dryer mud. When he had reversed out of the worst and up the hill to safety the Inspector then returned to the cars and untied the rope while the two drivers climbed out of their seats and shook hands in congratulations. The Inspector approached and Banks chose this moment to join them.

'Well, now that we have the car out, Drew I can drive you home while Frank and the Inspector go to the hospital with the body.' Banks barked orders rudely.

'Almost right, Sergeant,' the Inspector interjected, 'Drew, you can go home now. Get some sleep and we can talk again when you wake up.'

'Yes sir.' Drew replied wearily. He felt as if the games between him and Banks might be over now, the Inspector's arrival had changed everything.

'It's Inspector, you can just call me Inspector. Call me at Nettlewood station when you've rested, see you in a few hours.' Drew simply nodded, climbed back into his muddied car and drove away. The Inspector then turned to Banks.

'Sergeant Gates will give you a lift back to your car, then please return to your station, I am sure there are matters in your constabulary that need to be pertained to, we will talk again later.'

'Yes Inspector.' Banks' jaw was locked and he spoke through grinding teeth. He reluctantly turned and climbed into the back of Frank's car. The other two men followed him and climbed in.

'Sergeant Gates, if you would be good enough would you mind driving me to The Swan and Dove in Nettlewood where I will be staying.' The Inspector asked as he pulled his seat belt on. Banks reeled in surprise at this, but it made sense to Frank almost immediately. Presumably the murderer was someone in the town, so for the Inspector to stay close seemed logical.

'It's very nice at The Swan and Dove,' Frank remarked, revelling in the Inspector's casual air of authority over Banks.

'Is it?' the Inspector replied, intrigued.

'Yes a friend of mine stayed there. Very welcoming he said.'

'I am glad.' The Inspector liked rural police forces. The matters that concerned them were serious enough for the location but generally speaking, in the grand scheme of things, nothing of any real gravity took place. The freedom from such harsh realities as might be trivial in larger cities allowed the local forces time to appreciate a deeper knowledge of their area, the people and places in it, and they earned the respect of the people because of it. Towns like this were not supposed to have dead bodies appear in them, and the Inspector wanted life to return to normal for these kind people as soon as possible.

'So you're not going to just collect the body and go?' asked Banks, incapable of grasping the situation.

'No Sergeant, I am here to investigate its discovery in the copse, and to ascertain the reason for it to have appeared here. I will be here as long as it takes.'

'But you're not staying in Firestone Copse?' Banks asked.

'No, I am staying in Nettlewood.' The Inspector repeated, much to Banks' relief. Frank drove them down the thin path, which showed no signs of relenting under the barrage of cars. At the road Banks went to climb out.

'I can be reached at Nettlewood police station for now, should you need me,' the Inspector told him, his authoritative tone stopping Banks in his tracks.

'Yes Inspector.' Banks replied, shooting Frank a look of unhidden animosity.

'And I will need to talk to you once I've settled myself into the Hotel, so please remain at Firestone station.' Banks turned an angry red.

'Yes, Inspector.' He replied through his teeth. The Inspector ignored his hostility and allowed him to climb out of the car.

'Sergeant Gates could you spare a few men to come down and comb the area? They will need to go over every inch with great care so as to discover any evidence that we may have been left behind,' the Inspector asked.

'Yes Inspector, I'll come back down here later with a few men and scour the place,' he assured him. They pulled out into the road and headed back to Nettlewood.

The sound of the car engines slowly faded as the men drove away, leaving the area with the crater empty of all movement, save for the occasional stray leaf caught in the wind. The stillness remained, the dip in the ground continued collecting rain but otherwise it was empty. When they were sure everyone had gone, the trees began whispering to each other.

5.

At the exit from the wood on to the road Drew turned left. He drove the cars tyres through every puddle he could see to try and shake the mud out of their tread. The wet roads were slippery, and the going was slow at first. He daren't check his mirrors; the thought of seeing those lights again filled him with dread. He drove carefully, aware of his lack of sleep. The journey was quiet, and he unwittingly checked his mirrors out of habit. Driving close behind was Banks in his squad car. Drew ignored his closeness to the car's bumper and concentrated on driving, and soon houses began appearing along the road side. Amongst the trees cars could be seen in drive ways. Soon brick buildings outnumbered trunks, and Drew was back in Firestone. He took a left toward the western outskirts of the town, and saw Banks speed away along the northern road toward the station. Drew was exhausted, cold, and soaked to the skin despite his waterproofs. He pulled the car up outside his house and reversed it carefully into the drive. He left it at an angle, further away from the door than usual but safely parked, and let himself in. He placed his keys back on the table then trudged wearily up to the bathroom and started a bath running. He stripped in his bedroom, every movement causing him pain, every muscle crying for rest. By the time he had his clothes off a hot tub of foamy water awaited him. He turned the taps off and climbed straight in, laying his head back. He took a long sigh and allowed himself to relax. His eyes closed and there facing him were the eyes again, alone in the blackness behind his eyelids. He was too relaxed and too tired to open them, so he stared them out, searching them for a meaning. As he stared the road came into focus around them, and he drifted into a dream where he relived the previous night. He watched a car reversing toward him, battered and tossed by the storm. He began moving away from it as it approached, through the trees. The car stopped, paused, and turned up the path into the trees, following him. When he reached the clearing he stayed in the trees, and watched the car drive down into the crater. Looking through the branches were other eyes, all watching the car, all watching Drew. The light passed through the branches, illuminated through the wood. Staring, watching him discover the body.

Drew woke with a start. The water had gone cold, and the dream filled his mind, the eyes in the wood watching him, the reversal of perspective.

He pulled the plug and sat in the bath as the water drained away, rubbing his head and eyes. He towelled himself dry, pulled his pyjamas on and climbed thankfully into bed. He put the dream down to being just that; a dream, and tried to forget it. Now he was home, bathed, and in his own bed, he felt like the previous evening was a million years away. It had happened to someone else, not him. He took a bottle of aspirin out of his bedside drawer and took two tablets, then sat in bed and drank half a glass of water, before settling down under the duvet. He closed his eyes and there were the eyes waiting for him once again, and once again he began to relive the previous night, as he delved into a deep restful sleep.

6.

A voice battled against the darkness. The void it inhabited dropping and weaving giddily about it. It took all its effort to conceive a world outside as it flashed past. The voice struggled to form a picture of the world, struggling with new perceptions. It tried to gauge a meaning from what little flashed past it in the dark, like shadows cast across a wall through a window it couldn't see.

It knew where it was, it had been contained inside this one, and others like it, for longer than it wanted to be. This existence was not what it had planned, but better than the alternative; oblivion, but only just. Here it was trapped until a way out could be found. It had waited a long time, and had almost given up any hope. The prisons were temporary, weak, thought bound to matter. When all escape had become blocked it had been forced here, and now it had no alternative but to stay and hope the passage would be opened again. Now the voice had reason to try escape again; something had begun to make things feel different. Circumstances had conspired. Others like it were, it had discovered, forming ways to try and help, and had been for all of its incarcerated hell. This time, though, something was different. The fear was back, and through the window it sensed the cause. Another person, another echo of thought encased in flesh that threatened to reveal all.

'Is it time?' the voice screamed, disembodied, trapped, possessed. It wondered if its captor would reply, even if he could hear.

'No,' came a booming reply, and the voice cowered lower, fearful, writhing with the pain and the effort it took. How long had the reply taken? Moments? Eons? Such entrapment kept it lonely and desperate.

'I will stop it again.' The captor's voice boomed across the expanse of darkness, no form, no source.

The voice sank back into desperation. Its prison, this living tomb, had been responsible for its trap, and had prevented escape in the past.

'We've done it for three hundred years we can do it for three hundred more.'

'Not this time, you can't hide it this time.' With power it didn't know it had, the voice shouted its bravest reply. It took consolation from its bravery. It felt a return of energy, of its own purpose.

A deep mocking laugh returned, echoing, overpowering, and almost ridding the voice of the grain of hope it found. The voice returned to its silence, reserving its energy, and began to plan its escape.

7.

Banks tore his attention away from the reflection of his eyes in his rear view mirror. He swore constantly under his breath, muttering obscenities at the intrusion on to his patch and at the unwelcomed visitor. He left the Inspector and Frank at the wood, and had soon caught up to Drew, quickly becoming agitated at him for not driving faster.

'Damn him, you'd have thought he would want to get home quicker.' He swore to himself out loud. He was angry at the Inspector for embarrassing him in front of Frank.

'How dare he come into my town and talk to me like that?' he hissed to an invisible occupant. 'At least he's not coming here,' he reassured himself. They entered the town, and Drew turned left towards his house. A hint of paranoia crept into Bank's mind.

'I wonder what they were talking about in that mud,' he muttered. He had watched them carefully, but had been unable to gauge their conversation. They could have been talking about him. Drew, he thought, could have been going back to Nettlestone, to talk to the Inspector. Perhaps he was driving to Firestone as a distraction, to stop him from becoming suspicious. He took the next left away from the route to the police station and toward Drew's house. He drove quickly, having to make up distance along the longer route. When he arrived it appeared his suspicions were correct. Drew's car was not there. He stopped behind the van of Jenkins the window cleaner; close enough to see the empty drive but far enough away to remain unnoticed. He sat frowning and trying to think what his next move should be. Would the Inspector call the station to talk to him? How long did he have before he was missed?

He frowned a little harder and stared at the empty drive outside Drew's house. The sound of a car's engine droned up the road toward him, and on sight of it he breathed a sigh of relief. Drew pulled into his drive, locked his car, and went straight into the house. Banks still waited, watching the windows. He knew this house. He knew the bathroom and bedroom windows could both be seen from where he had parked, the bathroom a small rectangle on the side and the bedroom a large double window at the front. Both went on, and stayed on. Drew was home now, it was safe for him to leave, but suddenly more doubt crowded in on his mind. What if, he thought, Drew had seen him as he went into the house? What if he was waiting for him to go so he could make his way back to the

Inspector? He gripped the steering wheel, frustrated at the unknown, battling with himself for not knowing if he was worrying unnecessarily, or if his paranoia were justified.

He could wait no longer. He knew Drew was home, that was enough. He performed a quick three point turn in the road, and drove back the way he had come, this time heading for the police station.

8.
Banks climbed out of Frank's car and climbed back in his own, fuming. He felt as though he was being treated as a suspect, but had no idea why. He had parked his car awkwardly at a bit of an angle, without any hazard lights, making it a bit of an obstacle on the road. The Inspector and Sergeant Gates watched him pull off and race quickly back toward Firestone.

'Excuse me.' Frank leant over the Inspector's knees to the passenger side of the dashboard and opened the glove compartment. The Inspector angled his legs out of the way awkwardly, allowing Frank to retrieve a roll of police line tape. The Inspector placed a friendly hand on his arm.

'Perhaps it would be for the best if we kept the exact location our secret for the time being,' he suggested. Frank thought a moment.

'Yes, perhaps you're right.' He closed the glove compartment drawer again, and the set off toward Nettlewood.

'I appreciate the lift, Sergeant.'

'Of course Inspector, we'll all be more than happy to help any way we can.' He thought of Banks for a moment. 'This ain't the sort of thing folks round here are used to, you know. I just hope it's all cleared up as quickly as possible.'

'I also share that sentiment.' The Inspector nodded. 'Not that you haven't been welcoming, and I am sure your town is delightful, but there is always some satisfaction in leaving, knowing that the circumstances have been explained.'

'Do you mean when the crime has been solved?' Frank asked, unsure of the Inspector's choice of words.

'Yes, I suppose I do,' the Inspector replied, though he did not seem convinced that this was an adequate interpretation.

'So, Sergeant, perhaps you could explain something that I am confused about.'

'Of course.'

'I cannot quite work out why Drew contacted you. I am sure he was unaware that this area of the woods comes under your jurisdiction, so why go to you? You are not his commanding officer, you did not give the order.' The Inspector asked the question nicely enough, and Frank realised it was a fair point to ask. The Inspector studied the side of Frank's face as he concentrated on the road ahead. There was a flicker in his eyes, a twitch perhaps as his mind raced to think of an adequate answer.

'I can't really answer that, you'd be best off talking to Drew,' he replied, deflecting the question. 'But from what I understand Banks had been drinking with the Mayor. Drew spoke to him first, but he could barely understand a word he said so he called me.' He knew Frank was hiding something. He had told the truth, but not quite all of it.

'Has he ever called you before, when Banks has perhaps been incapacitated?' The Inspector saw a smile creep into the corners of his mouth, and knew this was because Frank was about to tell him something that he was happy to share.

'Drew and I talk a lot. He was based at Nettlestone, I used to be his commanding officer. We were close, and he still calls to ask me questions, I give him advice, that's all.' The Inspector heard a tinge of regret in his tone. This still hadn't completely answered his question, but it leant him to presume the answer to be 'yes'; Drew called him when Banks wasn't acting on the best judgement.

'How do you think he feels about discussing these sorts of things with Banks?' he asked, leadingly.

'Again, Drew would be the best person to ask on that one.'

'I just want your opinion.' Frank nodded and shrugged.

'Well would you want to ask Banks for advice? You must have picked up on his style of policing already. Sending Drew out in that storm last night, parking in the bus stop at the railway station, he's a bit of a joke with the surrounding towns.'

'Why's that?'

'Because he's got the smallest beat of all us, but he still does bugger all!' Frank laughed. 'Not really his fault though, I think that's just Firestone.'

'How do you mean? Does it have a lot of trouble?'

'Not exactly, it just don't seem to have much going for it, like with the railway being taken out by Beaching's lot. It's like it's trying to just vanish off the map or something. People don't want to be there. We never hear of bad things happening in Firestone, but it's getting smaller and quieter every year. Wouldn't surprise me if it don't just vanish into the trees one day.'

'So why did Drew go there?' the Inspector asked. Again that awkwardness came over Frank. He wasn't telling him the whole truth.

'Nettlewood had reached capacity, staffing wise, and there was talk of cutting one of the bobbies there. When Sergeant O'Ryan retired from Firestone Drew went over there in the hope it would be a more secure position. Banks is getting on. He's got better prospects of advancing up the ladder in Firestone.'

'Before the trees swallow it up,' the Inspector remarked, though Frank did not respond. They had arrived on the outskirts of Nettlewood. New estates lining the roads with modern houses adorned with well-kept gardens. Low fences allowed passers-by to admire their picture postcard perfection. As they approached the centre the buildings became older, and the architecture took a turn to the Victorian. Long thin houses stacked elegantly along the roads. A vestige of the towns Tudor past sat disguised as a pub beside a row of houses. They drove through the centre of town, a parade of shops burgeoning into side streets that boasted a shoe shop, a chemist, and even a Woolworths. They passed through the centre and shops became houses again, and just outside of the town they came to a public house. It was set back from the road slightly, with a well-kept lawn outside. This was only broken by a friendly path leading to the large front door and a gravel drive down one side which led to a car park.

When they had safely pulled up both men climbed out and between them they removed the luggage. They carried it inside, depositing it in the hall and the Inspector approached the reception desk. The hotel was understated, allowing the natural features of the old building to be appreciated. The carpet was new, still thick and soft with lack of use. A bell sat on the reception and the Inspector gave it two 'pings' to announce his arrival. After a moment or two a short and largely built lady appeared from behind a door which led from the kitchen with a welcoming smile.

'Good morning gents,' the lady said, nodding respectfully to the men.

'Good morning, Mrs Fothergill is it?' the Inspector asked.

'Yes, how did you know that?' Mrs Fothergill adopted a look of surprise.

'Your name is above the door as licensee,' the Inspector pointed out.

'Oh yes of course!' Abigail Fothergill blushed slightly at the logical answer.

'I was also briefed on the booking by my secretary this morning; she advised you had been most understanding on the telephone, despite the hour of her call. Please accept my apologies for such a rude intrusion at that ungodly hour.' Abigail Fothergill was surprised that such an officious looking man could be so unoffending in his approach.

'I am the Inspector, down from Scotland Yard.' He offered his hand and she shook it gently.

'Nice to meet you. Honestly sir it's no problem, I was relieved in a way that it was nothing more serious. A telephone call at that hour usually means bad news.'

'You are too kind, Mrs Fothergill, too kind. I look forward to a pleasant stay under the roof of such an obliging hostess.'

'Only too happy to assist Inspector, my guess is it must be something very serious for you to come down in such an 'urry?'

'Indeed madam, it would appear an unfortunate young man has been killed, his body was discovered close by last night.' Abigail took in a sharp breath in surprise.

'A murder? Here? Well I never. Not in all my years has any such thing come along,'' she told him, shocked to her core.

'Have you been in the area long, then?' the Inspector asked, pushing the conversation away from the body again.

'All my life, been running this place most for of it with Mr Fothergill. Do we know who the poor chap was?'

'We do, and you will be relieved to know that it was not a local man.'

'Oh, well that is a small mercy I suppose.' She thought for moment. 'But, I mean, what with you being here and all, do you suspect someone from the town is responsible?'

'I sincerely hope not, but that is what I am here to ascertain.' She bit her lip for a moment in a worried reverie.

'As much as the Inspector and I would like to stand about and discuss the case with you Abigail, any chance we can get this luggage up to the room and get on?' Sergeant Banks spoke up from behind the Inspector.

'Oh yes of course I'm sorry where are my manners.' She flustered uncharacteristically with the guest book. 'Here you are sir, if I can just ask you for a few details, will you be paying now, or on departure?'

'If you don't mind I will settle up when I leave.' The Inspector filled his details in the book. 'As the duration of my stay is obviously dependant on how quickly the case is resolved, would it be possible to keep the room on an ongoing basis for now?'

'Of course sir, not as if we're bursting at the seams this time of year any way!' She checked the book, then turned and faced a set of hooks on the wall. Each hook had a number, some also had keys. She took down a key and handed it to the Inspector.

'Here you go sir, best room in the house.'

'Thank you, there is an en-suite?'
'Yes sir, just as the lady asked on the telephone last night.'
'Marvellous. There is just one thing.'
'Yes sir?' Abigail asked, eager to assist.
'Please just call me Inspector, I always feel "sir" is so formal.'
'Of course, Inspector, now, I'll just show you up to your room, hold on let me get Harold to help with those bags.' She turned from them and poked her head through a door behind the counter that led to the kitchen.

'Harold!' she bellowed at the top of her voice. 'Come and help with the Inspector's baggage!' There was a muffled reply that neither man was able to catch, and after a moment a beleaguered figure appeared from the kitchen. He was shorter that his wife, with heavy bags under tired watery eyes. He looked as though he had the world on his shoulders and had been hard pressed by his wife for longer than he had been on Earth. He paid no mind to the men, not even to say "good morning". He picked up the biggest of the bags, giving an involuntary grunt under the weight as he did.

'Stop complaining and get on with it!' She snapped at him immediately. She lifted a part of the desk up that separated them and left the reception.

'This way Sergeant, Inspector.' She led them further down the corridor to a staircase that crept steeply to the higher storeys, followed by the Inspector carrying his briefcase, Sergeant Gates carrying the smaller of the cases, and Harold Fothergill struggling silently with the heaviest. The staircase was as thin as it was steep, Abigail's hips barely squeezing through the small gap. She made her way slowly up, her knees giving the occasion snap as her tendons struggled to carry her bulky form. Harold found the going difficult under the weight of the cases, and the sound of their scrapping on the walls followed them up the stairs.

'You be careful with those cases on my newly decorated walls Harold Fothergill,' she called out as they ascended. 'If you tear my nice new wallpaper you'll be sleeping in the chicken coop again.' Harold gave no reply other than a long resigned sigh, and the cases' passage up the stairs gave new meaning to the word "silent". The staircase, like the rest of the hotel, had obviously been recently refurbished. The wallpaper had a modern pattern repeating on it, like purple sand pouring through orange huge hourglasses from ceiling to floor. The pattern flooded the stairwell with bright colours. The clean soft carpet was covered with an intricate interweaving pattern of brightly coloured shapes, reds blacks and greens flowed together seamlessly. The brightly decorated walls remained unscathed as Harold trudged doggedly on. When they reached the first floor the corridor widened and they found themselves flanked by doors on either side, interspersed with tasteful unchallenging pictures. A bowl of fruit, a vase of flowers, the pictures were not there to be admired and so little thought had gone into their choosing. The bright hourglass paper followed them up and filled the space making it feel crowded.

'Here we are then, room seven, got a lovely view out of the window in here you have Inspector.' She unlocked the door and opened it wide. The view was indeed remarkable. Facing across the broad open fens that surrounded Nettlewood, the window afforded its occupants a sweeping expanse of the stretching hills and farmland. In this room the wallpaper was replaced with orange peel paint. Lime tinted curtains flanked the window.

'Well indeed that is a magnificent view, though I am afraid it will be wasted on me, as I shall be spending little of my time looking through the window,' he told her kindly. The Inspector left his entourage admiring the hotel's surroundings and instead made directly for the bathroom. He clicked the light on, then off again immediately. He wandered across the bathroom, pausing under the light to check the light bulb, then closed the door behind him. His hosts and the police Sergeant listened as he turned the light on and off, before re-emerging.

'Excellent facilities I must say,' he remarked on his exit. 'Has the entire establishment been redecorated recently?'

'Yes sir, just last month, we only reopened two weeks ago.'

'How fortuitous for me. Well, thank you so much for showing me to my room, however I'm afraid I must be moving on.'

'Of course Inspector, you'll no doubt be wanting to get on with your inspecting.'

'Indeed. Mrs Fothergill, the nature of my work often requires me to work long hours, would it be too much to ask for a front door key, to prevent any disturbance to you and your husband should I return to my lodgings in the small hours?'

'Oh, we don't have a spare, but I could get one cut for you, should you think it necessary.' She cast a worried eye at the set of keys in the Inspector's hand, as if she should have thought of that herself.

'I would be most grateful, and any costs will of course be reimbursed.'

'I'll get on to it straight away for you sir... Sorry, Inspector.' She turned to the downtrodden Mr Fothergill and shot him a look he was no doubt well accustomed to which was easily translated as "Get on with it".

'Wonderful. Now, Sergeant, we must be getting on. Lovely to have met you both, see you again later today, I hope, for dinner.'

'Thank you Inspector, yes, see you later.' The Inspector and Sergeant Gates left them in room seven and made their way back through the hotel and out into the grey morning.

'An interesting couple,' the Inspector commented to Sergeant Gates as they buckled their seat belts.

'They've always been like that you know, I think in all the years I've known them I've only heard poor Harold say half a dozen words, and all of those were when Abigail was out of ear shot.' The Inspector nodded with a small smile.

'Well they have a remarkable establishment. It would seem she runs a tight ship.'

'Got the staff living in fear she has, but that's why it's the nicest place hereabouts. Now, where next Inspector?'

'I think we should have a chat with the Major, there is a chance that he perhaps saw something more than just a fallen tree on the road last night.'

'As you wish.' The Sergeant pulled the car back out on to the road. 'He's back in Firestone,' Frank mentioned, hinting that they could have gone there first and so saved them the journey to Nettlestone and back. The Inspector appreciated the point he was making.

'Yes, I am aware of that, but I thought it best to allow him a little time to sleep, after all he did have a late night.'

'Sorry, I didn't mean to sound annoyed.'

'No apology necessary, I appreciate you taxiing me about the place.' They trundled along the twisting road that linked the two towns, the car disturbing dreamy puddles that reflected the cloud racing over their heads. As they approached the smaller town a drizzle attempted to start. It seemed to match Firestone in its dreariness. As they entered the buildings the drizzle petered out again, as if even the simple effort of falling from the sky was too much to endure. They came to Firestone's busiest crossroads on the outskirts of the town, which was governed by a roundabout of sorts. It was roughly twenty yards across, shaped like a square, with a row of shops lined against one of the opposite sides. It was covered in short hardy grass. At its centre, positioned at the peak of a small rise, stood a stone pillar. This protruded from the ground roughly four feet high, its width was about two feet by three feet. Its top face had a smooth channel carved from it, cutting the face in half across shortest path. It was a cold hard stump of rock, discoloured with a faded crimson.

'An interesting landmark,' the Inspector commented as they passed it. The Sergeant didn't notice what the Inspector was referring to; he was so used to its presence that it had merged into the scenery.

'What's that, sorry?' he asked as he drove them on toward the Major's house.

'The pillar on the roundabout, it's an interesting land mark,' the Inspector repeated, a little louder.

'Oh that, that's the Firestone that gives the town its name.' He replied airily.

'I say, how interesting. Why do they call it the Firestone?'

'If you look closely it has a red stain on top, like fire. If you believe the old wives' tales, and I should say that many around here do, the red comes from the blood of those that were beheaded on it.'

'My, what a ghastly story,' the Inspector thought for a moment, 'who was beheaded on it then? And why?' he asked, rather concerned.

'Story goes it was witches that lost their heads there,' the Sergeant informed him casually, as if the story was hardly worth telling.

'People say that back in the dark ages Firestone wasn't so much a town as a coven, a hot spot for magic and those that practiced it. The witches all worshiped, or did whatever it is that witches do, around the Firestone. One day the church came along and killed the lot of them, and to show they meant business they did all the killing on the object of their worship, their stone pillar. Since then it's been stained red, like fire, with the blood of all those that were killed on it. Over the centuries it became called the Firestone, and the town took the name too, sort of a warning to other witches.'

'For such a small town it seems Firestone has a dark past.'

'That it does, and it's a past that seems to hold on to it, like it won't go away and let the town forget what horrible things have supposed to have happened here.'

'Towns don't have memories, Sergeant, people do.'

'You're right, you know, and perhaps that's the problem, the people here all remember it too somehow. Like the memory is imbedded in everything, the people are just another part of it. The Inspector raised his eyebrows and pursued the matter no further. Frank tried to gauge what he was thinking, but it was impossible to penetrate the dark eyes, even when he wasn't driving. He was surprised at how much information, even personal opinions, that he had revealed to him with such little probing. He felt relieved to be revealing these things, as if the Inspector needed to know them.

They drove on into town, and out the other side again. The Major's house was on the furthest west point of the copse, a small bungalow buried in a cacophony of plant life. Frank parked up next to a Rolls Royce 1960 Silver Cloud and they stepped out of their car. The Inspector took a look around the Major's impressive mode of transport.

'Nice isn't it?' Frank called as he made his way round in envy.

'Yes, I'm sure,' the Inspector replied distractedly. Frank realised he wasn't interested in the car itself but the story told by its exterior.

'Looks like the Major did hit the fallen tree, but not with enough force to do any damage.' The Inspector picked away a stray twig that had fastened itself to the dirty grill. 'His wings are muddy, but not enough to suggest that he had driven into a muddy clearing. I think we can safely remove Major... what's his name again?'

'Hammond, Major Leonard Hammond,' Frank informed him.

'Thank you, Sergeant. We can remove Major Hammond from our list of suspects.'

'So do we still need to talk to him?' The Inspector was peering in through the driver's side window, admiring the interior. He glanced at his wrist.

'Indeed we do. What time do you make it?' Frank checked his watch.

'Just coming up to eleven.'

'Yes, that's what time I have. I think then it is no longer too early to speak to our Major.' He walked slowly past Frank to the door and knocked on it confidently. The Sergeant joined him at the threshold and they waited for a reply. After a few moments a loud voice came booming from the other side.

'Who is it?'

'Morning Major, I'm an Inspector, down from Scotland Yard. A body's been found, I was wondering if I could ask you a few questions.'

'I don't know anything about a body,' replied the disembodied voice sternly.

'Yes we know that Major, but you are inadvertently responsible for its discovery.' There was a pause, a lock snapped out of its latch, and the door opened a few inches. A face appeared in the gap. The Major noticed Frank and his eyes peered suspiciously at them both.

'You're not from Firestone,' he informed them resentfully.

'No, the body was discovered in Sergeant Gates' jurisdiction, next door in Nettlewood. Constable Drew found it after clearing a fallen tree last night at around one thirty, along Beaper Shute.' The latch was removed and the door opened.

The Major was wearing a full tweed suit with waist jacket, formal tie, and gleaming black shoes.

'I reported a tree down in the road last night, was it the same one?' he asked, trepidly.

'Indeed it was,' the Inspector confirmed.

'Well I suppose you had better come in.' The Major was flustered at the disturbance to his morning, and by the news of a body being discovered as a consequence of his actions. His bungalow was full of ornaments, every surface had a china animal perched on it, perfectly dustless. Despite the overcrowded feeling the house was neat and entirely spotless. Mozart floated through to them from a sitting room in the rear of the house.

'Would you care for some tea?' he asked, more out of resignation at the arrival of his unwanted guests than courtesy.

'Yes please that would be most agreeable, thank you,' the Inspector replied for them both.

'You go through to the living room, just follow Eine Kleine Nachtmusik. Make yourself comfortable I'll be through in a moment,' he told them with a sigh. While the Major busied himself in the kitchen, the closest room to the front door, Frank and the Inspector made their way down the corridor, passed the open door of a study come library, and into the living room. In the centre of the room two old but comfortable looking leather sofas sat in an 'L' shape, one faced a long glass door that lead into the back garden and the other faced a wooden cabinet containing a television. In the centre sat an oval table with an open copy of the day's paper on it. Around the walls stood cabinets full of more ornaments, a chest of drawers, and a gramophone from which came the magical tones of Mozart. The walls were adorned with blurry black and white pictures of soldiers, and dangerous looking swords.

The two men wandered about the room, studying the various photographs, trying to fathom the need for so many small ornaments in such a small place, protected so fiercely. Presently the Major joined them, with the tea on a tray large wooden tray. He placed it carefully down on the table atop the newspaper, and then moved round to lower the gramophone volume.

'Seems a shame to interrupt such beauty midway through,' the Inspector remarked distractedly. The Major sat and stirred the pot. He noticed the Inspector was looking at his war photographs, images of him in Africa in 1943, including one where he was in close proximity to General Montague.

'I'm the short one with all the hair,' he informed the Inspector helpfully. For a short time I was stationed directly under Monty. Hell of a leader. Did you see any action Inspector?'

'I was injured at Dunkirk,' the Inspector informed him in a business like fashion. 'I spent the remainder of the war behind a desk in Whitehall, so no such excitement for me.' The Major nodded.

'The war machine has many cogs, each as important as the other,' he told him condescendingly.

'Hmm,' the Inspector replied simply, coming to the table as if attracted by the clinking of the cups. Frank was too young to have fought in the war, but could tell the Inspector wasn't quite as proud of the Major's war efforts as the Major had hoped he would be. The Major stirred the pot.

'Sugar, Sergeant?' he asked Frank as way of inviting him to join them so their interview could commence.

'Two please.' Frank made his way to the sofa and sat down next to the Inspector. The Major dropped two sugars into a cup and turned to the Inspector.

'None for me thank you.' The Major poured hot brown tea into all three cups, and then poured the milk on top. Clouds blossomed and swirled into existence inside the china bowls, eddying into effortless beauty as the white milk and brown tea mingled. The storm's beauty was suddenly destroyed as the Major dipped in his spoon and stirred the cup's contents together. He passed each man his drink.

'Thank you so much.' The Inspector received his gratefully and immediately took a large swig. Frank accepted his with a nod and put it down on the table.

'Mmmm very nice,' the Inspector commented half to himself, as he replaced the cup in the saucer and put them on the table.

'So, Major, I just want you to understand that you are in no way a suspect in this investigation, I am of course interviewing you as a matter of procedure.' He reached into his coat and took out his notebook and pencil. 'Should you feel uncomfortable with my questioning or wish to have a solicitor present that is your prerogative, but it will delay the investigation and, if I'm honest, is totally unnecessary.'

'I understand, but I have nothing to hide Inspector, please carry on.'

'Indeed. So, could you please start by telling us what you were doing last night?'

'Of course.' He settled back in his chair comfortably. 'I was a guest at a charity ball raising money for wounded war veterans,' he told them proudly. The Inspector began scribbling.

'I see, and whereabouts did it take place?' the Inspector asked.

'North London, well Hemel Hempsted to be precise, just outside the capital,' the Major informed him.

'How did the fundraising go?' the Inspector asked with a smile.

'Very well. They were looking to raise two thousand pounds, and I believe they were close to the mark at the end. They had an auction, I donated a few of my wives' damned ornaments that are still cluttering up the place. The tickets were ten pounds a pop, it was a very auspicious occasion.'

'I am glad. And what time did the event end?'

'It finished at nine, I stayed a little later to talk to some of the organisers to whom I have a close friendship, and left about ten.'

'I see. And then you drove home, in the car that's parked outside?'

'Yes, that's right. I got home about one forty, phoned Banks straight away and he said he'd get one his of his boys to have a look.

'And what made you telephone Banks at that hour?' the Inspector asked.

'We have an understanding, you know, the men of this town,' he replied, eluding to his being a position higher than theirs, 'if we see trouble we let someone know about it,' he told them, as if this were all the explanation needed. He had quite a thick local accent and the Inspector struggled to understand everything he said. He had suspected there would be some ring of men, respected in the town that protected it in this way. It was not as uncommon as the Major hoped. The Inspector could tell from the Major's behaviour he had no interest in the body. Much happier was he to wallow in his status.

'How long does the journey usually take?' the Inspector asked.

'On an ordinary night I can be back in about two hours, but as I approached the midlands the weather turned and I couldn't travel as quickly.'

'I see, and so how long did it take you to get back?'

'Well as I say I left at ten, and I called Banks about one forty I suppose,' the Major informed him.

'So three hours to do a two hour trip, were conditions so bad that they added an hour to your journey?'

'Are you suggesting I had an hour to murder someone and hide their body in the copse on my way home?' the Major asked defensively.

'Oh my no, I am simply concerned about the time it took for you to get home. Never mind for now. You have an alibi for last night, as I imagined you would. I briefly cast my eyes over the exterior of your car and I am satisfied that it went nowhere near the site where the body was discovered. All that remains is for me to inspect the interior, with a particular interest in the clock, and we can leave you to finish your morning paper in peace.' The Major was rather surprised, as if he was escaping easily.

'Very good.' He wasn't sure how looking at the car's clock would help the investigation, but could see no harm in it.

'Wonderful, such marvellous automobiles,' the Inspector enthused.

'I'll just get my keys and I will show you out.' Major Hammond headed to his bedroom while the two policemen finished their cups of tea. Frank sat in quiet contemplation for a moment, trying to calculate the best way to ask the Inspector what relevance the clock may have had.

'Inspector....' he began, but before he could go any further the Major re-entered the room.

'Here we are then, gentlemen.' The Inspector and Frank rose and followed him back through the thin corridor and on to the drive where the Rolls sat. The Inspector walked around it again.

'Very good,' he said, though to no one in particular as he took one last careful look around the car. He peered in through the window.

'From the exterior of your car and I am satisfied that it went nowhere near the site where the body was discovered, I would just like to investigate the interior a little closer if you don't mind.'

The Major opened the passenger side door for him and he made directly for the clock. This was positioned on the door of the glove compartment on the passenger's side, and the Inspector studied it carefully. It was set safely and securely into the cabinet. He took the time from it.

'What time does your watch say, Major?' he asked. The Major looked at his watch.

'Ten Fifty,' he replied loftily, anxious to have the two men out of his car and out of his life so he could return to his paper and continue his morning.

'Hmmm, that is the same time that your car's clock says,' the Inspector replied, a concerned look on his face. The two men looked blankly at him. He noticed this, and so added an explanation.

'Your watch and the clock in your car are both seventeen minutes fast.' He held his own watch up for the Major to see. Indeed, it told anyone that cared to look that the time was in fact ten thirty three.

'Sergeant I am sure your watch will verify this?' the Major asked. Frank checked his watch.

'Indeed sir, although I keep mine a little fast, mine says ten thirty eight,' Frank agreed.

'Well, that's preposterous, what is the meaning Inspector?' Major Hammond asked in shock.

'Well...' the Inspector started, thinking aloud to himself. 'The only thing that could have caused something like this would be an electromagnetic disturbance that you probably experienced whilst driving home last night,' he stroked his chin thoughtfully. 'But for it to have pushed them both so far forward...' he shook his head. 'It would have to have been...' he trailed off, suddenly conscious of the men watching him, and where the train of thought was leading him.

'That is a very good question Major, and one I shall add to my gradually growing list of questions that require attention,' the Inspector told him confidently. The Major wasn't sure if that satisfied his question but let it rest. 'For now we can leave you to finish your morning paper in peace.' The Major wasn't sure he was happy to have the Inspector leave without a satisfactory explanation.

'Did you listen to the radio on the way home?' the Inspector asked suddenly.

'No, there's nothing on the air waves at that time of the morning,' the Major replied.

'Of course, excuse my ignorance. Would you mind turning the radio on for me?' The Major was too bemused to argue, so he climbed into the driver's seat, turned the ignition and switched the radio on. It hummed slowly into life, coming in midway through a Correli sonata.

'Wonderful, thank you, you may switch it off again at your leisure,' the Inspector advised, but for a moment the Major let the radio play and the woods around them filled with the subtle baroque tones.

The three men stood for a few quiet moments, studying the car. The trees began swaying as the wind picked up, and a chill whistled between them, as if urging them apart, pushing the policemen on with their investigation.

'Well Major, thank you so much for the tea, and I apologise for the interruption to your morning. I am satisfied, so Sergeant, let us leave Major Hammond in peace.' Without a word Frank headed for his squad car.

'Oh one last thing Major, if you do happen to notice anything else odd about the car, or think of something from last night that seemed odd, please call the station at Nettlewood so either myself or Sergeant Gates here can investigate.'

'Anything else odd? Like what?'

'I don't know, just anything odd.' The Inspector opened the passenger side door of the car, and raised his hat a few inches off of his head.

'Good day Major,' the Major stood still, rooted to the spot.

'Yes, good day Inspector,' he replied. He watched the men trundle away then returned to his paper with a shake of his head.

9.

Drew awoke with the uneasy feeling of having slept but not properly rested. His mind took a few moments to wake up, and he tried to remember why he was in bed so late in the day. When the memory of the previous evening surfaced he wished he could forget it again, and that it had all been part of some nightmare. He stayed in bed, staring at the roughly patterned ceiling, allowing his eyes to find hidden patterns in the ridges. This helped him to escape the image in his mind's eye of the body, the deepening pool of blood, and the eyes that had led him to the clearing. Eventually hunger got the better of him, and he pulled himself out of bed and into his dressing gown. He slowly traipsed downstairs barefoot, ignoring the pile of letters on the doormat, and he went through to the small kitchen. He switched on the grill and while it warmed up he cut two thick slices from a half loaf of bread which he placed under it. The kettle was switched on and he made himself a cup of tea. While it brewed he stood and stared out of the window, and was quickly lost again to the looping film of the previous night that played itself over and over in his mind. The weather had calmed from last night, and was in much the same mood as it had been when Banks and Frank had found him. It was only at this point that he remembered the third man, the Inspector. He wanted to know everything, "*No matter how strange it might sound*" he recalled were his words. Drew sighed and watched the trees blowing dreamily in the wind. Would the truth end his short career in policing? Would hiding the truth allow a murderer to go unpunished? He was only disturbed from the reverie when the smell of burning alerted him to the toast. He quickly removed the grill from the heat but it was too late, the bread was burned on one side and still pale and white on the other. He threw the wasted effort into the bin, sliced another two from the loaf, and tried again. This time he sat and watched as the bread slowly changed colour, turning it when the brown was warm, friendly, and smelt delicious. He then watched the other side slowly brown, the process was quite therapeutic, almost beautiful to watch.

He buttered the toast, sipped his tea, continuing his vigil out of the window and as he crunched through the first slice. He thought hard about the eyes. He needed to know what they were, even if the explanation sounded mad. It was this thirst for an explanation that had made him follow them into the copse in the first place, and he cursed his inquisitiveness. He cursed Banks for his lack of knowledge on basic police procedures. He cursed Frank for putting him here in the first place, but realised that there was no one to blame but himself. At any point in the past twelve months he could have said "no" to any of the requests that had been put to him, but he hadn't. He was too good a policeman, too dedicated to his job and the memory of his father to disagree with anything that was asked of him.

He realised that the only thing he could do was tell the Inspector everything and hope that he could offer an explanation to him as to what had happened, and what he had seen. The more he dwelled on what could have been the more explanations came into his head, and none of them favoured his sanity. He realised suddenly that he had stopped eating, he wasn't sure how long ago his hand had stopped moving back and forth to his mouth but the toast was cold and the tea had stopped steaming.

His kitchen clock ticked resolutely on, heading undaunted in the second half of eleven o clock. His mind had been made up, there was only one man he could talk to about his experience last night, and though the consequences of his honesty weighed on his mind, the thought of keeping his secret and slowly driving himself into madness weighed heavier. He put more water in the kettle to make a fresh brew, and while water slowly heated on the gas stove he went to the telephone in the hall way and called Nettlewood station to announce his readiness of an interview with the Inspector.

10.

'There's a fog forming,' Frank commented conversationally as he drove the two men away from the Major's bungalow. The Inspector gazed out of the window. Indeed a fog was forming, though it was still low, barely above knee height, as the meagre heat of the late morning forced the moisture from the previous night back into the air. The grey mist crept eerily up, whooshing into confused eddies as the Ford Anglia trundled carefully back along the road and toward Firestone.

'Indeed. It is quite beautiful after a tremulous night,' the Inspector replied. 'Although I fear the storm is far from over.'

Before the Sergeant had a chance to question the Inspector's analogous comment, the radio in his car suddenly crackled into life. Between shrieks of static a woman's voice could be heard saying;

'NW2 this is base, come in, over.' Frank picked up the receiver.

'This is NW2, go ahead Dorothy, over.'

'Morning Sarge, just had a call from Drew, he's up and about, says he's ready to speak to the Inspector now, over.'

'Roger that Dorothy, I'll get back to you when we know our schedule, over.'

'Right you are Sarge, you know where I am, over and out.' The radio spat static at them for a moment then went back to its previous silence.

'Well, no time like the present, shall we head for young Drew's house now?'

'It might be proper to warn him we're on our way,' Frank protested gently.

'Nonsense, I am sure he is as eager to speak to me as I am to listen to him. Let us get to him so as to ease his mind of the burden.' Frank frowned and failed to hide it from the Inspector, but did not follow up on the comment. There was no need to change their course, Drew's house was in a pocket of houses on the outskirts of Firestone but the Major's was further out, and so they trundled through the fog and between the trees toward Drew's small home. The Inspector left Frank in his thoughtful reverie, indifferent to the reasons for his silence. Frank thought about what the Inspector meant about the storm not being over, and the burden Drew carried. Shortly they reached Drew's house and Frank pulled up outside, parking across the drive. He had stopped the engine and unbuckled his seatbelt before the Inspector spoke.

'Thank you for your services as taxi Sergeant, I am aware that the task is, perhaps, a little below a man of your stature. I am sure you have matters of a more pressing nature awaiting you at Nettlewood station, so perhaps it would be best if you attend to them and leave me to talk to young Drew alone. No doubt he will be more than happy to drive me back to the station later.' He uttered the words with such finality as to not allow Frank any room for argument. Frank was eager to see Drew himself, to reassure him, and to receive a report on the events he had witnessed. As if conscious of this the Inspector continued;

'There will be ample time for you and Drew to converse, but for now I need to see him alone.' Frank wanted to see Drew but also found himself grateful to be leaving the Inspector behind. Though he gave a friendly air of openness, and was approachable and considerate of the situation that had fallen upon the town, he was also hugely intimidating. Frank wanted nothing more than to leave him behind and immerse himself in the familiar goings on of his small constabulary. He knew this meant leaving Drew to experience the strange effect this man had on people, and he felt guilt and self-reprieve at leaving him at the poor boy's doorstep unexpected and unannounced, but he also realised he was powerless to do anything else.

'Of course, please wish Drew my best, if either of you need me I will be at Nettlewood waiting for your call,' he found himself saying unwillingly. The Inspector swung open his door and stepped out into steadily thickening fog.

'Indeed, thank you again Sergeant, see you soon I'm sure,' he replied. Powerless to stop him, unable to probe the Inspector on this or any of his other leading comments, the Sergeant started the engine and pulled away into the misty morning as the Inspector walked up the drive and rapped his knuckles on the front door three times.

11.

Drew replaced the receiver and tapped the handset thoughtfully. He was aware he had no choice in what he had to do, but he still felt a twist of unease in his stomach at the events that would now follow. He returned to the kitchen and poured the boiled water on to the leaves into the pot, then slowly stalked upstairs where he brushed his teeth and dressed not in his uniform but into comfortable jeans and a dark red shirt. Somehow being dressed made him feel more confident, gave him a greater conviction in his story. He descended the stairs and finished making the tea, then passed into his living room where he switched on the wireless. He had it tuned, as always, to the world service, and he listened to an interview with the minister of farming while he waited for the News at eleven. Hearing the drone of the voices, the dullness of the subject, gave him a greater distance from the reality he faced. Outside of the woods, beyond the limits of the trees, the world continued to twist and turn with the daily traumas that people fought to overcome and adapt to. Now his own burden had been added to, and he wondered if he had the strength of mind to see it through to the conclusion, and what form that conclusion would take when it arrived. He wondered how it would shape him, where he would be when the end finally came. He blew air across the surface of his tea and watched steam as it drifted and dissipated into the room. Would this be the end of his career or set his reputation as a reliable Constable in stone? He sighed at the unknown. The right path might not lead him where he wanted but it remained the correct path. His mind was set, he would have to ride the wave and hope he found land. The News had started and finished without his attention being caught, and the radio now filled the air with the noise of a classical piece he did not recognise, but it still soothed his tired mind.

Three knocks at the door suddenly echoed through the building. He was caught unawares and stood absently, wondering who might be visiting him so late in the morning when he might ordinarily have been walking his beat, or sitting behind his desk writing a report regarding a stolen pint of milk or a missing cat. He had half a mind not to answer it; he was more concerned about when the telephone would ring to warn him of the Inspector's arrival. He was therefore unable to hide his surprise when he opened it to find him standing on the threshold.

'Good morning Drew, I understand you are now feeling sufficiently rested to allow me the opportunity to question you?' The Inspector explained with a comforting smile.

'Yes Inspector,' Drew faltered for a moment, flustered at the unexpected arrival of the future, of the lack of preparation he had been given. 'I was expecting a telephone call, you came awfully quickly.'

'My apologies, I admittedly took a chance on calling unannounced. I imagined you would be as eager talk to me as I am to listen to you.' Drew paused for a moment. The Inspector, though serious in his tone, remained approachable and Drew felt an overwhelming desire to trust him.

'Yes, of course. Delaying will only hold up your investigation, though I don't know what, if anything, you can learn from what I witnessed. Or think I witnessed.' The Inspector nodded reassuringly.

'Whatever you tell me will be taken in the strictest of confidence.' Drew stared at the hall carpet lost in his thoughts, the Inspector waited what seemed to be a polite amount of time, before asking;

'May I come in? It smells as though a fresh pot of tea has been made recently, perhaps you could make me a cup and we can chat?' Drew returned to the present with a shake of the head.

'Sorry, where are my manners, please come through.' The Inspector entered the house and was immediately hit by the sparseness of the place and the feeling of transience, of non-permanence that echoed from the bare walls and packing boxes. The Inspector removed his coat and followed Drew through to the kitchen where he made the Inspector a cup of tea. When they were both seated as comfortably as they could be on the creaking wood of the old chairs around the rickety table, they took a few sips of their tea.

'So, why don't you begin at the beginning, with the telephone call you received from Banks. I won't interrupt or pose any questions to you until you reach the point that you arrived back in your bed.' Drew took a deep breath, and told the Inspector everything. The telephone call, the slur in the Sergeant's voice. He let flow his feelings toward Banks, and the long list of jobs out of his jurisdiction that had led to his clearing of the tree. The Inspector nodded, sipped his tea, and listened intently. Drew could not hold his gaze for long, his attention would drift to the steam from his tea, to the trees outside of the window and the fog that was slowly encapsulating them. He explained about the weather, the atrociousness of the conditions that made him want to lock all the doors and windows and hide under his duvet. He found himself revealing these candid feelings that he had not even wanted to admit to himself. He found that saying them out loud made them easier to bear, until he reached the part of the tale where he saw the lights in his mirror.

'I wanted to move away from the turn in the road, to find a safe place to turn around, and as I pulled away I saw in my mirror...' He trailed off, and suddenly the movement of the branches outside his window became hypnotising. He drifted off, the Inspector remained silent, waiting, listening. He allowed Drew to find confidence.

'... two lights, I presumed them to be headlights, except...' he paused again, his mind fought with the words he knew he had to say, battling with his better judgement as he tried to turn the thoughts to words.

'... they were too high from the ground, they appeared in the exact spot I had just driven through, they weren't moving, and, I felt as if they were watching me, or more like I was being dissected, scanned by them. And although I was full of fear I found myself putting the car into reverse and backing up to them to try and work out what they were.' The trees swayed, and he found watching their rhythmic movement through mist helped him focus. They forced him on, forced him to relive the moment.

'As I got closer they moved, off of the road, into the trees, where they disappeared. I could just make out a track in my headlights, so I turned the car into the trees and followed them in. I lost control of the car as it slid into the centre of the mud. I got out and looked around, I looked all around the mud, around the trees, I took photographs to try and see what was going on in the light of the flash, it was brighter than my torch, but I couldn't see anything. Even if it was daylight I doubt I would have been able to see any movement, the trees were so thick there were a million places to hide. My mind played tricks on me, turning shapes between the trees into crouching figures, trunks became people hiding. The search was beyond me, it was an impossible task, but one thing I didn't see was anything that could have had head lights as bright as the lights I had seen in my mirror. There were no vehicles, no tracks, well you saw for yourself I was the only person to have driven into that place, perhaps the only person to have ever driven in there. Eventually I gave up through fear and exhaustion. I had already realised that I would be spending the night in that horrible place, so I returned to the car to settle down. It wasn't until I went to turn the lights off that I saw it, the body I mean, laying in the mud. As I told you earlier I hadn't seen it there before. I had been back and forth to the car, and the lights had been on the whole time, for what good they were, and I hadn't seen it. Then I radioed Banks to tell him, but I wasn't sure about what he told me, so I radioed through to Frank to tell him where I was and what I had found. He told me to stay there, he rightly pointed out that he had no chance of finding me in the storm and as long as I secured the car I was relatively safe. He said he would have to talk to Scotland Yard about what had happened and to ask for guidance, which is where you come in. I covered the body as best I could to try and preserve any evidence that might have been left behind, then I settled down in the back seat but I didn't really sleep much, I was too scared that whoever had put that poor man there was still around and would want to do something similar to me. I guess I must have drifted into a doze though because I woke just before you arrived with Banks and Frank. I heard you before I saw you, the branches scraping down the side of the cars made a hell of a racket. Then I suppose you know the rest, I showed you around the site, we got the car out, then I drove home. I had a bath and went to bed.' Drew realised he had been talking for a few minutes without stopping, he just stared out of the window at the swaying branches. The Inspector remained silent and waited to see if there was anything else that he wanted to share.

'When I woke up I had a cuppa, burnt some toast, then called the station.'

'Thank you Drew, that's a very helpful account of what happened,' the Inspector replied when he was sure Drew had finished. There was a moment of silence as the Inspector thought through the story. Drew reasoned that he was thinking on the lights.

'I know how some of it must sound, the lights, I mean. I've been trying to find a logical explanation for them, perhaps it was an odd reflection of the moon, I don't know.'

'They are indeed at the crux of your discovery, leading you so inexplicably as they did into the woods and to the body.' The Inspector shifted a little awkwardly on the uncomfortable chair.

'Rest assured that I believe you. I am not here to accuse you of anything. In normal circumstances you would be our prime suspect. It stands to reason. However, these are not normal circumstances. Perhaps I should explain a little about the sort of investigations that the department I work with are involved in. I work for the

Department of External Affairs. We deal with cases that have no apparent cause, or that are beyond the understanding of the local police. Missing persons, unexplainable appearances of persons, mysterious appearances of bodies, these things happen often enough to warrant their own investigative force. We are part of the yard, we have our own means of investigation, and we don't always find explanations that would fit with the conventional.' Drew sat and listened intently with the feeling he was privy to information not usually shared.

'I tell you these things because you are my prime witness. I will require you to work with me closely. Anything we see you must keep a close secret.' He reached for his case. 'And I need you to sign this.' He pushed a wodge of paper across the table toward him.

'You may have heard of the official secrets act, this is similar but goes a lot further. It is more thorough, and anything that we will report on will remain a secret. If the truth became public there is a strong chance that society would not be able to cope with the truth and the strange forms it takes in the shadows and whispers our senses usually ignore.'

Drew's eyes flicked through the incomprehensible language the document contained and he read a few points randomly.

"Events or non events that witnesses comprehend to be real or imagined are property of HM Constabulary."

"Any communication regarding any such events whether this be verbal, written or communicated psychically will be treated as an act of treason against the crown."

"Ways and means beyond the average understanding are shaping and defining the lives and realities experienced by the general public on a minute by minute basis and the undersigned recognises that any part of their lives affected thusly will remain unchangeable."

Drew looked up shaking his head in confusion.

'What does it all mean, what will it mean to me, and to my life, my career?'

'Excellent questions. Essentially it means that you no longer own the memories you are making. They belong to Her Majesty. Any attempt you make to share them with anyone other than myself, or any of our colleagues from the department will be taken very gravely.'

'That's all very serious,' Drew pointed out, flicking through the thick document he was expected to sign. 'What if I refuse?'

'Refusal is seen as a break in the contract. You're already in the loop, Drew. You're a young man at a crossroads not just in his career but in his life. Sign and you will discover that there is more to this world than you thought ever existed, don't sign and this path will be forever closed to you and you will always wonder what it is you said no to as you rot in a cell deep in the country's most secure mental institution.' Drew's jaw dropped in shock and fear, his eyes widened as his life flashed before them.

'Sorry, that last bit was meant to be a joke.' The Inspector smiled timidly, offering him a pen. 'If you don't sign then I take your statement, I walk out and continue my investigation without you. Honestly that's all.'

Drew took the pen and held it hovering over the dotted line, his hand steady and still. He found the invitation too interesting, and greatly desired to investigate it. He knew he was going to sign, but enjoyed the last few moments of normality before the ink was on the paper.

He then traced his signature and the date, slowly and carefully, across the dotted line. He passed the confusing document back to the Inspector, who placed it carefully into his bag.

'Thank you, now can you please relate as best you can the conversation you had with Banks last night after you discovered the body, and what he told you to do.' the Inspector asked. His words were stern, but diplomatic and business like. This was the professional side of the Inspector: logical, meticulous, and determined.

12.

The wind and rain battered his squad car relentlessly, adding to the feeling of abandonment. Drew picked up the receiver on his car's radio and waited for the operator to pick up his call.

'What number please?' Drew paused to consider. Banks was always first, that was the rule.

'Sergeant Banks 5945.'

'Please wait.' The line went dead for a second and the night felt a little darker. Drew switched his headlights back on to check the body was still there, and wasn't sure to be glad or not when he saw the man's back, arms out stretched, legs laying at awkward angles. Presently there was a ringing tone from the receiver. It rang for a long time before being picked up.

'Who the hell is this? What the bloody hell are you calling me at this hour for?' Banks yelled down the telephone. Drew pulled the receiver away from his ear and waited for him calm down.

'It's Drew, Sarge. I'm...'

'I told you not to call me you bloody fool. What is it?'

'I found a body, in the woods.' Drew spoke quickly, there was a silence from the other end.

'You, you've what?' Banks shouted. Drew could almost see the expression on his face as his brain tried to fathom the words. Banks faltered for a moment then surprised Drew by coming back to the mouth piece very quietly and deadly seriously.

'Listen Drew, we can't leave it out there all night. Put it in your car, drive over to my place, right now. I'll deal with it.'

Drew didn't know the correct procedure for discovering a body in these circumstances, but he was sure this wasn't it. Banks spoke with confident familiarity, as though he had done this before.

'Right you are Sarge.' Drew obliged the order knowing he wouldn't go through with it. This was what they had been waiting for. 'Small problem, the car is stuck in mud, I need someone to get me out.' He heard Banks swearing and coughing in the background.

'Stay where you are and I'll come and find you, where are you?' His voice was gaining volume again as the situation worsened. As he became angry his voice became gravelled and full of menace, like heavy boots down a stone path. Drew hung up the receiver. He picked it up again and waited for the operator.

'What number please?'

'Sergeant Gates, Nettlewood 7739.'

'Putting you through now.' The telephone rang but was answered a lot quicker this time.

'Hi Drew how are you?' Frank answered immediately.

'Not good Sarge, I've found a body.'

'A body? Bloody Hell mate what's happened?' Frank did little to hide his shock.

'Hard to tell, I'm in the middle of the copse, in an opening, I found it in here and now the car is stuck.'

'Jesus. Did you call Banks?'

'Yes, he told me to put it in the boot, and drive it to his house so he could deal with it.' Drew listened intently to the ear piece. All he could hear for a moment was Frank breathing to reassure him he was still there.

'What did you tell him?' Frank asked.

'I told him I would, then hung up.'

'Good work Drew. Listen, I'm going to call the Yard on this one. If you're stuck you best stay put until I can get out there. Tell me where you are.' Drew thought for a moment.

'About a mile south of the Firestone roundabout. There's a sharp bend in the road, turning west. What's left of the fallen tree will be about fifty yards up there on the left, and the gap in the trees about ten yards after that.'

'Ok, you understand it might not be tonight? You'll need to guard the body until we can get up there.'

'Yes Sarge, I guessed I'd be staying. You get on to the Yard, I'll stay here. See you in the morning,' Drew said bravely.

'Alright Drew. Stay safe,' Drew hung up the receiver, then took it off the hook again in case Banks tried to contact him. He grabbed his camera from his bag and climbed out of the car again. He took some photographs of the body then moved on to the trees, trying to pierce their darkness with the flash. The trunks blazed in to life with each click of the camera in the cold night. When he finally got back to his car he collapsed in to a thin sleep.

13.

The Inspector listened carefully as Drew retold the story, scratching his chin thoughtfully.

'Banks said he would deal with the body?' he asked, thoughtfully.

'Yes,' Drew replied, already wondering if the Inspector could be trusted, wondering whose side he would take.

'What did you think he meant when he said that?' Drew pondered for second.

'That he would take the body, and it would vanish. That it would never appear on a report, no one would ever know about it. It would be buried and all evidence of it would disappear.'

'And what about you, what do you think he would have done with you?' Drew shuddered at the thought.

'I would be silenced,' he replied darkly.

'Why do you think that?' Drew shifted his weight uneasily, he knew he had to reveal everything, that this was his chance, this was the town's chance, of having the wrongs of the past corrected.

'Because we have reason to believe that something like this has happened before. Someone discovered something that Banks was trying to hide, and they were silenced.' The Inspector lined the questions up in his head.

'By "We" I take it you mean yourself and Sergeant Gates?'

'Yes,' this was it, Drew knew, this was the moment that they had been waiting for all these years. They were about to discover if their hard work and sacrifice had been worth it.

'And what behaviour have you seen in Sergeant Banks that makes you think he has done something like this before?' Drew took a deep breath, the only other person he had ever discussed this with was Frank.

'Ten years ago Frank Gates' older brother Albert, my father, was made Sergeant of Firestone. He narrowly beat Banks to the post. Albert died six months later in a car accident. The car was scrapped by Banks before any mechanical checks were made.' Drew sighed, relieved to be getting the events off of his chest to someone who may be able to take some action.

'And I presume Banks then took up the vacant post?' The Inspector began seeing how the story would play out.

'Yes.'

'Is there anything else about Banks I ought to know?'

'Only what people say about him, or rather, what people don't say about him.' Drew paused to think how to communicate what he was thinking. The Inspector waited patiently.

'There are stories, things that are whispered, that people would never openly discuss. Banks is the third generation to hold the Sergeant post, his father and grandfather had it before him, so for the last 70 years or so there has always been a Banks as Sergeant at Firestone. Banks' father sold his farm, his business, his livelihood, in order to take up the post. He gave up everything to become Sergeant.'

'That does seem odd. What experience does a farmer have as Sergeant of a police force?' the Inspector pondered.

'Judging by how they have run the police force, none.' Drew replied. 'There's more. The stories say that they are hiding something.' Drew looked directly in the Inspector's eyes. 'That they are protecting the town by hiding the inhabitants from something in the trees.'

'Is that why you're here Drew, is that why you moved to Firestone, to try and find out what was going on?'

'Yes. It was my idea. Frank and I have been close since my father's death. He filled the void that my father left when I was fourteen. As I grew I learned more about Banks, and entering the police seemed the best way to follow in my father's footsteps.'

'Do you think your father may have discovered something about the Banks family, and this might have been why the current Banks didn't want the car examined?'

'The presumption has always been that there is something being hidden, there has never been any doubt in Frank Gates' mind that Banks was behind my father's death.' The Inspector held Drew's gaze.

'These are very serious accusations, based on little or no evidence. You and Frank have been right to be cautious.' The Inspector remembered the muddy crater, and Banks trying to get to Drew, he saw now why he wanted to whisk Drew away, perhaps to try and get him to change his story, perhaps for something worse.

'True. Admittedly, but you don't know him, or his reputation.'

'I will add Banks to my list of things to investigate,' the Inspector informed him. 'As a course of forward action I would suggest looking to see if your father kept any old records and reports, see if you can find any gaps, or anything strange.' The Inspector thought for a moment.

'It has been a challenging morning for you Drew. Shall we take a walk? A stroll might do you good.' Drew was surprised at the sudden change of mood.

'Is the interview over?' He glanced at his watch and was amazed to discover an hour had quickly past. He had found the interview emotionally exhausting.

'Yes.' The Inspector smiled, sitting upright and stretching. Their mugs were empty.

'I can piece together some of the events from where your story ends. It was then that Frank Gates put the call through to the yard, and I was brought into the investigation. I still want to chat about the lights you saw. I do believe that you saw them, as to what they are and how they are related to the appearance of our unfortunate Mr Berrow, I am still open to suggestions.' He stood and began putting on his coat. Drew took this as his cue and began to prepare himself for an outing into the cold of the early afternoon sun.

'Anywhere in particular you would like to go?' Drew asked as he pulled on his boots.

'Nowhere in particular, I would just like to have a walk. Perhaps if I get a feel for the town, meet some of its residents, it could open lines of enquiry I didn't know existed.' Drew pulled his coat around his shoulders and the Inspector opened the door. He braced himself against the cold and set off determinedly toward the small parade of shops the locals called town. Drew followed him downhill. The Inspector was remarkably quick for someone of his age. He walked as if he knew exactly where he wanted to go. As they walked, they talked.

'Let us pretend for a moment that we did not just have that conversation regarding Sergeant Banks. Should he ask you what you have told me, tell him you found the body by accident, and that you did not tell me about the orders he gave you. Hopefully this will be enough to persuade him that you have not switched sides, that you can still be trusted.' Drew thought for a second.

'Do you want me to see if I can get him to reveal anything else?' The Inspector smiled as he had guessed that Drew was intelligent enough to see his plan.

'Yes, if you get the chance, see if you can't get him to tell you why he ordered you to pick the body up take it to his house. I don't believe he would use being drunk as an excuse, although he might. If there is something else, another reason, he might tell you. Be brave, but be careful. He might only tell you because he is sure you won't get the chance to tell anyone else.' Drew thought of the implications of the Inspector's words. They had walked closer to the town's small centre, and there were more houses on the road side. They came to the end of the road and appeared at the short parade of shops that Firestone called a town. It consisted of a Fish and Chip shop, a general groceries store, a Tea Room come cake shop, a butcher's and a Fruit and Vegetables shop.

'Do you want to do some shopping Inspector?' Drew asked.

'Well I am rather partial to a cake, shall we pay a visit to the tea rooms?' the Inspector suggested. They strolled past the butcher's, with fresh joints hanging in the window and a fine selection of cuts displayed beneath. The sign above their heads read 'Johnson's Fine Meats' and a man in a bloodied apron stood behind the counter weighing out minced lamb for a po-faced old lady. Both turned and looked up as the men passed and the Inspector gave a friendly tip of his hat. All he received in reply was a pair of barely noticeable nods.

'That's Keith Johnson, inherited the business from his father, who probably inherited it from his,' Drew informed him.

'And the lady he was serving?' the Inspector asked.

'Ivy Cole, widow of Ron Cole, the milkman,' Drew replied as they strolled passed. 'All of them, the butcher, the husband and the widow, have lived in Firestone all their lives,' Drew continued.

'Ivy Cole, no doubt a fully-fledged member of the rumour mill?' the Inspector asked.

'Yes!' Drew replied with a smile. 'You could put it like that. No doubt we will meet some other members in the Tea Rooms.'

'Good.' The Inspector smiled, pushing the glass panelled door. 'Firestone Tea Rooms' was inscribed across the glass and printed ornately on the sign above the shop. A bell gave a pleasant 'ting' as they entered and the four patrons of the tea rooms looked up to see who had come to join them that afternoon. Five circular tables were set out neatly around the room, with four chairs around each. The floor was chequered black and white with tiles, and across the right hand wall stood a counter with a selection of pastries, sandwiches and cakes. The room was tastefully decorated, and gave every intention of being posh.

'Afternoon all,' the Inspector raised his hat in welcome. A finely dressed youngish couple sat at the table closest to the window nodded back, but the occupants of other table turned to each other with alarmed glances. The owners of these alarmed glances were a pair of ladies similar in age and appearance to Mrs Cole that they had seen in the butcher's, and the Inspector gauged that they were the members of the rumour mill he sought. He was also ready to bet that Ivy Cole would be joining them as soon as she could get out of the butcher's.

'Morning young Drew,' came a voice from behind the counter, where the proprietor stood over a fresh pot of tea. 'What can I do for you and your friend?'

'Morning Phyllis,' Drew replied with a friendly smile. 'This is an Inspector down from London.' The conversations in the room ceased as all ears turned to the visitor.

'Yes, good morning Phyllis.' The Inspector raised his hat again.

'Good morning Inspector.' Phyllis replied, politely, if a little reservedly. This was to be expected, and the Inspector was used to it. The people of the town knew that his presence must mean something serious.

'I was hoping I might buy some of your delicious looking cakes for some hard working policemen?' the Inspector asked.

'Of course dear, have a look, see if there's anything you fancy. I'll be with you in a moment.' She loaded a silver tray with fine china cups and the tea pot and moved round the counter and through the tables to deliver the tray to the couple by the window.

'Here you are my dears.' Phyllis placed the tray down. She was middle aged, quiet yet confident, and moved with the grace of someone happy with who they were. The Inspector and Drew studied the cakes behind the glass eagerly.

'They all look delicious, how is one to choose?' the Inspector asked out loud to no one in particular.

'Go for the one with the most chocolate on,' Phyllis advised, 'that's what I always do anyway.'

'A good tip,' the Inspector replied. Phyllis returned to the counter. 'I'll have an éclair if I may?' he asked.

'Of course dear, and you Drew?' Drew pondered for a second longer.

'A jam doughnut please, Phyllis.'

'Of course, are those to take away gents?'

'If that's agreeable?' the Inspector asked politely.

'Of course,' Phyllis pulled a couple of brown paper bags from underneath the counter. 'So what brings you to Firestone Inspector?' Phyllis began, 'if you don't mind me asking, like,' she checked herself quickly.

'Of course not, the more people who know the better as far as I am concerned. A body was discovered nearby last night by Constable

Gates here.' The room fell into a deeper silence. Phyllis gulped, and turned quite pale for a moment.

'In the copse?' she asked in a hushed whisper.

'What makes you say that?' the Inspector asked leadingly.

'Oh, well, my old nan always used to tell me tales of things in the copse,' she flustered. 'It's part of the town, but I never heard anything to back them up, you know, it's like I always expected someone to find something and they never have...' She trailed off rather worried.

'Please do not alarm yourself, I am sure the body's appearance does not mean that any ghost stories you were told as a child have suddenly come true.' The Inspector spoke carefully, gauging that all the occupants of the tearooms that day felt the same.

'I would like to know if you saw anything strange last night, anything out of place, any characters around town that you didn't recognise?'

'Last night? With that storm?' Phyllis stopped for a moment to think. 'Nothing springs to mind, but then I was locked up safe in the house most of the day hiding from the rain.'

'Of course, and a very wise thing to do too.' The Inspector nodded.

'But if you, or anyone come to that...' He turned to include the other occupants of the Tea Rooms who turned away and pretended they hadn't been listening. '...think of anything suspicious or that you think might be of use to my inquiries please do not hesitate to come to the station and tell an officer who will pass details on to me. Or of course if you feel you need to talk to me specifically please tell a member of the local force and they will get your message to me.'

The four customers all kept their heads down, refusing to reply or even make eye contact.

'Well, the invite is always open,' the Inspector informed them when it became clear that the response was going to be a resounding silence. He turned back to Phyllis.

'How much do I owe you?' he asked her.

'Oh, err, Two and Six please.' she replied, her mind on other things. The Inspector fished in his pocket and pulled out the correct change for her.

'Thank you, we'd best be off, good afternoon,' he raised his hat to her.

'Afternoon all,' Drew called to them and they headed for the door. As they left Ivy Cole came bustling in.

'Hello Ivy,' Drew welcomed her as they passed.

'Constable,' she nodded back curtly, and made her way quickly over to her blue rinsed friends to find out who the man was, and what she had missed. The Inspector and Drew made their way back out on to the street and the Inspector continued on his way along the road, cakes in hand.

'Well there you have a whistle stop tour of Firestone's shopping parade.' Drew informed him. 'What do you think, probably not much compared to London?'

'Oh, London is much the same, we just have more shops as there are more of us squeezed into the place.'

He stood facing Firestone roundabout and passed Drew his cake. They stood eating them for a moment while they waited for a couple of cars to pass, before the Inspector led them confidently across the road to the stone for a closer look. Drew obediently followed him.

'Tell me what you know about this stone,' he asked Drew. Drew regarded it.

'This is the stone they named the town after. It's called the Firestone because apparently the blood of all the people beheaded on it has stained the stone and it looks like fire, but I can't see it myself.' The Inspector took a close look at the top of the stone. There was a faded red hue to its appearance, but he decided this was due more to the colour of the rock than the amount of blood spilt on it. From a pocket in his briefcase he produced a small test tube and a sharp digging tool. He scraped a few grains from the rock into the tube, sealed it up and put it back in his case. He took a look along the base of the rock, feeling it gently with his fingers, studying the ancient growth of Lichen on the side. On the east facing side lay sporadic dark patches, scars left where long dead moss had clung to the stone.

'This stone hasn't always faced in this direction,' he pointed out. On the north facing side was a lighter patch of stone, revealing to the Inspector that this stone had once lain horizontally on top of another.

'It hasn't always been vertical either,' he studied the sides carefully and found an outcrop of moss hiding a dip on one side, like a bowl had been carved out of it.

'My look at that,' he said fascinated as he scooped the moss out and on to the ground. 'Interesting piece of stone. Any idea where it came from?' Drew was so used to the stone's presence that he barely gave it a second glance. The Inspector had found out more about it in two minutes than he had ever known.

'No, I never thought about it,' Drew admitted.

'Do you know anything else about it?'

'Like what?'

'Stories, myths, anything?' Drew thought.

'I don't think so.'

'A very enigmatic rock.' The Inspector opened his case to remove his map and started checking it closely. He marked the stones location on it then checked its position in relation to the body. It sat directly north of it.

'Interesting.' the Inspector muttered. Drew studied the map with the Inspector, following the familiar roads around the town, and the main road east out toward Nettlestone. The Inspector opened his case and took out one of the instruments that he had used at the scene of the body. He flicked a switch and the green light began to glow, and at such close proximity Drew noticed it also emitted a quiet hum. He started wandering around the roundabout with it, and gradually made his way out into the road, walking in a slow shallow spiral. He would occasionally retreat to the pavement as a car approached, and then continue from the same spot when the car had driven by. As he walked he scribbled in his note book, or marked his map. When he had walked as far out as he could he walked around the stone in a circle, continually checking the instrument or jotting down information in his note book. Drew simply looked on, not wanting to ask what he was doing for fear of disturbing his concentration. The instrument remained reasonably quiet during this time, giving the occasional change in pitch, but the light stayed green. When the Inspector had completed a circuit of the stone he walked in a straight line toward it from the east, then he turned at a right angle and walked away from it again, heading north. At the sudden change of direction the box immediately sent out a high pitched squeal, and the light turned from green to red. As the machine screamed its high pitched alarm the Inspector carefully traced a path heading south from the stone toward the body. Drew watched and listened, bemused or confused he wasn't sure. He suddenly became aware that he was not the only member of the Inspector's audience. On a corner of the road leading north from the roundabout, a man had stopped to watch. Drew recognised him as Firestone's Vicar Aldous Squires. Their eyes met, and Drew nodded to him to show he had recognised his presence. The Vicar crossed the road to stand with Drew on the roundabout and watch.

'Hello, Drew isn't it?' Aldous asked, his whisp of white hair flapping a little in the wind.

'Yes Father, nice to see you again.'

The pair had first met within a week of Drew moving to Firestone when Aldous had visited him at home to invite him to join the congregation on Sunday. Drew had politely refused, and their encounters since then had been the same simple nod of recognition that Drew had given today. This was the first time they had spoken since the Vicar's visit.

'Who is he?' Aldous asked.

'He's an Inspector, down from Scotland Yard,' Drew replied.

'What's he doing?' They watched him stalking his path, he had taken a second instrument from his bag and was comparing readings, then noting them in his book.

'Inspecting,' Drew answered, not sure how else to explain it. They watched for a few moments more.

'Why is he here?' Aldous asked, unable to fathom what he was doing.

'There was a body discovered last night in the copse. He has been sent to investigate.'

'A body? My word.' The Vicar was distracted for a moment, and Drew noticed that he had lapsed deep into thought. 'Did you notice anything last night Vicar? Anything you want to talk about?'

'No.' He answered immediately, but not entirely convincingly. 'I'm a very deep sleeper, I didn't even realise how bad the storm had been last night until I left the Vicarage a few minutes ago to walk into town. Parts of the roads are almost flooded.' He turned and pointed up the hill toward the Church and his small cottage. The Inspector stood on the pavement and continued taking notes, but the instruments were put back in the case.

'Were there any casualties, and damage anything like that?' Aldous asked, concerned there might be parishioners needing comforting.

'No reports I'm aware of. I'm sure if anyone needed your services they would know where to find you,' Drew replied.

'I hope so,' Aldous replied, distractedly. He was busy watching the Inspector, and Drew noticed what appeared to be a look of recognition on his face, as if the Vicar knew him but couldn't place where from. The Inspector put his note book away and walked back across to Drew and the Vicar on the roundabout where they had been watching him.

'Good afternoon.' The Inspector offered the Vicar his hand and he reached out and shook it slowly. 'I'm sure Drew has told about me. I'm an Inspector down from Scotland Yard.'

83

'Good Afternoon, I'm Aldous Squires, Firestone's Vicar,' he replied, studying his face carefully.

'Pleased to make your acquaintance,' the Inspector informed him, 'I'm here to investigate the appearance of a body in the woods last night, did you notice anything untoward between the hours of midnight and two am?'

'No,' he replied quickly, and a little less confidently. 'As I was just telling Drew here, I sleep quite deeply, I wasn't even awoken by the storm, which by all accounts was dreadful.'

'Yes, fortunately no one was hurt.' The three men stood for a moment in silence. The Vicar looked as if he wanted to say something, but it never came. He had stopped staring at the Inspector and now seemed agitated to go.

'An interesting stone, Father, any clues of its origins?' the Inspector asked, half in conversation, half in his investigative frame. Aldous was hardly listening, so eager was he to move on.

'Well, the stories I've heard is that it was used to sacrifice people, hence the red colouration, though I know little more of it than that,' he replied half-heartedly.

'Yes, this is all any one seems to know about it,' the Inspector replied, examining a piece of moss on the side. The three men stood quietly for a minute, the intensity of the Vicar's discomfort adding to the awkwardness of the silence.

'Well, nice talking to you Father,' the Inspector said, trying to hurry them on, 'if anything about last night does spring to mind, please contact me via the police station.'

'Hmmm? Oh, yes of course,' the Vicar replied thankfully.

'Well Drew, we'd best be off,' the Inspector prompted Drew into action.

'Indeed, and I have some matters at the Vicarage I must attend to. Goodbye Inspector, see you again soon I'm sure.' He turned and stepped into the road distractedly, only narrowly avoiding being hit by Mr Jones' empty bread van returning to Nettlewood after a delivery to the Tea Rooms. Mr Jones shot him a concerned look but drove onward when he saw he was unharmed.

'My goodness father, are you alright?' The Inspector rushed over to him.

'Yes, I'm fine, thank you,' he stood in shock for a moment, and then looked up at the Inspector. 'I'm... I'm sorry, I really must be off,' he told them with a shaking voice, then crossed the road quickly and hurried back up toward his cottage. Drew looked after him for a moment.

'Everything alright Drew?' the Inspector asked, noticing Drew studying the Vicar.

'Yes, I'm sure it's nothing, but he seemed to want to say something to you,' Drew replied. 'And he had just come down the hill from the church. He spotted you and headed straight back up there again.

'Yes, I noticed it too,' the Inspector looked after him as he hurried off. 'That is rather odd,' he agreed. 'We'll add paying a visit to Aldous Squires to our list of things to do,' the Inspector informed him, pulling out his notebook and scribbling some notes. 'But I do not think now is the time to do it. For now I am in need of more sustenance that can be offered from an eclair. Are you hungry Drew?' he asked jovially, tucking his note book back in his coat. Drew smiled back. The deductive persona was put to one side for a moment, and the Inspector rubbed his stomach.

'I could probably eat,' Drew replied. It was a marvellous change in the Inspector's demeanour, from the official procedure following law man he had been all morning to a real, hungry person. Somehow both suited him.

'Where do people go in Firestone Copse, Drew? Where would be a good place to hear what people think?' Drew knew just the place.

'There's a pub, The Green Man. It's seen better days, but that's where most people like to go.'

'So, to The Green Man it is, lead the way.' Drew led them back past the parade of shops, and up a slight hill. As they walked they passed an old man in a cardigan, brown slacks and slippers picking up broken slates from the road outside his house.

'Morning Ernie,' Drew called to him. 'Everything alright?' Ernie looked up.

'Ahh morning Drew. Yes, not too bad, my roof has seen better days though I'm afraid.'

'Oh dear not too serious I hope?' the Inspector interjected.

'Oh, sorry Ernie this is an Inspector down from London.' Ernie nodded at him in welcome.

'Afternoon,' he replied, more worried about his roof than the Inspector's presence. 'I'm afraid it is this time. Usually I just patch it up, but I've had to get roofers from Nettlewood over to fix the damage after the wind last night,' he said remorsefully, wondering how much it would cost him.

'Oh dear. Hopefully it won't be too bad.' Drew reassured him.

'No, hopefully not,' Ernie smiled. 'You blokes off somewhere?' he asked.

'Yes, we're just off to The Green Man for lunch,' the Inspector informed him. Ernie leant down and picked up more slate.

'Well don't let me get between you and your lunch fellas, see you later.' He urged them on as he added more broken slates to his armful.

'Yes, see you later Ernie.' Drew and the Inspector nodded respectfully and continued on their way.

'Charming chap,' the Inspector commented to Drew.

'Yes, old Ernie's a character round these parts.' Drew smiled. They walked a bit further along the road.

'So all those instruments you were using, what do they do?' Drew asked the Inspector as they traversed the hill. The Inspector smiled, pleased Drew was taking an interest.

'One measures air pressure, another detects electromagnetism, and I have a Geiger counter.' Drew listened intently.

'And why do you need to use them?' he asked.

'All in good time Drew. For now, let's worry about getting inside for lunch.' They continued awkwardly on the thin path, then down another wider road, at the end of which stood The Green Man. The exterior was welcoming, it showed all the signs of a building that had been there a long time, and was in no rush to go anywhere. It had almost shrunk into the surroundings, looking like it belonged there. It had the black beams and white facia of a Tudor design, and the entrance was lower than the street, the roads having been built on and improved since the building had been built. A sign hanging over the street swung in the icy wind. It was adorned with a man's contorted face, constructed from roots and branches, with a tongue of leaves protruding from his mouth, with the words 'The Green Man' in flaking paint underneath.

'Marvellous,' the Inspector muttered loud enough for Drew to hear as he pushed the door open and they went from being outdoors to being indoors.

The heavy door closed loudly behind them, and a few heads turned their way. They took a step down into the pub and removed their coats and hats placing them on hooks by the door, then turned to face the saloon bar. The interior was illuminated with low light from the two large windows at the front and from the lamps that dotted the walls. Through the yellow haze of cigarette smoke the Inspector could just make out the contents of an archetypal British public house. Placed upon a wall by the bar was a dart board framed by the pin prick holes of a million missed doubles. Nearby stood a fruit machine, displaying an impressive array of enticing flashing lights that distracted potential customers from the low chances of extracting from it more money than you had put in. Beer mugs nobody ever drank from hung on hooks above the bar between the landlord and the public. Scattered about the small bar area were dark wood tables surrounded by dark wood chairs with red cushioned back and seat. The green glass ashtrays advertised John Smiths Bitter, the beers mats advertised Strand Cigarettes. Once white walls were sandy yellow from nicotine, the once pristine white ceiling had become so stained over time it had adopted a muddy brown. Drew and the Inspector made their way to the bar, and the little man who sat behind it watching them over yesterday's copy of The Mirror stood from his stool to meet them.

'Afternoon gents,' he greeted them, almost cheerily.

'Afternoon Lionel, this is the Inspector down from Scotland Yard.' Lionel regarded him cautiously.

'Is it true then, about there being a body out there?' Lionel asked, nodding vaguely toward the door and losing a little of his joviality. What little conversation the occupants of the pub had been whispering to each other stopped and the pub became silent.

'Yes, I'm afraid so,' the Inspector answered. He was regretful in his tone, sympathetic at the trouble the body had caused. 'I'm here to clear the whole thing up.'

'Must be quite serious, to get the Yard involved,' Lionel reasoned aloud.

'Standard procedure I assure you,' the Inspector reassured him and his patrons. 'There isn't anything for you to worry about, no one in town is a suspect, I am just here to ensure all the clues we need to find are found.' The Inspector was calm, and spoke unhurriedly. Lionel unconsciously reached for a packet of cigarettes and lit one as the Inspector spoke.

'Well, that's good to know,' he conceded, blowing out a cloud of smoke as he spoke that added to the haze. 'What can I get you then?'

'Do you serve food?' The Inspector asked searching the bar for a menu.

'Of course, what sort of thing would you be after? We got soup, or we could do you some sandwiches, ham and mustard or beef. Mavis could knock you up some chips if you like?'

'Yes, that sounds fine,' the Inspector replied, 'and some tea.'

'What bit sounded fine? The chips?' Lionel frowned at the Inspector in confusion.

'All of it. Twice. I'm ravenous. And some tea, a pot if possible, enough for four.'

'Oh, are you expecting someone?' Lionel asked.

'No, I just drink a lot of tea. We'll be sat over there, is that alright?' The Inspector indicated an empty table by the front window with four chairs around it.

'Certainly, certainly, you sit yourselves down, I'll bring you your soup and start on the sandwiches. Ham and Mustard or beef?'

'Is there any Horseradish?' Drew asked Lionel.

'I could find some for you if you choose young Drew,' Lionel replied.

'Beef and Horseradish then please,' Drew confirmed.

'Make that two, please,' the Inspector asked nicely.

'Certainly gents. Anything else?'

'Yes, where were you last night from around midnight to two am?' the Inspector asked. The Landlord laughed.

'I was in bed worrying about how much of a pub I would have left standing in the morning!' All three men laughed. It was a question the Inspector had to ask, and he hoped spending a little money and using a friendly smile to ask a few simple questions would lead to honest answers.

'So there was nothing untoward other than the storm? Was there any one in you didn't recognise? Did you notice anything during the night perhaps?' the Inspector asked, seriously enough.

'Well,' Lionel leant across the bar toward them, and the three men formed a small conference on their elbows. 'Mavis said that old George was up and about during the night.' Drew smiled and nodded sternly. The Inspector awaited further explanation.

'Old George is what they call the ghost that haunts this place,' Lionel was kind enough to oblige the Inspector. 'Well, if you believe in that sort of thing. Mavis always hears him, can't say I've ever seen or heard anything I couldn't explain, but there you go.' He returned to standing upright. 'I'll get Mavis on to your soup, go make yourselves comfortable.' He wandered through a door at the side of the bar. The two policemen made their way over to the table, the Inspector wondering what Mavis might have heard. He noticed heads turning to look at him as he and Drew made for their table.

'Good afternoon,' the Inspector nodded to those that held his gaze for long enough. Mostly the locals wanted to study their drinks in silence, but a few heads nodded back. This afternoon's clientele was made up of a few local workmen who had slipped in for an afternoon snifter, and a couple of retired gents enjoying half a stout each.

The Inspector opened his case and removed his map, which was becoming increasingly covered in scribbled notes. He laid it out on the table, and noticed the two old men sat watching him, muttering to each other. The Inspector nodded to them, and they nodded back. He took in his surroundings, noticing the dull scene through the window.

'Not much to see out there,' He noted, nodding to the view. A damp road and a row of houses was all the window had to offer. Drew glanced out, but he knew the view, he had seen it before. The Inspector began studying his map, and Drew looked at it too, trying to fathom what all the markings and notes meant. Gradually the patrons of the bar grew used to his presence in the room, and a low murmur of conversation began again.

'Hmmm,' he hummed. Drew noted the marking of the body, the fallen tree, the line marked out along the route taken by the Major up the Nettlewood road and the time he was there. He saw the line that was his own route also taken last night, up to the body through to the corpse. He followed a line drawn across the map through the body, from north to south. The line crossed through the body from the south, struck through the town, and outwards to the north passed the Vicarage. Slightly to the right of the line was the Firestone, directly on the line sat the pub. There was also a line drawn across the map that cut through the body that went from east to west, the easterly end brushing through the north of Nettlewood. The Inspector checked his watch.

'Time to make a telephone call,' he told Drew. Drew didn't take his eyes from the strange notes and readings on the map. There were numbers scribbled over fields, circles and x's connecting readings and times to the map.

'There's a public telephone over by the bar,' Drew informed him.

'Yes I noticed on my way in, thank you.' Noticing Drew's interest in the map, he pushed it towards him. 'Here, have a good look, let me know what you make of it.' He walked over to the telephone and lifted the receiver. Having inserted a shilling he dialled a long series of numbers.

Drew spent a few minutes sat wondering at the Inspector's scribblings and began to try and guess their meanings. The numbers appeared to be higher in the clearing in the trees around the body, and at the points of the compass where the lines were emanating out. Presently the rotund figure of Mavis came rolling out with their bowls of soup.

'Just you Drew?' she asked as she placed the extra bowl down at the empty place. 'Lionel said you were with a chap from Scotland Yard.'

'Yes, that's right.' He informed her, suddenly distracted from his line of thought. 'He's just using the telephone.'

'Right you are, love,' she smiled and waddled back off to the kitchen.

Each time the Inspector dialled a number he had to wait for the number wheel to whirr back round to the start before he could dial another. When he had stopped dialling the receiver clicked, buzzed for a few seconds, and then rang once before being picked up.

'Rank, Number and Position please,' a man's voice asked immediately.

'Inspector, 99473. Scotland Yard, case 4199. I need to report a 183.'

'Hold the line please Inspector,' came the officious voice. The telephone clicked, hummed again, and then was picked up without ringing.

'183. Give the position of appearance please.'

'52.232802,-0.711735,' a pause.

'Thank you. Position confirmed. Condition and whereabouts of traveller?'

'Deceased, unfortunately. He is currently being examined by Doctor Ward.'

'Estimated distance of travel?' the man asked.

'Sixty to sixty five years.'

'Based on?'

'Date of Birth on driving license.'

'Name?' the man asked the Inspector.

'Matthew Berrow.' The man's pen scribbled, the Inspector could just hear it between the questions being asked and the answers given.

'We'll have a check ready for you on your next report.'

'That would be useful. I believe there to be a tangible cause, and that I might be able to find or even replicate it if I had could produce an increased magnetic field,' the Inspector informed him.

'Hold on,' the man paused again and the line went dead for a moment. 'I can have a Field Enhancer with you tomorrow morning for eleven. Where are you staying?'

'Well, now that would be useful. If you could have it delivered it to Nettlewood police station, the courier can collect my first report at the same time. Also, I think there is a possibility of a 347.' There was a pause while the man finished scribbling his notes.

'I'll put you through.' The telephone clicked and hummed for a little longer than before, as the first man explained the situation to the second. Eventually a bright voice came on the line.

'347, go ahead, Inspector.'

'One confirmed sighting, leading to the discovery of the body. No luck on a location for a point of origin, investigations continue.' The Inspector listened as more scribbled notes were made.

'Continue investigation, do not attempt contact. Send full report with your 347. Anything else?'

'Yes, can you put me through to Information?'

'Certainly, hold the line.' The line buzzed and clicked for a few moments.

'Information, go ahead Inspector.'

'Yes, I will need a full history of the town of Firestone Copse, details of the area, landmarks, maps, whatever you can find.'

'I'll have something delivered with the enhancer. Anything else?'

'Yes, I have a rock sample that I need an origin for. I'll include it with my report. Also I need to know as much as you can find out about the Sergeants of Firestone Copse, and the circumstances surrounding the death of one named Albert Gates.' The Inspector watched his soup cooling on the table.

'Noted. Anything else?'

'No that's all for now. My lunch is here, so I'll be off. Report ends.'

'Report received. Bye, Inspector.'

They hung up their receivers, and the Inspector walked over to his steaming soup.

14.
Drew was already chewing a mouthful of soup-soaked loaf and dipping for more before the Inspector returned.

'Wonderful.' The Inspector sat with an unhidden glee and began tucking in. He took one of the thick slices from the blue china plate and folded it in two, then immersed it in the soup for a few seconds. He brought the dripping slice up to his mouth, blew on it for a moment, then put it carefully into his mouth and chewed. The bread had the smell of being freshly baked that always made his stomach rumble in anticipation.

'Chicken and Leek, one of my favourites, 'he spluttered at Drew, who was also enjoying the meal.

'Warms you in this cold weather,' Drew replied through his mouth of soggy bread. Both men began spooning soup into their eager mouths and soon their bowls were emptied and the dregs were being scooped on to crusts. As both men sat back and took a deep satisfied breath Mavis reappeared to collect their empty bowls.

'Hello there, everything alright I hope Inspector?' she asked. Her smile suited her rounded features, she displayed all the affectations of a woman who enjoyed eating good food as much as she enjoyed preparing it. She waddled around under a voluminous dress, wearing an apron splattered with the scars of a busy day in the kitchen.

'Indeed madam, by far one of the most delicious soups I have ever had,' the Inspector replied as she stacked the bowls on to the empty bread plate. 'I believe you have the advantage of me madam,' he informed her.

'Really? How so?' she replied, a little concerned.

'Well, you seem to know who I am, but I do not believe I have had the pleasure yet.'

'Oh I see, yes, I'm sorry, I'm Mavis,' she told him blushing to be spoken to so politely. 'I run the place while Lionel over there sits on his arse all day!' she joked.

'Oi cheeky!' Lionel called back to her, and for a moment the bar was filled with a few howls of good hearted laughter.

'Well you certainly make a fine soup,' the Inspector complimented when the locals had calmed down a little. 'Oh, I am glad to hear you enjoyed it,' she replied, never losing her smile.

'Mavis this is the Inspector, down from London,' Drew informed her, in case she wasn't sure.

'Yes Lionel told me who you were here with Drew,' she replied appreciatively. 'Hello Inspector. You'll be here because of the poor chap in the woods then?' she asked.

'Yes, that's right.' the Inspector replied, amazed at how quickly news could travel in a small town. 'I was wondering if I could ask you about your uninvited guest.'

'Who's that then?' she asked, rather confused.

'Old George, is it?' the Inspector asked.

'Oh him!' Mavis chuckled, a little embarrassed. 'Yes, well he doesn't like a storm, always seems to upset him so he was busy last night.' She spoke of the unearthly visitor as if he were a member of the family.

'Well, let's hope the worst has been and gone. Does old George often make himself known if there's a storm?'

'Oh yes, all the commotion you see, keeps him up.' Mavis was pleased to have someone new to tell about him, everyone else had heard her stories a hundred times and believed her a little less with every retelling. Drew could hardly believe the Inspector was really interested, and wondered what he really wanted to know.

'Poor old George eh?' the Inspector was empathetic. 'Was there anything else you noticed last night? Anyone in you don't usually see?' Mavis thought for a moment, replaying the evening over in her head.

'No Inspector, nothing comes to mind immediately,' she replied, pondering.

'What about your clocks? All telling the right time this morning?' Mavis thought for a moment at the strange question then glanced behind the bar.

'Well, what time do you make it?' she asked him.

'Ten to one,' he replied. Mavis squinted at the old clock behind the bar.

'That one says five to,' she told him, then checked the small faced watch on her wrist.

'Same as mine,' she clicked the winding mechanism out and put it back five minutes.

'Why do you ask?' she wondered.

'Oh, just on a whim, I noticed they were fast is all, I'm a punctual sort of fellow.'

'I see,' she replied politely, not really seeing the relevance.

'Well, if you think of anything, let me know,' the Inspector asked her.

'Yes, of course,' she replied seriously. There was a moment where time seemed to hang, as if George himself had come to listen. Mavis came back to herself with a smile, as she noticed Drew lean back in his chair and rub his belly appreciatively.

'Now, will you still be wanting your sandwiches?' she asked.

'Oh, I certainly will, though I daren't speak for my colleague. What do you think Drew? Would a sandwich be too much on top of the Chicken and Leak?'

'Perhaps not quite yet Mavis, give me five minutes to let the soup go down.'

'As you wish my love,' she replied, and bustled off with the bowls. The Inspector turned back to Drew.

'What's all the business with old George then?' Drew asked quietly when she was out of earshot. 'Surely you can't be interested in Mavis's old ghost stories?' the Inspector shrugged.

'I am interested in discovering the reasons behind Mr Berrow appearing in the copse,' he replied casually, 'anything that happened at the time of the body's appearance that might be considered strange or out of place could give us a clue, no matter how unlikely it might sound,' he informed him. 'I doubt very much there is a ghost haunting the pub, but there might be something else causing the disturbance, and who knows how it could be connected?' the Inspector asked rhetorically.

'And what about the time?' Drew asked. 'That wasn't on a whim was it?'

'Well, that's something I noticed with the Major. The clock in his car was seventeen minutes fast, I'm still trying to work out why,' he pulled his notebook out and scribbled a few things down.

'Well, you're the Inspector,' Drew acknowledged, trusting the man's method.

'So, what did you make of the map Drew?' the Inspector asked, changing the subject. They leant forward to examine it together.

'I presume these numbers are readings from the instruments you were using earlier,' Drew pointed to where the Inspector had noted them on the map. He followed their trail around, pausing to consider the notations and crosses that the Inspector had neatly marked in various places. The Inspector remained silent, allowing him to consider their meanings. 'This cross refers to where I discovered the body, this one to the Firestone on the roundabout. This is the route taken by the Major,' Drew traced the line down the main road with his finger. 'And these numbers are the times and dates.'

'Very good,' the Inspector was impressed. 'There are increased levels of pressure along these lines, very odd, very small differences, but they are there. I want to see how far out they extend,' the Inspector explained.

'Why? What does it have to do with how the body got there?' Drew asked, unable to see the connection.

'How it is connected to that I don't know, I have to follow all lines of investigation open to me, and in a case like this there aren't many. I hope any relevance they hold, or not as the case may be, will be identified as the investigation continues,' the Inspector explained. He turned back to the map.

'I'd like to go here,' he motioned on the map a place where the east to west line interceded with the main road.

'Here.' Again, the line and a road crossed. Drew read the map and guessed where he might want to visit next.

'And here?' he asked, recognising the pattern, taking a chance.

'Yes, indeed, good man. I'll have to get readings at each spot, to see what we find.'

'Well they're a bit of a way out, it will be a long drive,' Drew warned him.

'Yes, you're right,' the Inspector conceded. 'Before we do that then we need to visit your Sergeant Banks, and see what he has to say about his actions last night.' Drew shuddered a little at the thought of Banks. The Inspector was thoughtful as he planned out all the things he needed to do.

'I would like to pay a visit to our fatality, to see if Doctor Ward has discovered something while inspecting the body that might throw some light on the reasons for his appearance.' The Inspector thought these words over for a moment then checked his watch. 'Though I doubt we will have time to reach the hospital today.'

'Doctor Ward?' Drew asked.

'Yes, a colleague of mine, a mortician from Scotland Yard. If I'm honest I suspect that any clues the good doctor discovers will raise more questions than they answer.' Drew frowned, and Mavis reappeared with their sandwiches.

'What do you think Drew, ready for the next course?' the Inspector asked as he spied the plates making their way to the table.

'My, I'm not sure yet.'

'No matter. I certainly am.' Mavis placed the plates down and put a napkin next to each of them as she had done with the soup. The Inspector's eyes widened in anticipation at the thickly sliced white bread and the generous filling.

'If these sandwiches are half as good as your soup I shall have to start eating all my meals here,' he commented as Mavis checked the table to ensure she hadn't forgotten anything. She chuckled at him appreciatively.

'Now, I haven't bought your tea as yet. I didn't think you'd want it with your soup, would you like it now?' she asked.

'Well that was most thoughtful of you, yes a cup now would be nice. I wonder, are the chips ready yet?' the Inspector ventured politely.

'Oh my word you do have a good appetite don't you!' she chuckled with a shake of the head. 'They're just cooking now, I'll bring them out as soon as they're done my love.'

'That is most kind, thank you,' the Inspector replied, and as she paced back to her kitchen he attempted to squeeze the doorstep of a sandwich into his mouth. He managed to take a large bite and brushed the crumbs from his moustache as he chewed. Drew could only watch in wonder.

'You must have hollow legs Inspector,' Drew commented with a smile. The Inspector swallowed.

'What's that?' he asked before taking another monstrous bite. Mavis returned humming a quiet tune to herself and balancing a pot and some cups on a tray.

'Here you are, everything alright?' she asked.

'Wonderful, thank you,' the Inspector replied at the end of his mouthful.

'Glad to hear it, chips won't be long,' she informed them before scurrying back off to the kitchen.

'Sorry what did you say Drew?' the Inspector asked before continuing to eat his sandwich.

'It's something my mother always says when I've eaten a big meal; "You must have hollow legs".'

'Ahh yes I see. You'll have to excuse my appetite. I tend to go for long periods of time without food, so when I do get the opportunity to eat, especially when the food is as good as this, I stock up.' He took another bite, and Drew gave into temptation and took a mouthful of his.

'So when did you last eat?' Drew asked through his mouthful.

'About five thirty this morning, just before starting on my journey here,' the Inspector replied carefully through his mouthful of sandwich. He was aware that although the murmur in the pub had returned to a more relaxed and natural level, the locals still regarded him cautiously, catching glimpses when they thought he wasn't looking, sneaking a look from the corner of an eye. He was aware of it, but pretended he was not.

'No wonder you're so hungry, you should have said I would have prepared you something at mine.'

'A very kind gesture Drew, and perhaps I will take you up on the offer another time.' He pushed the last mouthful of bread into his mouth and chewed.

'Quite delicious,' he said, taking a grateful swig of tea. A few eyes around the pub watched as the Inspector wiped the last few crumbs of sandwich from his bushy moustache. Mavis reappeared with a plate of chips in her hands and a bottle of tomato ketchup under her arm.

'Here you are then gents, hope you've still some room left for these!' They thanked her and tucked in, the Inspector liberally covering them in salt and pepper from the pots on the table. They made short work of them, the Inspector doing most of the eating. They sat and drank their tea and let their food go down for a few minutes.

'Are you ready for the off do you think?' the Inspector asked when the pot was emptied. Drew nodded with a satisfied smile. 'I'll just settle up and then we should be off.' The Inspector stood and made his way over to Lionel.

'I must congratulate your wife on a fine meal, sir.' He addressed Lionel who looked up from his paper as he approached.

'And I must congratulate you on eating so much Inspector. We had a sweep stake going to see if you would actually finish it all.' The Inspector chuckled.

'I hope I didn't leave you out of pocket?' he asked with a smile.

'No sir, I was backing you all the way!' He began pushing numbers into his till, and numbers popped up behind a glass enclosure on top. 'So, that comes to thirteen shillings six pence if you please.' The Inspector produced a leather wallet and handed over fourteen shillings.

'Please keep the change and give Mavis my best, I hope to dine here again before I leave.' Lionel's eyes widened at the generous tip.

'Well, you're always welcome here Inspector!' The till opened with a worn out 'ping' from its bell, and Harold deposited the notes. Drew stood by the door and handed the Inspector his coat.

'Thank you Drew, now, perhaps we should visit Sergeant Banks?'

'Of course Inspector.' Drew opened the door for him. The Inspector raised his hat to the locals as they cast one last analytical eye over him.

'Until the next time,' he called before leaving them all in a stupefied silence.

15.

The hearty meal gave Drew energy he had been lacking after his difficult night. The fine food was, he decided, exactly what he had needed, and they made short work of the walk to Firestone police station. The building was simple enough, a red brick house near the end of a row of identical terraces. The only thing that differentiated it from the others was the blue lamp outside the door with 'police' written in white on all four sides.

Drew and the Inspector entered the small station through the front door, the public entrance. Inside the difference between the station and an ordinary house was more pronounced. They entered a small room, painted clinically white and sparsely decorated with a few notices giving advice to the public about the importance of locking their doors at night and other such matters. It was furnished only with an uncomfortable looking wooden bench against one of the walls. Set into the wall at the far end was a hatch with a sliding window and to the right of this was a door. Behind the window sat a colleague of Drew's with his head resting lazily on his hand. His arm was perched on the desk in front of him and he peered down through thick glasses at his book. So engrossed was he that he didn't notice the two men enter the station until they were level with his window. He carefully, and with no sign of urgency, placed the open book down on to the table in front of him.

'Well Drew, who have you brought us this time?' the desk Sergeant asked, looking the Inspector up and down over his lenses and trying to calculate what crime he might be accused of.

'This is the Inspector Tom, down from Scotland Yard,' Drew informed him gently. He knew Tom would be as keen to have the Inspector here as Banks was. The Constable continued to look him up and down in disdain.

'Is that right is it?' he replied. 'And I suppose he's here to be answering all the questions about that body you found then, is he?' the man still addressed Drew as if the Inspector wasn't there. He was condescending, not even attempting to hide his dislike of having someone from the capital meddling in Firestone's affairs.

'Well we would hope so wouldn't we Sergeant? After all, it would appear you've got your hands full manning the front desk,' Drew replied. Far from being annoyed the man tittered quietly to himself patronisingly.

'I suppose you'll be wanting to come in then?' Tom made to raise himself from his chair, making it clear in his forced movements and slow reaction that he was unhappy at being disturbed.

'Indeed,' the Inspector addressed him. 'We're here to see Sergeant Banks, and we would like to see him sometime today.' He spoke politely with a gentle authority and Tom found himself huffing out of his chair as quickly as he could to let them in. The Inspector didn't have time for arguments with the local force, he found that combating the fights they tried to pick with a smile and manners made them feel they had won, and got them on to doing their job quicker.

'Course you are. Banks is in his office,' Tom told them defensively as he disappeared. A few moments later the adjoining door opened and he reappeared through it. He was shorter than the hatch revealed, and much rounder in the belly. He stood in silence as they entered, and as soon as both men were through he closed the door and locked it again then shuffled back to his seat. The door opened on to a corridor, immediately on the left was a doorway that led to the small office and reception desk where Tom had resumed reading. The Inspector followed Drew up the thin corridor to the main office of the police station. It was completely deserted, three desks sat empty between the sparse grey walls, slowly disappearing under paperwork. The walls were lined with filling cabinets, upon which sat folders gathering dust. The posters on the walls were frayed and brown, and a poorly looking spider plant sat by the window gasping for water. The Inspector glanced round the place disapprovingly before he rounded on the closed door to Banks' office.

'Shall we see if he's in?' the Inspector suggested, and gave the door two sharp knocks, causing the sound of movement to suddenly come from inside. The door opened and the figure of Banks appeared through it.

'Drew!' he exclaimed excitedly. 'It's good to see you finally, come in lad and sit down.' Banks began clearing a space in his office for the two of them to take a seat. Drew tried to hide his surprise at Banks' friendly reception.

'Inspector, any news on the body, any identification?' Banks asked as he shifted the contents of his desk from many small piles to one precariously high one.

'Yes I have identified him. He is not a local man, he is from Swindon. He has been taken to the hospital in Nettlewood for an autopsy and when they have been found he will be reunited with his family for a proper burial,' the Inspector informed him matter of factly.

'So it's nothing to do with Firestone Copse?' Banks asked. The Inspector heard in his voice the hope that he would be leaving him, and the town, alone.

'No, the victim was not from here, though I believe the reason for his appearance in Firestone to be related to the town in some way, and that is why I am continuing my investigations.' Banks nodded in understanding a little too enthusiastically, his eyes widened a little at the news. He breathed a heavy sigh and looked at Drew.

'You look very tired, Sergeant,' the Inspector pointed out.

'Course I look tired, I was out all night trying to find young Drew here. Worried sick I was.' His face was eager yet drawn. He looked directly in to the Inspector's eyes, and the Inspector found he was warming to him despite himself.

'Let's not forget why he was out there in the first place. You sent him out to do the job of the council workmen,' the Inspector reminded Banks, and himself. 'Did you attempt to contact them?' He remained impassive and business like, but whenever he looked in to his eyes, he got the feeling that Banks was being wronged somehow.

'Yes, I called Harry from this very telephone.' He defensively pointed to the telephone on his desk. 'He's the roads man over in Biddlecombe. He moved there from Firestone two year ago when he got made head of roads for the county. He told me that all the vans were already out clearing the roads because of the storm, but he would let them know and send someone over, but he couldn't say when that would be.' To Drew the alibi sounded rehearsed, and he blurted it out as if he had been waiting to be questioned on it. Drew was shocked, and a little disappointed to see the Inspector nodding sympathetically. 'When I realised how bad the conditions were, well, I was worried sick about Drew, poor lad stuck out there by himself. Especially with finding a body like that, it wasn't safe for him out there. So I drove around looking for him.' The Inspector had removed his note book and had begun to make notes.

'I see. And when Drew originally called you about the body, what did you advise him to do?' Banks turned from the Inspector to Drew.

'Drew, I wanted you to come back for your own safety, there wouldn't be much you could do out there all night by yourself. I thought bringing the body back would be best in those conditions,' he said firmly. 'I thought it best to get the body back, so we could preserve any evidence that might have been left on it. In that weather any clues might easily be washed away.' The tone was sincere, he was convincing the Inspector that his concern for Drew was genuine, and he even found himself believing that returning the body would be the best thing to do.

'What made you choose Drew for the job?' the Inspector asked. Banks stared deep in to the Inspector's eyes, and he felt him penetrating his mind. There was something about the way he was looking at him, something about his eyes, which made the Inspector feel that he could have told him anything and he would have believed it.

'Well he's been a real asset to the force, you only have to see his record over the two years to see that. He's reliable and properly suited to life as a rural police man.'

'Yes, well, really that's how you should be describing any policeman working these communities. Why send Drew?'

'It was a hard job, shifting a tree,' Banks replied slowly, looking deep into the Inspector's eyes. The Inspector felt as though Banks was trying some trick on him, and resisted it fiercely.

'Yes I'm sure. Why not the chap on the front desk?' the Inspector asked.

'Tom? He's not much good to anyone when he's on duty let alone off,' Banks joked, trying to keep the atmosphere jovial.

'Or one of the other Constables?' the Inspector asked. Banks gritted his teeth.

'Well,' he told them both gently. 'Drew is the only Constable I have that would have been up to it.' It was the truth, but it was hard for him to admit it. The Firestone force was aging.

'And so where were you last night when the body appeared?' the Inspector asked.

'I was having dinner with some friends.' he replied, looking in to the Inspector's eyes again. The Inspector's questions were not phrased accusingly, and Banks answers were slow and deliberate, as if answering a child.

'Whereabouts? Can I have a list of names of the friends you were with?' the Inspector asked nicely. Drew was a little concerned at the Inspector's tone. Was he falling under Banks' spell, as the rest of the town had?

'Really Inspector? Do you suspect me?' Banks was incredulous at the suggestion that he would have to prove his whereabouts.

'No of course not!' the Inspector heard himself saying. He then wondered what effect the Sergeant was having on him and checked himself. 'I need to ascertain everyone's whereabouts, Sergeant Banks. I won't know who the right person to suspect is until I find someone with no alibi.' Banks snorted derisively.

'Is it a problem for you to supply me with a list of names?' the Inspector asked in reply. Drew noticed the Inspector battling with Banks' answers, unsure of his replies or how to talk to him.

'I suppose not,' he conceded, almost triumphantly, knowing he could not possibly be a subject of investigation. He took a pen and paper from a drawer and wrote down four names which he gave to the Inspector. The Inspector studied the names on the paper for a moment then folded it and placed it into a pocket inside his jacket.

'Thank you. Well I think that answers all the questions I have for now. I trust we can find you here should I need you?' The Inspector stood. Drew wondered if he was perhaps being allowed to get away without being properly questioned.

'Of course, are you still basing things over in Nettlewood?' Banks asked hopefully.

'For now, they have a more active staff.' They stood and left Banks sitting in his office.

The Inspector not so much closed the door behind him as slammed it firmly. Banks got the meaning; stay where I can find you.

16.

Banks' eyes thinned and he winced in disgust at his own behaviour. It hadn't been easy toadying to them, he had been preparing himself mentally for it all morning. He sat motionless for a few minutes staring at the door, the clock on the wall ticked its way around mercilessly. He was unsure if his tricks had worked on him, he was stronger willed than the fools that filled Firestone he realised to himself. All he had to do with them was look deep enough in to their eyes until he found their minds. He could find them and use what he hid deep down to persuade them to his way of thinking.

'Of course they do,' he muttered to himself quietly. He sat motionless in the darkening room, listening, thinking. In the darkest recesses of his mind, a voice tried to break the silence.

'They don't believe you,' it screamed, over and over again. Banks could barely hear it, the voice was buried too deep. He unlocked the bottom drawer of his metal desk and pulled it open to reveal a packet of cigarettes, an ashtray, and a bottle of cheap scotch. He pulled out the scotch, ripped off the lid and took a long hard swig, straight from the bottle.

'Maybe you're right,' he told the unseen visitor, his voice thick with menace and mirth. The voice fell silent. Something about the way Banks uttered the words filled the air with fear. He lit a cigarette, took a long slow pull, and let out a massive cloud of smoke. He took his time in the silence, allowing the meaning of the words to vibrate around his mind; *'They don't believe you'*. He tried to fathom all possibilities, allowing their inevitable consequences to come to the fore, before realising what he knew he had to do. The voice cowered in the abyss, not wanting to know, hidden deep in the dark. Banks took another swig from the whiskey then reached into the back of the drawer and removed a hidden revolver and a packet containing twenty four rounds of ammunition. He placed the gun and the bullets down on the desk for a moment and looked at them as though any moment they would spring to life. When he seemed pleased enough that they were real, and that they weren't going to move, he slowly picked up the gun. He turned it over meticulously, a smirk lingering in an ugly corner of his mouth as he enjoyed the motions of loading it. When each chamber was loaded he felt its weight in his hand; three fingers gripped about the handle, one poised over the trigger. He stared down the barrel, aiming it at the door, remembering how much he enjoyed using it. He reached for the cigarettes and lit another, the dimly lit room slowly filling with smoke. He did not relinquish the gun but kept it in his hand, his eyes hardly leaving its dull grey metal.

'He's getting too close. We need to stop him,' he told the gun. He sat in silence for a minute or two, as the darkness crept in around him. He could control most of the town, but for some reason he couldn't fathom the accursed Gates family were immune to him. That's why Drew's father had to go. That's why he had allowed Drew to come to Firestone; so he could keep a close eye on him.

'Now that's true!' he suddenly guffawed aloud to the smoky air. 'Probably won't be the last neither!' He laughed long and loud, taking another pull on the whiskey.

'Well we know what to do, don't we?' he sneered, his eyes black and piercing through the dark. 'We waits till he's all by his'elf, then we takes care of him, don't we?' we asked the gun.

'All we has to do is keep our heads down, and wait for the right moment,' he sneered, staring at the door, waiting.

17.

Drew and the Inspector left Sergeant Banks in his office, and retraced their steps back through the police station.

'Well,' Drew said quietly when he was sure they were out of Banks' earshot. 'That's the nicest he has ever been to me.' He was surprised, and disheartened. Banks' behaviour went against everything he had told the Inspector.

'Do you think his previous behaviour toward you may have been his attempt at nurturing your policing skills?' The Inspector was impartial, investigative, and Drew was unsure by the tone in his voice what side he was taking. He hoped Banks hadn't gotten to him already. The Inspector sensed the need to elaborate. 'Some people find giving direct praise difficult. Perhaps by playing the role of the tough commanding officer he was trying to encourage you, allowing you to grow confidence in your policing?' the Inspector suggested, then suddenly heard his own words and wondered what he was saying, and why he would defend Banks over Drew. He reminded himself that Banks wanted to move the body, and that was enough to include him in his investigation. However he had to admit that the urge to side with him had been strong, and he wondered at just what he was capable of, and who he had managed to convince. The men reached the door and passed through without disturbing Tom from his book. Drew waited until they were through the waiting room, which was still empty, and out into the cold again before answering.

'No, I'm only there to do his dirty work. It's like an old boys' club and I'm the new blood. I've been working hard to prove to them that I'm not going to stir the water and threaten the easy life they have made for themselves policing a town like Firestone.'

'And how did you do that?' the Inspector asked.

'I played the part of the slow Constable, I did what I was told, but mostly I kept my mouth shut.' As they walked back toward town the light of the day was beginning to dull, night was already gathering around the fringes of the horizon.

'Is there much crime around here?' the Inspector probed. Drew nodded.

'Although Firestone is a sleepy little place, things still happen that require investigation. The usual drill is to visit the house and interview the person reporting the crime, tell them that we would let them know of any developments, and that would be it. The case would be dropped. No further action would ever be taken. Sometimes they would chase us up but we would easily talk our way out of it. It's a disgrace.'

'What sort of cases would you be called to?' the Inspector asked as they walked. The shops loomed into view, all closing up, the butcher slowly and carefully removing his display of meat from the window. He nodded to them as they passed his window.

'There are all sorts really,' Drew replied, 'missing cats, damaged cars, stolen milk. The reports all got filed, I'm sure Banks has got them all somewhere.' The Inspector nodded.

'Yes, all important things to those who reported them I'm sure.' He could see Drew was capable of better, and that he despaired at the way the police of Firestone treated the people they were there to protect. The Inspector removed the list of guests from his pocket and read it out loud to Drew as they walked. 'So yesterday Sergeant Banks spent the evening at the Mayor's house with Doctor Sparrow, Constable Atkins, and Charlie Hart.' He looked the list up and down. 'Drew, who are they, and where can we find them?' Drew leant over to see the list a little better.

'Well the Mayor lives up at the manor house, just outside of town. Officious man, he's very serious to his duty toward the town. Doctor Sparrow has his practice in Spencer Street. Family doctor, small family of his own. Constable Atkins is nice enough, his hearts in the right place even if his mind isn't sometimes. Charlie Hart…' Drew took a moment to try and place the name. The Inspector was impressed with how much he knew about the men on the list.

'I wonder if that's Charlie from The Black Prince. That's Firestone's other pub, it's not as nice as The Green Man,' he warned the Inspector.

'Shame, none the less I think we shall be paying it, and everyone else on this list, a visit,' the Inspector tucked the list back inside his coat.

'Can you think of anything that might connect these men?' Drew considered for a moment.

'Nothing comes immediately to mind, obviously the two coppers are connected. They all live in Firestone, not sure if they have all been in Firestone their whole lives, but it wouldn't surprise me. They are all about the same age, so if they have been in Firestone all their lives they probably all went to school together. The two men fell in silence for a minute while they walked along in the chilling air. They approached Drew's house and the car parked outside.

'Well, your list of places to visit has become rather long, where would you like to start?' Drew asked opening the passenger door for him.

'Well, I think we need to investigate these areas of interest I identified on the map first, that I hope will answer a few questions. We can leave the corroboration of Sergeant Banks' alibi until tomorrow,' he informed Drew, noticing the darkening sky on the horizon.

'Of course.' They climbed in, and the Inspector took from his case the map they had been studying at the pub. He also removed one of his instruments and switched it on. It began emitting a series of clicks, and a green light blinked rather randomly. The Inspector studied it closely, taking notes.

'What does that do?' Drew asked, trying to think what it could be.

'This device measures the electro-magnetism in the atmosphere,' the Inspector explained. 'Its readings can vary depending on various factors, such as the weather.' He looked out of his window at the grey murk that hung perpetually over their heads. 'However the readings can also be affected when a source of magnetism disrupts the normal flow.' A small needle on the dial, like that found on a set of scales, was wavering over the green light. The Inspector held it by a wooden handle.

'A source of magnetism? Like a magnet?' The Inspector welcomed Drew's questions.

'Yes, a magnet, or a battery, all sorts of things. I'll calibrate it to take into account your car's engine. Turn the key and I'll show you.' Drew obliged and brought the car's engine to life. The green intermittent light became focused and bright. The needles rose quickly. Drew's eyes widened.

'Is that normal?' he asked, trying to hide his worry.

'This is a normal reading for being sat in a running car,' the Inspector informed him, and then twiddled with a set of pegs at the back, as though he was tuning a musical instrument. With a few tweaks the green light returned to the flicker that it had exhibited earlier and the needle returned to its position.

'This however is not the average reading for your normal, everyday village,' the Inspector considered the wavering needle. 'It's a bit too high.' This was an understatement but he realised there was no need to alarm him. Drew looked at the green light, perplexed.

'What does it mean?' he asked, fascinated.

'It means Firestone is not a normal, everyday village,' the Inspector replied. He turned his attention to the map. The car had begun to warm up with the engine running and both began to thaw from the cold outside.

'Do you see this line?' the Inspector indicated the line that led east from the body and intersected with Nettlewood.

'Yes?' Drew replied.

'There were readings I took while at the body that suggested a line of activity stretching North to South, and East to West. This East to West line crosses a few places of potential interest in Nettlewood, namely this road here and these fields, here, that I showed you earlier.' The Inspector showed Drew places on the map he had marked with an 'X'.

'Shall we head for them now?' Drew asked.

'Yes, please,' the Inspector replied, pulling on his seat belt. 'Then we'll head back to my hotel, the day is drawing to a close.

'As you wish.' Drew was still looking at the map. 'Perhaps if we start with those that are further away, say this one, then this one.' Drew indicated two X's that were a few miles apart along the Nettlewood road, on its southern most border.

'Fine,' the Inspector complied.

'We could make our way over to this one, before driving into Nettlewood itself and seeing this one?' Drew suggested.

'Fine,' the Inspector repeated. The route was the quickest way round by far, and the Inspector delighted in Drew's ability to quickly choose it.

'It's a bit of a drive though, think I'll get some petrol before we set off,' Drew thought aloud to himself, wondering how many miles it would take them to zig zag across the country. Firestone had its own garage, with a single pump sat on a small forecourt. The garage was a large cold stone building that sat behind the pump, with trees hanging over it from behind. The building had a large door with flaking red paint peeling from it. Drew pulled up at the pump, running over a black lead that trailed away into the building. This caused a distant bell to emit two pings and announce to the proprietor, Gerald, that someone had arrived. He appeared through the door moments later, wearing overalls the colour of which was difficult to distinguish through the dense layer of oil that had accumulated on them.

'Morning Drew,' he called to them with a wave as he approached Drew's window. Drew wound it down. 'How much are you after?' Gerald asked.

'Might as well fill it up Gerald, thank you,' Drew replied.

'Right you are son,' Gerald took the pump and began filling Drew's Zephyr.

'I'll get this Drew, I don't wish to impede on the forces budget if I can help it.' The Inspector took out his wallet and removed three pound notes.

'If you insist sir,' Drew replied, pleased not to have to pay.

'Gerald certainly has a well-stocked yard.' The Inspector noted, admiring the premises. Various car parts were lined up against walls, presumably awaiting a home inside one of the cars that sat inside the garage. A pile of tires stood just inside the door, and 'Goodnight Midnight' floated out from a radio somewhere inside. Parked on the road by the pump sat a powerful looking tow truck.

'Yes, he's a busy man, being the only garage in town,' Drew told him. Gerald had filled the tank and made his way back to Drew's window.

'Two Pounds six,' he told Drew, who handed the Inspector's crisp clean notes over to Gerald's blackened oily hands. 'Thanking you.' Gerald poked the notes in his pocket then dived into a pouch on the front of his overalls for Drew's change.

'Here you are,' he dropped a few coins grubby coins back into his hand. 'Thanks Drew,' he said simply, and took a step back for them to pull away.

'Thanks Gerald, see you!' Drew called, and pulled out.

'A man of few words.' The Inspector commented as Gerald headed back to his garage.

'Yes, you can never get much out of Gerald,' Drew agreed. He put them back on course and as they travelled the Inspector continued to study his device and their route on the map. As they made their way out of the trees and Firestone disappeared behind them the needle on the device slowly sank, and the green light dwindled away to nothing. The Inspector marked the location on the map where the needle reached a normal level, then continued to watch it in case it began to move again. After a few miles he realised he was going to be disappointed. He turned back to the map contemplatively. Drew noticed he was deep in thought, so remained silent allowing him to concentrate. The road between the two towns afforded wide views of the barren moors. They were eerily misty, and empty of any life other than the thick bracken and heather which sprouted low to the ground. The rolling hills spilt out around them, a patch work of earthy greens and reds. They reached the summit of a low tor, and from its wide peak Nettlewood came into sight a short distance away. The first two X's were only accessible by driving to the far side of Nettlewood down a thin road that lead away from the town and on to a busy road going east and west. The drive was long, and the Inspector continued studying his device to see if it detected anything. It barely stirred. They brushed past the town of Nettlewood, the view opening up to a mish mash of farmland lying fallow during the winter. Beyond these fields hills stretched, greens and browns mingled, the fertile countryside surrounded them magnificently. Although the road was busy by comparison to the main road that connected Firestone and Nettlewood, it was quiet this afternoon. As the part of the road where the Inspector had drawn his 'X' approached, Drew carefully slowed the car down, putting his hazards and blue lights on as a precaution.

'It should be along here somewhere, I think,' Drew glanced down at the map on the Inspector's lap to try and gauge their position.

'Yes, you're doing fine Drew, just up here somewhere,' the Inspector didn't look at his map or the road, but instead kept a close eye on his device, looking for any indication of change. It soon became obvious that they must have passed the spot in question, and the contraption had made no sign of detecting anything. Drew pulled up at the side of the road.

'I think we missed it, would you like me to turn around? Circle back and see if we can see anything?' he asked.

'No, thank you. If there had been anything to see, I'm sure we would have seen it. Perhaps we should press on?' Drew nodded, checked his mirrors, and pulled out on to the empty road. Once safely on their way he flicked off the hazards and blue lights. The road they were on was bordered by a low stone wall on one side, which stretched along the road for many miles and must have been some feat to construct. The other side of the road was fenced with a rickety wood fence, and beyond this the moors ruled the land with their barren mystery. The road swept gradually south for a few miles. As it traced the border of a farm the road gradually curved round to the east, and Drew guided them along the quiet roads until he eventually took a sharp turn left on to a road that carried them northwards again back toward Nettlewood. They were soon approaching the next "X" that the Inspector had marked on the map, and again Drew slowed the car, turning hazards and blue lights on to alert fellow road users to his presence. He studied the side of the road, trying to see anything that might have caused the Inspector to want him to drive this way. The area they were looking for was soon passed with the same result. Drew stopped again, still slightly confused as to what it was they were searching for.

'Still nothing?' he asked.

'No,' the Inspector replied, not sounding either surprised or disappointed. 'Let us press on to the next one.' Drew pulled out once more on to the empty road, and continued north into Nettlewood. They approached on its eastern border, where the houses were sparse and the rolling hills were plentiful. It wasn't long before they were once more slowing down, crawling at the side of the road, and intently watching the instrument. Once again it remained silent. When they were passed Drew did not stop the car, but continued on to the next point on the map.

'Do you know what it is you're looking for?' Drew asked hopefully.

'Not entirely,' the Inspector admitted. 'A change in the reading from this thing would be a start, though even not receiving a reading is still helpful.' The Inspector's methods were well out of Drew's realm of understanding and he knew it, he simply drove on to the final "X" and hoped more of an explanation would present itself.

The last "X" was in the centre of Nettlewood and only a few minutes' drive from the Inspector's hotel, and was no exception to the others. When they had passed it the Inspector made a few notes and markings on the map. Drew drove them on and they arrived at his hotel just as the Inspector replaced his instruments and map in his bag.

18.

'Here we are then.' Drew brought the car to a halt, and climbed out. The Inspector followed suit.

'Thank you so much for acting as my chauffeur Drew. May I buy you dinner as compensation?' The sun had already set on what had been a busy day. Drew checked his watch and was surprised to discover it was six thirty.

'Well...' Drew considered his options. At home he faced dinner alone followed by a solitary evening listening to the wireless. His evenings usually ended with him falling asleep in his chair, waking in the early hours and taking himself off to bed. This change to the routine was quite welcome.

'...I'd be delighted, thank you Inspector.' The two men entered the Hotel together, and made their way directly to the restaurant section of the bar. This, like the rest of the hotel, had obviously been recently refurbished. The wall paper had a modern pattern that reminded Drew of purple sand pouring through orange hour glasses, flooding the room with bright colours. The clean soft carpet was covered with an intricate interweaving pattern of brightly coloured shapes, reds blacks and greens flowed together seamlessly.

A few of the tables were occupied, not by residents of the hotel but by locals enjoying an evening out. When Drew and the Inspector entered the quiet murmur of conversation turned a little more frenzied as heads turned their way and began gossiping.

'I'm afraid news of your arrival, and the circumstances surrounding it, seems to have reached Nettlewood,' Drew muttered to him out of earshot of those paying them so much attention.

'So I see. Not to worry Drew, let's have a look at some menus shall we?' They went to sit down at a nearby table when a voice from across the room called to them;

'Inspector! Care to join us?' They turned to the source of the voice to see a young lady sitting at a table with a rather embarrassed looking man who Drew recognised as being Doctor Collins from Nettlewood hospital. Drew did not recognise the lady, but she had obviously recognised the Inspector. The heads of those enjoying a quiet dinner turned to her and the Doctor's table at this fresh intrusion.

'Ahh, wonderful, Drew do you have any objections?'

'Of course not.' Drew smiled, interested to discover who she was, and how the Inspector might know her.

'Wonderful,' the Inspector replied. They abandoned the table and made their way over, Drew feeling rather conspicuous as all eyes watched their every move.

'Good evening Casey, wonderful to see you again,' the Inspector greeted her.

'And you Inspector,' Casey replied. She stood and they shook hands heartily over the table. She wore a pair of fashionable wide flared purple corduroy's, and a chunky woollen jumper to keep out the cold.

'This is Doctor Collins from Nettlewood hospital, he's assisting me with the study of your body.' The two men shook hands.

'Good to meet you doctor. Casey this is Constable Drew Gates, the Constable who discovered the body, he is assisting me with my enquiries.'

'Good evening,' Drew shook Casey's delicate hand.

'Hello Drew,' she replied with a smile.

'Casey is the mortician, here to conduct the autopsy,' the Inspector enlightened him.

'Oh, I see,' Drew replied, rather embarrassed to admit to himself that he hadn't been expecting a woman, nor one so young.

'Doctor Ward is one of the best I have worked with,' the Inspector continued.

'Well that is high praise Inspector!' she laughed infectiously and all the men smiled. The table they had chosen had four chairs, so the two new comers took the empty seats and made themselves comfortable.

'Well this looks as fine a place to eat as it does to sleep,' the Inspector commented. 'Have you ordered yet?

'Only five minutes ago.' Doctor Collins replied.

'They have quite an impressive menu,' Casey passed one to the Inspector to peruse. Drew took one from the centre of the table.
'I've gone for the Cod with potatoes and peas.' She informed them conversationally.

'Well, I must say this all looks rather good,' the Inspector replied, studying the choices with a hungry look in his eye. 'Have either of you eaten here before?' He addressed the Doctor and the Constable.

'I haven't been here for a while,' Drew admitted. 'Looks like Abigail has had a bit of work done on the place since I last came here.'

'Yes the work was only finished a couple of weeks ago,' Doctor Collins informed him. 'I come here quite a lot, it's easily the best place to eat in Nettlewood.'

'Splendid, then it would appear that we chose wisely,' the Inspector didn't look up from his menu. Drew was still digesting his lunch, which was larger than he would usually have had, however having had such a long day with the Inspector he found the list of food available very appetising.

'Doctor Collins, what would you recommend?' the Inspector asked.

'Well Casey and I are both having the fish, it's a speciality of the chef here,' the Inspector immediately closed his menu.

'In that case I will join you in eating the fish,' he said. Drew studied the menu for a moment more before realising the choice was too much for his tired mind.

'Well, perhaps I should try it too,' he conceded. 'Do we order here, or at the bar?'

'We ordered at the table, I'm sure someone will be out to see you soon,' Casey replied. 'So how goes the investigation Inspector?'

'Progressing, yes,' the Inspector replied amiably. 'We have just finished a tour of Nettlewood investigating some key spots of interest.'

'I see, and how did the tour go?' Casey asked.

'Very informative,' the Inspector declared to Drew's surprise. 'I discovered absolutely nothing of any use.' Casey laughed while Drew and the Doctor exchanged confused looks at his contradictory statement.

'From my investigation so far I can only deduce one thing; I am staying in the wrong town. Any information I am likely to discover about Drew's discovery is more likely to be found in Firestone, so it pains me to admit that tomorrow I need to move hotels.' Despite having spent all day with the Inspector this was the first hint he had given Drew that these were his plans.

'Casey I trust you are happy to continue on here?'

'Yes, it's fine with me, no point following you when I'm so close to the hospital. I have only really just started, I'm sure the bulk of the work will get done tomorrow.'

'Wonderful. How long before I can come and see what you have discovered?'

'I would leave it until the afternoon, give me a couple of hours to set up.'

'Very well,' the Inspector agreed. He decided to steer the conversation away from the body, as he was aware of the ears at the other tables pricking up at the slightest mention of a corpse.

'Doctor Collins, have you been at the hospital long?'

115

'Twenty years, getting on now,' he replied, taking a moment to work it out. 'Went over there when I closed my practice. Blimey that feels like a long time ago,' he admitted.

At this the conversation turned from the appearance of the body to a series of anecdotes from the doctor regarding the transition of his career to the hospital. Casey and the Inspector listened and seemed interested, though Drew felt this was more through politeness than through a genuine interest in the affairs of a rural GP turned coroner. As they discussed the Doctor's career, which he was eloquently vocal about, Abigail approached the table with two plates of Cod.

'Hello Inspector I didn't see you come in,' she greeted them with a smile.

'Good evening Abigail, this is Constable Drew Gates, from Firestone. He is kindly assisting me with my enquiries.'

'Hello Drew, lovely to meet you.' She paused for a moment. 'Are you Albert's boy?'

'Yes, that's right,' Drew replied with a smile. He liked meeting people who had known his father.

'Oh, I remember you, last time I saw you must have been twenty year ago, you were knee high to grass hopper!' Drew cringed in embarrassment and the Doctor, who was the only occupant of the table drinking from a bottle of wine, laughed rather too loudly. Casey suppressed a giggle, but the Inspector gave no sign of amusement, being more interested in ordering his dinner. Abigail seemed to detect that Drew was not in the correct company for her to embarrass him.

'Your Dad used to come in here a lot, you know. He was a really good copper, really cared about his town.'

'That's nice of you.' Drew smiled appreciatively, glad she wasn't pursuing her memories of his childhood.

'Such a shame the way he went,' she looked away, a melancholy look slowly creeping into her eyes.

'Would it be possible to order, Abigail?' the Inspector interrupted her thoughts and she sprang back to herself with a shake of the head.

'Yes, of course, sorry Inspector, what can I get you?' She pulled a note book from her pristine white pinny.

'I believe Drew and I will both try the cod.' He glanced at Drew who simply nodded for confirmation.

'Well that is a popular choice this evening,' she made a note on her pad. 'Any drinks?'

'I'll have a pot of tea, please.'

'Of course,' she noted this down before turning to the Constable. 'Drew?'

'I'll just have some tea with the Inspector,' Drew replied.

'Of course dears, I'll bring you a nice big pot. Anything else?' She looked about the gathered guests, who shook their heads.

'Nothing for now thanks,' the Inspector confirmed. 'Though I am afraid to inform you that my plans regarding the investigation have changed somewhat, and after tonight I will no longer be requiring a room at your fine establishment.' Abigail paused for a moment.

'Oh, I'm sorry to hear that, nothing we've done I hope?' She was obviously disappointed but did well to remain professional. The Inspector guessed correctly that her disappointment was caused by the loss in revenue during this slow season, the loss of having such a high profile guest, and the loss of having a source of local gossip at her fingertips.

'Oh no of course not!' The Inspector was quick to put the proprietor's mind at ease loud enough for all the locals to hear. 'However I think that the main thread of my enquiries will now be concentrated in Firestone, so I will be taking a room there for the remainder of the investigation.

'Well, whatever you think best,' she replied, remaining friendly. 'What about you young Casey, will you be remaining with us?' she asked, hopefully. Casey and the Doctor had both begun to tuck into their dinners with gusto, and she had to finish her mouthful before replying.

'Yes Abigail, I will be here at least two more nights. This Cod is wonderful.'

'Oh I am glad to hear that, about the Cod and you staying!' She let out a loud infectious laugh that all those sat around the table returned, even the Inspector.

'Now, I'll go and get these bits for you.' She bustled away back to the kitchen, and presently returned with a pot of tea.

'Your Cod won't be long,' she told them, placing the tea down. 'Oh, Doctor Ward, I was meaning to ask where abouts in London you lived?' she asked. Casey looked up with a smile.

'Well most of the time I'm walled up in Old Church hospital in Romford where I do the Yard's dirty work, but when I'm not there I share a house nearby with a couple of friends,' she replied. 'Why?'

'Well, now, I know it sounds silly but I have a niece living up there in Brixton and I wondered if you knew her?'

117

'London's a big place Mrs Fothergill but there's always a chance, what's her name?'

'Jocelyn Hooper,' she replied, half in question. 'Though I think nowadays she likes to go by Sky, or Star or one of those New Age type names. She got in with that hippy lot that you see on the television.' She added as if this might help.

'Well, I don't think I know any Jocelyn's or any Sky's I'm afraid, but I'll keep my eyes open for one.'

'Well as you say, London is a big place.' Abigail agreed. 'Thought I'd check on the off chance, you know.' She bustled off again, and the table settled comfortably into each other's company. Casey shared a look with the Inspector, and hid a smile.

'Do you get that a lot?' Drew asked.

'What's that, Drew?' Casey asked.

'I sometimes wonder if people forget that the rest of the world is unlike their sleepy villages and towns,' he told her. 'To some people living in the same place as someone means you must know them.'

'Yes, you're right it does happen a lot,' Casey replied. 'But there's no point being rude about it. I like that these smaller towns are like that. People can get lost in the crowded city, but in these small towns, you always seem to get found.'

The conversation lulled naturally as they gratefully tucked into their meals. By the time they had all finished and attempted a dessert the evening had passed seamlessly into night. The polite conversation flowed naturally, save for the occasional silence that the Inspector filled with pleasantries concerning the quality of the food they had eaten and the ambience of their surroundings. The doctor managed to quaff the whole bottle of wine, gradually becoming louder and laughing harder at his own anecdotes as the contents of the bottle emptied. It emerged he had taken a taxi over, and was planning to take one back, but Drew agreed to drive him home. Before helping Doctor Collins to the car Drew and the Inspector arranged to meet at the hotel at nine the next morning for breakfast. The Inspector settled the very reasonable bill and bid good evening to Casey, who returned to the table to read the paper before turning in. He then climbed the stairs, and returned to his room.

19.

The first thing he did once he was inside and the door was securely locked was remove from his case the evidence bags containing the items he had removed from the body that morning. This was the first chance he'd had to examine them alone and he was eager for a good look. He had kept them from the eyes of Drew as he had realised when he had first found them that they would not be something he would be able to provide an immediate explanation for. He placed them on the dressing table. He pulled his main case out from under the bed and opened it up to reveal its cleverly concealed treasures. He tilted a compartment forward from behind the tent, and a door popped open behind it. He removed the tent momentarily to reveal a shelf holding a concise microscope set with various lenses attached. He removed it and a small wooden case of tools and set himself up on the dresser, under the bright light atop the mirrors. He could hardly breathe as he opened the first bag, so afraid was he to damage the contents any further. Inside it was a slab of plastic approximately four and a half inches long by two and a half wide. The object was very thin, less than a quarter of an inch. All sides but one had been covered in white plastic. The one side that was not white plastic was jet black glass which had shattered into a web of cracks. On the back in the top left hand corner there were two circular holes, both very small, though one was half the size of the other. In the centre was an irregular grey circle, with a pointed oval coming from the top, and a small semi-circle missing from the right hand side. At the bottom was the word "iPhone" under which were the words "designed by Apple corp in California. Constructed in China. Serial Number…" There then followed a long series of letters and numbers. Under this were some symbols the Inspector could make no sense of, but looked as though they might be more letters; an F, a C, an X with an irregular rectangle incorporated into it, another C, an E. There was also an O with an exclamation mark in its centre. There were various holes around the edge and above the cracked glass front. The Inspector studied it carefully, pressing what looked like buttons on the top and sides, though this did not have any effect on the inanimate object. As to its use he could not even guess. It was unlike anything he had ever come across, gave no clue as to what it may be used for. He took from his box of tools a flat headed screw driver and put the thin blade along the edge, to see if he could open it up. He managed to find a small recess, and with a cautionary twist, he popped the object apart. The casing came off to reveal a detail of baffling complexity, and the Inspector placed the newly exposed interior under the microscope. When magnified the true extent of the object soon became obvious, and he realised that he was not best qualified to make this examination. The inside was a complicated map of green with pinpricks of silver solder connecting a network of circuits. He replaced the two separated pieces into the evidence bag and carefully placed them in a large envelope. He then took to writing down everything he had discovered for his report. When he was satisfied he prepared the next bag. The items contained therein were slightly easier to identify, as there were four of them in a bunch together on a ring, and at first glance they looked like a set of keys. However they were smaller and shorter than any key he had ever seen. They were constructed of a shiny silver metal, presumably stainless steel. Each had one smooth straight side and one side with a sharp jagged edge. There was a fifth item that shared the ring with the keys that really puzzled him though. This was a small black plastic rectangle with rounded edges. It was elegantly designed, being very light, smooth and comfortable to hold. On it were three buttons with small symbols embossed on to them which added to the mystery. He pushed two with no effect, however on pressing the third a long thin rectangle of metal sprung out from a hidden hole. This looked like a key of some kind, though why it was hidden he was unable to discern. He pushed the metal back into its hole, and pressed the button again to test the device. The key happily reappeared. Satisfied that he had discovered something about it, although what its use might be still eluded him, he replaced the keys in their evidence bag, placed them in the envelope with the first bag, and wrote the findings up for his report before moving on to the next bag.

This contained a handful of change. The Inspector presumed they were British coins, though there were no shillings or any other coinage he recognised. All had their denomination written on them, though strangely it was just numbers; a fifty, and two tens. He wondered what system of currency this could have been used in. There were another four that proclaimed to be Pound coins, though these were smaller than he recognised and made of a gold like substance. None of the coins bore the head of Elizabeth II but of William V, the monarch apparently being a bald middle aged man. Each had the same sovereign on one side and their own unique design on the other. The Inspector studied each carefully under the microscope. They were all exquisitely made, the detail on the monarchs profile was finely sculptured. He carefully recorded his thoughts about them before placing them safely in the envelope.

The last bag contained a black metallic cylinder and the man's wallet. The black plastic cylinder had a button on one side which, like black and white slab, made no signs of activating the device when pressed. It was slightly thicker than his fountain pen but shorter, and uniform in thickness. Like the plastic slab he could hazard no guess as to its purpose.

He returned to the wallet he had studied earlier and took more time to investigate its contents. There were three more plastic cards, the same size as the one proclaiming to be the man's driving license. One had the word "Natwest" printed on the side, and had the man's name embossed across it. Another was blue on one side with "Tesco Club Card" written in white on one side and on the other was a series of black lines under which was written a long series of numbers. The wallet also contained some bank notes, two five pounds and a ten. These were made of plastic, and were smaller than the notes he was used to. They seemed more like toy money. All the notes had intricate detail surrounding portraits of William V. Although mystified by all the objects he was certain that they were genuine. Creating such things had obviously taken a lot of mechanical ingenuity and so he ruled out the hypothesis that they were planted on the body to distract any investigation into the man's appearance. He placed the last bag into the envelope along with his hand written report, and it all went back into his case. The objects helped cement his original assumption regarding the man; he had been snatched from his own time and had appeared in the trees surrounding Firestone. The Inspector reasserted the task ahead of him; he needed to discover how he had appeared there and if possible why. More importantly, he had to stop it from happening again. He also had to consider the possibility that it might have happened before, and that the trip of any others may not have ended in such a grisly manner. Some may have survived.

He replaced the microscope and tools carefully away in the case and replaced the tent. He then opened a small drawer in the case and removed a red light bulb, and a length of string. Another compartment revealed two bottles of developing fluid and a sheaf of Lustre paper. These he took to the bathroom and carefully placed on the bath mat. He removed the light bulb and light shade currently dangling from the ceiling on their electrical wire and replaced them with his own red bulb. He removed the mirror over the sink and from the wall opposite it he removed a small picture of *Manneken Pis*. He hung from the exposed nails his length of string, so it was suspended like a washing line. He returned to the bedroom and retrieved the used film from his coat pocket and turned his bedroom light off. He then entered his makeshift darkroom. With only the red light to illuminate it the bathroom was dimmer, the shadows darker and more profuse. He emptied the development chemicals into the bath, ran a little water into the sink, and began to develop the films. He started with the roll from Drew's camera, containing the images he had taken the night before. As he hung the carefully treated sheets of paper on to the line, images began to slowly appear on them. When all were exposed he began studying them carefully, and even in the dull red glow afforded him by the red bulb it was obvious that there was something very wrong with the woods that surrounded Firestone.

Tuesday 4th November 1969.

20.

When the Inspector eventually turned in for the night, it was in the early hours of Tuesday morning. His report of the day's activity had been written, all the photographs had been processed, and copies had been made where he saw appropriate. Before bed he swallowed two small blue pills, which allowed his body to rest more fitfully and to sleep more deeply.

He awoke at eight fully rested, and began preparing for the day. He hadn't been resident in the hotel long enough to empty clothes from his case, so he dressed in items from his trunk that were still as well pressed as the day they were packed. When he was satisfied with his appearance; double breasted dark blue suit, waist coat, white shirt, red tie and well-polished shoes, he made his way down to the restaurant area of the hotel. He found Casey had already arrived and was enjoying a round of toast. Judging by the depletion of the jam from the jar, the consistency the butter had reached since being exposed to room temperature and the numerous crumbs surrounding her plate he took this to be her third round and that she had been there about thirty minutes. She sat comfortably at the same table they had dined at the evening before, partially eaten slice in her left hand, mouthful of grilled bread being slowly chewed in her mouth. A copy of the Telegraph was spread out in front of her, and as the Inspector approached she swallowed, and looked up.

'Morning Inspector, I'm afraid I've just drained the last cup out of this pot.' She nodded to the cold empty tea pot on the table. 'How did you sleep?'

'Very well, thank you Casey. And yourself?'

'Yes, well, it's very quiet here isn't it?'

'Yes, very peaceful.'

'Help yourself to toast, I'm full.' The Inspector nodded and began buttering one of the slices that remained on the rack. Casey reached the sports pages at the back of the paper, and as these offered her nothing of interest so she closed it.

'I've trawled every inch of the Telegraph and can find no mention of your body. This little corner of Britain seems to be well concealed in its quiet, peaceful, quaintness.' She offered the paper to him, and he accepted it.

'And that is how I would like it to remain, or at least, I do not wish for it to become known for such dark notoriety as has caused our presence here.' He added marmalade to the rapidly cooling bread. 'These things may seem as humdrum everyday events to us,' he studied the first page of the paper and immediately found a report of a murder in the East end of London. 'But here the loss of life still has meaning, and can still turn a town upside down.'

'Do you suspect any one from the town?' Casey asked. Her questions were not asked with the concern that came from a resident, but with the business-like nonchalance of someone who dealt with death every day. The Inspector paused thoughtfully before answering, considering the evidence that he had examined the night before.

'I think I require more time before I draw any conclusions as to the identity of those responsible for putting our unfortunate friend where Drew happened upon him.'

'Is that your way of saying you don't know?' Casey asked with a smile.

'I'm saying it's too early to tell, but it is unlikely that anyone here was directly responsible.'

Casey sipped her tea. These matters were really nothing to do with her line of the enquiry, she merely asked the Inspector to make conversation. She recognised his tentativeness at revealing too much regarding the case, and so did not pursue the matter further. She checked her watch.

'It's coming up to nine, Drew and Doctor Collins should be here soon.' She observed.

'Yes, I wonder in what state the thirsty Doctor will be in this morning?' the Inspector asked.

'He was a little worse for wear by the end of the night wasn't he?' Casey laughed.

'Indeed.' The Inspector shared a smile with her.

'Ahh morning Inspector,' Abigail approached their table with a tray and placed the empty tea pot on it. 'What are you two smiling about then?'

'Good Morning Abigail,' the Inspector returned her greeting.

'We were just wondering how the doctor's head will be feeling this morning.' Casey replied for them.

'Oh yes Alan knows how to put it away doesn't he! Strange to see him drinking so much on a work night you know.' She added quickly in his defence. 'It must have been the excitement of sharing a table with our two honoured guests.'

'Yes I'm sure,' the Inspector replied reassuringly. Casey smiled.

'Can I get you anything or are you alright with the toast?' Abigail set herself back to the task in hand. The Inspector cleared his throat.

'May I have two rashers of bacon, two sausages, two eggs, fried and with runny yolks, another round of toast and a fresh pot of tea please?' Abigail hurried to scribble everything down.

'Of course, love. Are you finished Casey?'

'Yes thank you Abigail.'

'Right you are then.' Abigail added Casey's empty plate and the last of the cold toast that sat on the rack to the tray.

'How did you sleep?' Abigail asked the Inspector.

'Wonderfully, thank you,' he replied.

'Still planning on checking out this morning?' she asked.

'Indeed I am, I hope Drew will be joining me for breakfast in a few moments, so would it be possible to have that order twice?' Abigail paused in her loading of the tray to scribble this on her pad with a satisfied smile at the amount of money the Inspector was spending in her hotel.

'Of course Inspector, it won't be long, I'll just fetch your tea.' She bustled away into the kitchen with her tray, and began to loudly bark instructions at her husband.

'Poor man,' Casey sighed at the continued harassment of Harold. 'All she's done this morning is order her husband around.'

'Well, apparently they've been together years, and they run a fine hotel, they must be doing something right,' the Inspector pointed out, playing devil's advocate more than defending Abigail's treatment of her husband.

'Yes,' Casey conceded before adding; 'But at what cost? Poor man is heading for a heart attack at this rate.' They ceased their discussion as Abigail reappeared with a fresh tray of tea things, and placed it down on the table before beginning to unload its contents with much clinking and scraping as cups were placed on saucers.

'I bought cups for Drew and Alan when they arrive,' she informed them without pausing or looking up.

'Your attention to detail is only matched by your delightful hospitality,' the Inspector informed her with a smile. She blushed slightly as she finished unloading, then vanished off toward the kitchen again. The Inspector stirred the pot.

'Drew seems like a fine fellow,' Casey mentioned airily.

'Yes he is indeed. A good policeman as well,' the Inspector agreed. 'Another cup?' he offered to Casey.

'No thanks, I've already had three this morning. Actually, will you excuse me?' Casey made her way to the toilet, and the Inspector poured himself a cup then turned his attention to the slowly brightening morning out of the window next to which their table was situated. The view was not as broad as that from the window in his bedroom. He faced out to the road across the well-kept lawn. He wondered if he would see either of their expected guests approaching, but the car park entrance was unseen from this view. He kept an ear open for the door, and presently heard it open and the familiar plod of Drew's feet approached the table.

'Good morning Inspector, enjoying the view?' he asked jovially. The Inspector turned with a delighted smile. Today Drew was dressed in full uniform, and though much more formal than his attire of the previous day, he looked relaxed and it fitted him naturally.

'Good morning Constable. Yes, just enjoying a fresh cup of tea as the day tries to struggle into life. How are you today?'

'Yes, I'm fine thank you. Have Casey and the Doctor already left?'

'No, we're still awaiting Doctor Collins's arrival,' he checked his watch; two minutes passed nine.

'I admire your punctuality, would you care for a cup of tea? I took the liberty of ordering you breakfast.'

'Well that's very kind of you Inspector.' Drew sat in the same seat he had been in last night, as had the Inspector and Casey, as if these were now forever their allotted places in the dining hall of The Swan and Dove. He helped himself from the pot and took a few grateful swigs from his cup.

'Did you sleep well?' Drew asked the same familiar pleasantries the Inspector had been through with Abigail.

'Yes, though I was up quite late, even after bidding yourself and the Doctor good evening. I presume you saw him home safely?'

'Oh yes, I'm sure he fell asleep in the passenger seat on the way home, but between you and me I was glad. There are only so many drunken anecdotes I can politely listen to in one evening.'

'My sentiments exactly,' the Inspector replied. 'Why people see the consumption of alcohol as an excuse to open a window to their past is quite beyond my understanding.' Drew nodded in agreement.

'Why such a late night?' Drew asked.

'It was only once I was alone in my room that I was able to write my report of the day's events and begin to develop the pictures we took.'

'It was an eventful day,' Drew agreed, his mind retracing yesterday's journey with the Inspector. 'Anything interesting from the film?' At this moment the Inspector heard the Ladies' toilet door closing, and Casey's familiar light step across the carpet.

'Ask me again later,' the Inspector confided before she was in ear shot. The two men fell into a suspicious silence in their conversation just as Casey reached them.

'Don't let me interrupt,' she remarked, noting their sudden silence. 'Unless you were talking about me of course,' she added with a hint of playfulness.

'No, of course not,' Drew replied, a little too quickly and a little too enthusiastically. Casey didn't try to hide a little smile.

'Still no sign of the good Doctor Collins then?' she asked, moving the conversation on.

'No, afraid not,' the Inspector replied.

'Tea?' Drew asked, picking up the pot to pour her a cup.

'No, thanks Drew, I've already had my fill this morning.' Drew topped his own up, and topped the Inspector's up without asking. Casey noticed and smiled.

'He's got you figured out quickly Inspector; Keep you topped up with tea.' All three of them shared a low chuckle.

'Tea and food. I've never seen anyone drink so much tea or eat so much,' Drew embellished. Abigail appeared from the kitchen carrying her tray, this time loaded with the two fried breakfasts that the Inspector had ordered.

'Ahh good morning Drew, the Inspector's ordered you breakfast, hope you're hungry.' She placed the plates in front of them, followed by knives and forks, then a bottle of red sauce and a bottle of brown. Drew's eyes widened rather hungrily at the sight of the plateful of food in front of him.

'Luckily I'm starving.' He picked up the brown sauce and gave the bottle an encouraging shake. Abigail looked about the table trying to work out if she had forgotten anything.

'Can I get you anything else?' she asked to make sure.

'No, that's great, thank you so much Abigail,' the Inspector replied, preparing himself.

'My pleasure,' she hurried off again and left the three of them alone. The Inspector and Drew immediately began tucking into their meal, while Casey looked through the window and out into the bleary morning.

'What is it like out Drew?' she asked. Drew finished his mouthful of egg.

'Cold, and rather over cast. No doubt there will be rain again later.'

'I don't think I've seen the sky since I arrived,' she continued conversationally.

'No, this area seems perpetually blanketed in cloud,' the Inspector added.

'I know. What a dreadful winter,' Drew agreed. Just as the men were finishing their food, the main door of the hotel opened and they were finally joined by the Doctor. Casey checked the clock over the bar; nine thirty.

'Ahhh, good morning Doctor,' Casey welcomed him warmly. 'Nice of you to join us,' she commented teasingly.

'Good morning all, yes, apologies for my lateness, had a hell of a time getting the car started this morning, it doesn't seem to like this time of year.' Despite his condition when they had last seen him the Doctor seemed in good spirits, and showed no ill signs of the previous evening's intake of wine.

'Well, I'm afraid you've missed breakfast. There may be a cup left in the pot, though it will be rather stewed by now.' The Inspector pointed at it with a forkful of egg.

'Not to worry. I'd rather get moving, if that suits you Casey?'

'Yes, that will suit me fine.' Casey stood. 'I just need to pop up to my room and get my coat and bag, I won't be long.' She made her way quickly out of the dining room leaving the three men alone.

'I presume you slept well Inspector?' the doctor asked. The Inspector was used to the banal repetition of polite conversation, though he still found having to answer the same questions several times a day rather tedious.

'Indeed, a very comfortable room,' he replied with as polite a voice as he could muster. 'I presume you also slept comfortably?' he added, a slight suggestion toward the doctor's alcohol intake.

'Oh yes, like a log,' the Doctor replied, not noticing the Inspector's tone.

'I am glad,' their breakfasts were now finished, Drew and the Inspector began readying themselves for the day.

'Now Drew, I need to collect my things from my room and settle up before we can begin our day properly, would you mind coming upstairs with me and helping with the cases?'

'Of course Inspector,' the two men stood just as Casey reappeared through the door to the dining room, coat on and bag in hand.

'Right you are Casey, shall we be off?' Doctor Collins asked.

'Of course. See you soon gentlemen,' Casey gave them both a smile and a wave, and they left.

'Well Drew, let's collect my things and we can be off too.' The two men made their way up stairs to the Inspector's room, where everything was packed and ready to go. There was no hint of the bathroom's conversion the previous night, save for a vague smell of developing fluid. Drew gave the air a tentative sniff, trying to place the odour.

'What is that I can smell?' he asked, unable to identify it.

'Developing fluid,' the Inspector replied simply. 'Oh, that reminds me,' the Inspector opened his case and removed the photographs he had developed the previous evening.

'Here are the photographs you took on Sunday night,' he handed them to Drew. At the sight of the first photograph, Drew's face turned pale. He walked uneasily over to the bed and sat down.

'I... those lights,' this was first the photograph he had taken that night, of the body laid on the ground. Steam could just be seen rising as the body quickly cooled. In the background, amongst the trees and barely discernible due to the angle, was not just one set of lights but dozens, all pointed ovals on their sides.

'Those are the same lights I saw, that led me to the body.' Drew had recovered slightly from the shock, but the fear from that night that he had been so determined to ignore had taken control of him, so shocked was he by the sight of the photograph. He went on to the next picture, another of the body. Again, hidden in the back ground amongst the trees were the lights. They were of varying sizes and arranged in pairs. Drew shook his head in shook, wanting to look away but compelled to look at every single picture he had taken.

'I can't shake the compulsion to say that they look like...' Drew trailed off, afraid to admit what seemed so glaringly obvious.

'Like what, Drew?' the Inspector asked. He had noticed the change in him, he could sense his fear.

'Eyes,' Drew admitted, though it was difficult for him to say it aloud. 'They look like eyes, watching me.'

'That was my first impression as well. You say you didn't notice anything when you were taking the photographs?'

'Nothing like this. The trees were far too dark to see into. The flash illuminated things for an instant, but I could make out nothing but trunks.' Drew turned to the next picture, this was one he had taken of the trees. Dotted between them were the eyes, all around him, all staring toward him.

'They were watching me.' Drew swallowed against the lump in his throat, trying to force it back to the pit in his stomach. 'I felt like I was being watched, but...' he trailed off again as his mind tried to put some kind of meaning to the photographs. 'Inspector, what are they?'

'That is the question. I have tried to fathom some logical explanation as to what they might be, but have so far not found one. The similarity to eyes is quite disarming. I am hoping this says something more about our psyche, I hope it is our minds looking to place a familiar tag on to something inexplicable, trying to give us an explanation no matter how unnatural it appears.' Drew could not tear his attention away from them. They were the same eyes that had haunted his dreams for the previous two nights.

'I hope you're right. The idea of there being something in the trees that night watching me fills me with dread.'

'Quite, Drew you are a brave fellow, and I have been most impressed with your demeanour since I arrived here.'

'Thank you Inspector,' Drew replied, somewhat taken aback by the sudden admission.

'With this in mind, and knowing how eager you are to help with the case and find explanations for the things you have witnessed, that I feel I must ask you to do something that you may not be completely willing to do. You are welcome to say no, of course.'

'Well, what is it Inspector?'

'We must return to the scene of the body, to the clearing in the wood, while we have daylight, to see if we can find any traces of what might have been picked up by the lens. We will take with us the same camera and a new roll of film, to see if we can again capture whatever it is that you didn't see, but that the camera saw.' Drew thought for a moment. The idea of returning to the scene would not have bothered him as much if he had not seen the pictures.

'The thought of returning does not immediately fill me with joy,' Drew admitted. 'However, I need to know what these things are. If you think there is a chance of finding out by re-enacting my actions, then so be it.'

'Capital. Drew, your conviction to uncover the truth surrounding these events is quite admirable, and I am sure it will stand you in good stead in the future.' The Inspector put on his coat and picked up his case. 'Firstly we must go to the station at Nettlewood. I am expecting a package. Shall we struggle downstairs with these? I feel poor Harold has been through quite enough this morning without me troubling him with this as well.'

The two men handled the luggage with some effort back down the stairs and to the reception, where the Inspector rang the bell for service. Presently Abigail appeared. With all the breakfasts served she had abandoned the pinny until lunch.

'Oh hello gents, I trust your breakfasts were alright seeing as there were two empty plates waiting for me?'

'Indeed, I will miss your cooking Abigail.'

'Glad to hear it, though it's Harold that does all the cooking, I'll pass on your compliments.' She spied the bags. 'So are you ready to check out now then?'

'I am indeed,' the Inspector replied.

'Very well,' she leant under the counter to remove the Inspector's bill then added up the few lines on it. 'That will be Thirteen pounds and eight shillings please.' The Inspector removed his wallet and took out fifteen pounds.

'Here you are, please keep the change, the least I could do for leaving you earlier than expected.'

'Well that is very generous of you,' she passed the visitors book his way. 'Could you just sign here for me please?' the Inspector obliged, leaving an illegible signature where indicated.

'Thank you, and here's your receipt,' she passed him a piece of paper. 'Lovely to have you stay with us.'

'Thank you, it was a pleasure.'

'Shall I get Harold to help you to the car with your bags?'

'Oh no need, Drew and I will manage. Good day, Mrs Fothergill,' the Inspector tipped his hat to her.

'Yes good day Inspector,' she replied, and the two men made their way to Drew's squad car.

21.

Nettlewood police Station was a short drive through the cold fog, along the quiet roads of Nettlewood. Drew was still a little shaken by the photographs, but he shook the feeling off and concentrated on the task ahead.

'Did you say you were expecting a package to be delivered Inspector?' Drew asked as he pulled up at a junction.

'Yes, I'm not sure if it will make any difference to the investigation, but it could give us a clue to the origin of the eye shaped lights. I am drawing up a hypothesis, and the package should help me determine if I am on the right track.' Drew waited for further explanation, but the Inspector took it no further. He wondered if he should press for more details, or if the hypotheses was still too vague, or too confusing, for him to understand it. Presently they arrived at the station. Nettlewood was a bigger town than Firestone, so the station was bigger, with a busier work force. They parked in one of the free parking bays at the front, next to another police car which the Inspector recognised. This station was a purpose built low red brick building with cells at the back.

'I see our friend Sergeant Gates is here,' he pointed out to Drew.

'You recognise the car?' Drew asked, he was surprised but realised he shouldn't be.

'Yes, let's hope he has the kettle on shall we?' They entered the police station to find a waiting room empty save for an elderly gentleman sitting on one of the benches. The walls were neatly lined with notices regarding property that had been found and was awaiting the arrival of its owner, and posters advising people to keep their doors locked at night and various other useful bits of advice. The window to the reception desk was currently unmanned, and as they approached it a door to the left of it opened and a Constable appeared.

'Oh hello Drew, nice to see you,' the man nodded to Drew respectfully. He was middle aged so had a few years advantage on him, and wasn't dressed in full uniform, but had a dark blue sweater over his shirt.

'Morning Geoff, we're here to see Sergeant Gates.'

'Right you are. Coming back to us finally are you?' Drew smiled.

'Not just yet, not now things are starting to get exciting over in Firestone.'

'Yes, bit of a turn up for the books all this isn't it?' Geoff smiled at the Inspector.

'Indeed it is, I'm the Inspector, down from the Yard.'

'Yes, I guessed you were. Glad to have you here to help Inspector.' Geoff held the door open for them and they passed through into the office area of the station.

'See you later gents,' he called as they passed through, and as the door closed behind them they heard Geoff address the elderly gentleman in the waiting room.

'Now then, Mr Harris, how can I help?'

The office had a low hum of activity buzzing around it, men sat at desks smoking cigarettes and writing reports, telephones rang awaiting an answer. A low haze of smoke surrounded the scene giving the impression that it was busier than perhaps it actually was. Drew led them to Frank's office, and knocked on the door.

'Come,' called a loud voice from inside. Drew opened the door and they stepped inside. Frank looked up distractedly from the report he was reading, and when he saw who was entering his office he immediately disregarded it.

'Drew! Good to see you lad, come in, sit down, how are you?' His concern for his nephew was palpable. This was the first time they had seen or spoken to each other since parting company the previous day so Frank was eager to make sure he was well.

'I'm doing ok Sarge thanks,' he told him reassuringly. Drew entered urgently and arranged himself with the air of someone who knew the room well. The office was well lit, the blinds over the frosted windows were pulled up and allowed the room to be filled with a bright natural glow.

Frank Gates' large wooden desk sat by the window facing the door. It had an "IN" tray filled with files that sat awaiting attention amongst the paperwork, and a desk tidy over flowing with pens. On one side of the desk sat Sergeant Gates' chair, and on the other sat a single chair for visitors.

'Good morning to you too Inspector, how is everything going?'

'Very well thank you. I am expecting a rather important package to arrive in a few minutes, could you please make sure you have someone at the front desk when it arrives?' he asked nicely.

'There should be someone on there all day, but I'll make sure it's not left.' Frank obediently picked up the telephone and dialled a number.

'Jack it's me, make sure there's someone on reception if Geoff's busy will you? We're expecting an important visitor.' Frank paused while the man on the other end spoke.

'Someone for the Inspector. I'm sure you'll know him when you see him, he'll have a package with him. Thanks.' He hung up again.

'Thank you.' The Inspector nodded to Frank.

'No problem.' Frank dismissed it lightly.

'Now, how did your search of the clearing go?' the Inspector asked.

'Not well I'm afraid, we found no traces of anybody, apart from those left behind by us, and Drew the previous night. No footprints, nothing.'

'Well, thank you for checking.' The Inspector sounded satisfied, as if this was the answer he had been expecting, the answer he had wanted. 'Could I trouble you for a cup of tea?' he asked.

'Of course, where are my manners,' Frank stood to go to the kitchen, but the Inspector waved him down with a calm movement of his hands.

'Please, allow me. If you point me in the direction of the kitchen I will make us all one,' Drew and Frank did little to hide their surprise.

'Out of the office, turn right, room at the end, next to the Gents loo,' Frank directed him in quiet shock.

'Wonderful, I feel I need to make a visit there as well. Back in a moment gentlemen,' he informed them, and made his way politely out of the office.

22.

'Well that was unexpected,' Frank commented as the Inspector closed the door behind him. 'Why do you think he went?'

'I told him all about Banks and Dad, he probably wanted to give us a few minutes to chat alone.' The two men sat down.

'Do you think so?'

'Yes, he's really quite intuitive.'

'Well, why did you tell him all about your Dad?' Frank asked, concerned.

'I'm not sure, he has a way of getting information out of people, almost as if he knows it already, but is waiting for you to say it.'

'What did he make of it?

'He thinks there's something in it. He wants me to check mum's house, see if dad left anything that might be useful.'

'Well that's good news. What did he make of Banks?' Frank asked.

'I don't know what he thinks, but I don't think he trusts him.'

'Well he has a strange way about things,' Frank told him a little bitterly. 'Getting me to check the area for clues, he seemed to know we wouldn't find anything.'

'I think he wanted that done to make sure, he knew you wouldn't turn anything up, but had to do it,' Frank shook his head.

'So what have you two been up to?' Frank leant forward on his desk, lowering his voice. Drew looked away, avoiding his uncle's eyes, and shifted awkwardly on his seat.

'He made me sign some papers,' he admitted grudgingly. 'I'm not supposed to discuss anything about it with anyone outside of the Yard, actually I'm not supposed to discuss it with anyone outside of his department.'

'His department?'

'Yes, he wasn't really clear about what his department is but it appears they investigate the cases where there is no easily accepted answer, the cases where nothing adds up to a normal explanation.' Frank thought for a moment. He was disappointed he couldn't get a full report on what had been happening.

'Well, I don't want you risking anything on my part,' he replied, understandingly. 'I am concerned for your wellbeing but that's more of a personal judgement than a professional one. Tell me what you can, if you want to.' Drew was relieved that he wasn't going to try and force anything out of him that would make the situation any harder for him.

'I want to tell you everything, but I don't want to endanger either of us. All I can say for sure is that there are things happening in Firestone Copse, in the trees, which I can't explain. Things I have seen, that I wish I hadn't. What they have to do with the body, I don't know. What they have to do with Banks, if anything, I couldn't even begin to guess. All we can do is put our trust in the Inspector, hope he knows what he is doing, and follow his orders.' Frank sat back in his chair and sighed.

'I'm sorry Drew. I can't help but feel it's because of me you're in this situation.' His concern was growing for him every day, especially with stories like these.

'Don't worry Frank. I have a feeling this situation was here long before either of us came along, it just took me to witness it, and your guidance, to bring someone in who might be able to make sense of it all.' Frank opened his mouth to say something else, but there was a knock at the door and the Inspector entered without waiting for Frank to invite him.

23.

'Here we are gentlemen.' The Inspector carried a tray with three chipped mugs and a steaming pot balanced on it. He pretended not to notice that the conversation had ceased mid flow at his reappearance. He placed the tray on top of some papers on Frank's desk.

'I must say your staff are most friendly and helpful,' the Inspector commented to Frank.

'I expect they would be to a man from the Yard Inspector, you should hear some of the back chat I get from them!'

'Yes, I often wonder if my presence brings out hitherto unseen wonders in officer's demeanour.' Drew picked up a spare chair from the corner and moved it over to the desk for the Inspector.

'Ahh thank you Drew,' the Inspector said gratefully. He took his seat and began to pour.

'Now while we wait for my package, I was wondering if there was anything you could tell me regarding Banks that you think I may find interesting. I'm sure Drew used your time alone to bring you up to speed as best he could?' Drew shot Frank a smile at his correct assumption.

'Well, he told me you were interested to know if there was anything his father might have left, in way of information about Banks.'

'Yes, oh how is that going by the way Drew?'

'I'm planning to call her this evening, it was too late to call by the time I got home last night.'

'Good show. Now, Sergeant, I know you hold a low opinion of Banks. Admittedly from what little I have witnessed of his means there has been little I have liked.'

'Yes, well, it's hard to treat any man you suspect of murdering your brother with any respect,' Frank's tone had taken a dark turn at the line of questioning though this was more at the subject matter than at the Inspector.

'Understandably,' the Inspector replied, picking up his mug. He had a way of brushing over people's personal feelings in order to get to the point at hand. 'Have you ever been given any other reason to think there may be more behind his behaviour?'

'Like what?' Frank asked.

'Well, you tell me,' the Inspector asked. Frank thought for a moment.

'Well, as I explained to you yesterday, he is seen as a joke with the neighbouring forces. Some of us question whether a force is even required in Firestone, as there's so little crime there it hardly warrants one.' The Inspector raised an eyebrow.

'Could this be because the force he has does such a good job?' the Inspector asked, knowing this wasn't a true proposition, but trying to urge Frank into revealing more.

'I feel it is more to do with the crime that is committed going unreported, or at least not reported any higher than Banks. The force is good at keeping things under wraps over there.'

The Inspector presumed he was referring to his brother's car crash.

'Well, I am planning to visit Sergeant Banks again today. I am also going to see the Mayor, so we can see if he can shed anything on to Banks' activities as Sergeant.

'The Mayor? Why?'

'The Mayor is the Sergeant's alibi for the evening the body appeared, it would appear he was having a dinner party for some friends, I just need to check this with the Mayor. Which reminds me.' The Inspector removed the list that Banks had written for him the previous day from his jacket pocket. These are the other men from Sunday evening at the Mayor's. Banks tells us they all went to school together, can you think of anything else that might connect these men?' Frank took it from him and studied the names.

'Nothing I can think of. I take it you'll be going to see all these people then?' Frank handed the list back.

'In due course,' the Inspector replied. The volume of their conversation had dropped to whispers, and they were suddenly interrupted by a sharp rap on the door.

'Ahh I wonder if this is for me?' The Inspector stood and opened the door, dispersing the atmosphere of secrecy that had descended over the room. On the other side of the door stood a balding middle aged Constable. Traditionally he was called into the room from the desk, he wasn't expecting the door to be opened and jumped slightly at the sight of the Inspector.

'Oh hello, you must be the Inspector. Your delivery has just arrived,' he informed him.

'So kind Constable, thank you.' The Constable nodded politely and hurried away.

'Drew would you mind if I put something in the boot of your car?' the Inspector asked with a light air. Drew was still consumed by the secrecy of their conversation and brought himself back to the moment with a blink and a shake of the head.

'No of course not Inspector,' he stood and the three men walked back through the station and into the reception where the courier was waiting for him. He wore a plain beige uniform which seemed to give the impression that he was a member of the forces, but surrendered no clue as to which force it might be.

'Good morning,' the Inspector welcomed him as they entered the room.

'Good morning, are you the Inspector?' Though the answer to this question may have appeared obvious, asking was part of the protocol that the Inspector and the courier adhered to.

'I am,' the Inspector replied, reaching into an inside pocket of his jacket.

'May I see some identification please?' the courier asked. Drew and Frank watched quietly. The conversation seemed natural, but there was a feeling of it having been rehearsed, both had repeated it over and over though not necessarily with each other.

'You can,' the Inspector handed over his wallet of papers. 'May I?'

'Of course,' he reached into his back pocket and pulled out his own wallet of papers. The two men studied each other's identification for a moment.

'That's great, thank you Inspector,' the courier replaced the papers and handed the wallet back to the Inspector.

'Yes, all seems to be in order,' the Inspector handed the courier back his wallet and with formalities over, both men relaxed.

'Now shall we see what you have brought me?' the courier nodded and led the men out of the police station to a large black van parked on the roadside. The courier opened the back and removed a large brown leather suitcase, not unlike the Inspector's large case.

'Where do you want it?' he asked.

'Could you put into the boot of Constable Drew's car for me?' the Inspector motioned to the Zephyr.

'Yes, of course,' he replied and followed Drew as he rushed round to the back of his car and unlocked the boot for the courier to place the case inside. He made lifting it look easy, despite its size it didn't seem to be overly heavy, and it was soon safely in the boot. Drew closed and locked it again.

'Thank you so much,' the Inspector thanked the courier gratefully.

'You're welcome. Were there some reports as well?'

'Yes of course. Drew could you open the car for me?' Drew obliged happily and unlocked the passenger side door. The Inspector reached in and removed his briefcase. He took out of it a brown folder full of papers, a brown envelope that Drew recognised as containing the pictures, and another brown envelope with strange bulges that left Drew wondering.

'There's also the information you requested,' the courier reached into the front seat of the van and removed a thick file for the Inspector.

'Thank you,' the Inspector quickly put the file in his case and replaced it in Drew's car.

'Anything else Inspector?' the courier asked politely.

'Not for now thank you, but I know where you are if I need you.'

'Very good, see you Inspector, gentlemen,' he nodded respectfully to the policemen who nodded respectfully back, then returned to the cab of the van and drove away.

'Wonderful. Well Drew, now I have what I came for, I think we should pay another visit to Firestone police station and see what else we can learn from Sergeant Banks.'

'Yes Inspector,' Drew replied, wondering just what it was the Inspector had put into his boot.

'Goodbye Sergeant, I will be in touch.'

'Yes, goodbye Inspector.' Frank replied, a little awestruck at the courier, the package, and the Inspector's demeanour throughout.

'See you Sarge,' Drew called to Frank as he climbed into his car.

'Yes, goodbye Drew,' Frank called after him, hoping for his safety, and wondering just what danger he had put his nephew in.

24.

They arrived at Firestone station in good time, the roads being clear under a sky darkened by gathering grey clouds. Drew parked his car outside the station, where another police car was sat.

'Another police car, but not the one belonging to Sergeant Banks,' the Inspector pointed out.

'No,' Drew replied. They sat and looked at the police car for a moment. 'Do you still want to go in?'

'Yes, let's see who is here,' the Inspector suggested, climbing out. Drew followed him into the station, where they were met by the desk Constable again, still engrossed in his book. The Inspector walked purposefully up to his window, but he did not look up.

'Good morning,' the Inspector said, rather loudly, disturbing his concentration and alerting him to the fact that he had company.

'Oh, morning Inspector,' he looked over the Inspector's shoulder. 'Drew,' he called to him as he stood to let them in.

'Good morning, we're here to see Banks,' the Inspector told him.

'Well you'll be disappointed then Inspector,' he fell back in his chair with a satisfyingly heavy lurch. 'He's not here.'

The two men in the foyer waited for more of an explanation, but it was not forth coming. Drew was sure he could hear the Inspector grinding his teeth as he tried to hold on to his patience.

'Would it be too much trouble,' the Inspector asked, his demeanour staying charming to the point of whimsy despite the Constable's lack of basic etiquette. 'To enquire where he might be found?'

'Who knows?' the Constable shrugged, indifferent to the Inspector's authority. 'Could be down The Black Prince, or at the bookies in Nettlewood, as far as I know we've had no calls come in that he would need to be attending to,' he was blasé in his betrayal of Banks, as far he was concerned these activities were the norm for the senior members of the police force. He neither realised nor cared that he might be compromising his superior officer.

'So he likes to drink at The Black Prince does he?' the Inspector noted. 'Perhaps you could allow us to enter a little further into the station, in order for us to await his return?' The Inspector smiled, assuming as polite a tone of voice as he could. The Constable sighed a guttural sigh of entrenched torture and began forcing himself from his seat once more.

'If I must,' he muttered heavily under his breath and heaved himself back up again. He disappeared through the door out of his little room, and after a moment the door next to the hatch opened and he reappeared through it. He stood and held the door open for them in a most unwelcoming fashion, heaving more sighs as they entered the station properly. He did not say a word to them as they crossed the threshold, when they were through he simply returned to his desk, picked up his book, and continued reading.

Drew and the Inspector shook their heads in shared despondency at the elderly Constable's rudeness and continued down the corridor to the main office where the three empty desks still sat. There appeared to have been no change to their state. The Inspector checked the desks, opened a few drawers on filing cabinets, and picked out some reports. He opened one and began reading. Drew watched him, a picture of calm as he casually pried into the business of the station.

'You don't really want to just sit here and wait for Banks, do you Inspector?' Drew asked, surprised at this rather static course of action.

'Indeed not,' he put the files back into the cabinet. 'I intend to break into Banks' office and have a look round,' the Inspector replied casually. He paced over to Banks' office and studied the door. He tried knocking on it, but there was no answer.

'Just in case,' he informed Drew. He tried the handle on the off chance that it might have been open, but as predicted it was locked tight.

'At least that is one piece of police policy he follows, albeit more likely for his own protection,' the Inspector said to himself. Drew nodded, and watched as the Inspector pulled from his case a set of lock picks. He studied the lock briefly, selected the appropriate pick, and made short work of the lock.

'Not that locking these doors makes any difference to anyone determined enough to gain entry,' he observed, and pushed the door open. He entered confidently without waiting for Drew, who loitered uncomfortably at the door.

'I'll just wait here in case anyone comes in,' he suggested. The Inspector carried on regardless. The office was poorly lit by dim sunlight filtering through closed blinds. The Inspector flicked the light on but it didn't make much difference to the cold dark room. He reached into his case again and took out a small torch which had a surprisingly bright beam. He used it to begin an investigation of the room. It was much like a smaller version of the office which led to it; a desk, a few filling cabinets, a dusty cactus sat on a windowsill. The room smelt strongly of cigarettes, the walls were grey. On one was a picture of the previous Sergeant, Banks' father.

The Inspector crossed the room and studied it. The two men were similar in appearance. The Inspector assumed the photograph was taken toward the end of his career, the greying moustache, the tired eyes, the drawn face. This could be a picture of the current Sergeant in ten years' time. He watched over the office, still influencing the movements within. The Inspector lifted the picture away from the wall and glanced behind, but it hid nothing. Actions such as these were more habit than an important part of the investigation. He was used to finding things hidden behind pictures, but this was hardly the place for such extravagance. He left Banks senior on the wall to watch him as he opened and closed the drawers of the filing cabinets. He pulled out a file at random and leafed through. It was a report of a stolen crate of milk from a milk float. The crate was later found, empty, by the road side later that week. No perpetrator was ever found, case was closed. He put it back and opened a few more drawers. They were all full of files with similar tales to the one he had pulled out, and the Inspector suspected they all had the same conclusion. He pulled another out at random, and read a few lines of a report about a dead cat found by the road side. The Inspector returned it, bemused. The files were sorted chronologically, and he flicked to the most recent entry; a brief report of a speeding car left a week ago. There was no report of the body, or a telephone call from Drew. The Inspector closed the drawer, unsurprised by the lack of detail to the biggest crime in the town's history. He flicked to the earliest records, which began twenty years ago, when Banks took over from his father. The Inspector wondered where the earlier files might be kept. He abandoned the filing cabinets for now, and moved to the desk. His eyes skimmed over the assorted untidy papers strewn across it. He found on the desk that Banks had written out part of a report form and had started to document the beginnings of an account of his actions on Sunday night. The Inspector read through it, there was no mention of what he had said during his telephone conversation with Drew. His report simply stated that a telephone call was received, who it was from, and what it had been about. He turned his attention to the drawers, retrieving his lock picks from his case and deftly picking their locks. The first drawer was full of stationery, and notepads full of scrawled notes that yielded nothing interesting. The next drawer down was fit to burst with paper, notes, pens, nothing of any relevance. The bottom drawer contained a bottle of scotch, partially consumed, and the evidence of a dedicated nicotine addiction. Empty cigarette packets, boxes of matches, and a filthy ashtray spilling its dusty contents were all that occupied it. The Inspector closed the drawer again and took a look around the dusty old room. He picked up the telephone and dialled a few numbers, Drew watched him and listened, intrigued as to whom he might be telephoning.

The Inspector dialled the same long series of numbers he had in The Green Man, then stood waiting for an answer.

'Rank, Number and Position please,' an authoritative man's voice answered almost immediately.

'Inspector, 99473. Scotland Yard, case 4199. I'm currently in Firestone Copse,' the Inspector said jovially. There was a pause, the line clicked and hummed.

'Good morning Inspector, I'm the operator who took your call yesterday, how can I help.'

'Good morning, I'd like to run a trace please.'

'Of course, from which number?' The operator asked.

'This telephone number, all calls between Saturday midnight and four am Sunday night,' a short pause followed while the trace was made. The Inspector took the opportunity to take out his notebook and a pen.

'No calls during that time.'

'Thank you. Now all calls for the last twenty four hours.'

Another pause as the operator began his search.

'He called 4678 last night at nine thirty, that's his home number,' the Inspector began scribbling it all down. 'He then called Biddlecomb roads office,' the man informed him. The Inspector's interest was held.

'How long was that one?'

''Fifteen minutes,' the operator replied.

'Hmmm....' the Inspector scribbled his notes.

'Can you put me through to that number? Can I talk to them?' he asked.

'Of course. If you need anything afterwards just hold the line and when the other person hangs up I will come back on.'

'Thank You,' the Inspector knew this but liked that the operators always told him. He waited and presently the drone of the dialling tone filled his ear.

'Roads.' The voice that answered was a little gruff.

'Hello I wish to ask somebody some questions about the road clearances on Sunday night. The person in charge, if possible.'

'I can help you there. What do you need to know?' The Inspector sensed a tone of unease settle into the voice at the other end.

'Oh wonderful. Were there many trees to clear up on Sunday?' The voice coughed and there was a pause as the person on the other end thought through their reply.

'Well what with the storm we had both our vans out most of the night clearing trees and debris off of the roads.'

'I see. So you were busy most of the night?'

'Yes, the conditions made things difficult to clear as well, it was mid-morning by the time they were back.'

'And did you receive many calls asking for trees to be cleared?'

'Yes, I even received one from the Sergeant at Firestone.' The man mentioned as casually as he could.

'My word. When did he call you?' The Inspector asked, pleased to hear Banks alibi backed up.

'At about half one.' The man replied without hesitation.

'I see. But they are all done now? The trees are all cleared?'

'Yes.' The man replied simply.

'I am glad.'

'And who would you be?' The man asked the Inspector.

'I'm calling from Scotland Yard. What was your name please?'

'Harold Barnes, head of roads.' Came the nervous reply.

'Thank you.' The Inspector had been scribbling furiously the entire time.

'That's alright. Will that be all then?' Harold asked, anxious to get off the telephone.

'Yes, goodbye,' the Inspector covered the mouth piece with his hand, moved it away from his mouth and turned to Drew.

'Goodbye,' Harold replied, nervously. He hung up his receiver and the line went dead.

'That was the man that Banks said he telephoned on Sunday night. He says Banks called him, but the call was made much later.'

'So he didn't call to have someone else come and take care of the tree?'

'No, at least not when he said he did. My guess is he pulled a favour with an old friend in an attempt to cover his tracks.' The telephone clicked back into life.

'Hello Inspector,' the operator came back on the line.

'Hello, were you listening to the call?'

'Yes,' the operator replied.

'Wonderful, could you put me through to the people who drive the vans he mentioned?' The Operator paused for a moment.

'I can put you through to the garage where they are stored, is that close enough?'

'Yes that would be marvellous, thank you.' The line went dead for a moment, and then the dialling tone returned. In a depo ten minutes' drive from Harold Barnes' worried face sat a fat middle aged balding man in dirty blue overalls in the cab of a flatbed truck. He turned the key. The engine stammered into life, then began ticking over. He had just pulled himself out from under the truck having been putting the engine back together from the oily floor. He lit a cigarette in celebration of his success, and just as he breathed out the first breath of smoke a harsh ring began to shrill out from the office telling him the telephone was ringing. He turned the engine off again and marched over to the stop the bell from ringing.

'Hello?' His voice was harsh and rough like smoke.

'Ahh hello, could I talk to the men who were clearing up the trees during the storm on Sunday?' the Inspector asked respectfully.

'Sunday night? You're having a laugh aren't you?' the man mocked, and the Inspector heard him take a drag from his cigarette.

'You didn't receive any calls for fallen trees?'

'Yeah course we did, and when we clocked in on Monday morning we went and cleared them.'

'But no one went out in the storm?' the Inspector asked just to clarify. The man sighed, beginning to lose his patience.

'No mate, like I said we were closed. You wouldn't get us out clearing roads in weather like that anyway,' the Inspector paused.

'Well, thanks for your time,' he said, and the man hung up without saying goodbye to go and make a cup of absurdly strong tea.

After a few seconds of dialling tone the operator returned.

'Anything else Inspector?' she asked.

'No that will be all for now, thank you.'

'No problem, goodbye Inspector,' the Inspector hung up the receiver again, and the bell gave a short 'ping' as it came to rest in its cradle.

'Well, we certainly have a few things to ask Sergeant Banks about now.' The Inspector took a look around the room.

'It would appear there is nothing more here of any interest. Perhaps we would have more luck at his home. Any idea where your superior lives?'

'Of course. He lives where he's always lived, in the Old Farmhouse,' Drew told him.

'The Old Farmhouse? Is there a new farm house or is it just an affectionate name?' the Inspector asked. Drew smiled.

'Yes there is a new one. When Banks sold his farm he built a new house for the new owner. He kept his and a little of the land around it.' As he talked the Inspector walked out of the office, closing and relocking the door.

'I'll take you there now.' Drew offered and led the way as they retraced their steps down the corridor.

'Thank you so much,' the Inspector replied. 'The questions are, will he be there, and if not, then where is he?' they went through the door out to the waiting room and back out on to the street without disturbing the desk Constable, who looked up briefly from his book to watch them leave.

25.

Banks awoke early, leaving his wife asleep in bed. He left the house without eating, he simply dressed and left. He drove through the dark morning. The town slept eerily in the early hours of the day. He arrived at Drew's house and parked a little way down the road where he had a good concealed view.

Then he waited. After being questioned by the Inspector the day before he had decided not to speak to him again. For now it would be easier to avoid him, only approaching when the time was right. A much deadlier plan had now entered his mind for the Inspector. He had decided to follow Drew, whom he had heard was playing chauffeur to the man from Scotland Yard, to the Swan and Dove. He would then keep an eye on them both, and see what they were doing. He hoped there would be a moment to get the Inspector alone, but knew the importance of remaining patient. His time would come.

When Drew finally emerged he looked fresh and ready in his uniform. Banks spat a few curses his way as he drove off, then trundled after him. He was in his own car, out of uniform. He followed him to The Swan and Dove, and waited on the road. A sinister grin spread across his face when he saw the Inspector emerge. He followed them to Nettlewood station, and watched the courier arrive, and deposit the package into Drew's boot. He wondered what it could have been, what he was up to.

He followed them into Firestone inconspicuously, and when they reached Firestone station he stopped his car a good distance away again. The police station sat near a T-junction, and after parking he walked back up the road to the turning where the police station was situated. By this time Drew and the Inspector had entered. Banks continued walking past the road with the police station on it until he found a spot where he had a narrow view of the station around the corner. He climbed through a gap in Donald Fothergil's shrub at 42 Hodges Lane and waited quietly in his front garden staring across the road, watching the station. The street was deserted. It was ten minutes before Banks saw anyone out as Sam Johnston strolled past on the other side of the road. He didn't notice Banks, he paid more attention to his dog Boris, a boisterous Jack Russell. Boris sniffed the walls, cocked his leg at every lamp post, and scampered happily along at his master's side. After another ten minutes the two men exited the police station. Banks watched them intently. They climbed back into their seats in Drew's car and drove away. Banks' mind began to divide as he wondered whether to continue following them, or to check in at the police station. He decided he could check it later, and hurried down to his car. He did a quick three point turn and sped back away after them. He drove quickly but cautiously, eagerly wanting to find them but not eager to give his pursuit away. He concentrated his thoughts, his mind reaching out around the town and the copse looking for them. He felt the direction they were moving in, and where they must be headed. Banks' gut lurched and he pushed the accelerator a little harder. The houses rushed by, but as he approached his house he slowed his pace to a crawl. When he saw Drew's car parked outside his heart sank. He tried not to think of what his wife would be telling them, what she was showing them, what the Inspector was seeing with his interrogating eyes.

He swore at Drew for his assisting the Inspector, but he wasn't surprised. Drew was smart, he had done well to get himself so integrated into the station. He saw now Drew's plan to become trusted. Banks swore at himself for using Drew so much. His mind screamed at him for letting him get close enough to find a body. He should have seen it would only be a matter of time.

Finding them here allowed one thing to become clear; they were looking for him. They had already gained access to his house. His wife would no doubt be serving them tea now, showing them his study. It was wise of him to be wary with them. He knew why they were looking for him, and he didn't want to answer any questions. He cursed Drew again for not just telling him where he was on Sunday night. All this could have been avoided if he could have found Drew that night, but there was no trace of him anywhere in that terrible storm.

Banks sat and watched the door. Now he knew where they were, and that he was their quarry, he began wondering if he had time to get back to the station. He wanted to assess what they might have seen, and wondered if they had taken anything. He rolled the thought over in his head until the urge to check became too great, and he abandoned his house, racing back the way he had come.

26.
The Old Farm House was the last house along the eastern road. After selling the land and splitting the cottage away from the farm the copse had encroached, and now surrounded the house. The farmland it used to be the homestead for was now cut off from it by trees. Beyond the trees the remainder of the farm stretched out for miles all around. The Banks' house was set back along a drive with a huge front garden that had, in the not so distant past, been used to park farm machinery. It had once boasted stables and even a pig pen. When Banks had relinquished his farmer status in favour of a career in policing he'd converted the land to a lawn that rose in a shallow incline toward the house, bordered with flower beds that during the summer bloomed beautifully, but at this time of year sprouted only the dull branches of plants that awaited the spring. The stables had been converted to rooms that added to the rambling nature of the house. Drew parked his police car on the empty drive and the two men approached the large red front door. A horseshoe hung on the left, and a hand bell to the right. The building was white, and single storied. A thatched roof sat on top, which seemed to be pushing the squat house into the ground. As they approached the door an older, but not old, lady opened it drying her hands on a tea towel.

'Mrs Banks I presume?' the Inspector asked as he approached her.

'Yes,' she replied, a little confused. Mrs Banks recognised Drew's face. 'Hello Drew, is everything alright?'

'Hello Mrs Banks,' Drew replied respectfully. 'We're looking for Sergeant Banks.'

'He's not at the station, we thought he might be here?' the Inspector continued for him. 'I'm the Inspector, down from the yard.' He held out his hand and she shook it, a little timidly, almost as if the mere action of shaking his hand would reveal to him some guilt she was unaware of.

'Well he's not here Inspector, he left so early this morning I didn't see him go. He doesn't come home during the day,' she replied, a tinge of worry slipping into her voice.

'I see,' the Inspector replied. He paused in thought for a moment, determined not to allow this line of enquiry to become a dead end. 'Would it be too much trouble to come inside, perhaps we could gain an idea of where he is by looking at his diary? Or at a calendar?' the Inspector asked casually. He did not want to cause her any concern as to his whereabouts, and wanted to gain her trust. He smiled comfortingly. She hesitated, wondering if there was anything her husband might be hiding that these two shouldn't see, then dismissed the idea with a shrug.

'Of course, I'll show you through to his study I'm sure you'll find something of use in there.' The two men crossed the threshold and entered the house. It was warmly decorated, even if the decor was little aged. This added to the feeling of homeliness the house exuded, making it feel lived in and welcoming. Though the building was quite large the rooms inside were small but comfortable. As they walked down the hall on their way to the study, they passed a living room with sofas, chairs, a television and an over filled book case crammed into it. There was a dining room, with a large table squeezed into the small space, and a rustic well used kitchen.

'I wonder where he could have got to?' she asked them. 'Did you try The Black Prince? He's quite pally with the landlord there you know.'

'Is he? Well perhaps we will try there next,' the Inspector replied as if he hadn't thought of it. When they arrived at the study she opened the door and she pushed it wide open for them. It contained a large dark wood desk covered in paper. It was not unlike the desk in the station in its content and appearance, though on this one Banks had made no attempt to hide the cigarettes or the whiskey. The Inspector could tell that Banks had not used the room recently, the smell of smoke wasn't fresh, and he guessed he had not been here for at least three or four days. He cast a quick eye over the paperwork. It was similar to what they had seen at the station, a few half written reports, forms awaiting completion. No one said out loud what they were all thinking; the room was a mess. The Inspector riffled through the papers on the desk, opened a few drawers but there was no sign of any diary. Mrs Banks watched powerless, feeling as if she should say something but not entirely sure if she had the power to stop him.

'Hmm, I can't see any diaries here,' his eyes turned to the walls. 'Any idea if he perhaps has a calendar?' They all looked about the room. The Inspector had been the only one of them brave enough to actually enter. Drew and Mrs Banks stood in the doorway as if held back.

'I've been specifically told that I'm not allowed in here,' Mrs Banks told him from the door way. 'Due to the sensitivity of information, you now, in his reports,' she motioned toward the desk.

'Indeed, very important to keep delicate details safe,' the Inspector nodded, eyeing the pile. 'Is there anywhere else he might keep a timetable of his movements? Perhaps the bedroom?' the Inspector suggested.

'No there's nothing in the bedroom, you could try the garage.' she suggested.

'The garage? Why would we want to check in there?' the Inspector asked, pondering casually.

'Well, he spends quite a lot of time in there. You know what men are like,' she answered with a nervous laugh.

'I guess it couldn't hurt to have a quick look. Please, lead the way'. Relieved that they were leaving the study, she relaxed noticeably as she led them back through the front door, and out to the garage. The larger main door at the front was shut and locked tight, so they tried the smaller side door. This too was locked.

'Evidently your husband is a man who likes to keep himself to himself,' the Inspector pointed out.

'That's strange, I never come out here so I always presumed it was left open. I don't think I've got a key to this door.' She thought for a moment. 'He must have it on his keys. He's got so many keys on there I'm sure he has a key to every door in town.'

The Inspector checked the thick garage door, giving it a gentle shove in case it was stuck, but it was definitely locked fast. He examined the lock, but it was beyond the ability of his picks. Without a key they would be unable to access whatever was inside. Mrs Banks looked worryingly at the door as she tried to calculate why he would be hiding something from her.

'Perhaps we could have a cup of tea and a chat?' She thought for a moment of the loneliness of waiting for her husband to return home.

'Yes, please come back in and I'll put the kettle on.' Happy for the distraction away from the locked garage and back to the chores of everyday life she led them back into the kitchen. Like the rest of the house it was warmly decorated. Patterns of faded flowers adorned the old wallpaper, pictures of family, recent and old, hung on the wall for happy reminisces. The sides, the table and the cupboards were all made of weathered oak. The Inspector and Drew made themselves comfortable at the old table while Mrs Banks busied herself with fetching cups and making tea.

'This is a lovely home you have,' Drew complimented, admiring the kitchen with its heavily laden shelves of homemade preserves, jars of herbs and spices.

'Why thank you Drew. It's a bit too big for my liking nowadays, lots of cleaning of empty rooms now the children have all flown the coop.' She pointed at one of the pictures hanging on the walls. 'That's our son and his daughter, they live down by Plymouth.'

'How delightful. Have you always lived in Firestone?' the Inspector asked.

'No I'm from Nettlewood originally, been here thirty six years, we moved here when we were married. It's been in my husband's family for generations.' She poured water into the pot and stirred.

'I believe it used to be the farmhouse?' the Inspector asked.

'That's right, when he got offered the Sergeant's job we sold the farm off but we kept the house. You can see how it used to look in that one there.' She stopped stirring and pointed at another picture on the wall with her spoon. This one showed the front of the property filled with horses, all stood on a dirt track. The house looked the same, but the surroundings of the picture were all foreign to the building now.

'So your husband has always lived in Firestone?'

'Yes, and his father, and his father before him.'

'How wonderful.' The Inspector portrayed genuine interest, and Mrs Banks began relaxing more into his company. Drew had noticed that the Inspector had a demeanour that could relax any situation, and bring anyone round to revealing what he wanted to know. He remained silent, allowing him to work.

'So does he ever talk about his policing?' the Inspector asked.

'No, not really, not that I don't ask.' She began moving the fruits of her labour on to the table; cups, tea pot, and even a plate of homemade biscuits.

'I always ask how his day was, and what he's been up to, but he always says he can't talk about it.'

'Why's that?' the Inspector asked, picking up one of the shortbread. 'Thank you,' he added, taking a bite.

'Well, he says it's private, you know, details of local crime and such.'

'Such a shame, I find that bending someone's ear at the end if a hard day can lighten the weight of a stressful day. Does he ever show signs of stress, there are some things we need to tell people, how our day went, how we are feeling, and I would have thought his wife would be the ideal person.'

'Well yes...' she trailed off as she remembered the locked garage. 'I wish he would tell me about it. He seems to have terrible dreams.'

'A sure sign of a weary mind. Does he tell you about them?' the Inspector asked, accepting a cup of steaming tea from her. 'Thank you,' he said again.

'No, when I ask he says he can't remember them. I hear him in the night, murmuring to himself. I can't tell what he's saying, but it seems urgent, like he's trapped, or in trouble.' She looked up suddenly, as if hearing something in the house.

'He talks to himself too. I don't tell him I know that, and I don't tell no one else either,' she informed them, as if there was an unspoken confidentiality between them.

'I hear him, sometimes when he's shaving. It sounds like he's talking to someone but I only hear his voice.'

'And does this worry you?' the Inspector asked, concern in his voice.

'A bit, but he's alright otherwise. It's like it's just his way. It's how he deals with things, and it seems to work, because he's alright otherwise.' Drew watched her as she drifted into thought, properly considering his behaviour to herself for the first time. Drew was sure that this was due to the Inspector allowing her to share her burden, asking her the right questions in the right way. The two men drunk their tea quietly and allowed her to think.

'Is that why you're looking for him?' she asked, seemingly coming to the decision that his behaviour wasn't normal. 'Has someone else noticed something and told you about it?'

'No, no one else has mentioned anything, but he should be helping me with my investigation, and I am unable to locate him. This is not the behaviour of a man concerned with finding the person responsible for leaving a dead body near his town.' She thought for a moment.

'Unless he was the person responsible for the body being there,' she reasoned absent-mindedly. The two men shared a surprised look.

'Do you think your husband could be capable of something like that?'

'Oh no!' she replied in his defence. 'He's just over-worked. He's very busy.' The Inspector and Drew shared another look.

'Does he say where he goes? What he does all day?'

'No, like I said, we never, well he never, talks about it. Not with me. I always ask but he never tells me much.'

'Well, I am sure he is fine and will be here again tonight. If he does come home could you please contact me at Nettlewood police station? They can then find me.'

'Yes. Yes I will,' she said determinedly. She realised that she too deserved an explanation as to his whereabouts, and only the Inspector was likely to get one out of him.

'Well Mrs Banks, as we can shed no further light on your husband's whereabouts, we shall leave you in peace. Thank you so much for allowing us to look.' At the news of their departure Mrs Banks stood politely.

'Well, no problem Inspector, I'm sure my husband will turn up, he can't have gone far.' She was reassuring herself as much as the policemen.

'Yes, I am sure he will. As I say, please inform him that I have been looking for him, and contact me as soon you see him.'

'Through Nettlewood station,' she repeated.

'Indeed.' The Inspector smiled. With no further hesitation Drew and the Inspector left, wishing Mrs Banks a good day on the door step. They walked back to Drew's car and climbed in.

'Well, do you want to try The Black Prince like she suggested?' Drew asked.

'Hmmm,' the Inspector replied thoughtfully. 'In good time, yes. Do you ever get the feeling that you're chasing your own tail?' Drew frowned.

'Are you saying that Banks doesn't mean to be found?' he asked.

'Yes, I wouldn't say this wild goose chase has been a complete waste of time.' The Inspector eyed the door of Banks garage. 'But I don't want to spend any more time looking for someone whom I feel is trying very hard not to be found. We will look, and we will find him, but perhaps not now.' The Inspector removed his notebook from an inside pocket and studied it.

'Perhaps we could gain more of idea as to where he might be by retracing his steps. We know where he was up until this morning, let us work back a little further. On the night of the body's appearance he called you to say he had been at the Mayor's house. Perhaps now is the time to visit the Mayor and ascertain what happened that night at his house.' Drew started the engine.

'Why the interest in Banks? It must be more than the business with my father,' Drew stated.

'It is. There were files missing from the cabinets at the station, that weren't in his study. I can't think why he would hide cases, but I suspect as they were not in the study that they are in his locked garage. Not to mention that he gave you orders about the body on

Sunday night that no decent officer would give,' the Inspector replied.

'Do you think she's right about him being able to murder someone? Do you think Banks is a suspect?' Drew asked.

'I believe he has a role to play in the body's appearance, though I am not sure yet what role that was, or the motives behind it. I don't believe Mrs Banks knows any more about it than we were able to get out of her.' The Inspector lost himself for a moment as all the possibilities played out in his mind's eye and his next move became obvious.

'Let us visit the Mayor, and see what occurred at his house on Sunday evening.' Drew nodded, put the car into first, and they drove away.

27.

Banks entered the police station through the front door, rushing past Tom reading his book, unlocking the door he guarded without disturbing him. He followed Drew and the Inspector's steps back down the corridor to his office door. He rattled the handle; it was still locked. He took out his keys, sorting through the bunch for the right one. Upon entering he could tell immediately that someone had been in there recently. Everything seemed to be exactly as he had **left it**; the drawers were all still secure. No item was out of place yet the Inspector's presence denied him. Banks followed his steps around the room, retracing his path, even his movements, as if having them dictated to him. He knew that the worst thing the Inspector was likely to have found in this office would be the **bottle hidden in** the bottom drawer, so his being here only disturbed him because he had been here. He had somehow gained access to his office, and now he had entered his house. He froze on the spot suddenly, as if hearing something.

'I must. He's too close,' he suddenly spoke loudly out into the air. 'No, you won't,' he called louder, as if arguing with someone. He knew what he would have to do. He would find a time when the Inspector was alone. Perhaps tonight he could sneak to his room. No witnesses. Before any reports were filed. He raised his head again. 'Then we will do the same thing to them,' he replied to no one. He took a cigarette from the packet in the drawer, and lit it with a crackling Swan Vista. He inhaled the first drag with a sharp intake of air and had poured himself a scotch before he exhaled the smoke, satisfied. He reorganised the papers on his desk, took some more out of the cabinet and put them on top. When the cigarette was finished he stubbed it out and lit another one, then put the scotch and the matches back in the drawer and locked it. He left the room with cigarette in mouth, locking the door again behind him. He hurried out of the station, the desk Constable not once looking up from his book. When he was back in his car he looked up into his mirror and said, very calmly;

'**I will. There will come a time,**' before he drove away back towards his house.

28.

Drew drove his squad car down the road toward Firestone copse, but took a left heading north before they reached the town. The closer they got to the Mayor's house, the thicker the roof of trees over their heads became. The roads thinned and became more difficult to traverse.

'What can you tell me about the Mayor?' the Inspector asked Drew as they drove.

'He provides all the mayoral duties as you might expect. Opens fetes, judges vegetables. He attends the monthly council chamber meetings, though I've never attended myself so I couldn't tell you what if any role he plays in them.'

'What about his private life? Anything you know about him outside of his official duties?'

'Well, he drinks in The Black Prince occasionally on a social footing, but more often attends various dinners with members of the local council in various places around the county. They are very formal affairs. Apart from that I couldn't really tell you much I'm afraid.'

'What do you know about his relationship with Banks?'

'That's something I have always puzzled about,' Drew admitted. 'Nothing I can think of that connects the two, other than in a professional capacity. I presume the Sergeant of the local force and the Mayor would be required to discuss some matters together, security, crime rates, but outside of this I'm not sure what they have in common.' They turned down the private lane where the mayor lived and a grand old house loomed into view ahead.

'Is this the residence of all the Mayor's, or is this his own private house?' the Inspector asked Drew.

'As far as I know this is his own house. He's been Mayor for as long as I can remember, and he has always lived here.'

They pulled up on to the gravel drive in front of the impressive front door. Huge and over bearing, the door was far from welcoming. It was as if the doors themselves warned them not to enter. Drew stepped out of the car and shivered against the cold and the feeling of trespassing. Whether the Inspector shared his feelings was unclear as he stepped purposefully out of the car, barely noticing the chill, and walked confidently to the door. Drew stepped up behind him, inspired by his confidence. The Inspector pulled the bell cord and from somewhere deep inside the house they could here its distant ring. The men stood and waited patiently. The house stood in a clearing in the trees, its grounds protected on all sides from the long ancient branches by a low and ancient looking red brick wall. Eventually the door was answered by the Mayor, dressed in suit trousers, shirt, waistcoat and untied tie, but no jacket. Instead he wore an official looking red gown over his smart attire. He looked rather affronted at the sight of a policeman at his front door.

'Good morning gentlemen.' He eyed them up and down distastefully. 'Is there a problem?'

'No sir, sorry to bother you, I'm an Inspector from Scotland Yard, I was wondering if I might ask you a few questions?' the Inspector asked with a polite smile.

'Do you have a warrant?' the Mayor asked immediately.

'Well, I don't really need one, I'm just wanting to ask for a few details,' the Inspector did not allow himself to become riled by the Mayor's attitude.

'Concerning what, exactly?' the Mayor was offish, and suspicious as to what they would possibly want to question him about. Someone of his stature was not used to being questioned by the law on his doorstep.

'Well, as I hope you are aware, a body was discovered in the woods not far from here. As one of the leaders of the town I wondered if talking to you might help me understand the community, and you could perhaps help the investigation by keeping the community calm in such difficult times.' The Inspector smiled a sycophantic smile.

'Well, yes of course.' The Mayor remained rather uppity, but bowed under the Inspector's logic and compliments. 'Yes of course, please come in. I'm afraid I'm just preparing to go out so I can't give you very long.' This seemed to be his excuse to them for his offish behaviour, however no apology was forthcoming. The two men stepped across the threshold and into a large cold flag stoned hallway. The Mayor kept them there; he did not allow them to enter any further into the house.

'So if you'll excuse me I must dispense with the same questions I have to ask everyone,' the Inspector explained.

'Please go on Inspector.' The Mayor, realising he was having to accommodate the visitors on a professional level had developed a slightly more welcoming tone.

'Firstly, where were you Sunday night?' The Inspector asked kindly, every part the guest, respecting the Mayor's hospitality.

'Well I was here, entertaining guests,' the Mayor replied.

'I see, and who were these guests?' the Inspector asked.

'Well, there was Sergeant Banks, Constables Atkins, Charlie, and Doctor Sparrow.'

'And what did you all do?'

'We played cards, drank port, smoked cigars, and reminisced on our old school days together,' the Mayor replied curtly. 'What would you expect us to be doing? Scouring the street for urchins to murder? Really Inspector we are pillars of the community.'

'Were there any other witnesses to their being here? Perhaps your wife witnessed you all playing cards?

'My wife? Oh no my dear man, card nights are strictly men only.'

'I see, of course, how silly of me. So the only people who can ascertain for certain that the five of you were here all night will be yourselves?

'Is that not enough then?' the Mayor's demeanour was slipping again and he was becoming quite agitated. 'The head of the local police force, the Mayor and the Doctor do not hold enough authority for you? What is the meaning of these questions, are you suggesting that I, we, are suspects?'

'No of course not,' the Inspector replied calmly. 'And so what of Banks, how was his behaviour?' he moved swiftly on with the questions, not seeing a need to defend himself.

'The same as always, he was amiable enough, he won a few hands, lost a few hands, and was delightful company as always, in other words he was his normal self. He stayed later than the others as he usually does and we discussed the price of houses, err, the maintenance of the park, general local issues that interest us.'

'And how do you all know each other?'

'We were all at school together, and have made the effort to stay in regular contact throughout the years. Everyone else we went to school with has I believe moved from Firestone a long time ago. In those days we had our own school, it has since closed due to declining numbers of course.'

'Would you mind perhaps writing me a list of everyone that was here Sunday night?' the Inspector asked. The Mayor thought for a moment, then shrugged.

'Very well,' he replied, apprehensively, not knowing why the Inspector might need it. He entered one of the rooms that lead off of the hall through a heavy dark wooden door and returned with paper and a pen. He leant against a table in the hall holding a plant and jotted down the names. Every action he made was defiant, from the crossing of the 't's to the fullness of each stop. When the names were written he tore the sheet from its pad and handed it to the Inspector who studied it briefly before folding it and putting it into his inside jacket pocket.

'Well, thank you for your time, please don't allow us to keep you from your preparations any longer.'

'Is that it? No more questions?' he asked, surprised. He opened the door for them gratefully.

'No more questions for now, thank you,' the Inspector informed him. He turned to the Constable. 'Well then Drew, shall we be off?' he raised his hat in farewell.

'Good day,' he said, and they returned to Drew's car leaving the incredulous Mayor staring after them.

29.

The Mayor closed his front door behind them and moved into the room at the front of the house to watch them through the window. The two men crunched across the gravel drive, climbed into their car, and drove away in full conversation. He had no doubt they were discussing him and his answers to their questions. He imagined them talking about his house, and how impressed they were by him, his clothes, his surroundings. He wondered if his answers were what they had been expecting, if they had learned anything new from him. He wondered exactly what it was they were trying to discover, as he had nothing to hide, and neither did any of his guests. When they had disappeared from his view he walked back to the room he had entered earlier for paper. It was a large study, with an imposing desk sat in the middle of the room surrounded by shelves stacked with old volumes and books. As he passed it he replaced the paper pad in its place on the desk. On the same wall as the door, the wall that the desk faced, was a mirror. It was large enough to allow a full reflection of the head, shoulders, and most of the torso. He stood in front of it, watching himself for a few minutes, searching his eyes. He looked at himself amongst the books, the fine surroundings. He tilted his head this way and that as if listening for something. Eventually he stopped, and walked through the house down a sprawl of corridors to the back garden. He let himself out, and walked for a minute or two to a quiet spot at the back of the grounds looking out on to the copse. He stopped, apparently not feeling the cold biting wind or the splatter of rain that began soaking into his fine clothes. He stood quite still, tilted his head, and listened to the whispering of the trees.

30.

'Well, what did you make of him Drew?' the Inspector asked when they had buckled their seat belts. The car spluttered into life and Drew pulled away once more into the cold day. A mist of spit filled the air, and the windscreen wipers screeched across their view of the road.

'I don't think he was too pleased at being questioned like that, but he sounded genuine enough. Are you still going to check out the other guests?' Drew began to move the car away from the house.

'Yes, I think we'd better. There's something about the story I don't like. These men are all from very different walks of life. The doctor, two policemen, a pub landlord and the Mayor. Even if they were friends at school why should they still meet up regularly like that?' The Inspector thought for a moment and wondered if they were even aware they were hiding something. He removed the list of guests from his pocket and studied it for a moment before comparing it to the list Banks had given him.

'All in the same order,' he commented to Drew. 'How odd,' he thought for a moment. 'Drew, out of those who attended the Mayor's that night, who would you say was, well, the slowest? Perhaps someone whom might be more open to us asking questions the Mayor would not have liked?' Drew smiled at the Inspector's method.

'It would be Atkins, the Constable.' He replied knowingly.

'Perhaps we should start with him, lead the way young Drew.' Knowing which direction he now needed to head he picked up speed and took them back down the lanes toward the house of Constable Atkins. The quickest way back to town took them towards the small parade of shops, and as they approached Drew noticed a figure walking to his car.

'That's Doctor Sparrow.' He pointed him out to the Inspector.

'Well what a stroke of luck, shall we stop and have a quick chat?' the Inspector suggested. Drew obliged, and pulled the car up at the next space he saw, on the opposite side of the road. The two men were quickly out and had caught up to the Doctor before he'd had a chance to get in his car.

'Doctor Sparrow!' Drew called to him as they approached. He turned to face them, car keys in hand, and was surprised to see an officer of the law approaching.

'Good afternoon officer, is there a problem?' Of all the men on the list, the doctor looked the youngest. He was dressed in casual blue slacks, a light beige coat and had hair of a longer, more fashionable, length.

'Hello Doctor. I'm Constable Gates, from Firestone constabulary. This is an Inspector from Scotland Yard, we were wondering if we could have a quick word?'

'My yes, this sounds serious.' The Doctor was relaxed, comfortable in the knowledge that he was an innocent man, and that their search was not for him.

'Thank you so much,' the Inspector thanked him. 'Could you tell us where you were on Sunday night, between the hours of say, nine o' clock at night and one a.m.?'

'Yes of course, I spent the evening at the Mayor's house with some friends, I left at around eleven, and went straight home,' he was happy to tell them everything, he yielded to the questioning obediently.

'I see. And what did you do at the Mayor's house?' the Inspector asked.

'We... drank port, played cards, and reminisced about our school days together,' the Doctor replied airily.

'And who else was there?' the Inspector asked, taking out his notebook.

'Well there was Sergeant Banks, myself, your colleague Atkins, and Charlie.'

'I see, thank you,' the Inspector passed the Doctor his notebook. 'Would you mind writing them all down for me?' The Doctor placed his case down on the pavement.

'No of course not,' he replied, casually taking the book from him and writing down the names in a messy hand. He passed the Inspector back his notebook with a smile.

'Thank you so much for your time, doctor.'

'No problem, is there anything I should know? Is one of my friends in some kind of trouble?'

'Not at all, we are simply following up a few lines of enquiry following the discovery of the body on Sunday night, eliminating people from our enquiries.'

'I see, yes I heard about that, my patients have been talking about it all day. Anything I can help with?' the Doctor offered kindly.

'Oh that is a thoughtful offer, but we have everything in hand. Thank you so much for your time. Please don't allow us to hold you up any longer.' The Inspector tucked his note book safely back into his coat pocket.

'No problem. I have few more house calls to make but I'll be back for the afternoon surgery about three.' He opened his car door. 'Should you need me for anything else,' he added, before climbing in.

'Yes, I will bear that in mind, good day.' The Inspector raised his hat and Doctor Sparrow drove off to his next appointment. Drew and the Inspector watched him drive away before returning to their car.

'The same story again,' Drew pointed out. 'Almost to the word,' he fired up the engine and rubbed his hands together for warmth.

'Yes, and the same list, in the same order.' The Inspector compared the three lists.

'Let us see what Constable Atkins can reveal shall we?' Drew obliged, and they continued on their way.

31.
Doctor Sparrow drove his car away from the policemen and toward his next appointment. He wondered why they were interested in his movements on Sunday night, and then wondered if it wasn't his movements, but the movements of another of the Mayor's guests. Without noticing he drove past the turning that would have taken him to Mrs Smythe, his next appointment. Instead he continued away from the houses, and into the copse. He pulled his car up along a quiet lane and, without consciously realising that he was doing it, climbed out of his car. He walked a few yards into the copse until he was out of sight, surrounded by trees, and he began to listen to the branches swaying in the wind. On the road where he had parked his car a figure watched him, hidden between the trunks.

32.

Atkins lived in a small two up two down house on an estate near the old train station. Originally built for the men working on the railway, they were cheaply made, and cheaply maintained. There were two streets of these houses, all identical. Their occupants were largely those who lived alone, without the income nor the need for anything larger. The Inspector knocked on the thin wooden door, and immediately the two men heard an outburst barking, followed by the gruff sound of a man shouting at the creature responsible to shut up. After a few moments struggle to put the dog somewhere safe the front door was opened a crack and a face appeared.

'Alright Drew? What's up?' Atkins asked, a hint of suspicion in his voice. He wasn't used to uniformed officers visiting him at his door.

'Hello Gerry, this is the Inspector, down from the Yard. He wants to ask you a few questions if you're not busy?'

'Oh.' Atkins paused. 'No, of course not. Hang on.' The door closed again briefly while the chain was removed, and then it was fully opened.

'You'd better come in then, it's too bloody cold to be standing around with the door open today.' He led them into the house. The front door opened directly from the pavement on to the front room.

'Shall I get the kettle on? Think you'll be here long enough for a cuppa?'

'Oh, I believe there's always time for a cup of tea,' the Inspector replied as he crossed the threshold. The room they entered contained a small settee, a smaller chair, and a television with a football match being played out on its grainy black and white screen. A flight of stairs led directly off of it leading, the Inspector presumed, up to a small bedroom and bathroom.

'Right you are, back in a tick, have a seat.' Atkins left through the only door out of the room, struggling as the dog contained within tried to escape. It whimpered and gave a few barks, and Atkins replied in kind with swearing and threats.

'I don't mind if the dog wants to come in,' the Inspector called from his seat as Atkins wrestled his way through the door to the kitchen.

'Are you sure?' Atkins called back. 'She can be a bit of a pain.'

'No of course, please, it will be easier for you, and more pleasant for her I'm sure.' With permission granted Atkins gave up his fight and a large Alsatian bounded excitedly out of the kitchen and up to the two men, who had made themselves comfortable on the small and rather worn out settee. The dog was friendly, displaying her affection by attempting to lick both men's faces simultaneously, jumping around in circles, and giving small excited barks at them. The Inspector stroked her head and back, making calming 'Shhh' noises. She immediately took a liking to him, sitting at his feet and staring at him expectantly. He studied her name tag.

'There there Cara,' he told her, using a tone soothing enough to calm a storm. 'There there, shhh, shhh.' Cara soon calmed and made her self comfortable at his feet, enjoying the attention. Atkins appeared presently with three chipped and dirty cups full of tea. He struggled out of the kitchen with them, holding two awkwardly in one hand by the handles.

'Well who's a little hussy then?' he asked Cara, who looked up at him indifferently. 'Here you go lads, a nice hot brew.' He dished out the cups and they all sat sipping the tea and watching the game.

'Did I miss anything?' Atkins asked.

'No, though United need this game to stay up don't they?' Drew replied.

'Yeah, they also need Newcastle to lose, not much chance of that when they're playing at home though.' The Inspector sipped his tea.

'I'm very sorry to interrupt such an important game,' he apologised sympathetically. 'But I do need to ask a few questions.'

'Yes of course,' Atkins eyes did not turn away from the screen.

'Where were you on Sunday night, between the hours of nine in the evening and one in the morning?'

Atkins thought for a moment, retracing his steps.

'Sunday? I was having dinner with the Mayor and a few old friends, up at his house,' he replied rather proudly.

'Sounds nice,' The Inspector replied. 'Who else was there?'

'Banks, err, Doctor Sparrow, me, and Charlie.'

'Well, seems like an eclectic collection of friends, how do you all know each other?' the Inspector asked.

'We were all at school together, and we all sort of stayed in touch over the years. A lot of people from Firestone move away as soon as they're old enough, not much here to keep them around. We all stayed, so we all meet up about once a month.'

'I see. And what made you stay here, if so many of your friends moved?'

'Well, my old mum, she was very ill and needed me to stay. Then I got the Constables job which I really like, so I stayed here.'

'And when you go to the Mayor's house, what do you do?'

'We play cards, drink port, and reminisce about our school days, people we knew.'

'And you meet up on a Sunday? Didn't you all have work the next day?'

'Yes, but it's not always easy to find a day when we're all free, especially the Mayor.' The Inspector sipped his tea.

'Well, I think it's wonderful that you have all stayed in contact for so long. I can't say the same for anyone I went to school with.'

'Small town like this it's not that hard staying in touch,' Atkins pointed out. 'Everyone knows everyone else's business anyway.' The Inspector stroked Cara's back, Atkins stared, hypnotized, at the television. Drew and the Inspector exchanged looks.

'And what of the Mayor and Banks, what's their relationship like?' The Inspector asked.

'It fine I suppose,' Atkins replied. 'They're the most-well off of us all, bloody rolling in it the Mayor is, you should see his house. Banks ain't doing too badly for himself either I reckon.'

'What makes you say that?' the Inspector asked.

'Well, it's like a competition with him and the Mayor, you know, whose got what, or how many of these. He makes a fortune from renting the farm out I know that much.' The Inspector raised an eyebrow in interest.

'Rents? I was led to believe he had sold it?' he asked.

'Oh no, still owns it, just rents out the land and the new house to the bloke up there, what's his name?

'Colin Underwood,' Drew replied.

'Yeah that's him.' Atkins took a mouthful of tea. 'Oooh bloody hell, come on united!' he suddenly shouted as his team missed a goal. The Inspector and Drew had drained their cups.

'Well, thanks you for the tea, but I feel we must be off.' The Inspector informed him.

'You're welcome to stay and watch the match if you like gents?' There was a hint of loneliness in his voice, as if the company was appreciated, even if it was on an official level.

'Well that is a very kind offer, but we must be getting on, hope the game turns out in your favour.' They stood to leave, and Cara immediately began pacing the room, whining after them. The Inspector patted her on the head.

'Right you are, see you then.' Atkins opened the door for them, and they stepped back out into the chilly afternoon.

'Well he was a nice chap,' the Inspector noted as they walked back to the squad car in the cold afternoon light. 'Hard to see him still being friends with Banks after all this time though, seeing as none of his other mates are.'

'No, I suppose not,' Drew replied, and opened the car. 'Next on the list is Charlie, who should be at The Black Prince. We pass the station on the way, shall we head in and see if Banks has appeared?'

'I think we will leave Charlie for now, we can drop in to the station before stopping for a spot of lunch. I am eager to see how Dr Ward is progressing so then we'll head to Nettlewood'

Drew nodded in understanding and drove them back to the police station, and they entered to find the front desk unmanned. Drew rang the bell, but no one came to answer, so he leant into the open reception desk window and removed the key from a hook on the wall. He unlocked the door and let the Inspector in. In the staff room they found the desk Sergeant, eating his sandwiches and reading the paper.

'Did you hear us ringing Sergeant?' the Inspector asked indignantly.

'Yes, I was just getting up when I heard you let yourselves in,' he replied defensively through a mouthful of ham and cheese sandwich.

'We could have been anybody,' Drew pointed out.

'You weren't though were you?' he mumbled, shrugging off the young Constable's approach.

'Any sign of Banks?' Drew asked. The Inspector was noticing Drew taking a more confident tone with him and did nothing to stop it.

'No, no one's been in since you left,' he replied, standing defensively. Neither man backed down. The Inspector sniffed the air.

'I think Banks might have been in,' he pointed out.

'No, I didn't see him,' the desk Sergeant replied. They walked away from him, leaving him bruised and bewildered and made their way up the corridor to Banks' office. The Inspector checked to see if the door was open but was disappointed so picked the lock again. This time Drew followed him in.

'Can you smell the cigarette smoke?' the Inspector asked rhetorically. The odour filled the air.

'Never saw the appeal myself,' Drew replied. The Inspector studied the desk and cabinets.

'These papers have been moved. He has been here, and he wants us to know he's been here,' the Inspector surmised.

'Why would he do that?' Drew asked.

'As an alibi, as a game,' the Inspector checked the files on the desk, no changes had been made recently, the crime detailed on them merely served as a prop in Banks' game. 'Come Drew, I feel I need some food. Let's get up to The Green Man again.' The Inspector paused at the staff room and the Desk Sergeant with a mouth full of fresh sandwich.

'Should Banks come back to the station please inform him that I am looking for him and that he should contact me in Drew's car immediately, do you understand?' the Inspector's tone was severe, the man looked at the Inspector in fear, suddenly conscious that he may have more power than he bargained for.

'Yes Inspector,' he replied timidly.

'I want the desk manned every minute that the station is open. I don't mind if you eat your sandwiches while you are there however I am sure you have better things to do than read your book,' the man swallowed a lump of fear that had lodged in his throat.

'And I want a list of everyone that comes through that door, the time they came in, the time they go out, and what they want in this building. Do you understand?' Drew was pleased to hear the Inspector taking the man to task, it had been a long time coming.

'Yes Inspector,' the Constable repeated, picking up his lunch box and obediently heading out to the front desk. The Inspector glared at him displeasingly, and he squirmed under his powerful eyes. When he had returned to his desk the Inspector considered the station disapprovingly.

'This place is not up to scratch,' he informed him thoughtfully. 'I want at least two officers here at all times. I want you to find the location of all the other officers and get some of them to come into help you cover,' the Inspector told him firmly. The man nodded obediently.

'How am I supposed to find them?' he asked the Inspector timidly.

'You're a police officer, I am sure you will work something out.' the Inspector informed him. He turned to Drew and with a nod they disappeared outside, leaving the Desk Constable scratching his head.

'Drew, to The Green Man if you please.' He asked the younger Constable nicely, and they headed for the car.

33.

Drew found a convenient space to park a short walk away from the pub, and they hurried along in the dreary afternoon to the warmth of the Saloon bar. The Inspector went in first, and as had happened the previous day, the conversation trailed off when the patrons realised who it was coming in. The Inspector pretended not to notice and headed for the bar.

'Pint of Bitter Drew?' the Inspector asked.

'Not while I'm on duty Inspector, I'll join you on a pot of tea though,' Drew suggested jovially.

'Very good,' The Inspector replied, and waited patiently for service. Presently Lionel appeared from the kitchen.

'Ahh hello again Inspector, Drew.' He welcomed them to his establishment with the grin of a man who knew he was about to become a little better off.

'Hello Lionel, any change to the menu, or can we just have the same as we had yesterday?' the Inspector asked.

'Of course, take your seats gents and Mavis will bring you some soup over shortly.' He told them gleefully.

'That's great. Also, while I have your attention, I noticed your 'vacancies' sign outside, and was hoping I might be able to book a room with you.' Lionel's smile grew a little at the corners.

'Of course, Inspector. We have all the rooms free at the moment, so you can take your pick.'

'Do you have a room with an en-suite?'

'Yes, no problem.'

'And could I possibly have a key to the front door, so as not to disturb you too much should my investigations run into the small hours?'

'Yes, I think we have a spare somewhere,' Lionel replied, eyeing an unseen board of keys hidden behind the bar.

'Wonderful. Well, perhaps after lunch I can move my things in?'

'Of course sir, not a problem.' They retired to their table with their steaming pot. Presently Mavis appeared with a beaming smile and started fussing over them. The food she delivered seemed to have only improved over night, and the two men ate their lunches eagerly; it had been a busy morning. As they ate the mood in the bar lightened. The locals were becoming more accustomed to the sight of the Inspector and Drew in their establishment. Not to mention their admiration of his appetite. The news of the Inspector's change of location caused their tongues to wag a little more ferociously, and, the Inspector hoped, would make them a little more likely to approach him with any information they may have. When they had finished their meal Mavis came and began clearing away their plates. The two men sat drinking the remainder of the tea and relaxed for a few moments.

'Another impressive spread,' the Inspector noted, rubbing his belly appreciatively. He took a large gulp from his cup.

'Washed down with a cup of tea. The perfect way to prepare for the afternoon ahead,' he stood and approached the bar. Lionel spotted him coming and immediately jumped to his feet.

'Everything all right Inspector?' he asked.

'Yes, again, a most excellent spread, thank you.'

'Our pleasure,' Lionel replied happily.

'Well we're all finished, perhaps if I am staying I could start a tab and add today's bill to it?'

'Of course, hold on I'll tally it all up now and get you started,' Lionel began punching numbers into the till, and when it was all done he opened up the guest book and added the receipt to it.

'Here you are then Inspector, if I could get you to add your details here.' Lionel passed him the book and the Inspector dutifully filled out his details.

'Many thanks, now, would you like to see your room?'

'Yes, shall we get the cases from the car first?' he asked Drew from across the room. Heads turned and voices lowered.

'Can do,' Drew replied, enjoying the theatrics of the scene. 'Perhaps you could give us a hand Lionel? They're a bit heavy.'

'Yes 'course, I'll just get Mavis to come and watch the bar.' Lionel replied, begrudgingly. He glanced around as if looking for an excuse not to leave his beloved pub, but when nothing appeared he went into the kitchen in search of his wife, returning with her a few moments later.

'So I hear you'll be staying with us a while Inspector?' She asked, doing little to hide her pleasure at the news.

'Indeed Mavis, your good husband here was about to help me in with my cases, if we may borrow him for a few minutes.'

'Certainly, don't let me hold you up, be good to see him doing a bit of work for a change,' she added with a smile.

'Oi, you watch it cheeky!' Lionel laughed, leaving the bar and its tittering occupants. He followed Drew and the Inspector outside and along the road. Before taking the cases the Inspector removed from them a few items he would need for the rest of the day's activities, namely his Wellingtons and a pair of waterproof trousers. He stowed these in the boot next to the Drew's Wellingtons. Drew then struggled with the heavier of the two cases, leaving Lionel and the Inspector to carry the others. Soon they were back in from the cold and they made their through the bar and upstairs.

The rest of the pub was decorated in a similar manner to the main bar area, a little out of date but with a friendly homely feel. The corridor upstairs had shadowy corners, a red carpet shirked beneath their feet, cream walls skulked in the background. 'Here we go then.' Lionel said, opening the door. Room six was warm and comfortable. The bathroom was smaller than that at The Swan and Dove, but it had all that the Inspector required. He went through the same routine as he had at the previous accommodation, of closing the door and testing the light. He emerged quite satisfied.

'Well, this will do fine,' he told Lionel. 'Thanks so much for putting me up at such short notice,' he thanked the landlord gratefully.

'You're very welcome Inspector,' he replied. 'Shall we leave you to unpack?'

'No time for that now I'm afraid. We must be off to Nettlewood hospital.'

'Very well. Would you like to book a table this evening for dinner?' Lionel asked.

'Capital idea. I'll take a table at seven.'

'As you wish. The one by the window?'

'That would be perfect.' The men descended the stairs, the Inspector locking the door behind him.

'Well, see you this evening then Inspector,' Lionel called after them as he took his place again behind the bar.

'Indeed, good day,' the Inspector called back, and they made their way out into the cold. As soon as the door was closed behind them the bar erupted into heated discussion.

34.

Banks left the station and began the drive back to his house, but already knew he wouldn't find them there. He spat and swore aloud in the car, staring at his own front door. The Inspector would have turned her against him, or he would have tried. He didn't want to go inside just yet, he sensed that his wife had been instructed to telephone the police as soon as she saw him. He concentrated for a moment, using the trees and the power within to locate the Inspector. He felt him in town, nearby, and tore himself away from the house. He drove toward the centre of town and found them outside The Green Man, struggling with the Inspector's cases. Banks stopped a safe distance away. He gawped at the luggage, and he turned into a rage. He screamed and swore at them, in complete shock that he had come to stay in Firestone. He took a deep breath, opening the window to get some air. The trees blew quietly in the breeze around him, and suddenly he sat up and looked out. In a state of panic he started the car and sped off to a quiet spot he knew in the trees. He parked his car where he thought it couldn't be seen, then walked a few paces into the foliage. He came to a clearing, quiet and peaceful, where he stopped and listened intently to the whispers in the trees.

35.
Has he seen us all? Does he know us all?
No, he has not found me yet
He asked about you
Yes he asked us about you
It doesn't matter, he isn't interested in me
Then who is he interested in?
The one that stops us all. The one that blocks the escape.
He came back, he must know something.
So we will be freed.
No, we cannot leave, we must stay.

The new voice again, silencing the rest, spreading fear they tried to hide. This voice had changed a long time ago, it was no longer like theirs.

This could be our only chance.
We have to stay, hide in town, we must protect it, hide it.

The voices drifted away at this intrusion. The trees swayed and buckled under the wind, each branch shimmering. The voices listened, waiting for each other, wondering if they were alone, or if the other was still listening.

We should meet, without him, in secret.
The Black Prince, tonight.
Yes. The Black Prince.

36.

When Drew and the Inspector reached the hospital they left the car in the small car park at the front and walked across the patchwork of puddles to the main building. From the front the hospital gave the misleading appearance of being quite small. The original building had been converted from a mansion house, with red brick and a high tiled roof. Time had now decorated its exterior with sprouts of moss. Hidden behind the grandness of the mansion stood the main building of the hospital; a modern construction of bland grey concrete and windows. The buildings, old and new, were set in a landscape of trees and fields, with gardens set aside here and there for patients to sit into aid their convalescence. They entered the grand hall of the older building and approached the unmanned reception desk. The Inspector 'pinged' the bell on the desk to alert the staff to their arrival. Presently a matron appeared, as tall as she was round, with an officious face and a frightful demeanour. She looked the two men up and down as if she wanted them out of her hospital; she could tell they were trouble.

'Good afternoon, we're here for Doctor Collins, I believe a colleague of mine is here already? I'm an Inspector, from Scotland Yard.' The Inspector cut through her dissection of them with a polite rise of his hat.

'This way,' she replied through tightly clenched teeth, giving them the impression she knew exactly who they were and what she needed to do with them. The Inspector was more impressed with her than she was with him. She dashed off at speed and they were shown briskly through a winding maze of identical hospital corridors, all white tiles and whited out windows. Eventually she delivered them to the door of the morgue, and knocked twice. After a few moments the bald little shape of Doctor Collins answered it.

'Hello Nurse McCole what brings you to my door?' he asked her rather warily.

'This gentleman is from London, he's here to see the Doctor that you have in there from London.'

'Yes, about a man from Swindon, I believe. Come in Inspector. Casey is just through here.'

'Thank you so much for your help,' the Inspector called to Nurse McColl's back as she hurried off to more important things. They entered the cold white morgue and followed Doctor Collins in at a much more comfortable pace. This ward was much like the other wards in the hospital that they had just raced through, but was much quieter.

'I trust you chaps are well, how goes the investigation today?'

'Very well, thank you doctor. How goes the dissection?'

'You'll have to speak to Casey about that, she hasn't really let me be much help,' he replied, hiding his disappointment. They pushed through a set of double doors and into the colder section of the morgue. 'All I have really done is fetch her lunch.'

'Well, I am sure she has appreciated being left to do her job.' The Inspector tried to put the Doctor's mind at ease.

'Yes, well, I'm happy to let her get on with it, shall I put the kettle on for you? Three teas?' Doctor Collins asked.

'That would be capital, thank you Doctor,' the Inspector replied gratefully.

'Right you are, she's just through there.' He waved toward another set of double doors for them before scuttling away to prepare them all tea.

They followed his direction and pushed the double doors open to find Casey in the operating room with a naked dead man spread out on a stainless steel table in front of her. She had on a tray to her right a collection of hair cuttings and skin scrapings chosen for further inspection. On a tray to her left was a collection of mediaeval looking tools, all stained red with their part in the dissection of the man's remains.

'Casey, how good to see you again. How are things going?' Casey removed the mask over her mouth, and the green surgical hat.

'Ahh Inspector. I should have expected a body like this from you.' She smiled at him, as one might welcome an old friend.

Drew approached the cadaver, recognising it from the hole through the centre of the chest. Spread on the table in this manner he was no longer a person but a piece of evidence, to be cut away at and scrutinised. He gulped nervously at the body.

'Afternoon Drew, hope he's not working you too hard?' Casey had about her an indifference of being a woman in what was traditionally a man's workplace. Drew did his best to hide how impressed he was with her.

'He's doing a good job at keeping me busy,' he replied simply.

'Yes, he has a habit of doing that.' Her mouth edged up at the sides into a pixie-like smile. The Inspector chuckled, amused at being discussed as though he wasn't there. Doctor Collins then entered, carrying a tray and four mugs.

'Ahh, thank you Alan.' Casey moved away from the body, covering it with a green cloth. They took their mugs and stood sipping the hot tea for a moment.

'So I suppose Nettlewood is a bit of a change of pace to what you're used to in the city Inspector?' Doctor Collins asked.

'Actually I spend a lot of time travelling the county investigating various cases,' he explained. This surprised Drew, who had always just presumed the Inspector worked mainly in London. 'Nettlewood and Firestone aren't that dissimilar to a lot of rural towns, though each is of course different in their own way.'

The room fell quiet for a moment, and Alan seemed to notice they had stopped talking when he had entered the room.

'Well, if you'll excuse me.' Doctor Collins raised his mug to them and strolled purposefully back to his desk politely. Casey waited for a moment, and when it became clear to her that the Inspector would not be asking Drew to leave with the Doctor, she gave a pleased smile.

'Well then, Drew, Inspector, let's think about this poor chap,' Casey continued as soon as he was gone. 'Time of death I would estimate to be at about one thirty Sunday night, judging by the rate of rigamortis.'

'About the time you discovered him Drew,' the Inspector pointed out. Drew nodded with a shiver.

'He was a non-smoker, I would say thirty two years of age,' Casey continued. 'No distinguishable features, no tattoos, no wedding ring. In fact there is nothing odd about this gentleman apart from the two things you are here to determine Inspector, the two things I will be totally unable to help you with. Namely, how this chap came to be where he was, and what caused that hole to appear in his chest.'

The Inspector ruffled his moustache with his hand in thought.

'There are no bruises or markings to suggest he was involved in any type of struggle. If he had been dragged or carried we would see bruising or scratching on the body where it was dragged, however he is clear of any injuries, apart from the obvious, not even a razor cut. His clothes are clean, recently washed, perhaps even clean on the morning he was killed. I have taken some cuttings of his hair, and some swabs inside his mouth and of his arm pits. They are currently sitting in test tubes in the other room, awaiting results, hopefully we should have something in another eight hours or so.' She motioned out to the other room with a wave of her hand.

'Now for the good bit,' she told them with a smile. 'Typically of your cases, and the reason I thought it best that the good Doctor left room, there are some odd things about this corpse.' She lifted up an evidence bag and handed it to the Inspector. It looked empty. Drew exchanged a look with the Inspector at the empty bag.

'Look closer,' she advised. The Inspector held it up to the light and the two men were just able to discern two barely visible tiny plastic disks with curved edges, like shallow miniature transparent bowls. The Inspector studied them closely.

'Fascinating.'

'Aren't they?' she agreed. They all peered at the bag, trying to fathom them. 'I found them on his eyes.' Casey informed them.

'On his eyes?' Drew asked, astonished. 'Like miniature lenses?' he suggested. Casey suddenly screamed.

'Yes of course!' she laughed. 'It seems obvious now, but I couldn't work it out for the life of me.' Drew blushed a little at her reaction.

'Yes good spot Drew well done,' the Inspector informed him a little more restraint.

'Let's move on to the cause of death.' Casey pulled the green sheet off of the body again. 'It is I would hope fairly obvious to you what has caused this person to die, however the wound itself is rather odd.' She passed the Inspector a magnifying glass and he leant down to examine the wound with it.

'You'll notice there are no exit or entry marks on the skin. Usually there would be some kind of dragging or tearing of the skin.' She looked away from the wound to Drew. 'As a cutting instrument like a knife, or saw, enters a body it stretches and drags the skin,' she mimicked a saw cutting through her arm. 'Even the sharpest of blades leave their mark behind. We can use it to work out what kind of weapon made the cut.' Drew nodded, turning his attention back to the hole in the poor man's chest.

'But this skin is intact,' Casey continued quietly. Her subtle tones echoed about the room. 'It was not cut, it is as though the skin next to it was unhooked, and the two parts were gently separated. This pattern is copied as you follow the wound through the body. Through bone, organ, muscle, all in the same pattern. No cut marks, no dragging or tearing. The bones haven't even cracked or splintered.' The Inspector looked up at Casey, rather mystified.

'Any ideas what may have caused it?' she asked him. 'I've never seen anything like it, have you?' The Inspector stood up straight and passed her back the magnifying glass.

'No, sorry, never seen anything like it,' he informed her. Casey wondered if this was the truth but didn't press him further. 'I have a lot more work to do before I'm any closer to working that out,' he added.

'Yes, and I will need more time to see if there's anything else I can find out about him,' she informed him, finishing her tea and placing the mug on a rare patch of empty work surface. The Inspector took the hint.

'Very well, we'll leave you to it and pop by tomorrow.'

Drew and the Inspector bid the two doctors goodbye, and made their way back along the corridors of the hospital and out into the cold air. Drew would have easily become lost along the maze of identical repetitive white tiled walls and floors, but the Inspector lead them quickly back to the entrance as if he had walked the path all his life. They returned to the car without seeing the severe matron on reception.

'Now, what's next?' the Inspector asked out loud, fishing out his note book and skipping through a few pages. 'Oh yes, let's return to the scene, see if we can pick anything else up on that camera of yours,' the Inspector suggested.

'If we must, though I must admit I'm not looking forward to it,' Drew confided.

'No, neither am I,' the Inspector replied honestly. 'We'll try and get it over with as quickly as possible,' he assured him.

37.

The road was deserted; theirs was the only car making its way along the puddle strewn tarmac in the rainy twilight of early evening. They arrived at the entrance to the clearing where the body had appeared, and Drew shuddered involuntarily at returning to the scene. He had found it easily enough, its location etched into his mind with the events that had occurred there. He turned the car into the gap between the trees with trepidation. It seemed to be narrower than yesterday, as if the vegetation was closing in, once again hiding the secrets of the Copse.

The clearing no longer had the look or feel of a forgotten corner of the world as it had on Sunday night. The mud was criss-crossed with the boot prints left behind by the Constables of Nettlewood during their fruitless search for evidence. Tyre marks sliced through the terrain, and in the centre of the low dip the painted outline of the body was still visible, clinging on despite the elements. Drew parked the car at the top of the dip, in the tyre marks of Sergeant Frank Gates' car, and the two men clambered out. Once their Wellingtons were on, they began to study the copies of the photographs that Drew had taken on Sunday evening.

'We'll start at the middle and make our way around,' the Inspector informed him. 'We'll try and follow your trail as best we can, it looks as if you took a clockwise path around the edge.' The eyes stared back from the pictures, chilling Drew to the bone. The Inspector took from his case his electromagnetic sensitive reader, and switched it on. The needle sat low on the dial, and the Inspector frowned.

'Here's your camera back.' He handed Drew his camera. 'I've put a fresh film in there. You make your way around, I shall be making my own way around, taking pictures and checking this for any change.' He indicated his device with a nod of the head. He then took his own camera out of his bag. Drew pulled his jacket closer around his shoulders. The cold seemed more intense here, it bit a little closer to the skin, and all the layers in the world could not keep it from gnawing at him.

'Yes, Inspector,' Drew replied, trying not to show how little he enjoyed being in this place. He immediately started to walk toward the centre, each step reliving the memories of the night he had spent stranded here, alone. The Inspector followed him through the mud, checking the unresponsive needle as he walked, taking pictures of Drew and the trees surrounding the area. Drew made his way quickly around the perimeter, clicking away at his camera, pointing it into the trees without looking, fear stopping him from studying the space between the trunks. When he had completed a circuit of the perimeter of trees he briskly walked back to the centre and waited by the outline of the body for the Inspector in the encroaching dark. He returned shortly afterward, notebook in one hand, inactive device in the other.

'It would seem all is quiet here this evening,' he informed Drew, looking disappointedly at his notebook. 'I have one last place to check, follow me.' Drew found being in this place exhausting, as if his energy was being physically drained from him. He silently obeyed the Inspector, who led him back to the edge of the opening.

'Please wait here, and take pictures as I go,' he informed Drew, and then he left the opening, and stepped into the trees. This took Drew by complete surprise, the wall of trees had seemed an impregnable barrier, and now seeing it broken was unnatural. He immediately began taking pictures of the Inspector, and noticed he was holding something in his hand, which he held up, as if comparing it to his surroundings. It was then that Drew suddenly realised what he was doing; he was trying to find the location of the eyes. Drew watched as the Inspector compared his surroundings to the photograph he held until he stopped behind a tree, and began fiddling with his device again. He looked up into the bare branches, scuffed his shoes about in the fallen leaves, and traipsed this way and that looking for anything that could have caused the abnormality in Drew's pictures. He checked his device, noted a few things on his map and notebook, and then began fighting his way back through the trees toward Drew. The afternoon was drawing to a close now, and evening was setting in. A fresh flurry of rain begun splashing down on them, and Drew was keen to get away from this place.

'Well, there's nothing of any interest in there,' the Inspector told Drew when he had reached him in the mud. This did little to put his mind at ease. 'Let's get back to town. I'll get these films developed and let you know what, if anything, appears on them.' They began walking over the mud again.

'Yes Inspector.' The Inspector could tell Drew was beginning to flag, it had been a long day for both of them.

'I'll let you get back home and freshen up Drew,' the Inspector said once they were safely away from the clearing and heading back to Firestone.

'I'd appreciate that,' Drew admitted. 'I could do with a bath.' Leaving the clearing had changed Drew's demeanour, he could feel the life coming back to his bones.

'We still have Charlie we need to chat to, how do you fancy meeting up later for a pint in The Black Prince?' the Inspector asked.

'Can do, though I hope you're not expecting much, it isn't much like the Swan, or The Green Man come to that,' Drew informed him.

'Oh, well, we can't have everything can we?' the Inspector replied.

'I suppose not, I'll drop you back at the pub.'

'That would be wonderful, thank you Drew. I should have just enough time to develop these films before dinner.' They arrived at The Green Man, and the Inspector climbed out, collecting his belongings from the boot.

'Well, see you at The Black Prince about eight?' he asked through Drew's open window.

'Yes Inspector, see you there.' He wound his window up again and drove away, leaving the Inspector alone on the roadside.

38.

Before heading home Drew drove to Correy's Fish and Chip shop and picked up a portion of Cod and Chips with mushy peas to take away. Correy was friendly enough, preparing Drew's dinner while providing his usual mix of small talk and banal gossip. After giving him a roundup of who he had seen in his shop that day and everything they had told him he turned to more serious matters.

'So I hear you found a body in the copse,' he told Drew in his untactful manner as the chips fried.

'Yes that's right Correy.' Drew paused for a moment, before adding; 'Where were you between the hours of twelve and one a.m. on Sunday night?' Correy laughed the question off.

'You can't suspect me?' he replied, feigning a slightly insulted demeanour.

'Don't worry Correy, I'm sure you have an alibi?' Drew asked, smiling.

'Yeah, you can check with the Mrs to make sure I was here for her to nag!' Correy replied jovially.

Drew was in no mood for small talk this evening, his return to the clearing in the trees was playing on his mind. He paid for his dinner and took the newspaper packaged food home as quickly as he could before it went cold. He ate it on his kitchen table from the paper using a wooden fork from Correy's counter. When he was finished not a morsel was left in the paper, which went into his kitchen bin.

After a long soak in the bath he finally felt as though he had washed the day from his bones. Drew prepared himself for an evening out with the Inspector. He dressed casually in a pair of dark blue slacks, and a red shirt under a black jumper.

Before leaving the house he picked up the telephone and dialled a familiar number. The telephone rang for a moment before being answered by a cherished voice.

'Nettlewood 452,' she said politely, if a little confused.

'Hello mum, it's Drew,' he told her.

'Oh hello Drew. I recognise your voice you know, you don't have to tell me who it is.'

'Well, I always think it best, as you usually get me and Isaac confused.'

'Well you both sound so alike! Any ways, how are you? When are you coming to see your old mum and let her cook you a proper meal. I bet you just had fish and chips again tonight didn't you?' Drew wondered at his mother's ability to know these things about him.

'Yes, but I've had a busy day.'

'Oh surely not too busy to make yourself a proper dinner son.'

'Actually yes, and it's not over yet. I have to go out again.'

'Down the pub with your mates?' she asked. Drew marvelled at her.

'Down the pub yes, but it's on business. I've been helping out the Inspector, from London.'

'Oh yes, with the terrible business about this body you found.'

'Yes, I was wondering if I could come round for dinner tomorrow, perhaps have a look through dad's old stuff, see if there's anything in there that might help.'

'Might help with the body in the copse? How so?' she asked a little worried. Drew took a deep breath.

'The Inspector thinks Banks is hiding something, something he knows about the body. He thinks perhaps dad was getting close to working out what it was.' His mother went quiet for a moment. The mention of Banks always had an effect on her. Drew gave her a moment, allowing her to regain her posture.

'Really? Do you think there's something in there Frank might have missed? Something your dad knew about?' she asked, calmly.

'Well I'm sure if there was something in there to be found then Frank would have found it when he looked, but the Inspector wants me to look again, just in case I suppose.'

'Well you know you're always welcome love, see you tomorrow about seven?'

'Ok mum, look forward to it.'

'Me too. Love you, see you tomorrow.' They hung up their receivers. Drew pulled on his wax jacket and shoes, and went out into the cold foggy night, heading towards The Black Prince. His mother turned the wireless up again and continued with her knitting, a pleased smile on her face.

39.

Once he saw Drew away safely up the road the Inspector made short work of the walk to The Green Man. He made his way around the empty tables across thin carpet, wishing Lionel a good evening behind his bar as he pushed open a door marked 'Staff and Guests only'. Once upstairs he deftly converted his bathroom into a dark room and processed the films from his and Drew's cameras. While the prints dried he turned his attention to the package he had received from the courier that morning, but before he could make any headway into the documents his appetite got the better of him, and noticing the time was already past seven, he made his way downstairs to eat.

The bar was now reasonably full, considering that it was a Tuesday night, and though a few of the patrons heads' turned as the Inspector entered the room and approached the bar, he was pleased to see that the locals were apparently becoming used to his presence in their establishment. He propped himself against the bar and awaited service, Lionel having disappeared for the moment. Presently Mavis appeared from the kitchen wiping her hands and greeted him with a smile.

'Evening Inspector, what can I get you?'

'Good evening, what do you have in the way of food this evening?' he asked.

'Well, there's Beef stew with dumplings, or I could do you a mixed grill, and sandwiches of course...' the Inspector held up a hand for her to stop.

'No need to go any further, the stew sounds delicious.' She noted this down in her little book.

'Right you are. Pot of tea to go with it?'

'That would be capital,' he replied happily.

'Of course. Make yourself comfortable and I'll bring it all over to you,' she told him, and hurried off to the kitchen. The Inspector retired to the seat by the window where he and Drew had sat earlier and waited patiently, smiling at any faces that turned his way. After a few minutes an elderly gentleman stood and walked to the bar, and Mavis welcomed him.

'Same again Bert?' she asked.

'Yes please Mavis,' he replied, fishing in his pocket for a handful of coins, and passing over a few to her. She rang them into the till and passed him a glass of frothy beer. All through the transaction Bert glanced over toward the Inspector, who noticed, and sat watching him expectantly. When he had his beer safely in hand, Bert approached the Inspector warily.

'Good Evening,' the Inspector welcomed him. 'Would you care to join me?'

'Aye,' he replied in a broad country accent. 'You'd be that Inspector then, up from London?'

'Yes, that's right, and you are?'

'Bert Cobblestone, I live out by Banks' farm, on New Road.' Bert wore baggy green thick cotton trousers, a lose fitting white shirt with wide collars under a well-worn green woollen tank top. His hair and sideboards were snowy white.

'Well, pleased to meet you Bert.'

'And I you.' Bert leant in closer across the table, the Inspector leant in too. 'Rumour round here is young Drew happened upon a body, in the trees,' he confided, nodding toward the door. His bushy clouds of eyebrows danced expectantly.

'Secrets don't stay secrets long in a small town like this,' the Inspector replied. 'Did you see anything that night that you want to tell me about?'

'Not that night no,' Bert replied cautiously. 'But I can tell you a few things about those woods.' He glanced around the room. His visit to the Inspector's table hadn't gone unnoticed.

'Like what?' the Inspector asked.

'Most don't like talking about it, like in case just mentioning it makes 'em come out.' Bert's voice was hushed, his eyes stared into the Inspector's.

'You've no need to worry, any information passed to me will be taken in strictest confidence.'

'It's not just me what's seen 'em,' he continued in a rambling fashion, as if finally revealing a secret that had been baring down on him for decades and not really knowing where to begin. 'My old dad used to tell me he saw 'em too. Told me not to go near the trees, even in the day.'

'And what was it that he saw?' the Inspector asked, lowering his voice so they were now both conversing in whispers.

'Other folks will tell you they ain't there, or there's nothing to see, but there is you know.'

'Slow down, what is it that you and your father, have seen?' the Inspector asked. Bert shifted in his seat and took a deep breath. He lit a cigarette, trying to compose himself. His hand shook as he lit the match and held it up to the blunt brown tobacco.

'There's something in those woods,' Bert revealed, avoiding the Inspector's eye, glancing into the darkness that lurked outside of the window. 'Something that don't want to be there,' he paused and took a long drag of his cigarette before continuing. 'My dad was told by his dad, who was told by his dad before him. They been there hundreds of years. They tempt people in, see. Then when they're in, they make 'em vanish, they take 'em, so the people, they get stuck in the trees.' He raised his pint glass up to his mouth and took a shaky swig.

'Do you know of anyone that has vanished recently?' the Inspector asked Bert. He looked at the Inspector determinedly.

'You don't believe me, do you?' the Inspector smiled politely. He could smell the alcohol on Bert's breath.

'I can't investigate a missing person report without knowing who the missing person is,' he replied. 'I need evidence, I need something to corroborate your story,' the Inspector was apologetic in his tone, he needed more information regarding the body, he wanted to win over the trust of the locals, but old wives' tales were not going to help the Investigation.

'No one's gone in those woods for years,' Bert replied. 'And they won't go in because of what I just told you. And I can't give you a name of someone what's gone missing because no one's gone in there to not come out again, if you get my meaning.' Bert frowned, realising he might not be making much sense. 'But that body being found, well I reckon it's got something to do with it.' He stubbed his cigarette out.

'And I thought you ought to be told, because if you go in those woods looking for something you might not come out again, and this town needs you.' Bert took a swig of beer. 'I like living here, but I'm fed up of living in fear of those trees. If the people give up on this place, the trees will win, and Firestone will just up and vanish, see?' Bert shook his head.

'Look, I'm not thinking all that straight. Perhaps I had a few too many of these waiting for you to turn up to tell you all that. I been running it through me head all day trying to work out what to say, and now it's all come out wrong.' Bert laughed. 'But now I told you any way. Make of it what you like, but the woods hereabouts ain't right, everyone knows it but no one talks about it.' He took the last swig of beer. 'So now you know, and here's your dinner, so I'll leave you to it. Good night, Inspector.' And with that he pulled his coat on and headed out into the night. Mavis placed a steaming plate of delicious smelling stew down in front of the Inspector, and placed a knife and fork on the table.

'Everything alright Inspector?' she asked as Bert made his way hurriedly out of the door. The Inspector looked anxiously after him.

'I think so, Bert had a few things on his mind, but I'm not sure I could help him.'

'Strange to see Bert in here on a Tuesday,' she commented, picking up his empty glass. 'Especially drinking that much, he usually comes in on a Sunday for a quiet one in the afternoon like, but I never seen him put it away like that.' She left this in air, and walked back to the kitchen, pushing an unoccupied chair back under a table on her way. The Inspector began to eat as his mind turned over what the kindly old gent had divulged to him.

40.

Banks watched from his hiding place deep in the shadows as the Inspector finally left The Green Man. The mere sight of him caused Banks teeth to grind. The hatred he felt for the man from London pulsed through his veins, and it was all he could do not to spring out from the darkness and attack him. It had been building up inside since his visit to his office. He took deep breaths, calmed himself, and followed him into the night. There were few people out so late, the streets were deserted and cold, but he found no chance to apprehend the Inspector safely. The Inspector headed off indifferent to the darkness. Banks followed behind, not close enough to raise the Inspector's suspicions, but close enough to attack him, should the opportunity present itself. Banks kept to the shadowy corners, wondering where he was going. When he rounded the corner to The Black Prince he realised where his destination was, and slowed his pace. He would have to wait until he reappeared and follow him again, so for now he re-entered the shadows, and kept a close eye on the door of The Black Prince.

41.

Drew arrived at The Black Prince, walking along the cold deserted street, looking about him as he stalked quietly along the pavement.

'Evening Drew,' the Inspector welcomed him from the shadows, taking him by surprise and making him jump.

'Inspector!' he cried involuntarily. 'Good evening!'

'I trust you ate well, and are feeling rested?' the Inspector asked him.

'Yes, just a fish supper but the bath has restored me. Yourself?'

'Indeed, I can recommend the stew at The Green Man, most invigorating.'

'Yes, Mavis is rather a good cook isn't she?'

'Indeed she is, now before we go in, a quick briefing. Although we are officially on duty, we are trying to make it look as though we are not. So we can drink, smoke if you so wish, do whatever it takes to put the patrons of this place at ease, feel more comfortable, and hopefully reveal something of some use.'

'I understand,' Drew replied calmly.

'Good. Now, let us see what we can garner from the proprietor of this establishment.'

The exterior of The Black Prince was dark and unwelcoming. Placed high on the outside wall over the small front door was a full suit of armour, painted black. This stood guard over threshold, doing its best to warn potential customers away.

'Not the most welcoming of places,' the Inspector noted.

'No, I've only been in here once myself,' Drew replied. 'That was enough.'

'Can't say I blame you.' The Inspector pushed open the front door and they stepped inside.

The bar of The Black Prince was propped up by a scraggly haired old man who stood looking forlornly at a glass that was almost but not quite half emptied of whiskey. Besides the sole costumer the only other human presence was that of the Landlord, sitting on the other side of the bar with a scowl on his twisted face, waiting for the man to finish his drink and order another. The door opened with a shrill squeak and the pub's occupants shared a look of surprise and turned to face the door. No one else usually came into The Black Prince on a Tuesday.

The two policemen ignored their enquiring stares and glanced around the room looking for somewhere to sit.

The closest seat to the front door was a sofa under the front window. It dipped in the centre and appeared bereft of all comfort. It sat in the same spot it had occupied for the last twenty years, looking as though it might finally collapse were anyone to actually sit in it. Too connected to the space to be noticed anymore, it blended in so completely that it was now ignored, walked around, and disregarded by all. To those laying eyes upon it for the first time, like Drew and the Inspector, it offered a seat so utterly uncomfortable in appearance that they chose instead one of the four sets of chairs and tables that filled the small main room of the pub. These did their best to hide the dirty sticky carpet, stained by decades of decadence and decay. The once colourful pattern muted to a monotone of brown. The men removed their coats and put them on the backs of their chosen seats. Every move was scrutinized by the men who usually frequented the pub. The sight of someone else occupying the space so appalled their senses they could not look away. These people were here, and they looked like they were making themselves comfortable. The two men felt the eyes boring into them, doing all they could to make them feel unwelcome.

'I'll get these, what'll it be, Drew?' the Inspector asked jovially, and rather loudly, ignoring the staring eyes and the men's confusion.

'Pint of bitter please,' Drew replied, picking up the tone of the Inspector and carrying it on, regardless of the two men's shock at seeing them there. The Inspector approached the bar, the landlord looking away as the Inspector made eye contact. His customer wore a large grin at seeing someone else there.

'Good evening Gentlemen,' the Inspector said.

'Good evening,' the man drinking the whiskey quietly slurred. He wheezed from a tatty roll up that filled the air with the smell of cheap tobacco.

'Good evening,' the Landlord replied quite gruffly. He made every effort to make it clear to the Inspector that serving him was an inconvenience. He sighed, leant irritably on the bar, then suddenly remembered that the optics that needed cleaning and began wiping all of them down with a dusty tea towel.

'What'll it be?' he called over his shoulder distractedly.

'Two pints of bitter, please,' the Inspector asked. The Landlord waited until he was convinced that the optics were as clean they were going to get before turning to the beer pumps. A glass appeared in his hand from a shelf under the bar, and he began to pour bitter into it. He made no attempt at conversation, neither with the Inspector nor his forlorn regular. As the landlord pumped the dark brown liquid frothed and spat itself out of the tap. He only managed to fill a quarter of the glass before the pipe was empty. He placed the pint glass on the bar, muttered a curse under his breath, then without any explanation walked out of the bar area through a door in the far wall. He left behind him three bemused men.

'He'll have to go and change the barrel,' the old man explained.

'Yes I'd guessed,' the Inspector replied. 'He didn't seem too happy about it did he?' he asked him.

'Ahh don't mind old Charlie. He's only happy when he's got something to be miserable about. Makes me chuckle it does listening to him going on.' He smiled at something to himself for a moment, then turned to the Inspector.

'So what brings you gents into Charlie's on a cold Tuesday night then?' he asked quietly.

'Well, I'm staying in town for a few days and I thought I would ask my friend Drew here to show me around.' The old man was quite acutely drunk, but in a thoughtful, controlled way. He swayed on his feet a little, he couldn't quite keep his eyes still when he looked at you, but he was lucid, thoughtful, and remarkably polite now he was becoming used to their presence.

'Not much to see around here, except the trees. About all there is to see.'

'Yes, it ought to be called Firestone Forest,' the Inspector quipped.

'Yes!' The man rose his glass. 'Firestone Forest,' he toasted the air and drank a small sip from his drink.

'Well, I have to say, it's not often we have new faces in here. My name is Sam. People call me Sam.' He held out and his hand and the Inspector shook it.

'Nice to meet you Sam. This is Drew, he's a police Constable. I am an Inspector down from Scotland Yard.' The man nodded, as if pulling together some answers in his head.

'I suppose you're here about the body folks are talking about then?' he asked. Drew approached the bar.

'That's right. What were you doing Sunday night?' the Inspector asked, politely. The man shrugged the indifferent shrug of someone with nothing to hide.

'Sundays I have dinner with me mum, then I usually come here for a couple, then when he shuts I go home. Lamb she made this week. Don't like it myself, always find it a bit greasy, plays havoc with my duties. Don't like to say anything though, you know, because of all the trouble she goes to.'

'You say you usually come here, did you come here this Sunday?' Sam thought for a moment, swaying as if the room was moving around and he was trying to stay upright.

'Now you mention it no I didn't, he was bloody closed! I had to go home and have a dram there.'

'Did you see any suspicious activity, anybody around that isn't usually around?'

'Nope, I didn't see anything apart that bloody storm.'

The landlord chose that moment to appear through the door again, huffing and bright red in the face. He breathed exaggerated breaths and began pumping the tap again. He was rewarded with more froth and air, but he kept at it.

'This here is an Inspector, down from London,' Sam informed Charlie. Charlie puffed and panted his cheeks back to a healthier colour before answering. The fresh bitter had begun appearing through the tap, frothy and sputtering he filled the first glass with an undrinkable mass of bubbles.

'That right is it?' he replied, eyeing him up and down with suspicion.

'Yes,' the Inspector informed him. 'Where were you on Sunday night?'

'Yeah, where were you?' Sam asked. 'I came here to get a drink and you were closed!'

'I was up at the Mayor's' he replied defensively. 'Dinner and Port.'

'Sounds delightful. Just the two of you?' the Inspector asked innocently.

'No it was me, Banks, Doctor Sparrow, and your mate Atkins.' He stared at Drew. 'So you can ask any of them where I was, they'll back me up.'

'Of course, no need to check I'm sure, hopefully you understand we need to check everyone to eliminate them from our enquiries.'

'You got no suspects then?' Sam asked.

'Unfortunately not,' the Inspector replied candidly. 'It's quite a mystery of how that poor chap ended up in the copse here. '

'In the forest here,' Sam corrected with a raise of his glass.

'Well I doubt if it's got anything to do with anyone from round here,' Charlie informed them, but he didn't seem to have any reasons why not. The pipes were finally cleared and he poured two fresh pints and passed them to the Inspector.

'That'll be eleven shillings,' he demanded rather rudely. 'And one for yourself of course,' the Inspector insisted, ignoring his tone. 'And for Sam.'

'Well, that's very kind of you,' Sam nodded appreciatively. Charlie poured another whiskey for Sam, and poured himself a pint of bitter.

'A pound then,' Charlie told him, holding out his hand. The Inspector handed over a pound note, and they took their drinks and departed back to their table. They sat and the Inspector took a mouthful of beer.

'This really is a good pint landlord,' he called across the room, and raised his glass in appreciation.

'Bloody ought to be the effort I had had to go through to pour it for you,' the landlord muttered back.

'So, The Black Prince... interesting name for a pub,' the Inspector noted.

'Aye, stupid more like it,' Sam commented.

'Oh yes, why is that then?' The Inspector asked, trying to stir up conversation.

'Named after The Black Prince of Firestone, before it was even called Firestone.' Sam continued amiably despite his body's alcohol level. The landlord looked on unamused. 'Came here to clean up the town he did, what did he get for it? Murdered by the people what lived here.'

'That's not what I heard,' the landlord joined in with a huff. 'I heard he came here and began teaching people magic, dark stuff like. They didn't like it so they killed him, buried him in the woods.'

'Yeah an' if you're out late and you walk in the trees you might see him in there, still walking about looking for someone to teach his magic too.' Sam laughed, finishing the story for him. 'That's what I got told anyway, sixty bloody year ago in school.'

'So does anyone know if he really came, or what happened to him?' Drew asked, wondering how long these stories had been told, passed down by one generation to the next.

'No idea,' Sam raised his glass. 'Whoever he is, and for whatever reason, he had a bloody pub named after him.' He drank his first whiskey down and turned to his fresh one. Drew and the Inspector took a slug from their pints.

'But I heard he was the first to lose his head on the bloody Firestone.' Sam paused for a moment and turned to Drew and the Inspector.

'No pun intended,' he added to them with a wry smile.

'Oh that bloody thing,' the landlord retorted, not getting Sam's play on words.

'They would be better of moving it if you ask me,' Charlie continued.

'But it's part of the town's heritage that is, part of its history,' Sam conjectured. He didn't seem particularly swayed by his own argument.

'Yes, but it's a murderous one, one that doesn't do us any favours. What's the first thing you see as you come to town along the main road? An old stone where hundreds of people were murdered,' Sam scoffed. 'It should be moved, even just in respect of them. Put up in the church yard or something.' The landlord shook his head, looking at the floor.

'That stone ain't never being moved,' he told his audience with the wisdom of a man who has spent too long living in a town stuck in perpetual static. The Inspector sensed this was not the first time the two men had voiced these opinions.

'Well, I must say, this town certainly has a chequered past,' the Inspector noted.

'Yes, if all the old stories are to be believed,' Sam said. Drew had been looking around the room as they spoke. It was a dark space, the corners receded away into almost blackness, as if the dim light was too lazy to reach all the way to edges of the room. The walls were, as far as he could tell, a dark cabbage like green. The pub did not look as if it had ever seen daylight, it seemed as if it could only exist in the night.

Drew and the Inspector turned casually to their drinks, and after a moment the other two men lapsed into their earlier fug. They stood forlornly in silence together, so much shared between them over the years that now there was nothing left to share but the silence.

'He gave us the same list again, in the same order,' Drew whispered over the table when he was sure they were being ignored.

'Yes, as we expected,' the Inspector whispered back.

'I feel we've probably learnt all we can from this place,' the Inspector informed Drew as they sipped their pints. 'Shall we drink up and leave them to it?' Drew did not need convincing.

'Yes, I must say it's not the nicest of places is it?' Drew thought of their meal the previous evening in Nettlewood, and of the hospitality they had been afforded in The Green Man.

The two men finished their drinks without haste, and bid the occupants good evening before heading outside.

'I'll walk you up to The Green Man if you like, it's on my way,' Drew offered.

'Yes, please do,' the Inspector agreed.

'So what next?' Drew asked as they walked.

'Well, tomorrow we shall continue our search for Banks, tonight I shall finish developing the photographs we took earlier, and see if they can bring anything to the investigation,' he told him. Drew nodded. 'My, this town is quiet once the sun goes down isn't it?' the Inspector commented noticing the deserted streets.

'Yes, well, there's not an awful lot to do once it gets dark,' Drew pointed out. They soon reached The Green Man.

'Care for a night cap Drew?' the Inspector offered.

'A nice thought, but I feel my bed calling, I had best be off,' Drew replied gratefully.

'Well Drew, see you in the morning.'

'Yes Inspector, shall I drop by and pick you up?'

'That would be wonderful, see you about nine?' he suggested.

'Sounds good, see you then.' The two men then went on their separate ways, Drew heading home and straight to bed, the Inspector back to his hotel room to study the photographs he had taken, and the paperwork delivered by the courier that morning.

42.

Finally the Inspector emerged from The Black Prince with Drew in tow, and the hatred welled up in Banks again. He followed him up the road, seething that Drew was with him, once more hindering him. He knew he would have no opportunity to follow through on his plan tonight. He followed them back to The Green Man, standing outside and waiting for a light to come on. When it did, he noted to himself what room was the Inspector's, and decided to come back the next night, to break in during the early hours, and do away with him. He stood and watched the window for an hour, hoping he might re-emerge and save him some time, but he stayed awake late into the night, and Banks eventually gave up and headed home.

43.

The Green Man was slowly emptying of people when the Inspector arrived back.

'Evening Inspector,' Mavis called to him as he walked through the bar.

'Evening Mavis, I'll be heading up to my room now, see you in the morning.'

'Right you are Inspector, see you in the morning,' she called after him, preoccupied with the wiping of tables.

He made his way upstairs and into his room, where he took down the now dried photographs and began to carefully study them. They were all devoid of anything out of place, the dark trees had kept their secrets in these photographs. He placed them into a folder and into his case. Disappointed but not disheartened he then turned to the file of documents that had been passed to him that morning, and opened them out on to the bed. The thick file delivered by the courier contained a mass of documents all about Firestone, and by the light of the dim lamp he began a journey back through time, through the history of the town in maps and land ownership documents, dating back hundreds of years.

He poured for hours through deeds, reading through hundreds of pages of hand written scrawl detailing the splitting and selling of estates. Slowly a picture of the town's land ownership began to become clear to him, however the documents he had been provided with were scarce, and many decades unaccounted for. The deeds came to a complete stop at around the turn of the nineteenth century, and it was clear that there must be more documents hidden somewhere, and he had to think about where these documents may be to complete the picture. The oldest map he found, the first ordinance survey of the area, showed what appeared to be the outline of large house in a quiet corner of what would, in later years, become a dense corner of copse. The house vanished from the next map, made some decades later though no explanation of what it was or what had happened to it could be seen anywhere in the papers. This, he thought, would be a good place to pay a visit to the next day, to try and ascertain what if anything remained of the place. In the early hours of morning it became clear he could not find anything new from the documents, and fatigue was finally beginning to get to him. He tidied the papers away neatly into their folder, keeping out the map showing the old building. He moved over to the window to close the curtains and call an end to the day, when he noticed moving through the streets a figure, hunkered down into his coat against the wind and the cold. The Inspector peered through the dark at him to try and see who it was, and what he might be doing out at such an unsociable hour. The man looked familiar somehow, and he suddenly realised it was Doctor Sparrow who he had briefly interviewed earlier. He quickly pulled his coat and shoes on, and headed out of the door after him.

It took him less than two minutes to get out of the front door of the pub, carefully creeping through the front door so as not to disturb anyone. He began walking in the direction he had seen Sparrow heading, keeping to the shadows and treading lightly. He caught up just in time to see him disappearing into The Black Prince. The Inspector approached carefully, hiding in the darkest corners he could find, waiting in the dark for a few minutes whilst deciding his next move. As he considered, another figure appeared. This man had a German Shepherd with him on a lead, and also let himself into the pub. He recognised the dog as being Cara, who lifted her head to the wind for a moment and sniffed, before being tugged inside by Atkins. The lights inside, upstairs and down, were off. The pub sat in darkness. The Inspector waited for another five minutes before advancing toward the pub and risking a glance through the window. He could just make out through the glass the bar area where he and Drew had sat earlier. It was now empty, no guest or landlord sat at the bar.

Wanting to try and see what the occupants were doing, the Inspector moved around the building to the side, where he discovered a tall fence hiding the beer garden. With a quick glance round to ensure he was not being watched, the Inspector raised himself on to his toes to peer over the top and see if the back garden would be safe to climb into. His glance over the top revealed a circle of people, facing inwards. There stood Atkins, Charlie, the Mayor, and Doctor Sparrow. They stood in silence, eyes open, unmoving, seemingly impervious to the cold wind. The Inspector stood and watched them, trying to garner a clue as to what they could possibly be doing. Try as he might nothing came to mind. After twenty minutes the circle suddenly broke, and the men silently moved inside. The Inspector crept back to the window at the front of the building where he watched the men being given pints of beer by Charlie, which they drank chatting quietly. As their glasses emptied they made their way out one by one. The Inspector hid on the other side of the road and crouched behind a car, watching the men exit the pub and go their separate ways home.

The last to exit was Atkins, with a tired Cara in tow. The Inspector followed him silently through the dark streets. He walked home at a weary pace, and quietly let himself and Cara in. A light went on briefly upstairs, and then off again, and the Inspector presumed this was Atkins settling down to sleep. Confused at this turn of events, the Inspector made his own way back to The Green Man. He quickly added what he had seen to his report, then got himself ready for bed. Before turning in he took a small bottle of blue pills from his bedside cabinet and swallowed one with a pint of water. He then settled down into a deep sleep.

Wednesday 5th November 1969.

44.

The Inspector woke naturally at eight, his body clock well-rehearsed at waking at this time. He dressed, and made his way downstairs for breakfast with his case and his coat. The pub was yet to open, but Mavis was already up and about, preparing for the day.

'Morning Inspector, can I get you some breakfast?' she asked, tucking a cloth into her pinny and removing her notebook and pencil.

'Yes please, two rashers of bacon, two eggs, two sausages, two slices of toast and a pot of tea,' he asked. Mavis scribbled all this down.

'Well that's a good start to the day, anything else?'

'Do you have a copy of today's Telegraph?'

'Oh, no I'm not sure we do, I'll send Lionel down to the newsagent for you to pick one up.'

'Only if it's no trouble.'

'Of course not it's only down the road. Have a seat I'll get your breakfast started.' She wandered into the kitchen, and the Inspector made himself comfortable. A moment later Lionel appeared.

'Morning, I'll be back in a mo, Telegraph is it?' he called cheerfully as he walked toward the door.

'Only if it's no trouble,' the Inspector replied.

'Oh of course not, won't be a tick. If you want it every morning I'll get Bill to have one of his boys deliver it, be even less trouble then won't it!' he laughed.

'That would be good actually, much appreciated.' Lionel simply waved and disappeared out of the door. The Inspector tried to gauge the weather through the window when Mavis appeared with a tray of tea things.

'Here we go then, the breakfast won't be long.' She unloaded the tray, noticing him looking at the sky. 'Bit of rain later they said, but then they always say that!' They shared a chuckle before she rushed off to her next job. As he poured a cup her husband reappeared, looking very cold.

'Here we are,' he announced with a shiver, passing the cold paper to the Inspector.

'That was very quick,' he told him, astounded.

'Well he's not far, nothing is in this town!' Lionel laughed.

'Well much obliged,' the Inspector thanked him as he walked back toward the kitchen to help get the pub ready for the day. He spread the paper on the table and began reading, catching up on the happenings of the rest of the planet before concentrating on the affairs of Firestone. Mavis soon reappeared with a plate of food, which the Inspector devoured while flicking through the paper. He took his time in reading, reaching the sport pages at the back just as Drew knocked on the door. Mavis appeared to answer it.

'Someone's keen, shame I've got to turn them away.'

'Actually it might be Constable Gates for me, would you mind if he came in and joined me for a few minutes?'

'Yes that's fine, I just thought it was someone trying to get in wanting a drink.' She unlocked the door and Drew came in from the cold.

'Morning Drew,' she welcomed him. 'Cup of tea?'

'Mavis you're a wonder,' he answered as she rushed off to the kitchen again. He noticed the Inspector waiting for him.

'Ahh morning Inspector,' he began removing his coat. 'All well I trust?'

'Yes, are you wanting breakfast of have you eaten?'

'Oh, I've eaten thank you.'

'Good.' Mavis reappeared with a hot mug of tea for him.

'Thanks.' Drew took a grateful swig.

'Thank you Mavis, could you add it to my bill?'

'Of course Inspector,' she nodded and hurried off to the kitchen again.

'Now Drew, before we leave, I wanted to show you this.' He opened his case and removed the map with the disappearing house on it, handing it to him. Drew could tell immediately from its browned paper and antiquated writing that it was quite old.

'My, look at this,' he exclaimed, fascinated. 'Well, I say, there's a lot less copse, and a lot less town, on here than there is now.'

'Yes, but what I really wanted to show you is this.' The Inspector pointed to the outline of the grand house he had noticed the previous night. Drew studied it carefully.

'How curious. It's along Manor Road, just outside the copse, or at least, back then it was just outside the copse.' He traced a line round the building with his finger.

'The trees stretch out past in now. As far as I know there's nothing there anymore.'

'What do you suppose happened to it?' The Inspector asked. 'Seems like too big a building to have just been forgotten.'

'Hard to say, I don't recall anyone ever mentioning there being a building there. We could ask Bill, he lives in a cottage down that way.' The Inspector checked Drew's mug, it was empty. He stood and made for his coat, hanging by the door.

'Well, let's start there.' Drew stood and began pulling his own coat on.

'You think this building has something to do with the body?' he asked, trying to find a connection.

'Everything is connected in some way,' the Inspector informed him. 'How it is connected I don't know, but it is certainly part of the town's mystery, don't you think? Houses do not simply disappear, and search as I might through the records delivered to me I was unable to find any mention of any building there.'

'How far back did the records go?' Drew asked.

'Oh they went back far enough,' the Inspector replied. 'But they didn't go as far back as I would have expected.' He opened the door, turning briefly to see if Mavis was in earshot so he could bid her good day, but she was not in sight.

'I suspect there to be further records, though I don't know where they might be.'

'You could try the library?' Drew suggested. 'They have all the old land ownership records in there.' They closed the door behind them and stepped out into the cold grey morning.

'Thank you Drew, I will endeavour to discover what I can from there.' The two men walked briskly to Drew's car, and climbed in.

'To Manor Road then? Old Bill?' Drew asked. The engine revved reassuringly into life.

'Yes, a quick visit there to see what we find,' the Inspector replied. 'There was something else I wanted to tell you about,' he informed Drew.

'Oh yes?' Drew asked as he skilfully navigated them out of town.

'Yes, last night I saw Doctor Sparrow walking out in the cold, so I followed him.'

'My word, what time was that?'

'About one thirty.'

'Where was he off to at that hour?' Drew asked, wondering what the Inspector was doing up at that time, and wondering at his bravery for going out at that hour to investigate.

'I followed him to The Black Prince. Then I saw Atkins arrive. Indeed, it transpired that all of the people on our lists, bar one, went to The Black Prince last night.'

'Banks?' Drew guessed.

'Yes,' the Inspector replied, impressed Drew had worked that out.

'Well that is odd. I wonder where he's got to then. Did you get to see what they were up to?' he asked.

'Yes,' the Inspector replied remembering the scene and trying to think of an explanation for their behaviour.

'Well, what were they doing?' Drew asked outright.

'They were in the back garden, stood in a circle. My guess is they were there about half an hour before they went in had a pint, and went home.'

'What were they talking about in the garden?' Drew asked.

'There was no talking, they all had their eyes open, they were stood in silence, and then with no cue they all went inside,' the Inspector informed him.

'Well, what were they doing?' Drew asked.

'No clue, sorry. I was hoping you might have a revelation,' Drew thought for a moment.

'No, sorry, I haven't a clue either.' Drew shook his head in confusion, mystified at their behaviour.

'Perhaps we should go back to Atkins' house and ask him?' Drew suggested.

'Yes, that can go on the list of visits we need to make.' The Inspector found his notebook and scribbled down a reminder. As they approached the residence of Bill it was more obvious that the copse had indeed grown beyond the border drawn on the older map as Drew had pointed out. Manor road was once surrounded by fields, now those open spaces were over grown with trees. Drew slowed the car down as they approached a short thin gravel track that led into the copse. He steered them along it and to the cottage that Bill called home. On arrival the two men climbed out of Drew's car and had a look around the enclosed driveway.

'From what I can tell,' the Inspector announced, studying the map. 'The house was not far from here, in that direction.' He pointed into the trees, and stalked the border between the cottage grounds where they grew, trying to see a way in.

'Perhaps if we spoke to Bill before we go traipsing through the trees he could shed some light on it?' Drew suggested. He was not eager to enter the trees on a hunt for something that might not be there at all.

'Yes, let us see what Bill knows,' the Inspector agreed. Drew approached the door and gave it two firm loud knocks.

'I see Bill in town occasionally when he's getting his shopping. He's quite deaf,' Drew explained to the Inspector as he knocked again.

The Inspector nodded understandingly. After a short wait the door was opened by a bent old man with a wisp of grey hair poking out from under a warm looking hat. He peered at them through glasses. He wore several layers of thick clothes to protect against the cold.

'Hello Bill.' Drew spoke in a raised voice. 'How are you doing?'

'Eh? Who are you?' he asked in a wheezing whisper.

'It's Constable Gates, from Firestone,' he explained.

'Yes? What do you want?' Bill asked, as if he knew that already. He seemed rather perturbed at the intrusion to his day.

'I hope we're not disturbing you,' the Inspector answered for Drew. 'I'm an Inspector from Scotland Yard, I was hoping you could help us with our enquiries?' Bill opened the door.

'Well come in come in,' he wheezed as he began to shuffle down the hall way. 'What's all this about then?' The entrance hall was piled high and all about with a lost lifetime of belongings, that spread into the rest of the small cottage. They followed him into the cold building to the living room, which like the entrance was awash with piles of dusty keepsakes.

'What a lovely cottage,' the Inspector commented, making small talk and hoping to charm Bill on side.

'What's so lovely about it?' Bill replied. 'It's too small and costs me a fortune to heat. And it's miles from town,' he grumbled. He slumped himself into a worn out armchair next to the fire. The chair was facing a window that looked out onto the trees. On the floor next to the chair was a paper, opened on to a partially completed crossword. The Inspector decided to avoid taking the conversation any further and instead pursued the reason they were here.

'I was wondering if you could look at this map for me?' the Inspector asked, 'and perhaps shed some light on something.' He took the old map from his case and placed it on Bills lap. He then moved round to be next to him and crouched down to the same eye level.

'Bloody hell where did you did dig this old thing up from?' Bill swore as he studied it. The Inspector was pleased to hear a spark of interest in his voice.

'It's from the national archives,' the Inspector explained vaguely. 'Here you see, near to this very cottage, it looks as if there's a building of some kind, but it does not appear on any later maps,' the Inspector pointed to the outline the cartographer had carefully etched all those years ago.

'Well that's probably my manor house,' Bill replied casually. Drew and the Inspector shared a confused look.

'Come again?' the Inspector asked, not sure he had heard him correctly.

'It's not called Manor Road for nothing you know,' Bill replied. 'Been there hundreds of years, but it got too much work for my granddad, so he moved his family and anything he thought was worth any money into here. Suppose whoever made the later maps didn't get to see the house, by then it was empty and the copse had grown round it.'

'Oh.' Drew replied, slightly taken aback.

'Do you think we could see it?' The Inspector asked, amazed. Bill thought for a moment.

'If you like. Not much to see mind.' He handed the map back. 'Suppose you want me to come with you and show you where it is?' He rose from his worn out chair with extreme effort.

'Well, it would be useful to have you guide us if you could,' the Inspector replied hopefully.

'Alright, hold on I'll get my boots on.' He made his way hobbling out of the room by a different door that led to the bedroom. The two men were left alone amongst the relics of Bill's family, relocated to the cottage to collect dust safely around him.

'Have you ever heard anything about a Manor house in the area?' the Inspector asked Drew quietly while they were alone.

'No Inspector, never,' Drew replied. 'Not exactly the sort of thing you lose though, is it?'

'Indeed not,' the Inspector replied. 'How fascinating. I wonder what sort of state we will find it in.'

'Come along then,' came a sudden call from the hall that took them both by surprise. They returned to the front door to find Bill with his coat and boots on waiting for them.

'It's a fair walk, hope you lads are feeling fit,' he remarked, before stalking out of the house. He kept a good lead on them, they were never quite able to catch up on him despite their best efforts and Bill's apparent lack of health and dexterity. The gravel drive that had led them from the road carried on around the cottage, passed the back of the house which boasted an impressively sized small holding, divided into segments for vegetable patches. The Inspector wagered that beneath the white frost sat carefully tended fertile earth poised and awaiting spring. Amongst the patches sat a large greenhouse, its clean glass reflecting the cold grey clouds that bustled above their heads. They followed Bill up to the end of the drive, which stopped at the trees that circled the cottage and its grounds.

'This is as far back as I can keep the trees,' he informed them over his shoulder as he slipped between the trunks through a small gap. 'I spent most of last summer cutting the new shoots back. No doubt when the weather changes and we start getting a bit of sun they'll start growing back and I'll just start the whole thing all over again.' He sounded stranded, as though this were his battle and he alone was there to fight it. The thick line of foliage on the edge of the copse was deceiving, and once inside they found the trees grew thinner and further apart. The gravel track was still discernible despite the growth of the occasional weed and the scores of trees breaking through its surface. Bill followed it, marching staunchly through the indifferent branches he fought so hard to control. The snapping of branches and crunching of stones beneath their feet echoed eerily around them, the sound ricocheting through the branches and bouncing back. Drew felt similar emotions as he had on Sunday, as though he shouldn't be here, a feeling of trespassing that caused him to creep as quietly as he could, while Bill and the Inspector trampled and barged their way through, disturbing a centuries old peace. They seemed to walk for some time, before suddenly the building was upon them. It appeared out of the trees like a grey monolithic monster, towering above them. They came to it not at the front but to one side, the corner of the easterly wing.

'Here we are then.' Bill admired the impressive building looming out of the trees at them. The trees grew almost up to the walls but not quite, allowing the men to skirt around the gap between the building and the trunks. Here and there vegetation had taken a hold between the bricks and grown into the walls, cracking them and causing cladding to fall. Bill's grandfather had taken the wise step of covering the windows before abandoning the place, so as to try and preserve the interior as best he could, in case some future generation of descendants found themselves in a position to occupy the building once more. As they hiked around it looking for an entrance, more and more of it appeared through the trees as if appearing through mist. It had many corners and hidden recesses that Bill ignored as he guided them around the edge. Finally they reached the front, and awaiting them stood a grand entrance of impressive double wooden doors, sat atop a set of twelve stone steps. Leaves had blown into every corner they could, and the trees needed little encouragement to begin their attempted invasion.

'How old would you say the building is, Bill?' the Inspector asked as they all paused on the threshold to catch their breath and admire the building. Bill considered for a moment.

'Well I reckon it must have been here at least three hundred year,' he replied. 'Though it's been added to over the years, you know, and improved upon, by different generations.' He took from his pocket a set of ancient looking keys, attached to a rusty loop of metal.

'I usually try and get up here once or twice a year, make sure the old place is still standing like, not that it would make much odds to me if the whole place fell down one night. Would be a weight off if it did, any road...' He ascended the steps to the door, and slipped the biggest grandest looking key into a hole above an ornate handle. With some effort the key was turned, the handle pushed, and the door gave. With a heave of Bill's shoulder the old oak entrance yielded, and with a teeth wrenching creak that echoed between the inside of the house that waited, and the trees that stood around them watching, the old door opened.

What dull light there was crept through the trees and found its way inside to illuminate a narrow view of the interior for them. All they could discern was a dusty wooden floor, covered with a huge worn rug. The smell of damp began to drift out as though waiting for release, looking for a way out of the dark lonely house. The three men stood at the door, as if waiting for the building to let them in, for it to invite them inside.

'Well here you are then gents.' Bill broke the silence. He did little to keep his disdain of the building from his tone. 'This is what you wanted to see, come on I'll give you the tour.' Stepping over the foreboding threshold ahead of them he vanished instantly into the dark. The Inspector fished inside his ever present briefcase and brought out his torch, switching it on and sweeping the beam around the grand entrance hall. Bill reappeared moments later with two oil lamps, and handed one to Drew.

'Here, help me light these, he ordered politely, fishing a dirty brass petrol lighter out of his pocket and flicking a flame out of it. After a few misfiring's and burnt fingers he and Drew had the lamps lit, and despite their damp wicks they spat a flickering light out into the room which only added to the eeriness of the house. The Inspector and Drew took a long look around the large room in their dim light, awed by the size and grandeur. The hall was flanked on both sides by a pair of impressive dark wooden staircases, leading up to a wide balcony. Any features the balcony hid were shrouded in darkness, the dim light of the lamps could not penetrate far enough to reveal its secrets. Under the balcony large unidentifiable shapes hid beneath ancient sheets. The shapes cast shadows against walls, hiding corners. A closed door could just be seen on the far wall under the balcony, and two more led off on either side of the hall.

'If it's history you're interested in I'll take you through to the library, there's enough books in there to keep you happy for a year,' he informed them, opening the door to their left and leading them through it.

'Bill, this place is very impressive,' the Inspector admitted, as Bill led them through a long dark corridor. Their lamps illuminated the world around them for about ten feet, otherwise they were blind as to what was around them. A row of tall windows flanked the left wall, boarded up on the outside, but from the inside they revealed ornate iron work. The right hand wall had a row of pictures, covered by more dust sheets. The Inspector paused to lift the sheet on one and shone his torch under to get a better look. Under a thick layer of grime he saw a landscape smattered with fields, and a few classically dressed figures draped forlornly about a tomb.

'This is a wonderful piece,' he called to Bill, quite overwhelmed.
'Early renaissance, similar to the work of Jean Fouquet. Do you have many examples like this?' Bill didn't stop to chat.

'Can't say I ever bothered looking,' he called back indifferently as he continued down the hall. 'If there were anything in this place worth a penny my grandfather would have sold it.' He reached the end of the hall and opened the next door for them. The Inspector resisted the urge to look under every sheet along the wall and tried to keep up with Bill.

'I honestly think it would be worth your while getting a few of these valued,' the Inspector advised when he reached the door where Drew and Bill waited.

'Aye, if you say so.' Bill replied absently, continuing into the next room. This was, as far as they could tell, devoid of any furniture, decoration or carpet. It was desolate, and their footsteps echoed emptily about them as they crossed it diagonally to another door. Bill led them through the house, down corridors, through rooms, some empty, some containing long forgotten furniture with only thin cotton sheets to protect them from the ravages of damp, dust, and age. Drew and the Inspector followed dolefully. Drew did not want to lose their host and become lost in the labyrinth of rooms, but he suspected the Inspector could find his way out again without

Bill, perhaps without even the aid of his torch. After a long walk through a wasteland of forgotten spaces Bill opened a door where all sound was muffled. They walked in and could immediately feel this room was different from the others. Bill found an extra lamp on a desk and lit it, helping to illuminate their surroundings. This room was the largest yet, dwarfing even the impressive entrance hall. Crowded into the centre of the room were row upon row of dust sheet covered book cases, lined up uniformly and disappearing into the dark recesses of the library.

'Whole history of my sorry family is in here,' Bill revealed, 'and a lot about this town and all. My family owned some of it, and the land here abouts, for hundreds of years, till they started selling it all off.'

'How long ago was this? the Inspector asked.

'Centuries ago, hang on I'll find the land sale records and we can work it out.' Bill carried his lamp off and the Inspector followed. Drew shuddered against the cold and stayed by the door. His eyes followed the path of the men through the book cases by watching the lamp light illuminate the shelves around them, and the ceiling high above their heads.

At the far side of the room a glass cabinet held the family records, and Bill opened it carefully. He took out a large thick heavy book, bound in think worn red leather. He opened it to the first page where, written in a swirling almost unreadable hand, someone had written;

'These pages herein do lay forth the goods and appropriations that, by the providence of God, hath been so hard fought for by the perseverance and good fortunes of the Brockenhirst family and their squires. Let it be a true and accurate record, for the goods and receipts of what goes traded from their lands, and what comes into them, in the name of His Majesty King George II in this year of our lord, 1750.'

The Inspector marvelled at it, and began flicking through the delicate parchment.

'And these records show your family's land, and dealings, for the last three hundred years?' he asked, astounded.

'That's right, it's all there, every deal, every pig that's been bartered, every inch of land sold. Can't rightly say what year it goes up to, I've never written a word in there me-self, nor my father as far as I know. All what's left of the estate now is this house and the bit of land it's on, with the cottage. Even that's been taken over by the trees now. Goodness knows what'll become of it all when I'm gone'

'Have you no family? No children?' the Inspector asked as he carefully studied the first page of entries.

'No, I never did marry you see. My sister had kids though, suppose it will all go to them.' The Inspector leant in closer to the ledger under the lamplight, asking his questions with an air of feigned disinterest.

'And what about them, are you in contact? Do they know what they are due to inherit?'

'My sister died ten year ago, I haven't seen or heard from her kids since we buried her.'

'Well, perhaps it's been long enough?' The Inspector suggested casually. 'I'm sure they'd love to know their family history.'

'No, they wouldn't want to be bothered by me,' Bill replied gruffly. The Inspector turned to the next page, and studied it carefully.

'Oh, I'm sure you're right. It's not as if you need the company, or the help, now is it?' the Inspector asked. Bill fell silent as the Inspector read. 'You can go back to your cottage, and live out the rest of your days in peace there. I'm sure they wouldn't be interested in learning about the Brockenhirst family estate, which it seems only you know about.' The Inspector suddenly closed the book and placed it carefully back on the shelf next to another similar one. There was a row of these oversized volumes, detailing the estates fortunes over the centuries. He picked out the next in the row and began to read.

'It seems your family were very successful, owning land, and either farming it themselves or renting it out to be farmed,' Bill was lost in thought, the Inspector's earlier words circling around his head, as the Inspector hoped they might.

'Aye,' was all he managed in response as the thought of living the rest of his years alone in the cold cottage played out in his mind.

'These volumes are fascinating,' the Inspector enthused. The detail given was exquisite, with the price that the land had originally been paid for, how much income it had brought the estate in the year, what had been grown on it, the names of the workers, most of whom lived on the land they worked. Whenever a sale of land or property occurred a map of its location accompanied the sale details. He flicked through the next volume, then returned it to the shelf. He then picked out the last one.

'This one is dated 1859, I suppose your great grandfather must have started it off?'

'Is there a name?' Bill asked, pleased for the distraction from his train of thought. The Inspector flicked his eye quickly over the page.

'Harold William Harlock.' He announced.

'Aye that'll be my great grandfather. Though he died not long after this book were started then.' The Inspector flicked to the end.

'Yes, the last entry is 1865, with the selling of two acres of arable land to the Banks family.' A map showing the location of the land that had been sold had been carefully inked next to the price. The Inspector fished out his map of the copse.

'These books concur with what I had discovered last night,' he informed Bill.

'Oh aye? What's that then?'

'Sergeant Banks owns Firestone Copse. Every inch of it. The fields, the buildings, the land, it's all owned by him, passed down over hundreds of years. He even still owns the farm that everyone thinks he sold. He's just rented it. Everyone at one point or another sold up to the Banks family. Well, apart from you, Bill.'

'He can't do,' Bill replied disbelievingly. 'If he owned that much he'd be a millionaire, why would he be working? Especially as head of police, can't be an easy job.' The Inspector wondered just how much work there was to do.

'The question I feel isn't so much why he works, as why he doesn't do something with the land. Or why none of his family have ever done anything with the land either. Over the years the Banks family brought all your family's land, and I discovered last night they have slowly brought everyone else's too. Yet all they have ever done is leave it to grow wild, to allow the copse to spread into it unchecked. The two men descended into their thoughts, trying to find some logic in the Banks' actions, when suddenly a loud crash echoed through the building.

'Drew!' the Inspector exclaimed, and dashed off in the direction of the noise, leaving Bill standing dazed.

45.

Drew watched the light from Bill's lamp illuminate the space around him as he headed into the shelves of books with the Inspector. He could just make out their muffled voices in conversation, but he could not tell what they were saying. He decided not to follow them, if the Inspector needed him he would have asked him to follow, so instead he began to look around the library. He looked about at the covered shelves and wondered what tomes filled them, unseen for decades, perhaps centuries. He checked under the sheets, shining his lamp on shelves filled with ancient books. He wasn't sure why he felt the need to check, but was glad he did.

He read a few titles;

'The Prelude', 'The Scarlet Letter', 'Concept's Dust', he did not recognise any of them, nor the authors, though he wasn't surprised. He continued around the edge of the library, walking slowly around the wall. The bottom half of the wall, the first five feet or so, was decorated with large dark wooden panels that had stood the test of time well. An ornately carved border adorned this, separating the flaking paint from the dark stained wood. Pictures hung on the cracked wall, dust sheets hiding their artistic treasures. At the first corner he came across a door, or rather, a door handle. It was disguised well and looked like part of the ornate decoration of the border. It was betrayed however as it extended out from the wall slightly further than the rest of the decoration. Drew gave it a hopeful turn, and sure enough a door appeared miraculously from the wall, cleverly disguised as a wall panel. He had heard of such doors within old buildings built to allow servants to come and go from their quarters without using the main corridors and so removing the risk of embarrassing the man or lady of the house by having to be seen by them. He held the lamp up to shine the light down it to see where it led, and was faced with a long bleak corridor. He took a few heavy books from the nearest shelf and used them to prop the door open, then entered the corridor to see where it lead. It was low and thin, much lower than the library ceiling. The corridor stretched out before him. He wondered about telling the Inspector, but didn't want to disturb him with distractions. He stepped in, leaving the library behind. He walked bent over to stop from hitting his head. The air got colder as he delved deeper into the dark. At the end of the corridor he was presented with a small door. Drew tried the handle and was disappointed to discover it locked, or stuck. He thought of the Inspector with his lock picks, carefully opening Banks' office door, and wondered how quickly he would get this door open. Drew opted for the lock pick of the bobby on the street, and gave the door a sharp kick with his heel at the handle. It gave remarkably easily, the wood around the lock being old and rotten it fell off its hinges and rattled to the ground. He held his lamp up to the dark space beyond the fallen door and revealed another room, small and dank, with no windows. It was large enough for his lamplight to evaporate before reaching the far wall. A pile of wood sat in the corner by the door, he studied it under the lamplight and saw that at one point it had been a table and chairs, but they had disintegrated with age and neglect. He considered going back to inform the Inspector but decided that if he needed to, the Inspector would be able to find him. He looked around the strange room, the sound of his boots echoing into the darkness as he investigated the forgotten room. The damp surrounded him, and the cold seemed to intensify. His breath steamed in the light of his flickering oil lamp, which showed him only damp grey walls and floor. He walked into the dark bravely, though the fear of not knowing what awaited filled him with dread. He stepped carefully and slowly, and found the room to be quite small and full of the slowly decaying remains of wooden furniture. At the far end of the room stood an old water pump and basin along with an ancient looking decrepit stove. The room fascinated him, a hidden room within a hidden mansion, and he examined every inch of it carefully, studying each wall in turn, though what he was looking for was not clear to him. The wall with the entrance showed no sign of anything strange, though he did find nails, as if at some point in the rooms past something had been hung there. He continued on around the room, finding more nails, but nothing of any interest. It was only on closer inspection of the wall opposite the door that he noticed it was different from the others. At one end there was a small section that differed from the others. While the rest had a smooth finish this section of wall had been plastered in a hurry. Drew studied every point where it met the ceiling, the floor, and adjoining wall. It soon became obvious to him that this section had not been built at the same time as the others, and that it had, for whatever reason, been added at a later date. He checked carefully across the top of the wall where it met the ceiling and saw a sliver of a gap in one corner where they did not quite meet. He stared at the gap, wondering what he could do, what it meant. He reached up to it and pushed at it, causing the weak plaster to crumble away beneath his fingertips. He pushed a little harder, and the hastily placed bricks fell away, dropping inside, behind the wall. With a rush of adrenaline Drew squared his shoulder up against the wall, and gave it a soft shove to see how strong it was. On doing so the weak wall tilted, crumpled, and with a deafening crash and a suffocating cloud of dust, collapsed in on itself with Drew somewhere in the middle. The noise echoed loudly all about and Drew collapsed, coughing terribly in the dust.

46.

On hearing the noise the Inspector tore away from Bill, quickly finding the hidden door and rushing down the corridor. He burst into the room before the dust had settled and rushed into find his spluttering colleague. Bill, in a state of surprised shock, was still standing in the library not quite knowing what to do for the best. The Inspector found Drew on the ground sitting up. His legs were covered in bricks, and he gasped for breath between coughing up lungs full of dust.

'My word lad what happened here?' The Inspector rushed over to him, pulling him out of the rubble and brushing him down. Drew wasn't quite ready to start speaking yet, he kept coughing and wheezing while the Inspector, satisfied that was wasn't seriously hurt, lifted his lamp up to survey the damage. Despite himself, his jaw dropped a little as he put the scene together. Behind the wall Drew had brought down lay the remains of several bodies, decomposed beyond the flesh. All that remained of them were bones making it difficult for the Inspector to see how many sets of remains he was faced with.

'What have you stumbled upon here Drew?' the Inspector asked.

'Looks like some kind of hidden tomb,' Drew had recovered enough to reply in a broken voice. The Inspector shone his torch on the scene to examine the remains of the bodies that lay scattered around.

'How did you find it?'

'I was looking around in the library and happened upon the door,' Drew croaked. 'I followed the corridor down here and noticed this false wall.'

'And you deduced that there must have been something behind there worth seeing?'

'Precisely.' The Inspector scanned the destruction. He was glad he had decided to leave Drew alone in the library, his investigative capacities were quite impressive.

'Well, you were right to pursue your inquisitive nature, but I do wish you'd have come and gotten me first, who knows what might have happened to you, or what evidence you may have inadvertently destroyed.' The Inspector looked Drew up and down, his uniform was a mess but otherwise he seemed quite unharmed by the experience.

'I'm glad to see you still in one piece though. You did give me a fright.'

'Sorry, I really only gave it a little shove to see how strong it was, I didn't expect the whole thing to come crashing down on me.'

'Well, not to worry, as long as you're uninjured that's the main thing.' He knelt down to take a close look at the remains. 'What a surprise this house is. I think we need to get some pictures, and then contact our friends Jim and Andy to come and deliver these poor souls over to Nettlewood hospital for Casey to look at.'

'Do you think Casey will be able to find much out from what's left of them?' Drew asked, a little surprised.

'Oh, I'm sure she can learn much from so little. Her results always surprise me.' He stood and they left the room together.

'My camera is in my briefcase, which I left with Bill when I dashed off. Poor man I wonder what he thinks is going on.'

They found Bill still standing by the bookcase of his family's history, looking rather anxious.

'Everything alright?' he asked when they reappeared.

'All fine, I'm pleased to announce,' the Inspector reassured him. 'Drew here was doing a little investigation of his own and seems to have come across a hidden corridor.'

'Really, whereabouts?' Bill asked, intrigued, giving Drew's filthy clothing a look up and down.

'Well we are just on our way back down there now if you would like to see?'

'I would indeed. I thought I knew everything there was to know about this place.' The Inspector picked up his case, and walked back toward the door that Drew had discovered.

'My word lad, what have you been up to?' Bill asked, rather worried about what Drew had to go through to discover this hidden corridor.

'The corridor was not the only thing that was hidden,' Drew revealed. 'We found the remains of some poor souls bricked up in a recess in one of the walls.' Bill stopped in his tracks and drew a surprised breath.

'Here, in my house?' Even in the dim light they could see his face turn white.

'Yes, but judging by what little of them is left, I would say they had been there a hundred years or more,' the Inspector consoled him. This seemed to calm him a little.

'Now I am intrigued,' Bill admitted. They reached the door to the corridor, still propped open by Drew's pile of books. Bill studied it with wide eyes.

'Well I never, all these years I've never known any of this was here, you chaps are here for an hour and already you've found a secret corridor and some dead bodies. What else have you got in store for me?' he asked rhetorically. They continued down the corridor, and to the door Drew had unceremoniously kicked open. The smell of damp emanating out gave Bill an ominous feeling that he tried to ignore. On reaching the collapsed wall the three lamps together illuminated the room a little better, and the men stood and stared at the scene as the cloud of damp dust gradually thinned. The Inspector removed his camera from his briefcase, attached a flash cube, and began taking photographs. The skeletons, as that really was all that was left of the bodies, lay intermingled with each other. The Inspector did a rough guess at the number and came up with four. Judging by their positions it appeared they had been stacked one on top of each other, in an undignified pile. He took photographs, changing the flash cube twice, until he had no flashes left.

'There we are. Now to contact Jim and Andy.'

'Would you like to use my telephone?' Bill asked.

'Yes please, I'm sure we'd all like to get out into the light and the fresh air.' Bill and Drew nodded in agreement and Bill led them back through the house and into the trees. The Inspector paid a little closer attention to their route on his way through the trees this time, trying to see if perhaps an ambulance might squeeze through the branches over the ground. He noticed a vague trail of stones through the trees.

'I take it this used to be a drive way?' the Inspector called out to Bill, who had gotten a lead upon them again. He turned and came back to where the Inspector stood, kicking away dead leaves from the ground to reveal a buried layer of gravel.

'Yes, before the trees invaded,' Bill confirmed.

'Well, shame we won't be able to get the ambulance along here really. Not to worry I'm sure we will be able to find our way through the woods with a few bags of bones.' The men continued through the trees and soon reached Bill's cottage. Bill opened the door and led them to the telephone which sat on a table with a built in seat in the hall. The Inspector picked up the receiver and dialled 100. Presently the operator answered.

'Yes, Nettlewood Hospital please.' There was a pause. 'The Morgue please, Doctor Collins.' Another pause. 'The Inspector, from Scotland Yard.' He turned and smiled at the two men watching him while he waited. 'Any chance of a cup of tea?' he asked Bill. 'We may have to wait a while for the ambulance.' Bill started suddenly as if he had forgotten something fundamentally important.

'Yes of course, I'll get the kettle on.' He rushed away. His demeanour had changed dramatically from the curmudgeonly old man sat in his chair when they had arrived. He was now positively animated, wanting to do whatever he could to aid the Inspector.

'Ahh good afternoon Doctor, I trust I find you well? Oh glad to hear it. I have a favour to ask, I am with Drew at a Cottage on Manor Road.' He paused to listen to the Doctor.

'Yes, Bill's cottage that's right. We have discovered some bodies, would it be possible for you to arrange an ambulance, preferably with the same chaps that collected the body on Monday, to come and collect them?' There was a pause while the doctor fired questions at the Inspector.

'I think about four, but we should get them all moved in one trip, due to the state of deterioration they are in. Yes, please do. The number here is...' He paused to study the ticket on the telephone where Bill had written the number in biro. '211. Could I speak to Casey please? Thank you. Yes see you soon.'

There was a break in conversation while the telephone was passed over.

'Good afternoon Casey. I'm afraid I've found some more work for you. Drew has discovered a few more bodies. Well lucky is hardly the word I would use, but I see what you mean. Yes, we'll need them all examined, with a profile of each, and a cause of death. Yes, Doctor Collins is arranging that we'll wait here for the ambulance and accompany it back to the hospital. Right you are, see you soon.' He replaced the receiver.

'All well?' Drew asked.

'Yes, the good Doctor Collins will be contacting me shortly regarding the ambulance. When they arrive we can assist them with the bodies and get over to the hospital to brief Casey properly.' Bill arrived with three cups of hot tea on an ornate silver tray.

'Here we are then, ambulance on its way?'

'Presently, yes.' The Inspector took a steaming cup form the tray and took a deep grateful mouthful.

The ambulance arrived fifteen minutes later, parking on the gravel drive next to Drew's car. Andy climbed out of the driver's side door and greeted Drew and the Inspector like old friends while Jim, still rather shy, made his way to the back of the vehicle and started removing the trolley.

'I don't think there'll be much use for that today,' the Inspector called to him. 'Did you bring the bags?'

'We did,' Andy answered for them. 'I know you said there was four but I brought six, just in case.'

'Casey's idea?' the Inspector guessed.

'Yes, she suggested it.' Andy smiled. 'Is there really more bodies hiding in there?' he asked, nodding in the direction of the trees. Andy joined them with an armful of bags, looking as worried as his colleague about what the Inspector had in store for them in the copse.

'There are, I estimate, four bodies to recover, but don't worry gents, they aren't in quite the same state as the poor chap we met on Monday morning.' The Inspector saw their trepidation, so thought full disclosure would only be fair. 'The bodies are in a large house hidden in the trees so please try to stay close, we'd hate to lose you.' The two glanced at each other and tried to remain resilient. Jim shared his burden of bags with Andy and they entered the trees following in the Inspector's footsteps as he traipsed back through to the manor house. Drew thought he must have taken a different route, as they seemed to arrive quicker than they had the first time.

'My word!' Andy exclaimed in awe when they approached the first wall. 'Look at this place. I had no idea this was here.'

'Almost no one did until a few hours ago, only Bill,' Drew replied.

'Well he's kept this well-hidden,' Andy stated. 'Shame too looks like a beautiful old place this.'

They soon reached the front of the house, the newcomers making more sounds of wonder at the magnificence of the main entrance. The men made their way through the corridors, Drew and the Inspector becoming somewhat accustomed to the building's darkness, to its smell, and to the atmosphere of trespassing that being inside it forced upon them. The ambulance men however followed timidly behind, following in the lamp light, as if at any moment an unseen occupant would leap at them from behind one of the sinister shapes shrouded in old dusty sheets. Their mood did not improve when they entered the library, with its rows of book cases hiding unknown terrors deep in the darkness.

They were led down Drew's corridor, and into the dank unwelcoming room. The bags were put in a pile by the door way.

Andy and Jim were quite obviously in a state of confusion regarding the whole affair, but Andy kept them on a professional focus.

'Well I see what you mean about them being in a different state than the last one we saw, eh Jim?' Jim nodded enthusiastically, relieved that the task would not be quite as sanguinary as he had been preparing himself for.

'Let's clear this rubble and see what we can find shall we?' the Inspector suggested. He began carefully removing bricks away from the scene, and his three companions joined in. The bricks were slowly and carefully moved to the far side of the room, and stacked neatly, revealing a tangled mess of bones that spread under the wall that Drew had brought down. Occasionally the Inspector would pause to take a few photographs, recording their progress as the scene beneath the bricks was slowly revealed. As the Inspector began picking up bricks from the edge he suddenly stopped, putting the bricks he was holding back where he found them.

'I think that will do, the main area is cleared, let's begin clearing the remains,' he told them. Though a good deal of bricks remained, they could access all the bodies so they started work. The skeleton closest to them seemed the best place to start, so Andy prepared a bag and with Jim's help they carefully lifted the delicate frame into it. The bones were still connected into one fragile piece, tissue that had once bound it through muscle and skin had fused the bones together as it decayed. With the carcass safely zipped into the bag, the men started on the next set of bones. These had broken from the spine just above the hip bone. This half was mostly complete, but an arm was missing. The legs were hidden in the dust. As others were in a similar state it was impossible to say which arm, or which legs, belonged to this individual. Andy pointed out the problem to the Inspector.

'Any thought on whose bones are whose?' he asked, showing the Inspector the partial corpse in the bag. The Inspector looked around at the confusion of bones.

'Let's just make a best guess of it shall we?' the Inspector suggested. 'My colleague Doctor Ward can make a more informed judgement at the hospital morgue when she studies the remains.

'Right you are,' Andy replied, and he and Jim began carefully removing bones that, as best as they could tell, matched the rest of the body. They then zipped the next bag up, placed it next to the first, and continued with their grim task. Drew and the Inspector joined them, their shadows casting dark shapes against the wall, the lamps flickering and hissing as they moved all the corpses into the bags. Drew felt as if he were being watched, but buried the feeling deep in his gut. The Inspector had been right in his count of the bodies, there were indeed four set of remains.

'Can we get out of here now Inspector?' Andy asked hopefully as soon as the last bag was zipped.

'Yes, indeed we can,' the Inspector replied gratefully. If you chaps take the bags up to the ambulance I just want to look through the remaining rubble and ensure we haven't missed anything. The men agreed so Andy took two of the bodies, Drew and Jim one each, they then made their way out of the house, leaving the Inspector alone in the dark. Bill had been sat looking out of the window of his front room waiting for them the whole time, and when he spotted them through the trees he came out to see them.

'How goes it then?' he asked. 'Did you get them all out?'

'Yes, all out. We'll just wait for the Inspector then we'll get them to the hospital.' Andy opened the rear doors of the ambulance for them and they placed the remains carefully in the back.

'Anything I can do to help?' Bill asked hopefully.

'A cup of tea while we wait would be good,' Drew suggested. 'Warm our bones a little.'

'You're not wrong there Constable,' Andy agreed.

'Come on in then, I'll get the kettle on,' Bill told them, and they followed him inside.

47.

Drew and the others made their way back through the library carrying the bags they had filled with bones, leaving the Inspector alone in the cold darkness. Although they had cleared the debris away from the bodies, the small room still had a few piles of bricks around its edges that the men had left. The Inspector returned to the pile he had been clearing earlier and removed the bricks that he had started to clear. Beneath them he had discovered the remains of another body, with an object attached around its wrist. He presumed it to be a watch of some kind, however its face was one piece of jet black glass, with an array of buttons around its large display. There were no hands, or numbers around the edge of the clock face. He carefully removed it from the skeleton's wrist over the hand without undoing the clasp on the strap, and placed it into an evidence bag which made its way swiftly into his briefcase. He then began a thorough search of the mysterious hidden room. He studied the layer of brick and dust that remained for any shapes that were at odds with the ancientness of the room, carefully lifting bricks and placing them with the other chunks of wall to search for items that ought not to be there. He was not disappointed, as he soon uncovered a rectangular object, similar to that he had found on the body of Matthew Berrow. As with the original object, one side of this one also seemed to be made of a dark glass. There was only one button, on top. There were a couple of holes in the sides but there was nothing obvious that betrayed what the holes were for or indeed what the object was used for. It was slightly thicker than the other, but otherwise they were so similar in appearance it led the Inspector to reason that they were two different types of the same thing.

There was something about this object that differentiated it from the first; one of the corners was missing. It had been cut in a perfectly curved line making a quarter of a circle. Moisture had penetrated the gap and had rusted away some of the metal around the wound, but from what the Inspector could make out through the small gap in the dim light, there was circuitry inside. He placed this new object into a fresh evidence bag, and continued his search. He began moving the bricks away and slowly revealed more of the body. Jim had left the two remaining bags behind, so the Inspector carefully lifted the remains and placed them into the bag. With the body safely stowed away he continued searching through the bricks, and soon came upon a much decayed and fragile scrap of cloth. He could just make out, etched across it in deep red, a rambling scrawl. He carefully picked the item up, and tried to read what was written on it, but the writing was too faded and the light too dim. He carefully placed it into an evidence bag, and then into a protected compartment of his briefcase to prevent it suffering any further damage. He continued digging through the bricks, becoming quite dusty in the process. After an hour the area was completely cleared with no further finds. He picked up the last body and his case with the strange evidence, and feeling somewhat tired and dishevelled the Inspector finally escaped the dank room.

48.

Drew, Jim and Andy headed inside for a cup of tea, when Drew realised they had not all been introduced.

'By the way Bill, this is Andy, and Jim.' Bill stopped at the threshold of the house and the men all shook hands.

'Nice to meet you chaps, come on in and I'll get the kettle on,' he said as he opened the door and welcomed them inside.

'Thanks Bill,' they all replied.

'So you've been helping out in the Manor have you?' Bill asked Andy.

'Yes, that's right,' he relied.

'What's the Inspector up to then?'

'He's still down there doing a little investigating on his own, he'll be up soon I'm sure,' Drew replied.

'Funny old business this, bodies being found in the Copse, don't you think?' Bill asked them.

'Well, they sent an Inspector down from the Yard, that shows you how serious it must be.' Andy pointed out.

'I've never seen anyone from the Yard before,' Jim confided to them.

'Neither have I mate,' Andy told him. 'Like I said, it's got to be something serious.'

'He doesn't seem too bad though,' Jim admitted. 'I thought Inspector's would be more, bossy.' They shared a chuckle at his innocence and enjoyed their hot tea in the comfortable chairs all the more for their time in the cold dark basement. They sat and made small talk for a while, before the Inspector returned, announcing himself with a loud knocking on the front door. Bill clambered out of his chair and let him in.

'Ahh thank you for waiting,' the Inspector told them gratefully. 'I found another body under the uncleared bricks would you believe.' The men all gasped in surprise.

'Well, good job you decided to stay behind then then,' Andy pointed out.

'Yes, quite fortuitous,' the Inspector agreed. 'I've already deposited the bones in the ambulance.

'Would you like a cup of tea Inspector?' Bill asked, making for the kitchen.

'Thank you no, now we have all the remains in the ambulance, we should be getting them back to the hospital,' he replied. They bid Bill goodbye and drove back to the hospital, Drew and the Inspector following the ambulance in the squad car. The ambulance led them to a large ambulance bay close to the main entrance of the building.

Jim parked up and Andy jumped out of his door just as a burly man appeared from a large door that serviced the bays. Drew put his car in the next bay along then he and the Inspector joined them at the ambulance.

'Hello, alright?' the burly man from the hospital called to them in welcome. He rushed up to their ambulance excitedly. 'Let's have a look at this delivery for Doctor Collins then.' Andy pulled the door open and revealed the pile of bags, much to the burly man's amazement.

'Blimey, you blokes have been busy. Well you'd best come straight through then.' Jim pulled out a bed trolley from the ambulance.

'Let's see if we can fit them all on here shall we?' he asked them. Jim climbed in and began passing the bodies out while they balanced them carefully on the bed. When the bodies were all on Andy pushed them through to the hospital, the burly man holding the door open for him.

'Thanks Adam,' Andy said appreciatively, heading inside. They all followed Jim as he pushed the trolley through the wards and corridors, down the endless maze of white tiles that led to the morgue, where Doctor Collins and Casey were waiting for them.

'Good afternoon,' Doctor Collins welcomed them in, opening the doors wide to allow them through with their bed of bodies.

'Hello Drew, Inspector,' Casey welcomed them back to the morgue. She took the pile of bags and wheeled it into the area she had been working in. Drew and the Inspector followed her, leaving Jim, Andy and Doctor Collins waiting for the kettle to boil. Casey's room had been rearranged to accommodate the extra bodies, with three more examination tables added to store them on. With the doors closed behind them they began unloading the bags on to the empty examination tables.

'Well, it looks as though I'll be staying longer than I thought with all these to look through,' Casey said, opening the bag nearest to her to get a better look. 'My, not much left of these chaps is there?' Drew shook his head.

'No, we're also not sure if all the bodies are together in the right bags, it was a mess down there.'

'I can see that by the state of you,' she informed him. 'Well then I really do have my work cut out for me.' She continued, looking through the bags grotesque contents. 'Luckily I've booked myself in for the rest of the week at The Swan and Dove.' There was a moment where Drew tried to hide his pleasure at this news and she searched his face, looking for his reaction. Both of them noticed it and blushed with a little laugh.

'I'm sorry to be keeping you so busy, how long do you need?' the Inspector asked, not seeming to notice that anything had passed between them but breaking the moment none the less.

'Give me ten minutes while you go and drink a cup of tea and I'll tell you what I can about this bag,' she told them, holding up a dirty yellow hip bone and admiring it under the light.

'Yes of course, come Drew, let's keep the others company for a few moments and allow Doctor Ward to work.' The men left her to her bones and returned to the others.

'Is there any chance of a cup of tea?' Drew asked when they found them, perched against a low bench in the friendlier area of the morgue, well away from the smell of death. They stopped their conversation mid flow.

'Yes of course, might want to refill the kettle though,' Doctor Collins stood and showed them the way.

'Casey getting on alright in there then is she?' Doctor Collins asked.

'Yes, she has a very thorough process,' the Inspector informed him as they entered the kitchen area. 'She's extremely determined.'

'I image she is,' Doctor Collins agreed. The kettle seemed to take an age to boil, but when it finally clicked itself off and steam stopped filling the room, Doctor Collins retrieved a box of tea bags from the cupboard by their feet.

'Sugar chaps?' he asked, shaking the sugar jar.

'No thank you,' the Inspector replied.

'Not for me thanks.' Drew held a hand up.

'Could you make one for Doctor Ward as well?' the Inspector asked. 'I'm sure she'll appreciate one after all the work we are giving her today.' Doctor Collins obliged understandingly.

'Yes of course, good idea.' He took another mug from the cupboard and poured hot water into all three. After a few minutes chatting over their tea, the Inspector lost his patience.

'Come Drew, let's return to see what Doctor Ward has discovered.' They bustled back into where Casey was working, Drew carrying his and Casey's cooling tea with him. Casey removed her mask and gloves and Drew passed it to her.

'Well Inspector, as if five mixed bags of remains weren't enough you surprise me again,' she said as way of welcome. She took a mouthful of tea and the Inspector smiled with delight.

'Casey you never fail to amaze me, what have you found.'

'Well, in this first bag I opened.' She motioned toward it with her usual air of exuberance. 'So far I have discovered it contains the remains of three individuals, one leg is of a male that I would estimate to be in his forties at the time of death, the other leg is a female I would guess about twenty at the time of death, and the rest of the torso is of a second female aged about thirty. I presume I will be finding similar contents in the rest of the bags as I make my way through, and I will of course put them altogether as best I can as I go.'

'Thank you, if you saw the circumstances these bodies were found in I'm sure you'd understand.'

'Oh no need to thank me Inspector, I can tell by the state of your and Drew's clothes that removing these remains wasn't much fun.'

'Have you discovered much about the bones you have had a chance to look at?'

'A little,' she revealed, with a wry smile. 'Looking at the quality of the bone, the size and strength of the bone tissue, and the teeth, I can tell what year almost to the date that a person lived and died.'

'That's amazing. How do you do that?' Drew asked. Casey smiled, pleased to have an audience.

'Good question Drew, thank you for asking. By comparing bones that we know to be from the same era and looking for similarities. Using these similarities as a general pointer, and bearing in mind I've only had the contents of the bag for a couple of minutes, I would say the origins of the individuals in this bag range in date from a remarkably well preserved 3rd to 5th century left leg, a right leg from the 17th or 18th, and a torso from, I would estimate, the 15th century.' She waved a finger over the bones as she spoke.

'What is wrong with this picture, Inspector?' He looked over the remains carefully.

'They are all in the same state of decay,' he said. Drew frowned.

'Exactly,' Casey replied. 'These remains have all been decaying for approximately three hundred years, meaning your left leg hasn't been decaying for long enough, and your other leg and the torso have been decaying for too long.' She looked at the Inspector, who was nodding, and not in the least surprised by the seemingly contradictory information she had given him. She looked at Drew who was showing signs of being a little more overcome with the information.

'You found all that out in the time we were gone?' Drew asked, amazed. Casey simply smiled.

'I told you she was good,' the Inspector told him.

'Am I to presume that I will find similar oddities in these other bags?' she asked.

'I presume you will, yes.'

'In that case, I think you should study the chest a little closer.' The Inspector raised his eyebrows apprehensively and bent lower to the table for a proper look.

'Does this look familiar to you?' she asked, pointing at the chest cavity where, in the centre of the ribs, a perfect circle had been cut away. The bone around it was not chipped or cracked.

'I presume this wound matches the wound on the body I found?' Drew asked intuitively.

'From what I can tell Drew, yes it does. This person from the 17th or 18th century died in exactly the same way as that man did.'

'Can we also presume then,' Drew asked the Inspector. 'That she appeared in similar circumstances?' The Inspector ruffled his moustache thoughtfully with his fingers.

'I try not to ever presume anything,' the Inspector replied thoughtfully. 'But I think it would be a fair hypothesis.'

'That's all I've got for now, give me more time and I'm sure I will find something normal about one of them,' she promised wryly.

'Well, time marches on, let's allow the Doctor to work.' The Inspector nodded to her politely, and made for the door.

'See you soon Drew,' she called after them. Drew turned and smiled then followed the Inspector back through to the other men.

'Well gentlemen, thank you for your help today, let's hope we don't need to call on your services again.'

'Well I hope not, but it is nice to be helping you out, makes a change from the usual day, you know,' Jim replied, putting his tea down. They left Doctor Collins to his morgue, and retraced their steps back to the ambulance bays.

'Well, goodbye chaps.' The Inspector raised his hat to them, then he and Drew returned to his squad car and they headed back toward Firestone.

'Will you be joining me for dinner this evening Drew?' the Inspector asked when they arrived at The Green Man.

'Not tonight, though thanks for the invite. I'm going to see my mum tonight, as you suggested. I'm going to have a look through my dad's old things, see if there's anything there that might give us some clues about Banks.'

'Capital, well done. I feel we became rather distracted today, albeit for a worthwhile cause. No doubt Banks feels he has escaped our clutches. First thing tomorrow we shall see if we can locate him.'

'Right you are,' Drew replied as the Inspector opened his door and climbed out.

'See you for breakfast then, about nine?'

'Of course, we can catch up on what, if anything I find out from mum's house,' Drew agreed. 'See you in the morning.'

'Yes, good night Drew, good luck.' The Inspector closed the door and Drew headed home for a bath.

49.

Following a long soak in a hot bath Drew dressed in brown cords, red shirt and warm black jumper before driving to his mother's house. He didn't knock, nor did he require a key. He simply turned the handle to the front door and walked in.

'Hello Mum!' he called into the apparently empty house.

'Hello Love, I'm in here!' Came the muffled reply. He followed its direction to the kitchen, where his mother was up to her elbows in a sink full of foamy bubbles and pans. She wiped her hands on a filthy apron around her waist and rushed to meet him, embracing him tenderly.

'Hello Drew my love,' she held him with the closeness that can only be shared between a mother and her son. She was at least eighteen inches shorter than him, and rather rounded about her middle.

'I'm sure you've grown since I saw you last,' she felt him around the middle. 'And gotten a bit thinner. Are you eating properly over there in Firestone?' Drew laughed off the fuss. She didn't so much walk as waddle back over to the sink to finish the washing up. Her dimming eyes sat behind thick spectacles, her hair sat in a neat grey bun at the back of her head. Traits that had been slowly imposing upon her over the last twenty years or so, as she crept out of middle age and into the realm of the elderly. When they were apart Drew's mind's eye showed her as she looked when he was a toddler; thinner, taller, brown hair hanging about her shoulders. It was only seeing her again after a period of absence that made him fully appreciate how time had changed her, and so how it must also be changing him. He wondered if she still saw him as her little boy, bumping knees and scraping elbows as he ran about the house causing mischief.

'Well to make sure you get some good food in you I've made your favourite, roast beef and Yorkshires.'

'On a Wednesday?' Drew exclaimed. 'You didn't need to go to all that trouble.' He protested though he knew it was useless, and that his mother enjoyed preparing such extravagant meals for him.

'Oh nonsense!' she laughed in reply, wiping her hands again. 'It won't be ready for a while yet, so why don't you tell me all about what you've been up to?' She sat with her son at the table, satisfied with the mountain of clean pans and plates that slowly lost their water on the drainer. She poured them a cup of tea each from the streaming pot that waited between them.

She had lived in the cottage since marrying his father, they had moved in shortly after their wedding day. Drew and his brother had been born and raised here. It sat in the middle of generous plot of land, which, while his father had been alive, had seen a vegetable patch, fruit trees and a greenhouse all carefully tended and heavily laden during the summer months. Since his father's passing his mother had found caring for it all too much, and had put it all back to lawn. Now a gardener came to the house once a month to mow the grass and keep the bushes in check. The cottage was two low storeys, under a slated roof. The kitchen sat at the back of the house, the window looked out on to the dark garden where Drew had spent his childhood summers daydreaming.

'Well, usually I would say what I always say, "Not much going on, things are rather quiet."'

'And that is what I always hope you'll say! I don't want you to be mixed up in any trouble.'

'I'm a policeman Mum, it's my job to sort the trouble out, not get involved in it.'

'Well you know what I mean. If you say it's quiet I know you're safe.'

'Yes, well, as I was saying, usually I would say that things were quiet and that there was nothing much to talk about.'

'But there's been that body you found over there.'

'Yes, I told uncle Frank about it, and he got the yard involved, so now I'm working with the Inspector they sent to try and work out who the poor bloke was, where he came from, and how he managed to end up in the woods.'

'Scotland Yard? Well it must be serious.'

'Well, someone has been murdered Mum.'

'Yes I know, never heard of anything like it before, not in these parts,' she told him, glancing at the window with a shudder.

'The man was from Swindon, and the Inspector doesn't seem to think that he was murdered by anyone from around here,' Drew paused for a moment, preparing himself for what his Mother's reaction would be to what he said next. 'Do you remember that I said he is interested in knowing about Banks? He seems to think Banks and his cronies might be involved somehow, though he's not sure how.'

'Banks,' she spat the word out of her mouth like a bad taste. 'What could that man have to do with it?' At the mention of the name his mother's tone and mood changed dramatically, as if Drew had deeply offended her.

'Well, that is the question he is trying… we are trying…' Drew corrected himself '…to work out.'

'Is that why you wanted to come over for dinner tonight? To see if I could help?' she was confused as to what she could possibly know that could aid their investigation.

'In a way, yes,' he replied. She shifted her position uncomfortably.

'I better check on dinner.' She stood and went to the oven, opening it up and being enveloped by a cloud of steam. It slowly cleared and she looked inside. 'Oh yes, this is all looking rather good now.' She pulled the tray out and put it down on the surface next to the hobs. A joint of beef, some roasted potatoes and some parsnips all sat in the roasting tray sizzling appetisingly. Drew didn't interrupt her, but was determined not to allow her to skim over the subject of his father's death and Banks' connection to it. She dished the contents on to two plates, and then put the joint on to a separate plate with a carving knife. Drew helped her move it all on to the table, then he sat down and began carving the meat as his mother poured a saucepan full of gravy into a gravy boat.

'The Inspector would be very impressed with this spread Mum,' he told her as he sliced comfortably through the perfectly prepared meat.

'Oh yes?' she asked, grateful to be off of the subject of Banks.

'The man has hollow legs. I've never seen anyone eat so much.'

'What's he like then, this Inspector chap?'

'Surprisingly nice,' Drew placed the cut meat on their plates.

'Not too much for me love,' his mother protested.

'Well I can't eat all this by myself!' he laughed.

'No but I thought you could take anything that's left with you and reheat it during the week. Or make sandwiches with it.' Drew took some of the meat from her plate and put it on his.

'You are funny Mum,' he shook his head in wonder.

'Well I have to make sure you're eating properly!' she defended herself.

'The Inspector's making sure of that at the moment,' he laughed.

'Oh yes, go on then, what's he like?' they began tucking into their food.

'He's very good, very thorough. He has a way with people, everyone immediately trusts him. People want to talk to him. They want to tell him everything they know, even if it doesn't make sense, or has apparently nothing to do with anything. I'm not sure why they are telling him these things, but he always listens.'

'Is he nice then?'

'Yes, as long as you're nice to him. Even when he's rubbed the wrong way he maintains this calmness, this professionalism. And some of his methods are very strange. He has a suitcase full of all these contraptions, they look for radiation, atmospheric pressure, magnetism...'

'Radiation?'

'Yes.'

'Is it safe?' Drew considered for a moment.

'Yes it must be. I'm not sure he's actually detected any yet anyway.'

'Well what's all that got to do with finding a murderer?'

'I don't know. He has extraordinary means. I'm not even sure he is trying to find out who murdered him. I think the Inspector is just trying to work out how he ended up there.'

'Well, wouldn't the murderer have put him there?' his mother asked.

'Well, there was no one else there, only me.' Drew thought of the lights on the road, their eerie stare penetrated through his memory and into his waking life for a moment, so he quickly buried them into his psyche again. 'It was as if the body, well, just appeared.' His mother considered for a moment.

'How was he killed then?'

'He had a hole in his chest, here, like this.' He traced a circle on his chest in the approximate position of the man's wound.

'Well, no question what killed the poor soul then,' his mother deduced. 'Could he not have fallen, from an aeroplane or something?'

'I'm sure I would have heard a plane over head, or heard the body land. And the landing would have disturbed the mud, and caused more damage to the body. The coroner said the body was fine, fully intact and healthy. Apart from the wound in the chest.'

'So how do you know he was from Swindon then?'

'The Inspector found his wallet. Someone else from Scotland Yard is going down there to find the family and inform them.'

'Well it all sounds like ever such a queer business to me Drew. Bodies appearing in the woods, strange wounds.' Their food slowly disappeared from their plates as they talked. Drew was relieved to be speaking to someone other than the Inspector or his uncle about the affair, and his mother was interested to hear the details. She was reminded of conversations she'd had with Drew's father.

'And you think that man Banks has something to do with it all?' she broached the subject, knowing where the conversation would eventually head.

'Well, I don't know.' Drew was pleased she had mentioned him first. 'I told the Inspector everything about Dad and Banks, about them both going for Sergeant and the car crash. He said I should look through Dad's old papers, see if I can find anything that might help.'

'You told him all about that?' his mother seemed surprised.

'Well, it's like I said, he's easy to talk to, you feel you want to tell him things, even if they don't seem to matter, or aren't relevant.' Drew shook his head. 'It's difficult to explain.' Drew watched her for a reaction. She looked away, pensive for a moment, before sighing.

'Oh, well, it can't do any harm. We might even get some answers.' She thought for a moment. 'I don't know what there is of your Dad's old stuff, or if it would be any help. Your uncle Frank put all his things up in the loft after he died. I didn't have the heart to throw them away, but I couldn't stand having them about the place, you know?' she blushed for a moment and bravely fought back tears.

'Don't worry mum. We'll finish up here and then I'll go up and see what's what.' He reached out a hand and she held it for a moment with a smile, before she returned to her dinner.

'This was your Dad's favourite as well,' she said jovially, the smile back on her face.

'There was this one time when you were about five when you came in from the garden covered in mud...' They finished their meal with Drew allowing her to retell the same story she always retold whenever he went to her house and they had roast beef. It made her happy, and allowed him to contemplate what he might find in the loft space. He wondered if his father had stored anything relevant up there, safely away from the eyes of Banks and his cronies.

With dinner eaten, and the dishes washed up and put away in their cupboards, Drew began preparing himself for the loft.

'Cup of tea before you go love?' his mother asked, filling the kettle.

'No thanks mum, it's getting late and I don't know how long it will take me to sort through what's up there.'

'Oh yes, I'd forgotten about you going up there.' Drew strongly suspected she hadn't forgotten and was hoping that he had, but he let it slide. 'The ladder's in the garage, I'll get you the key.' Gathered on one of the kitchen walls were a row of hooks with keys on, and from this she took an old rusty padlock key. Just the sound of keys rattling brought back to Drew memories of his father, it had been

237

the workshop he had used for projects around the house, or for tinkering with his old squad car. Drew was forbidden to enter without his father, and even then entry was on the strict understanding that he wasn't to touch anything.

'Thanks.' He took it from her and felt the passing of responsibility, the inheritance of the space, of his new place in the family. Although it had been years since his father's passing, he was only now realising his new position in the household. His mother seemed to sense it too, and viewed her son with a new sense of pride. After his father had died the garage had been locked, and the lock had barely been touched. Over the years he and his brother had forgotten it was even there, having no need to enter it. The large brick building had merged into the surroundings, becoming as vague a part of the background as a hedge or fence.

'You'll find a torch out there too I should think, though the batteries might not be much good.'

'Thanks Mum.' He pulled his coat back on and walked out into the cold night, while his mother looked on and tried not to compare him to his father.

The evening was dark, and what little light there was barely penetrated into the garage once he had the door open. The door was stiff but despite years without use it opened with a little determination. Inside the garage Drew fumbled around on the wall for a minute before finding the light switch. It was lower than he expected, and he reasoned that this was because the last time he had been out here he had been much smaller. A dim bulb flickered into life, illuminating a space much smaller, and tidier, than he remembered. No car sat in the middle of the floor in a stage of dissection. There were no oil stains spoiling the grey cemented floor. The tools were all tidied away in drawers. These were not the only things that were missing. The most conspicuous thing to be missing was his father. To be back in the garage again was one thing, but to be here by himself felt disrespectful. He tried not to think about how much he missed him and set about removing the extendable ladder from its coupling on the ceiling. He removed it with only a small amount of fuss, then set about searching the drawers for a torch. These yielded rusting spanners and rotten hammers, and a large metal torch. He tried it but it failed to light, and on checking saw the batteries had leaked and the acid had furred up the points beyond rescue. He slung it back in the drawer, and remembered he still had one in the boot of his squad car. He retrieved it, and returned for the ladder, noticing the smell of burning dust as the bulb began to warm up. As he headed back to the door at the rear of the house his mother opened it and let him in.

'Everything alright then love?' she asked as he trudged carefully back into the kitchen.

'Yes, although the torch had seen better days, luckily I still had mine in the car.'

'I'm trying to think of the last time anyone might have been out there, I don't think even Isaac has been out there.'

'Well then I doubt anyone's been up in the loft for a while either have they?' he asked.

'No, well you can tell by looking at the state of that ladder.' Drew looked at the long heavy thing properly for the first time and realised it was covered in a tangle of dusty cobwebs that gave testament to the years it had lain idle.

'You're traipsing dust all through my house young man!' she suddenly realised, and ushered him out of the kitchen and towards the stairs with a flutter of her tea towel. 'If you insist on going up there then get on with it!' Drew laughed and hurried as best he could with the cumbersome steps. At the top of the stairs was a small landing with three doors heading off from it. In the ceiling above, a hatch awaited him. Drew extended the ladder by four rungs then pushed it open with the high end by pushing up against the opening. He then climbed up, his mother watching anxiously from the landing trying hard to stop herself from saying "Be careful!"

He pushed back the hatch and entered a window on to his childhood. The roof was low, but he could stand stooped under the highest point. He switched the torch on and in a hushed awe flashed its beam about. Before climbing the ladder he could not have told her what he was expecting to find, but now he was here the memories he had of this space came flooding back. His father had insulated and added flooring, and then transferred the possessions he had inherited from his father, Drew's grandfather, from his loft space to this one. He then began adding to it, and so a family history had slowly accumulated, passed from generation to generation. From loft to loft. All that history was now confined to the dozen or so cardboard boxes stacked neatly around him. One he recognised immediately, and went to it. Opening it up he found it full of the toys he had played with when this was still his home. Old Matchbox cars sat heaped, paint flaking and rust round the edges, with die cast metal soldiers, a snakes and ladders board, and a smattering of familiar items he used to love and play with every day. Once he wondered how he would live without them, now they sat abandoned in this dark corner of the world. He began digging through the box on a reminiscent whim before stopping himself and turning back to the task at hand. He turned to the next box, and found it full of old photographs. He could not help but look through them. At the top, in colour, were some photographs of his family; he and his brother as young boys growing up, as babies nestled at their mother's breasts. As he went further down he found photographs of them being held in their young father's arms, then as bumps under their proud mother's clothes. As he dug the photographs soon went from colour to black and white, and the faces became unrecognisable; family long gone, friends forgotten, moments immortalised on celluloid for future strangers to find and wonder over. As he dug deeper the photographs became older, greyer, the pictures fading almost to nothing, like the memories of those that they depicted.

Behind the box of photographs he found a box containing his father's toys, much the same as his had been, cars, toy soldiers, metal cowboys, their paint chipped and faded. He also found school books, all of a deep red, all containing neat looping handwriting that he could hardly read. Here too were mementos from his mother's school days, stories written, pictures drawn, another lifetime ago, another child's memories forgotten as the pressures and responsibilities of a dawning adulthood took precedence. He continued through the boxes, finding a box of saucepans, which he wondered if anyone apart from him even knew were there. He elected to take them downstairs with him and moved the box over to the hatch.

He searched through the other boxes, finding more photographs, more mementos of his families past, until he eventually came to the object of his search. A plastic container, hidden under and behind other cardboard boxes, sat at the back of the loft space, as close to the tiles as its shape would allow. Drew recognised the container as it was not unlike the containers used by Nettlewood to store evidence in. He had not seen one ever used in Firestone. He prised open the lid, releasing the all too familiar smell of police paper work; old cardboard, smoke and spilt tea. The top layer consisted of folders, full of commendations for his father's police work, certificates he had gained through training, and his diploma. Beneath this were some old copies of the Nettlewood Herald Newspaper. Drew presumed they contained some stories regarding some work by his father, and so put them with the box of pans to be taken downstairs. He continued through the box, finding nothing that might be of any use, until he reached the bottom of the box, where a thin unlabelled file lay unassumingly. He pulled it out and began to read under the light of his torch. On the first page was a letter;

Dear Albert,

I wanted to write you this letter following something you brought up with me at the last district meeting. I said I was very busy on the day and I promised to try and find some time for you later, but I didn't. I was dismissive, and I apologise.

The truth is I didn't want to discuss it there and then. There are ears everywhere, listening to everything we say, and the risk was too great.

You wanted to speak to me about a certain Sergeant, at a certain village. You mentioned that you were suspicious of him, and things were not being investigated as they should.

The truth is that you are not the first to mention such things. We want to take this further but the opportunity never seems to arise. I would ask you not to mention this to anyone, in fact to destroy this correspondence as soon as you have read it.

If you want this matter investigated it must be done with the upmost tact and in complete secrecy. I am aware of the situation, but I cannot take the matter any further without evidence. I would recommend;

Keep a journal of times, dates, events, no matter how insignificant they may seem, to show what the officer is doing.

Where possible obtain reports from others pertaining to the officer's behaviour.

Keep any evidence you find hidden. Send me correspondence c/o Head Office. I will arrange with you a time and a place that it can be handed over to assist us in developing a case.

Best of luck.

KB

Drew read the letter over and over in the light of the torch. He had no idea who it might have been from, but he did have some initials to work on as a lead. It was obvious who the Sergeant mentioned in the letter was, and he wondered if his father had collected any evidence, or kept a journal as the letter suggested, and if so where it was now.

He continued looking through the thin file, which also contained a report he had made of a body being found in the copse. It was a body of a female, approximately thirty years old. It had a date of the discovery, and a brief description of where she was found. There were no other details he might have expected, for example what had happened to the body. He searched carefully through the rest of the papers but there was nothing of any use, or seemed relevant. He went to refill the container with the files he hadn't found interesting, when he noticed a clean white square against the dirty grey bottom. He removed it, and upon studying its hidden side discovered it to be a picture of him and his brother as babies in their father's arms. Their father looked down at them smiling, they were both sound asleep. He placed it carefully in his pocket. He put the file with the newspapers and the pans, then repositioned the boxes back into their original places. With the area back to how he had found it he climbed back down the ladder, precariously carrying the box with him. When it was safely on the ground he climbed back to the hatch, resealing the loft and its contents again. His mum heard the hatch being shifted back into place and appeared at the bottom of the stairs.

'Any luck love?' she called up to him.

'Sort of,' he called back. He carried the ladder down first, and she noticed the box at the top of the stairs.

'What's in there then?' she asked.

'Go and have a look if you like, I'm just going to pop this back in the garage.' He carried the ladder out, putting it back on its hooks, then left the garage and its memories behind a locked door again. When he was back inside his mother had carried the box downstairs and was poking through the pans.

'I think these were my mothers,' she informed him, holding one up to investigate it. 'I didn't even know we still had them.'

'I wondered if you did. Do you mind if I have them?'

'No of course not love, be sure and give them a good clean before you use them though.'

'Yes of course,' Drew agreed. There was no need for his mother to give him such advice but he liked that she did.

'And what are these other bits? Is that what you were after?' She indicated the pile of papers on top.

'I'm not sure yet, I'll have to have a good look through the newspapers, see if there's anything of any interest there, and show them to the Inspector, he might see something I miss.' Drew thought for a moment.

'Any idea who KB might be mum?' he asked.

'KB?' she replied, a little mystified.

'Yes, there were some initials at the bottom of a letter I found. KB.'

'No sorry love, I don't think so.'

'Oh well worth a try.' He checked his watch; ten thirty had crept up on him.

'Cup of tea love?' she asked out of habit more than out of any desire to make or actually drink one herself.

'Thanks, but it's been a long day, I'd best be getting home.'

'Right you are dear,' she stood and hugged him without any arguments. He picked up the box of paper and pans, and they walked to the door where they kissed each other goodbye on the cheek.

'Nice to see you love, drive safe.'

'Will do, night mum,' he bid her farewell and drove back to Firestone and back to his small cottage. Once there he made a cup of coffee, opened the old newspapers, and began to study each article closely.

50.

The Inspector watched Drew drive away, then returned to The Green Man and made his way directly to his room where he too ran a deep hot bath. Before undressing and getting in he took some blue pills, designed to help his muscles recover from a hard day's work. An hour later, scrubbed and feeling fully refreshed, he adjourned to the lounge bar of the pub to eat. He ordered steak and kidney pie with new potatoes and green veg, which was delivered quickly, was hot, and delicious. He made short work of it. He then relaxed with a pot of tea in the saloon bar, which was busier and a little livelier. A few locals turned their heads his way, even nodding in welcome and bidding him good evening. He was, it appeared, becoming a feature of the bar that people were growing accustomed to. This pleased him greatly. The more used they were to seeing him, the more likely they were to impart information. Within half an hour he was approached by two men carrying partially consumed pints of flat dark amber liquid. The Inspector looked up from the paper he had been half reading to welcome them.

'Good evening,' he said.

'Evening,' they replied, standing close to his table and not making eye contact.

'Would you care to join me? This newspaper is not interesting me particularly. It's nearly time I was off to my room, but it would be nice to have some company.' He folded the paper in half and placed it on to the table. The two men nodded and each took a seat opposite the Inspector, looking quietly into their drinks.

'So, are you both from Firestone?' the Inspector asked in an attempt to make conversation.

'Yes,' one answered for both. The men were both greying, with wrinkled frowns on their tired faces. The older scratched his long sideburns, as if searching for something for his worn hands to do.

'Have you lived here long?' The men were a little surprised with this line of questioning. They had expected to be asked immediately about the body, what they knew, why they wanted to speak to him. The Inspector engaged them in casual small talk, and tried to make them feel more comfortable in his presence.

'Lived here all my life,' the younger one replied. He had undone the top button of his wide collared shirt, the glowing fire gave sweet relief to the cold outside.

'Aye, me and all,' the older added. The Inspector guessed they were brothers, perhaps a little older than Banks. Not only did they look alike they were dressed alike too.

'Well, you must have seen a few changes over the years?' the Inspector asked. This was somewhat a loaded question; he knew little had changed in Firestone, perhaps for centuries.

'Not much changed around here,' the older told him.

'No, people come and go but the town seems to stay the same,' the younger agreed.

'Well, the appearance of a body must be exciting news, if nothing of that sort ever happens,' the two men exchanged a brief glance. Anyone else might not have noticed it, but to the Inspector it was full of meaning.

'Nothing of that sort ever happens,' one replied, leaning in close to the Inspector, 'what the likes of you ever gets to hear about.'

The Inspector leaned in close too, enveloping the secrecy, ignoring the smell of ale and smoke on the men's breath.

'There's stories, things we want you to know,' the older man confided.

'What things, and why do you think I should know them?'

'Because there's something ain't right about this town. All the folks round here know it, but none want to say nothing about it.'

'Like what, for example?' the Inspector asked.

'Like the things what live in the trees,' the younger man revealed. 'Things we can't see, but we know they're there. We can feel them, watching us.' The Inspector thought of the conversation with Bert the previous evening, and of the photographs Drew had taken.

'You chaps aren't the first to tell me about them,' the Inspector informed them. They looked relieved. 'But I can't be seen running around the trees chasing things no one can see. I need a bit more evidence before I can go looking for something you only feel is there,' he explained patiently. 'How do you know these things exist, who has seen them, where's the proof?'

'Well, don't suppose there is any, not like you would need,' the younger man admitted.

'There is the Firestone though,' the older one said, mentioning it casually.

'Well yeah there is the Firestone.'

'What of it? What has it to do with these alleged creatures in the woods?' The Inspector probed.

245

'Well, on dark nights, and I mean really dark nights, they say that if you look at it right, you can see the Firestone, sort of, glowing.'

'Glowing?' the Inspector repeated.

'And it's the glowing what brings them out, the things in the trees.' the older one went on.

'Not that anyone I know has ever seen it glowing,' the younger one continued. 'Our old mum used to say about it, but don't know if she ever saw it either. No one ever goes to look nowadays. Just an old rumour.' he added, as if justifying the tallness of the tale.

The Inspector considered the stone, its locality directly above the site where the body was discovered, the high electromagnetic readings he had picked up around it.

'Well, it's certainly worth looking into,' the Inspector informed them airily. 'I appreciate you coming to tell me, obviously if anything else should come to mind, please don't hesitate,' he stood, his tea finished.

'I do beg your pardon gentlemen but I have had a long day, I think perhaps I should retire for the evening.'

The two men nodded, and wished the Inspector good evening. He disappeared through the door leading upstairs.

'Do you think he believed us?' the younger asked the older, who he had always looked up to, and always seemed to know what to say.

'Let's hope so. And let's hope he can do something about it too,' the older replied, draining his glass of beer and making toward the bar for another.

51.
The Inspector returned to his room and removed from his bag the faded parchment he had recovered from the Manor house earlier. With infinite care he placed it on the desk in his room, angled the lamp over it as best he could, and began trying to decipher the writing. Two painstaking hours later, he had jotted down his best guess at what it said;

7,2,1594

Forgive me oh lord, for I have failed, and now I can only wait alone in the dark for death to come. My name is Kirk Yetholm, I am a traveller, tradesman, I have travelled the scope of this fair isle. I have seen many a thing, and I never thought my time on your sweet Earth would end in such a manner. Allow me the ---- undecipherable----

---- Let me use my own life's blood and the cloth from my back to record what has become of me save I am erased from history's memory forever along with the truth of this place. My captors left me a candle, so to allow me to see the bodies they claim I am responsible for in my last moments, though the light will fail long before I am gone. When it is, there---- undecipherable ----- and onwards.

The bodies here with me are those I have found, along with their strange abundances. This town harbours some evil, some bloodthirsty thing that takes bodies from abroad and brings them to the town, scattering them in the fields. The people about here know of it, and fear it, but they hide it also. To the south of the town is a patch of holy ground, consecrated, the site of a church long destroyed. All that is now left is a huge circle of mud where the trees can't grow. I couldn't fathom that circle in the trees, till I found, to the north of ---undecipherable --- In-between them the stone, used to such bloody ends in their lust to satisfy the beast and prevent more bodies coming. This seems the key, somehow, though to what I had no chance to see.

Let these things be known, if only to me and this shirt from my back, and to you Lord. Let whoever might find these words know that I was betrothed to my Heather, that I loved her, that I was once loved.
Kirk Yetholm

The scrawls red texture was, evidently, due to it being written in the poor man's blood. Here the Inspector had the last record an unfairly condemned man could make before the candlelight was exhausted, and all that was left for him to do was sit and wait for death to take him. The Inspector sighed, moved by his bravery, and by a life taken so unfairly.

He wondered what had been found to the North of the town, and studied his maps to see if anything was marked there that might give him a clue. He deduced the circle of mud to be the area where Drew had discovered the body. The most northerly building on the maps was the church, and a small cottage next to it. The Inspector decided that perhaps he should pay a visit to the Vicar, but it would have to wait until morning. He then thought of the Firestone, of the brothers' stories of it glowing, of the readings he had taken around it. He then thought of the package he had received form the courier. The Field Enhancer lay hidden under his bed. So far he had been unsuccessful in finding a suitable time and location to use it. He walked over to the window and looked out at the cold unforgiving night.

52

Despite the biting December wind and the occasional bluster of sleet, Banks stood in the dark unabashed by the onslaught of the winter. He had been standing, watching The Green Man, waiting for the Inspector for hours. He had seen him return earlier in the evening, and he now stood waiting for all lights to be extinguished so he might find his way in, find the Inspector, and do away with him. He had been watching him all day, always knowing where he was, like an instinct he had inside to know what he was doing, as long as he was near the copse. When he left town he vanished from his radar. He was surprised that he spent so much time in the woods up by Bill's, and wondered what he had been up to. He had stayed clear of him, waiting for him at The Green Man.

The Inspector's bedroom light was still on, and Banks began to wonder if he ever slept. He stood motionless and silent in the shadows, watching the lights of the town go out as the night had drawn in. The Inspector's light finally went out just before two in morning, and Banks could finally begin preparing himself to break into the hotel and get to him. He had chosen his route while waiting in the cold, deciding to shimmy up a drain pipe up the side of the building, climb through the Inspector's bathroom window, and sneaking through to his room.

He tried to image one of the others trying such a thing at their age, the ailing Mayor probably wouldn't make it up the curb. He stifled a laugh at the thought of it.

If only they knew what power they had hidden inside, if only they knew what they could be capable of.

He had decided he would wait an hour before going in, to give the Inspector plenty of time to get settled into a deep sleep. He waited, the countdown ticking away slowly in his head. As he waited he thought back to the day he had seen his dying father, how in his last moments he had brought him close, and passed the voice on to him. He had felt the life pass from his father to him, and a few minutes later he was gone. He knew it wasn't any spirit, or a possession by his dead father. It was another lifeform, something that his father, and goodness knows how many other Banks generations before him, had kept hidden and used for their own gains.

The voice told him little, it was so quiet now that he could barely hear it, yet its power was still within him. Banks dreamt of immortality, he was sure he could live forever as long he was controlling it. Long ago he'd decided that he would not be passing it on to his son, the fool would waste such power.

He had been shocked to find there were others with voices inside them like his. He had discovered them, quite by accident, one night when he was out in the copse. He had heard them talking to each other, whispering in the trees. The voice inside him had heard them and thought it was rescued, but Banks had other ideas. After much torturing he forced the voice to tell him what was happening, and the voice told him that they had come to find it. Banks harassed further, and it admitted that it and another voice had left the trees long ago, and taken two bodies as their hosts. How long ago Banks couldn't determine, but by all account it was centuries. They were trapped in the copse, these voices in the trees, and wanted to use the men to try and free themselves from the copse. Their departure had been so long ago that a search party had been sent to look for the two missing voices, and these were the voices he discovered.

Banks mind had plotted and planned, his twisted mind turning the situation to his advantage, to his control. He revealed himself to the new comers as one of their missing, and told them that he would help find the other missing voice. They had believed him, more evidence, Banks thought, of his power and ingenuity.

The voices had not been able to choose their hosts, not many were brave enough to venture deep enough in to the woods for the voices to find as they floated about their nowhere world between the trees. But they had been lucky with the boys they had found, daring each other deeper in to the woods, following the whispers that taunted and tempted. When Banks discovered the voices had been hiding in his friends all those years, he was dumfounded. Now he could begin trying to control them as well, slowly tightening his grasp on the copse.

He searched for the second voice across Firestone and Nettlewood. He could not risk whoever it was discovering they possessed the same power. With such small towns to search it was not long before he found his quarry, Albert Gates was not aware of what he carried, like the rest. The voices attempt to control their hosts to bring about their escape from the trees had failed miserably, their power was not strong enough to control the hosts they chose. He had done away with Gates when he began to get too close to the truth, as he would do away with the Inspector tonight.

He checked his watch; another twenty minutes and he would find him asleep. Suddenly the front door opened quietly, and the

Inspector stepped out. Banks hunkered down deeper into his dark spot, merging with the shadow, the power of the voice helping him disappear into the darkness. He watched the Inspector standing in the grey night, studying the dead silence of the night to see if anyone else was out. As well as his usual briefcase he also had a large heavy looking suitcase, and Banks wondered what he was up to coming out so late. After a few moments glancing up and down the deserted silent street he seemed satisfied that no one was about, and began to walk up the road. Banks followed. To his surprise he headed toward the Firestone, out of town. When he reached the roundabout he began setting up various objects from the suitcase. Banks hid behind a car and settled down to watch. This was the moment he had been waiting for. The Inspector had spared him the trouble of breaking into the hotel, this opportunity had been handed to him. The nosey old man wouldn't be bothering him anymore. He slowly rose from his hidden spot and pulled his gun out from inside his coat. He leant his arm across the car roof, and took aim at the Inspector.

53.

The night was deadly still. There was no moon, just a deep darkness, and in Firestone Copse all was shadow. The dull houses and empty roads were dusted with the harsh sleet that had been falling listlessly from the sky all day. The night robbed everything of colour, leaving tones of bleak grey and ashen black. The Inspector's reflection looked into his room from the window. He saw the maps, the bed, the desk, the dim red light from the bathroom posing as a dark room. He leant forward and closed the curtain to hide the night. He turned to the bed and pulled out from beneath it the case he had received the previous day containing the Field Enhancer. He clicked the locks open, and pulled the lid up. Inside, sitting in beds carved out of protective foam sat the Field Enhancer. It consisted of ten long metal rods with sharp pointed ends. These were twelve inches long and about two inches in diameter. Connecting each of these at the flat end was a thick black wire. These actually took up little of the large case. The main bulk of which was actually a heavy battery that sat at the bottom. He closed the lid again, put on his coat and hat, picked up the case, and headed out of the door. He crept silently through hall, though he was certain there were no other guests. Once downstairs he made directly for the front door, bearing no mind to the empty bar. He passed through, opening and closing the front door with infinite care, so as the latch would pass silently back into its housing. Three miles away the town clock in Nettlewood's central square struck the hour of two. Firestone had no church clock to ring the hours of the day. The Inspector heard the bell's drifting across the tops of the trees, but he already knew the time. The wind had abated, adding starch calm to the cold town. It was frozen in the night, still framed like a photograph. The Inspector slipped through it, hidden between the shadows, stalking his way to the Firestone. He passed through the streets quickly, keeping to the darkest paths. He saw no other creatures, human or otherwise, brave enough to face the night. This feeling of solitude made the footsteps he heard following him rather a confusing surprise. He noted their presence but walked on as if he hadn't.
Under the bare hidden trees the air was filled with the whisper of their branches, driven by some unfelt breeze between their ancient arms. The Inspector took his torch out of his bag and shone it around the scene a moment, illuminating around him the skeletons of the trees, huddled together. He knew now what the brothers had

meant about their being something in the trees watching. He wondered if the eyes were there, hidden from him. He took out his camera and took some photographs as he walked.

Soon he reached the stone, where he stopped and rested, sitting on the case for a moment. He listened intently for the footsteps, but could hear nothing. When his breath was back he began setting up the electrodes, pushing the pointed ends into the ground. When he had created a wide circle around the stone he took a few photographs of the equipment ready to use. In the dark the stone stood dim, lifeless and frozen. He took some readings from his instruments and was pleased to see them all read high; there was an area of increased pressure and magnetism around the stone. This convinced him he was close to something, so he plugged the Field Enhancer into the battery, switched it on, and waited. The equipment was designed to slowly build the effect so he walked about the area, taking more readings, and watching as all the instruments reacted to the enhanced magnetic field produced by the enhancer. If the stone was connected in some way to the higher readings, he hoped the Field Enhancer might allow him to discover how. He returned to the stone, stepping into the ring of electrodes that surrounded it. His presence inside the electrodes had an immediate effect on the stone, and as he watched it began to lose the darkness around it, and instead attract a shimmering light. The Inspector went to reach for his camera, but found the light was too hypnotic, too enchanting. Unable to stop himself he found his hand reaching out to the stone, wanting to feel it, to experience the eerie light that danced about it. Caught up with its beauty, powerless to resist, the Inspector's hand gently touched the cold hard rock, filling him for an instant with satisfaction. At the moment skin met stone, between a breath, inside an infinitesimal moment, the Inspector vanished; disappearing into the darkness completely.

End of Part One.

Part Two.

Monday 3rd November 1969

54.

Hunkered down upon the hill, the Vicarage slept nervously in the storm. The last remnant of flame spluttered out, and the fireplace fell cold. Soon the chill of the night encroached on the cottage. Eventually the cold stirred the Vicar, Aldous Squires, from his sleep. He lifted his head, trying work out where he was. He then tried to work out why he was asleep in the front room. He noticed an unfamiliar lump in front of the remains of the fire, and the events of the night were returned to his tired mind. He sleepily rebuilt the fire, piling on more coal once the flames were settled. He found extra blankets which he loaded on to his visitor before returning to his own bed. Once he was settled again he lay awake, unable to sleep despite the hour.

He prayed long and hard for an answer to the man's riddle. Part of him was excited. The unexpected visitor injected a much prayed for chance for doing good, and he thought perhaps his prayers had been answered. The strangeness of his appearance on his doorstep could be a sign, he thought, he hoped.

Another part of him however, the part that spoke louder, was his responsible side. He was, or wanted to be, a respected member of the community. Housing a potential criminal, however well-tailored their suits might be, was not the behaviour of such a respected person. He resigned himself regrettably to the conclusion that in the morning he would have to go into town and find a policeman.

As he lay in his gradually warming bed he played the next day out in his head over and over. He pictured giving his statement to the policeman, and what he would say. He replayed the events of the night over in his mind and rehearsed his story to ensure he could recall every moment. As he did so his eyes drifted closed, and the night crept on.

He only realised he had drifted off to sleep when he woke up again. From the grey out of his window he could see it was late morning, the day was as bright as it would get. This time when he awoke he remembered the man as soon as he opened his eyes. He dressed as quickly as he could and rushed down to the living room. White embers at the end of their reserve glowed in the fire place, and before them, still snoring, was the blanket covered man. He was drier, as were his clothes, though they would require washing before he could wear them again. Aldous ate a half a slice of toast watching him sleep, wondering what had happened. When he was ready he strolled down into town, and quickly happened upon a man, stalking around the Firestone roundabout suspiciously. He watched him for a while, trying to fathom what he might be doing as he dodged cars and scribbled notes. He then noticed Drew on the roundabout watching him, and nodded to him in recognition.

Drew was an enigma to him. He knew the stories of his father, and had even heard the rumours about Banks' part in his death. He wondered what sort of dangerous game he was playing under the scrutiny of Banks, and wondered if he needed a friend. Drew seemed cold and unapproachable, but he decided to make an effort none the less.

'Hello, Drew isn't it?' Aldous asked, admiring his tall helmet.

'Yes Father, nice to see you again,' Drew replied, though the Vicar doubted he meant it. Drew was a little unapproachable, though he did everything he could to display a professional demeanour.

'Who is he?' Aldous watched as the man stomped here and there, producing strange looking objects from his bag.

'He's an Inspector, down from Scotland Yard.' This didn't quite satisfy Aldous' curiosity.

'What's he doing?' he asked. Suddenly the Vicar saw something familiar about the man.

'Inspecting.'

Aldous watched him skirting the road, reading his instruments. He had seen him before but could not fathom when.

'Why is he here?' Aldous asked, trying to place him.

'There was a body discovered last night in the copse. He has been sent to investigate.' Aldous froze. Could the man asleep on his living room floor be responsible? He studied the Inspector again, and suddenly realised who it was he reminded him of. He shook his head in disbelief. How could this be?

'A body? My word,' Aldous said, trying to hide his train of thought for a moment.

'Did you notice anything last night Vicar? Anything you want to talk about?' Drew had noticed, he was a sharp one, Aldous realised.

'No.' He realised that he had been right from the start. Something was happening, and he should help the man without police assistance. He couldn't quite work out what brought him to this decision, but he knew it was the right one. Despite the risks, and the body.

'I'm a very deep sleeper, I didn't even realise how bad the storm had been last night until I left the Vicarage a few minutes ago to walk into town. Parts of the roads are almost flooded.' He indicated back up the road toward the Vicarage, but his attention did not leave the Inspector. The familiarity was uncanny.

'Were the any casualties, and damage anything like that?' Aldous asked, playing for more time to clarify his instinct.

'No reports I'm aware of. I'm sure if anyone needed your services they would know where to find you.' Drew wondered what he found so fascinating.

'I hope so,' Aldous replied, the more he saw of the man, the more sure he was he was right. The Inspector approached finally, and suddenly Aldous felt nervous speaking to him.

'Good afternoon.' The Inspector shook Aldous' hand. 'I'm sure Drew has told about me. I'm an Inspector down from Scotland Yard.'

'Good afternoon, I'm Aldous Squires, Firestone's Vicar,' Aldous replied, staring into his eyes.

'Pleased to make your acquaintance.' The Inspector shot a look at Drew, noticing the Vicar's behaviour. 'I'm here to investigate the appearance of a body in the woods last night, did you notice anything untoward around the hours of midnight and two am?'

'No,' Aldous replied, a little too quickly he thought. Paranoia began to edge into his mind and he realised he needed to get back to the man on his floor. 'As I was just telling Drew here, I sleep quite deeply, I wasn't even awoken by the storm, which by all accounts was dreadful,' he said quickly, wanting to go.

'Yes, fortunately no one was hurt.' The three men stood for a moment in silence. Aldous was now too scared to flee in case it looked suspicious.

'An interesting stone, Father, any clues of its origins?' the Inspector asked. The Vicar baulked a little. He regarded it briefly.

'Well, the stories I've heard is that it was used to sacrifice people, hence the red colouration, though I know little more of it than that,' he informed him, hoping this would suffice.

'Yes, this is all any one seems to know about it.' There was an awkward silence, and Aldous wished he had the courage to leave them and walk back to his cottage.

'Well, nice talking to you Father.' the Inspector finally released him, and the Vicar sighed inwardly. 'If anything about last night does spring to mind, please contact me via the police station.'

'Hmmm? Oh, yes of course.' Aldous felt he would have agreed to anything at that moment to escape.

'Well Drew, we'd best be off,' the Inspector informed him.

'Indeed, and I have some matters at the Vicarage I must attend to,' Aldous told them gratefully. 'Goodbye Inspector, see you again soon I'm sure,' he told him quickly. As he stepped into the road Mr Jones' empty bread van raced past nearly knocking him off his feet.

'My goodness father, are you alright?' The Inspector was first on the scene as the van sped away.

'Yes, I'm fine, thank you,' he lied. Aldous felt as though the last few hours excitement was perhaps all a little too much for him.

'I'm... I'm sorry, I really must be off,' he managed to blurt out, before he finally escaped and raced back up the hill a little shaken from his near collision with Mr Jones the Baker. He walked in a daze, dumbfounded and confused.

'It couldn't be,' he muttered to himself shaking his head. He scuttled up the path, the street was bordered on both sides by lazy cottages, set back from the road with gravel drives and neat gardens.

'Hello Aldous,' Mrs Tarbuck called to him as they passed. She stood, empty wicker basket in hand, and watched him pass her.

'Yes, hello,' he managed to reply, along with the conventional smile and nod. His pace didn't slack, he continued up the road unabated.

'Well I wonder what's gotten into him?' Mrs Tarbuck muttered to herself as she hurried down to the shops. The grey sky hung overhead, and an icy chill occasionally flustered down Firestone's quiet streets. Aldous' attention was distracted, his mind awash with questions. He reached the Vicarage and hurried through the squeaky gate of his cottage. As he rushed down the path of the well tendered garden he fumbled in his pocket for his key. He reached the low slung building and quickly let himself in. He closed and locked the door behind him, drawing the curtain that hung behind it to block any draft. He went through all this as an act of concealment; he was trying to hide the cottage's contents. Now safely back he suddenly realised how exhausted he was and stopped to catch his breath. His old bones felt the effects of exertion more than they used to, and his pace up the hill had been quicker than usual. His walk had been accelerated by the confusion that swam around his mind, and his eagerness to check on the strange visitor that had arrived during the night that he had left sleeping on his living room floor. The likeness between his visitor and the Inspector he had just met was eerie. He felt as though he was being made a fool of, or his sanity was being severely strained. He took off his hat and coat and hung them on their hook behind the door. He strained his hearing, listening to the humble cottage, trying to sense if the man was still there. He walked softly and gently down the low corridor to the lounge where he had left the man sleeping. Much to Aldous' surprise the man was no longer asleep, but sat bolt upright looking about the room in a dazed fashion. Aldous cautiously sat down in his usual chair, behind the man's line of sight.

'Hello,' he said as confidently as he could, trying to hide the shaking in his voice. Suddenly he felt very nervous about having this man in his house, an intruder inside his solitary world. The man turned slowly to face Aldous.

'Hello,' the man replied. His voice was coarse and weak. He was grey, washed out, his eyes sunken. The room was small, like all the rooms in the ancient house. The man and his makeshift bed almost filled it.

'Who are you?' Aldous asked, gaining a little confidence at the sight of the bedraggled man. He open and closed his mouth, rubbing his dry tongue against his mouth's roof, trying to create some saliva for his dry throat.

'I'm afraid,' he replied wearily. 'That I have no idea of whom, or where, I am.' Aldous frowned doubtfully.

'Well you look uncannily like a chap I have just had a conversation with at the Firestone roundabout. An Inspector, apparently, down from Scotland Yard.' Aldous held his ground, his bravery gathering.

'Inspector? Hmm... yes that sounds familiar.' A moment of recognition flashed across his face. 'What is he here to inspect?' the man asked.

'Well, I'm not entirely sure what he was inspecting at the roundabout, but a body was discovered in the copse last night and you, I mean, the man at the roundabout, is here to investigate it.'

'Why do you think that he is me?' The man thought for a moment, trying desperately to find reason. 'How is that possible?' He seemed genuinely confused to Aldous, who studied him closely. Although holding an undoubted similarity to the Inspector, the two men did look slightly different. Besides having a layer of facial hair this man was greyer, his features were drawn out. His face was longer and his eyes were set deeper, and had a morose expression.

'Well, you look similar, that's all,' Aldous replied after a moment of thought. Doubt began to creep into the edges of his mind as he considered the impossibility of it all. The man seemed to have already forgotten about their conversation, his eyes had begun wondering disinterestedly about the room. Another difference Aldous noticed between them was that the Inspector was obviously keen eyed and intelligent, whereas this man acted as if drunk or heavily sedated.

'Perhaps I could get you something to eat?' Aldous offered kindly.

'Alright,' the man replied, not quite seeming to know how to react, or indeed what Aldous even meant. Aldous put together some ham sandwiches and a poured him a glass of water. As he was feeling peckish he decided to have a sandwich too. The man studied the food on his plate, not picking it up. It looked to Aldous as if he wasn't sure what to do with the sandwich at all. The man watched Aldous eating a few mouthfuls then tried it for himself. He soon got the hang of it, and quickly devoured the sandwich as if he hadn't eaten for days.

'Is there more?' he asked desperately when every crumb had been cleared from the plate.

'Yes, hold on.' Aldous returned to the kitchen and prepared some soup from a can, which he gave to the man with half a sliced loaf. He wolfed the lot down eagerly. Aldous brought him more water, his heart softening toward him. When he had drunk a gallon almost without taking a breath, he looked up at Aldous.

'I think I need to lie down again,' he informed him.

'You can sleep upstairs, there's a spare bedroom.' Aldous stood to try and guide him up, but the man staggered back to the living room and collapsed on to his makeshift bed. He was asleep before his body hit the cushions. Aldous watched him for a few minutes, but he did not stir. When he was sure the man wasn't going to rise again Aldous cleared up the plates and bowls, washing them and replacing them in their cupboards, before returning to the living room. He sat in his chair and waited for him to wake up, but the man remained unconscious for the rest of the day. Eventually Aldous grew tired, and slipped off to sleep himself. He awoke in the evening and rebuilt the fire. He had dinner and read a book as he did most evenings. He left the man to rest. He managed to stay awake until ten before he gave in. He stocked the fire generously then took himself off to his bed, leaving the comatose man alone again.

Tuesday 4th November 1969

55.

Aldous awoke early the next day. He quickly dressed, and descended the stairs to find the man still asleep on his floor. He had half hoped, half expected, for him to have been gone this morning and had mixed feelings about seeing him still there. Seeing him still asleep on his floor made him wonder just what kind of trouble he might be in, and what he might be letting himself into. He left him to sleep and went through to the kitchen where he began making bacon and eggs. He closed the cupboards with a little extra vigour, he rattled plates and cups, however despite the racket he created the man didn't stir. As the bacon fried it filled the house with the most delicious odour, and as Aldous began to busy himself with eggs, the man suddenly appeared at the kitchen doorway in his dirtied but dry clothes. Aldous was quite startled to see him suddenly stood there and jumped at the sight of him. Without a word he walked in and sat down at the kitchen table. The sensation of having someone else in his house was a little unsettling to Aldous, but he tried to put these feelings aside.

'That smells good,' the man said simply.

'Would you like some? I've made enough for you,' Aldous told him.

'Oh, thank you,' the man replied hoarsely.

'You're welcome.' Aldous studied him. He was beginning to recover his colour a little, the food and water yesterday had obviously done him some good.

'I've never seen someone sleep for so long, or so deeply. Are you a drunk?' The man looked about him, as he had done yesterday. He didn't seem to have heard Aldous.

'How long have I been here?' he asked.

'You arrived Sunday night, well, very early Monday morning to be precise. It is now Tuesday morning.' Aldous paused. 'Do you know where you are today?' The man's eyes thinned suspiciously.

'Have we already spoken? Have I been awake already?' His glance darted around the room as he tried to recognise something.

'You don't remember waking yesterday? You don't remember speaking to me?' Aldous asked, a little concerned.

'No.' His guest replied morosely, leaning his elbows on the table and burying his head in his hands. He massaged his tired eyes with his palms. Aldous stood and began cooking the eggs.

'Well, what is the last thing you can remember?' he asked him as the eggs and bacon from Johnsons Butchers fried enticingly. The man looked around the kitchen.

'Waking up in there a few minutes ago,' he gestured toward the living room.

'Do you know who you are?' There was a moment of silence, while the man tried to recall something about his identity.

'No, nor exactly where I am, except for being in your house,' he replied eventually with disdain. Aldous took pity on him.

'You're in the village of Firestone.' He reminded him. 'And you are recuperating from whatever has happened to you in the Vicarage of Firestone.' Aldous paused in thought for a second, and the man picked up a fleeting moment of doubt.

'What? What is it?' he asked him, dreading what else he could have to contend with.

'Well, it's just that there is already someone visiting the town, someone who looks very similar to you. I met him yesterday on my way to the police station to inform them that I had a strange man asleep on my lounge floor.'

'Oh,' the man replied, then realised who he meant. 'Oh,' he said again, rather more forlornly.

'I didn't however make it as far as the police station before I met young Constable Gates, and your doppelganger, taking some kind of reading at the Firestone. When I saw how similar the two of you looked, something told me that I shouldn't tell the police, so I came back to check on you.' He looked the confused man up and down.

'I hope I made the right decision.' Aldous studied the man's face, his build. As he recovered from whatever ordeal he had been through he was beginning to look more like the man he had met yesterday, save for the hair sprouting from his cheeks, neck and chin.

'But that would be impossible,' the man replied, not sounding wholly convincing to himself or to Aldous. 'How can I possibly be in two places at once?'

'Well, indeed. That appears to be the question.' Aldous was confused, but convinced that they were the same person. The men were too alike in too many ways for him to accept they weren't the same man, no matter what the consequences of that might mean. He presented the Inspector with a plate full of eggs bacon and toast, which he immediately began to devour. He made short work of it, pausing only to glug down water from a jug that Aldous had placed on the table. When he had finished Aldous picked up his plate. The food was obviously doing him good. He sat for a while rubbing his stomach, looking satisfied.

'Would you like anything else?' Aldous asked when he noticed he had gained some colour in his cheeks. The man thought for a moment.

'Yes, err... sugar. Do you have sweets, chocolate, anything like that?' he asked, his voice a little brighter. Aldous rummaged in a cupboard above the worktops for a moment and eventually produced a white paper bag of Kola Kubes.

'These have been in the cupboard a while, please help yourself.' The Inspector began putting them in his mouth two at a time and crunching them.

'Would you happen to have any tea?' he asked when he got through half the bag.

'Of course,' Aldous replied, as if he should have thought of it himself. He stood and filled the kettle then placed it on the stove. Within a few minutes the two men were holding steaming cups of strong sweet tea.

'That's better,' the Inspector informed him in between mouthfuls. When he wasn't drinking tea he sat chomping on Kola Kubes at a leisurely fashion.

'You seem to have a good appetite, and a sweet tooth,' Aldous noticed.

'I think I have lost a lot of my body's natural sugars,' he explained, feeling much more like himself. 'Judging by how I feel and how emaciated I am I would say that I haven't had anything to eat or drink in about four days,' Aldous gawped.

'Why haven't you starved to death?' he asked a little surprised.

'There are ways of preventing these things from happening,' the Inspector replied vaguely.

'Well you certainly look like you've not eaten for a while. How was the food?'

'Delicious and much needed.' He glugged down a mouthful of tea then threw more sweets into his mouth. 'I presume whatever caused my absence from food and water also caused my amnesia, though things are slowly beginning to come back to me.' The Inspector suddenly stopped crunching.

'What day did you say it was today?' he tried to hide his trepidation at the answer.

'Tuesday,' Aldous replied. For a moment the Inspector lost his colour again, before recovering and continuing to crunch his sweets thoughtfully.

'The eleventh?' he asked hopefully.

'No, the forth. Have you remembered something?' Aldous asked. 'Something important?' The Inspector had realised that he had been thrown three days into the past, and that it had taken him about four days to get here. The Inspector sat, eyes closed, and tried to work out what he was going to do. The Vicar saw he was buried deep in thought, so poured them both another cup of tea, and pushed one towards the ruminating Inspector. Finally he opened his eyes, and turned to face the Vicar.

'How rigid is your view of the world we live in, Father?' the Inspector asked kindly. Aldous did not know how to reply, this was not quite what he had been expecting. He opened his mouth but when no words were forthcoming the Inspector elaborated.

'As a man of the cloth you may fall into one of two categories; on the one hand you may be open to new ideas, fresh views on a beautiful if not bewildering world. Or you may be so distracted by the word of your holy book that you squeeze all occurrences, no matter how fervently against your beliefs the evidence suggests they might be, into an explanation that fits the scripture but isn't entirely comparable with the apparent evidence.' The Inspector paused for Aldous to answer. The Vicar thought carefully.

'I think I may sit somewhere in the middle,' he replied after a cautious pause, feeling somehow a trap was being set.

'I don't believe that everything can be explained by the Bible.' He continued. 'But I do believe that all natural things, no matter how cruel or incomprehensible they might seem to human eyes, have come from God. He has a plan for it all, a plan so massive and intricate that to try and understand it would drive you to madness. It has come, after all, from the mind of God.' He paused to point a finger at the ceiling. 'No mortal could ever hope to understand it.' Aldous smiled, satisfied that this summed up his opinion, and his way of life. The Inspector nodded, satisfied. This was his faith, this was his life, and the Inspector had no intention of taking that from him.

'Well, let us imagine for a moment that you are right.' The Inspector suggested, rather jovially. 'I work for a government department that tries to comprehend that plan. We, mankind, have created a society that allows us the time and the intelligence to observe and study the world we live in, our environment. Call this study what you will; biology, geography, they are the sciences we use every day. We use these sciences to write rules that nature appears to follow, to the best of our observations.' He waved a hand in the air as he took another drink of tea. 'And we can use the rules to formulate, and make predictions about what will happen in the future, like...' He thought for a moment. 'Like weather forecasts and the movement of the planets.'

'Yes, I see,' Aldous nodded, his attention captured.

'There are times, as we seem to have discovered, when nature decides not to follow these rules, or we stumble upon new discoveries awaiting explanation. In this instances I, or a colleague of mine, will be sent to investigate the occurrences and try to discover what has happened, so that the observations of nature's behaviour can be extended to include the new occurrences. The rule book has not finished being written yet.' Aldous nodded.

'So you are trying to unravel the plan of God?' Aldous asked.

'We are trying to make sense of the universe,' the Inspector replied with a smile.

'That's all very interesting I'm sure, are you trying to explain to me how you are in two different places at the same time? I presume that is what you have realised now?' the Inspector thought hard for a moment.

'I guess what I am trying to explain is that the universe can be a vast and unnervingly confusing place if you look at it for too long,' he continued with a smile. 'I do not wish to distract you with my pursuits. I am, to be honest, still not entirely sure how I can be here, and somewhere else, at the same time.' This was true, it was still a mystery how he had gotten there. The Inspector needed to keep the Vicar onside, but didn't want him to know too much.

'Not that I don't believe you saw me at the Firestone,' he hastened to add. 'My mind, my body, and my memory are slowly recovering from whatever happened but I am still weak. I still don't know what has happened to me, but I would like to try and find out,' the Inspector informed him.

'I should think you would you poor chap,' Aldous replied. Though confused himself, he couldn't begin to think how his poor guest was feeling. The Inspector rubbed his thickly sprouted beard thoughtfully.

'Father, may I ask your name?' the Inspector asked, realising that if he did know it he couldn't remember it.

'Aldous,' the Vicar replied. 'Aldous Squires.'

'Aldous, there are different perspectives on the importance of asking for favours. What may be of vital importance to the person asking may be of little importance to the person being asked,' the Inspector mused.

'Well, yes, quite,' Aldous stuttered, wondering what the Inspector was about to ask of him.

'It is with this in mind that I must ask of you several things, and I list them in the order of inconvenience I consider they will cause you.' Aldous, feeling he was now embroiled in something beyond his comprehension, tried to remain business like, unsure how to react to the Inspector.

'Go on,' he encouraged him, cautiously.

'Firstly, may I stay at your house until Wednesday night?' Aldous leant back in his chair, looking thoughtfully out of the window at the movement of the trees.

'Do I have any choice?' he asked. The Inspector raised his shoulders into a half shrug.

'You must decide if you have a choice or not, I will not force you into anything. We all have choices in life.' The Inspector hoped Aldous was a decent enough man to find he was unable to choose "No".

'What are your other requests?' Aldous asked, wanting the full list before making up his mind.

'Well, secondly may I borrow some clothes and perhaps some Wellingtons? Third, I must ask that you keep me and my whereabouts a secret, never to be revealed to anyone, not even me, unless I should broach the subject. And lastly, could I have a pen and some paper? I need to write a few things down.' Aldous' gaze had not drifted from the swaying of the branches, but now he turned to look the Inspector in the eye.

'Well, I think before I can answer any of those requests I must ask you some questions.'

'Of course, please do,' the Inspector replied without hesitation. He was asking rather a lot and expected some conditions.

'Well, how can I be sure that you are not an imposter, sent to thwart the attempts of the man I met at the Firestone, and all this is not just some elaborate hoax?'

'An excellent point. You can't,' the Inspector conceded. 'Though you can also not be sure that he is not the imposter, and that I am actually the real Inspector.' Aldous thought for a moment.

'Well, yes I suppose you're right,' he thought for a second. 'So you admit that you and he are the same person?' He asked.

'Yes, we are,' the Inspector replied frankly.

'And your being in two different places at the same time is part of the trouble with the body you're investigating?'

'It is,' the Inspector replied. Aldous thought for a moment.

'And do you have any idea how, or why this is all connected?' he asked incredulously.

'No, I haven't worked that out yet,' he admitted.

'So you are as in the dark about what you are doing here, and how you got here, as I am?'

'I am.' It was dawning on the Inspector that Aldous was as astute a fellow as he could have hoped to have found in his current circumstances.

'Well then yes, of course you may stay here,' he replied without a moment of deliberation. 'You look as though you've been to hell and back. I will do all I can to help you recover, and to help you work out what in God's name is going on. As to the clothes, I'm afraid I might not have anything to fit you, but I will see what I can find. As to mentioning you to anyone, rest assured your stay here will not go any further.'

'And the pen and paper?' the Inspector asked eagerly.

'Yes of course.' Aldous hurried out of the room and returned with a sheaf of paper and a fountain pen, then leant on the table and tested the pen. After a few shakes and a couple of scribbles the ink began to flow. He replaced the lid and left the pen with the paper.

'Here, seems to be working alright.'

'Thank you.'

'Well, now, shall I show you upstairs to the spare room? You may be a little more comfortable there.' The Inspector nodded and let Aldous led the way.

'I would have put you in here yesterday, but I hadn't the strength to get you up the stairs.' The Inspector followed him up the small staircase that led to a short hallway with three doors.

'This is the bathroom.' Aldous pushed the door on their right open to reveal a small green tiled room with a bath, sink and toilet. 'This is my room.' Aldous introduced him to the door, but did not open it. 'And this is where you will be sleeping.' He pushed the spare room door open. It was simple enough, a double bed was pushed against a wall with a wooden dining chair next to it acting as a bedside table with a lamp balanced on it. A wardrobe stood lazily in one corner.

'This room isn't used very much, I don't often entertain visitors,' Aldous explained. 'I'm afraid it's become somewhat a dumping ground for items I cannot find a home for anywhere else.' A box of hymn books sat under the window gathering dust, along with a large black refuse sack full of clothes.

'This is left over from our last jumble sale.' Aldous picked it up looking rather embarrassed. 'Which must have been over two years ago. Firestone Copse moves at a somewhat slower pace than the rest of the world.'

'That is no bad thing,' the Inspector pointed out. 'Have you ever considered that perhaps the world moves far too fast, and Firestone is actually travelling at just the right pace?'

'An interesting thought, perhaps you're right, I do appreciate the speed here,' Aldous replied thoughtfully.

'Indeed,' the Inspector agreed. 'Sometimes I feel it is a shame not to appreciate what you have, the grass is not always greener, you know.' Aldous smiled.

'Well you may find something in here that fits you.' He lifted the bag of jumble on to the bed. 'Otherwise there are some old clothes of mine in the wardrobe, hopefully you can find something that fits. Feel free to try some things on, I'll leave you to it.'

'That would be most welcome. I cannot tell you how eager I am to get out of these dirty clothes. Perhaps I could also trouble you with a bath, and a towel?'

'Oh of course, there are towels in the airing cupboard, in the bathroom. I'll turn the hot water on for a bath, you may want to give it ten minutes.'

'I will, thank you,' the Inspector replied gratefully.

'Right we are then.' Aldous took his cue to leave and hurried off. Before the latch on the door had clicked shut the Inspector had the black sack open and had begun searching through. It carried the faint musty air of material that has spent too long without human contact. He found it full of men's clothing, of a rather older style. There were shirts, trousers, a thick dark blue woollen jumper, and some ties. All the clothes were the same size, as if all belonging to one person. The Inspector deduced that the previous owner of these garments had probably died, and a grieving widow had donated her deceased spouse's better clothes to the church. The thought of them being a dead man's clothes did not bother the Inspector. He chose a pair of red corduroy trousers that fitted in the waste but were slightly too long in the leg. He swiftly solved that by rolling them up slightly at the ends. With these he wore a plain white shirt that was a little baggy and a little too long in the arm, and the blue jumper. He also found a flat cap, and he picked out the warmest looking scarf from a pile at the bottom of the bag. In the wardrobe were Aldous' old clothes, all of which were slightly too small for him, but he did find an old sheepskin coat that he could squeeze into.

Satisfied with his new ensemble he removed it again and took a quick bath, shampooing his new beard thoroughly. He also took the opportunity to wash his under wear, which he placed on the radiator in his room to dry. He would have to forgo the extra layer for the moment. When he was refreshed he dressed again, and descended the stairs, finding Aldous in the kitchen drinking tea. He looked him up and down.

'You look very smart, a new man,' he complimented, genuinely surprised at the difference that a bath and a change of clothes could make.

'Thank you, these are so much more comfortable than the dirty suit.' The Inspector was pleased to have found something that had fitted.

'If you give your clothes to me I'll have them cleaned for you,' Aldous offered as he poured out a cup for the Inspector.

'Most kind, thank you,' the Inspector replied, slightly overwhelmed by the offer. 'They are in the spare room, I will see that you are reimbursed on Thursday for any costs incurred.'

'Oh no need,' Aldous insisted with a fluster, and the let the matter drop. 'Well, why don't you relax in the living room? It might be more comfortable than these old chairs,' Aldous suggested, indicating the dining chairs.

'A kind offer, but if you'll excuse me I feel I need to take a walk. I hope a spot of exercise may clear my mind, help me think. I hope I might also recognise the area and recall how I came to be here.'

'Of course, good idea, though are you not worried you may be recognised?' Aldous asked with a little concern.

'I don't plan to go anywhere near the town, and with my new facial hair and these clothes I doubt anyone will look twice.' He put his hat on and pulled it low over his eyes.

'Well, if you're sure.' Aldous didn't want to stop him, and just hoped he would come back. He found his shoes still near the fire and pulled them on, they had dried nicely and were warm from the flames. Aldous walked him to the front door, drawing back the curtain and unlocking the door.

'See you soon Father.' The Inspector tipped his new flat cap to him and strolled out into the grey afternoon.

'Yes, don't be long,' Aldous urged, admitting to himself that he was rather concerned for his welfare.

With a belly full of good food a walk was exactly what the Inspector needed to kick start his metabolism, and get the energy flowing. The same questions kept circling around his mind; how had he gotten here? What had happened on Wednesday night? He set about trying to see a way of calculating what had happened and lapsed into a steady march in concentration. He stomped determinedly up the hill away from town with his head down, deep in thought for about ten minutes when he happened upon a car parked beside the trees. He stopped and stared at it. Somewhere in the tangled fog of his subconscious he recognised it, but what relevance it held he did not know. He glanced around for the car's owner and noticed, almost completely hidden amongst the trunks, there stood a man watching the branches, listening to the trees. The Inspector recognised the man as someone he had spoken to, and stood looking at him, trying to place his face. The man stood stock still, save for the occasional sway as the wind blew. The Inspector watched him, perplexed as to what he might be doing, though the scene was somehow familiar. The man's identity evaded him, his memory was still struggling to recover. The man suddenly broke the pose, and strolled back to his car casually. He climbed in, turned it around, and drove away. The Inspector crouched inconspicuously, remaining hidden from him at all times. When he was passed the Inspector rose, and traced his steps into the trees. He found the space the man had been stood in and searched around the trees thoroughly, peering into the branches to try and fathom what he might have been doing, or what he might have been looking for. As he looked the trees began to look familiar, and he felt as if he might have been there before. He suddenly remembered the woods, racing through them in the dark, and a memory of the night before was released. He hung on to it for a moment, replaying the brief scene in his mind. He could see the dark, he could feel the cold unwelcoming trees, and he felt the blind panic, the fear. He remembered the want of escape, and the entrapment of the trees. He came back to the moment and realised the events of Monday night were coming back to him, and that he must hurry back to the Vicarage to try and capture them before they faded again.

56.

On returning to the cottage the Inspector knocked three times, and Aldous answered almost immediately.

'Hello, did that help any?' the Vicar asked as soon as he was over the threshold.

'Some thank you,' the Inspector replied, removing his coat and hat.

'Would you care to join me for a cup of tea?' Aldous asked hopefully. 'I have just made a pot.' He led him through to the kitchen where a fresh pot stood steaming.

'I would very much appreciate the tea, but I must get on with writing my report on the events of Wednesday night and Monday morning, or rather, the events that I can recall.' Aldous poured a cup of steaming brown liquid and passed it to him.

'Have you remembered anything before this morning yet? Do you remember appearing at my door?' The Inspector nodded.

'I think the walk may have dislodged a few memories, yes. There is a rather large gap in my memory which I am hoping will come back to me. I tend to find that as I mentally retrace my steps my memory opens up on scenes I thought I had forgotten.' The Inspector took a swig of tea.

'Well, I wish you luck,' Aldous informed him.

'Thank you father, for now I shall be upstairs, see you later.' He picked up the pen and paper from the table.

'Indeed Inspector, I shall be down here pottering around should you need anything.'

'Most kind, thank you.' The Inspector took his leave, and ascended the stairs. Once in his room he sat on the bed, back against the head board. The bed was old, soft, and very comfortable. He took a deep breath, and began to write.

Date; Tuesday 4th November 1969.

I awoke yesterday, Monday 3rd November 1969, at The Vicarage in Firestone Copse, where I am still currently resident. I was awake for about an hour in the afternoon during which I ate and drank, I then fell back into unconsciousness. I do not recall this incident, I was told of it by the sole resident of Vicarage, Aldous Squires. I remained unconscious until this morning, when the full situation became evident to me.

Upon waking this morning I had no memory of where I was, or how I had gotten here. I did not know who I was, and could barely fathom anything. Aldous kindly fed me again, and slowly things have begun to come back to me. My last memory before waking this morning is leaving The Green Man late on the night of Wednesday the 5th. I believe the hour was sometime around one am. I recall being outside, and of being at the Firestone. There was no moon. I had the enhancer with me, and once activated the stone took on a glow in the dark. I recall speaking to some locals who told me stories of the stone, where it was seen to be glowing, and is not difficult to see how these legends may have begun. As I write more memories are coming to me. I remember now I had the Field Enhancer set to full, and the glow of the stone was significantly enhanced. I now remember having the overwhelming need to touch it, to feel the stone to experience the power that seemed to be emanating through it. On touching the rock, all my senses were lost, as if I was suddenly plunged into water.

'Yes!' he exclaimed aloud, closing his eyes as the memories suddenly flooded back. He tried to concentrate and began furiously scribbling.

All around me all I could hear was the most incredible rushing noise, deafening beyond sound, it was beyond loud, as though a thousand people were screaming at me all at once. The noise was unbearable, from all around yet with no definite source. I felt a pressure all about my body, as though I was being crushed from all directions. My eyes were closed in defence and I daren't open them, they remained locked shut. I had no feeling of gravity, no sense of up or down, I could barely tell what my own shape was any more. I tried to move my arms, then my legs, but felt no sensation of any movement at all. I could no longer feel my body, yet the pain was incredible. The longer it went on, the greater the pressure against my body. I finally braved opening my eyes, to attempt to make sure I was still in one piece, to try and ascertain some idea as to where I was and what was going on. Upon opening them I saw I was surrounded by swirling flashing lights. They were dizzying, as if on a merry go round. The view did not change, no matter what direction I looked in. It took every ounce of ounce of energy I could manifest to concentrate on what was happening around me. I felt that if my focus lapsed for a second I would be ripped apart by the sheer force of the environment I had appeared in.

For a moment, through the dizzying view that surrounded me, I caught a glimpse of trees and a starry sky high above. It flashed across my vision, like a series of photographs splayed out in front of me, skimming quickly past, each picture slightly different as the trees fought the wind. They faded in and out as the indeterminable surroundings encircled me. I could not tell how long I was there, it felt like it never ended, but now I look back it seemed to be over in a moment. Despite these differing perceptions by my estimations it lasted five to seven days. I was sure that I would die at any moment, the pain was perpetual and agonising. As the lights swirled the pictured trees reappeared in front of me again, scattered in an infinitely long line stretching beyond my comprehension. They were bigger this time and closer. Each image was slightly different, each was a moment captured in still frame which span past me, only to be replaced by another, and another. As they were the only thing I could perceive in this nightmarish place I gathered every atom of energy I could muster and headed for them. I seemed to make headway through the ghastly din, and as I approached the images raced around me faster. Their dizzying race span about me until the many images moved so quickly they merged, becoming one constant animated vision, and I fell into it.

He stopped, gathering his thoughts.

It is here that my memory fails. I cannot penetrate what happened between then and this morning.
He remembered the corpse Drew had found, and the circumstances of its arrival in Firestone.
My theory is that whatever it was that caused the body in the copse to appear here, I believe I may have experienced it too. I wonder if perhaps the appearance of the body saved me, returning me to the copse, or if in some way my actions triggered its appearance. We were both victims of the energy that the copse attracts. I presume my success at interacting with the energy came from some protection I gained from the enhancer. I have this to thank for my survival.

He thought for a moment.

My presumption is that there must be a correlation between the distance that a person is away from Firestone and the length of time you spend going through the…

He paused, trying to think of what he should call the environment he had experienced that had brought him here.

Vortex? Singularity? Worm Hole? I know not what it was, I can only retell my experience for the official record, and hope that any evidence I find can be used to help determine what it was. I put my survival down to a short trip, as I was so close, and the protection that I must have had from being inside the Field Enhancer. What caused the man from Swindon Drew found, or those we discovered in Bill's Mansion, to have appeared here I know not.
He considered the readings he had taken around the town.
One possibility, I realise, is that there could be a build-up of electromagnetic energy around the town, centred on the Firestone. I have been registering high readings of pressure, of electromagnetic energy, and I believe these are due to the unknown energy that lit the Firestone and delivered me here. This build-up of energy could occasionally be released, like two opposing sides of a fault line slipping against each other, causing a quake of energy to escape out like a wave. Judging by my experience this wave could travel four dimensionally, through space and time. Anyone unlucky enough to be caught in the quake of energy would be pulled from their place and time and dragged here, to its epicentre. My theory is that this would have caused the wounds we have seen on the bodies, the strange holes in their chests being a consequence of the energy finding them and moving them into the…

He stopped again, searching for words to describe things hitherto unseen to human eyes. His head ached a little, and his wrist was strained from the constant scribble he dashed across the paper.

I am only thankful that the Field Enhancer saved me from such a fate. I will of course have to confer to my readings, but of what I can remember of them, there may be some credence to this idea. I hope I can now piece together some explanation from the few clues I have in order to calculate why the energy is building up, and find a way to stop it.

He closed his eyes and rubbed his pupils through the eye lids. He began to read back through what he had written and tried to focus on what had happened, to see if he could recall anything new. As he read he replayed everything in his mind over and over until his head began to hurt. Eventually he was unable to keep his eyes open, and the pure escape of sleep finally claimed him.

Wednesday 5th November 1969

57.

The Inspector suddenly sat upright in bed. The morning had crept up on him, the previous evening had slipped away. Sleep had at some point taken him but he couldn't recall when, so waking surprised him. He allowed himself to wake slowly.

Spread about him on and in the bed were the crumpled sheets of paper that he had been writing on last night, and in the dim light of the morning he collected them up and read back through what he had written. The hurried scrawl made him question if what he had remembered had happened at all, or if his was mind trying to fill the gap in his memory and this was the best it could do. As he read he remembered falling through the stream of pictures, but anything after that still eluded him. He knew that in a sudden rush of air he had left the pain and spinning behind, but what happened next was still a mystery. He recalled appearing somewhere utterly opposite to the nightmare he had left behind, but equally as confusing. He stared out of the window as a grey sky was slowly and painfully illuminated. He could see the tops of the trees from where he sat, and as he watched them swaying hypnotically in the wind, a memory was opened and he began scribbling furiously again.

On entering the picture the spinning ceased, though my head still span and I still ached. There was still a pressure bearing on me but it was static. I now could not move, my limbs were stiff, as though ceased up, but I could feel my body again. I could also no longer breathe. I struggled and found that I could gain some give against the resistance, and with every effort I gained a little more advantage. I could also now tell that I was facing upwards; the feeling of gravity had returned. I began forcing myself up and it was as if I swimming in thick, almost solid liquid. It did not take a lot of effort, thankfully, for my head to break the surface. When it did I rested, took deep thankful breaths, and then began the struggle to release the rest of my body from this strange prison. Wherever I appeared was as dark as can be imagined.

The Inspector paused for a moment, the remembrance of the struggle making him realise why his body still ached today. It had taken every inch of his strength to force his way out of his entrapment and his muscles ached from the effort.

Once free, all I can recall is running as best as I could, though I do not know from what, from where, or in which direction. I simply followed my instinct, blindly, through the dark. The journey didn't seem to lead anywhere. The terrain was completely black, and I simply stumbled on. Obstacles unseen blocked every turn I took, and I began to wonder if I had completely escaped from the strange place I had entered on touching the Firestone, or perhaps I had escaped from one place and now found myself trapped in another. On I raced, my limbs ached, my head swam, and I felt as though it might implode with pain at any moment. I do not remember finding Aldous' cottage, I do not remember him bringing me in. Therefore the logical thing to do would be to attempt to discover where I was taken when I touched the Firestone, and what happened between there and here. So today I shall enter the copse to retrace my steps, and track my path through the copse to discover the start of the trail.

The Inspector paused for a second to rest, he allowed his mind to relax. When he was ready he continued writing, as much to satisfy his own mind of the events than to record them.

Yesterday morning I awoke, emancipated, with approximately seven days growth on my cheeks. I discovered that it was Tuesday, and when my memory returned I realised it should have been Thursday. Although the experience between touching the rock and falling through the picture only seemed to last a few moments, and despite having reappeared three days before I left, I appear to have aged by several days, perhaps even a week. Certainly I was malnourished enough to support this hypothesis, though I may never know. My watch is broken, it has not just stopped but has been rendered completely useless by the experience.

I believe that the falling through the vision of the tree swaying in the wind against a starry sky was me returning from where ever it was that the touching of the stone took me. I have now only one day left before the event of my disappearance reoccurs. During this time I will have to remain unseen. I will return to The Green Man tonight, and follow myself to the Firestone so I can pick up exactly where I left off, so to speak. Perhaps I may find some clue as to what happened if I witness myself vanishing. I can then collect the Field Enhancer, my bag, and continue my investigation.

The Inspector carefully placed the papers of the report together and folded one corner. He then lifted a rug that the covered the wooden floor, and slipped the paper into the gap between two floor boards, anchoring it with the folded corner to stop it from falling through completely. This he hoped would keep it safe from any prying eyes. He doubted whether Aldous would believe it, but as security for the next few days would be an issue, this was the best he could do.

Teasing the memories from his tired brain had taken its toll, and his body still ached from the experience. His mind was weary with the effort of trying to recall the events, so he decided to allow his mind the opportunity to rest, settling back down into bed, and allowed slumber to once again take over his mind and body.

58.

He awoke again a few hours later with the grey sky framed through the small window. The clock on the bedside table read half past ten. With an extended sleep he felt suitably refreshed, and was starting to feel like he was recovering from his ordeal. He thought about what his original movements had been today; the discovery of the old manor house. His travels had not brought him this far north in the town and he was, he hoped, without risk of being seen whilst he entered the copse and tried to retrace his steps in an attempt to discover where exactly he had appeared. He went to the bathroom, washed, and brushed his teeth with a squirt of paste on his finger. He studied the hair covering his cheeks, deciding against a shave as keeping it might decrease the chances of his being recognised. He then descended the stairs to see Aldous, who was quietly reading a Maigret in the front room. The fire he had woken in front of on Monday was lazily licking at the remains of a log. A cat had appeared and was curled up comfortably in front of it. The cat and Aldous both looked up as he entered the room, the cat returned to its slumber indifferently, Aldous stood up excitedly.

'Ahh good morning Inspector, can I get you anything? Perhaps you would like some breakfast?'

'Having missed dinner due to my exhaustion I am once again extremely hungry and a hearty meal would be most appreciated, actually Aldous. Thank you.'

'Of course.' He thought for a moment, thinking through the contents of his cupboard. 'Will eggs and bacon be alright again?'

'That would be most appreciated, yes, thank you.' Aldous stood and made his way into the kitchen, the Inspector following him.

'So, may I ask what your plans are?' Aldous asked as he began preparing the food. The air quickly filled with the sound and smell of frying bacon.

'Of course. I must make the most of this extra time that has been afforded of me to try and discover where I appeared, and why. After eating I will be going out again in an attempt to see if I left any kind of trail.'

'Have you somehow been travelling through time?' Aldous blurted out. The Inspector had presumed the matter must have been pressing on his mind. Aldous had recovered a little from the experience of having a strange man appear on his door step, and was growing accustomed to the Inspector's company. He felt more confident in asking some of the questions that had been raised in his mind.

'You understand that any conversations we have over the matter must remain completely confidential? Tomorrow afternoon I will return to see you and you will need you to sign a document to show that you agree with the conditions I told you about. I'm sure I needn't explain that such occurrences as this have massive implications for national security.'

'Of course, as you mentioned earlier I should not discuss this with anyone, and I fully intend not to. Do I take it then that you travelled back to Sunday night from Wednesday?' Aldous dished up the eggs and bacon, placing a full plate in front of the Inspector.

'Thank you.' The Inspector began gratefully tucking in and spoke through a mouth full of food. 'Well, as far as I can see there does not seem to be any other explanation currently presenting itself. Thus I intend to trace my steps back from your door, to where I appeared in the early hours of Monday morning. I have deduced that it must have been somewhere in the copse. The weather has been wet since I arrived, and judging from the state of my clothes and shoes I must have left quite a trail through the trees and mud. If it would be agreeable to you I would like to borrow some Wellingtons, a torch, and if possible a camera.' Aldous shook his head.

'Well, actually I already checked and you are two sizes too big to fit into my Wellingtons.'

'Ahh.' The Inspector paused in his eating to consider for a moment. He wanted to curse the air at this stroke of bad luck but held his tongue.

'So I rummaged through some more of the left over jumble I had in the church, and I found a few pairs, and a few odd ones, that might fit you.' Aldous leant on the table to help himself out of his seat and pottered off to the hall. He returned with a bulky black sack, fit to burst with boots.

'My, I had no idea the church were so keen on Wellingtons,' the Inspector quipped with a raised eyebrow.

'The result of old age getting the better of me I'm afraid. Too many jobs to do and I haven't the speed or the strength to do them all.' He placed the bag on the kitchen floor. 'Luckily for you!' he joked back with a whispery laugh. The Inspector rooted about in the bag, and after a few tries he managed to find a boot to fit each foot; a red boot for the right foot and a blue boot for the left.

'Not a perfect match,' the Inspector admitted.

'Not that it matters, as we will be the only people to see them,' Aldous pointed out.

'Yes, let's hope so,' the Inspector agreed.

'Now a torch and a camera, let's see.' Aldous hurried off thoughtfully, while the Inspector removed the boots and continued to scoff his cooling breakfast. After a few moments Aldous returned with an armful of things. He placed them all down carefully on the kitchen counter, then changed the batteries in a small torch.

'I'm afraid the torch isn't very powerful, but it should do the job.' He switched it on and off to check it worked. The Inspector chewed. Aldous rifled through a drawer and produced a spare roll of film. 'The camera is a bit old, but it was quite advanced in its day.' He passed them both to the Inspector, who admired the camera. It had an adjustable shutter speed, to allow more light into the lens for longer exposures. It also had different settings should the environment be dark, light, or the subject be moving.

'Indeed, a very nice piece of equipment,' he agreed.

'Yes, I used to quite enjoy photography in my younger days, haven't used it for an age though. There's still half a roll in there you can use up, I'm afraid I only have one spare but I can pick some more up for you if you wish.'

'I'm not sure if that would be necessary, and I would hate to put you to any more trouble. I'm sure what we have here will suffice,' the Inspector informed him gratefully. Aldous placed the camera on the table and stood looking at the Inspector as he ate.

'Is everything alright, Aldous?' the Inspector asked, suddenly feeling rather self-conscious.

'Yes, well, I can't explain it. I have been feeling as if your arrival in Firestone has lifted a weight from my shoulders.' He looked out of the window thoughtfully. 'I've always felt that there was something about this town that didn't fit quite right. Part of the reason I have stayed so long I suppose. I felt as though I was needed here, to try and protect the town.' He shook his head, and smiled, he wasn't sure what he was saying made sense. 'Whatever it is, it's beginning to lift. Can you feel it? Can you feel the town suppressing something? Holding something back?' The Inspector shook his head.

'No,' he said simply. 'There is no doubt something about the town that does not quite fit, my presence here testifies to that. Perhaps if I were here longer I would feel this oppression that you, and others I seem to recall, experience. But I am a man of reason, and logic. My role as an Inspector depends on it. I have no doubt that places, areas, can take on an atmosphere but this atmosphere is, in my experience, in the eye of the beholder. It stems from their perception of the place they are in. For example during the day your cottage is no doubt a delightful, picturesque little building. However I am sure that during a dark stormy night it could take on a completely different feeling. It could seem menacing, haunting, full of mystery. We are raised listening to ghost stories where these traits are associated with these emotions. In reality the cottage and its surroundings are indifferent to what they look like, or what time of day it is.'

'Yes, I see what you're saying, but Firestone is different. There's something dark here, something that seems to be lifting since you arrived.'

'Well, my presence here is evidence that there is certainly something about this area that differs from the norm. I am sure there is a perfectly reasonable explanation for it all, even if it is one that we have not come across before.' Aldous smiled at his words.

'Of course, there you go again, trying to fathom God's magnificent plan,' he commented wryly. The Inspector remembered the hospitality that Aldous had offered, and did not want to offend his opinions. He decided to skirt around the subject.

'Well, I certainly hope I can be of help, in whatever way possible.' He stood and put his new boots and coat on. The pockets of his sheep skin were generous, and he placed the camera in one and the torch in another.

'I think perhaps I should make a move. The breakfast was excellent, thank you.'

'You're very welcome. I shall be doing a stew for dinner, there will be sandwiches for lunch. I will leave the bread and ham out for you. I have a few errands to run today so I may not be here when you return, but I was hoping we could have dinner together, before you leave.'

'I am most grateful. I don't know how long I will be but dinner sounds wonderful.'

'Good. I will leave the back door open for you in case I'm not here, let me show you.' The back door to Aldous' cottage was further down the main corridor, beyond the kitchen and living room. Aldous unlocked it and showed the Inspector out into a ferociously cold morning, with a biting wind that showed no mercy.

'I admit I don't envy you in the slightest Inspector, traipsing through the muddy copse in this weather,' Aldous told him from the warmth of the threshold. 'But I do wish you luck.'

'Thank you Aldous, see you for dinner this evening.'

'Agreed. Stay safe, and see you later.' And with that the Inspector turned and headed out into the cold day.

59.

Aldous gratefully closed his back door, leaving the Inspector alone with the cold. He made a cursory check for tracks, or any kind of trail. The only prints he could see belonged to Aldous and his cat. He made his way around to the front of the building, eyes down, searching for anything he might recognise as his own. On the paving at the front of the building he recognised the Vicar's prints coming and going over the last couple of days. Although the rain had made a good attempt at cleaning them away, there was still a faint trace of his own footprints leading to the front door. By the angle of the step and the sliding clumsy print, he could tell that they had been made in a state of beleaguered confusion. They led away from the cottage, and he followed them across the lawn toward the gravestones as the canopy began to bruise and darker grey clouds rolled over the sky.

Following the trail was an odd experience for the Inspector, he had no memory of making it, of ever being here. It was as if he were retracing someone else's tracks, not his own. The trail through the gravestones was haphazard, he had obviously fallen blindly through them, tripping often. The grass was disturbed, the muddy prints lead this way and that. He had not travelled in a straight line, but wandered across and between the stones, with no fixed direction or destination. The Inspector wondered again at the miracle of arriving at Aldous' door, and what might have become of him had he simply collapsed between the trees. He followed the tracks and approached the woods, the trunks so close together and so overrun with brambles and nettles that he could hardly believe he had come from them. The trail was lost for a while as the Inspector carefully searched for a clue as to where he had appeared from the trees, and come to the graveyard. He eventually found it when he spotted a path had been forced through the undergrowth. Nettles lay battered and bent, branches snapped. He slipped through the path in between the trunks, and once again the copse surrounded him. He fought his way through the brambles and nettles that protected the line of trees, tripping on young saplings that were sprouting as the copse continued to expand its territory.

Stepping into it was like stepping into a different world. Here the wind behaved differently as it whistled between the trunks. Sound echoed and bounced about the trees, the diverted path delaying its course, distracting its source. The canopy, despite being bare, still offered a protection from the dim light of the sun, so it surrounded him with an eerie darkness that felt all encompassing. The bare branches shattered the sky into a million fractured pieces. The dank and damp filled his nostrils with a smell of decay and death, as the leaves of a thousand autumns slowly rotted under foot. He turned his attention to the leaves and quickly spotted, in the thick layer of decay beneath his feet, a path of clumsy footprints staggering through the trees.

The trail led directly away from the graveyard, but as he followed it he found more gravestones in the trees. The copse had spread, showing no respect for the sacred ground, slowly taking over the graveyard. As he followed the trail through the trees he saw a space where the tree's grasp hadn't taken control. Their growth skirted around a dark structure trying to hide in the trees. He was unable to make out its full shape, and he had to resist investigating what it might be and continue to follow his path. He saw scuffs in the leaves where he had fallen or bounced off of trees and generally the trail was one of a hurried step. Despite himself the Inspector crept along, as if trying not to disturb some hidden occupant of this strange world he had entered. The gravestones continued to appear, in some cases just their peak broke through the fallen leaves. At the gravestones limit he found a low stone wall that skirted about the graveyard, a protective barrier that the trees had ignored. He skirted along it, finding some freshly disturbed bricks which he took as being the place he had climbed, or fallen, over it. Once over the trail continued into the copse between the dark trees. He followed it in. Occasionally he would hear a branch snapping, or a disturbance in the leaves, though from what distance and from what direction it was hard to tell. He put the noises down to the wild residents creeping through the trees, though he saw no other trails crossing his own, as if no life wanted to be here. He pressed on, surprising himself when he suddenly found he had left the copse and had appeared out on a road. He glanced about, looking for a landmark to help gauge what road it was. As he had headed north he determined that he must be on the same road as the church, the road where he had witnessed the man's strange behaviour in the trees the day before. He wondered where he should head next, and after a few minutes search he decided to follow a vague track he found that crossed the road. A few cars passed without seeming to pay him any mind, while he traipsed along the border between the road and the trees on the opposite side looking for a disturbance where he might have emerged from the copse. After a few minutes cautious searching he came across a wide gap in the brambles where something large had forced its way out on to the road recently. As this was the best lead he had found, he decided to pursue the trail and forced his way back into the copse. This was a much older collection of trees, the trunks were larger, and were thankfully further apart making the going easier. His trail continued, falling and tripping around clumps of ancient and twisted bark. The path was hard to see in places and the Inspector had difficulty following it but continued on, following the clumsy trail.

After an hour tracing his way down false starts and dead ends, he finally found what he had been looking for. He was concentrating so intensely on the trail in the leaves that he hardly noticed when the trees parted and he found himself in an opening, standing in front of a huge mound of dark sticky brown mud. It towered above him, he guessed it stood thirty five feet at its highest. The sides were steep and slippery, scarred with landslides. He stomped around it, the trees had not managed to grow on it but grew right up to its edge. He measured it in steps, taking photographs of it on the way round. He estimated the circumference as being about one hundred and fifty yards. He carefully studied its sides and at one point found a trail heading up to the top. He studied it closer and realised that it was actually someone's quick decent which had caused the disturbance in the mud. With a slight shock he recognised the foot prints as being his own, and that it was from the top that the trail started. He could find no footsteps leading up, only the clumsy fall down. Carefully, and with a few falls, he began to climb up the steep side. On reaching the top, he was afforded a completely different view of the copse. From here he could just see over the tops of the surrounding branches. Finding this view from the mound enlightened him as to the mounds success of being undiscovered for so long. Its peak only slightly edged over the tallest branches that surrounded it. Its position, hidden deep in a forgotten corner of the copse, meant it was not viewable from anywhere other than when you were stood up close to it. He took a few photographs of the view before continuing his search. It did not take long to discover the scene of a struggle. The ground on atop the mound was mostly flattened by the wind and the rain, but in the centre the mud was disturbed, as if something had recently appeared from within. This, the Inspector realised, was where he had appeared the previous night. He now realised what had caused the sensation of being trapped that he had experienced when he had fallen into the picture of the trees; it was of being buried, and the pressure of the mud pressing against his torso. He used this elevated view from the summit and began to try and calculate his position. He could see the steeple of the church, and it was closer than he expected it to be. The twisting path through the trees he had followed had caused the journey to seem longer, but he was sure he would not have found the place at all if he hadn't followed the trail. He took a best guess at how far he had travelled from the church, and at his proximity to the road he had crossed. He guessed that it would be quicker to head directly back to the road and make his way back to the church along the easier path it would give him, so decided to head in that direction. He carefully descended and began searching through the trees for an easy trail, slowly stumbling his way through the trunks toward the road. Eventually he found his way out, and snapped a few branches around his exit from the trees as a marker for later. He then began the trek down the road back to Aldous' house. As he walked he was cautious of any oncoming cars, turning his face away from them to prevent being inadvertently recognised. It was whilst performing this manoeuvre that he noticed, hidden amongst the trees on the same side of the road as the church, a squad car. Intrigued he cautiously retraced his steps up the road, finding an entrance into the trees, but only because of a few broken twigs at the sides where something big had been forced through it recently. There was a thin parting of mud through the trees, similar to that Drew had found. Down this fresh tracks and battered grass had been created, by his calculations, within the last half an hour. He stalked cautiously along the path, and up ahead he saw the squad car. From what he could tell there was no one sat in any of the seats, but someone could of course be laying down, or be in the boot. He continued to approach with the upmost of caution. When he reached the car he glanced in and found it empty. Just beyond it he noticed a thinner path, just wide enough for a person to fit through. Whatever the owner of the car was doing in the trees, it appeared he was doing it down there. The Inspector slowly made his way along it, keeping low to try and avoid being seen. He eventually came to an opening, a rare patch where no trees grew. Stood in the centre of this patch was Sergeant Banks. He stood stock still, looking out at the tall branches around him, listening intently, just as the man had been the day before, and as the others had been in the garden of The Black Prince. The Inspector quietly found himself an inconspicuous spot, and settled down to see what the elusive Sergeant would do. As his watch had been stopped on Wednesday night, the Inspector could not know the exact time, but after what he judged to be approximately half an hour Banks suddenly turned and marched back down the path. He had not moved save for the occasional sway in the wind in all that time but had simply stood, staring. The Inspector watched him traipse ignorantly passed where he crouched in the undergrowth, and waited until his footsteps had disappeared out of earshot before removing himself from his hiding place and walking carefully back down the path. He heard Banks reverse his car back out on to the road again and drive away. By the time he emerged from the trees he had gone. He then began walking back towards town, towards the church, still no closer to being able to fathom what Banks or the man he had seen yesterday had been doing in the trees. The afternoon wore on in a flurry of cold wind, and the Inspector hurried his pace along the road. He finally returned to Aldous' house, entering through the unlocked back door and removing his boots before making his way into the kitchen. Aldous appeared from the living room where the Inspector had correctly deduced he would be reading with his feline friend.

'So what happened?' he asked excitedly. The Inspector couldn't hold back a smile at Aldous' enthusiasm.

'I believe I have discovered where in the copse I appeared, though how I got there requires further investigation.'

'Where?' Aldous asked, breathless with excitement.

'I discovered a hidden mound. I appeared in it,' the Inspector replied, sitting down on the sofa to rest.

'A mound?' Aldous tried to fathom the situation. 'How big must it have been for you to appear in it, where is it?' Aldous asked, unable to stop himself firing questions.

'Approximately thirty five feet high. It is huge,' the Inspector answered. 'As to its location, that might be better answered with a map.'

'Did you say thirty five feet high? How can something that big go unnoticed?' Aldous asked, confused.

'Perhaps by understanding its location we can begin to piece together the answer to that. Hold on a moment.' The Inspector bounded upstairs, surprising Aldous with his agility. He returned shortly with his pen and paper and quickly drew a map of the area surrounding the Vicarage.

'It is hidden deep in the copse, here.' The Inspector indicated the section of copse on his hastily drawn map where he had discovered the mound. 'It is too far back from the road to be seen through or over the trees. It has become a forgotten corner, untouched for a long time.'

'My goodness, you're good at this Inspecting aren't you?' Aldous half asked, half told the Inspector. He was suddenly very impressed with the time travelling stranger that had happened upon his house.

'I also discovered that your graveyard is a lot bigger than I realised, it goes back at least another ten yards, and there appears to be a hidden tomb in the trees,' the Inspector continued casually, as if he hadn't noticed what Aldous had said. Aldous' eyes widened in shock.

'Really? Oh my!' He covered his gaping mouth for a moment, then leapt out of his seat and began pulling on his own Wellingtons. The Inspector watched for a moment, then stood and walked to the back door to put his own boots and coat back on. When both men were prepared in hats and coats, Aldous turned to face the Inspector.

'Could you show me?' he asked.

'Of course,' the Inspector replied. 'Follow me.' Aldous followed him out of the back door and they walked to the bottom of the cemetery, where Aldous peered through the gloom between the trunks.

'I can see gravestones in there,' he admitted. 'I can't see any tombs though.'

'It is much further back. Do you think you can walk through the trees?'

'I'll certainly try,' he replied, and with the Inspector leading the way they entered the trees. They carefully made for the closest stone to them, it was dirty and had almost been pushed completely over by roots. The Inspector scraped the moss away with his boot to reveal the barely visible engraving.

'Doreen Clarke.' The Inspector read the name. 'Devoted wife, mother and grandmother. Died in her sleep. 08.12.1890 – 17.4.1957.' The Inspector glanced back at the edge of the trees and calculated a distance.

'So the trees have encroached at least six yards in, say, the last twelve years,' he estimated. Aldous nodded, seeing his logic.

'Left unchecked, they have been slowly encroaching upon your graveyard.' He considered for a moment. 'And indeed the whole town. Let's press on.' They climbed carefully over fallen branches and trudged through deep leaves and after a little effort chose another tombstone deeper into the trees to study. The Inspector peeled back years of moss to get a better look at the inscription.

'William Beaufont.' The Inspector read from the lichen covered stone. 'Dearly Missed, 12.09.1794 – 15.03.1844'.

'I had no idea these graves existed,' Aldous admitted. 'It is amazing how quickly they became hidden.'

'Not to worry, I think there lies something of even greater interest further in, do you think you can make it a bit further?'

'I'll certainly try,' he replied, and they traipsed onward into the woods, the Inspector having to help him here and there where the going was tough. They passed a few more tombstones without paying too much attention, and eventually they found what they were looking for. It was an ancient tomb, as the Inspector had thought. It was still standing despite nature's attempts at pulling it down. It was covered in vines, its walls were cracked and moss covered. Its door stood at an angle, as if pushed open from within. All in all it presented a rather ominous shape protruding from the trees, but this did not stop the men from approaching it.

'Well, now how fascinating,' Aldous commented enthusiastically. He made his way over to the building, which stood in a small bare clearing. 'It appears this old cemetery has a lot of secrets.'

They made their way round it, trying to find a name or dates. When they could find no trace the Inspector began removing some of the ivy that had attached itself to the stone above the door. Eventually he found a name; 'BROKENHIRST' was engraved in deep foreboding letters.

'Brokenhirst,' the Inspector murmured, trying to place the name. 'Oh of course, Bill,' he realised suddenly.

'You recognise the name?' Aldous asked.

'Yes, Bill up at the Manor. His family were Brockenhirst's, in the 16th Century.'

'Well it appears we may have stumbled upon some of his family history then,' Aldous said, leaning wearily against a nearby tree. The Inspector noticed his host's condition.

'Shall we head back?' he asked him. 'I think the weather is starting to turn, certainty there can't be much daylight left.'

'Yes, if you think so,' Aldous replied, the sound of relief showing in his voice. They trudged back to the cottage, where Aldous collapsed in his chair and was soon dozing. The Inspector allowed him to sleep while he wrote up his report of his day's findings, he then woke Aldous with a fresh cup of tea. The old man stirred gently awake at the Inspector's gentle shake.

'I'm sorry Inspector, it must have been the long day catching up on me,' the old man apologised as he rubbed his eyes. 'I think that stew must be about ready by now, I'm just about ready for some food. Thank you for the tea.' He took a grateful mouthful.

'You're welcome,' the Inspector replied, sipping his own cup.

'What time will you be leaving tonight?' Aldous asked.

'I need to be at The Green Man for about one am, so I will give myself plenty of time and aim to leave here at about twelve.'

'I see.' He sipped his tea. 'And will I see you again?'

'Of course, I shall be back tomorrow with some papers for you to sign.'

'Ahh good. Well then, shall we eat?' They made their way into the kitchen where they ate heartily. They then sat in the lounge and chatted, Aldous managing to keep himself awake until eleven 'o' clock, when he admitted defeat.

'Well, I really must be off to bed,' he said through a long yawn. 'Good luck tonight, and I will see you tomorrow.'

'Yes good night, and thank you again for your hospitality. I will reimburse you for your trouble in the morning.'

'There's really no need, you are welcome. It's the most excitement I've seen in...' he had to think for a moment. 'Actually it's the most excitement I've ever seen. Thank You.' Aldous was genuinely grateful.

'You're welcome, good night.'

'Good night Inspector.' Aldous took his leave and slowly and carefully took his tired body upstairs. The Inspector listened to him preparing for bed, and waited. When he was sure that Aldous was quite asleep he took a pair of scissors from a kitchen drawer and made his way up stairs to the bathroom, where he removed the beard that covered his face, and trimmed back his moustache. He then changed back into his own clothes that Aldous, good to his word, had freshly cleaned. When he was finished he double checked his appearance in the bathroom mirror, and was satisfied that he was back to looking as he normally did. He walked downstairs, put his shoes back on, and then headed out of the door and toward the Firestone.

60.

The chill of the night pushed him along, wanting him to hurry, to get tonight over with so he could return to some form of normality. As he approached The Green Man he slowed, suddenly recalling that he had heard footsteps following him on his way to the stone. He wondered if it had been his own that he had heard, the footsteps he was about to make as he followed himself, or if someone else had been out in the night. He ducked low behind a parked van, and waited for his earlier self to come out into the night. He glanced around the scene, trying to peer into the darkest corners, looking for the slightest movement, but saw nothing. Suddenly the front door opened and the Inspector caught sight of himself for the first time. As he watched a twinge of nausea filled him at looking at himself, the experience was quite odd. His earlier self checked each dark corner and hiding place, as he had just done, before walking away toward the stone. He held back for a moment before following to see if anyone should appear, and noticed Banks emerging from the shadows. He waited a moment longer, then set off following Banks. Banks' usual heavy gait was gone, now he walked quickly, with agility. He slipped in between the darkness, occasionally disappearing completely and causing the Inspector to wonder if he had lost him. Eventually they reached the Firestone, and he watched as Banks settled down behind a car to watch his earlier self busy around the Firestone. To his horror the Inspector watched as Banks produced a gun from inside his coat. The Inspector quietly knelt down behind a tree on the edge of the copse and picked up a large sturdy branch, then quickly snuck up to Banks, who watched mesmerised as the Inspector stepped inside the Field Enhancer's metal poles, and the stone began to glow. He held out his gun and took aim just as the Inspector reached out and touched the stone, and vanished. Banks stepped out from his hiding place dumfounded, looking at the stone in disbelief. Suddenly, from behind him, he heard;

'Banks,' in a raised voice. He spun round to find himself face to face with the Inspector.

'Inspector!' he cried in shock.

The Inspector simply nodded in greeting, and then hit him across the head as hard as he could with the heavy stick, knocking him unconscious. He lay on the floor, unharmed but quite asleep. The Inspector bent over him and searched his pockets. He removed his keys and his wallet, and retrieved the gun from the floor where it had fallen. He immediately removed the bullets and placed them and the gun in separate pockets of his coat. He stood and worried for a moment over why Banks would want him dead. The only explanation he could think of was that he was getting close to whatever it was he was hiding that connected him to the body. When he was satisfied that he wasn't going to stir, he left him in a heap behind the car and walked to the Firestone to retrieve his things. He picked up his hat from where it had fallen off his head and replaced it with a satisfied smile; he had felt rather naked without it. He packed up the field enhancer quickly and silently, wanting to be out of the cold dark night and back to his room at The Green Man. He realised he would have to drag Banks back to the police station before he could go back to his hotel room, and he began to wonder if he should disturb Drew and ask for his assistance.

Within ten minutes all the rods and wires were packed away with the battery in the case. As he had pulled the rods from the ground he noticed they were all burnt out, singed around the wires and where they had broken the surface. Closer inspection also revealed that the battery had shorted out. When he was satisfied that everything was safely packed away he hid the box that contained it all behind a tree at the side of the road, as he would not be able to lift the case and Banks at the same time. He then prepared himself for the hauling of the Sergeant's dead weight. However when he arrived back where he left Bank's unconscious body, he was surprised to find he had gone. He glanced about the scene, looking around and up and down the road to try and see any sign of him, but he had fled. The Inspector thought for a moment, feeling as if he was missing something about where Banks would be heading. He suddenly noticed a thin trail of blood on the floor from where he had left Banks laying, and he followed the trail to the edge of the thick copse. In desperation or out of fear the Inspector knew not, but Banks had run into the copse. He peered into the dark woods but the Inspector knew from experience that if Banks was between the trees in the dark, then finding him would be impossible. He retrieved his equipment and walked doggedly back to his hotel. He let himself in and snuck back to his room, glad to finally be back to the here and now. He looked out of his window, out into the bleak night at the swaying trees of the wood in the dim light. He wondered where Banks was, what he was doing out there, and where he was going. Tomorrow he would start a man hunt, but now had to rest.

End of Part Two.

Part Three

Thursday 6th November 1969

61.

The trees around the copse shifted uneasily, their tangled branches pulling against each other in the cold wind. Night blanketed the town in an unreproachful blackness, spilling into every corner, blurring every line. The Mayor awoke suddenly, disturbed by a forgotten nightmare. He rose and snuck secretively out of his bedroom, leaving his wife snoring quietly. He wandered aimlessly, not really paying any mind to his destination, but soon found himself stood at the backdoor looking out at the abyss of the night. He could just make out the shapes of the trees that stalked the bottom of his extensive gardens, and he wondered if they had permeated his dreams and drawn him down here to be stared at. He peered into the night. It was black beyond dark, as though even the night itself was afraid to come out. Despite the warmth inside his house he shivered at the bitter cold beyond the glass. He stood and watched, perplexed by the trees. Something about them was different. Barely visible, he could just make out their branches dancing as the wind passed through. Shapes flitted amongst them, jumping from branch to branch, from tree to tree. The thin twigs at the tops of the branches moved as if slowed down, as if they could control time. He unconsciously pulled his boots and coat on and took a few steps outside into the cold. The wind was strong but all was silent save for the wind hurtling through the trees, whistling through the branches. Tormented by the wind the trees swung and swayed, whispering, almost talking. He leant his ear toward them trying to catch a word, a syllable, but it was all just out of earshot, nothing seemed to make any sense. He crept closer, trying to hear, always missing a word behind the snap of a branch or a gust of the wind. Before he knew it he had made his way through the long thick grass to the back of the grounds, and was close enough to see into the trees. He peered fearfully into them and wondered if perhaps it wasn't the trees making the noise, but someone in-between them. He crept forward, hideous shapes in between the shadows of the swaying trunks morphing and moving, like figures between the ancient bark. He crept in, slowly penetrating deeper. A memory stirred from the darkest recesses of his childhood, a vague memory, reduced to raw emotion by time. He tried to recall what it meant, but the noise of the copse soon distracted his line of thought. The voices evaded him but with every careful step he kept following, slowly being enveloped by the dark, entwined into the branches, and absorbed by the copse.

62.

Drew arrived at The Green Man just before nine, announcing his arrival with three heavy knocks on the large front door. Mavis bustled out of the kitchen wiping her hands on her apron and let him in from the cold.

'Morning Drew,' she smiled in welcome as he entered the warmth of the pub. As soon as the door was closed behind him she hurried back to the kitchen without another word. Drew smiled at her new familiarity with him. Walking into the bar was an eerie experience; the lack of people at this time of day changed the atmosphere of the space, as if they were part of the décor, and the room was incomplete without them. He removed his hat and coat, and glancing around noticed the Inspector's coat, hat and suitcase carefully arranged on a chair at what was becoming his regular table. A fresh pot of tea sat on it, with two empty mugs and a copy of the Telegraph. He sat and poured himself a cup and began to scan the front page for anything of interest, when he suddenly heard the Inspector's voice. Looking up he noticed him on the telephone, deep in conversation. Mavis chose this point to appear through the kitchen door with two plates loaded with fried food.

'Inspector's ordered a breakfast for you, hope you're hungry.' She placed the plates down in a flurry.

'Lovely, thanks,' he replied. She smiled happily and returned to her kitchen, Drew poured some brown sauce on to the edge of his plate and began to eat. He was chewing his first mouthful of egg and sausage when the Inspector appeared.

'Drew!' he exclaimed happily. He beamed with delight at seeing him.

'Morning Inspector, you seem in good spirits, did you have a good night's rest?' Drew asked him through a mouthful.

'Eventually, yes,' the Inspector replied, eyeing the food and sitting down to tuck in.

'Eventually?' Drew enquired, popping another forkful into his mouth.

'I went for a late night walk and I got a little distracted whilst I was out. I bumped into the elusive Sergeant Banks,' he informed him as he cut up the bacon.

'Banks!' Drew almost yelled. 'Where is he?' In the excitement he struggled to keep his food in his mouth.

'I'm afraid I lost him again, though I did get these from him before he vanished.' He removed Banks' keys from his briefcase and placed them on the table triumphantly. 'With these we may be able to reveal some of Banks' secrets.

'His keys?' Drew thought for a moment. 'The locked garage?'

'The locked garage,' the Inspector confirmed. 'I'm hoping one of these will open the lock and let us in for a look around.'

'What of Banks?' Drew asked. 'Are we still looking?'

'The search for Banks has now officially become a missing person investigation. As has the case of the missing Mayor.'

'The Mayor? When did he disappear?' Drew asked.

'His wife reported him missing this morning, he vanished sometime in the middle of the night last night. I was informed during my daily call to Head Office' He replied. Drew stopped eating to think. 'Do you think the disappearances are related?' he asked.

'Yes,' the Inspector replied, stifling a proud smile at Drew's intuition. 'We will need to visit both of their wives this morning.' He continued eating.

'Of course,' Drew replied. 'Do you think Banks has the Mayor?' he asked.

'I don't think so, though there is a chance they are together. It would appear our investigations over the last few days are starting to pay off.' Drew wondered how two missing men was progress but didn't ask. 'I have contacted Sergeant Gates at Nettlewood and informed him of both the missing men, he is organising a man hunt. He is sending a few men over to meet us at the Firestone at nine thirty, so we had best eat up. Your colleagues Constables Matthews and Johnston will be there to assist us, what are they like?'

'They're alright actually, wouldn't say there were the hardest working pair of policeman you're likely to meet but they are not as bad as Tom Blanchard the desk Constable,' Drew told him.

'Good. How did it go at your mother's last night?' The men talked in turns while the other ate, so Drew finished his mouthful quickly as the Inspector grazed on the feast in front of him.

'Good, I didn't find much, but I did find this letter to my father, it seems he attempted to raise the alarm on Banks.' Drew removed the letter from his pocket and placed it on the table for the Inspector, who read the small writing carefully from the frayed yellow paper.

'KB?' the Inspector asked when he'd finished.

'Yes, not sure who it is, and my mum didn't seem to know either.'

'Well, I'll put a call in, see what we can dig up,' the Inspector assured him. 'We could also ask Sergeant Gates if he recognises the initials.'

'Yes, sounds like a good idea,' Drew agreed.

'I'll need to hold on to the letter,' he explained to Drew. 'As evidence against Banks.'

'Of course Drew replied,' pleased to have found something useful for the Inspector.

'Did you find anything else?' He carefully placed the letter to one side.

'Only some old newspapers. I read a couple last night cover to cover, the only connection I could find in them was a couple of mentions of fires, or the remains of fires, being found. One was in a farmer's field, the other by the side of the road.' He brought one of the newspapers out and showed him. The article was squeezed amongst others on WI knitting circles and local Scouting achievements. It read;

GYSPY'S BLAMED FOR SPOILED CROPS
The remains of a campfire were discovered by Reginald Banks in fields to the north of his cottage on Saturday night. Nettlewood Fire Brigade confirmed no reported fires during the night and are not treating it as suspicious. Banks confirmed seeing a Gypsy caravan the previous day and suspected they had used his field to camp before moving on. Although some damage was caused to the surrounding corn he is not looking to press charges.

'I would love to know the whereabouts of these fires,' the Inspector said, considering carefully. 'Did the other article mention what road it was found on?'

'It just says Beeper Shute, no other clue I'm afraid. I bought this article for you to read as it seems everyone just believed Reg Banks, Banks' father, about what the fire was and how it got there.' Drew informed him with hushed breath in the empty bar.

'What's wrong with that?' the Inspector asked, playing devil's advocate to Drew's theories.

'Well, what if he was hiding something, and it's the same thing Banks junior is hiding, or seems to be hiding.'

'Then whatever it is has been hidden well for a long time,' the Inspector replied.

'Like those bodies at Bill's,' Drew pointed out. The Inspector rubbed his chin, preferring it clean shaven.

'It's a very interesting theory, but we still don't have anything to connect Banks to the body, or to the bodies in Bill's house,' the Inspector pointed out factually. 'Nor can we provide any evidence to disprove Reg Banks' explanation for the fire.' He paused. 'We need evidence,' he added, to encourage Drew. Drew looked at the Inspector, then at the keys. He finished his last mouthful of breakfast, just ahead of the Inspector.

'Well, then we best be off,' Drew suggested before downing the last of his tea.

'Yes my good man, we shall,' the Inspector agreed. 'I feel today will be extremely busy,' he warned him. The Inspector put the papers and letter that Drew had found safely into his briefcase, and they prepared into their hats and coats before exiting quietly into the cold morning.

'To the Firestone first?' Drew asked as he led them to the car.

'Yes, the Firestone,' the Inspector confirmed. It was only a short drive, and the Inspector was pleased to see that the officers from Nettlewood and Firestone had already arrived and were huddled together in conversation. Drew parked the car and they approached them, walking comfortably side by side.

'Good morning gentlemen, thank you so much for coming on such a cold morning.' At the sound of the Inspector's voice they broke off their meeting and turned to face him.

'No problem Inspector,' the bravest muttered back. Judging by his distaste for the cold the Inspector guessed that it probably was a problem for him, but he didn't press it.

'Inspector this is Constable Matthews and Johnston from Firestone.' Drew introduced them in turn and they shook gloved hands.

'I'm Jim Moir from Nettlewood Constabulary.' Constable Moir introduced himself and motioned to his partner with a nod of the head. 'And this here is Constable Bob Renwick,' he informed him.

'Well thank you all for coming.' the Inspector replied kindly. Matthews and Johnston were noticeably older than the Nettlewood officers, who were pushing forty themselves. 'Have you all been briefed?' the Inspector asked, his words puffing out in clouds of steam in the cold.

'Yes Inspector, I had the call from Frank this morning, we're here to look for Banks,' Matthews replied through chattering teeth.

'Indeed. We also have a second missing person on our hands, the Mayor is now also missing.' The men shared a concerned look.

'Now, I last saw Banks here last night at about one am.' He pointed at the spot on the ground where he had left him. The car he had been hidden behind had now been driven away, leaving the road stark and empty in the pale morning light. The thin trail of blood could still just be seen on the road.

'When I left him he was unconscious. I was gone for about ten minutes, and when I returned he had disappeared. I followed this trail of blood that led me to believe he had made his way into the copse, over here. They followed the trail together, the Inspector taking photographs of it on the way, which led them to the side of the road where the trees vied for space. 'We have forces in the surrounding areas all keeping an eye out for him, however it is my presumption that he is still somewhere in here.' He motioned to the trees.

'Do you want us to search for him in there?' Constable Johnston asked, not attempting to hide the trepidation in his voice.

'Not exactly. I have a little experience of trying to walk through the copse, and it is not easy. I want you to see if Banks could have made his way through the trees, and perhaps find where he might have come out of them again. Also some door to door enquires might be a good idea, and perhaps a look through peoples sheds and gardens.' They all nodded respectfully throughout, putting their minds to the task at hand.

'Please report anything you find immediately to Nettlewood, I will be there later and will be looking for an update. Any questions?'

'No Inspector,' they all called back, setting themselves for the grim task ahead.

'Wonderful, hope to see you all later. Drew, shall we pay a visit to Mrs Banks?' They left the men to their thankless task, returning to their car and quickly setting off once more.

63.

The door to the Banks' house was opened by a forlorn Mrs Banks, whose poor face fell a little further when she saw the two policemen at her door again.

'Oh, good morning Inspector, Drew,' she greeted them feebly.

'Morning,' Drew replied politely with a reserved nod.

'Good Morning Mrs Banks,' the Inspector said the quickly and respectfully. 'Have you seen or heard from your husband this morning?'

'No, Inspector, I haven't.' Her voice was nervous, she was obviously scared. 'He went out after dinner and didn't come home last night.'

'I see. Tell me about his actions yesterday, from coming home to going out again,' he asked kindly.

'Well, he came home late from work, I had already made dinner and had started eating mine. He came in and took his out of the oven, and we ate mainly in silence.' She sniffed back a tear. 'I asked the usual questions, how his day had been that sort of thing. He said it had been fine, nothing out of the ordinary. I always ask after the Constables, but he said he hadn't seen them all that day, mostly they had been out on their beats when he was in the station. I told him about you coming to look here for him, that you couldn't find him.'

'What was his reaction to that?' the Inspector asked, jotting notes down into his little book.

'He said he knew you'd been here, and that he knew you had been looking for him. Seemed dead pleased with himself about it and all.'

'I see,' the Inspector replied, more calmly than Drew thought he might have.

'Did he mention where he had been at all?' The Inspector was the epithet of calm, his voice was soothing and smooth, he used his years of practice to put her at ease.

'No, he said that he couldn't understand why you couldn't find him, as he had been around all day.'

'I see.' He paused to scribble notes. 'And what did he do after dinner?' he asked with a quiet understanding.

'He finished eating and left the house again straight away. I asked when he'd be back and he just said "Sooner or later".'

'Do you have any idea where he might have gone? Perhaps he had arranged another evening with his friends?' he suggested, hoping that perhaps he had met up with the Mayor. She shook her head defiantly.

'No, he always tells me if he's going out with them, and he always comes home even if he is usually a bit late.' The Inspector nodded reassuringly.

'Well I am sure he is fine, we have launched a search party and we will keep you informed should we find him.'

'Thank you Inspector.' She nodded appreciatively.

'Whilst looking for him, we discovered his keys,' the Inspector informed her gently. Her bottom lip quivered a little at the thought of her husband without his keys but she managed to keep herself from crying.

'Drew and I were hoping to have a look around the garden, and the perhaps in the garage? You never know, something there may cast light on his whereabouts.' The Inspector mentioned it airily, almost casually.

'Of course, help yourselves,' she replied, her head hung remorsefully.

'Please try not to worry. You should stay here by the telephone in case he returns or tries to call you.' She nodded absently in agreement.

'He's not a bad man, you know,' she said suddenly. 'He don't always treat me right, but he's not a bad man.' She didn't look up from the path, and her head kept nodding, as she tried to reassure herself. Drew restrained himself professionally, he knew she was trying to justify her emotions, trying to justify why she missed the man she had feared all these years. She closed the door without another word, leaving Drew and the Inspector feeling a little sorry for her.

'Now, let us see what is hidden inside the garage shall we?' The Inspector turned to Drew and removed the keys from his case. They walked around to the side of the house and to the large garage door where the Inspector tried the handle. A solid rebuff confirmed it was still locked, so he tried each of the keys in turn until one fitted. After the third try the lock suddenly shifted open with a satisfying clunk. There were another two locks at the top and bottom, and the Inspector found the keys for them all next to each other on the keyring. Finally the door gave with a hard shove, and opened a crack to reveal little more than the room was going to be dark and musty.

'Wonderful, we're in.' The Inspector smiled happily as he peered into the bleak darkness behind the door. Drew held him back a moment.

'Inspector, how can you be sure that we won't find Banks hiding in here? He might have had a spare set of keys hidden away somewhere,' he warned. 'He could be waiting for us.'

'We can't, but let's hope we do. I honestly doubt it.' The Inspector pushed the old door open the rest of the way with a barge from his shoulder. It was oaken and heavy, not the sort of door you might expect to find on a garage. After the initial shove the door swung open remarkably easily to reveal a deep darkness within. The meagre sunlight did little to illuminate it, so the Inspector fished his torch out of his case and broke through the blackness with its beam. He began surveying the interior walls under its halo of light for a switch.

'Ahh here we go.' Drew spotted it and flicked it on. The bulb that hung in the centre of the ceiling cast a dim light around the room that revealed piles of boxes cluttered at the edges, huddled together as if protecting themselves from the light. The Inspector removed his camera from his bag and took a few pictures inside the garage. The flash filled the dark room with light for an instant with each picture he took. Strange shadows danced in the corners, shapes lurched out of the darkness at them.

'Now, shall we see what these are hiding?' the Inspector suggested. Drew nodded, and they began opening boxes. The first one Drew opened contained old sheets, damp and mould ridden. The second contained mostly pots and pans, but also had a collection of mouldy worn out shoes at the bottom. The Inspector began by opening the closest box to him and found an ancient pile of books, the pages swollen with age and damp, the covers frayed from years of abandonment. He pulled a few out and tried to study their titles under the thin light. A thick layer of dust had gathered on top of the boxes which slowly filled the air as they searched.

'I have a question,' Drew informed the Inspector.

'Yes?' he replied from behind a swollen copy of 'Treasure Island'.

'Why would someone want to keep worthless rubbish such as this under lock and key, and carry the keys around with them every day on an already full key ring?'

'Very good questions,' the Inspector agreed. 'And why would he not allow his wife to have access?'

'Yes,' Drew replied in agreement. 'If he was coming in here, what was he doing? If he wasn't coming in here, where was he going?' The door was suddenly blown closed by the wind which sent dust up into the air with a flurry. The smell of damp was strong, and with the door closed the smell intensified. The Inspector opened it again, propping it open with an old woodworm infested spade he found tied to a wall by spiders webs. The light was barely bright enough to see, and Drew found himself having to pull items out of boxes and angle them to the bulb to try and get a better idea of what he was looking at. The Inspector pulled a dust covered blanket away from one corner to reveal a pile of furniture crudely stacked.

'He is certainly not coming in here sort through his belongings,' he mentioned. They continued to search, yielding little that was of any interest. Drew was about to suggest they gave up when he opened a large wooden crate hidden away at the back.

'This one's empty,' he called to the Inspector who was studying some old car parts on a shelf. It was too dark to see the bottom clearly, so the Inspector shone his torch inside.

'Interesting, it doesn't seem to have a bottom.' The floor of the garage was hard cold concrete, however the floor under this box consisted of wooden planks. There was also a latch.

'It looks like a trap door to me,' Drew pointed out. The box was deep, neither could reach the bottom.

'Hold on a moment.' The Inspector leant into a box he had been searching through and pulled out a walking cane.

'I found this earlier, might just do the trick.' He lowered it into the box, hooked the latch with the crooked end, and pulled. The door was heavy and awkward to lift, but together they heaved it open. Inside a stone staircase led down into a dark cellar.

'Well, it would appear we have found what we have been looking for.' The Inspector aimed the beam from his torch inside but the light was lost to the depth of the stairs.

'Hello?' the Inspector called down. 'Sergeant Banks? Are you there?' The Inspector's voice echoed back to them from the dark depths in reply.

'Well, shall we get down there and have a look?' the Inspector suggested after a few seconds of eerie silence. 'Drew, could you help me up?' With a short struggle the Inspector climbed over and into the box, then stepped awkwardly down on to the staircase. He helped Drew over as best he could, and they began to descend the stairs into the gloom. The light of the dim bulb on the garage ceiling was lost within a few steps. The Inspector's torch valiantly tried to show the way, but its light failed to pervade usefully through the bleak darkness that awaited them.

'What do you think is down here?' Drew asked, doing well to hide the mix of fear and excitement in his voice. Their voices echoed strangely in the unseen space. The Inspector was as calm and collected as always. This was, Drew presumed, the sort of thing he did all time.

'Whatever it is Sergeant Banks has gone to a lot of trouble to hide it from the outside world,' the Inspector replied. The staircase was narrow and cold. Damp clung to the walls and as they descended deeper their breath began to steam in front of them. They soon came to an ancient door, with a thick heavy bolt that slid from it into the cold damp wall. The bolt was secured tight with a shining modern stainless steel padlock. On the door itself was an ornately carved face, old and haggard. It had been carved to look as though it was in the process of screaming, eyes wide and tongue out.

'My, what an ugly fellow,' the Inspector commented jovially, trying to keep the atmosphere light. They both knew the carving was there for more than decoration, it was clearly there to strike fear into the hearts of any unwelcome visitors. The Inspector took two photographs of it.

'Yes,' Drew muttered back, trying not to let the door's warning have an effect on him. The Inspector began trying keys in the lock.

'Here let me hold that.' Drew realised he could be more help than he was, and took the torch from him to shine on to the keys. The padlock was heavy, and was not going to be easily removed if they couldn't unlock it. He began trying the smaller keys but they were abundant, and rather fiddly. After a few failed attempts the Inspector gave up and produced his lock picks, which opened it in a few seconds.

'Wish I had done that in the first place,' the Inspector shrugged. They gave the door a shove, but it didn't budge. He looked carefully around the edges. 'Ahh, there appears to be more locks, these are too cumbersome to pick but the keys should be easier to find.' The Inspector studied the bunch in his hand, and chose a clean new one that didn't look as though it belonged to this door at all. It did however unlock the first bolt. There were two similar keys with it on the bunch, and these opened the next two locks. Though the keys were new looking the locks were stiff with age and were a struggle to open. Eventually all the locks were free from the wall, and with a combined effort they pushed their way through. It was hard to tell how large the room they entered was due to the lack of light, but by the way the sound of the door opening fell into the space they could tell that it would be large. Drew shone the torch into the room, but it was too dark for the light to penetrate far. The Inspector noticed under the dim torch that the walls had candles in holders placed on them, so he pulled a zippo from his case and began lighting them to little effect.

'I feel we may need more than candle light to show us the way. Drew, would you be good enough to get your torch from the squad car? I will light these, and continue the search.' Drew nodded, grateful to be getting back to the light for a few moments. He climbed back up the stairs into the garage, leaving the Inspector alone in the darkness. When he returned the Inspector could not be seen, but candles had been lit around the walls, revealing the space to be high as well as wide and long. Drew swayed his torch around him to get an idea of what the room was like. It was supported here and there with thick wooden beams, and strange symbols were drawn out on the floor in thin white lines. Somewhere in the darkness ahead he could hear the familiar clicking sounds made by the Inspector's camera. He then noticed the flash penetrating the darkness briefly, and followed its direction. He was led down a corridor and ahead Drew could just make out the dim light of the Inspector's torch, illuminating him making careful notes in his note pad. Drew approached the Inspector who didn't seem to have realised that he had returned, but suddenly and without looking up he said;

'Ah Drew, thank you for getting the torch, it's much better than my little thing here.' He switched it off and placed it in his pocket.

'I had two at home and put them both in the car a few days ago, I thought you might want one for yourself.' Drew passed him the spare one.

'You are an enterprising and thoughtful young man, thank you.' The Inspector switched it on, the light being brighter than his own. He noted down a few more readings in its light, then turned to Drew.

'This strange underground lair of Banks' has several rooms leading off of it, would you feel able to investigate one way while I went another?' Drew didn't like the feeling of the place they had found themselves in. It was not quite fear, but a feeling of the ominous. A feeling that something was just outside of his view, hiding in the shadows beyond the range of his torch. He swallowed his irrationality down into his gut, and tried to ignore it as he had on Sunday night.

'Of course, we could get this over quicker then.' He shivered at the cold. It penetrated his clothes, biting at his skin. They took their torches and followed a wall each, the Inspector continuing along the wall he was already exploring, lighting candles as he went. Drew retraced his steps back to the door, and continued past it and down a long corridor leading in the opposite direction to the Inspector. He plucked a lit candle from the wall and began lighting candles as he found them. These had obviously been used fairly recently, there was no damp to hamper their lighting, and there had not been enough time for dust to settle on them. The candles began to illuminate the bare walls around the room with a constantly shifting orange glow, but neither their heat nor their light managed to infiltrate far into the room. The two men made their way down their thin corridors leading off from the main room, and it wasn't long before the candles stopped appearing on the wall. With a heavy heart Drew bravely shone his torch ahead to begin investigating the darkness.

The Inspector followed his corridor from the main room, stalking down it carefully. The walls were white, and wet with chalky water. The blackness was complete, it penetrated the thin corridor completely. As he continued on his way he almost stumbled over more steps, which led down to a second chamber. The Inspector followed the steps down into the new depths. There weren't as many steps here as there had been leading down from the garage, so he soon reached the bottom and began to cautiously stalk along another thin corridor. The Inspector shone his torch ahead, and noticed that recesses had been dug into the wall, three high, each about two feet in height. They stretched along the walls out of sight into the darkness, beyond the beam of the torch. He walked up to the first recess and shined the light in, squinting at the contents to try and make out a familiar shape. When he realised what he was looking at his eyes widened in shock. He moved his torch beam into the next one, and the next. Each contained the same thing.

'Drew!' he called at the top of his voice, turning and running back up the stairs. 'Drew!' he called again as he sped quickly back along the corridor and up the stairs. He followed the route Drew had taken, and discovered that the tunnels were symmetrical, and so he followed the corridor along and down another flight of steps and found Drew looking into a recess similar to the one he had found. He turned to the Inspector.

'Its fine, Inspector, I'm fine,' he reassured him. The Inspector nodded, and realised he needn't have worried.

'It's the same the way I went. There must be at least fifty or so sets of remains down here,' he told him, panting in the cold dark. He shone his torch inside to confirm that the contents were the same as he had found; corpses in the advanced stages of decay. Despite the Inspector's panic Drew was not as distressed as he expected.

'I also happened upon this,' Drew led him further down the corridor passed more reclusive recesses to a filing cabinet sat in the dank darkness, perfectly out of place. The Inspector immediately whipped a drawer open.

'Unlocked, of course,' he commented to himself. 'These look like the reports missing from the station, or at least some of them.' He read from one for a moment, and Drew watched intensely, waiting for the Inspector's analysis.

'Yes, this one's about another strange fire, like the ones we saw in the paper.' The Inspector thought for a moment. 'We'll have to get this out with us as well.' He eyed the heavy looking metal cabinet.

'Well, is this enough evidence do you think?' Drew asked.

'Indeed. Our need to track down Sergeant Banks becomes more pressing,' the Inspector replied. 'Well, these poor souls aren't going anywhere for now. Let's lock up and get over to see the Mayor's wife Mrs Cardwell,' the Inspector suggested. 'We'll come back with Andy and Jim to collect these remains later.'

'You won't hear any arguments from me,' Drew reassured him, eager to escape the dark. They headed back up to the surface, leaving the bones behind.

64.

For the second time that morning a distraught wife opened her door to find the Inspector and Drew at her doorstep. Mrs Cardwell's face fell at the sight of two policemen at her door, as it defined the seriousness of her husband's disappearance.

'Good morning Mrs Cardwell, I'm here about your missing husband,' the Inspector informed her calmly with a tip of his hat.

'Oh, good morning Inspector,' she nodded to them both quietly. 'I woke up this morning and he was gone, I'm sick with worry,' she explained, shaking.

'Was he home last night?' Drew asked. 'When was the last time you saw him?'

'Yes he was home. We went to bed about ten, and he was there when I went to sleep, but when I woke up to go to the toilet at about four he was gone,' she sighed deeply, her eyes wide with worry. 'That's when I called the police,' she explained.

'May we come in?' the Inspector asked kindly.

'Yes of course.' She held the door open for them and the two men entered the house.

'Is there anything of his missing? Any clothes you think he might be wearing, shoes, coats, anything we can use in a description?' The Inspector asked Mrs Cardwell gently as they entered the impressive hall where they had stood a few days earlier. She sniffed sadly into a handkerchief.

'I don't know, I'll take you to where we keep our things.' She sighed, and led them along a series of grand corridors to the rear of the house where they came to a large kitchen with generous oak worktops and cupboards. A huge table sat in the middle and an aga filled the room with a comforting heat. Along one wall were set large windows looking out on to the grounds at the rear of the property. At the edge of the grounds stood the trees, huddled together, guarding their secrets. She led them to the back door where a row of pegs held a collection of coats. Under this a selection of footwear sat paired neatly in a row. A conspicuous gap indicated immediately that one pair was missing.

'His Wellingtons are gone,' she suddenly gasped. 'And his coat.' She looked out of the windows into the gardens with watering eyes.

'What colour are they? What brand, what style?' the Inspector asked.

'He's got a big blue wax jacket, down to his knees, and the boots are green Wellingtons, just, ordinary Wellingtons,' she told them, wishing there were more of a description to give. The Inspector noted this down in his note book.

'Would you mind if we were to cast our eyes around the garden?' he asked gesturing through the window to the blustered grounds. 'Perhaps we might find some trace, some clue as to which direction he may have headed in?' She nodded at them, and tried to unlock the back door.

'Oh!' She exclaimed suddenly. 'It's already unlocked. He must have gone out this way.' She looked out at the garden, feeling lost.

'Well, Drew and I will have a careful look round to see if there's any trace. Please wait here, we won't be long.' The two men left the fretful Mrs Cardwell at the door and walked out into the cold of the garden, the Inspector's eyes looking carefully around for any sign of recent movement across the overgrown tufts of grass. He didn't have to look for long.

'Drew, look.' He pointed the footprints out to him. The grass was long, and the Mayor's feet had trampled it down as he traipsed through.

'Well spotted Inspector. Which way do you think he went?' Drew asked, casting his eye around their feet for more tracks.

'Let's find out shall we?' The Inspector had his suspicions as to where they would lead them, and began to carefully track them across the boggy lawn. They headed, as the Inspector had thought, in an almost straight line toward the trees. When the two men reached the edge of the trunks they looked forlornly into the tangled mass of wood.

'So from what I can tell,' Drew sighed. 'We have two missing persons. Both disappeared during the night, both were present here on Sunday night, and the last known whereabouts for both men was in the copse.'

'Yes, that would appear to be the situation,' the Inspector agreed. 'There isn't the time for us to search in there for him now, let us get back inside and lie to the worried Mrs Cardwell,' the Inspector suggested. They returned back to the house where she had been watching their every move through the window.

'No trace of him I'm afraid,' the Inspector informed her. 'I will send a man down from Nettlewood to take your statement in due course, for now stay in and stay by the phone, in case he tries to call.'

'Yes Inspector,' she agreed sadly. 'Can I offer you some tea?' she asked.

'Usually I would jump at the chance,' the Inspector replied. 'Unfortunately I have a prior appointment. We will of course keep you informed of any developments, and should you think of any further details, or hear anything from him please telephone Nettlewood station immediately.

'Of course,' she agreed, and walked them back to the front door. She stood on the threshold and watched as they drove away.

'You have a prior appointment?' Drew asked as he came to the road. 'Where are we off to?'

'There comes a time when matters are too much for one man to tackle alone young Drew, even with your invaluable help. I have requested some back up. I am to meet them at Nettlewood station at ten thirty. If we go now we may have time for a cup of tea with Sergeant Gates before they arrive.' The Inspector was as vague as ever, but Drew was learning that the details of the Inspector's means became clear in time. The two men left the Mayor's house, and his distressed wife, behind them and set off for Nettlewood station.

65.

On arriving at Nettlewood they found the station in a busy state, with ringing telephones going unanswered and Constables conferring with each other. A haze of cigarette smoke filled the room with a low hanging cloud that made it seem bigger than it was. A figure briskly approached them through the smog.

'Inspector, good to see you.' Frank held out his hand and the Inspector shook it. 'Morning Drew.'

'Morning Sarge,' Drew nodded.

'Sergeant, any leads regarding the missing men of Firestone?' the Inspector asked.

'Err, no,' Frank replied forlornly. The Inspector nodded, as if this was unsurprising. He checked his watch.

'I am expecting some company at ten thirty, I was hoping there might be time for a cup of tea before they arrive,' the Inspector asked hopefully.

'Of course, go and make yourselves comfortable in my office, I'll get the kettle on then you can fill me in on what you've been up to. I'll be down shortly.' Frank made his way toward the kitchen at the back of the station while the Inspector followed Drew down the corridor to the Sergeant's office. The door was open, and the two men entered and sat down, the extra seat still positioned where the Inspector had left it. Presently Sergeant Gates came into the room carrying a tray of mugs and a pot of tea. He placed it on his desk, and began to pour.

'So Inspector, are we any closer to discovering anything about the man Drew found in the woods?' Steam filled the air as tea filled the mugs.

'Well, we know he is from Swindon, a colleague of mine is there looking into his past, investigating his family and so forth.'

'Will we be having someone along to identify the body?' Frank asked. The Inspector accepted a mug and sipped at the piping hot liquid before continuing.

'I don't think that will be happening. I predict my colleagues' search of Swindon will not be successful, and that no one will come forward to claim the body.'

'I see. So are your investigations over?' The Inspector smiled and Frank began to back track. 'Sorry, err, I didn't mean I wanted rid of you.'

'Of course, no offense taken I assure you. I am as eager to wrap up the case as you are for the two towns to return to normality. However there is still the matter of how the body arrived in the trees, and the case of the missing Banks, and of the Mayor. I believe the disappearances are related to the body's appearance. I also am led to believe that as the two men were together on the night of the body's appearance there is a link between them, and all the people at the Mayor's house last Sunday night, to the body. What that connection is I am still trying to determine.' He paused to sip his tea. 'It would appear however that the body Drew found is not the first to have appeared in the woods. We may know who the victim is and where he is from but we still know nothing of why, or how, he appeared where he did. That is why I am still here, and why I have requested some extra help in finding out.'

'Extra help?' Frank asked.

'Yes. Once I have set them to work Drew and I will revisit the other members of the Mayor's party and question them further.' Drew and Frank shared a confused glance. 'That reminds me, may I ask for some of your men to follow the Mayor's guests to ensure we don't lose track of them as we have Banks and the Mayor?' the Inspector asked so politely it hardly sounded like a command at all.

'Well, I will have to see who we have available.' Frank stood and walked over to the door.

'Carl can you bring in this week's rota?' There was a reply inaudible to Drew or the Inspector but Frank seemed satisfied. He returned to his seat.

'So do you have any theories as to what links Banks to the body?' Frank was unable to hide his interest in Banks' involvement.

'I have been investigating Banks over the last few days. He has been avoiding me ever since I questioned him, no doubt he realised that I was going to discover something he would rather remain hidden. Drew has been delving into his father's past and more about his involvement with the body has become clear.' The Inspector paused for a moment.

'You will have to excuse me if I am a little vague with details, Sergeant. The trouble is that my investigations often need to remain a closely guarded secret, and the fewer people that are aware of them, the better chance there is of the secret remaining a secret and my investigations remaining uncompromised. From what I have discovered you were right to harbour your suspicions of Banks. Our priority now becomes finding him, ensuring he is safe, and bringing him to justice for his actions over last thirty or so years.' Sergeant Gates physically sighed.

'So you believe Banks was involved in my brother's death?' he asked, gratified.

'I believe your brother was on the same trail that I have discovered, and Banks stopped him before he discovered too much. Banks attempted to stop me, but fortunately I was able to thwart him before he was successful.' Drew and Frank looked shocked.

'He tried, tried to kill you?' Frank could barely believe what he was hearing.

'Yes, he did. It was immediately after this attempt that he vanished.' Frank and Drew tried to digest the situation.

'There's something else I wanted to show you.' He reached into his case and retrieved the letter Drew had discovered. He passed it to Frank who read it studiously.

'Ok.' He looked up at the two men sat opposite him. 'Who is KB?'

'We were hoping you might know,' Drew replied for them.

'Well whoever it was, it looks like your dad was trying to tell them about Banks,' Frank told Drew, and fell into thought for a moment. A knock at the door interrupted him.

'Here's the rota you asked for Sarge.' The man passed a piece of paper to him. 'You alright?'

'Err, yes, thanks Carl.' He regained his composure and tried to study the rota. Carl left them to it, but before he had left the room another Constable knocked on the door.

'Cor it's like Piccadilly bloody Circus in here today!' Frank swore.

'Sorry Sarge, there's a bloke here asking for you, well, actually he asked for the Inspector, Morning sir, Drew.' He nodded respectfully to both men.

'Ahh, it would appear the cavalry has arrived,' the Inspector downed the last of his cooling tea and stood up. 'Gentlemen, we must be off.' The Inspector waited for them both to put their coats and hats on then they made their way back through the station to the public waiting room. Standing at ease and reading the notices on the board was a man in the mossy green camouflage of an army uniform. He wore a green beret, and on hearing the door open he turned to face the three men.

'Inspector?' he asked the one man not in police uniform.

'Yes, Major Sheppard?'

'That's right sir. Before we continue do you mind if I ask to see some identification? Protocol,' he explained curtly.

'I understand, I commend you for your keenness to detail,' the Inspector removed his wallet and took from it some papers which he showed the Major. He studied them carefully.

'Very good sir, thanking you,' he handed them back to the Inspector who replaced them carefully in his wallet. The Major seemed amiable enough, though serious and business like. He had a row of different coloured ribbons over his right breast and crowns sewn into the shoulder tags of his uniform.

'Of course. Thank you for coming to my aid at such short notice,' he replied with a grateful smile.

'The barracks isn't far, and it's always good to get the lads out on some exercises.' Frank and Drew exchanged more confused glances.

'There are more of you?' Frank asked, somewhat surprised.

'Indeed Sergeant, I have a bus full of my finest outside awaiting the Inspector's order's.' The Major informed the shocked policeman.

'Well let's have a look at them shall we?' the Inspector suggested, and led the way with the three men following closely behind.

66.

Parked by the kerb outside the station stood a stout blue bus being battered by a fresh shower of icy rain. The engine ticked over filling the air with a noisy clicking and the smell of diesel. The four men entered the bus and climbed the steep steps up to where the occupants sat waiting. Sat on the bus were thirty chattering young men in uniforms identical to their commanding officers, save for the crown on the shoulder and the row of ribbons on the breast. Frank and Drew were completely taken aback. At the appearance of Major Sheppard and the others the men quietened down and turned their attention to the front of the bus.

'Settle down lads,' Major Sheppard called to them, and soon the bus was a dead calm.

'This is the Inspector we were told about,' he announced. 'For the time being he will be giving the orders, through me. We do as he says quickly and as safely as we can and we can all get back to the barracks and running around the parade ground in the cold and wet.' The Captain was commanding, yet respected enough by his men to joke with them, and a small ripple of titters echoed between them.

'As it is I don't think he's got anything nice planned for you, but I'm sure you'll make the most of it. Inspector?' He offered him the floor. The Inspector stepped forward.

'Good morning gentlemen, I am indeed the Inspector from Scotland Yard as the good Major pointed out. I am also giving the orders, as Major Sheppard rightly pointed out. The task at hand is not a pleasant one. We will be mostly digging.' The men shuffled about in their seats but kept their thoughts on the subject to themselves. Frank frowned in confusion; he had presumed they were there to search the copse for the missing men.

'There is a good chance while we are digging that we will find human remains in various states of decay. What else other than that we might find I have no idea, however it is imperative that whatever you discover does not get shared with anyone outside of this regiment. Before we make our way to our destination I must ask that you all sign this.' He reached inside his briefcase and brought out a document Drew recognised. It was passed around with a pen and the men all began adding their scribbles to it.

'This is a document, a lot like the national secrets act, which you are signing to show that you agree not to tell anyone,' the Inspector informed them simply. He had full faith in them, and their abilities. He knew, as they did, that this was part of the protocol for these situations. The Inspector kept speaking as the men passed it round adding their individual signatures.

'We will also be chopping. We need to clear a path through trees big enough for the mechanical diggers that are arriving tomorrow morning to help us dig. I am informed that there are some here licensed to drive them?' he asked the attentive faces.

'Yes sir,' a few of the men spoke up with raised hands.

'Splendid. Before you begin using the diggers tomorrow we will assess the situation and see what we need you to dig.' The wodge of paper with everyone's signature reached the front, and the driver, Captain Sheppard, and Sergeant Gates all signed it too.

'Wonderful. Drew, if you could please follow us in your car, Sergeant Gates, I will be back just after lunch. Please could you contact the hospital and arrange for Andy and Jim to meet us here at one with Casey and one of your police vans?' the Inspector asked.

'Yes, of course,' Frank nodded. 'Who's Casey?' he asked, fishing out his notebook and beginning to write it all down.

'Call Doctor Collins in the morgue, he'll be able to sort it all out for you,' Drew told him. Frank kept nodding and made some scribbles.

'Well then, shall we?' the Inspector suggested. Drew and Frank disembarked, and the driver closed the folding door behind them. They stood and watched the bus drive away towards Firestone.

'Digging?' Frank whispered to Drew on the roadside as they watched the bus vanish round a corner. 'How much digging is he expecting to do with that lot and some diggers?'

'Quite a bit by the looks of it,' Drew replied, equally as mystified.

'Do you know what he's going on about?' Frank asked, still unable to fathom the situation.

'No, but it's not even lunch time and I have already had a very strange day. Something tells me it's going to keep getting stranger,' Drew told him. He hurried over to his car.

'See you later Frank.'

'Yes Drew, see you later. Take it easy out there, ok?' Frank called as Drew ducked into his car.

67.

The Inspector and Major Sheppard took a seat behind the driver and the Inspector called out the occasional direction for him.

'Head left out of here, and follow the road until I say turn right.'

'Yes sir,' the man replied. The bus trundled out of Nettlewood and through the fields, and after a few minutes the men on the bus began chattering quietly amongst themselves again, discussing their objective and what they might find. Before long they were entering the trees around Firestone.

'Turn right here, then pull up on the left hand side just past the church,' the Inspector called as they approached the Firestone roundabout.

'Yes sir,' the man replied simply again. They were soon past the church, and as instructed the driver pulled into the side of the road, hazard lights flashing orange against the trunks.

'We're here,' the Inspector stood and informed the bus passengers. 'When we get off the bus please can we split into two teams depending on what side of the bus you are on. If you are on this side of the bus I will leave you in the hands of Major Sheppard.' He indicated the right hand side of the bus. 'Please can you begin clearing the trees where I enter them, and keep clearing them until you find me again.

'If you are on this side of the bus you are with me, we will fight our way through the copse and I will show you where I need you to begin digging.' The Inspector looked about at their young faces, they looked back expectantly.

'Any questions?'

'No sir,' came a resounding reply.

'Very well. Shall we get started?' the Inspector asked rhetorically, and climbed down the stairs. The men were very quick at retrieving their equipment from the side compartments of the bus. The panels were quickly opened and the equipment dished out. Drew pulled up behind the bus and switched his blue flashing lights on to warn oncoming traffic of the obstruction, then walked over to join the Inspector.

'Ahh Drew, splendid, we're just organising ourselves.' The men were lined up in their two groups with equipment in hand within ten minutes. Drew watched mesmerised by the men's energy and organisation while the Inspector opened Drew's boot and put his Wellingtons on.

'Right lads, this way.' The Inspector called when he was sure they were all together. 'Drew, stay close to me.'

'Yes Inspector,' Drew replied, rather awed by his casual authority over the regiment. They marched up to the trees, and for a moment the Inspector was lost as he searched by the side of the road for the markers he had left.

'Ahh! Here we are!' he exclaimed suddenly.

'Ok diggers, all together please, and here we go.' The Inspector headed in through the trees, the fifteen soldiers and the policeman close behind. As he fought his way through the undergrowth he heard Captain Sheppard beginning to bark orders at the remaining fifteen soldiers, and soon the sound of chainsaws began echoing through the trees. The men tripped their way haphazardly through the trees after the Inspector, making a decent path for their colleagues to follow. Soon the mound loomed through the branches at them surprising the party, including the Inspector who had been looking out for it. The men all filed out of the trees and sized up their task. Drew approached the Inspector, who was fishing in his bag for something. Drew's jaw dropped when he laid eyes upon the mountain of mud.

'How did you find this?' he asked, rather mystified. 'What do you think it is?'

'I found it whilst on the walk I took last night,' he replied casually. Drew thought for a moment and tried to fathom how he might have found this place alone, in the dark. 'As I said, I got a little distracted,' the Inspector explained, though this still didn't satisfy the policeman. The Inspector removed his electromagnetically sensitive device from his bag and switched it on while the men prepared themselves.

'As to what it is, I am hoping that's what these chaps will help me discover.' The needle on the machine immediately shot up, and it started to emit a high pitched squeal in to the air. The Inspector raised an eyebrow and quickly turned it off again. He replaced it in his bag and cleared his throat.

'Right gentlemen,' he spoke up so they could all here him clearly. 'I want to find out what is in here. We are really a scouting mission, a reconnaissance. Our task is to gauge just how hard a job it is going to be to clear this mud. There are a few spaces in the trees about us we can use to fill with the mud we will remove. Please begin as soon as you're ready,' he asked them politely, and they all began to spread out along the face of the mound, tenderly prodding the soil with their spades and pick axes, summing up their options. They began talking amongst themselves to decide on a tactic to tackle the mountain. Drew and the Inspector looked on anxiously, the Inspector taking the occasional picture of the men, the mound, and the trees. One of the soldiers prodded the mound tenderly causing some of the soil to shift, which quickly gave way to a small avalanche of mud from the top. A few men leapt out of its way but no one was hurt, and the task had begun. They dug their spades into the fallen soil and began to shift it in to into the trees.

'Splendid!' the Inspector called excitedly. Soon a chain of men had formed, slowly transporting the mud from the continuing avalanches into the trees. The men shifted spadeful after spadeful away under the Inspector's watchful eye. Drew looked about the trees, unable to shake the feeling that they were being watched, dissected and scrutinised by some unseen object dwelling within. The copse was not used to having people amongst its trunks, and now the group of men digging and chopping were disturbing something in trees.

'Drew!' the Inspector called to him, disturbing his reverie.

'Yes Inspector?' Drew called back, his attention drawn back to the mound. The Inspector stalked through the trees and joined the Constable where he stood looking into the copse. He noticed his attention was drawn to the trees.

'What is it?' the Inspector asked him.

'Nothing, just thinking how long it has been since anyone was here, I don't think the trees like it,' Drew replied.

'They have become accustomed to not changing, of standing undisturbed. It must seem strange for so many people to be walking amongst them and invading their space,' the Inspector mused.

'Yes, it is,' Drew replied, feeling the strangeness himself.

'Well, for now I think we may need some help from Firestone constabulary. Would you be kind enough to head into town to see if you can find any of your colleagues? I think our arboreal exercises could attract some attention from the villagers and it would be good to have some uniform present to distract them and allay any fears.'

'Of course, leave it with me,' Drew agreed with some hesitation. He was hoping to see what the men might reveal, but accepted his orders obediently and headed back out of the trees to his squad car.

68.

Drew returned an hour later having finally located two officers from Firestone. They had followed him to the site in their squad car. Once both cars were safely parked he approached the two men who surveyed the situation suspiciously.

'What's all this about then Drew?' Constable Hanson asked, rather surprised at all the commotion. He was in his forties, greying, and pleased to be able to help the man from London.

'All part of the investigation into the body I found on Sunday,' Drew replied vaguely. He hadn't much of an idea himself what it was all about. 'All you chaps need to do is stop anyone trying to get into the trees to poke about, and stop them disturbing the men from the barracks,' he explained. The two Constables goggled at the sight of the men working in the trees. They had already cleared a large space, opening up an area large enough to move the bus off of the road.

'The Inspector is overseeing the whole thing, I'm sure he'll be out to explain it all to you soon.' The two men shook their heads in wonder at the operation. Drew left them by the side of the road and walked toward the noise of the chainsaws. The men had split into several teams; while some chainsawed their way through the trunks others attacked the stumps that they left behind with pick axes and ropes. More still carted the debris away and had started a stack of fallen trunks at one side of the clearing they had created. A wide uneven path was gradually forming through the trees, which were powerless under the might of the men and their machines. Drew spotted Major Sheppard as he picked his way carefully along the path and the two men nodded respectfully at each other as he passed. He eventually reached the Inspector, and found that after an hour of hard work the mound had lost no discernible height, despite their being heaps of mud throughout the trees around them. The regiment were beginning to lose momentum at the unthankful task, and the ground beneath their feet was becoming clogged with fallen earth. It was as if the copse was fighting back at the change, not allowing the men to alter years of stasis. It had become stuck rigidly in its undisturbed undergrowth and it stubbornly refused to change.

'Ahh Drew you're back, you were successful I presume?' the Inspector asked hopefully as Drew approached though the trampled mud.

'Yes Inspector, two Constables are stationed by the road to put the fears of any passing pedestrians at ease.'

'Splendid,' he replied, pleased with Drew's luck.

'How have things been here? It looks as though you've been working hard, but I can't see much of a change to the mound,' Drew pointed out.

'Quite,' the Inspector agreed. Knowing he was beaten, he made a decision.

'Thank you gentlemen, if you want to stop there,' he called. With an audible sigh of relief the men stopped what they were doing and made their way to where the Inspector stood.

'It is clear to me, as I am sure it is to you, that for all your hard work we do not seem to be making much progress.' A low murmur of agreement echoed between them.

'So I think we should wait until the digger arrives tomorrow before we continue. For now, I suggest we adjourn to The Green Man where I have arranged for you all to get a good feed.' The men's spirits immediately brightened at the thought of a trip to a pub.

'So let's head back to your colleagues and superior and see what progress they have made, then jump on the bus and head into town,' the Inspector informed the happy men. They headed into the trees toward the sound of chainsaws that had been gradually approaching as the morning had gone on. On their arrival the Inspector studied their progress with glee.

'Well I am pleased you have made such headway Major,' the Inspector informed him.

'They're good lads these,' the Mayor replied with a hint of pride in his voice.

'Indeed they are. We didn't have much luck clearing the soil I'm afraid. Shall we break for lunch? I've arranged for some refreshments at a local pub, if you think that would suffice?' the Inspector asked.

'I think you'll be very popular with the lads, I'll let you tell them,' the Major replied. The Inspector nodded.

'Thank you gentlemen, you can all break there,' the Inspector called to them with a smile. The sound of chopping gradually ceased, and the two teams began swapping tales of their hard work.

'Thank you. You have all worked spectacularly hard this morning, and to show my gratitude I would like to take you all into town for a pint and some sandwiches.' A barely suppressed cheer echoed around the trees.

'So if we can all jump back on the bus and we'll get you down there.' The men didn't need much convincing, and all piled on to their transport. As they did the two Constables approached.

'Does that include us then?' Constable Hanson asked.

'Ahh good afternoon gentlemen,' the Inspector welcomed them jovially. 'Unfortunately you will need to remain here to ensure we don't have any trespassers disturbing any evidence or tampering with the equipment. We should be back in an hour or so, perhaps you could contact Firestone station and see if any of your colleagues are available to come and relieve you later.

'And what are we to tell anyone that should ask what is going on?' The Constable asked.

'The truth, or at least, a watered down version of it. This is all part of the investigation into the body that was discovered Sunday night, and that this area of the copse is temporarily out of bounds while we search for evidence.'

'Have you found another body?' Hanson's colleague Constable Presley asked.

'Not yet, but that's not what we are looking for. No need to give too many details away Constable, simply inform them that these activities are part of our ongoing investigation, is that clear?' the Inspector asked. The two men were making it fairly clear that they were would rather be coming to The Green Man with the soldiers.

'Yes Inspector,' they replied grudgingly.

'Splendid,' the Inspector replied. 'See you later.' And he climbed on to the bus. The driver made short work of the drive to the pub, his pace no doubt encouraged by the thought of a free beer and lunch. When the men arrived at The Green Man the few locals that had come out for a beverage that afternoon sat open mouthed at the seemingly never ending line of soldiers that traipsed in and made their way directly to the bar. Lionel stood rubbing his hands together eagerly. On hearing the commotion of thirty men filling the small space Mavis came rushing out of the kitchen to greet them.

'Good afternoon Inspector!' she called over the din.

'Ahh hello Mavis, please put anything the men order on to my tab,' he called back.

'Will do! Your lunch is all set up in the lounge bar, make your way through when you're ready.'

'Thank you so much.' The men all slowly made their way from the bar to the lounge carrying foaming pints of beer. Good to her word, Mavis had put together a generous spread, and they tucked in eagerly. The food was soon devoured, and the men made themselves comfortable in the warm surroundings while they digested the food. It wasn't long before Mavis appeared and began clearing away plates and glasses.

'Oh dear,' she said to the Inspector. 'I fear I might not have done enough if they've eaten it all.'

'Oh fear not Mavis, I am sure you've done yourself proud,' he replied to put her mind at ease. She nodded respectfully, though she wasn't entirely convinced.

'We will be leaving shortly, could I possibly have two flasks of tea to take with me? I will of course return them later.'

'I should think that could be arranged,' she agreed with a nod and hustled away to search for a couple of flasks. The Inspector glanced about the room and noticed that the men had all finished eating and drinking, so he addressed them again.

'If I could have your attention for a moment please gentlemen,' he called above their din, with little effect. Major Sheppard noticed, and called sternly;

'That's enough lads, quieten down.' This had the desired effect, and their voices were quickly silenced.

'Thank you Major. Now, I hope you're all refreshed and ready for an afternoon of work. If we could all file out and back to the bus please, and when we return to the copse please split back into the two groups you were in earlier.'

'Yes sir,' came the hearty reply, and the men filed out of the pub obediently with the Major, the Inspector, and the Constable following close behind.

'Inspector!' Mavis called as they passed through the bar. 'Don't forget your flasks!'

'Thank you Mavis, I am sure you have just made two bored bobbies very happy.' She smiled, though she wasn't at all sure what he meant.

'Good day, I should be home in time for supper.' He raised his hat to her, and made his way unhurriedly after the others. The shocked occupants of the bar began swapping stories and rumours about what the men might be doing, and some followed the men out to try and fathom where they might be going.

69.

At the copse the bus pulled up into the pot hole covered area of trees that the men had cleared, and they began to disembark. Once out they began filing into their two teams again, while the Inspector approached the two policemen in their car. They saw him coming and Constable Presley, who was sat in the driver's seat, wound down his window.

'Good afternoon gentlemen. Here, I thought you might appreciate some tea.' He passed them the flasks which they accepted gratefully.

'There's a couple of Constables from Nettlewood coming to relieve us in an hour,' Hanson informed the Inspector.

'Perfect. We'll keep going while we still have the light,' he informed them. 'Perhaps you could arrange a rota with your colleagues at Nettlewood, I'll need someone back here first thing, looks like we could be here for a few days, lots of work to do.' They nodded back, glad to be part of the investigation. The Inspector left them to their tea and went back over to the men who were lined up and awaiting orders.

'Gentlemen, thank you so much for arranging yourselves so quickly.' The men fell silent and all turned to listen. The cold drizzle that had begun to cover them was a far cry from the cosy warmth they had left behind in the pub.

'I think a swapping of tasks might be in order,' he informed them. 'Could the men who accompanied me into the copse earlier please assist Major Sheppard with the task of clearing the trees, and the men that were clearing the trees please follow me, we are going to pay a visit to a friend of mine across the road.' Drew raised an eyebrow and wondered who he meant.

'Drew, would you care to come along?' the Inspector asked.

'Of course Inspector, where are we going?'

'To the Vicarage, it's not far,' he replied. 'We will return later Major.' He informed him.

'Yes Inspector, no problem,' the Major replied, beginning to wonder himself about the Inspector and what it was they were all doing out here in the cold and wet. Satisfied, the Inspector stomped off in his Wellingtons down the road toward the Vicar's' house. Drew followed obediently, the soldiers formed a line behind them, and they all marched down the road.

'So the Vicarage?' Drew asked rather confused as they walked. 'What are we doing there?'

'There is a large section of the graveyard hidden in the copse,' the Inspector informed him as they walked. 'I'd like to clear it for a better look.' Drew frowned.

'And you discovered this, I presume, whilst on your walk last night?' Drew asked.

'I did,' the Inspector informed him casually. 'There's not enough space in the trees up there for all these men just yet. So we'll put them to good use somewhere else while we wait for the area to clear a little.' Drew didn't take the Inspector's choice of route for his evening stroll any further. If he wanted him to know, Drew reasoned, he would already know. They arrived at the small cottage of the Vicarage, and the Inspector announced their arrival with a short series of raps at the door. It was presently opened, and Aldous' face lit up at the sight of his visitor.

'Inspector!' he exclaimed, his smiling face quickly turning to surprise at the sight of the men behind him. 'What are all these chaps here for?' he asked.

'Good afternoon Aldous. These gentlemen are from the local barracks, they are here to assist us with revealing what secrets the graveyard might hold.' Aldous glanced over the Inspector's shoulder.

'Oh my, such a lot of them!' he gasped, rather impressed.

'You remember Constable Gates?' The Inspector introduced Drew formally.

'Yes, good afternoon Constable,' Aldous smiled to him and Drew nodded back, not quite sure how or when the Vicar and the Inspector had become so informal with each other. The Vicar's behaviour was far removed from what he had seen Monday morning, he was much more relaxed in the policeman's company.

'Give me a moment I'll pop my boots on and walk you round.' He began pulling his boots and coat on and Drew turned to the Inspector once more.

'He seems pleased to see you,' Drew noted. The Inspector nodded, but did not give any more of an explanation. Soon enough Aldous was leading them around the side of the cottage's flint walls. The thorny rose bush climbing up one side of the cottage did nothing to elude to the beauty it would exude in the spring. The path was bordered by empty flower beds, the garden sat in stasis as it awaited the spring. At the back of the property they were faced with the slowly disappearing gravestones, and the encroaching copse.

They all filed into the space between the house and the trees, standing amongst the stones.

'Well gentlemen,' the Inspector faced the men. 'Hidden amongst these trees is the rest of the graveyard, it extends approximately thirty yards into the copse, where a small stone wall stands. While we wait for your colleagues to clear a path through the trees to the mound we will be helping the Vicar to clear his graveyard. We have hidden in the trees hundreds of years of Firestone's history, and we need to clear it as carefully as we can. Any questions?'

'No sir,' came the resounding reply, the orders were painfully simple.

'Wonderful, I will leave Drew here with you to field any issues you might come across, I will be stepping inside with the Vicar for a few moments.' Drew did his best to hide his continually deepening confusion, and as the men began readying themselves for an afternoon of hacking and sawing at the trees Aldous led the Inspector inside.

'Well I am pleased to see still you in one piece, how did it go last night?' Aldous asked the moment the door was closed behind them. He wasted no time in asking questions, or putting the kettle on.

'Not well,' the Inspector replied as positively as he could. 'Banks tried to kill me then he disappeared into the copse.' The Vicar looked up from the sink where the kettle was slowly filling with water.

'Banks tried to kill you?' he asked in a shocked awe. 'Why?'

'Because it would appear that I am getting close to whatever it is that he and his family have been hiding for the last hundred years or more. Now he has disappeared, and I'm afraid I may never get the opportunity to question him.

'Well, shouldn't you be out looking for him?' the Vicar asked.

'Oh rest assured we have men searching across the county for him. Some are searching the copse, some are conducting a door to door search. I don't think they will have any luck, but we'll see.' The Inspector was removing paperwork from his briefcase and arranging it on the table. The Vicar soon joined him with two steaming mugs of tea.

'So, I suppose this is the document that you wanted me to sign?' he asked, picking the bundle of papers up and examining it anxiously. 'My word it certainly seems very thorough.' He fished out some fragile looking reading glasses from his shirt pocket and began reading, but gave up after a few sentences. 'Could you perhaps give me the drift of what it is I am signing?' he asked.

'Of course, it can be a rather daunting document,' the Inspector conceded. 'Essentially you are signing to say that you agree not to speak to anyone regarding the information you have about the case. What you know can never be shared.'

'As we agreed on Tuesday morning?'

'Yes exactly, as we agreed on Tuesday morning. This just makes it official.'

'Well, I have no issue with signing that.' Aldous skipped to the last page and slowly scrawled his signature across the line. 'There.' He passed it back to the Inspector. 'Now, how did you get so many men so quickly?' the Vicar asked.

'Oh, well, such is the need to get the case wrapped up as quickly as possible, the department I work with has far reaching powers.' The Inspector informed him cryptically.

'I see,' Aldous replied, not sure if he did really understand. 'What department is it you work for exactly?' I'm not sure if you ever told me.'

'I work for the Department of External Affairs,' the Inspector informed him purposefully. Aldous frowned.

'That sounds sufficiently vague,' he complained. The Inspector smiled.

'Usually the vagueness and the authority end the questioning there,' the Inspector admitted. 'The department is there to look into the things that other departments don't want to know about. Affairs that are external to other government departments, that are external to the generally accepted world view.'

'Things that don't fit into God's plan,' Aldous commented, referring to their earlier conversation.

'If there is a plan, then your god has gone to great lengths to conceal it,' the Inspector informed him kindly. Aldous smiled knowingly. He could sense the difference of opinion and didn't want to test their blossoming friendship.

'I was hoping I might pop up to your spare room, I have a feeling I may have left something behind,' the Inspector asked airily.

'Yes please help yourself, though I did check and I couldn't see anything, apart from the camera and the rolls of film,' he remembered, opening a drawer and handing the film to him. Aldous was glad of the change of subject.

'Thank you, but I will just have a double check.' The Inspector left the film on the table and ascended the stairs quickly. He opened the spare room door and saw that since his departure Aldous had somehow made the room look even tidier than when he had left it. He retrieved his reports from under the carpet where he had left them, then returned to the Vicar's kitchen.

'Ahh I see you found it,' Aldous remarked, rather surprised at the papers in his hand. 'I'm sure I would have noticed something like that.' His eyed thinned a little in realisation that the Inspector must have hid them from him.

'Yes, thank you.' He opened his case and concealed the papers and film inside. He faced Aldous with a smile. 'Now there was just the matter of reimbursing you for the food and cleaning of my clothes.'

'Oh really Inspector I assure you there is no need, I was pleased for the company, and to have a little excitement added to my otherwise quiet existence.' Aldous began a fluster of hands in objection which the Inspector ignored.

'I appreciate that, but still, Her Majesty's police force insists.' He reached into the inside pocket of his suit jacket and produced a prewritten cheque which he passed to the Vicar. Aldous studied it and the sum made his eyes widen.

'My, this is too generous.' He shook his head, unable to tear his eyes from the amount he had been given.

'Oh please, you were a perfect host in an imperfect situation. This is to show how grateful the Yard is for your cooperation.' The Vicar blushed slightly.

'Well, if it was coming from your own pocket I might have put up more of a fight, but if you insist, how can I turn down such generosity?' Aldous' mind turned for a moment to the leaking roof in the small chapel next door. He stood and put the cheque safely away in a drawer.

'Wonderful. Now, if it suits you I will leave the men here to continue with their clearing for now. I'm hoping they can get it all cleared, but I doubt if it will all be done today. I may be able to spare them in the morning.'

'Of course, anything they can do is appreciated. I must say I am grateful, it will be wonderful to see the copse coming back under control again.'

'Indeed. The other half of the men are busy clearing a path to the mound I discovered, we can then begin trying to fathom what purpose, if any, the strange thing has.'

'Any ideas yet?' Aldous asked. The Inspector had a few, but he couldn't share them with Aldous.

'I have a few theories based on the readings I have taken, but the only way I'll know for sure is to dig up the mud unfortunately.' The Inspector swigged his tea. 'There was one other thing.'

'Yes, of course,' Aldous replied, eager to help.

'I need to arrange a funeral, I was wondering what your plans were on Sunday?'

'Well, I usually run a few errands on a Sunday after the service, I should be free around three 'o' clock though.'

'Marvellous, I shall see you on Sunday then, just before three. I'll leave it up to you to choose the site of the grave, ask the army men to dig it where you think best, but in a quiet corner somewhere inconspicuous would be preferable.'

'Of course, may I ask whom you will be burying?'

'We have discovered some other victims in the area during our investigations,' the Inspector revealed.

'Oh my!' The Vicar exclaimed in shock. 'Who?!'

'Unfortunately we have no way of identifying any of them, their remains are decayed beyond identity but I thought they at least deserved a decent burial.'

'Yes, very good,' the Vicar nodded, pleased to be able to help in any way he could.

The two men finished their tea then donned their boots and coats before heading back out into the cold afternoon to see Drew and the soldiers. To avoid feeling like a spare part Drew had decided to lend the army men a hand, and they found him sawing through a fallen trunk. When he saw them coming he placed down his saw for a well-earned rest.

'Everything alright Inspector?' he asked, brushing the sawdust off of his hands. His jacket and hat were off, his sleeves were rolled up ready for action.

'Yes thank you Drew, shall we be off? We must get to Nettlewood station.'

'Yes of course,' Drew replied, wiping the sweat from his brow and rolling his sleeves down. 'What of the men?' he asked.

'They will stay here for now, not much we can ask them to do at the mound, there's not space enough for them to help with the tree clearance. And we shall need the graveyard before the week is out.' He cleared his throat. 'Gentlemen, if I could have your attention for a moment,' the men stopped what they were doing and turned to face the Inspector.

'Drew and I will be leaving you for now, please continue your hard work here. I see you are making great headway into the trees, and I greatly appreciate it. The Vicar here will be more than happy I am sure to furnish you with cups of tea and the like.' He turned to Aldous.

'Oh yes,' he replied to them all excitedly. They let out a friendly chuckle.

'Wonderful, in that case I will leave you in his capable hands. I have asked him to ask you to dig me a hole,' the Inspector said, slowly and clearly. 'As we are in a graveyard it shouldn't take you long to work out what that hole is for. The Vicar will show you where he wants it dug. If during the clearance you reach the low stone wall at the rear of the graveyard then you will know that you have gone far enough. Please try and clear as much as you can of the trees within the walls. I will relieve you later.'

'Yes Inspector,' came the rousing reply.

'Well now young Drew, shall we make our way to Nettlewood and see what luck, if any, our search party have had?'

'Yes, let's hope they've found something,' Drew replied, smiling at the Inspector's ease of speaking to such a raucous and intimidating collection of large men.

'Good afternoon Aldous,' the Inspector tipped his hat.

'Yes see you soon Inspector, Drew.' Aldous waved them off. They returned to the car and were soon on their way. Drew's head was buzzing with questions that he knew he would already know the answers to if the Inspector wanted him to. He thought of the Vicar, wondering how and when the two men could have become so friendly. As far as he could see the Inspector had had little time for developing such friendships.

'So, if you don't mind me asking, why have the army invaded Firestone?' Drew asked, hoping he at least deserved an explanation for this.

'A good question Drew,' the Inspector replied, glad he had asked. It showed confidence. 'I'm in a bit of a hurry. I believe that under that mound is the secret behind what is causing the bodies to appear. If my readings are correct there is a chance that another body may appear soon. I need to reveal what the mound conceals before that happens, and try to stop it from happening ever again.' The dull grey day hung over their heads ominously, the trees rushed past them, their branches hanging morosely over the road. The Inspector was glad to be away from the closeness of Firestone and into the open country that separated it from Nettlewood.

'And you have the power to, just, call the army in whenever you want to?' Drew kept the conversation moving, wondering just how much the Inspector was willing to tell him.

'Not whenever I want to no, just whenever I need to. Whenever circumstances dictate that their help is required.' Drew nodded.

'And we need them to clear the Vicarage?' Drew asked, slightly confused.

'Yes, and the path to the mound,' the Inspector replied, looking distantly out of the window. They soon reached the station and briskly entered, the Inspector eager for an update from the Constables searching for Banks.

'Why don't you go ahead and see the Sergeant, Drew?' he suggested. 'Let him know we're here, ask him to put the kettle on.'

'Right you are Inspector,' Drew replied and hurried off to find his uncle. The Inspector wandered toward the back of the station, and found the officers he had met earlier in a smoky staff room, tucking into their sandwiches.

'Ahh hello Inspector,' Constable Moir spoke up as he spotted the Inspector entering. They were all sat together and were relishing the warmth and the rest.

'Good afternoon, what luck have you had?'

'Well, we checked out the copse as best we could, but most of it was impenetrable. Banks couldn't have gotten in far there, the brambles were just too thick.'

'I see,' the Inspector replied, rubbing his chin thoughtfully. 'And the door to door enquiries, any luck there?'

'We did a few of the surrounding roads, checked some sheds as you asked, no trace at all I'm afraid.' The Inspector nodded.

'Well, I am grateful, when your lunch is eaten please resume the search, and keep going until something turns up, thank you men.' They all nodded in silence. The Inspector hurried onward to the Sergeant's office where he found Frank and Drew talking to a white haired man in an impressive blue uniform.

'Ahh you must be Chief Constable Fairclough.' The Inspector reached a hand out in welcome.

'Indeed I am, and you must be this Inspector I've heard so much about.' He shook the Inspector's hand and the two men shared an anxious smile.

'Yes, thank you for coming at such short notice, and sorry to bring all this down on you Chief Constable. Your advice would be most welcome, the Firestone station is in a dire way with no Sergeant.'

The men began arranging themselves on chairs around the room.

'Not at all, I've been meaning to get down here and see how it's all going. The question is, what do we do about the Firestone force? I'm not sure any of them over there are capable of filling the position, not in these circumstances certainly.' The Inspector nodded in agreement.

'It could be a good opportunity for someone to act up to the position though,' the Inspector suggested. 'Someone from Nettlewood perhaps?' He looked to Frank for any suggestions.

'Well there is Hemming, one of the other Sergeants here. We could spare him for a while,' he suggested.

'Hemming?' Fairclough scoffed into the air. 'Nice enough bloke but not sure he's up to it. You need to get down there Frank, leave Hemming up here to look after this place,' he told him affably.

'Yes sir, that's actually a good idea.' Frank stood and made his way out of his office in search of Hemming. 'Won't be a mo.'

'What about men, do you need any of the Nettlewood boys to come over?'

'Well actually I've already commissioned a few of them to go over to Firestone and help out with the search,' the Inspector admitted.

'Ahh good man,' the Chief Constable concurred. 'What have you got them doing?'

'Currently they are eating their lunches down the corridor, but after that they will be doing door to door searches looking in gardens and the outhouses and the like for any signs. So far no luck.'

'Hmm. What are the Firestone boys doing?'

'There's the desk Sergeant at the station, though it's quiet in there from what I've seen,' the Inspector informed him. 'I've got a couple stationed in the copse with the chaps from the barracks to speak to any curious civilians. Some are searching the copse near Banks' last known location looking for any signs of where he might have headed.'

'The barracks?' Fairclough asked. 'What have you got those blokes doing?'

'I discovered a mound in the copse, I believe it to be related to the body's appearance and I need to discover if there is anything buried in it. They are kindly clearing a path ready for some heavy digging equipment I have arranged to come tomorrow.' Fairclough raised an inquisitive eyebrow.

'Well, whatever you think Inspector, it's your investigation.' He thought for a moment. 'I think you'd be better off swapping some of the men round. You might do better having local bobbies going door to door, a bit of local knowledge, a friendly face, you know.' The Inspector nodded in agreement.

'You could be right, I'll give them the good news before they head back over there,' the Inspector informed him.

'Good work,' Fairclough nodded. Frank re-entered the office with Hemming.

'Morning all,' Hemming smiled as he entered. He was one of the younger men in the station, and although technically the same rank as Frank, it was Frank who controlled the force.

'Morning Mike, how are you doing?' Fairclough asked.

'Very well thank you Chief Constable,' he replied cheerfully.

'Good-oh. I'm sending Frank here over to care-take Firestone while we work out what we're going to do about Banks.' Hemming nodded.

'Right you are,' he replied.

'So while he's away we're leaving you in charge here, understand.'

'Yes of Course Chief Constable,' he nodded in understanding.

'Good. I want you to send a few more Nettlewood officers over to help search for Banks and the Mayor. I want that copse scoured.'

'Yes sir.' Hemming nodded, finding a notepad and scribbling it down. Frank began pulling his jacket on.

'You'll be in charge over there during a tough time Frank, what with the body and now two prominent members of the community missing. Think you're up for it?'

'Should be fine Chief Inspector, just hope the boys over there are ready to do some work.'

'Well, that's what you'll be there to do. Keep them in check, make sure they're where they're supposed to be. There'll be a major shake-up round here when all this blows over, but for now we just have to maintain the peace, do we all agree?' he asked the room in general.

'Yes sir,' they all replied. The Inspector nodded satisfied.

'I think it might be best if I stuck around for a while Inspector. I'll set myself up here, seems there's a lot going on I could be helping out with,' Fairclough advised.

'I'm sure the men will be pleased to have the extra help,' the Inspector replied. There was a rap at the door and a head poked round.

'Sorry to interrupt gents, but there's a couple of blokes from the hospital here for the Inspector.'

'Ahh, Andy and Jim, wonderful. Thank you Constable.' The policeman nodded and disappeared back into the station again.

'Drew, this is our cue to leave. Sergeant Gates, I presume it is still alright for us to borrow your police van?'

'Of course Inspector, see Harry on the front desk for the key.'

'You're taking the van?' Fairclough asked. 'Planning to round up a few local criminals for us while you're here?'

'Not this time I'm afraid, this is an evidence gathering mission. Drew and I conducted a search of Banks' property and found fifty or so very decomposed corpses.' Fairclough and Frank reeled in shock.

'So Banks is the killer?' Fairclough asked.

'No, I don't believe he is, though he obviously has a connection to the body, as I am sure these corpses will prove. I think he and his family have been covering up the appearances of bodies for some considerable time. What I would like is to apprehend him so I can interview him and ascertain, if possible, why they have been doing it.'

'Well, you better get off then,' Fairclough exclaimed.

'Indeed. There was just one other thing, Sergeant.'

'Yes?' Frank asked.

'Would you have a female officer that might accompany us to the Banks residence? I feel Mrs Banks may need some comforting when I inform her of her husband's secrets.'

'Yes of course, I think Jill should be out there, Drew you know Jill, Jill Fields. Take her out with you, she's a good lass.'

'Right you are Sarge,' Drew agreed.

'Good to meet you Chief Constable, speak to you soon I'm sure,' the Inspector shook his hand again.

'Yes Inspector,' he replied. 'Good luck.' With that Drew and the Inspector made their exit, leaving the remaining men in a state of shocked confusion. They walked through the station to the staff room, where they fortuitously found Jill talking to the men that had been doing the door to door enquiries in Firestone.

'Ahh here you all are,' the Inspector interrupted their conversation. 'I want you Firestone chaps to head back over to Firestone and continue the door to door enquiries, see if you can have a look round a few gardens, alright?' Johnson and Matthews nodded.

'Yes sir,' Matthews replied.

'You Nettlewood chaps, I want you to continue searching the copse, head to the Mayor's residence, and start with the trees at the rear of his property.'

'Yes Inspector, of course. We were just heading back over there now.' They stubbed out their cigarettes and prepared themselves for their tasks. The Inspector turned to the female officer they had been talking to.

'You wouldn't happen to be Jill would you?' he asked politely.

'Yes sir, yes I am,' she replied, a little taken a back at being addressed by the man from the capital.

'Wonderful. I am about to give a lady some rather bad news about her husband, and was wondering if you could accompany us to offer her some support, and perhaps try and garner any further information from her regarding her husband.'

'Oh, yes of course, give me a moment I'll just grab my things,' Jill smiled.

'Of course, we'll meet you at reception,' the Inspector replied as she made her way quickly away to her desk. Drew and the Inspector made their way to reception where they retrieved the key to the van from Harry. The key had a fob attached upon which was written the van's registration number and a telephone number. They then walked through to the reception where Andy and Jim were sat quietly and patiently waiting.

'Hello again Inspector,' Andy stood and shook the Inspector's hand. 'I was hoping we wouldn't meet again under these circumstances, but you seem to have quite a knack at finding dead folk for us.' Andy was jovial and friendly as always, his attitude toward death bred from an over familiarity that came with his choice of career.

'Hello again Andy, Jim,' the Inspector nodded to the younger man, who nodded nervously back.

'My apologies for calling on your services again, but I feel now that you have been involved in the case, and realise the severity, I would like to keep using you. Saves me having to explain the situation over and over, I hope you understand?'

'Of course, just pleased we can help, aren't we Jim?'

'Yes Andy,' he replied. 'Bit more interesting than what we usually end up doing and all,' he admitted.

'Wonderful.' The Inspector handed Drew the van key.

'Drew, I'm presuming you'll be alright driving the van?'

'Yes of course Inspector, no problem,' he replied. He was not overly excited about returning to Banks' hidden morgue, but hid it well enough. Jill exited the station into the reception room and joined them.

'Ahh good, our party is complete,' the Inspector smiled at Jill in welcome, and she smiled back.

'Afternoon lads,' she said to the ambulance men.

'Afternoon Constable,' Andy replied for them.

'Good. Well Jill if you would like to come with us, gentlemen, shall we meet you there?'

'Sounds like a plan,' Andy agreed, and they set off to their vehicles. The ambulance was off first leaving Jill, Drew, and the Inspector huddled in the cab of the black police transit van. Drew set off, and as they passed the row of shops that marked the start of Nettlewood's town centre the Inspector held up a hand.

'Drew would you mind pulling in here for a moment?' he asked politely. 'I just need to pick up a few supplies.' Drew obliged and with a sense of wonder he was becoming accustomed to he pulled the van into the first space he saw. The Inspector jumped out and hurried into Jones' Haberdashery.

On entering a bell behind the door gave a friendly peal to announce his entrance. The Inspector surveyed his surroundings. Stacked from floor to ceiling, on every inch of shelf space, was a myriad of useful household necessities. Here was a place one could pick up a shoe lace, a light bulb and packet of clothes pegs with change from a pound. A man in a plain brown overcoat, white shirt collar just visible above the neck line, suddenly appeared from below the cashier's desk and stared at him.

'Ahh good afternoon,' the Inspector raised his hat.

'Afternoon, up from London are we?' the man asked, with a friendly smile.

'Indeed I am, is it that obvious?' the Inspector asked, wondering just how he could tell.

'You could say that. Folks that ain't from around are usually up from London,' the shopkeeper told him. 'And I don't recognise you from round here.'

'You're quite right Mr Jones, I am up from London. I presume you are Mr Jones?' the Inspector checked quickly.

'That's right, I'm Mr Jones,' Mr Jones told him with hard earned pride.

'And this is your wonderfully stocked haberdashery that I find myself in on this dreary November afternoon?' the Inspector asked.

'Aye that's right it is,' Mr Jones nodded assertively.

'Marvellous, could you help me? I'm looking to buy a few bits,' the Inspector asked, eager not to have an ambulance parked outside of Mrs Banks house for too long.

'Oh aye, no problem, what is it you're after?' He leant forward on the counter.

'Four pairs of braces, four torches, and all the batteries you've got that will power them.' Mr Jones raised an eyebrow.

'Blimey, well isn't that an interesting shopping list?' Jones laughed. Let's have a look shall we...' He fished a step ladder out of a hidden cupboard and began scanning the walls.

'Ahh there we go, let's see how many pairs we have.' He climbed the steps and reached to a corner where a row of suspender braces were hanging. 'My last four pairs, lucky you,' he called down, carrying them down the steps. 'Torches are...' he moved his steps round and climbed back up them again. 'Over here.' He took four good quality torches down.

'Will these do you?' he asked, showing them to the Inspector who studied them carefully. They had long silver handles of just the right thickness to be held comfortably in the hand.

'Yes, these are just right,' the Inspector informed him.

'Champion, now, batteries are behind the counter, so...' he moved over to his counter, leaving the steps out for the moment. He totted the total up on his till then pulled out a large selection of batteries.

'If you don't mind me saying sir you look like the sort of gent who would be wanting these,' Mr Jones produced a packet of Ever Ready batteries. 'They're a bit more expensive than the rest, but there's a reason for that, if you get me, sir, they last a lot longer.'

'You'd be right on the money there Mr Jones, I'll take all you have of those.'

'Very good sir.' He added the batteries to the total. 'That will be two pounds then please,' he asked. The Inspector produced his wallet and handed over two pound notes.

'An absolute bargain, thank you Mr Jones.' Mr Jones rang the money into the till.

'You're welcome sir,' he informed him, putting the Inspector's torches, braces and batteries into a large brown paper bag for him.

'Good day.' The Inspector tipped his hat to him and disappeared out of his shop, leaving Mr Jones two pounds better off.

70.

When the police van arrived at the Banks' residence the front door was open and Mrs Banks was approaching the ambulance looking rather distressed. She saw the Inspector arrive and changed course to the dark blue police van.

'Inspector? Have you bought him back?' she asked, eyeing the police van and ambulance and wondering which one her husband could be in.

'Unfortunately not, and can I presume from your question you have not seen or heard anything from him?' the Inspector asked as he carefully climbed out of the van.

'No,' she answered rather crest fallen at the lack of news. 'What are you doing here then?' She asked, rather dumbfounded.

'Well Mrs Banks, during our search of your husbands garage earlier we discovered a rather large amount of evidence in a hidden cellar.' Mrs Banks gawped for a moment.

'A cellar?' she asked, not sure whether to believe him or not. 'Where? We don't have a cellar.'

'Beneath the garage, behind the door you did not have a key for,' he informed her. Andy and Jim had left the warmth of their ambulance to join them, and she took a step back toward her front door nervously.

'What sort of evidence?' she asked, valiantly holding back tears.

'Bodies,' the Inspector answered bluntly. 'Dead bodies Mrs Banks.'

Her jaw dropped as quickly as her resilience. She finally succumbed to the weight on her shoulders and released a sob. She composed herself after a moment.

'Then, it was him? Who murdered the man Drew found?' she asked bravely, producing a tissue from her sleeve and dabbing her eyes with a corner.

'Actually no, I don't believe it was,' the Inspector informed her kindly. 'But I certainly think he knows more about it than he let on.' This didn't seem to make her feel any better, and she allowed herself to be consumed with years of suppressed worry. The men behind the Inspector shifted awkwardly at the sight of Mrs Banks' grief, and the Inspector turned to Jill.

'This is WPC Fields,' he introduced her to Mrs Banks. 'Why don't you two go indoors and have a cup of tea.'

'Yes, come on love let's get the kettle on,' Jill suggested. Mrs Banks simply nodded and allowed herself to be led back inside.

'Poor woman,' Drew shook his head sympathetically.

'Yes. She is finally free of Banks' grip over her, but the irony is she won't know what to do with her freedom and will probably defend him,' the Inspector mused. 'Well gentlemen, we have a lot of bodies to move. I thought it might help if we used these,' he reached into his bag from Mr Jones' shop and removed the braces and torches, handing them out to the men. They stood and looked at what they had been given, rather confused.

'Err... Inspector?' Drew asked, not quite knowing how to phrase the obvious question. The Inspector smiled knowingly.

'Allow me to demonstrate,' he suggested, and wrapped the elastic braces around his head so they looped under his chin and over his crown several times until comfortably tight, securing them in place with the clips. He then slid a torch under the braces on top of his head, so the braces held it in place on top, the beam facing forward.

'This will allow us all to have both hands free, and be able to see what we're doing.' He switched the torch on, and his companions smiled at his ingenuity.

'My, that's awful clever,' Andy enthused, and put his on. Drew and Jim followed suit, and they all switched their torches on.

'Splendid, don't we all look smart?' the Inspector studied them all and smiled. His idea worked well, even if they all looked a little ridiculous.

'Now, shall we start getting these bodies into the ambulance? When that's full we'll start putting them into the van.' They all nodded in agreement.

'Shall we begin by moving these boxes out of our way?' Drew suggested. 'Might make it easier getting in and out.'

'Splendid, yes,' the Inspector nodded, and they all began piling the boxes together in the corner furthest from the hidden hatch. With the added space the Inspector had room to try and shift the crate that hid the hatch, but Banks had secured it firmly to the floor. Drew approached him, carrying a rusty axe he had found amongst the forgotten debris.

'Shall we try this?' he suggested. The Inspector smiled.

'Capital,' he nodded, taking a step back as Drew swung the axe at the ancient wood. The first blow sent an ear piercing crack through the garage, causing the Inspector and the ambulance men to put their hands over their ears. Drew swung again, and the wood split and buckled. With a few more swings Drew reduced the box to firewood, and the men helped clear it away to reveal the hidden door.

'Drew, would you mind staying here while Andy, Jim and I bring up the first load?' the Inspector asked. Drew didn't have to be asked twice.

'Of course Inspector. See you in a minute,' he replied thankfully. They returned to the ambulance for some body bags, then descended into the hole. Andy and Jim turned white with worry as they carefully navigated the stairs down into the dark. Drew wandered over to the door and looked out at the bleak surroundings, a shower of rain soaking everything for what seemed like the hundredth time that day. He soon heard the sound of footsteps ascending back to the light and turned to find they had reappeared carrying two bags each, which they deposited on the floor. They all took a moment to catch their breath.

'It's not nice down there,' Andy told him, shaking his head. 'How many bodies do you recon Inspector?'

'Another five or six trips should do it,' the Inspector replied. His pleasure at being above ground was palpable.

'Well let's get going then, try and get it over with,' Andy suggested, and they returned to the underground morgue. While they were gone Drew carried the first batch of bodies to the ambulance. As he returned from moving the last set of bones the three men reappeared with six more bodies. The Inspector noted Drew's handiwork.

'I think we have struck upon a good technique here Drew,' the Inspector told him. 'Jim why don't you stay up here and move these into the ambulance. Give you a bit of a break. Drew you can come down with us and give us a hand.'

'Yes that's fine,' Drew agreed, switching his torch on and rolling up his sleeves. Jim brushed himself down and tried to hide the relief of not having to return to the hidden rooms below.

Almost an hour after they had arrived the remains had finally been removed. The men then set about trying to extract the heavy filing cabinet from the hidden basement and getting it in to the van.

'Thank you all so much for your hard work,' the Inspector said when the van door was finally shut. The men were all tired and hungry. He removed the contraption from his head and switched the dimming torch off. 'One last task and we can all sit down with a nice cup of tea. Let's get these poor lost souls to the morgue, I'll drop the filing cabinet back at Nettlewood and arrange it's collection.'

'Right you are Inspector,' Andy agreed, removing the torch from his head and wiping the sweat from his brow.

'I'll just check how WPC Fields is doing, we may need to make a stop at the police station to drop her off.' He knocked at the front door, and presently it was opened by Mrs Banks.

'Hello Inspector, all done in there I hope?' she asked. She was visibly shaken, with red eyes and pale face. 'I can't believe the time, it's flown by.'

'Yes, time did get away from us a bit didn't it? You will be pleased to know that we have searched the area thoroughly and I am quite happy that there is no more evidence to be found, please feel free to examine the cellar should you wish to.' She looked rather disparagingly at the dark inside the garage.

'I'd rather not,' she replied. Jill appeared behind her.

'Ahh, WPC Fields, we are about to head back to Nettlewood station. I presume you're ready to go? I could always have a squad car come over to collect you if you would rather have more time?' he offered to them both.

'That's very kind Inspector, and Jill has been ever so nice, letting me chunter on about all my problems,' she blushed.

'Don't you be worrying about that now,' Jill reassured her with a friendly rub of the arm.

'I'm sure she didn't mind at all,' the Inspector replied with a kind empathy.

'No of course not, and I'm happy to stay if you'd like,' Jill told her.

'That's kind of you dear but I'd really like a little time for myself. I'm thinking I might go and visit my sister over in Birmingham for a few days. I need a rest after all this.'

'I understand, but may I ask you remain here for the time being, at least until we have found your husband?' the Inspector asked.

'Oh yes, don't worry, I'll not be going anywhere until he turns up.' She flushed in the face a little, but it was in anger, not fear. 'I'll be wanting to give him a piece of my mind when he reappears.'

'Well, should you find him before we do, please remember that I need to question him when you're done with him.'

'Yes Inspector I understand, don't worry I won't hurt him,' she smiled.

'Splendid, well, we shall leave you in peace, please call Nettlewood should you see him.'

'As you wish Inspector, good day.' She stood on the door step and waited for them to leave.

'Yes Mrs Banks, good day.' The Inspector raised his hat to her politely, and his party returned to their vehicles.

'Andy if you could head over to the hospital Drew and I will meet you there once we have WPC Fields safely returned to Nettlewood station.'

'Right you are, see you at the morgue,' Andy agreed, and headed back to his ambulance. They were on their way through the drizzle before the others had their seatbelts on. When his passengers had all settled down Drew revved the van into life and they headed after the ambulance back through Firestone.

'Well Jill, you seemed to work wonders on Mrs Banks back there,' the Inspector noted.

'Yes Inspector, she was quite upset when we went indoors. It appears she has suffered an unhappy marriage at the hands of Sergeant Banks, though not a violent one, his was a cruelty of the mind.'

'An all the more vicious cruelty if you ask me,' the Inspector warned. 'Bruises heal, but a psychological wound can torture a person beyond physical pain.'

'Indeed,' Drew agreed. 'Did she reveal anything you think we might find useful in apprehending him?' he asked.

'I don't think so, she spoke of his long brooding moods, of his secretive personality, of how it all began when his father had died, she said that's when he changed from being a loving kind man and began the change to the man we are now searching for.' The Inspector lapsed into thought, stroking his chin as Firestone zipped past them. Soon they were crossing the broad shrub lands that separated the two towns, and Nettlewood edged into view.

71.

With Jill safely returned to her station and under orders from the Inspector to write a full and frank report on everything that Mrs Banks had revealed, Drew drove them to the hospital. On reaching the morgue they piled the van's contents on to two hospital beds and wound their way through bright white tile to the morgue, where they found their paramedic friends sharing a hot cup of tea with Casey and Doctor Collins in the small kitchen space of the morgue.

'Good afternoon Drew, Inspector,' Casey welcomed them with her usual mischievous smile. 'Nice of you to finally join us, these two gentlemen have been filling us in on your underground exploits.' Both men gawped at the young lady's demeanour with the authoritative Inspector.

'Well, then they have saved me the job,' the Inspector brushed off Casey's brash attitude with a cool ease that she had become used to. 'I hope you at least made the tea in thanks for all their hard work.'

'Actually no I did,' Doctor Collins informed him.

'Why am I not surprised?' The Inspector shook his head with a playful frown. 'I knew it wouldn't take you long to charm these unsuspecting fellows into becoming your servants.' They all shared a laugh at the banter between the two, the Inspector genuinely enjoyed working with Casey, and the energy she injected into the grim surroundings. With their teas quickly drunk, the ambulance men stood to leave.

'Well Inspector, we'll let you get back to it.' Andy shook his hand.

'Thank you again for all your hard work today gentlemen, I shall be sure to mention your efforts to your superiors.'

'Thank you Inspector, see you later.'

'Yes see you Andy, bye Jim.'

'Bye Inspector, Drew, Doctors.' Andy nodded to each, and then followed Jim out of the door.

'Well, I suppose I should get back to my office.' Doctor Collins began picking up their mugs and putting them in the sink. 'That paperwork won't do itself you know.'

'Of course Doctor,' Casey nodded.

'Yes, speak to you soon.' The Inspector removed his hat and coat and placed them on a hat stand by the door. When Doctor Collins had departed and his office door was safely shut, Casey addressed them both.

'So, shall I show you what else I have found in the haul from Bill's house?' she asked.

'Oh yes, lead the way,' the Inspector enthused, and she led them down to the end of the corridor to the lab and its huge freezers. She opened the big steel doors and entered for a moment, returning with a partial skeleton on a metal bed.

'I would say this specimen died in her late nineties,' she informed them as she emerged from the foggy cold. She pulled up a light for them to examine the cadaver closely, and they gathered round to hear what she had discovered. 'The cause of death appears to be from the same sort of wound as the man Drew discovered, am I right in thinking I will find the same wounds on the bodies from Banks' house?'

'Yes, all the bodies we bagged up had the same cavity in the chest,' the Inspector confirmed, having checked each body carefully. Casey nodded.

'Well let's begin with this lady.' She pointed at the skeleton's head. 'She was in extremely good shape. Usually with the bones of older people you find they are weak or cracked, age takes its toll on the body's ability to regenerate, so we weaken,' she informed them, more for Drew's benefit than the Inspector's. Drew nodded, eyeing the skeleton cautiously.

'However this person's bones are all very healthy. They are strong, so they lived an extremely good life. It gets really interesting though, when we look at the teeth. She moved up closer to the head and opened the mouth.

'These teeth at the front, from what I can tell, are all original teeth. They have a consistent amount of wear and tear. They also look as though they have been artificially lightened. There is no discolouration that you might expect to see. Even the most careful of brusher would still accumulate some staining of the teeth, but these are all whiter than you'd expect.'

'Very interesting,' the Inspector agreed.

'Ahh, but my dear Inspector, it gets better.' She directed their attention to the teeth at the back of the mouth. 'From what I can tell, these teeth are all newly grown.' The Inspector frowned, and Casey noticed.

'Sorry, let me be a little clearer. These teeth are newer than the teeth at the front. They aren't Wisdom teeth either. These aren't the original teeth, they are in too good condition. It would appear that the original teeth fell out, or were removed, and these were put in their place but they are not false. They have a root, they have been grown in the skull. Here, I have some x-rays.' She walked purposefully over to a light screen with the blurred blotchy grey transparency of an X-ray pinned to it. She switched the screen on to illuminate the interior of the skull, and the newly grown teeth were clearly visible as clear white imprints in the dark jaw.

'Could they be implants do you think?' Drew asked, moving over to study the image closely.

'Good idea Drew, and for all I can tell yes they are,' Casey told him, impressed at his intuition despite herself. 'However I can't explain how an implant was grown into the skull. Here you see the front teeth, though they seem outwardly healthy they have smaller gums. Age has decayed them. The back teeth however cast bright white shadows on the jaw.' She leant into the picture for a closer look.

'So, whilst this is all very interesting, what do you think this tells us?' the Inspector asked her.

'It tells us that this lady had an excellent dentist,' Casey told him. 'So good in fact that his techniques are, I would say, hundreds of years more advanced than today's. Somewhere around the standards of Mr Berrow's optician you might say,' she pointed out. 'This body was killed, or at least, walled in after dying, about two hundred years ago. She also died in the same way as Mr Berrow,' she reminded them, pointing at the chest.

'And what do you think this means?' the Inspector asked.

'That's not what you want to ask, or at least, that is not the question you want me to answer,' she replied frankly. The Inspector's moustache twitched.

'What do you think am I trying to ask you?' he replied.

'You are trying to get me to say that you and Drew are gradually making a collection of corpses from various time periods, future and past,' she replied. 'But you want to ask the question in such a way that you feel safe that you didn't put any words in my mouth. That I came to this conclusion of my own fruition.'

'And did you?' the Inspector asked.

'Despite the impossibility of it all I have to admit to that being my conclusion. Or at least, that is what the evidence points to. Should other evidence present itself that refutes that proposition I will happily change it to something more...' she stalled for the word.

'Plausible?' Drew suggested, a little baffled by the conclusion.

'Thank you Drew. Something more plausible.'

'Well implausible or not, that is the conclusion I have also come to,' the Inspector informed them.

'So what now Inspector, do we try to work out how they all came to be here?' Drew asked. 'And how all the bodies in Banks' cellar came to be here?'

'Well, that is your problem, all these bodies are mine,' Casey pointed out. 'What exactly do you want me to do with them all?'

The Inspector carefully studied the remains of the poor soul from somewhere in the future.

'Essentially what we have here is a collection of missing persons,' he informed them. 'Some of these cases have gone cold and will never be solved. Put these bodies to one side, they will be buried here in Firestone. Some of these poor souls are yet to go missing,' he pointed out. 'In fact, some of these people may not yet have even been born.'

'True,' Casey nodded, eyeing the skull with the mysterious teeth.

'So please can you identify as best you can the remains which might fall into this category, and take them back to London with you where you and your team can try and get as much detail from them as you can. This way we might, I hope, be able one day offer a distressed family some kind of closure.'

'Yes, this I can do,' Casey nodded, solemnly. The Inspector had a certain melancholy in his voice that made her remember something she too often forgot; these remains were once people, with lives, and loved ones who would miss them. They seemed to all realise this, and for a moment silence was allowed to echo through the characterless room.

'Well, do not allow us to hold you from the task at hand,' the Inspector said quickly, breaking the silence and the mood.

'Well, I do have a lot more work to do now, try to keep the inspecting to a minimum for a few days would you Inspector? I don't think the freezer can hold any more.'

'I will do my best not to find any more remains for you Casey, I assure you,' the Inspector replied dryly.

'Very good,' she nodded with a smile. She escorted them down to the kitchen where they began putting on their coats. Casey opened the refrigerator that sat buzzing under the work top and took out her sandwiches.

'Ham and Cheese,' she informed them. 'Abigail does a nice sandwich.'

'Well if they're as good as the rest of the food from The Swan and Dove then I would agree with you,' the Inspector replied.

'Say, why don't you two join me for dinner tonight?' she suggested. 'It gets boring eating by yourself every night you know.'

'Sounds good to me,' Drew accepted the invitation quickly, much to Casey's obvious delight.

'A kind offer, but I'm afraid I have too much to do and am usually far too tired to be able to spare the time or the energy for a trip beyond the dining area of The Green Man,' the Inspector declined politely. 'Drew I'm sure you would appreciate a night of not having to cook, you go ahead without me.'

'If you're sure Inspector?' Drew asked.

'Yes of course,' the Inspector nodded.

'Well that's settled then, meet you at the bar of The Swan and Dove about seven?' Casey asked, blushing a little.

'Yes, about seven, look forward to it,' Drew replied, a little nervously. 'See you later.'

'Splendid!' the Inspector enthused. He raised his hat. 'See you, Casey.' And the two men left her to her sandwich.

72.

Drew's car approached the site of the mound clearance as the last rays of the sun set on the distant horizon. For a few minutes it shone, huge and orange, in the gap where the cloud ended and the land began. It silhouetted the tips of the trees across a tired grey sky, and with its parting, so the light followed, and the end came to the soldier's merciless conflict with the earth. Their activity had not gone unnoticed, an ensemble of village folk had gathered at the mouth of the newly cut path into the trees. They gawped and nattered, they shared what they knew to whoever would listen. The Constables that acted as crowd control had been forced to leave the warmth of their car, and now stood behind a line of blue and white police tape, chatting casually to the people whose curiosity had gotten the better of them. The Inspector approached the police tape, which was raised for him by the Constable from Nettlewood.

'Evening Inspector,' he nodded respectfully.

'Evening Constable, I trust you've not had any trouble?'

'No sir, folks just wondering what's going on that's all. The crowd is slowly getting smaller as the sun goes down. Not many want to be out in the copse at night like.'

'Good. Well you're doing a sterling job men, well done.' He marched on toward the trees, and found the men starting to pack their equipment back into the bus.

'Ahh Inspector, you made it back just in time,' Major Sheppard welcomed him with a hand shake.

'Yes, hello Major. How goes it?'

'Very well, I believe we will be ready for the heavy equipment tomorrow.'

'Capital. I can't say how appreciative the Yard is of all the hard work.'

'You're quite welcome. I'm thankful to you for giving the lads a bit of a break from the barracks. It's always nice to have them out doing something to put their skills to the test.'

'Well, get them back for a well-earned dinner,' he insisted, peering round the Major for a moment to do a quick head count. 'It looks as though the contingent I sent to the Vicar's residence have returned. How went their task?'

'Hold on I'll get Sam over here to fill you in.' The Major turned to the shifting shape of men lifting equipment in the encroaching darkness. 'Ramey!' he yelled loudly.

'Yes Major!' came the reply through the thickening black. A few moments later a familiar face had appeared next to them.

'Oh, hello Inspector, sorry I hadn't seen you arrive.'

'No problem Private Ramey. Tell me, how did the clearance at the Vicarage go?'

'Very well, we thinned it down, even reached that wall you mentioned at the back.'

'But not quite a complete clearance?' the Inspector enquired.

'No sir sorry, we just didn't have the time.'

'No problem I assure you. I am just grateful to you for helping. I trust the Vicar treated you well?'

'Old Aldous?' Yes, don't think I've had so much tea and biscuits in my life!' he replied with a smile.

'Wonderful, yes he does like to spoil his guests. Well, thank you private, don't let me keep you from your work, and thanks again.'

'Yes Inspector, sir.' He shot Major Sheppard a quick salute before joining his colleagues on the bus.

'Well looks like they're all done, see you in the morning Inspector?'

'Yes Major, I'll be here,' The Inspector confirmed, raising his hat.

'Very well, have a good evening gents.' He shot him and Drew a salute and joined his men on the bus which was quickly on its way. Night had now well and truly consumed the trees.

'Shame it's too dark to see, I'd really like to examine the clear path to the mound,' the Inspector informed Drew, staring into the dark void that cloaked the new path.

'Well, I wouldn't recommend it. Even if the path is clear, the ground is very rough. I just hope we can get the digger over it tomorrow,' Drew informed him.

'Yes, well, tomorrow is another day,' the Inspector replied jovially, and turned to face the road. The crowd had all dispersed, leaving just the two policemen. Drew and the Inspector walked toward them.

'Well gentlemen, thank you for a good day's work,' the Inspector called through the dark as he approached.

'You're welcome. Will you be needing us tomorrow?' the Constable asked.

'I will indeed. As early as possible, sunrise or before would be preferable.'

'Blimey, you're a hard task master!' he commented.

'Tomorrow will be a shorter day for you, I will arrange for you to be relieved before lunch, I understand you have put in the effort today and I thank you for it. For now, please get yourselves off home, and I'll see you here in the morning.'

'Yes Inspector,' they replied, looking forward to getting in front of their fires and discussing the day's events with their wives. They wandered off into the darkness, and after a minute Drew and the Inspector heard their car rev into life. They then watched as the lights came on, illuminating the area around their feet. The light then swept round affording them a brief view of the path into the trees, before it disappeared into night and headed back to Firestone.

'So Drew, that just leaves you and I. If you would be so good as to drop me back to The Green Man, I will let you head home and prepare for your evening at The Swan and Dove with Casey.'

'Of course Inspector.' They made their way back to Drew's car.

'I wonder what Mavis has on the menu tonight,' the Inspector mused to himself.

73.

The Inspector ate a quick dinner and retired to his room with a pot of tea. He took the films from Aldous' camera and from his own and set up his darkroom to develop the pictures. The red glow was warm, and while the pictures developed he sat and drank tea, taking a blue pill while he waited. The photographs showed the mound, the view over the trees, his path through them, and the gradual chopping back of the trunks. He was pleased with them, and checked each one carefully for anything that didn't ought to have been there. His eyebrows raised at some of the shapes in the trees, and he decided to debate them in the morning with Drew.

He wrote up his report of the day, ensuring to commend Andy and Jim for their continued help, as well as the Major and his men.

He concluded that, although the searches for the missing men were of course necessary, they would reappear from the copse soon.

By the time he was finished it was beyond one in the morning, so he gratefully turned in for the night.

74.

Drew arrived at The Swan and Dove at ten minutes to seven in an attempt to surprise Casey when she came down from her room, however she'd had the same idea, and Abigail was already pouring her a glass of red wine when he entered the almost empty bar. He quickly ordered a pint and Casey insisted on paying. The only other occupants in the restaurant that night were a local elderly couple sipping halves of mild in a corner and the hotel's only other staying guest. This, Abigail had explained to Casey, was a busy night for a Thursday. The second guest sat by himself in the middle of the dining room at a table for two hurriedly scoffing down steak and kidney pie with the all the trimmings.

'Don't look,' Casey warned Drew. 'But do you see that man over there?' She was barely whispering, and the hush of her voice in the quiet pub made her more conspicuous than if she'd been shouting.

'What about him?' Drew asked, not looking.

'He says he's a salesman,' she confided to him quietly. They were staring quite intensely into each other's eyes. Drew subconsciously glanced over her shoulder at him.

'I said don't look!' she hissed at him. Drew quickly looked away, and returned to attempting eye contact with Casey.

'He's got a case full some really weird stuff,' she told him, confiding in him as though this were a dark secret. Drew was struggling to stifle laughing at her childish ways.

'Like what?' Drew asked, playing along with her game. He casually took a sip from his bitter.

'Err, well, there was a big plastic thing about this big.' She mimed a shape roughly the size of two house bricks side by side. 'It only had two buttons, and a ball that you could spin around. He said you could control a computer with it.'

'What?' Drew laughed shocked. 'Two buttons?'

'I know. He also had a calculator,' she informed him. Drew nodded, wiping a moustache of white bubbles from his upper lip. 'Those things they have at the bank?' he asked.

'Ahhh, no, you see that's what I thought he meant too but this thing was much smaller. It would fit in your hands.' She delicately placed her wine glass down on the bar and held her hands together to give him an idea of the size. 'It was tiny. He says every house will have one someday.'

'If I hadn't seen the contents of the Inspector's case I might not have believed you,' Drew replied.

'You've seen inside his case?' Casey asked excitedly. Dickie Valentine floated out of the radio behind the bar, crooning about a 'Finger of Suspicion'. Casey wondered for a moment if The Beatles music would ever arrive in Nettlewood or Firestone. The slow steady beat however seemed to fit the ambience of the sleepy bar.

'Well, only the things he takes out of it, but some of it is pretty strange,' Drew admitted.

'Like what?' she asked.

'Have you never seen anything out of the case?' Drew asked, surprised. Casey shook her head, ruffling her crop a little.

'You have to remember that I spend all day in a cold room trying to find clues on dead people, I never get to see him...' She struggled for a moment to find the right word, and decided on; '...Inspecting. So tell me what he's got.' Engelbert Humpledink began asking someone to please 'Release me' from the radio, and Drew wondered if it would be rude to ask Abigail to retune it to Radio 1.

'Well, there's a Geiger counter, to detect radiation,' he told her, ignoring the music for now.

'Boring!' she declared. 'Bloody hell Drew even I've got one of those!'

'Well maybe in London every household has one, but up here in the sticks they're a rare sight!' he replied, making her snort with laughter.

'Yes, well, ok, what else has he got? This better be good,' she directed a playful finger at him encouragingly.

'Ok, well now I'm not sure if this is strange or not, but he had something that could measure air pressure.'

'Air pressure?' she thought for a moment. 'Like a barometer? Like that one over there?' she pointed teasingly at a wall by the door where a grand brass circular face with a needle told anyone who cared to look that the weather outside was 'Changeable'. Drew shook his head.

'Not exactly like that, no,' Drew replied, trying rather hopelessly to defend himself. She giggled at his squirming.

'Sorry Drew, goodness I am awful. Sorry I'm just teasing.'

'That's alright, you're right anyway, it was essentially a glorified barometer but it was hand held, like this.' He sketched its rough shape on to the bar in spilt beer.

'And it had aerials he pulled out of the top.' He added antennae on to the sketch in the appropriate place. 'And it didn't tell you what the weather was like, it gave out a reading, like numbers and letters, which he wrote down on a map, at the position he took the reading.' The teasing had stopped and she was listening carefully, mesmerised.

'What else did he have?' she asked, suddenly quite serious.

'The only other one I saw detected electro magnetism, he did the same thing with that, writing down the readings he took on to his map.'

'And what do you think all the readings mean?' she asked. Drew looked away nervously, only managing to answer with a vague shrug.

'What's the matter?' she asked, worried.

'He made me sign something,' he explained. 'He said I wasn't allowed to discuss the case with anyone.' She smiled and shook her head.

'Well I'm pleased you were paying so much attention to that document you signed,' she laughed at him shaking her head. 'It actually says not to speak to anyone else about the case unless you are investigating it with them.' Drew thought for a moment.

'Yes, you're right, he said not to talk to anyone who wasn't directly associated with the case.'

'Right, which is why he asked Doctor Collins to leave but you stayed, remember? So spill. I want to know everything.'

'Actually, it would be really good to speak to someone else about it,' he admitted. 'The numbers he wrote down, whatever they mean, were high around where I found the body, but have gradually faded since Sunday night.'

'Did he take a reading from the Geiger counter?' she asked, suddenly concerned.

'No, he tried but there was no reading.'

'Good, I have used mine on the body, Matthew Berrow, and the other bodies you found, but there's been no radiation.'

'So the electromagnetism and the air pressure are higher over there. That would explain the weather,' she thought for a moment.

'But it doesn't explain what's causing it,' he pointed out.

'No,' she replied, but this hadn't been what she had been wondering.

'How did you find the body?' she asked, realising there could be more behind his discovery.

'I found it amongst the trees, in a dip in the ground, in a clearing in the copse.' She paused, nodding, sipping her Burgundy.

'And did you see anything else?' she asked lightly, trying to avoid suggestion.

'Do you know about that then?' Drew asked, confused as to what was and wasn't common knowledge.

'It's just that I know a little of what the Inspector's cases are like, and there is usually something, well, odd about them.'

'Are all his cases like this?' he asked. She leant on the bar, and leaned her face in close to his, multiplying the intimacy, encouraging the sharing of a secret.

'What sort of a case is this, Drew?' she asked. He did his best not to flush under her gaze.

'Mysterious bodies found in woods, ancient corpses, are all his cases the same?' he asked again, being more precise. She thought for a minute, realising that for her, locked away with her body's, all the cases were quite similar. A low voice mumbled inaudibly on the radio, then Elvis began describing a 'Devil in Disguise', and both were pleased with the change in tempo.

'Let's just say that all his cases are the same, in that they are all different,' she laughed at her own vagueness, giving a sudden burst of life to the quiet bar.

'The truth is Drew I don't really have much of an idea of what his cases are really like. I only see them from my point of view, just as you will only see this one from your point of view. What really goes on, what he really discovers, I don't think any of us will ever know.' Drew nodded, knowing what she meant exactly.

'So what did you see, Drew?' she asked him again. 'To make you go in to those woods.' Drew avoided eye contact and instead talked to last of his beer.

'I saw a pair of lights, like eyes, shining in the night. I followed them into the trees and they led me to where I discovered the body.'

'What do you think they were?' she asked, fascinated.

'I really don't know. I've never seen anything like them.' She nodded understandingly.

'There are some things that are too big for us to ever understand them, or hope to know what they mean,' Casey told him, and Drew got the feeling she had often pondered on these points. 'That's where the Inspector comes in. He doesn't always exactly solve cases. He is more here to, to close them,' she finished carefully. 'He might not even find out what it was that killed the man from Swindon, or any of the others, but he will ensure it doesn't happen to anyone else.'

'Well, that's the real point I suppose,' Drew replied thoughtfully.

'So what else is there I ought to know about your side of the case?' Casey asked, steering them back to the conversation.

'Well, there is mounting evidence that Banks was responsible for my father's death,' Drew informed her. Casey's jaw dropped.

'He killed your father?' she asked, quite shocked. Drew nodded, and gave her a brief history of the Gates family. She nodded intently throughout, basking in Drew's honesty, mesmerised by the sad tapestry of his past. When his tale was complete they stood quietly for a moment, with only the mumbling DJ bridging the silence. His low tones were quickly replaced with the sultry sound of Bob Dylan's voice asking to be sung a song by the Tambourine man. Casey didn't quite know what to say to Drew.

'I still need to sort through a pile of old newspapers for some more evidence though,' he broke the silence for her.

'Old papers?' Casey enquired, her attention suddenly ignited. Before Drew could explain any further Abigail approached them, and noticed their empty glasses.

'Would you two like another drink?' she asked.

'Yes please Abigail, and we're going to be eating as well, can I have the cottage pie?' Casey asked. Abigail took her notebook out from her pinny and jotted down her order.

'Of course love. And what about you Drew?' Abigail turned to Drew who was studying the specials board behind the bar.

'Can I have the liver and onions please Abigail?' Drew replied after a moment's thought.

'Of course dear. Will you be at your usual table Casey?' Abigail was already pulling Drew a fresh pint.

'Yes Abigail, over by the window,' Casey replied with a smile.

'Right you are love. Go and get yourselves sat down I'll bring these over for you in a minute. Your dinners won't be long.'

'Thanks,' Drew said, and they walked to the table. Casey took the long red bench by the window, looking into the bar, and Drew sat on a new and comfortable wooden chair facing her and looking out of the window. The table seemed much larger with just the two of them sat at it.

'So you mentioned some papers?' she asked Drew as soon they were seated.

'Yes, I found them in the loft at my mother's house. I think they probably all have an article in them that my father thought was relevant. He was trying to build a case against Banks,' he explained.

'Have you had much of a chance to go through them yet?' she asked.

'No, they're still in the boot of my car as it goes, I took them with me this morning when I went to meet the Inspector in case he wanted to have a look.' Her smile widened.

'You have them here, now?' she asked excitedly.

'Yes, why?'

'Well, we could look through them couldn't we?' she suggested shyly. 'I love looking through old papers, it's like a window on to the past, do you know?' she was coy, realising that she was revealing something about herself that no one else knew.

'Yes, I do.' Drew agreed, without hesitating or judging. 'When I looked through a few of them last night it was interesting to see what was newsworthy twenty years ago.' He stood to leave, and a look of worry passed over Casey's face for a moment.

'Where are you going?' she asked.

'To the car to get the papers,' he explained. 'There are quite a few so we may be here a while,' he warned her.

'Suits me,' she replied, struggling to conceal a content smile. When Drew returned with the dusty old box a fresh pint was waiting for him on the table. Casey was sipping her red wine and the other people in the bar were watching him wondering what they were up to.

'Here we go. Did I miss much?' Drew woke her from a reverie.

'Oh, just the general comings and goings, you know. The salesman has retired for the evening, the elderly couple ordered another round of drinks.' She eyed the box. 'How many are there?' Drew placed it on the table next to her.

'I'm not sure, thirty I guess, collected about twenty years ago.' She opened the top and took the first one out.

'Should we start by putting them in date order?' she suggested, pulling out a few more and studying their dates. She was in her element and Drew sat back to watch.

'You're obviously very good at this sort of thing,' he pointed out to her after a few minutes.

'Ha!' She screamed, with a laugh that Drew was realising Casey used to distract people from the real her. The person who she hid under her boisterous persona. He suddenly saw that her boldness was a defence mechanism, the shy girl overcompensating. 'The truth's out, I'm really a bit of a boring egghead,' she laughed, but Drew could see it wasn't a joke. She kept her concentration on the papers, now avoiding eye contact, waiting to see how he would react.

'Egghead maybe, but there's nothing boring about that,' Drew informed her warmly. She relaxed a little; this was a good answer.

'As you're so good at the organising, why don't I start reading?' he suggested.

'I like a man with a plan, Drew.' She passed him the oldest paper she had found so far. 'Here, you can start with this. It was a copy of the 'Nettlewood Herald' dated 5th May 1949, yellow and fragile. Drew placed it carefully on the table in front of him.

'They don't print this anymore,' he informed her. 'Can't remember the last time I read a Nettlewood Herald.' The headline on the front page read 'Farmer Home' and the story attached to it was of a man finally returning from active service following the end of the war. Drew took a few sips of beer as he read through the story, and then continued into the paper.

'They don't go any further back that that at the moment,' she told him looking at her piles of carefully organised papers. 'There were thirty six in total.' She picked out one of the papers. 'I'll start with the most recent, and we can meet in the middle somewhere,' she suggested.

'Sounds good,' Drew agreed readily, looking up from the Herald. Casey glanced over his shoulder and noticed Abigail wobbling out of the kitchen.

'Perhaps we should start properly after we've eaten,' Casey suggested. Drew turned just as Abigail placed his steaming dinner down on the table.

'Ahh wonderful,' he said, discarding the paper carefully to one side on the large table. 'I'm starved.'

'You sound more like the Inspector every day!' Casey informed him with a smile, shifting herself into position where the landlady was placing her cottage pie.

'My word look at the mess you two have made of this table!' Abigail smiled, trying to hide her disdain at her restaurant being made a mess of.

'Don't worry we'll tidy it up behind us,' Casey piped up in their defence.

'Very well, would you like some more drinks?' She noticed their almost empty glasses. Drew downed the end of his pint.

'Yes please that would be good,' he passed her his empty glass.

'Yes I'll have one too,' Casey hadn't quite finished hers so Abigail hurried off.

'I thought she was going to tell us off then!' Casey leaned in to whisper to Drew. Drew tried to hide a laugh as Abigail returned with his glass and a fresh one for Casey. She scuttled off without a word, and as soon as she was out of sight they both burst into laughter. They tucked into their dinners, Casey shooting a wishful look at the piles of papers every few minutes.

'You're eager to get started aren't you?' Drew asked, noticing.

'It's good to be helping out in a way that doesn't involve scratching around through piles of old bone,' she explained. 'It's also nice to have some interesting company for dinner,' she added, blushing a little.

'You do know we may not find anything of any interest don't you?' Drew warned. 'For all I know he collected them for a completely different reason.'

'Yes I know,' Casey nodded in reply through her mouthful of mashed potato. 'But it'll be worth a shot.'

With dinner quickly eaten they set about their task eagerly. Within two hours they had spread the contents of the box across the table in some kind of order. They had, in one corner, placed all the papers in which they had been able to find something that they considered might be of interest to the Inspector, with the pages carefully marked out. In another corner were the articles that were of possible interest, but they could see no clear connection, and back in the box were placed the papers where there did not seem to be any connection at all. Now, both were feeling a little too drunk to carry on, their glasses having been refiled a little too often.

'Well I think the Inspector will be pleased with our hard work,' Drew informed her. His sleeves were rolled up, but his eyes were beginning to ache.

'I hope so,' she replied, stretching. 'That was fun Drew, thank you.'

'Yes, it was actually wasn't it?' Drew replied smiling. He checked his watch; it was getting late. He stretched his arms wide, sitting up straight. She picked up her wine glass and swirled the last of the evening's wine around its base, watching him, hypnotised by his every move. He looked up from the newspaper on the table and their eyes suddenly entwined.

'So,' she purred, her pupils twinkling at him over her glass. 'What shall we do now?'

Friday 7th November 1969

75.

Drew gave a knock at the door of The Green Man, a little flustered and out of breath; he was half an hour late. He had been rushing all morning to make it here in time and in uniform. The door was presently opened and he was surprised to see the Inspector there to open it for him.

'Ahh good morning Drew, I hoped it would be you.' Drew nodded.

'Morning Inspector. Apologies for my lateness.'

'Oh that's quite alright, I trust Casey didn't keep you up too late?' Drew coughed nervously.

'We were up quite late, she was very keen to look through the old newspapers I told you about.'

'The ones from your mother's loft?' the Inspector asked. 'Did you find anything of any interest?'

'Yes, we think we may have discovered the identity of KB.'

'Wonderful, well, come and sit, please share.' He led the Constable over to his table where an empty pot of tea sat with two cups, only one used.

'I'm afraid I've already finished my breakfast, but I'm sure Mavis will be happy to rustle something up for you.'

'Oh no thank you, I already ate breakfast,' he paused for a moment, unsure how the Inspector would receive the next piece of information, 'with Casey.'

'Ahh good. Most important meal of the day you know. Now, what did you find?' He asked as they sat down. Drew, relieved with the Inspector's lack of interest in his spending the night with his trusty pathologist, put the newspaper he had been carrying on to the table. It was a copy of The Times dated sixteen years ago.

'This one stuck out a mile from the rest as it was the only national broadsheet out of the pile, all the others were local,' Drew explained. 'So we went through every page meticulously, and I spotted this...' He began carefully opening the pages, skipping straight to the page he needed.

'Here we go.' He turned the paper round for the Inspector to see. The headline read; "Midlands police mourn Chief Inspector." A grainy photograph of an elderly gent in police uniform accompanied the article, with a date of birth and date of death printed ominously below. The Inspector wagered he could guess what the rest of the

365

article contained but continued reading in case some vital clue revealed itself.

"Locally renowned in his home town of Arkwright, Chief Inspector Kieron Bramble was pronounced dead in Sheffield Infirmary last night (15th) after suffering a heart attack. Bramble retired from the force ten years ago having made his way up from desk Sergeant in his local station to Chief Inspector in Swindon, helping to ensure that the Midlands streets were safe to walk at night. He retired back to his home town where his career had begun, becoming an outstanding member of the community championing a Neighbourhood watch scheme and helping to raise many hundreds of pounds for his local church. He is survived by his wife Margaret and their two sons. A private ceremony will be held in All Saint's Church in Arkwright next week."

'Well, such a shame we will be unable to question him regarding his conversation with your father, he would have been a powerful witness against Banks,' he informed Drew, handing him the newspaper.

'Yes,' Drew agreed, pouring himself a cup of tea.

'I have already been in contact with Nettlewood and with Scotland Yard and there are no reported sightings of Banks or of the Mayor,' the Inspector informed him. 'This means that they are either extremely skilled at escaping the outstanding police forces of the surrounding area, which I doubt, or they are still at large somewhere around here, probably hiding in the copse, which I find more likely.' Drew nodded.

'Which means at some point, they will have to reappear,' he guessed.

'Indeed. At some point they are going to get hungry. They are probably already cold and wet due to the atrocious weather this town seems to attract. It is only a matter of time before they are forced out of hiding in search of food. I am still not sure at this point if they are together, and as the Mayor was not a suspect I am rather mystified as to why he might have disappeared. However, we have all available forces searching for them, so we must for now trust in my hunch that they will at some point reappear, albeit it a little worse for wear.'

'And until then?' Drew asked.

'Until then we continue with our investigation at the mound. Today the digger arrives, and I hope some of the mystery will be revealed.'

The Inspector leant down and removed something from his briefcase.

'Here, look at these.' He passed Drew a few of the photographs he had developed the previous night. The first one was of the men digging at the mound in the trees. Drew moved on to the next photograph, which was the same scene but with more trees than men. Drew looked up before going any further through the pile.

'What am I looking for?' he asked. The Inspector took the top photograph from him gently and placed it on the table in front of them, so they could both see it. He gave Drew the benefit of having the photograph the correct way round as he had already studied it very closely.

'Here, and here,' the Inspector pointed a long thick finger gracefully in two places on the photograph. Drew looked closer and could just make out, vaguely, on the outer edge of the picture, on the horizon of trees, two figures standing and facing him. Or was it? He held the picture to the light as best he could.

'I can't tell if it is just trees, or if the men are there.'

'Yes, these shapes are easily anthropomorphised.' The Inspector mused, adding; 'It is easy to see people there if you look for them, though you may be creating them yourself,' for Drew's benefit. Now he knew what he was looking for, Drew looked through the rest. In each picture a cryptic shape hid in the darkest corner. Drew stopped at the last one. In the centre was one figure, out in the open, amongst a patch of tall pines. Drew shook his head in confusion.

'What is it?' he asked.

'Good question. I also took these.' The Inspector passed Drew three more pictures, and in these the lights had returned. Drew turned a little pale as studied them

'What do you think it means?' Why are these things appearing on the photographs?' Drew asked.

'Well, because we are close to something. I don't know where the men are, I don't know if that is them in the photographs or just shapes that happen to look like them,' the Inspector replied. 'That's why I thought you should see them. We are close.'

Drew handed the photographs back to the Inspector and he put them carefully back in his briefcase. He then swigged the last of his tea and stood to put on his coat.

'You will need to take half the soldiers to where you discovered the body and help them to cut back the trees so vehicles can easily use the path to the clearing.' He explained, though gave no explanation as to why.

'Alright,' Drew agreed. 'May I ask why?' The Inspector nodded.

'We will be moving the soil there from the mound,' he explained. 'I want the scene clear of soil and easily accessible.

'As you wish,' Drew replied, and they left the warmth of The Green Man and ventured into the unforgiving cold of the morning.

When they arrived at the site the Inspector was pleased to see that two of the Firestone officers were chatting to some locals at the police tape, and that the soldiers had already begun work on the trees. He nodded at the officers at the tape who nodded respectfully back.

'Would you mind checking on your colleagues while I chat with the Major?' the Inspector asked Drew.

'Of course not,' Drew replied cheerfully, and made his way over to them. The Inspector made directly for Major Sheppard who was talking to some of his men as they tackled a large tree trunk.

'Morning Major,' the Inspector called.

'Ahh morning Inspector, well, what do you think now you can see it in the daylight?' the Major asked.

'Well, I surely have to commend your men on their efforts, this is an amazing feat.'

'Good, pleased you are pleased,' the Major smiled, proud of his men. 'Still more work to do this morning, it's the oddest thing.'

'What is?' the Inspector asked.

'Well this morning when we arrived the path was, or seemed, narrower. It's the damnedest thing, as though the trees on the edge had grown back overnight.'

'Well, that is odd,' the Inspector agreed. 'I trust we still have enough space for the digger to fit through?'

'Oh yes, plenty of room for that,' the Major reassured him.

'Wonderful.' The Inspector removed his camera from his briefcase and began taking pictures. The path through the trees was very definite, made more so by the density of the trees along it borders. The men had done extremely well. The Major looked about the newly created path as the camera's click echoed around them.

'I shall just brief the men quickly before the digger arrives,' he informed the Major as he put the camera away. The Major nodded and the Inspector cleared his throat. 'Could I have your attention please?' he called to them and they all turned to listen.

'In a moment the digger will arrive, during which time it won't be easy for us to work around the mound, so if I could ask you to split into the two teams again, one half of you will go with Drew in the bus to begin clearing another path through the trees, and the other will remain here to assist the digger.'

As he spoke, a large flatbed truck arrived with the digger riding piggy back on it. It pulled up on the side of the road in the space the soldiers had cleared at the entrance to the path.

'Well, looks like your diggers arrived and we can start getting some of that mud shifted,' the Major informed him. The Inspector turned.

'Marvellous.' he enthused. 'That will be all for now men, please get yourself into your teams,' he requested nicely. 'Major could you locate the Private trained to drive it and send him over to the truck for me?'

'Of course Inspector no problem.' The Major began searching the men for the driver while they began arranging themselves in two their teams. The Inspector approached truck.

'Morning!' he called up to the drivers cab.

'Morning,' the driver replied. He opened his door and climbed down, revealing a short man in grubby oil stained dark blue overalls. 'I take it you're the Inspector I'm supposed to find then?' he asked in a broad northern accent.

'Yes that's me, everything alright? Are we ready to go?' the Inspector asked him.

'Yes sir it's all yours, I'm supposed to stick around, help you move some earth you've got is that right?'

'Yes, that would be much appreciated, one of the chaps here is going to move the digger, ahh here he is now.' The Major approached them with a young man in his twenties.

'This is Private Jenson, Inspector. He's going to get this digger going for you,' the Major explained.

'Wonderful, well Private, I am presuming you can guess what I want you to do?'

'Yes Inspector, you want me to shift all that mud on to the back of this truck,' Jenson replied intuitively.

'Indeed. As carefully as you can as we have no idea what is hidden under there. May I suggest you get the digger down and drive it up to the mound while, sorry what was your name?' the Inspector asked the truck driver.

'John,' he answered simply.

'While John reverses the truck up the path so you can begin loading it with soil.' The Inspector informed Private Jenson.

'Yes sir,' Jenson replied, and he and John began freeing the digger. Within a few minutes the hoists were loose and John lowered a ramp from the truck for the digger to drive down. A small cry for joy went up from the soldiers and the small gathering crowd when the digger's engine erupted into life. Jenson carefully drove the digger down the ramp and up the path through the trees, its tracks making short work of the rough terrain. The Inspector followed Jensen's careful driving, arriving at the mound just behind him and his digger.

'Now, if you could start to carefully removing the soil from here,' the Inspector called over the din of the engine, indicating a side of the mound close to the path through the trees. 'And slowly make your way round the edge I would appreciate it. Careful being the operative word here Private.'

'Understood Inspector,' Jenson called back, and he began to carefully tease the soil into the scoop at the end of the digger's long arm. The men had all stopped their preparations and hiked up the path to watch, breath baited, as the first scoop of earth was picked up. The digger's arm was carefully pushed into the soil, causing avalanches to cascade down to the ground. The truck slowly approached, getting as close as it could on the rough broken ground before the first scoop of soil was dumped unceremoniously on to the back. Jensen continued to carefully lift more mud from the mound while the men split into their groups. They all stood and watched the digger at work for a few minutes before half of the man drifted down to the coach ready for their next assignment, and the other half returned to clearing trees from around the path and mound.

'I'll be off then,' Drew announced once the digger was well under way.

'Yes, thank you Drew, shall we reconvene at The Green Man at one 'o' clock for lunch?' the Inspector suggested.

'Sounds good, see you then,' Drew agreed, and hurried to the coach, which pulled out and went on its way.

After thirty minutes of careful digging it was clear that the digger was having much greater effect on the mound than the men could. As they watched mesmerised by it a car arrived unnoticed by the side of the road. Its lone occupant approached one of the officers at the entrance to the path, who escorted him to the Inspector.

'Excuse me Inspector.' He called over the sound of the digger as he approached.

'Yes Constable?' the Inspector asked, clicking away with his camera at its progress through the mud.

'There's a man here to see you, says he's from the Museum in Telford, says you asked for him,' the Constable replied with a shiver against the cold.

'Ahh yes, our archaeologist has arrived.' The Inspector tore himself away from the digger to welcome his guest. 'Good morning, thank you so much for coming.' The Inspector and the archaeologist shook hands.

'My pleasure, Doctor Samson at your service. My word what have you found here?' he asked immediately. Doctor Samson was dressed in tweed trousers with high green Wellingtons and a well-worn wax jacket. He was greying with small spectacles over keen black eyes. He wore a flat cap and looked every part the archaeologist.

'It's an earth mound, I would say approximately seven hundred years old, I doubt if it is a ritual burial mound, there are no entrances as you might expect, I suspect it could contain remains, but I think its purpose is to actually hide something else,' the Inspector informed him.

'What?' Samson asked intrigued, and a little impressed at his knowledge.

'That I am not sure of,' the Inspector replied honestly. 'What I think you would find interesting for the moment is on the back of that truck.' The Inspector motioned toward the gradually heightening pile of earth. A couple of the soldiers had jumped on the back of the truck and were beginning to spread the soil around to even out the weight.

'The soil from the mound?' Samson asked excitedly. 'There could be anything in there,' he realised.

'Indeed,' the Inspector agreed. I hoped that perhaps you could do me a favour and sort through it to see what, if anything, is in there?'

'Well yes of course, I only brought myself though, I'll need some help from my museum.' Samson began to redden with excitement.

'Of course, please, as many hands as you think you need,' the Inspector agreed.

'You do realise that by destroying the mound like this you could be compromising hidden artefacts?' he asked, a little aghast.

'A necessary risk I'm afraid Doctor. It is part of an ongoing investigation into a body that was discovered here a few days ago,' he explained. 'Whatever is hidden underneath it holds a vital clue to the body's appearance, and it is paramount I discover what it is as soon as possible.' Samson nodded distractedly and dropped the subject.

'I need to get to a telephone and make some calls,' he informed the Inspector excitedly. 'There is a lot of soil here, I will need some help.' He glanced about him constantly at the movement around the site. The Inspector sensed his urgency.

'Of course, if you head across the road to the church you will find in the Vicarage a very kind gentleman by the name of Aldous. If you tell him I sent you, who you are, and that you need to use his telephone I am sure he will be pleased to oblige you.' Doctor Samson nodded.

'Yes I saw it on the way here, just over the road. Thank you, I won't be long.' He hurried off back to his car, and the Inspector returned his attention expectantly to the mound. The truck was soon at capacity, and Jenson stopped digging and switched the digger's engine off.

'Truck's full,' he called as he climbed out of the cab. Although the mound was visibly shrinking it was still obvious that the task was taking a considerable effort. It was not as low as the pile in the truck suggested it should be.

'Well done Private, very good work,' the Inspector thanked Jensen. 'Have a break for a while, you've earned it. I might be a while, when you're ready to start again leave the soil you remove here.' The Inspector indicated to a spot near where he stood with a pointed finger.

'We can load it in the truck on our return.' Jensen nodded and lit a cigarette gratefully. The Major approached.

'Where's all this going then?' he asked.

'There's a sight on the other side of Firestone, I believe it is where the soil was taken from in the first place, we are putting it back.' The Major nodded.

'Right you are, see you soon,' he said, and busied himself with his men.

'Wonderful. Now, John,' he turned to the small man in the blue overalls who sat in his truck's cab keeping warm.

'Yes Inspector?' John answered.

'Shall we get rid of this soil?' the Inspector suggested. John nodded.

'Right you are, jump in,' he called down, and the Inspector made his way round to the passenger side and climbed in next to him. They were quickly off, John making his way carefully out on to the road. The small crowd had become a little smaller, no doubt due to the persistent cold spit that fell sadistically from the sky.

'The path we're going to is quite narrow, you'll need to reverse up it, do you think that will be manageable?' The Inspector asked.

'Depends how narrow,' John pointed out, unabashed.

'Good point, by my estimations you should have a foot gap or so each side,' the Inspector informed him.

'That should be fine, squeezed it in tighter places believe me!' he informed him with a rasping cough of a laugh.

'Good. Right here,' the Inspector informed him, and he took a right turn out of town and in a few short minutes they had arrived at the path to the clearing. A large pile of cut wood had already appeared at the side of the road, making it obvious for John to see where he was expected to go. He gave two quick blasts on his horn to inform the soldiers he had arrived before pulling up at the side of the road. The Inspector jumped down from the cab and strolled purposefully toward the opening. The soldiers, having heard the truck's horn, began filing out of the trees with Drew close behind them.

'The first load is here,' the Inspector informed them as they appeared. 'Could you all step out from the trees for a moment to allow the truck down there safely?' The men all shifted out of the way and the truck, under John's skilled piloting, began to slowly edge backwards through the trees.

'Blimey you weren't joking when you said it was thin!' John exclaimed to the Inspector through his window as he passed, but he doggedly reversed his way down the path, the men following slowly. They had made a good start at clearing the trees, but as he travelled deeper into their branches the familiar piercing sound of branch on metal erupted again. This time it seemed to have more vigour, as if the trees knew what was happening and would stop at nothing to prevent the truck leaving its load. The truck however was unstoppable, and despite a few slips as the tires struggled to find their grip it made it to the dip without issue. The paint that had marked the location of the body still remained, though a little faded and beginning to be covered by leaves. The men gathered about the truck as John activated the control in his cab that caused the flat bed at the rear of the truck to rise, and as it did the earth slipped rather gracefully from it and on to the ground, creating a large neat pile. The flat bed was then returned to its normal position, and the

Inspector jumped back into the cab with John. As they pulled away the Inspector asked him to stop near Drew.

'You're doing great work here, Doctor Samson will be down later with some colleagues to begin working their way through the soil, have them fill the dip with the soil they no longer want, and gradually we will have it filled in,' he instructed.

'Yes Inspector will do, see you later.'

'Yes, The Green Man at one 'o' clock for lunch if I don't see you sooner.' The Inspector tipped his hat at the men and the truck made its way out of the trees and back toward the mound. When the Inspector returned with the empty truck he was surprised to see that all work had ceased. A small pile of earth had appeared where he had requested, but the digger stood motionless, its claw hanging lifelessly in the air. The men stood about the mound, anxiously awaiting the Inspector's return. The Inspector, immediately sensing that something had happened and fearing the worst, jumped out of the truck as it reversed up toward the mound, easily out-manoeuvring it and getting there quicker. When he arrived at the scene his mind was put to rest as he could immediately see why the men had stopped.

Protruding upward through the mud, tall and proud, stood the peak of a huge rock monolith. All about it the earth was still piled high. It was only slightly shorter than the mound had been at its tallest; the Inspector estimated its height to be at least thirty feet with most of it still being hidden in the mound. The soldiers were obviously amazed to see it. They stood gawping, unsure of what to do next.

'My word!' the Inspector gasped loudly, running to the mound to inspect it closer. 'Good work Jensen! Not a scratch!' He called to the driver, who put a hand up in recognition of his efforts. The Inspector carefully walked as close to the revealed stone as the mound would allow in the wet mud. The rock still had a thin layer of dirt that remained from its burial but the persistent rain slowly washed it away, revealing a shimmering grey surface. For a moment the Inspector, like the soldiers, was too awestruck by the sight of it to know what to do. It was too regular in shape and in too strange a place to have gotten their naturally, it was clear that it had been carved by men, moved here by men and then, for whatever reason, hidden by men. The Inspector considered for a moment, gathering his thoughts, before he began directing the soldiers.

'Well, it would appear we have found what we were looking for,' he informed them. 'We still need to have the entire site cleared though, who knows there may even be more rocks hidden away in the remaining soil.' The men began gathering around him. 'I think for now the safest way forward would be to clear the soil with spades, and add to the pile over by the truck, which we can use the digger to fill.' The men all nodded, and soon they were all digging away at the soil. After an hour of digging they were joined by Doctor Samson again.

'Inspector!' he gasped, awestruck, when he saw what they had discovered. 'This is incredible!'

'Yes, it is rather marvellous isn't it?' he replied. 'Tell me, what do you think it is?'

'Do you mind if I get a closer look?' he asked.

'No of course, please be my guest.' Doctor Samson sped carefully over the mud and made his way up to the stone, the men that had been on the mound working leant him a hand to help him up.

'Fascinating, it seems to be rock similar to that used at Arbor Low, not far from here,' he called down.

'Arbor Low?' the Inspector asked from the base of the mound. 'What's that?'

'It's the remains of an ancient stone circle, in the Peak District,' Doctor Samson replied. 'These stones are still standing though. There's a dome on top of this one. Fascinating, that suggests there could be more stones in here you know.'

'Yes that's what I thought, I'm hoping we will find some others hidden in there somewhere.'

'Well, I am quite amazed,' Doctor Samson admitted. He glanced around suddenly as if remembering something. 'Where is the rest of the soil?' It could be filled with artefacts,' he asked excitedly.

'It has been moved to the site where I believe it was removed from originally. I was hoping you and your colleagues would be happy to set up camp there, as things are getting a little overcrowded here. You are of course welcome to come and watch the progress.'

'Splendid, they should be arriving shortly, providing they can find the place of course. Firestone Copse doesn't lend itself to being easily found,' he informed him. 'I must have driven past the turning several times before eventually getting here.' The Inspector smiled.

'With the discovery of this rock I have a feeling this town is about to become a well-known destination for historians and sightseers alike. It is about to become a lot easier to find,' the Inspector said. 'When are your colleagues joining you?'

'They should be here within the hour, they are bringing some tents to shelter under and some more equipment. I brought some in my car but had no idea there would be so much work.' Doctor Samson's eyes had barely left the rock, he was in complete awe of such a major discovery.

'Well you are welcome to wait here with us, I am sure you would like to watch the digging process, to see if any other rocks are discovered?'

'Oh rather!' he enthused excitedly. 'Any chance of joining in? I have a spade in my car.'

'Of course, the more the merrier,' the Inspector replied encouragingly, and the archaeologist rushed off to fetch his equipment. The digging continued with spades, the men carefully tossed the soil on to the ground where it was slowly moved into a heap near the truck. Doctor Samson quickly returned, climbing back on to the mound and starting his work around the first stone. The soldiers helped him back up and began helping him dig. Before long Doctor Samson could be heard shouting fervently;

'Ahh! Here! Another one!!' Once again all work stopped as everyone approached the scene to witness the second stone being revealed. Doctor Samson found it approximately five feet away from the first, standing just as tall. Now all the men began helping around the two rocks, and after another hour of hard work both were half exposed. As the men dug the rest of the archaeologists arrived, approaching the remains of the mound dumbfounded at the discovery. When Doctor Samson saw them arrive he jumped down from the mound and ran up to them. As they walked to the stones he briefed them frantically on the situation. The soldiers gave them some space, allowing them to study the rocks closely. Doctor Samson's colleagues were middle aged men in old boots and scruffy trousers. They were wrapped up warmly against the cold in worn out old coats that fitted the men rather comfortably. All were bespectacled and had smiles that only archaeologists could have at the prospect of sifting through mounds of old mud. One of them began taking pictures, at which point the Inspector interjected.

'Gentlemen, I fully appreciate the need for recording the moment, and as such could I request to develop your films for you, and take copies for my investigation?' the Inspector asked friendlily. He needed to check the photographs in case they revealed anything lurking between the trees, but he saw no reason to reveal his ulterior motives.

'Well that's a kind offer, thank you.' They nodded.

'You're welcome, please give me your films as you finish them.'

'Of course. Well then, we have a lot of work to do, don't we gentlemen?' Doctor Samson asked them, and then continued excitedly without giving them a chance to answer. 'I'll show them round, then if it suits you we'd like to make our way to the other site,' he requested.

'Of course, we need as much information as you think you might be able to give us.' The Inspector made his way over to the stones with the archaeologists.

'What would you like to know?' Doctor Samson asked.

'Well, how long do you think the stones have been there? Why were they buried? Could there be any more buried in the area and if so, where might we expect to find them?' the Inspector asked. The archaeologists had a collective scratch of their individual heads.

'We'd need to sift through some of the soil to try and answer all those properly,' one of the older men replied. 'And study the stones themselves, but if these are like some of the others that we have dotted about the area of this size, then the rocks have been here around five thousand years,' he told him. The Inspector nodded.

'Perhaps some of you could stay here and help us with any further discoveries?' the Inspector suggested.

'Yes that's a good idea,' Doctor Samson agreed.

'As to your question regarding where to dig for more stones.' another of his colleagues spoke up. 'Although the obvious searching point for now needs to be the remaining soil here, I would also suspect that you might find more stones in amongst the trees. These relics often have avenues of smaller stones leading to them, you may find some remnants of them in the trees.'

'Yes of course good thinking Charles,' Doctor Samson nodded in agreement.

'Look gentlemen the afternoon is nearly upon us,' the Inspector informed them, feeling the wind pick up a little. 'Why don't we show you to the site where the soil is being taken and you can make a start?'

'Yes ok, Charles and I will stay here, you chaps go down to the site and start setting up, we'll swap over later.'

'Very well,' a bearded chap agreed for the others.

'Wonderful. I will come down with John in the truck, I can catch up with the others then and learn how the clearance is going. Follow us, it isn't far,' the Inspector instructed them.

'Well see you all later then,' Doctor Samson called after them as they hurried in the Inspector's footsteps.

'Yes, see you later Roddy.' They waved goodbye and returned to their cars while the Inspector disturbed John who was sitting in his cab reading a paper listening to the radio. He folded it away as the Inspector climbed back in and they drove out of the sight. As the policeman removed the blue tape for them to exit they noticed more people gathering at road, word had obviously gotten around that something big was happening.

On arrival at the site of the path clearance things were quieter than at the mound. None of the townsfolk had noticed the commotion that the quiet clearing in the woods had attracted. The men had cut and cleared almost the entire path, the sound from their chainsaws ricocheting around the trees clumsily. The men required little attention, they were quite happy to continue with their task unsupervised, which pleased Drew as he was able to allow them to do what they had been ordered to do and occasionally lend a hand. He soon became distracted though, finding himself staring into the trees, and wondering if somewhere between them one, or both, of the missing men were watching him.

John parked the truck on the side of the road again, the archaeologists pulling up behind him in their Volvo Amazon. John gave a couple of blasts on his horn and soldiers exited the path up to the clearing to allow him to reverse up safely. When the soil had been deposited and the truck was safely out of the way the archaeologists carefully drove through the trees. The path was clearer now, a definite track through the trees had been carved. The Inspector joined the archaeologists at the site, and watched as they began to set up their things. They had two large shelters under which they set up folding tables, and on these they optimistically placed large blue plastic tubs for their finds. They then began to process the mud, carrying it by the bucketful up to the tables where the unenviable work began. As if by habit the Inspector removed his camera and began taking pictures. The scene was so unlike his first visit here. That occasion had been sombre and had a sense of finality about it. The atmosphere was now charged and exciting at the prospect of change. Drew approached him muddied and tired, but optimistic.

'Strange to see so much life here after Sunday night,' he observed to the Inspector, who nodded.

'I was just contemplating the same thing,' he agreed. 'We are beginning to make some headway to a solution, Drew, I am sure of it.' Drew smiled, thinking of Casey's words the night before. The Inspector wasn't there to find out what had happened, but to stop it from happening again.

'Well, now our friends seem to have settled themselves into their task, I say we make our way back over to what remains of the mound. I suspect they'll all be wanting their lunch.' He checked his watch, the time had just past twelve.

'Gentlemen,' he called to the archaeologists who were already covered in mud. They looked up at the Inspector.

'Lunch at The Green Man in town from one 'til two if you're interested,' he informed them. They nodded in thanks and eagerly got back to their work.

'Drew perhaps you'd like to ride in the truck with me?' he suggested, and they made their way back to John in his cab and then headed back to the stones.

As the truck approached the site of the path through the trees toward the stones the Constables standing guard ushered the small crowd to one side for safety and then removed the blue tape across the opening. John, with the upmost skill as he had demonstrated whenever he was behind the wheel of the large vehicle, positioned the truck carefully across the road and began reversing down the path, checking his side mirrors as he did to ensure he was making safe passage.

The Inspector also looked in the mirrors, marvelling at John's careful work, when his attention was suddenly distracted by the pair of monoliths protruding into the air. They were more pronounced than earlier, standing proud amongst piles of dirt that once hid them. As the truck approached the stones, the Inspector noticed something about them that he couldn't fathom, and it took every ounce of his self-control not to react to it.

Moving eerily between the stone pillars, connecting them and connected by them, was an iridescent film that shimmered like an oil spill or the surface of a soap bubble. It shone dimly, an eerie glow emanating from it which was barely visible under the dull grey sun. As soon as the truck had stopped the Inspector leapt down from the cab to face the stones and study it, wondering why no one else was marvelling at it. When he faced the stones however he found that the film had vanished. Downhearted and confused he slowly climbed back into the cab and slammed the door shut, baffled. John watched him climb back in, then grabbed his paper and carried on where he left off. The Inspector looked again in the mirror, and to his amazement the iridescence had returned. He quickly removed his camera from his case and took some photographs of its reflection in John's mirror, much to John's confusion. He then climbed out of the cab again and began taking pictures of the stones. He also removed from his bag his instruments, and began taking readings rather frantically. Drew had exited the cab and on seeing the stones for the first time his jaw had dropped in astonishment. He could do nothing more than stand in wonder and watch the Inspector going about his investigation. His movements also caught the attention of the others working at the site, and realising that he was being watched he stood up on a mound of nearby earth to address the men.

'Well gentlemen thank you so much for your hard work this morning.' Those that hadn't stopped already turned to face him. 'I think you all deserve a break so why don't you all head off to the pub for lunch.' The men happily downed tools and made their way out of the area to the bus.

'John, why don't you leave your truck there and get a lift in the bus with the others?' he called to him. John jumped down without hesitation and fished out his keys.

'No need to lock it,' the Inspector assured him with a trusting smile. John shrugged and followed the others out of the woods. The Inspector stood thanking those that passed him on their way, waiting for the area to clear.

'Well you were right about there being something hidden in the mud,' Drew congratulated him.

'Yes, wasn't quite expecting this though,' the Inspector informed him. 'You might as well head off to the pub as well Drew, I will meet you there, go ahead and tuck in,' the Inspector advised him when all the others had gone.

'If you're sure Inspector?' Drew asked.

'Oh yes thank you, the walk into town will do me good.' Drew nodded and made his way after the men, wondering what the Inspector was up to.

The Inspector waited a moment for Drew to make his way out of the area before continuing to take his readings, and jotting down his findings. He took more pictures of the stones, and jumped back up into the cab and watched the strange shimmering carefully for a while. A theory began to form in his mind, and with it came a plan of action. He jumped down from the truck's cab again, and hurried out of the copse, his destination set.

76.

In the front room of the Vicarage, Aldous dozed lightly in his arm chair. The cat had forsaken its spot by the fire and had instead taken residence on his lap, curled up and fast asleep. Aldous had spent a tiring morning in the back garden of the Vicarage, continuing the hard work that the soldiers had begun in clearing the graveyard. His rusty shears had made the work harder than he had imagined and now with lunch eaten he was taking a well-deserved rest. The cat purred lightly in his sleep.

Suddenly their rest was disturbed by three loud bangs at the door. They both jumped awake, Aldous rubbing his head while the cat pounced casually and elegantly back on to the floor.

'Oh my, we must have dropped off Samuel,' Aldous addressed the indifferent cat, who began cleaning himself. Aldous rushed to the door to see who it might be.

'Ahh Inspector, what a nice surprise,' Aldous welcomed him in with a warm smile when he saw who was behind the door. 'I had a visit from a friend of yours earlier, the archaeologist, what was his name?'

'Doctor Samson,' The Inspector replied.

'Oh yes, nice chap. He wanted to use my telephone,' he scratched his sleepy head. 'May I ask why there are excited archaeologists descending on Firestone Copse?' the Vicar said.

'You can, and I will answer your questions, but first I'm afraid I must ask to use your telephone as well.'

'My, I should start charging!' Aldous joked. The Inspector thought for a moment.

'I am happy to pay, I do apologise for the inconvenience, it's just yours is the closest phone to the site.'

'The site of what?' Aldous asked excitedly.

'In a moment Aldous, in a moment!' The Inspector hurried to the telephone and lifted the receiver. He began entering a long series of numbers.

'Well, I'll get the kettle on shall I?' Aldous suggested, suspecting the Inspector wished to keep the telephone call private, and he plodded sleepily through to the kitchen. The Inspector waited as patiently as he could for his call to be answered, but the truth was that he was short of time and eager for the line to be picked up.

'Rank, Number and Position please,' a man's voice asked as soon as soon as the call was answered.

'Inspector, 99473. Scotland Yard, case 4199. I am in Firestone, and I need to report a 111,' the man on the end of the phone paused for a moment.

'Just confirm that for us please, what are you reporting?'

'A 111,' the Inspector replied. 'And I need to do it quickly, as I believe there may be a chance I could exit through the 111.' The line went quiet, the operator seemed to reel for a moment though the Inspector of course could not be sure.

'Judging from previous reports that would be, inadvisable,' the man explained. 'Please give justification.'

'I understand your misgivings, following from my earlier experience I believe if I had sufficient protection and correctly aligned field manipulators I could enter, and this time perhaps make contact with the potential 347.'

'Go on,' the operator urged him. The Inspector wondered who else was listening in on the call, and decided to give the full details behind his theory.

'It appears that the energy I was detecting was being blocked, and it was this blockage that caused the body's to appear. The energy would build to a certain level, and then it would burst, sending a charge through space-time, much like an electrical charge for a lightning strike. It would grab whatever poor person it happened to strike, from whatever random place and time they happened to be in, and drag them to Firestone Copse. None survived, and it was this movement through the 111 that gave the bodies their distinctive cause of death. I wouldn't swear to it, but I imagine if we were to find where they were snatched from, we would find the missing flesh that was cut from the centre of their body's. With the removal of the blockage the energy is no longer building up, so the cause of the appearance of the body's has been stopped. My theory is that the missing men have entered the 111. However if the energy dissipates completely the men will be lost inside. I may have solved one problem, but the missing men have created a new one.'

'What of the 347?' The voice asked.

'I believe the 347 used the 111 to travel between places before it became blocked. When the mound blocked the energy it also blocked its way in and out. Actually there is every chance that there are more 347's,' the Inspector added. 'Now that the blockage has gone they should be able to use it again to...' he thought for a moment. 'Exit the trees, and return to wherever it is they have come from.' The Inspector could hear the operators pencil scribbling.

'Hold please,' he said, and the line went dead. The Inspector held his breath and waited impatiently.

'Inspector?' the voice returned after what seemed like an eternity.

'Yes?' the Inspector asked eagerly.

'I have confirmation that you are to proceed with your plan,' came the reply.

'Good, in that case I will require a suit.' Another loaded silence.

'I can't give you authority to go ahead with that, hold please.' The line clicked and whirred again while he was transferred. The line was answered again quickly.

'Suit Control, good afternoon Inspector.'

'Good afternoon. I'm trying to gain access to a suit.'

'When?' The man asked.

'Tonight would be good,' the Inspector told him hopefully. He heard Suit Control looking through some papers.

'Use of suit has been authorised, it will be delivered to the stones at midnight tonight. You have it for six hours. Suit will be collected at six am tomorrow morning from the same position.' The Inspector could not help but smile at the news, despite the extreme danger he had placed himself in.

'Understood, though I am unsure of how long I will be gone for, or where I might end up after my visit, so I can't guarantee I will be able to have it back for you at the collection point at that time.'

'In these cases an indicator has been fitted that can be activated on your return. It will act as a beacon, and the courier will be able to track you to the new location,' the man informed him.

'Marvellous, I'd hate for it to be left outside for too long.' The Inspector thought of the inquisitive locals at the site of the mound. 'I will report in as soon as the suit is activated as per the protocol.'

'A full report will be expected on your return,' the operator told him.

'Yes I understand,' the Inspector nodded.

'Anything else?' the voice asked.

'Yes, I will also require another Field Enhancer, I'm afraid the first one was destroyed on Wednesday night.'

'Of course, I'll let them know, it will be with the suit,' Suit Control assured him.

'Thank you,' the Inspector replied. 'That is all for now.' He hung up the telephone and paused for a moment, pondering his actions, contemplating the next twenty four hours of his life and where they would leave him. He then turned, and walked to the kitchen.

Through the window he could see Aldous in the garden, and he walked through to speak to him.

'Ahh Inspector.' Aldous placed his shears down and picked up a cup of tea from the ground nearby and passed it to him, hand gloved in green stained white cotton.

'All well I hope?' he asked, referring to the telephone conversation.

'I hope so too, we shall soon see,' the Inspector replied, taking a grateful swig. 'I see you've been working hard out here,' he pointed out.

'Well, I was put slightly to shame when the lads from the barracks cleared most of it. I hadn't realised how bad it had gotten, so thought I should make the effort.' The grounds had expanded significantly, the old tomb now a prominent feature.

'We really should get Bill up here to have a look, I'm sure he'd be interested,' the Inspector mentioned, nodding toward the dilapidated structure.

'Yes, I'm sure,' the Vicar replied, noticing the Inspector seemed distracted but not wanting to pry.

'What plans have you today?' he asked, making conversation.

'I shall be heading down to The Green Man shortly for lunch with the men, I am hoping Doctor Samson and his colleagues will be there to fill me in on their progress. Then back to the mound to continue the clearance and this evening...' He trailed off, wondering again just what would become of him that night. 'Well, I guess we shall have to see.'

77.

Atkins closed and locked his door behind him, and set off into the cold wet afternoon, Cara jumping excitedly about his heels.

'Down girl!' he snapped sharply at her, pulling at her lead. She gave an excited bark but did as she was told, and walked next to him obediently. Her ears were pricked up, her mouth open with tongue lapping out to one side, her hot breath filled the air with short lived clouds. Atkins enjoyed his beat, enjoyed having Cara with him to keep him company as he walked it, and despite its problems he even enjoyed living in Firestone. He knew the streets well, and having lived there all his life he also knew most of the residents as well.

'Afternoon,' he nodded a welcome to Mrs Grimes, whose husband had at some time over the past twenty years repaired the plumbing of every household in town. She nodded a welcome and carried on her way with a basket full of fruit from McColl's fruit and veg shop on the High Street. The McColl's had run the shop since his father was a child, it was now being passed to the third generation of McColl boys. His beat took him away from the main streets in town and around its perimeter, where the trees met the roads and buildings, and the town gave way to copse. Usually his only concerns along these back roads were the odd fallen tree, or an animal hit by a car that might need clearing. Today he peered into the trees anxiously searching for any sign of his missing friends. As he walked along the roadside Cara suddenly gave out a bark, and the hackles stood up on the back of her neck.

'What is it girl?' he asked, peering into the dark trunks to see what might have caused her alarm. He stared into the trees, hoping to see them appear suddenly. For a brief second he thought he saw a movement behind a tree buried deep in the darkest region of the copse. It was over in an instant, a brief shifting of light, a bending of shadows. Cara yelped, her bravado had disappeared, and she began tugging on her lead to get away.

'Hold on girl, what is it?' He asked her, taking a step closer to the trees, crossing the line between road and undergrowth. Cara did not follow. She remained by the road, pulling at her lead trying to stop him taking another step. Again Atkins saw the barest of movements and it seemed, for a second, as though the trees suddenly stopped. The wind ceased, their branches stood still, and from within them came another noise, a different whisper, like a voice shouting from so far away that he couldn't catch the words. He dropped the lead, releasing Cara who ran full sprint away. Atkins took another step further into the trees, then another, and another, and slowly he became enveloped by them, and disappeared amongst them.

Atkins looked about the trees searching for the movement again, trying to trace it, but every time he thought he saw it, it had moved a little deeper into the trees. He slowly crept inwards, as if walking out to sea, not wanting to get out of his depth, not wanting to get too far from the safety of the road.

He was distracted for a moment by a memory awakening from the dark recesses of his mind. He suddenly felt as though he had been here before, a long time ago. Then, suddenly, the trees were everywhere, and he found himself surrounded. He glanced back but the road was gone, now all was trees. He went to turn and run back where he had come, but found he was paralysed. His legs were rooted to the ground, his body was frozen still. He tried to scream, but no sound came. Then his legs began to move uncommanded, and he lurched forward involuntarily. He began to panic as his body stalked quickly and clumsily through the trees. All he could do was watch, an unwilling spectator. The woods seemed darker than ever, the trunks stood like ancient pillars, propping up a decayed roof. Space and light flitted around nervously, the trees would suddenly seem two dimensional, like a picture in front of his eyes, and then bounce out to three dimensions dramatically again when he tried to focus. Shapes oozed through the thick nothingness that was the space about and around him.

He was aware of something else with him, off to his left. It walked with him through the trees. It was aware of his presence, but did not bear him any mind. The knowledge of its existence was not helped by his ignorance of whom or what it was. As the two of them marched another joined them, and another. Atkins strained to see what they were, following him through the trees. He could just see in the very corner of his vision the Mayor, still in his pyjamas. He reeled in shock, realising he had found one of the missing men, but was totally powerless to help. He then realised who the others were, and that he too must now be one of the missing men. He looked around as best he could and managed to see Doctor Sparrow, and Charlie. He couldn't see Banks, though he knew that didn't necessarily mean he wasn't here. He was consumed with fear, but all he could do was watch and wait. He had the distinct feeling they were looking for somewhere, but he could not begin to guess where. As they stomped flailing and stupefied along things trickled and flashed around the trees, unfathomable shapes beyond the realm of his senses. One of the incomprehensible shapes that haunted the world they had stepped into came forward, and approached them. They could not move, nor could they react. The bodies of the men all stopped walking. They were lost now, silent vessels, yielding witnesses to events beyond their understanding. The shapes that approached flitted effortlessly through a myriad of wavelengths before settling upon bright burning white. They stopped, two bright white lights burning amongst the pillar-like trunks.

'Welcome back my friends.' The voice came from nowhere, yet echoed everywhere. Despite this the men all knew what was responsible, and that it was them being addressed.

'Thank you,' came a chorus of voices in reply, again from nowhere. The men could not understand where the new voices were coming from.

'Where is the last?' the eyes asked.

'His vessel... rebelled,' the voices chimed in reply. Atkins tried to listen for the source of the other voices, but sound travelled in odd directions in the trees.

'Where is it now?' the lights asked.

'It also came here,' the voices informed it. Atkins heard the voice clearly, and realised it was his own, and that he and the other men were conversing with the lights.

'We must find it,' the lights told them. 'The time is upon us.' Atkins tried to fathom what they were talking about.

'Yes, we must take it to the man. He will free the last.' He heard his own voice say in tandem with the others. He wondered at what was making him talk.

'Yes, come, I will take you to the door,' the lights told them, and the men found themselves following the eyes, as they slipped into the trees. The eyes led them deeper and deeper into the trunks, the space becoming smaller, the light fading. When all was almost dark, when they were hidden deep in the trees, a bright light started to appear ahead.

'It has begun,' the eyes told them. They surrounded the door, which consisted of two huge bright monoliths standing proudly in the dark.

'Yes. It is the new man, he has opened it again, but it is not ready. The lintel is gone.'

'He will need to find it.'
'We must tell him.'
'Yes, he will find a way,' the eyes told them. 'He sees us. He will free us all,' the eyes informed them, as around them shapes of different sizes and consistency emerged from the trees to study the visitors to their limbo world. The men all struggled for escape, but all they could do was stand and allow themselves to be studied as the shapes shifted and oozed around them.

78.

The Inspector arrived at The Green Man to find everyone had just about finished eating and were enjoying their drinks. The pub was full to the brim, not just with soldiers and policemen, but also with Firestone residents who had learnt of the daily lunchtime meet and had come along to learn the latest from the site. The entire population of The Green Man seemed to turn and greet him, pleased to see him, as if they had been worried about where he had gotten to. He smiled and nodded to those that said hello as he made his way through. The Inspector was pleased to see so many of the townsfolk there, glad to see them taking an interest in what was happening in their hamlet. He was sure that the discovery of the mound was going to change the town forever, and the smoky air was charged with excitement. The pub was hot and sticky from all the wet clothed men, and he noticed behind the bar a bustling Mavis serving drinks.

'Mavis!' he called. 'Any chance of some tea?' She nodded to him in reply as she poured a pint with one hand and took money with the other. She handed the drink over and set off at once to get the kettle on, leaving a wide grinned Lionel to handle the bar. A group of soldiers standing at the bar turned and nodded to him respectfully.

'Thank you for all your hard work,' he enthused to them, though they seemed to need little more thanks than to be treated to an afternoon in the pub.

'Ahh Inspector.' The Major approached with a glass of brandy in hand. 'You'll have to stop spoiling the men like this, they'll start getting used to it!' he laughed.

'Just my small way of showing my appreciation,' the Inspector replied, pleased to see his efforts having the desired effect. He made his way through to the dining area and was surprised to find there was still some food remaining. He grabbed a plate and piled it high with sandwiches and crisps, which he began to devour gratefully. He noticed Doctor Samson and his colleagues sitting in one corner in their muddy clothes and made his way over to them.

'Ahh Inspector good to see you,' Samson welcomed him as he approached through the sea of activity.

'And you, what updates can you give me?' the Inspector asked through a mouth of prawn salad sandwich.

'Well, lots of finds in the soil from the mound, no remains yet, not sure if that is a good result for you or a bad result.'

'It fits my new hypothesis,' he informed them, starting to eat another sandwich as Mavis arrived with his tray of tea.

'There you are Inspector!' she flustered, placing the tray down on the table. 'Enjoy!' she called to him as she rushed off to see to another customer.

'Thank you!' he called after her. He began pouring a cup of tea when Drew approached.

'Inspector, everything well I hope?' he asked. Their voices were raised over the din of the pub's occupants as soldiers and villagers rubbed shoulders comfortably.

'Yes Drew, all well. How goes things here?'

'Yes, the men are just about ready to leave but I thought I had better warn you, there's a journalist asking a lot of questions.'

'Wonderful, local or national?' the Inspector replied to Drew's surprise. He wasn't used to having media interest in cases, and had always presumed it to be a negative thing.

'Well, there's a chap from the BBC desperately trying to get someone to talk to him, but no one seems sure what they can and can't tell him so they're all staying quiet.'

'Good to hear. Point me in his direction and I shall field the questions,' he finished his sandwich and picked up his mug of tea, then Drew lead him over to where the man from the BBC stood trying to casually bribe some information out of a group of soldiers by offering them cigarettes. One of them saw the Inspector approaching.

'He's the bloke you want to talk to,' he informed him, accepting the cigarette and lighting it quickly.

'Indeed, I am the bloke you want to talk to,' the Inspector informed him.

'Finally,' the journalist sighed. 'John Harper BBC, what exactly have you found in the woods?' he asked immediately.

'Your cooperation in this would be most welcomed,' the Inspector informed him, ignoring his question.

'We have discovered a major archaeological site. Hidden in the woods are some standing stones, and we are currently busy clearing them for viewing by the public. Unfortunately the site is not yet safe, however I have prepared a statement and have some photographs for you...' He reached into his ever present case and removed a brown envelope which he held out to the journalist. The man took hold of it, but the Inspector did not let go. The two men stood looking at each other, holding the envelope between them.

'Journalists will be allowed access to the site, once we have finished with it, which should be within the next few days. This will then be a story of national interest,' the Inspector continued. 'So I congratulate you on getting here so early.'

'Has this got anything to do with the missing men? The Mayor and the Sergeant, what's his name, Banks?' the journalist smiled, hoping to rile the Inspector by showing how much he knew.

'It is indeed connected to the disappearance of those men, and to the appearance of a body in the woods near here a few days ago,' the Inspector nodded. His tone had changed, he was suddenly quiet yet domineering. 'The case is nearing its conclusion, which is why it is vitally important that I must ask you to...'

'Not file the story until the case is over,' the journalist finished for him. He realised suddenly the authority the Inspector carried.

'Indeed. Please do not publish any details until the case is finished and I am gone,' the Inspector asked him commandingly. 'Doing so might compromise my investigation. This is a case of top secrecy, do you understand?' The journalist swallowed, suddenly feeling a little out of his depth.

'Yes sir,' he replied, trying to keep up the pretence of confidence.

'All is explained in the here,' the Inspector finished with a smile, letting go of the envelope. He returned to his usual self, much to the relief of John Harper.

'Are you going to tell me anything else?' he asked.

'I am not,' the Inspector told him simply, displaying his usual mix of overarching authority and friendliness. Knowing when he was defeated, the journalist nodded, accepting the situation.

'Well, at least that's better than nothing' he conceded. 'Thank you, err...'

'Inspector. You may call me Inspector,' the Inspector informed him.

'Well, thank you Inspector.' He tapped the envelope and made his way through the throngs of people to the door. Drew and the Inspector watched him leave.

'Do you think he'll be back for more details?' Drew asked.

'Hopefully,' The Inspector replied. 'If he's a good journalist he will. My bet is he's on his way up to the stones now.' Drew did little to hide his surprise.

'You want this open to the public? You want people here?'

'My dear Drew, it is the secretiveness of this town that has caused all this to be hidden in the first place. By opening up to the outside world we can stop the stones from ever becoming lost again.' Drew pondered this for a moment and realised he had a point.

'I expected a bigger fight from the town's people,' the Inspector informed him. 'All these strangers descending on the place, but they've been nothing but welcoming.

'They are all tired of being held captive by the copse,' Drew replied.

'Yes, and hiding from the ghouls they have created for themselves that dwell within it,' the Inspector added. He was still holding his tea and he took another swig.

'They are welcoming the change because they know, like I did, that your arrival here would mean no more hiding. The secrets of the copse are finally giving themselves up,' Drew told him. They stood in contemplation for a moment while the Inspector enjoyed his tea.

'So do you think there are ghouls hiding in the copse?' Drew asked.

'There certainly is something in the trees,' the Inspector admitted.

'And tonight I hope we can find out what it might be,' he revealed.

'We?' Drew asked, a little reservedly.

'I will need your help yes. If you could see your way to meeting me at the stones tonight at about half past midnight and we will see what we can see.'

'Of course, I will be there,' Drew confirmed with a nod, though he did wonder at the strange hour. Just then they were approached by the Major.

'Afternoon gents,' he said.

'Major,' the Inspector welcomed him with a smile.

'The men are all ready to head back, so we'll be off in a few moments,' he informed them.

'Excellent,' the Inspector replied. 'Drew, I will get a lift up the road with you if that's alright?'

'Of course,' Drew agreed.

'Well, see you up there.' The Major nodded and turned to his men.

'Ok lads let's move out,' he called to them, and the men marched noisily out, halving the population of The Green Man. They left in their wake a much quieter and emptier place.

'Ready when you are Inspector,' Drew informed him, lowering his voice in the new hush that had covered the bar.

'Of course,' the Inspector finished his tea and they followed the soldiers outside. The bus was already making its way toward the site when they exited out into the cold wet air.

'The cars just over here,' Drew informed him, but before they could cross they were met by a fretful and frightened Cara, on her lead but with no Atkins in sight. She made her way directly to the Inspector and cowered behind his legs, whimpering and shaking.

'There there Cara it's alright,' the Inspector stroked her gently as he spoke.

'Odd to see her out without Atkins, he's usually so careful with her,' Drew remarked, immediately fearing the worst.

'Well perhaps we should return her to him,' the Inspector suggested. He picked up her lead and walked her over to Drew's car. She jumped in without any need for coercion and took up residence on the back seat. The Inspector and Drew climbed into the front and within a few minutes they had reached Atkins' small house. The Inspector took Cara and knocked on the door. Cara barked and scratched to be let in, and after a few minutes with no reply the Inspector returned with her to the car.

'Best get in contact with the station, see if Atkins has reported in today,' he told Drew.

'Right you are Inspector.' He picked up the radio and called in.

'Any news from Atkins today?' he asked the Constable who was operating the station radio.

'No not since lunch, he usually does his beat along the Copse Road about this sort of time if you're looking for him.'

'We are, and we have Cara here with us, there's no sign of him,' Drew informed them. He glanced to the Inspector who had a look of concerned contemplation on his face.

'I hope Atkins hasn't become our next missing person,' he informed Drew calmly. 'We should go and check, then drop in on Doctor Sparrow and the others.' Drew nodded.

'We'll drive up the copse road where he walks his beat,' Drew informed the Constable on the radio. 'Then the Inspector and I are going to check on Sparrow.' The radio crackled and fizzed.

'Understood, I'll let them know over at Nettlewood.'

'Over and out,' Drew told him

'Roger, over and out.' The radio fell silent again and without a word Drew started the car and drove them toward the back road out of town. It wasn't too far, and Drew slowed as they prowled the outskirts of the trees. Cara hid on her seat, not daring to look out. They drove with the upmost care, keeping watchful eyes on their surroundings.

'No sign?' Drew asked.

'Nothing,' the Inspector replied, though he wondered if that's what they should have expected. 'Let's head over to the Surgery.' Drew put on his flashing blue lights and sped them back into town. At their arrival they leapt out of the car and ran to the Surgery to be greeted by a hand written note taped to the glass inside the door. It read;

'All appointments cancelled today, surgery closed.'

'Not what I was hoping for,' the Inspector said, trying the door but finding it locked.

'No, this is ominous,' Drew agreed. The Inspector rapped on the glass and a lady appeared with a scornful face that vanished when she saw Drew's uniform.

'Mrs Howes, the receptionist,' Drew informed the Inspector quickly while she unlocked the door.

'Are you here about Doctor Sparrow?' she asked nervously.

'We are,' the Inspector informed her. 'I'm an Inspector, down from Scotland Yard. I presume from the note and your face that he is missing?'

'Yes, I haven't telephoned the police though, I thought you might be here to give me some awful news,' she told them, stifling a worried sob.

'No, we have no news, but we are looking for him, don't worry,' he reassured her with a warm smile. 'For now wait here, and report to us immediately should you see or hear from him,' the Inspector asked gently.

'Of course,' she replied, glad to have a purpose of sorts toward the Doctor's recovery.

'We'll need to get back on to the station and let them know,' the Inspector informed Drew. Drew nodded and they returned to the car, where Drew called in the situation.

'Go ahead Drew, over,' came Frank's voice. It was full of trepidation. He had come to the radio for updates when the Constable had passed him the news.

'Confirm we now have two more missing persons, Atkins and Sparrow both now unaccounted for, over.' The line went quiet for a moment.

'Roger that Drew, we presume the Inspector is aware of this? Over.' Both men could hear the Sergeant's concern.

'Roger, He's with me now, looking for them,' Drew replied. 'We will need to get someone round to Mrs Sparrow's house to get a statement from her,' Drew informed Frank. He turned to the Inspector suddenly.

'If that's alright with you Inspector?' he double-checked.

'Yes that's top work Drew,' he replied. 'Could you check if any of the men Sergeant Gates sent to follow the members of the Mayor's party have reported in yet?' the Inspector asked hopefully. Drew nodded.

'Anyone reported in regarding the other suspects Sarge?' The radio crackled between the gaps in their conversation.

'Yes Drew. One's back now hold on.' There was a break in the conversation while Frank hollered for his colleague to come to the radio.

'Barnes here sir,' came a new voice when the radio crackled back to life. 'I've been trying to track you down for the last hour and a half.' The Inspector took the radio receiver from Drew.

'I apologise, the Inspector informed him. 'We were at The Green Man, please tell me what you saw of Atkins.'

'Yes sir, he walked his beat, then went home for lunch. Nothing strange there like. Then he went out again and I followed him. Then he takes a turn into the woods, and promptly vanished. No trace at all, weirdest thing I've seen. I did start into the woods to see if I could spot him, but he was gone.' The Inspector thought momentarily.

'Whereabouts did he enter the trees?' he asked.

'Down the Copse road, if you turn left out Collyers Avenue he went in down there on the right about 'undred feet.'

'Thank you Constable.' The Inspector scribbled the location down in his notebook. 'Please could you track down your colleagues and have them contact Drew with the whereabouts of the men they are following?'

'Yes sir can do,' came the crackled reply.

'Thank you, over and out.' The Inspector hung up the receiver. 'Well Drew, let's head back to the stones quickly, see what progress they have made.' Drew had hoped they would keep looking for Atkins and the others, and wondered at the importance the Inspector was putting on the stones in the trees.

79.

The body of Sergeant Banks fell over clumsily and then stood again, pulling itself laboriously to its feet before continuing to trudge slowly and painfully through the trees.

'Where?' he sobbed weakly. 'Where? Where?'

'We must find that man. He will be amongst the trees,' he replied to himself in a loud, clear voice that was not his own. What remained of Banks' mind watched as his body was carried against its will through the trees. The energy that inhabited his body had finally overcome him, and he was no longer in control. The voice he imprisoned, that his family had imprisoned for generations, had broken free. Banks now could only watch helplessly as the energy that had been trapped within searched the copse for their means of escape. Banks saw the copse flit and skirt about them, it faded in and out like in a haze. The pain of possession racked him and tore him apart. He knew not how long he had endured this torture, how much longer he could endure it, nor how much longer there was to endure. He wept and wept, defeated, overcome, hijacked and raped.

'No, no, why...' he cried, trying to scream, hoping to find help, but knowing that ultimately it was useless. The trees stretched on and on, a corridor of trunks without end, without day or night, without conclusion or meaning. Through it tripped the bloody body of Banks, its new possessor grappling to control it after such a long time suffocated under Banks' will.

The woods skimmed passed them, out of sync, out of time. They wandered through a world between the trunks, on a different angle to trees. The woods were empty and unceasing, like their search.

80.

Drew and the Inspector returned to the mound, where they found the man from the BBC talking to the policeman at the tape.

'Drew, can you wait in the car for any radio contact regarding the missing men? Come and find me if you hear anything.' Drew nodded, rather glad not to be trudging through the rain and sticky mud back to the stones.

'Of course Inspector, if you insist,' Drew replied. The Inspector opened the door and the rain immediately began trying to blow into the car. The Inspector sighed.

'I will be back as soon as I can,' he informed him as the cold bit his cheeks. 'I just need to get things ready here.' He climbed out and closed the door, then opened the back door.

'I think I have a job for you Cara, come on girl out you come.' Cara jumped out of the car with the Inspector, leaving Drew alone with his thoughts and the radio.

'Afternoon!' the Inspector called to the journalist, who looked utterly fed up standing in the rain, failing to get information from two very quiet policemen. The Inspector signalled for them to follow him and they moved back from the line to talk privately.

'Afternoon officers,' he spoke to them quietly. 'No trouble I hope?' he nodded surreptitiously toward the journalist.

'No Inspector, this lad's from the press,' he pointed him out to the Inspector. 'BBC no less.'

'Yes we met earlier. I trust you've told him everything you know?' the Inspector asked with a smile.

'Well, that ain't going to be much!' the older one joked and they both shared a laugh. 'We've only told him some stones have been found and that you're excavatin' them. Is there more to tell then?' he asked the Inspector. The Inspector pulled out a brown envelope for them from his case.

'This is the press pack I gave him earlier. I asked him not to open it but I am sure by now he has digested the contents. This is everything he knows, so tell him no more than this.' The men nodded.

'Finally something to do,' the older one joked again, removing the sheets and beginning to read.

'I have something else for you,' he informed them, handing the younger one Cara's lead. 'Some company.'

'Well hello Cara,' the older man said, recognising her. 'Where's our Atkins then?' he asked rather surprised.

'Missing,' the Inspector informed him shortly. 'Along with the Mayor, the Doctor and the Sergeant. That is something we will not be informing the man from the BBC,' he informed them. 'Though he already knows about the Mayor and Banks.

'Right you are,' they nodded in understanding, more than a little concerned about the missing men. The Inspector gave Cara a playful stroke of the head and then left them to it. Cara looked up at him adoringly with lively black eyes and wagged her tail excitedly. He stalked up the path through the trees, his Wellingtons squelching through the mud. When he reached the stones he found a widespread operation of clearance, as little by little the mud that covered the site was gradually removed.

'Oh no, this will never do,' the Inspector muttered to himself.

'Gentlemen if I can just have your attention for a moment,' he called to the men around the stones. The men stopped what they were doing and turned to listen.

'It is time we concentrate our efforts on clearing the two standing stones, and clearing a path to them through these remaining piles...' He indicated the piles he wanted removed with a pointed finger. '...and clearing the path out of the trees,' he informed them, indicating with his arms the course that he wanted the path to take.

'I need this path cleared before you can all go home tonight,' he called loudly to them, his voice echoing eerily between the trees, as if they too were listening, wanting to know what the next move would be. The men muttered reproachfully to themselves as they judged the amount of work they had to complete that evening. The Major stepped in and cut off their misgivings in an instant.

'You heard the man, don't just stand there looking pretty let's see some movement shall we?' he yelled at the top of his voice at them. They immediately jumped into action, quickly forming a busy line between the stones and the truck and shovelling soil toward it and on to the back. It began to fill with earth and the Inspector approached the Major.

'Do you think this amount of work will be an issue for them this evening?' he asked, rather worried it might be too much.

'We might need to break out the torches in a couple of hours when the sun sets, but we'll be able to get you your path,' the Major informed him. He studied him closely for a moment.

'Can I ask why the sudden need for a clear path to the stones?' he asked. 'And why the hurry to uncover them? They've been hidden hundreds of years so why the sudden rush now?' The Major, despite himself, was impressed with the Inspector and how he had handled the men over the last few days. He was intrigued as to what it was exactly that this man did, and what he had done to wield the power to arrange all that he had so quickly and effortlessly.

'If I'm honest with you Major,' the Inspector said quietly, as if sharing a secret. 'Do you promise not to tell?' The Major took a step closer.

'The truth is; I actually have no idea what is going on,' the Inspector told him quietly. 'Or what these stones are for, why they are here or how they are connected to the body. I really don't know or understand any of it.' The Major nodded, his attention captured.

'But I am very good at finding these sorts of things out, and I suppose that is why we have our hurry. I have to find out what it all means before some other poor soul meets his end in the copse,' he informed him. The Major smiled, glad to have had a moment with the Inspector he could call his own.

'If you want to know why, the real why, then the answer is that we are here in the interest of public safety. We are here for National Security.'

'And I suppose that's as good an explanation as I can ask for,' he replied. The Inspector smiled.

'Inspector!' came a call from the other end of the path. The Inspector turned to see Drew waving to him from the road side.

'Must be off.' He patted the Major on the shoulder and rushed off to Drew. The Major saluted him as he disappeared again.

'What news?' he asked as he approached. Drew waited until they were both in the car.

'The men have all come to the station with similar stories. One of them, looking for Charlie, hadn't seen him all day. When he failed to open up he went and checked, only to find he had gone. The back door was wide open so he thinks he might have slipped out through the back of his garden, which...'

'... Leads directly on to the woods,' the Inspector finished the sentence for him.

'Well, now I have set things in motion here we can start to check the points in the copse where the men vanished. Let's start with Atkins.'

'Of course,' Drew replied. He started the car, and they set off along the cold wet road.

81.

As Drew drove the Inspector removed one of the instruments from his bag, and upon flicking the power switch the needle quickly rose to the red. As they headed away from the stones it slowly sank down to the green and almost zero. The Inspector carefully noted the falls gradient on his map. He watched the needle intently and as they approached the area where they thought Atkins could have had entered the trees it slowly rose again.

'Here we go Drew, this is close enough,' the Inspector informed his unwitting partner, and Drew pulled up on the side of the muddy road. Before he exited he flicked a switch and the car's blue lights began spinning, so to warn other road users of their presence. They climbed out into the cold afternoon and began stalking along the trees, the Inspector flicking between the slowly climbing needle on his instrument and the border between the trees and the road. The needle suddenly jumped up, and the Inspector spotted some nettles bent back, as if someone had not long entered the trees.

'There was certainly some activity here recently.' he informed Drew, indicating the trace he had found.

'Oh yes.' Drew crouched down closer to get a better look. They both looked into the trees, but there was no sign of any movement.

'Shall we take a look?' the Inspector suggested, and began to carefully tread into the trees. Drew followed closely behind but was not quite as eager. Within a few yards the road was lost, and the trees surrounded them with their eerie presence.

'The reading is fading the deeper we go,' the Inspector mentioned, half to himself, as he fished the map out of his case and noted the time and location on it.

'What's causing it?' Drew asked.

'That I am not sure about, but it would appear that at the time of his disappearance, there was a huge surge of electromagnetic activity here. Let's have a quick look around before heading back to the car, you never know we might spot him.' The two men began walking further into the woods, the Inspector checking his instrument every few yards, but otherwise he kept his eyes closely on the ground and the trees about them in the hope of noticing something that might act as clue as to Atkins' location.

'Spotted anything?' he asked Drew hopefully.

'Nothing,' Drew replied.

'As I thought,' he nodded, not looking particularly surprised. 'Well let us not dwell here, we can head down to The Black Prince and see if the readings are similar. Drew nodded and they began heading out of the trees, but he realised that he had quickly become disoriented and relied on the Inspector to find their way back to the road. When they emerged he found they had travelled further through the copse than he had thought, and they had to trek back to the car. They were soon back in and on their way, and at arriving at The Black Prince they found Sam knocking at the door and peering through the glass.

'I'm afraid he will be shut for a while,' the Inspector informed him as they approached.

'Ahh, it's you again,' Sam replied quietly. He looked as though he may have already had a few before arriving. 'Where is he then?' he asked them with a smile and ruddy cheeks.

'No idea I'm afraid, but we are looking and I am hoping to find some clue here. Any idea how we can get into the back garden without clambering over the fence?' The Inspector asked.

'Yes, there's a gate round the other side, here I'll show you.' They followed him round the side of the pub and down an alley between it and the house next door. He leant an arm over a high fence at the back and after a moment of fiddling managed to slide a bolt to one side and let them in.

'Ahh thank you, you have saved me a lot of effort,' the Inspector said.

'Oh, no problem,' the man replied a little forlornly. Drew and the Inspector entered the garden and Sam followed them in, looking through the back door of the pub and not seeming to know what to do with himself next. The Inspector offered a friendly smile.

'You know, The Green Man is still open, they're very welcoming,' he informed him.

'Yes, I suppose,' Sam replied vaguely, and wandered back down the alley distractedly.

'Oh dear I do hope he'll be alright,' the Inspector said as he wandered away. 'Let's see what we can find then shall we?' he suggested, removing his device and beginning to traipse about the small garden. It was full of long grass, but the lawn was patchy and overgrown with weeds. A bench leant against one wall that looked as though it might collapse if anyone were to actually sit on it. The needle on the instrument slowly climbed, but did not make it very far on the scale. The residual energy was beginning to dissipate, the Inspector concluded.

'It would seem that Charlie entered the woods at roughly the same time as the others.' He marked his findings on the map, which was by now becoming covered in lines numbers and dates.

'I don't think we will garner anything else from visiting all the sites of disappearance,' the Inspector told Drew.

'And it's getting too dark to be able to see anything that might have been useful,' Drew pointed out.

'Indeed.' The Inspector thought for a moment. 'Shall we head back to the stones for now, I am hoping the concentrated efforts of the men up there will have prepared the ground for tonight and am eager to see their progress.'

'Of course,' Drew replied, glad to be heading out of the untidy garden. On the journey back the Inspector watched his instrument nervously, waiting to see if the needle would crawl up as they approached the stones. When it began moving again he breathed nervously, the reading was higher than before. He watched it until they parked, satisfied that the energy was still there. On their arrival at the stones they saw the men were beginning to fill their coach with their tools in the drizzle that had done its best to thwart their efforts all day. They were all worn out through their efforts, moving slowly and carefully through the encroaching dark. Drew and the Inspector soon found the Major rounding up the last of the men from around the stones.

'Ahh Inspector, hope this meets your satisfaction?' he asked. The Inspector began pacing the path out, getting an idea of its width. He whipped out his torch and flashed it around the cleared ground.

'Yes, this seems fine, thank you I appreciate the extra effort this evening.'

'Happy to help. See you in the morning.' He waved them goodbye and stalked off to the coach.

'Well Drew, I think that will do for today,' the Inspector announced. Drew was also clearly feeling the pressure of the long day they had had. 'I was hoping you might join me for dinner?' the Inspector asked.

'Well actually I had planned on meeting Casey at The Swan and Dove,' Drew replied then thought for a moment. 'But I am sure she wouldn't mind if you joined us.'

'That would be most agreeable. I will of course telephone her first to ensure she doesn't mind.'

'That would be appreciated,' Drew replied. Shall I pick you up in an hour? I'll need time to get home and change.' The Inspector checked his watch as they began walking back to the entrance.

'Yes that sounds good, see you at The Green Man about seven?' As they approached the path they heard the coach pull away into the night.

'Seven it is,' the Inspector agreed as they ducked under the blue police tape. The dark night and the unrelenting weather had finally forced all the spectators home, even the journalist had made an escape from it. The two Constables were sat in their patrol car at the side of the road, trying to keep warm. Their windows were open and both sat fitfully smoking cigarettes.

'Evening gentlemen,' the Inspector called to them as they approached.

'Ahh evening Inspector,' the elder Constable greeted him. 'Drew,' he called over his shoulder.

'You're welcome to finish here now, head off home,' he informed them.

'Are you sure sir?' the older one asked.

'Yes of course. It's an awful evening I am sure that you would rather be at home in the warm.'

'What do you want us to do with Cara here?' the younger asked, nodding to the sleeping dog in the back seat. The Inspector frowned, unsure exactly what he could do with her.

'I could take her if you like?' the Constable suggested. 'Kids would love a dog for a bit, until Atkins is found,' he added quickly.

'Of course, that would be most appreciated. Poor Cara, let's hope we can get Atkins back soon for her shall we?' the Inspector asked hopefully. 'Well good night gents.' The men nodded, chucking their cigarette butts away into the night and rolling their windows up. The Inspector and Drew stood for a moment and watched as they went on their way down the cold dark road toward their homes.

'Come on then Inspector, I'll drop you back at The Green Man,' Drew said, and they wandered back to the squad car.

82.

Drew's timing was impeccable, unlike that morning, and he and the Inspector both entered the bar of The Green Man simultaneously at precisely seven 'o' clock.

'Drew good evening!' the Inspector welcomed him with a surprised smile.

'Inspector hello, did you manage to speak to Casey?' Drew asked immediately.

'I did, she says she doesn't mind sharing you for one night but wants you all to herself tomorrow.' The Inspector replied with a knowing smile. 'Glad to see you two getting on so well,' he added. Drew could barely stifle his grin.

'All in the name of improving relationships with colleagues in other departments,' Drew replied seriously but with a hint of humour.

'Good man, very important we are all working together,' the Inspector smiled. He had noticed immediately that Drew had made more of an effort in his appearance tonight. He was dressed in quality shirt and trousers, the sort, the Inspector guessed, that were only worn for special occasions.

'While I applaud your efforts, I hope you don't feel too upset when she inevitably has to return to London,' the Inspector warned friendlily. Drew smiled, appreciating his consideration.

'Inspector I promise that you are worrying unnecessarily. I am bound to this town, just as she is bound to London. She has her world and I have mine, but we met, and we found something, so we are making the most of it while we can,' Drew replied happily.

'Well, as long as you two have things worked out then it's none of my business,' the Inspector nodded and left it at that.

'Shall we get going?' Drew suggested, obviously eager to see her again. They made their way outside and quickly located the car. The clouds were still brewing overhead, hemming the town in. The atmosphere felt crowded and claustrophobic.

'Did you explain that we would be continuing our investigations this evening?' Drew enquired as they climbed in.

'I did,' the Inspector replied, studying the clouds and hoping optimistically that the rain might stop for them.

The weather did not improve for their journey, and they arrived at The Swan and Dove wet and blustered by an incoming icy wind. On their arrival they removed their wet coats and made directly for the bar.

'Good evening Inspector, nice to see you again,' Abigail welcomed him warmly.

'And you,' the Inspector replied with a smile. 'What can I get you Drew?' the Inspector asked him.

'I think I had best stick with Coke tonight,' Drew replied.

'Right you are love, ice and a slice?' Abigail asked.

'Yes please,' Drew replied with a smile.

'And for you Inspector?'

'I'll have a pot of tea please,' the Inspector told her.

'No problem.' She opened a bottle of Coke for Drew and filled a glass with ice from a plastic container behind the bar. She put them both on to a clean dry towel on the bar advertising Guinness, and a small avalanche of fizz scurried down the bottle.

'I'll bring the tea over for you, I presume you'll be sitting with Casey?' Abigail asked nodding to Casey's regular table by the window. She fished a slice of lemon out of a jar for Drew and dropped it in on to the ice in the glass.

'We will indeed, thank you,' the Inspector confirmed, and they made their way over to the table. Casey was lounging nonchalantly in her chair flicking disinterestedly through a newspaper and sipping her wine. She looked up as they approached.

'Good evening Drew, Inspector,' she nodded to them. 'Nice of you to join us Inspector, to what do we owe the honour?'

'Oh, no particular reason,' the Inspector replied, making himself comfortable. 'Though an update would be nice, I just felt like a little company this evening, I hope you don't mind my gate-crashing your dinner.'

'Not at all, I'm interested to hear how the case is going,' she replied. Drew studied her carefully. He had been hoping they could have the evening to themselves, but she genuinely didn't seem to mind the Inspector's presence so he relaxed a little. He still half wished he could have had her to himself, but was happy to have the Inspector for company.

'Well, more men have disappeared without a trace,' the Inspector informed her.

'Oh dear, who's missing now?' Casey asked, rather shocked.

'So far today we have lost Constable Atkins, Doctor Sparrow, and Charlie the landlord from The Black Prince. Add these to the currently missing men and we are now missing everyone from the list of guests at the Mayor's house last Sunday night,' the Inspector informed her.

'And you think the men have gone into hiding? Are they connected with the body?' she asked.

'I don't believe they have gone into hiding, and they are connected to the body that Drew discovered, though I still am not sure how,' the Inspector admitted.

'We also discovered a pair of standing stones hidden in the copse,' he added lightly. Casey did a double take for a moment.

'Standing stones?' she asked, a little confused. 'How do you mean?'

'We found two standing stones, hidden under a pile of earth amongst the trees.' Drew told her.

'Like Stonehenge?' she asked, agog.

'Yes, but nowhere near as many stones,' Drew nodded.

'At least not yet,' the Inspector interjected. 'Who knows what they might find up there.'

'They're huge,' Drew continued.

'Who found them?' Casey asked.

'The Inspector found the mound, in the middle of a forgotten corner of the copse, whilst out on a walk,' Drew informed her with an eyebrow raised doubtfully that the Inspector pretended not to notice. Casey stifled a giggle.

'Well, that sounds very exciting, any chance I could get up there and have a look?' she asked hopefully.

'Yes of course, why don't you come up tomorrow?' Drew asked. 'If that's alright Inspector?' he checked respectfully, not wanting to get above his station.

'Well, tomorrow's events depend on how things go tonight, but you are welcome to come and see the site, the stones are a wonder to behold if you think you can spare the time.'

'Well, fascinating as the decaying bodies you have provided me with are, I am sure an hour out of my day would not make much difference.'

'How goes the search for bones to bury?' the Inspector asked.

'I've sorted through them all. There were a few I want to look at before Sunday but otherwise they are ready for you,' she told the Inspector, pleased with herself.

'Well why don't I telephone you at the morgue tomorrow when we know how the time stands and we'll arrange a pick up?' the Inspector suggested.

'Good idea,' Casey agreed, just as Abigail arrived with the Inspector's pot of tea. She set it on the table for him.

'Well my dears, are you eating with us tonight?' she asked Drew and

the Inspector.
'We will be yes,' the Inspector replied for them. 'May I have the roast lamb with all the trimmings I noticed on your specials board?' he asked.
'Of course my love,' she whipped out her notepad and began scribbling.
'What about you two, what can I get you?' She turned to Casey first.
'I'll have the liver and onions please,' Casey replied without having to study the menu.
'And I'll have the lamb with the Inspector I think,' Drew replied.
'A good choice,' the Inspector concurred, nodding.
'Right you are my dear, it won't be long,' Abigail smiled and made her way through to the kitchen where she barked instructions to her long-suffering husband. The food was with them in record time, piping hot and smelling delicious. The dining area was quiet this evening, the salesman had moved on to new hunting ground, the only other patron with them being a lonely local sat in his regular corner nursing his pint of ale and smoking roll-ups.
'So how long have you been in the force, Inspector?' Drew asked as they tucked in. He realised suddenly how little he knew about him, and was feeling confident enough in his company now to pry further into his personal life.
'Longer than I care to remember,' the Inspector replied, as vague as ever. 'I started off in a similar position to you Drew, local bobby on the beat, so to speak.' His eyes clouded over dreamily for a moment as he was lost to a reminisce.
'Funny isn't it, how time changes us?' he asked abstractedly. 'Such subtle movement, such small changes, building day after day. Then you turn around and you suddenly see behind you all the changes at once, all the people you have been, the young man you used to be, that you had forgotten. Left behind in the pursuit of growth, in the hurricane that is our continual wish to improve ourselves and the society we are thrown into. The casualties in this fight are ourselves, or at least, our former selves. The people we used to be are a foundation on which we blindly build, not knowing what will become of us, or where our adventures will lead.'
Both Drew and Casey had stopped eating for a moment to listen, it was as if the Inspector had let his guard down for a moment, as if he had forgotten where he was and whom he was talking to.
'The best we can hope is that in our short time we can add a little of ourselves to the hurricane. That it is a little calmer, or at least it is a

little easier for the next generation to cope with. And yet our lives will flash past us before we even realise we are here.' He smiled an ironic wry smile for a moment and they all fell into thought.

'I could of course advise you two to not let it happen to you. Advise that you should enjoy every moment, embrace life and the challenges it throws your way, but alas, I am afraid that the wisdom of the young would overshadow any guidance I could pass on. You are of course already walking paths of your own. All I can offer is what little I have learnt on my path.' He spoke as though he might never see either of them again, and these might be his last words. He paused to chew appreciatively on his dinner.

'I think lamb has always been my favourite food,' he told them suddenly. 'It is good to take moments to enjoy the things in life that mean something to you. Good food, good company.' He waved a hand at his company.

'Such a shame that it is only through experiencing life's monsters that we come to appreciate the beauty.' It sounded to Drew as if perhaps the Inspector had experienced more monsters than anyone.

'The trick of course is not to allow them to take over. You have to stop and see the beauty, or they win. They can shape the small, seemingly insignificant changes that shape us, and before we know it we are monsters too.' He put down his fork and poured another cup of tea. He spoke airily as to keep the atmosphere light and friendly.

'And we wouldn't want that,' Casey interjected raising her wine glass elegantly as means of a toast.

'Quite,' Drew agreed. 'To not becoming monsters.' They raised their glasses and cup, and relaxed into the evening. The Inspector didn't take the conversation any further. He spent the evening taking great pleasure in watching Drew and Casey enjoying each other's company. They all chattered and laughed, the Inspector surprising Drew and Casey with his occasional bursts of openness. He allowed his guard to be lowered and the evening was happier for it. After what seemed only a fleeting moment the Inspector was complaining that his tea was cold, and on checking his watch Drew realised the hour had slipped to ten 'o' clock.

'We'd best be getting back Inspector,' Drew informed him regrettably. He was unwilling to leave the company of Casey, and nervous as to what lay ahead for him in the remainder of the night.

'Yes, we should indeed Drew thank you,' they stood and prepared for the off. Casey stood with them and waited for them to get ready.

'I'll put dinner on my tab, Inspector,' Casey informed him as he pulled on his coat.

'Ah yes, thank you. I'll just visit the gents, won't be a moment Drew.' The Inspector headed off leaving the two of them alone. There was a moment while they waited for the toilet door to close, before they turned to each other in silence, which was immediately broken by a nervous laugh from Casey.

'Should we take this opportunity to embrace life, and the opportunities it throws our way?' she suggested, moving closer to him and slipping her arms around his waist. Drew smiled but she didn't give him a chance to reply, kissing him gently on the lips. It was over all too quickly for Drew's liking, and as she pulled away and stood apart from him, the toilet door opened and the Inspector returned.

'Well gentlemen, an absolute pleasure as always,' she informed them. 'Hopefully we shall see each other tomorrow.'

'Yes, we shall be in touch,' the Inspector agreed. 'Good night Casey.'

'Good night Inspector,' she nodded to him and he turned to go.

'Good night Abigail,' he called to the bar as they walked passed.

'Yes, good night Inspector,' she called back from her crossword behind the bar.

'Good night Drew,' Casey called after him as he left. He turned to see her dark sparkling eyes staring at him for one last moment before heading out into the cold winter air.

'Well that was a fine meal,' the Inspector noted as they pulled away into the night. He looked out at the bleak sky between Nettlewood and Firestone.

'I wonder what the weather will hold out for us tonight,' he mused to the blackened canopy. The cars heater did little to warm them against the chill.

'It might clear later,' Drew offered optimistically, but it was difficult for him to add any enthusiasm to the idea.

'What is it exactly I will be doing tonight? he asked as the car trundled through the desolate landscape.

'Well, you will be my guardian, of sorts,' the Inspector explained. 'I will be attempting to do something that will help me calculate what is happening in the woods around Firestone. I have tried something similar a few days ago and I got into a little bother. This time I'm being more careful, but it is likely that I may need some assistance following my attempt. More will become clear later, I hope.'

They arrived at the Firestone roundabout and headed straight on toward town. The streets were hollow and empty, the town had lost all colour. A sickening grey had swept over, leaving it ashen and cold. They arrived at The Green Man in silence, the cold bearing into the car with them. The Inspector opened his door and climbed out. He turned to Drew.

'Meet you up there,' he said with a comforting smile through the dark.

'Yes, see you later then Inspector,' Drew replied. The Inspector watched him drive off into the black night before entering the pub. A few of the locals remained even at this late hour, though as last orders approached they realised they would soon be forced out into the cold dark night. The door creaked shut behind him, and Mavis appeared behind the bar from the side door as if she had heard its slow whining closure.

'Oh good evening Inspector what can I get you?' she asked with a smile as she manned the bar.

'Oh nothing at the moment thank you, I just wanted to warn you that I will be heading out tonight quite late, and returning even later. I will do my best not to disturb you of course but wanted you to know in case you wondered what I was up to.'

'Well thank you for letting me know, we have heard you creeping out on a few nights, we are beginning to wonder if you sleep at all!' she half joked.

'Well Her Majesty is a strict time keeper I have to say,' he quipped back. She humoured him with a polite laugh. 'Hope I didn't disturb you too much.'

'We don't mind you coming and going, all I ask is you make sure the doors locked tight behind you when you go out, which you obviously do any way.'

'Of course, I wouldn't dream of doing anything otherwise,' he replied. 'Now if you'll excuse me I shall be in my room,' he smiled.

'Yes Inspector good night.' Mavis nodded and he made his way up to his room. He was comfortable enough now with the lay out of the building to be able to move silently along its corridors without switching the lights on. He hated disturbing his hosts with his late night investigation and much preferred to move about at night without making any noise. Safely in his room he made straight for the bathroom and poured himself a pint of water, which he drank down in one go. He then drank another, and another. He then moved to the dresser in his room, and opened a drawer, inside which were a selection of pills in bottles. He took two blue tablets from a small orange bottle and put them in his mouth one at a time, washing them both down with a pint of water each. He then took two red ones from a separate bottle. He then sat studying his map and carrying out some careful calculations as to his chances of exiting through the 111 later.

83.
The trees around the stones shook and split. They watched and ached, expectant, wanting. The stones stood tall and proud, defying their hiding place. Suddenly, through the black cold trees, an engine roared. Sliding across the muddy path a van's wheels skidded and scraped as it made its way to the standing stones. The van stopped, the sound of its engine spreading out amongst the trees. From the cab two men exited, leaving the motor running. They leapt down and slammed their doors behind them. The noise echoed horribly amongst the branches. The trees studied and probed them, but their step was brash and determined. No fear stood between them and their job. They marched to the back of the van and threw open the doors. It was a large van, not unlike one a removal firm would use. They were dressed all in black, and with their black van their shapes were barely visible in the night. One of the men climbed into the back of the van and carefully wheeled a large wooden crate on to a loading platform that the second man was preparing. The crate was larger and heavier than the man, standing eight feet tall and four feet squared. When the platform was prepared the man positioned the crate on it, and the second man pressed a button on the side of the van. The platform's electric engine emitted a high pitched hum as it struggled under the weight, but it slowly began to lower itself toward the ground. The man then moved the large crate awkwardly through the mud with his colleague's help. When it was positioned securely the two men returned to the van and put the platform back to a safe position. They then returned to the cab of the van and drove away back into the darkness. The trees returned to silence, but now something new stood between them. Something unknown, but they would not have to wait long to discover what it was.

84.

Drew arrived at the site earlier than he had arranged to, his neatly pressed uniform under Wellingtons and wax jacket. He followed his torchlight up the muddy path toward the stones, the rain that had battered him persistently from the moment he had closed his front door had thankfully retreated. The clouds gathered about the copse, as if being kept at bay by an unseen foe. The moon suddenly emerged from behind a whisp of vaporous cloud, a thin sliver of silver in the sky. For a moment Drew was taken back to Sunday night and a vision of the body flashed in front of him on the dark mud for a moment, doing little to raise his enthusiasm for his night in the copse. He stalked carefully and silently up the path, resisting the urge to turn back. Crouching and creeping he slowly approached the stones, unsure if he was hiding in the trees or from them. As he approached the rock columns that protruded so unnaturally from the Earth he noticed the flash of a torch, and saw up ahead a point of light bobbing about the stones. He approached carefully and quietly, the feeling of trespassing creeping in again, as if he was unwelcome. The Inspector heard him from a distance despite his care at being quiet, but he waited until he was closer to welcome him. He stood now and turned to greet him.

'Evening Drew, so glad you could join me,' the Inspector welcomed him in a loud voice. 'I appreciate your punctuality.' The sounds of his words echoed and clattered amongst the trees.

'Evening Inspector,' Drew whispered back, relieved to find the Inspector there. He shone his torch at the equipment the Inspector was setting up. 'What's all this then?' he asked. He flashed his torch at the area around the stones to see that the Inspector had been placing a series of spiked metal tubes into the ground. The tubes were connected by a thick cable that came from a heavy looking battery pack. The Inspector had arranged them in a large circle around the two stones.

'It is a Frequency Modulator,' the Inspector explained. 'Also known as a Field Enhancer. It will, I hope, ease the current erratic nature of the surrounding frequencies and create one large and safe enough for me to exit through.' Drew thought for a moment.

'I'm afraid I don't fully understand,' he replied honestly, looking about him. 'Where are you going?' he asked.

'I am not sure, but I have a feeling that the missing men have been pulled somewhere beyond here, beyond the trees, and these stones.

A place separate to the copse, yet bound to it. The trees anchor it here somehow. It is a phenomenon of the same energy that is causing all the bodies to appear; the energy I have been detecting on my devices. I am hoping if I can enter this place beyond the trees I may learn how to stop it.' Drew still did not fully understand, but assumed the Inspector knew what he was doing. If anyone other than the Inspector had explained such things to him he would have thought them mad. The Inspector stopped preparing the Field Enhancer and turned to face him.

'Why do you need me here? How can I help?' Drew asked, realising this might be more useful information.

'Well, first of all you can help me get this open,' the Inspector suggested, a mixture of excitement and trepidation lined his words. He flashed his torch into a dark corner of the area and illuminated a huge wooden crate that Drew hadn't noticed hidden in the background.

'My my, what's in there?' Drew asked.

'A suit,' the Inspector replied, and casually leant down to his case. To Drew's surprise he removed a crowbar, and headed over to the crate. Drew followed, and watched as the Inspector used the crowbar to begin prising open one of the sides from the large wooden crate. Drew helped and with their combined strength the side was off after a few minutes work. They propped it up against the crate, and Drew tried to make out what the strange shape was lurking inside where it was too dark see.

'I have been through something similar to this before, and when I emerged I was, unwell,' the Inspector explained when they caught their breath. 'I was under nourished, dehydrated, and exhausted, but I had been unprepared for the journey. This time I have taken some very serious precautions by arranging for this suit. Part of those precautions is having you here.'

Drew nodded, hoping he would soon learn what he was to do.

'If my calculations are correct I should disappear and reappear in the same place.' He pointed at the space between the stones. 'There should not be more than twenty four hours between those two events. If there is, I need you to call this telephone number and make them aware. They will help.' He pulled a card from his faithful briefcase that stood nearby.

'Keep this number safe,' he urged him. For a moment they both held the card. The moment lingered, Drew stared deep into his eyes.

415

'I will, Inspector,' Drew replied nervously. The Inspector let it go with a nod and Drew stashed it in a waterproof pocket of his jacket. 'When I reappear I do not know what sort of a state I will be in,' the Inspector informed him. His tone was serious, business-like. 'Please ensure I get back to my room at The Green Man safely, and that I receive medical attention from Casey, should I need it.' Gone was the moment of openness they had shared over dinner, now the Inspector had work to do.

'Of course,' Drew replied, accepting the responsibility without hesitation, still mystified as to what it all meant, but determined to take care of this man should he need to. The Inspector stood and studied the rods he had entered into the ground, then referred to a page of complicated calculations that he produced from his pocket. He measured out the rods carefully with a tape measure, and took several readings from one of his devices. He studied the batteries and turned some important looking knobs.

'Yes, I think that all seems to be in the right place,' he muttered to himself, satisfied everything was how it needed to be. 'Let's switch it on shall we?' he asked Drew.

'Yes, I'm eager to see what it will do,' Drew replied with a nod.

The Inspector flicked a switch, and the power from the battery began to emanate through the thick wire and down into the rods. As they warmed they began to glow an eerie orange. Drew watched them, wondering if this was what the Inspector had been expecting.

'Yes, look, it's working!' the Inspector suddenly gasped. Drew looked up and realised he wasn't talking about the rods but about the stones, or rather the space between the stones. A film had appeared between them. The oil slick that the Inspector had seen earlier had returned. It was ever changing, flowing. It glowed ultra violet, slowly growing in brightness. Drew was transfixed, he had never seen anything so beautiful in his life. The Inspector removed an instrument from his bag and began taking measurements.

'Yes, as I'd feared, it is growing again. If we don't act fast we might not be able to stop it from bursting.'

'Bursting?' Drew asked.

'Bursting, or striking. I am not sure how to describe what it does,' the Inspector informed him. 'But this I am sure is what is causing the bodies to appear in the copse. The energy builds up, it has nowhere to go. It is blocked. I thought that by removing the soil we would allow it to be released, but in fact it is now just building up quicker, because the soil held it back.

'So now you plan to enter it to see if you can find out why it is still blocked?' Drew asked, shocked.

'That is my main reason for entering. I should make it clear Drew, up to now this sort of phenomena has only been only theoretical. For it to come into existence is extremely improbable. There is something about the stones in the copse that draws an energy. It interacts with the magnetic field, it causes air pressure to drop, and it allows this to happen.' He gestured at the iridescent film between the stones that they had both been marvelling. He took a moment to enjoy its beauty, before reaching for his camera and beginning to take pictures.

'We have no idea what it is or where it came from, or how it got here,' he informed Drew meaningfully. 'It is what we call a 111. The Department of External Affairs has been aware of their theoretical existence for a while, and we have prepared for them. As far as I know this is the only one that has ever been recorded, and we are all rather excited about it.'

'Do you think you would know if there had been another one? Would they tell you?' Drew asked. This was a poignant question and the Inspector had to think for a moment.

'I think they would have told me by now if there had ever been another case like this. Any information they could give that would increase my chances of going out through it, and coming back again, would have been passed my way already. As they have not shared any such information with me, I think it is safe to say this is the first.'

He began fiddling with something in the crate, and Drew held his torch up to help, illuminating a large white object, of such an odd shape he wasn't sure if it was one large thing or many small things stacked up.

'This 111 seems to be accompanied by several 347's,' the Inspector told Drew. 'A 347 is a set of circumstances that seem to suggest some as yet unidentifiable sentient consciousness.' Drew digested these words for a moment.

'A lifeform?' he asked. 'Alien life?'

'Yes, sort of,' the Inspector said, pleased Drew had worked it out. 'We call them 347's for short.' He had finished his preparations.

'I'd stand back if I were you, I haven't driven one of these before,' the Inspector warned. Drew nodded and put greater distance between him and the crate while the Inspector fiddled for a moment with something unseen, then a door swung down revealing a small opening, and releasing a bright white light out into the area around the Inspector. It cast his shadow large and looming about them, like a giant black creature filling the area, carpeting the mud and the creeping up the trees. The Inspector took a strong grip of something on the outside of the object, then pulled himself into it, the door closing automatically behind him, robbing the area of light again and plunging Drew once more back into darkness.

Drew waited for an anxious moment, wondering if he should do something, but lost as to what that something should be. As he waited, the object began to emit a low hum that echoed quietly around the area. Drew strained his eyes through the dark, shining the torch beam toward the crate to try and see what was happening, when small pinpricks of light started to illuminate the inner crate, and the unidentifiable shape within suddenly gained meaning. It suddenly revealed itself as a protective suit of monstrous proportions. It filled the crate completely, with the back facing him. As Drew watched the suit was becoming more active, then to his amazement it rose from the ground and floated in the crate. Drew stood in shock and watched as the Inspector piloted it out of the crate and turned it to face the stones. At the front was a large domed windscreen. The surface was mirrored and Drew wondered how the Inspector was able to see through it. The suit was perfect gleaming white. It looked plastic to Drew but he could not tell what it was made of. It had bulbous legs and arm compartments, marked with black rings around the elbows, knees and hips where the different sections met. He had watched, along with the rest of the world, the moon landings just a few months ago, and the similarity between the astronauts' suits and this one was obvious. It seemed to Drew however that this suit seemed much sturdier, and much more advanced. Drew reached into the Inspector's case and found his camera, and began taking photographs. Although he hadn't been asked, he presumed the Inspector would want the moment recorded. As he snapped the suit began moving again, heading straight for the stones. Drew walked to the other side of the stones and took pictures of it slowly approaching. As he watched it reached the thin film, but it did not stop. The Inspector guided the suit carefully, and as Drew watched he exited through the space between the stones.

85.
The Inspector opened the hatch on the back to study the interior of the suit and found inside two large holes for his legs. He pulled himself up and dropped his legs in, finding two hard flat surfaces at the bottom for his feet to stand on. He shifted his weight and tried to get comfortable on the hard red leather seating, and as he did he noticed the door close automatically and seal him in with a satisfying 'pssst' sound. He studied the spacious cockpit with an impressed air. Inside was cool and bright. There were holes that he could put his arms into enable him to control the arms of the suit, but there was space enough in front of him to control the dashboard. Different coloured flashing buttons were set into the white plastic around a huge glass window. A small screen afforded him a view of the copse behind him, and he could just make out Drew peering through the dark wondering what was going on. The dashboard was awash with levers, dials and buttons. There were choke like devices protruding from the centre, to regulate speed and altitude. Around the levers were dials and screens giving readouts as to the wellbeing of the suit, and its occupant. More dials showed the condition of the environment inside and out. He opened a drawer on the underside of the dashboard and removed a set of laminated cards with instructions on them. He studied the first, and began pushing buttons in order as instructed. As he pushed the buttons the suit began to hum, the dials began to shift, and he felt the suit lift a few inches from the ground. He checked a few dials, and seemed satisfied. He flicked a switch and held a button down.

'This is a systems test. Control can you hear me, over?' he called into the air. He depressed the button and a quiet screech of static filled the air for a second.

'This is control, good evening Inspector,' came a stilted reply.

'Good evening control, how are things looking your end?' the Inspector asked, pushing the button down again.

'All good here, good reception, we are showing all systems are operational and you are currently good to go. How are things your side?'

'Yes, all fine all systems are showing as operational here as well. We are good to go.'

'Roger that.' The voice faded off again and the Inspector continued pressing buttons according to the laminated instructions. The lights blazed on suddenly and the view outside of the huge visor was illuminated, to show the inside of the crate. After a few more careful checks of dials and read outs the Inspector pressed a large red button, and using the levers on the dashboard he carefully piloted the suit out of the crate. He guided it carefully to a halt a few feet away from the stones, the film between them still eradiating ultraviolet light out amongst the trees. The Inspector studied the cards, flicked a few switches and carefully turned a dial, as if looking for a radio station on the wireless, and slowly the view through the windscreen changed, so the colours were brighter, more vibrant and pronounced.

'Ready control,' he called into the air, pressing the radio contact button.

'Roger that all good here,' came the quick reply. The Inspector took the suit forward toward the stones, and passed through the film.

The surrounding black of night was replaced by a bright swirling light for a few seconds, then he found himself cast adrift upon a bottomless abyss of black. His stomach turned at a sudden attack of vertigo, but he brought himself quickly back under control. He pressed the radio button.

'Control,' he called into the air. There was no static hiss, no reply was forth coming. 'Control,' he tried again. The lack of reply was daunting, but unsurprising. 'Control, I don't know if you can hear me, but I'm through.' He checked the rear view camera and saw a bright doorway floating in the darkness in the spot he had emerged from. He pressed the communications button again.

'All systems appear to be operating normally. Attempting to locate missing men.' He began turning the wireless dial again, and as he did the view outside began to change, the darkness slowly focused and refocused itself, until the environment around him began to gain shape, and he peered out trying to fathom what he was looking at. He glanced occasionally at a series of dials directly above the visor; they were all moving a lot quicker than he would have liked, meaning he did not have a lot of time. Shapes around him slowly came into focus, and the Inspector found himself surrounded by columns reaching into the sky. He peered up but they seemed to have no end. They surrounded him, and he realised these were the trees protruding into this world. He cautiously moved the suit slowly on and amongst them. The light was dim, as if he was in a black fog. He checked the cameras were operating, he did not have time to stop for pictures. He moved about, looking for life, looking for a sign of the missing men. He searched about him, avoiding the trees, and suddenly he spotted the figure of a man up ahead. He approached carefully, and found it to be the Mayor. He stood stock still, gawping aimlessly. He checked the dials and moved towards a heat source nearby, discovering it to be Atkins, also standing in a similar state. He slowly toured the area locating more of the missing men. They stood, looking in different directions as if not even noticing the other's presence. The Inspector realised they had not recognised his existence there, and moved toward Atkins to study him closer. He looked drained and empty, his eyes were weary and distant. He studied the Mayor, and Charlie, then realised that one man was still missing. Banks was not amongst them. As he glanced about him he saw between the trees a flickering, a movement. He twisted his dial slightly and as he travelled through the different frequencies the shapes loomed in and out of view. All were stuck here, all needed the energy to begin to flow again. None of them seemed to recognise his existence there, so he moved on, trying to see how far the trees would go. After a while the suit stopped, as if the way was blocked. He focused on the path in front, and through the dark he could see the view beyond was blocked and blurred. He knew time was short, but he wanted to make the most of this opportunity while he could. He decided to see how big the area he could access was, so went back on himself as far as he could, and found after thirty yards or so his path was blocked in the other direction as well. He began working his way around the edge, finding a roughly semicircle shaped area. As he approached the middle of the flattest edge he realised he was returning to the stones, where he had emerged. He turned the wireless dial, adjusting the light frequency filters on the suit's visor, and the stones came into focus. On the other side, through the stones, he could see the other half of the path, and realised there was something wrong with the stones that was causing the doorway to not operate as it should. The two halves of the energy field were blocked from being connected through the stone doorway, and this he realised was trapping the poor lifeforms in the limbo between the trees. The Inspector kept twisting the dial, pushing the suit's receptors to their maximum. As he did something above the stones flashed into view. It had a black centre, and flashed darkness in all directions like smoke from a dark inferno. From what he could see it was ten feet long, and about the shape and thickness of a tree trunk, though the edges were straighter. Here was the missing link, here was the blockage, though what might bridge the two stones he knew not. He glanced up at the dials above the screen and saw that the suit's energy had nearly been exhausted, and that it was time to return.

He headed back toward the doorway, skimming back through different frequencies on his dial, causing the blackness to fade and die, returning it to the frequency he had entered through. Slowly he saw ahead of him the feint glow of the door, and a light began to glow, the Inspector saw the space between stones alter and flicker, and the light between them that he had entered through returned. The change of frequency had drained the suit's energy significantly. He pressed the controls forward, suddenly realising that he had perhaps left it a little too long. His body suddenly sagged under the effort, he had expended too much time here, and needed to get back through quickly. He pushed on, moving back into the light, out of one darkness and into another. The trees around him became static, the shapes shifting between them vanished, and the world around him swirled back to something more recognisable. Standing in front of him looking more concerned than the Inspector might have liked was the welcome sight of Constable Drew Gates. He did a few calculations from the dials at the top of the visor and calculated that he had been gone approximately 46 hours. Now he had returned to a frequency that his body and perception was used to he began to regain his energy. The suit landed itself, and the door at the rear opened with a hiss. The Inspector carefully and painfully lifted himself out, before collapsing under his own weight. Drew rushed forward, laying the Inspector on his side. He offered him some water, which he accepted gratefully, carefully taking a few sips from where he laid on the ground.

'My pocket... some sweets,' the Inspector croaked. Drew searched his coat and pulled out a packet of Kola Kubes. The Inspector began munching them two at a time.

'How long was I gone for?' How long did it take? What year is this?' he asked desperately, trying to focus his tired eyes on Drew's face.

'Relax Inspector you didn't go anywhere,' Drew explained, trying to calm him.

'What do you mean?' the Inspector replied, he was losing consciousness but tried to hold on. 'I've been gone for days,' he informed him incredulously.

'No, you just floated through the stones, and out the other side. You didn't go anywhere.' The Inspector began to wonder to himself as to how much of it had been real, and what had really happened in the space between the stones.

'It's broken, we must fix it!' the Inspector yelled suddenly, wild-eyed. He had begun to lose his fight with unconsciousness and the world drifted away from him. He didn't seem to see Drew anymore, he stared right through him at stones, then suddenly pointed at them. He had to communicate what he had learned with Drew before the encroaching blackness took him.

'The Firestone!' he cried with a gasp of realisation, and lost consciousness. Drew checked his pulse and his breath, and he seemed to be fine. He studied the suit, and saw its gleaming white exterior was now blackened and burnt. Drew watched the Inspector under its dimming lights, which suddenly switched themselves off. Not sure of what to do he lifted the Inspector's body and carried him uncomfortably to his car and drove him to The Green Man.

86.

Drew could hear Lionel swearing from his bedroom all the way downstairs and to the front door that he had banged on so hard few minutes ago. His car was parked on the road outside, the Inspector lying down on the back seat.

'This had better bloody well be good,' he rasped at Drew angrily as he flung the door open.

'Sorry to wake you Lionel, the Inspector has fallen ill, I need to get him up to his room,' Drew explained apologetically. Lionel immediately changed his attitude when he saw the desperate young Constable on his doorstep.

'Oh my goodness, yes of course. Where is he?' Lionel asked.

'He's in the back of the car.' Drew informed him, and showed him the Inspector unconscious on his backseat. The car was pulled up on the pavement awkwardly. They heaved him out together and carried him inside, standing him up and each taking one of his arms over their shoulders. When they reached the bar Mavis appeared.

'Oh my, what's up with him?' she asked when she caught sight of the Inspector's dead weight being carried between the two men.

'He's just had a very busy night,' Drew informed her calmly.

'He looks terrible,' she told them. 'What could he have possibly been up to out there?'

'Stop nosing and get the key to his room would you Mavis?' Lionel asked with a raised voice.

'Oh yes of course, hold on.' She raced off and re-emerged shortly with a set of keys.

'This way then,' she said, and led them quickly up the stairs. They got him on to his bed, made sure he was comfortable, and left him to rest.

'Shouldn't he be in the hospital?' Mavis asked, looking worried.

'I don't think that's necessary,' Drew reassured her. 'But I will get a Doctor to him. Can I borrow your telephone?' he asked urgently.

'Of course Drew, this way,' Lionel said, and led him quickly back down the stairs, through the bar and to the office.

'Here you go,' he told him.

'Thank you,' Drew said, then lifted the receiver and dialled 100 for the operator. The few seconds he had to listen to the dialling tone felt like an age.

'Operator how can I help?' came the prompt answer.

'Can you put me through to The Black Swan in Nettlewood please?' he asked urgently.

'Thank you hold the line please.' There was a click, then the dialling tone filled his ear again. The phone rang for longer than he liked, but it was eventually answered by Abigail.

'Black Swan Nettlewood,' she said in a daze.

'Sorry to wake you Abigail, it's Drew Gates, from Firestone police. I need to talk to Casey urgently.'

'Alright dear hold on and I'll go and see if I can rouse her,' she informed him sleepily.

'Can you get her to call me urgently at The Green Man? The number is 442,' Drew informed her, reading the number from the centre of the number wheel.

'Right you are dear, is everything alright?' Drew thought for a moment how best to reply.

'The Inspector has fallen ill and is asking for her,' he lied. 'Probably nothing to worry about but we'd best get him seen to.'

'Right you are dear,' Abigail replied, a new sense of urgency entering her voice. She hung up and Drew spent an anxious few minutes pacing around the office waiting for Casey to call him back. Suddenly the shrill bell began to ring and he leapt at the receiver.

'Casey?' he asked as soon as he had the receiver to his mouth.

'Yes, Drew, what on earth is the matter?' she asked, unable to hide her fear.

'The Inspector has fallen ill, he asked if he you could come and see him,' Drew replied, not wanting to give away too much.

'Of course, but how will I get over there?'

'I'll come and get you, I'll be there in ten minutes.' There was the sound of a yawn as Casey tried to wake up.

'Alright, yes, I'll be waiting outside.'

'Great, see you soon,' Drew replied, hanging up and running out to the bar where Lionel and Mavis waited.

'I'm just off to get the Doctor, I'll be back in about twenty minutes,' Drew told them.

'Right you are Drew, we'll be waiting,' Lionel reassured him, and Drew raced out to his car. He made it to Nettlewood in good time with blue lights flashing but no siren, the roads were quiet enough at that time of night not to warrant it. When he got to The Swan and Dove Casey stood by the side of the road with a briefcase similar to the Inspector's and Drew pulled up next to her.

'So what's happened?' she asked as she climbed in. Drew swung the car around and began racing back to Firestone. Casey noticed Drew's speed and put her seat belt on.

'He has fallen ill, I'm not sure how much I can tell you, but he's unconscious.' Casey did little to hide her shock. 'He looks gaunt and frail, he was conscious for a while and I think he was hallucinating. He's in his bed resting, we've made him as comfortable as we could.' Casey watched as he spoke and could see he was worried and pretending not to be.

'We?' she asked.

'Lionel and Mavis, at The Green Man where he's staying,' he told her.

'How much do they know?' she asked.

'Not much, I just told them he had fallen ill,' Drew replied, concentrating on the road ahead.

'Good,' she replied coolly. 'What has he been up to, or can you not tell me?' she asked.

'Best not, not until he wakes up then he can fill you in where he can.' She nodded understandingly.

They were soon back at The Green Man, and nodded to the proprietors as they rushed through the bar and raced up the stairs as quickly as they could. Drew led Casey up to his room where the Inspector still lay fully dressed, his breathing shallow.

'My goodness, yes he's very pale,' Casey remarked as she walked in. She sat carefully next to him on the bed to open her case and removed a stethoscope. She leant round to undo his shirt buttons to enable her to hold it against his hairy chest.

'His heart beat is slow, but strong,' she told Drew, a trace of concern in her voice.

'Good,' he replied simply.

She checked his temperature with an open palm to the forehead.

'He's very hot, and probably dehydrated.' Her voice was determined, professional, even more so than when she was in the morgue. She wrapped up her stethoscope and replaced it in her bag thoughtfully. She then removed from her bag a machine, and attached part of it to the Inspector's left index finger. It looked like an elongated black thimble, and was attached to the main part of the mechanism by a thin black wire. The main machine consisted of a black box, about the size of a shoe box. On top a sat a small screen surrounded by an array of buttons. She switched the machine on, and a light on the part attached to the Inspector's thumb began to flash green.

'Well that's a good start,' Casey said. Drew watched as the screen came to life, and slowly filled with text, though it was too small for him to see what it said.

'Well he's not in a good way, but it looks like he took a few precautions before attempting whatever it was that caused this.'

'What is that thing?' Drew asked, amazed by her equipment.

'I honestly don't know Drew,' she laughed. 'They taught me how to use it, and I helped with the design and helped them to improve it, but they never really explained what it was, or how it worked. I use it to get some really good results about a person's health, and I can use the information to give them a prescription to aid their recovery.' She reached into her bag and removed a small leather bound box, which opened up to reveal a syringe and some sterilised needles. She then removed a small plastic case, which she carefully opened to reveal a row of bottles containing various liquids. Each had a label with a detail of its content typed across it, which Drew could read but did not understand.

Using a pipette she began taking liquid from some of the bottles and collecting them in the syringe.

'What are you doing?' Drew asked.

'I'm creating a very specific remedy using the data from the Health Monitor,' she rolled up one of the Inspector's sleeves, 'and administering it to him.' She pierced his arm with the needle of the syringe and injected the cocktail into him.

'It might take a day or so, but he's going to be ok. We should let him rest for now.' She rolled his sleeve down again and pulled a blanket over him. She carefully packed all her things away again, Drew wondering if he should ask about it, but quickly realising that there was always going to be something that he didn't understand. They backed carefully and quietly out of the room and closed the door on the sleeping Inspector.

'He's really out for the count,' Casey whispered to Drew as they crept along the corridor.

'Yes, he asked for you specifically, before he…' Drew paused for a moment. 'Fell ill. He said I should call you if anything happened.'

'You did the right thing Drew,' she reassured him as they entered the bar. Mavis stood suddenly as they entered making them both jump.

'Sorry Drew, Doctor,' she apologised quickly.

'No bother Mavis,' Drew reassured her. They all spoke in whispers.

'How is he?' she asked, obviously worried.

'He's going to be fine,' Casey replied, authoritatively but kindly. She had a bedside manner that Drew wasn't expecting.

'I'll come back in the morning to check he's ok, as long as Drew doesn't mind coming over to the Hotel to pick me up again?' she asked.

'No of course not,' Drew replied, mirroring Casey's reassuring tone.

'Has he been in some kind of trouble? Has he found the killer?' Mavis was still a little fretful around the edges, understandable due to the late disturbance. 'Wouldn't he be better off in hospital?'

'Oh there's no need for that, he has just fallen ill, nothing a good night's sleep won't heal,' Casey told her calmly.

'You see, there's nothing to worry about,' Drew endorsed Casey's words and they offered a combined front. 'We'll be back in the morning but you can call me if he stirs, here you go.' He took his notepad out of his pocket and scribbled down his home number. 'We'll be off, let you get some rest.'

'Alright my dear I'll see you out and lock up behind you.' They walked to the door and Mavis opened it for them.

'Thanks Mavis, now you get off to bed. We'll see you in the morning,' Drew assured her.

'Yes, alright my dears, goodnight.' They stepped into the cold night and heard the door lock behind them. Drew led Casey down the deserted street back to his car in silence, both were a little too shocked to speak. They were quickly in his car and out of the cold and Drew started the engine. He paused for a moment, swallowing a balloon of fear that had got caught in his throat.

'You know, you don't have to head back to the hotel,' he told her, more seriously than he had intended.

'How do you mean Drew?' she asked, a little reproachful. She was worried about the Inspector and was unsure what she needed at the moment.

'Well, I live five minutes away. We don't have to share a bed if it would make you feel uncomfortable. I have two rooms. I just, would rather not be alone at the moment.' She was quiet.

'Why wouldn't I want to share a room with you?' she asked, also serious. Drew was rather surprised by the question, and thought he heard a little sense of tease in her voice.

'Well, I didn't want you to assume that just because I am taking you home that anything was going to happen.' He took a risk at humour to try and lighten the mood. 'I'm not that kind of boy.' They shared a welcome laugh that unwound the atmosphere a little.

'It's been a long night,' Drew informed her. 'I need to get some rest, but you're welcome to come and rest with me.' He offered the open invitation with no hint of commitment. The choice was hers.

'Well that sounds perfect to me.' She reached out and squeezed his hand. 'Thank you Drew.'

'It isn't much I'm afraid,' Drew informed her as they drove back along the dark roads, slightly concerned at the state of his house.

'I'm sure it's lovely.' She smiled without turning her gaze from the road ahead. She leant her head against the window, and relaxed into Drew's company.

87.

With Drew and the Inspector gone, the clearing around the stones returned to a state of dark indifference. The branches swayed, forever reaching into the bleak sky. The rain flittered and fell through the cold harsh air. The suit sat amongst it, as out of place as ever an object could be, its power almost exhausted. And so it remained for several hours, until cutting through the eerie chill came the sound of a diesel engine, disturbing the silence. The black van reversed up the path through the trees, snapping and crunching over the muddy stick-strewn ground. When it arrived at the suit it stopped, and the two men got out again. One of them removed a small device from his pocket, which he used to control the suit. He pressed a button, and it suddenly came out of its reverie and was once more alive. With another button pressed it floated into the air, then with the push of a lever he directed it back into its crate. It landed carefully back on the wood, and with a satisfying sound of pressurised air escaping it landed and the man switched it off. Its lights dimmed back to black and it was lifeless once more. The two men reaffixed the panel that the Inspector and Drew had removed, filling the trees with the sound of hammer blows as they nailed it back into place. They then wheeled the crate back into their van over the uneven mud, and put it back in place inside.

They then retrieved the Field Enhancer, placing the rods carefully back in its box. They did not need to speak a word, they knew exactly what they were doing and how to do it, their actions well-rehearsed. Finally they drove away, the sound of the engine fading into the distance, once more leaving the trees in the dark with the stones.

Saturday 8th November 1969

88.

Drew awoke to the sound of china clinking from his kitchen, and it took a moment for him to remember he had company. He wondered blearily how long Casey had been up, then quickly rose to head downstairs. He went to put his dressing gown and slippers on, only to find they had gone. He stalked downstairs in his pyjamas and found her sat at his old kitchen table drinking tea and looking out of the window at the trees.

'Morning,' he said. She turned to face him with a warm smile.

'Morning,' she replied, pleased to see him awake.

'Did you sleep alright?' he asked, rather concerned at his lack of hospitality. 'You're up early.'

'I'm just an early riser is all,' she explained 'I've only been up long enough to make tea. Would you like some?'

'Yes, if there's enough in the pot.' He took a seat at the table and she poured a tea for him into a cup she had already prepared.

The first thing that struck Casey when she had crept downstairs that morning and seen Drew's house in the light for the first time was the number of boxes stacked all about the place. Some were open with contents spilling, others piled hither and thither accumulating dust.

'Are you moving out?' she asked. Drew sipped his tea and wondered at how good she looked in his dressing gown and pyjamas.

'No, I've only just moved in,' he replied, though as he said it he began wondering just how long he had been there.

'How long ago?' she asked, noticing his doubt. He thought for a moment.

'About two years,' Drew replied, with an embarrassed smile. 'This was never intended to be a permanent home, I had always intended on moving back to Nettlewood,' he explained. 'So I didn't unpack as I didn't want to stay.' Casey nodded understandingly.

'Does it not feel like home here?' she wondered. Drew had to think about this.

'Actually, it does now. I've become so caught up with the goings on of the town that I have become a part of it, I guess I just never wanted to admit it to myself,' Drew found himself saying.

'There are worst places to find yourself in than Firestone Drew,' she told him. 'I think I actually quite like it here.' Her cheeks flushed red she and looked back out of the window again.

'Would you like some toast?' he offered, feeling his belly give the familiar tug of hunger.

'That would be nice,' she replied. He nodded and switched the grill on.

'Our first home cooked meal together Drew, I hope you won't disappoint,' she teased with a smile. Drew laughed out loud nervously, he still found her a little intimidating. He tried not to read too much into her use of the word "first". He was soon dishing up a round of perfectly browned toast, along with a dish of butter, some strawberry jam, and some orange marmalade. She was impressed but didn't let on.

'We'd best get over to The Green Man as soon as we can, check on the Inspector's progress,' he told her as they crunched. She finished her second slice and took a sip of tea.

'Yes, you're right. I'll pop upstairs and get dressed. Would you mind if I used your toothbrush?' She asked. Drew could not deny her anything, even if he had wanted to.

'No of course not. You can use the bathroom first, I'll be up in a minute.'

'Ok,' she replied simply, and skipped off happily. He listened to her pottering around upstairs while he ate his third slice with marmalade. When he heard the toilet door open again he made his way upstairs and he found her in the bedroom putting her shoes on.

'Well I see you're dressed and ready to go, I'd best get dressed myself,' he told her, rather surprised. 'Aren't you a fast mover?' Drew asked, impressed.

'Well aren't I just?' she replied smiling. He quickly began dressing into his uniform.

'Who's this?' she asked, noticing a few pictures poked into the side of the mirror on his dresser. He glanced up.

'The lady is my mother, the two boys with her are me and my brother,' he told her, trying to hide his embarrassment.

'You were cute,' she told him matter of factly.

'Is this you and you brother being held by your Dad?' she asked, noticing the photograph that he had found a few days earlier.

'Yes, I found that in the loft in with my Dads things.' He walked over to join her.

'So this was the photograph of you and your brother that your dad carried around with him?' she asked.

'Yes, probably.' They stood and looked at the picture for a minute.

'That's nice Drew,' she told him. She turned and started to button up his stiff blue police jacket.

'Where's your brother now?' she asked.

'He moved away, got a good job over in Selford. Wife and kids, he's doing well.'

'And what about your mum?' she asked, straightening his tie.

'She's still in Nettlewood, in the house we grew up in,' he told her. She admired him proudly.

'She's lucky to have such a good son,' she told him.

'Thank you,' he replied, not sure whether to take her seriously or not. 'What about you? Do you have any brothers or sisters?' he asked. He tried to find a stray hair to flatten down but she looked perfect. He stroked her hair anyway.

'Parents alive and well and living in the Isle of Sheppey,' she told him. 'Retired. My family's a bit normal. I'm an only child, so no embarrassing photographs of me and my siblings I'm afraid.' She thought for a moment, remembering something. 'I do have this though...' She found her case and removed her purse from it, pulling a picture out to show him. It was about the size of her palm and had rounded corners. Still visible, though it was tattered and torn, were three people, a little girl and what Drew presumed were her parents.

'This is me and my parents,' Casey confirmed. 'When I was six we went on holiday to Butlin's and I won a talent contest. I sang 'Wake up little Suzy.' I was adorable, and it was the happiest day of my life,' she told him. He realised she was sharing something special with him. 'This picture helps me remember it.' She told him. 'When times aren't so good, it helps me through.' Drew took her hand and they looked at the picture together for a moment.

'Now you don't have to feel so embarrassed about me nosing at your photographs,' she told him with a smile. 'We're even.'

'Thanks,' he said. He studied the photograph a little closer. 'You weren't so cute then though, were you?' he teased. She laughed and pushed him away playfully.

'Alright that's enough from you Gates. Get me back to the Inspector and let's see how he's doing shall we?'

They headed out to the car and were quickly away. When they arrived at The Green Man Drew gave a good hard knock at the door.

'They're usually in the kitchen and don't always hear,' he explained to Casey, who seemed a little concerned with his heavy handed knocking. The door was soon opened by a red faced Mavis.

'Come in my dears.' She ushered them inside to the warm and closed the door on the cold morning.

'Any movement from our patient today?' Casey asked.

'No I haven't heard anything from his room,' she informed them, worry still filling her voice. 'I haven't been in to check, but I did put an ear against the door to try and hear any movement. Didn't hear anything though,' she told them.

'Great, well we'd best go up and check on him,' Casey told her, and she followed Drew through the bar up to his room. They found he still slept, having hardly moved since the previous evening. He didn't stir as they entered, nor when the cold surface of the stethoscope was placed on his chest.

'His pulse is still strong, he's made of tough stuff this one.' She placed a hand on the back of his neck.

'His temperature has come down too. He's certainly recovering from whatever it was.' He remained in his deep slumber despite their conversation. She removed her contraption from her bag again and attached the Inspector's finger into the large thimble. She switched it on, and the green light flashed again. The screen began filling with text, which Casey studied carefully.

'He's doing well,' she told him with a smile. She took the small box of bottles from her bag and made a cocktail from them which she injected into the Inspector's arm.

'He'll be awake soon, and he'll be ravenous.' She removed the instrument from his finger and began packing away her things.

'Let's warn Mavis, she might be able to get some lamb on for him.

'Yes, if you think so,' Drew nodded, his anxiety at the Inspector's condition easing with the news of his recovery. They made their way back downstairs where Mavis waited nervously for them.

'How is he?' she asked. 'Is he awake yet?'

'No, still out for the count I'm afraid, but he is recovering nicely and will be awake soon,' Casey informed her with a kindly smile.

'Oh good, what should I do?' Mavis asked.

'We'll leave him for now, when he wakes up he is going to extremely hungry, do you have any lamb you could prepare for him, with roast potatoes and all the trimmings?' Casey asked.

'Well, I don't think there's any lamb, but we need to stock up since the Inspector's been bringing all these people into my pub every night, so I'll pop down to see Keith now and get some,' she told them, pleased to have something she could do to help.

'Brilliant. He'll no doubt contact us when he's ready, but any problems call the station and they will get on to us,' Casey smiled, trying to put her at ease. 'He just needs rest, he'll be up and about and eating you out of house and home again before you know it,' she consoled her gently.

'If you say so Doctor.' She looked nervously at her hands. 'Can I get you a cup of tea my dears?' Drew and Casey exchanged a glance and a shake of heads.

'That would be nice Mavis but I need to get up to the stones and make sure everything is ticking over up there,' Drew told her. 'We'd best be off.'

'Right you are dears,' she smiled and bustled them back out on to the street again before heading back to the kitchen to put her coat on and head into town. Drew and Casey returned to the car, marching quickly thought the cold damp morning. They climbed in and Drew quickly headed off.

'You continually surprise me,' he informed her as they slowly warmed under the cars heating.

'Good!' she replied as they drove away. 'What have I done this time?'

'Are you a doctor as well as a mortician?' he asked, impressed.

'Well I was a doctor for a few years after graduating, then a surgeon, now I do pathology.' She watched through the window as the houses gave way to trees. 'I don't mean to boast but I'm qualified enough to do most things. Sounds a bit yuck but I find pathology sort of fun. It's like a puzzle and you have to find the clues on the body to solve it.'

'Well you're obviously brilliant at everything, which makes it even stranger that you want to hang around with me,' Drew half joked. He was pleased she did, but couldn't work out why. They arrived at the turning through the trees leading to site where Drew had discovered Mathew Berrow from Swindon, and he turned up it. Casey was distracted from any reply by the sudden change in direction.

'Is this the way to the stones?' she asked, peering into the dark trees nervously. Even with the track cleared the way still seemed narrow, the trees jostled for a view in at them as Drew piloted the car toward the clearing.

'No, this is where they're bringing the soil from the stones,' Drew told her. 'This is where I discovered the body.'

'Really?' She hid her excitement well, but Drew noticed it.

'There isn't much to look at you know,' he warned her. 'I want to check on the archaeologists to see if they've found anything.' The trees opened up and they entered the clearing, which was now full of activity, the area could not have looked more different to when he had last seen it. A mound of dark brown mud had been piled in the centre where the body had appeared, and some basic shelters had been arranged around it. Several smaller piles of dirt were slowly diminishing as the archaeologists painstakingly sifted through it for anything of interest. Drew climbed out of the car while Casey eyed all the mud with unhidden misgivings. One of Samson's colleagues spotted them pulling in and began making his way over through the mud.

'Perhaps I'll wait here,' she decided with a smile.

'Yes, I don't blame you,' Drew nodded back.

'Morning officer,' the archaeologist welcomed him. 'Sorry, I don't remember your name.'

'Gates, Constable Drew Gates,' he informed him, and they shook hands. 'Oh yes. I'm Roderick, Doctor Samson's colleague.'

'Good morning Doctor, I was just wondering if we could speak to Doctor Samson?' Drew asked.

'Oh sorry Constable he isn't here, he's up at the other site, up at the stones,' Roderick told him regrettably.

'Well we are heading there next so I shall see him soon. How are things here?' Drew asked.

'Very slow actually. For a while we were having a lot of luck, but as the soil gets closer to the centre of the mound, the fewer artefacts we find. After a few feet all traces are gone, and all we have is mud.'

'What does that mean?' Drew asked thinking. 'Was the mound made very quickly?'

'Yes this could be an answer,' Roderick agreed. 'We see a few relics but we think they are more recent than the time the mound was formed. It's as though the mound was created and then completely forgotten about for centuries.'

'Is that not a possibility?' Drew asked.

'Well, yes, but it would be so uncommon. Stones like these are landmarks, they take a great amount of workmanship, and not to say a great amount of effort, to put together. These sorts of projects would unite a community, it was a part of the culture of the land, it brought people together. It was a symbol of wealth and power. Even if we don't know exactly what it was used for, we can be sure that for it to have been hidden in such a fashion, and then swallowed up by the copse, is very strange indeed.'

'Yes, it is,' Drew could only nod and agree. 'Well, thank you, I'll head up to the stones and see if I can find Doctor Samson,' Drew told him.

'Ahh yes of course, see you later Constable.'

Drew clambered back over the mud to his car and drove them back to the road.

'So, to the stones?' Casey asked hopefully.

'Yes, and on the way we will pass the Firestone, see if you can work out why the Inspector was so distressed by it last night.' Drew sped up the road but slowed as they passed it.

'There you go,' he pointed it out to her as he rounded the roundabout. He checked his mirrors, and carefully slowed so she could get a good look. Casey stared out of the window as he navigated around it.

'It looks like a standing stone, is it like the others?' she asked.

'It is much smaller,' he commented. 'The others are much more impressive.' Drew headed up the hill past the church.

'Let's hope Doctor Samson can offer us some clue to its relevance,' Drew mused as he drove them to the site of the stones. As they pulled up the area was a hub of activity, with soldiers bustling around, busily flattening out mounds of gravel that had appeared. John's truck sat on the side of the road with the digger perched on its back. Drew parked the car up at a safe distance from the entrance and they climbed out.

'Seems rather busy up here,' Casey pointed out as she raced to keep up with him.

'Yes. I wonder what's going on,' Drew replied. As they approached the police tape was opened for them, the policeman gawping slightly at the sight of Casey accompanying Drew.

'Morning, how are things?' Drew asked.

'Bloody busy!' the Constable swore back, rather rudely. 'We've had a truck up here this morning full of gravel laying a path. Did you know about it?' Drew looked up from the entrance down the path toward the stones where a neat, if rather bumpy, gravel track was slowly being created out of piles of stone by busy soldiers. The truck was still tipping gravel out at the stone end, and all around it men heaved and hauled at it with rakes and spades to lay it out into a fine flat surface, making the path up to the stones look and feel more permanent.

'I suppose the Inspector had something to do with it,' Drew replied. 'He didn't tell me anything about it.'

'Well, it's made the journey back and forth a bit easier. It was turning into a bit if a mire,' the Constable remarked.

'Yes. Is Doctor Samson up there?' Drew asked.

'He's up there somewhere, he's eager to get the digger up there to clear some of the soil that's accumulated, but he's waiting for the gravel to finish being laid.'

'Hopefully he won't have to wait too long. We'll trek up there and see if we can find him.' Drew led the way and Casey skipped along after him, flashing a smile at the policeman. She looked ahead hungrily for the stones.

The gravel crunched awkwardly under their feet, it was still fresh and needed time to settle. The site of the stones was a hub of activity, as all around them the army men shifted the stone piles flat. The trees had been cut further back, extending the area into the woods. The clearance of the soil had revealed more stones that had been hidden by the slick mud. These were smaller, and laying down flat at odd angles from the standing pair. There were pockets of excited historians gathered around them, and while Casey marvelled at the standing stones Drew began making his way around in search of Doctor Samson.

'Morning Doctor,' Drew called to him when he spotted his familiar form hovering over a patch of freshly revealed stone. Samson looked up.

'Ahh morning Constable Gates.' Doctor Samson left the stone to his colleagues and made his way over to Drew. He made his muddy hand cleaner slightly cleaner by rubbing it on his grubby trousers and the men shook hands.

'My colleague and I were wondering if you could spare some time to come and have a look at something for us?' Doctor Samson immediately looked interested.

'I should think so, what is it?' he asked, turning away from his nearby colleagues to afford them a little more privacy.

'It's a monument to our town's dark past, a stone, much like these, but rather smaller. We were wondering if it might have some relationship to the stones.' Doctor Samson's interest was captured and he smiled excitedly.

'Well it sounds very mysterious, I'd best come and have a look.' He turned back to the man he had just been working with, who now stood with his arms elbow deep in mud trying to reveal more stone.

'Simon? Simon!' he yelled at him. Simon looked up from what he was doing and squinted through his spectacles to see what he wanted.

'I'm just popping off with the Constable here for a while,' he called to him. Simon replied with an inaudible mumble and a dismissive wave.

'Well, looks as though he has things under control,' Doctor Samson remarked. 'I say this gravel was rather a good idea don't you think?' he asked Drew. 'Makes things much easier.'

'Indeed.' Drew looked round for Casey as they stomped away from the stones.

'Casey!' Drew called for her. She looked up and waved, leaving the conversation with the archaeologist she had found to rejoin Drew. The gravel truck dropped the last of its load as they left the stones behind them. 'Ahh thank goodness for that, now we can get the digger back down here and clear some of this earth,' Samson muttered as they stomped away.

'They're amazing!' Casey enthused to Drew.

'Yes, they are rather aren't they?' Samson agreed. 'Are you also helping Constable Gates with his enquiries?' he asked politely.

'Yes, I'm down from Scotland Yard as well, I'm a colleague of the Inspector's.' She told him. They shook hands as the gravel scrunched under foot. 'Doctor Ward, Casey Ward,' she told him.

'Doctor Christopher Samson, pleased to meet you,' he told her.

'The Inspector is a very nice chap.' Samson smiled. Drew had charged ahead, keen to keep them moving through the cold afternoon.

'Yes, he is,' Casey replied, realising she was just one member of a bigger community of experts and helpers that the Inspector surrounded himself with.

'Where is he today?' Samson asked, looking about for him.

'He's fallen ill,' Casey replied, trying to hide the worry in her voice.

'Oh dear nothing too serious I hope?' Samson replied, sounding a little more concerned.

'Oh I doubt it, he'll be back on his feet before we know it,' Casey replied with a smile. They reached the car and Drew opened the back door for Doctor Samson.

'Mind your head on the way in sir,' Drew told him out of habit.

'How exciting I've never ridden in a police car before!' Samson told them excitedly. They were soon at the Firestone roundabout and Drew pulled up on the road that headed toward The Green Man.

'Where is this monument of yours then?' Samson asked excitedly.
'We just drove passed it actually, it's over there.' They all climbed out and Drew led them back along the road and over to the roundabout.

'Oh yes I see, well...' Samson walked about it for a moment then approached and studied it closer.

'Well, this is very interesting.'

'Oh yes? How so?' Drew asked.

'Well, it is hard to tell as some of it is buried, but this appears to be a lintel from the site of the stones.' He studied it again.

'It could even be the lintel that's missing from the two stones that are still standing that we uncovered,' he informed them a little awe struck, his excitement visibly growing.

'I never expected it to be so obvious, out here exposed. The others are all so well hidden. I wonder how it ended up all the way down here?' He shook his head and tried to imagine what could have possessed the ancient inhabitants of Firestone to perform such acts. He took a good look around the stone, measuring it up, calculating its potential size.

'It certainly seems to be the right sort of size to be the lintel,' he nodded to himself thoughtfully. And these lighter patches of stone suggest it spent many centuries sat upon something of similar dimensions, though it's impossible to tell of course as its partially buried.' He pointed out the part of the stone he meant. 'Thank you for bringing it to my attention. What sort of things did you want to know about it?'

'I think you have answered all my questions with what you have discovered.' Drew studied the stone with Casey and Samson.

'I'll take a few measurements of it and then we could head back up there and see if we can confirm our theory,' Samson suggested.

'That would be interesting,' Drew agreed. In the absence of a tape measure Doctor Samson began taking rough measurements with his hand span.

'These types of structures are made very precisely,' he told them as he totted up the size of the exposed stone.

'Which means if we take just a rough guess at its length...' he measured his way across each edge. 'I can make a pretty good guess to see if it would fit across the stones.' He scratched his head. 'Right, I think that should do it.'

They all bundled back into Drew's car and he returned them to the stones. They ran up the gravel, the lorry that had laid it had now moved on, and the truck and digger were working hard shifting the pile of mud around the stones. Samson walked up to them quickly. They were now completely free of the mud and stood staggeringly tall. Their fallen comrades laid about them, slowly being revealed by the careful hands of the army men and archaeologists. They were joined by Simon who began talking him through their finds.

'Look, you can see where the stones used to be a circle.' He looked about the fallen stones, pointing to the ground where they had been toppled. Two were pushed inward, four more were pushed outward. 'Whomever did this then attempted to smash them to pieces.' In the centre lay a scattering of rocks slowly being revealed from below the last pile of mud.

'Here, look at this.' Samson took them into the woods.

'This one was toppled and pulled away into the trees.' He indicated to the soldiers hacking their way around a fallen monolith.

'These two.' He indicated the only two stones still standing. 'I suppose they couldn't topple, or wouldn't.' He regarded the two stones.

'Fascinating Simon, but you'll never believe what Constable Gates has just shown me,' Samson interrupted, unable to hold his excitement any longer.

'Oh my, what now?' Simon replied.

'The lintel, that used to sit across these two, we think,' Samson replied eagerly. 'Now, let's see.' He began measuring the width of the stones, and the distance between them. Simon stood in an awed daze.

'What, here, on this site? How could you tell?' Simon asked, rather shocked.

'No, it's just down the road.' Samson explained. 'I'm just trying to work out if my rough measurements add up,' he explained. 'The exposed part of the stone comes up to here.' He drew a deep line in the mud with the heel of his boot. 'If it is the lintel, then it means there's still about another two thirds of it buried, about six feet. That would make it about 9 feet in all.'

'Fascinating, but what does it mean?' Casey asked. 'What should we do?' Drew thought he had an idea what the Inspector would want to do, but he didn't know how exactly he would go about it. As they considered the stones one of the policemen from the entrance came running up the newly gravelled path toward them.

'Drew!' he called, out of breath and panting. 'Alright George what's up?' Drew replied.

'We just had a call through from the station. The Inspector is awake and asking for you.' Casey practically jumped with glee.

'Well, we best be off to see him then, thank you for the tour gentlemen, we shall return with the Inspector, see what he makes of it all,' Drew informed them.

'Right you are Constable, Doctor.' Samson nodded to Casey respectfully again.

'Doctor,' Casey nodded back, and followed Drew back to his car.

89.

Casey and Drew burst into the bar of The Green Man to find the Inspector tucking heartily into a roast lamb dinner with a pleased looking landlady standing behind him watching. He looked up momentarily from his food to see them enter and waved them over to join him while he chewed.

'Good afternoon,' he greeted them as they sat down.

'Good afternoon Inspector, how are you feeling? Casey asked.

'Still a little weak, Doctor,' the Inspector admitted. 'I hope I wasn't too much trouble? Mavis advises me that I've been out for the count for about twelve hours?'

'No, you weren't really any trouble, you were asleep for most of it,' Casey replied, instinctively taking his wrist to check his pulse.

'How long have you been awake?' she asked.

'About an hour, I've been coming too slowly, and drinking lots of sugary tea. I've literally just sat down to eat five minutes before you came in.' Casey studied the remains of the food on the plate, most of it had already been eaten.

'You're very hungry I see,' she pointed out knowingly.

'Yes, I feel as though I haven't eaten for days,' he admitted. 'I would like to thank you both for taking care of me while I was ill,' he said seriously.

'You're welcome,' Drew replied humbly.

'And also thank Casey for suggesting roast lamb for my lunch,' he commented to Mavis.

'Yes, well done me dear!' Mavis laughed, and left them to it now the Inspector had some company.

'Well, I wanted to encourage you to eat. Any memory of what happened?' Casey asked. 'Any idea as to what might have made you pass out?' The Inspector chewed his mouthful thoughtfully for a moment. He knew exactly what had caused him to pass out, it had been the effects of the world he had visited on his body, but he wasn't about to tell them that.

'Nothing comes to mind immediately,' he told them blankly. 'I seem to remember something to do with the Firestone.' Drew and Casey glanced at each other.

'What can you remember about it exactly?' Drew asked. 'It was the last thing you said before you passed out. You stared at the standing stones and shouted "The Firestone,"' Drew informed him. The Inspector nodded.

'Well, I knew there was something about that stone. I took some samples and I received the results a few days ago. I suspect the rock will be an exact match to the stones at the site, but I would like to ask Doctor Samson for a second opinion.' Drew smiled.

'No need. While you were recovering Casey and I asked the good Doctor to have a look at the Firestone. He immediately recognised it, and took some measurements. He agrees that it is from the site. In fact he suspects, as I think you do, that it is the lintel that once connected the two stone pillars,' Drew explained.

The Inspector paused for a moment, and took a slow look around The Green Man public house. He considered his options, and what they meant for Firestone. He considered future victims of the energy's reach, yet to have been swept away from their homes and dragged through time and space to find their end in the trees of Firestone. He thought of the eyes Drew had seen, and that had appeared in his photographs. Travellers that had become lost, and were now trapped in the trees. He thought of the missing men of Firestone, caught up in it all and trying to get home.

'Well then it is clear what we have to do,' the Inspector informed them. He knew what needed to be done, and judging by the readings he had been taking since he had regained consciousness, he had to do it soon.

'It is?' Casey asked. She glanced between the Inspector and Drew, who sat nodding knowingly to each other.

'We have to put the Firestone back where it belongs,' Drew told her, much to the masked delight of the impressed Inspector. 'We have to replace the lintel.' It took a moment for Casey to realise what he meant.

'Move the stone?' she said, aghast. 'Is that, how?' she stammered, flabbergasted. Both men were pleased to see her speechless for once.

'We should get up to the site,' Drew informed the Inspector coolly. 'Speak to Samson and his team.' The Inspector nodded in agreement, he had been shovelling food in to his mouth the whole time and his big lunch was almost finished.

'If we're to shift the stone we'll need the army men, the digger, all the help we can get,' Drew continued seriously. 'Let's get up there.' The Inspector finished his last mouthful and stood purposefully.

Casey, who had been sat in a stupor, suddenly realised they were preparing to leave and leapt up to pull her coat on. So shocked was she at what they were going to attempt that she had failed to notice the men donning their coats. She chased after them as they flurried out into the street, leaving the pub quiet and peaceful behind them. The drive to the stones was quick, Drew was purposeful, fuelled by the sense of urgency exuded by the Inspector. He pulled up by the tape and they all jumped out. A Constable pulled back the tape for them and they all nodded politely to him as they passed.

'Nice to see you up and about Inspector,' one of the men called as they rushed past.

'Thank you.' The Inspector nodded politely back. Their feet crunched over the gravel, the hard stone giving the route into the trees a confident permanence.

'Ahhh, I see the path I ordered a few days ago has finally been laid. Wonderful,' the Inspector announced with delight as his feet dug into the stone. Drew and Casey exchanged an impressed glance and they trudged towards the stones. As they approached Drew spotted the truck parked up and John the driver reading his paper in his cab. The digger was carefully piling mounds of earth on to the back. They navigated carefully around the commotion and the Inspector quickly found Doctor Samson, who practically yelled with excitement to see him.

'Inspector!' he rushed up to him and began shaking his hand. 'How are you feeling?'

'I'm much better thank you, how are things here?' the Inspector asked.

'Very busy, and exciting! Let me show you what we have found, I have to say the men are extremely helpful.'

'Wonderful, I see that there has been a lot of action here since my last visit.' The Inspector, Drew and Casey looked about the site. It had developed even since they had last seen it, with more trees removed around the site, allowing for the digger to move freely to pick up soil from around the stones.

'Yes, as you can see a lot more stones have been found under the soil.'

'I believe you had a chance to look at the Firestone while I was recovering?' the Inspector asked.

'Yes, fascinating, I think it once connected the two remaining stones you know.'

'Yes, that was my theory,' the Inspector informed him. 'I took some samples, I'll see you get a copy of the results. I'd like to take some samples of these stones as well.'

'Already done,' Samson informed him.

'Good work, thank you,' the Inspector smiled.

'Now, the next phase of the site will be to have it cleared so we can begin a serious excavation for more artefacts,' Samson informed them.

'Apologies Doctor, but I am not quite finished with it,' the Inspector informed the excitable man with a friendly smile.

'I see, sorry Inspector, so what is the next step for the site?' he asked, wondering what else they could possibly do with it.

'We need to return it to some of its former glory,' the Inspector informed him. Samson's face adopted a confused look, as he awaited an explanation.

'We need to return the lintel to its rightful place,' the Inspector told him. 'We need to put the Firestone back atop these two monoliths.' Doctor Samson's face did not lose its look of confusion.

'You can't mean...' was all he managed before the Inspector left him and weaved his way through the men and climbed upon a newly uncovered stone. The men all began nodding and greeting him as he passed, aware that the Inspector had been unwell and glad to have him back up and at the site with them.

'Good afternoon everyone can I have your attention?' he called about the space. The men immediately downed tools and made their way toward him. Major Sheppard was glad to see him back.

'Alright lads, here we go,' he called to them in encouragement as he downed his spade and they all gathered around the stone that the Inspector stood upon. The digger stopped, and even John poked his head out of the window of his cab to see what was going on. The Inspector waited for everyone to assemble, and quieten down. A low hush spread across them, even the trees leant it to listen.

'First of all I want to say a big thank you for all the hard work you have done here, it looks truly impressive, especially compared to what we were faced with just a few days ago. As you can see this is a site of major historical interest, however it is not complete,' the Inspector called to them.

'There is a piece missing, and today, we are going to put it back.' There was a murmur of wonder amongst the men.

'I refer to the lintel, the stone that once sat between these two stones.' He motioned to the giant monoliths that dominated the space. 'It sat there for thousands of years, then a few hundred years ago some vandals removed it, and it now sits on the Firestone roundabout.' The Inspector paused to allow the gathered men to chatter for a moment, allowing them to digest the news.

'Today we make more history, by returning it to its rightful place.' There was a collective gasp that echoed around the open space between the dwindling trees.

'If you could all pick up your tools and get on to the bus, I will meet you all at the roundabout.' The men exchanged amazed glances at this sudden turn of events, then the area burst into a hive of activity. They abandoned the stones and began picking up anything useful and marching down toward the entrance. They took off like a well-oiled machine, even before the Major began yelling at them.

'Well then you lot, you heard him let's get this sortie moving!' His voice was brash amongst the branches. 'Archie, Felix, get down to the bus and get the doors opened. Carl help get these tools shifted back down there.' The Inspector grabbed Drew.

'Best get down to the tape and warn everyone that we're coming out,' he told him. Drew nodded. They started off, but the Inspector stopped him in contemplation for a moment.

'You might as well go ahead in the car and prepare the Firestone roundabout. I'll follow with the digger. I'll have to take it down to the other site and get rid of all this soil, but that'll give you time to make the site secure, and maybe get a diversion around the roundabout. Get on to Firestone Station and get all available men down to the Firestone roundabout. News is going to travel fast, let's hope we can get it over with as quickly as possible. We might need to ask Nettlewood nicely if they can spare a few more bobbies. We're going to need to keep people back from the site while we try and dig it up and move it.' The Inspector was thinking aloud, but Drew paid close attention.

'Yes, you're right, see you soon,' he told him, and confidently raced off toward the entrance to the trees. While the Inspector raced off toward the digger, Drew looked round and saw Casey chatting to an archaeologist. He quickened up to her.

'Look, I'm going to be a bit busy, will you be alright?' She smiled a rather contented smile at having such a fine man checking on her.

'Yes, I'll be fine. You get to work we can catch up later.' Drew nodded gratefully and raced off toward the small crowd of people trying to grab a glance of the stones from behind the police tape. As they approached people began to call questions at him.

'What's happening Drew?' one of the assembled townsfolk called out to him. He put up a hand up as hello, but made his way to the two officers that stood on the line.

'There's about to be a lot of activity coming this way,' Drew warned them. 'The Inspector is moving the men.'

'Where are they going?' the Constable asked.

'They're going to the Firestone,' Drew informed them quietly.

'They're going to dig it up and move it up here.' Their jaws dropped in shock but Drew kept talking. 'Then they're going to try and put it on top of the other two stones.' The two men stood, mouths agape. Drew kept talking, time was short. 'You'll need to stay here, but every officer on duty has to get down to the Firestone to stop people getting too close to the digging. Get on the radio and see who's about and send them down there. If you can't find anyone get on to Nettlewood,' Drew instructed him.

'Yes Drew,' he replied simply, and rushed to his car for his radio.

Drew raced off to his car and headed down the hill.

90.
Drew sped down to the Firestone and arrived before anyone else. The space was deserted, and rather desolate. The shops were open, but the weather was too cold and too wet for many people to brave going outside. Drew parked his car up on the roundabout and looked anxiously up the road towards the stones. A few moments later Jim Moir and Bob Renwick from Nettlewood appeared in their car, and parked up behind Drew. The climbed out, pulled on their helmets, and slowly stalked towards him, arms behind their backs.

'Afternoon Drew, what's occurring?' Jim asked as they approached.

Drew waited until he was closer before speaking in a hushed voice.

'The Firestone is about to be exhumed,' he informed him quietly. 'There's about to be a lot of men and dangerous equipment coming down here from the site of the stones. We need to secure the roundabout, and see any cars that might appear have safe passage through,' Drew quickly told the nodding men. 'You two take up position at the other two roads, stop them at the junction, check it's clear before sending them through.'

'Bloody hell they're shifting this thing?' Jim interjected quietly.

'Yes, though how we actually do it is another question.' Drew realised, seeing the stone now made him wonder if they were perhaps being a bit ambitious.

'Aye, best of luck getting that out of there!' Jim nodded at it doubtfully.

'Well, come on Jim let's get to us post,' Bob told him. 'He's got a bus fully of squaddies coming down the hill to help 'im. I'm sure they can manage without us.' They wandered off to their posts with Jim shaking his head. Soon more policemen arrived, and Drew assigned them to gaps along the perimeter of the roundabout. Soon a line of men had appeared around the edge, as was a slowly gathering crowd as people visiting the shops paused to goggle at what was happening. Mrs Lancaster stopped to wonder what was going on, and she was soon joined by Sarah Hollis from the green grocers.

''Ere there's a lot of bobbies appearin' up there,' Sarah told her.

'Aye, what are they up to?' Mrs Lancaster asked.

'I don't know, I just spotted them now.'

'Do you think it's another body?' Mrs Hollis asked her.

'I don't know dear, but there's definitely something going on over there.' Their heads bobbed up and down as they tried to catch a glance of what could be causing so much excitement. A few cars drove slowly past, helped along by Jim and Bob. For a minute, all was quiet, and those gathering at the roundabout held their breath in anticipation for what would come. Drew had been stood at the junction, staring up the road, straining his ears for the slightest hint of coach engine. Finally he saw the familiar blue bus chugging down the hill.

'Alright gents, here they come,' he shouted to his colleagues in warning.

'Looks like somethings about to happen,' Mrs Lancaster said, nodding at the policemen as they began preparing for action. Word travelled around the few shoppers that had assembled, and when the coach appeared on the roundabout a small gasp of awe escaped from them. It pulled up on the side of road next to the roundabout and the army men piled out and followed the archaeologists over to the rock.

'Well I never look at that lot!' Ivy Cole exclaimed.

'Yes,' Mrs Lancaster replied nervously. 'Must be that lot up the road, they found some old stones you know.'

'Some stones, yes.' Ivy Cole was caught between rushing off to get her friends and staying to see what would happen. She decided to rush off and find Mrs Tolhirst, and told everyone she saw on her way about the events unfolding. The few people that had been vying for a view of the stones up the hill slowly trickled down behind the coach, and after a few minutes a small crowd had gathered to watch from the roundabout's perimeter. When the men began examining the stone Drew joined them.

'What do we think?' he asked Samson, who stood examining it with the Major.

'Well, if we start digging a little further back, I reckon from about here.' He stood at a side of the stone where the ground was lower. 'And make our way forward, like this,' he waved an arm from where he stood toward the stone. 'Being careful of the stone of course, then we should be able to reach the bottom fine,' the Major told him. 'We could probably lever it out from there.'

'Good, let's get going then.' Drew told them. The Major nodded to his men, and they cleared a space for the pickaxes to swing.

'Here we go,' Mrs Lancaster tapped her friend's elbow, and the collection of people watched in wonder as the first pickaxe stuck the cold hard ground.

91.

The Inspector arrived at the site with the truck and the digger a little later than he would have liked, but was pleased to see that work had already begun. John had to park the truck further up the road to prevent any hold ups forming, and the Inspector left him there and rushed over to dig.

'Drew!' the Inspector called as he approached.

'Ahh hello Inspector,' Drew called back. He approached the Firestone and studied the progress, pleased to see the hole around it was deepening quickly. The ground was hard and old, unwilling to give up its prize. As the men dug there was a commotion at the perimeter, and a policeman approached the Inspector with a rather bothered looking Simon, the archaeologist from the stones.

'Ahh good afternoon,' the Inspector welcomed him, recognising him from the day before.

'Stop this!' he yelled at the men, ignoring the Inspector. The men bore him no mind and continued unabated. Simon realised he was a little powerless to stop them so approached the Inspector instead.

'You have to stop this! You are destroying a historical site! You can't just remove it!' he shouted indignantly.

'Yes, true, it is a historical site,' the Inspector replied quietly. A few murmurs echoed around the crowd at Simon's intervention, just as he had wanted.

'But it is also the scene of historical vandalism,' the Inspector continued, calmly. 'The stones were buried, and we have revealed them, would you rather have had them remain hidden to respect it as a historical site?'

'Well that's a bit different,' the flustered man erupted.

'What's he doing?' Mrs Lancaster asked her friend.

'Who is he?' asked Mavis from The Green Man who had rushed down when she had heard what was going on.

'I don't know, but he's not happy,' Phyllis May from the Tea shop commented.

'I think he's trying to stop them,' Ivy Cole had returned in time to see the events unfolding.

'Stop who?' Ernie had taken a break from offering the roofers from Nettlewood tea to come and see what was going on.

'The men, he's trying to stop them from moving the stone.'

'Oh is that what they're doing?' Mrs Lancaster replied in a hushed voice. 'I never thought I'd see the day.'

'Where are they going it to move it anyway?' Mrs Earnshaw pondered out loud.

'Why are they moving it then?' Jerry from the barbers asked.

'How should we know?' they replied in unison.

'Finally, that horrible thing is being moved,' Jerry told them.

'Shush!' someone else interjected, bending their ear toward the conversation.

'The Firestone is in the wrong place,' the Inspector was telling Simon. It should be returned to restore the stones to their historically accurate design.' There was a ripple of applause from the assembled crowd of Firestone residents who had heard what the Inspector had said. Doctor Samson suddenly noticed what was happening and left the work at the Firestone to interject.

'Simon, it's fine.' He tugged at his friends arm to pull him away. 'Look, come and watch them removing it, this is real history, were righting an ancient wrong.' Seeing Samson assisting with the stones removal, Simon stood down. He was not so much admitting he was wrong, as bowing to the pressure of the crowd. The army men dug down until they found the end of the stone, and as Samson had predicted it was at least ten feet long.

'Now we have to work out how we are going to get it out of the ground,' Samson informed his disgruntled colleague Simon, the soldiers, the Inspector, and Drew.

'We still have the digger at our disposal,' The Major reminded them.

'And the truck,' the Inspector looked about the stone.

'Do you think we could get some rope attached, lift it out with the digger and place it on the truck?' he asked the Major. The Major was also looking down at the stone and the same plan was forming in his head.

'I believe that is probably our best bet,' he agreed. 'But I don't think it's going to be easy.'

'Unless we had some sort of brace above it, we could put a rope over it and pull it out,' Drew suggested. The Inspector eyed the scaffolding that had been half erected around Ernie's house.

'I believe I might have just the thing,' he told them.

92.

Between the trees, shapes danced. Unseen by the crowds, hidden in the dark, they oozed. They squeezed and squashed, ebbing for a view, watching the crowd, watching the men digging at the Firestone.

They felt the change. They felt the flow releasing, changing direction. They felt the bubble of energy slow, and its expansion ease. They saw, they felt, and they waited, as they had for so long, except now they knew. Now they knew they would not have to wait much longer.

93.

While the Inspector stalked off to try and convince Ernie's scaffolders to help them, Drew took the men that weren't digging back to the bus to collect all the rope they could find. They returned with arms full to find the Inspector carefully guiding a truck full of scaffold poles over to the stones. The truck's doors advertised them as being the Brake Brothers. When the truck was parked safely they jumped out of the cab, and a conference began between the Inspector, the Major, the Brake brothers, and the archaeologists.

'It'll need to be high enough to get the stone in the air and the truck underneath,' the Inspector explained. The scaffolders looked about the place and did a quick calculation.

'How are you going to lift it out?' the older brother asked. The Inspector motioned toward the heap of rope Drew and the soldiers had gathered.

'I think we'll need more than that,' the Major shook his head doubtfully.

'And I don't think your truck will take the weight,' the younger scaffolder informed him, adding to the woes. 'There's a good twenty five ton of stone there.' The Inspector stopped for a second, suddenly realising he was going to need another plan.

'Doctor Samson, how would the stones have been moved originally?' he asked.

'Ah, well, interesting question Inspector,' he informed him, pleased his time to contribute had finally come. 'And a matter that is up for debate. While some believe the stones were moved by water from their home in south Wales, others say the stones' weight would have been too heavy to float. Another theory is...' The Inspector held up a hand.

'How would they have got the stones across land, if they wanted to move them a few hundred yards up the road?' the Inspector narrowed his question down for the excitable doctor.

'Oh I see, well yes, still an interesting question, the general consensus is that they would have been rolled along on logs, as the logs rolled underneath the stones they would have been passed back to the front.' The Inspector studied the stone, thought about the distance it had to travel, and how easy it would be to do.

'That would use a lot less rope,' the Major informed him.

'And you could use the truck to pull it up the hill,' the scaffolder nodded. 'We could use some of our poles to push it out, on to the trunks,' he suggested. 'All we need is some trunks.'

'Yes, but we will still need you to construct something to lift it on top of the stones,' the Inspector informed them, thinking aloud. 'If you could head up there and start constructing, I would be most appreciative. I will reimburse you of course for your help.' The men nodded eagerly, caught up in the excitement.

'Major, take half your men and look for large trunks of a similar circumference in the piles of wood up near the site that we can roll the stone on. You'll need to trim them down to ensure they can roll comfortably. The other half can keep digging here, and we'll try and work out how we get the stone out of the hole and on to the trunks.' The men all nodded and made their way off to their tasks.

'Do you think the rope will be strong enough to lift it? Drew asked, marvelling at its size.

'No, I think we'll need something stronger,' the Inspector admitted.

'I could go up to Gerald's garage, see if he could help?' Drew suggested.

'Yes, good thinking,' the Inspector agreed. 'I'm going to remain here for now, try to keep things moving,' the Inspector told him. The entire area had descended into bedlam as different people began coming and going, preparing themselves. Drew headed off to the garage while the scaffolders removed a few poles to use to try and pry the stone out, then drove carefully through the crowd to begin constructing a frame to lift the lintel on to the standing stones. Samson and Simon stood over the men as they hacked at the soil, anxious that the stone didn't get damaged, and that any other artefact hidden under with the stone remained intact.

Almost as quickly as the soldiers left to find trunks, they began returning with them. After about an hour a pile of twenty trimmed down trunks had accumulated, and Drew returned to the roundabout with Gerald in his tow truck, laden with chain. By this time the rock was well exposed on one side, and the men began carefully freeing it from the remaining soil. The mud had only been removed from one side, to allow it to be lifted and carefully tipped on to the trunks on its side. The accumulating trunks were laid out, Gerald's truck was positioned and the chains were carefully attached to the stone. The long scaffolding poles were poked under the end of the stone, with men queuing up to help lever the stone out.

'Here we go then,' Doctor Samson gasped to Simon, neither men could believe what they were witnessing; it was all happening so quickly. The Inspector checked everyone was ready, then with a wave of his hand the task began. Gerald slowly pulled forward with his truck, the chains straining under the weight. The men all pulled at the poles, the weight seeming too much for their combined efforts at first, but gradually, slowly, the stone began to shift from its hole. As it rose it slowly tipped, then almost gracefully it slowly dived ground ward, until it was horizontal for the first time in several hundred years. As it landed on the trunks the ground reverberated with the powerful thud it made. The crowd strained for a view of what was happening, and when it hit the ground a small ripple of applause flittered amongst the assembled people. A flutter of rain erupted on to the scene, but undeterred the Inspector prepared everyone for the next phase.

'Gerald, you are doing a marvellous job, please wait there while we arrange ourselves,' the Inspector called to him. Gerald raised a hand to show his understanding and awaited instructions.

The Inspector made his way over to the stone, where the men were laying the logs out behind the truck in preparation.

'Marvellous, yes, that's it.' The Inspector was pleased the men were able to organise themselves so efficiently. The Major mingled in between them to hurry them along, ensuring the logs were evenly spaced.

'I think we're ready Inspector,' he called when all the logs were in place.

'Thank you Major,' the Inspector called back. A group of men stood at the rear of the stone, ready to begin lifting the logs to the front of the line. The atmosphere was alive, the excitement in the air was tangible, and the crowd watched on in a hushed awe.

'Thank you Gerald, let's begin slowly up the hill shall we?' the Inspector called to him, and the truck began to inch slowly forward. The men jumped into action, the logs were moved quickly and carefully, and the stone began its journey rolling on logs to the stones with an entourage of almost a hundred people.

When they reached the stones, almost an hour later, the edges of the horizon were beginning to darken. The scaffolders had done the Inspector proud, having constructed a huge frame that towered around the standing stones. The men were still active but their energy was waning. The policeman stood at the mouth of the path into the copse to hold the crowd at bay for their own safety. The stone was rolled into position under the frame, and more ropes and chains were tied around it to help guide it into place. When all was prepared, and the chains reattached to Gerald's powerful truck, everyone one stood waiting, ready for the next instruction.

'Everyone ready?' the Inspector called. A general murmur of readiness echoed about the trees.

'Gerald?' the Inspector called to the truck, and a hand appeared to indicate he was ready.

'Right, slowly then please, here we go,' the Inspector called, and the truck moved slowly forward. The stone began to rise into the air. The men also had ropes attached to help lift and angle it correctly. They all took the strain, keeping the stone steady, and guiding it as it in ascended. With much shouting and pulling the men bravely tackled the heavy load and the lintel was carefully, slowly, and precisely placed upon the stones. When it landed in place a satisfying thud echoed around the space. For a moment dead silence hushed around the men, as everyone held their breath and hoped the stones would hold the weight, followed by a stammer of relieved applause when the monoliths stood firm. The men then began to walk around the stones, talking and chattering excitedly to each other, marvelling at what they achieved.

'Well, it's a marvellous sight,' Simon conceded, finding Drew and the Inspector with Doctor Samson. 'There's no doubt that it should have been put right, my apologies for my interference gentlemen.' He was humbled to have been present at such a prestigious occurrence, and embarrassed by his behaviour.

'Oh no bother Simon,' Samson waved his apology away. 'Your heart was in the right place.'

'Indeed,' the Inspector agreed. 'It takes a brave man to stand up for what he believes is right in the face of such opposition. I applaud you for it.' Simon was pleased to have the Inspector's blessing, and to have been a part of the day's activity.

'If you're alright Inspector we'll remove the scaffold now?' one of the brothers approached and asked.

'Yes of course, I cannot thank you enough for your help,' the Inspector replied gratefully.

'Oh not at all Inspector, historic moment this, glad we were a part of it,' he informed him. 'I'll drop the bill into Firestone police station as you said.

'Of course, and they will forward it to me,' he told Drew who nodded in understanding.

The brothers made their way to the stones through the throng of people to the carefully constructed frame to begin dismantling it. The army men began lending a hand, and before long their truck was once more laden with metal poles. They then set off back to the roundabout to collect the last of their poles from the hole so they could carry on with Ernie's roof. By now the sun was beginning to set, the sky was muddying behind the thick cloud. A splatter of rain began to fall icy and hard on to the crowd, and this seemed to be the last straw. The men all resigned to leaving the stones behind and began to slowly trickle away from the clearing, and towards the town, gravitating toward The Green Man.

The Inspector and Drew followed them out of the area and down the path.

'So, now do we look for the missing men?' Drew asked, wondering what the next step would be.

'Not quite,' the Inspector informed him. 'We must return tonight, and watch the stones. If I am right, the men will come and find us,' Drew replied with a puzzled look, which the ever observant Inspector noticed. 'Come and have some dinner, I shall explain,' the Inspector advised.

'Only one more night to keep watch chaps,' the Inspector called to the policeman on guard merrily as they passed.

'Oh really?' one replied, relieved, though a little confused. They watched the crowds dispersing.

'Yes, and you'll have some company tonight. A couple of ambulances will be sat here with you while Drew and I search the woods for the missing men.'

'You're going out looking for them tonight?' The other asked, not quite believing what he was hearing. Darkness hovered over them perilously. A splatter of rain lashed them and the cold bit in a little deeper. 'Do you really think you'll find them then?'

'Well, let's hope so,' the Inspector replied, rather confidently. They made their way back to Drew's car and drove quickly to The Green Man. They entered to find it bursting at the seams with excited and slightly drunk town's people. At the sight of the Inspector a cheer erupted.

'It would appear you are some kind of hero,' Drew called to him over the applause that followed. The Inspector began shaking the hands that were thrust at him as he fought his way to the bar.

'Whatever for?' he asked them all, though Drew was the only one listening.

'For moving the stone, it was a dark piece of our history for a long time, you burst into town and its moved in a week, and you discover the stones to boot,' Drew informed him.

'I'm just doing my job,' he informed them all modestly, refusing the pint of beer that someone was trying to push into his hand.

'Oh not for me, not while on duty,' he brushed the brimming glass away politely. 'I will have a cup of tea though please Mavis, and two lamb roasts when you're ready. Perhaps we'll eat in my room, Drew?' he suggested over the ruckus.

94.

Drew and the Inspector made their way up to the Inspector's room, where the Inspector immediately began tidying away his things to make space on the dresser so Drew could put the pot of tea down.

'The lamb here really is delicious,' the Inspector said over his shoulder as he filled drawers with folders and paperwork. The first thing Drew noticed on entering the room was the odour of developing fluid.

'Well it's all local, probably from old Benson's farm, between here and Grantham,' Drew replied, entertaining the small talk. 'So, what should I expect tonight?' he asked. 'Are we going into the woods?'

With the dresser cleared he could put the tray of tea things down, and the Inspector immediately began to pour two cups. Drew stood by the window and looked out upon the swaying of the trees behind the dim roof tops.

'No, I do not wish to enter those trees again,' the Inspector replied. We shall be sitting comfortably in your car.' He opened a drawer and pulled out a folder.

'Here, look at these,' he suggested.

'More photographs?' Drew asked, picking up the folder.

'Yes, taken over the last couple of days.' Drew opened it up and took them out. The first was a view of the trees from the stones. At first glance it seemed a rather dull photograph, but as Drew looked closer he saw stood to one side was a dark shape of a man, like a tall shadow, half exposed, half empty. Drew studied it carefully.

'What is it?' Drew asked.

'That is what I am not sure of. But there are more.' Drew continued to look through, and on each picture a vague shape appeared.

'It looks like the missing men,' Drew informed him after close examination. 'I don't understand,' he admitted. 'How did you take these?'

'Just with my ordinary camera,' the Inspector replied. 'I also developed these.' He opened a second folder and passed the photographs to Drew. 'These were taken by the archaeologists.'

Drew sat quietly for a few moments and studied the photographs.

'Sorry Inspector, what am I looking for?' he asked, unable to see the relevance.

'Exactly. The strange shapes only appear on the photographs I took. I think it means that the men are trying to contact me, to tell me something.' He looked at the photographs from his camera again. 'I hope it means we are doing the right thing, and that replacing the lintel will bring them back,' the Inspector informed him just as there was a knock at the door.

'Room service,' came a friendly call from behind it. Drew pushed the photographs back into the folder, and the Inspector stood and let Mavis in.

'Thank you for this Mavis I do appreciate it,' the Inspector welcomed her warmly. Drew moved the tea tray so that she could put their dinners down in its place on the dresser.

'Oh not a problem Inspector, I don't blame you wanting to come up here and get some peace.' She bustled her way in and put the dinners down. She instinctively grabbed Drew's tea tray from him.

'Enjoy gentlemen,' she called to them as she flurried out again.

'Oh, Mavis before you go.' She stopped in her tracks and spun round.

'Yes Inspector?' she asked, eager to please.

'This may seem a little odd, but I was wondering if I could borrow some mirrors from you?' She thought, for a moment, not sure how to react.

'Mirrors Inspector?' Whatever for?' she asked, rather confused.

'Oh it is just part of the investigation,' he told her vaguely.

'Which ones, the ones in the bathroom?' she asked, glancing anxiously round the doorway at the strange smelling red room.

'Yes, and one from the bar if possible. You won't even notice that they're missing, all will be returned before you awake in the morning.'

'Well alright then,' she replied. 'Just be careful with them.' She bustled away again, leaving the men to their food. They perched on the end of the bed facing their dinner on the dresser, and the makeshift arrangement sufficed as a dining table. They began to eat. After a few mouthfuls, the Inspector paused to take a sip of tea.

'So, do you have a theory around where the men are, about what is happening in Firestone?' Drew asked, though he wasn't sure if he would understand the answer.

'Well, Drew, the best theory I can formulate with the evidence I have obtained is that Firestone seems to be attracting energy sources in many different forms, like the increased magnetism, and the lower pressure, but also energy in forms we have only really theorised about before. Whether this is because of the stones, I know not. It could be that they are in some way emanating this energy, or it could be that the stone circle was built there because the early residents were aware of the energy that surrounds this area and constructed the circle as some kind of monument to it. Either way, the energy and the stones are now connected. The energy itself was being used as a pathway across a myriad of dimensions by other energy forms.' He paused for a sip of tea and a mouthful of food. 'Then, as we know, the energy was rediscovered a few hundred years ago and the townspeople destroyed the stone circle in fear, in an attempt to eradicate the energy. In doing so they managed to cause a blockage that trapped these energy forms in the trees.' Drew could barely believe what he was being told, it all sounded too fantastic. 'On the most part the energy became lost in the trees, however I think that some of the energy that became trapped in the trees made the leap from tree to man, and it has been inhabiting the bodies of the men that were at the Mayor's house for decades, perhaps even inhabiting their fathers before them. My best guess is that they found a way into the bodies in an attempt to reopen the blockage, but something went wrong, or they found themselves unable to do anything, and so they have been trapped in the bodies of men ever since. Where the others lived quiet lives, eking out an existence through the generations, I think something went awry with the Banks line. They somehow became able to use the beings that had possessed them, exploiting them to build up power and influence, and using that influence to continue to keep the secret of Firestone hidden. Hiding the stones and stopping them from being repaired. That is why your father died, that is why others have died in the past at the hand of the Bank's family. As people discovered the secret, they were silenced.'

Drew nodded, dumbfounded.

'I expect that when it gets dark enough whatever the energy is that inhabits those bodies will make their way to the stones, and travel through them back along the unblocked path, opened now that the Firestone is back in place. There are likely to be other 347's that inhabit the trees, and I am hoping we might see more of these lifeforms through the mirrors.' He glanced nervously out of the window at the rapidly encroaching darkness.

'Time moves on,' he said, swallowing a mouthful of potato. Drew had stopped eating while the Inspector had been explaining his theory. Both men now tucked into their meals, the explanation rolling around in their heads. The Inspector had been purposefully honest with Drew, he had wanted him to hear the full theory but knew he would need time to digest the information. When they had finished their food, they relaxed as best they could on the bed.

'How does all that sound to you Drew?' the Inspector asked, interested to hear what he thought of it. Drew sat back on the bed, looking out of the window.

'If it had come from anyone else I might have thought them mad. But over the last week I have seen some strange things. I would never have believed it if I hadn't been with you throughout your investigation,' he admitted. The Inspector smiled.

'Luckily I have enough evidence to back up the theory, but we are yet to see it in practice. That is, I hope, what we will be witnessing tonight. Let's grab those mirrors and get head up to the stones,' the Inspector said excitedly heading into the bathroom. Drew stood and put his coat on.

'Does Mavis not mind you transforming her bathroom into a developing room?' he asked.

'She hasn't mentioned it,' the Inspector replied, lifting a mirror off of the wall and not understanding why it might be of any inconvenience. Drew grabbed a second smaller mirror from over the sink and they headed out of the door. They fought their way through the crowd, who helpfully carried the third mirror out to the police car for them. They laid them carefully in the boot and the backseat, then headed off up the hill.

95.

The approach to the stones was dark, and all around them the trees swung about in the wind and rain in defiance of what they had witnessed that day. As they approached the entrance to the woods Drew's headlights picked out two ambulances parked at the side of the road.

'Ahh the ambulances are already here,' the Inspector said with surprise. Drew piloted the car up to the police line, and one of his colleagues jumped out of their car and into the cold night. He pulled the tape back and allowed them through. Drew and the Inspector gave a wave of thanks then headed up toward the stones.

'Do you think you could turn the car around?' the Inspector asked, looking about the space in the dark evening.

'Probably,' Drew replied, beginning a tricky manoeuvre in the odd corner of wood that he had found himself in. He managed to squeeze the car around, so they faced back down the newly gravelled path and toward the road. The Inspector fetched the mirrors from the backseat and set them up on the dashboard in front of them blocking their view forward.

'So what are we looking for?' Drew asked, staring into the dark behind them at the stones reflected in the mirrors. The Inspector peered carefully at the newly replaced Firestone, and as his eyes adjusted to the dark, he saw what he was hoping for.

'There, it's beginning already,' the Inspector pointed at the space between the stones and sure enough a dim light had begun to illuminate the air. Drew turned around quickly and glanced about the dark space that surrounded the stones.

'I can only see it in the mirror, like the eyes on the night I discovered the body,' Drew realised. The Inspector nodded.

'We must watch carefully for the men, I'm not sure how long it will take them to appear.' As they watched the light between the stones slowly grew brighter, illuminating the space around the stones. Soon the night was darkest black around them, but the light shone through it, brighter than white. The glare shone around the space, illuminating shapes, picking out things that were ordinarily invisible in the darkness. From the trees came a waft of fog, a light whiff of vapour that caught the light and reflected the spectrum through it and out amongst the trees. The vapour paused, circling round and moving about the stones, studying the light. Drew and the Inspector watched open mouthed.

'A visitor from another plane, another dimension,' the Inspector whispered to Drew as if he might startle it at any moment.

'Stranded by the blockage. It must depend on low frequency light waves for its means of travel, hmmm,' the Inspector took a few photographs of it in the mirror as it wafted around the space, it then shot through the stones, vanishing between them.

'Very interesting,' he mused to himself. He checked his watch and studied a few instruments, then noted it all down on his notebook. Drew sat and watched the reflection of the invisible scene behind him, mesmerised. Soon another shape shifted itself out of the trees. It was black, and flat, and was only visible because of its contrast against the white of the light. It moved like a square wheel, its sides flexing, shrinking and growing as it rotated. The shape headed straight for the light emanating from the gap without hesitation, like a scared rodent darting for safety. It was gone before the Inspector could get his camera to it, but he scribbled the time and a description down in his book.

As the darkness of night sunk deeper into black the light between the stones grew ever brighter, as if drawing its energy from the dark. It illuminated the view of the woods around them in the mirror, revealing lost visitors hiding between the trunks. All had been washed up in the woods around Firestone when the circle had been destroyed. When the sky reached its darkest at around three in the morning, the shapes that flowed through the light and between the stones were indistinguishable from each other. An endless stream of startling shapes darted through whisping smoke trails and slipped through a spectrum of wavelengths as the lifeforms skipped through space and light before disappearing through the stones back on their way to their own dimensions. The trees too were affected by it. They were shrinking, thinning, losing energy. As the energy dissipated so the readings on the Inspector's instruments slowly faded. He checked them regularly all night, carefully noting down every change in them. The spectacle was like nothing Drew could ever imagine. Creatures he could barely comprehend were flitting past behind his head. It was like watching dreams being formed, being dreamt, and being released. The shapes hurried past for a while, but suddenly their course slowed and they began coming indeterminately, until through trees and into the light came floating shapes that Drew was more familiar with. They moved sideways, side by side through the trunks, burning above all the other shapes. The eyes were powerful and piercing. They stopped in their tracks in the clearing and stared into the mirrors and straight into Drew and the Inspector's eyes. The men stopped in shock. For a moment, everything slowed down. The light paused in its flow, hanging trails in mid-air. The eyes stared at them and they were caught in their piercing glare that penetrated through the night. Then the eyes were on them and in them, and they were a part of them, and of all the mysterious lifeforms that was passing by, and they could feel and know and see all the explicit and unending gratitude that the beings felt for the release that was finally theirs. And then the eyes released them, their message delivered, and they moved on through the stones and on their way. The night returned around them and time resumed a direction and speed they were more accustomed to. For a moment the two men were motionless, as their minds raced to comprehend what had happened. Before they could move or speak or even blink, another disturbance came from beyond their field of vision. This one was much more solid, and human. The body of Atkins crashed abruptly out from the trunks, tripping and falling on to his face then springing unnaturally back up again. Drew jumped from the car but the Inspector called him back.

'Drew! Not yet, let him go through the stones.' Drew looked out into the trees to try and spot his friend and colleague, but all about the trees was dark. The area remained deserted, just as it had been when they had arrived, blanketed in an insidious night. He climbed back into the car, to continue his vigil by the mirror. Now he saw where Atkins stood, twitching and convulsing in the light of the stones. He then limped, leapt, and finally sprinted his way at the stones, leaping through them headfirst, and to the relief of the Inspector and Drew, shooting straight through to the other side as one might expect. They looked into the mirror at the body of Atkins, lying motionless on the cold wet ground.

'Right, let's go,' the Inspector yelled and leapt out of the car. He and Drew sprinted over to Atkins, and found him lying face down in the mud. They rolled him on to his side, and the Inspector checked his pulse.

'He's still alive!' he cried in joy. 'Do you think you can get him down to the ambulance?'

'Yes, I'll give him a fireman's lift,' Drew replied.

'I'll stay here in case any of the others appear,' the Inspector said. With a little struggle they managed to get him up right and on to Drew's shoulders, who carefully carried him down the path toward the ambulance. The Inspector returned to the car and continued the vigil. After a while Drew returned, this time with one of the folding beds from an ambulance.

'I thought this might make our lives a bit easier,' Drew told him.

'Good thinking Drew,' the Inspector replied with a nod. 'How are things down at the road?'

'Quiet, thankfully,' Drew replied, climbing back into the driver's seat. 'We don't seem to be attracting any attention from the town's people, probably a bit late for them to notice anything.'

'Good. And the men? In good spirits?'

'All fine, they have set themselves up in the back of one of the ambulances and were playing cards and drinking coffee. It looked like Andy was winning. They were surprised to see me appear with Atkins, they gave him the once over and he seems to be fine, but dehydrated. They asked if they should take him back to the hospital but I asked them to wait,' Drew asked, checking he had done the right thing.

'Good. The rest of the men should start appearing now we have the gateway reopened. We want them all taken to the hospital together if we can.'

As if on cue another disturbance came crashing through the trees from behind them and the shape of a man appeared in their mirror.

'Who's this?' the Inspector asked, peering through the dark trees. The figure lurched and limped over to the stones, and upon reaching them stopped, then fell through them. They raced over and discovered the Mayor, his pyjamas torn and ripped. His breathing was heavy and wheezing but he seemed alright otherwise. They lifted him on to the trolley and Drew raced him down to the ambulance. Drew returned with his trolley within ten minutes to find Charlie had appeared. They loaded his unconscious body on to the trolley.

'Perhaps we should get these three to the hospital now, we shouldn't keep them from medical help for too long. I have arranged for them to have their own ward so they should all be together at the hospital.'

'Right you are Inspector,' Drew replied and raced off. A few moments later the blue light of the first ambulance began spinning, and with a roar of its engine it sped off towards Nettlewood.

Drew returned to his seat and they continued to watch the invisible lights in the mirror, hypnotised by its beauty for a few minutes, before the sound of breaking branches through the trees once more announced the arrival of another of the missing men. The body leapt awkwardly through the stones and the two policemen raced to his side with the trolley being pushed awkwardly on the newly lain stone path. The body of Doctor Sparrow lay dirty and sweating in the mud, and without needing to discuss what was needed they lifted him on to the trolley and Drew raced him down to the ambulance.

'Now we just have to wait for Banks,' the Inspector informed Drew when he returned, and they settled back into their dark vigil. The night crept on, and as morning hesitantly broke over the trees the ebb of light slowly dissipated, and began to flurry like a rainbow of snow in the wind. From the trees suddenly emerged the stumbling body of Banks.

'Here he is at last!' Drew yelled. In the dim morning light they could just see that his clothes were torn and caked in mud, his face gaunt and ill. They watched Banks walk to the centre of the circle, the flow of light circling and enveloping him. He appeared to be resisting, where the other men had positively rushed for the stones Banks fought the urge, and the eerie mist seemed to be coaxing him into the light. Slowly, painfully, he was pushed, pulled and otherwise forced along, until finally he made it to the stones, and after a fight he was through.

Drew and the Inspector jumped out of the car and rushed over, but Banks had not appeared on the other side. They walked around the stones again and again, waiting, in case he suddenly reappeared. After a long wait it became obvious that he was not going to appear, and they returned to the car.

'Sorry, I don't understand,' Drew admitted. 'Where is he?'

'He could be anywhere,' the Inspector informed him, rather downheartedly. 'He might not reappear ever again, or perhaps he will appear somewhere around here, in the same way that the other bodies have appeared. Or perhaps he has already reappeared, at some point in the past, and his remains sit amongst those we found in his garage, or in the Manor house,' the Inspector replied.

'But, why did he not just pass through the stones, like the others?' Drew asked.

'My best guess, and I have nothing more than guess work to go on here I'm afraid, is that his mind and that of the energy that he hosted were too intermingled, too closely attached to be separated. When he passed through the stones the lifeform was unable to leave, so he had to take Banks through with him. What his fate will be, I am afraid we may never know.' The two men lapsed into thought, and watched the last few drifts of mist evaporate through the stones before the sun broke over the horizon, and they vanished.

'Well, I think the show is over,' the Inspector informed him remorsefully after a few minutes. He removed the mirrors and carefully placed them on the back seat.

'That was the most beautiful thing I have ever seen,' Drew admitted. 'Does this mean the bodies will stop appearing?' he asked.

'Actually not quite,' the Inspector advised. 'There is still a chance that more bodies will appear. Just because we've opened the gateway, doesn't mean there won't still be bodies caught in a historic wave that could still appear at some time in the future. There could be none, there could be, well, a hundred, who knows?' the Inspector admitted. 'Let's inform the men at the gate that they can go home, then we can all go and get some well-earned sleep,' the Inspector yawned. 'We can meet at the Vicarage tomorrow at three to inter the remains of our anonymous victims. Drew realised how exhausted he was and nodded obediently, starting the car and driving them out of the trees.

Sunday 9th November 1969

96.

The Inspector woke just before noon, keen to get moving following a long rest. He was quickly dressed and downstairs where The Green Man was host to a few regulars, and a few new faces examining maps. The excitement of the previous day still hung in the air, despite the reduction in patrons.

'Afternoon Inspector, I presumed you were out,' Mavis greeted him with her usual smile. 'Would you like your usual breakfast?' she asked, checking her watch.

'Yes please,' the Inspector replied simply. 'And tea,' he added. 'Don't forget the tea.' Mavis nodded.

'As if I could forget your tea!' she joked and carried herself off to start cooking. The Inspector turned to face the room and found his usual seat was taken, so took a seat nearby and patiently waited for his breakfast, gazing out of the window at the blue sky over Firestone. Shortly Mavis trotted out with a tray plate of steaming delicious food and tea.

'Ahh marvellous thank you,' the Inspector beamed.

'How are you feeling today then?' she asked.

'Like a new man, thank you,' he replied. 'I was wondering if you might order me a taxi Mavis?'

'Yes, I can give Dave a ring see if he's about, where are you off to?' she asked.

'I need to visit Nettlewood hospital but I don't want to disturb Drew, I've put him through rather a lot this last week and I thought he deserved a day off.'

'Of course, about half an hour do you think? Give you time to eat your food?'

'That would be ideal, thank you,' the Inspector told her, and tucked in. He was soon fed and watered, and returned to his room briefly for his hat, coat, and case. He then sat and waited for his taxi, which pulled up and gave a short beep from the pavement. He left the pub and embraced the new day. The fresh air breezed lazily over his face, beating off the unseasonal heat of the high sun. He took a moment to bask under it, allowing the sun to warm him slowly. He had become accustomed to the cold cloud throwing freezing water at him. It had seemed the sun would never shine in Firestone again. He climbed into the front and Dave welcomed him.

'Morning, you this Inspector everyone's been talking about then are you?' Dave asked with a smile.

'Guilty as charged. All good things I hope?' the Inspector checked.

'Well, you moved the Firestone, so you've made a few friends there,' Dave told him. 'Hospital is it?' he checked as he pulled away.

'Yes please,' the Inspector replied, and Dave took off. They arrived at the hospital quickly, the Sunday roads bereft of traffic. The hospital car park was a little fuller with the cars of friends and relatives visiting their loved ones. Inside the hospital the sound of squeaking shoes on the cold white tiles filled the air. The Inspector paid Dave's very reasonable fare then headed inside. He gave the reception bell a 'ping' and presently a Matron appeared, a little younger and less fierce looking than the lady they had been greeted by during the week.

'Hello, can I help you at all?' she asked.

'Ahh good afternoon,' the Inspector welcomed her, removing his hat. 'I'm here to visit the missing men who were brought in last night? I believe they were given their own ward?'

'Oh yes hello, you must be the Inspector, this way I will take you there myself.' She stalked off down the shining corridors and the Inspector followed, close on her heels. The men were situated on the first floor, in a quiet corridor. The hospital's occupants that they passed along the way were all relaxing in their beds. Those that weren't trying to entertain guests read under dim lamps or listened to the hospital wireless. The Matron delivered him to the door.

'Shall I get the nurse to bring in some tea?' she suggested.

'I am sure that would be most appreciated thank you,' the Inspector replied. On entering the private ward the Inspector found the Mayor to be asleep, but Doctor Sparrow, Atkins and Charlie had gathered around a bed and were playing cards for matchsticks on the stiff starchy sheets.

'Look gents, our saviour has arrived,' Charlie spoke up for them, and they all turned their heads to look.

'Good afternoon gentlemen, good to see you all looking so well after your ordeal,' the Inspector enthused as he entered. Even the snoring Mayor was looking well. The Inspector removed his notepad in readiness of taking notes. They all looked pleased to see him, and Doctor Sparrow pulled a chair over for him.

'Thank you.' The Inspector sat down. 'I was wondering if you wouldn't mind answering a few questions about what happened?' he asked them.

'Well, we can try,' Doctor Sparrow told him. 'But we've all been asking ourselves and each other the same questions I imagine you are about to ask,' he warned him friendlily.

'Well, let's begin with what you can remember,' the Inspector proposed. 'Charlie, let's start with you, talk me through what happened, starting when you woke up on the morning of your disappearance.' They turned to the landlord and he shrugged.

'I'm really sorry Inspector, but I really don't know what happened. I remember I had just got out of bed, must have been about eleven o' clock or so. I had eaten some toast and was thinking about getting the pub ready for opening, but then it all goes blank. Next thing I knew I was waking up here wondering where the bloody hell I was.'

'You have no memory of entering the copse? Or why you went in?' the Inspector asked, just as the tea arrived, carried by a busy looking nurse.

'Here you are gents,' she threw the tray down and disappeared again. 'Thank you sister,' the Inspector called after her, and took a swig. She nodded as she hurried out again.

'So Charlie, do you have any idea what took you into the woods?'

'No I don't,' he told him flatly. 'We've all been racking our brains trying to work out what happened. It's as though my memory has been wiped, or as if it wasn't remembering while I was out, if that makes sense?' he asked. 'Because it doesn't really make sense to me,' he added quickly. The Inspector nodded, jotting everything down in his book.

'I see. And Doctor, you are in the same position? No memory of what happened to you while you were in the copse?'

'No Inspector I'm afraid not,' he shook his head, the worry of the unknown creeping in.

'And Constable Atkins, how are you feeling today?' Atkins nodded.

'I feel fine, almost like a weight's been lifted, the best I've felt in years,' he shook his head. 'I can't explain it.'

'But no memory of what happened, what made you go into the trees, or of what happened while you were there?'

'No, sorry,' Atkins said, a little remorseful. 'Last thing I remember is walking my beat with Cara...' he trailed off suddenly. 'Oh my God Cara! What's happened to her?' he cried out in anguish.

'Relax, it's fine, I found Cara shortly after you disappeared, she is being cared for by one of your colleagues, I am sure she will be pleased to see you when you are discharged,' the Inspector reassured him. Atkins looked relieved.

'When will we be discharged?' Doctor Sparrow asked. 'We are all feeling fine, could we not be allowed home now?' he hoped.

'I would rather you were kept in for observation for a few days,' the Inspector explained. 'You may be experiencing shock or some other hidden side effects, I want to be sure you are all better. We will also need to run a few tests, take blood samples and the like, to try and see if we can work out what caused your... episode.' He studied the Mayor.

'And how has the Mayor been?' he asked them. 'The same I presume?

'Yes, he's been sleeping a lot, he's not generally in good health anyway by all accounts. I think the ordeal has had a greater effect on him,' Doctor Sparrow informed him professionally, 'but otherwise the same, no memory of what occurred.' The Inspector jotted a few more things down in his notebook, and then finished his tea.

'Well gentlemen the nurses here will be keeping a close eye on you. Let them know immediately if you have any illness or pain. Should anything come to mind regarding your experience please let me know immediately via Drew Gates at Firestone police station, he will relay the news to me.'

'Will we ever know what happened?' Atkins asked.

'Well, I think it was some kind of fit, or paralysis, which could have been brought on by a virus. You were all together at the Mayor's house so there is a good chance you picked it up there. As you may have heard Banks is still at large, but there is a good chance he was not as lucky as you, and perhaps succumbed to the elements whilst in the copse,' he told them.

'Oh,' said Charlie, downheartedly, 'poor old Banks.' They all looked rather gloomy for a moment, and the extra bed in their ward that no one had slept in seemed that much emptier.

'But we do still have hope that he might appear alive and well. We have people looking for him all over the county. We won't stop looking until we find him, believe me.' The men seemed to take some comfort from this. The Inspector felt it was best not to mention that if Banks was found he would be put on trial for the murder of Albert Gates.

'Well gentlemen, the day presses on and I'm afraid I must say goodbye. So glad to have got you home safely, and I hope your recuperation continues,' he told them kindly.

They all shook his hand and thanked him again, before the Inspector took his leave and headed back to the reception desk. He exited the hospital and found a lonely taxi waiting in the short rank outside. He climbed into the front passenger seat. The car had cold black leather seats, not unlike Drew's squad car. It stank of cigarette smoke, a haze hovered around it.

'Afternoon, where to?' the driver asked with his broad Northern lilt. He folded his paper up and stashed it on the backseat.

'The Old Farmhouse, on the other side of Firestone,' the Inspector informed him.

'Right you are.' The car blasted into life and he pulled out.

'Nice to have the sun out for a change isn't it?' the driver asked.

'Indeed it is.' The Inspector agreed with a satisfied smile.

97.

The Inspector arrived at Mrs Banks' house and gave a knock on the door. She answered it quickly, and did not look pleased to see the Inspector.

'Oh, it's you,' she said forlornly. It was as though she already knew what the Inspector was there to tell her. 'Here with more bad news I suppose. Well you had better come in.'

'Are you expecting someone?' he asked, noticing her displeasure at seeing him.

'Yes, my son is on his way here with the family for a few days,' she told him. 'It will be good to have some company.'

'I am glad to hear that. How is he handling his father's disappearance?' The Inspector asked. She walked to the kitchen and he followed behind.

'He seems alright, but you never know with kids do you? They never seem to want to talk to their parents, once they're all grown up.' She sniffed into a handkerchief.

'I suppose you're here to tell me there's still no sign of my husband, and that he probably won't be coming home,' she told him as she sat at the table.

'Almost right,' the Inspector replied kindly, sitting down opposite her. 'Last night I managed to relocate Doctor Sparrow, Constable Atkins, Charlie and the Mayor. From what I can tell they had independently gotten lost in the copse. Perhaps due to suffering from some illness that they had picked up while at the Mayor's. The search for an explanation goes on, they are all recovering from their ordeal in hospital.'

'But you didn't find my husband?' she asked, tears welling up in her eyes.

'No,' he told her flatly. 'I did see him, briefly, but he once again escaped my clutches.' She let out a little sob. 'I do apologise. I thought I should let you know the situation myself. I find his ability to elude me quite… frustrating,' he admitted.

'I am only sad because he keeps getting away,' she told him with a sniff. 'It's not that I particularly want the sod back again now.' She dabbed her eyes. 'I just want to see him back safe, whatever happens to him. No doubt he's got himself in all sorts of trouble,' she motioned at the Inspector.

'Well we will keep looking. And though it is true that there's now no sign of him, there is still hope,' he informed her. This had a small effect on her though she still looked downtrodden.

'I am actually here to give you some other news,' he told her. 'Which I hope is good news.' Her look perked up a little in interest.

'During my investigations I discovered that your husband and his ancestors have accumulated a large area of the land surrounding the town.' He took out his map from his case and placed it on the table to show her. She marvelled at the notes and scribbles that she could not fathom. The Inspector took his pen and indicated all the areas about the copse he had discovered to be the property of the missing Sergeant Banks.

'He owns all of this? Well, that's almost the whole copse!' she cried in shock. 'What's he done buying all that?' she asked him.

'Well, that is the question, as I say it has been in his family years. Centuries. There is a good chance that he was not even aware that he owned most of it,' the Inspector told her.

'Well, what am I supposed to do with it?' she asked, a little worried. 'I can't look after all that. I wouldn't know where to start, what would I do with it?'

'Indeed, well, I have been instructed to make you an offer,' the Inspector told her. 'Up to you completely but under the circumstances, what with the owner missing, and the land being overgrown and under-used, it has been suggested that the land be donated to The National Trust. They will then tend to it, it will be managed and accessible, and open to the public once more,' he advised.

'Well, I don't know, this is all rather a shock,' she told him, looking a little red in the face.

'Yes of course I understand.' He took out his note book and tore out a piece of paper for her. 'Here is the number of a lady that you can talk to, if you want, once you have had a think about it.' She accepted it and read the number over and over again.

'There is no pressure, the choice is yours,' he told her reassuringly. 'Speak to your son, I am sure he will help you make up your mind.

'Well, I will consider it,' she nodded. 'Would you like some tea?' she asked, out of habit.

'A kind offer, but I am afraid my visit today will need to remain short.' He stood to leave, and she showed him out.

'Thank you Inspector,' she said at the threshold. 'Thank you for exposing my husband. You've set me free in a way, you know. I thought when he went missing it would be a bad thing, but it isn't. Thank you.' She was still dabbing at tears, but the Inspector saw that she cried them in mourning of her old life, and in welcoming of a new one.

'My dear Mrs Banks, you are most welcome and I assure you, the pleasure was all mine.' He shook her hand and stepped outside into the sunny afternoon.

'I will be in touch when I find him,' he told her, tipping his hat and going on his way. He walked back to town, enjoying the sunshine and the warm air. The trees about him danced in the breeze, sun dappled and dashed between them. The red hue of the leaves littered on the ground made the copse shine warmly, and as he approached the town the Inspector felt his walk was over before he'd had a chance to fully enjoy it.

He headed down the hill, heading straight for the roundabout and the scene of the Firestone's removal. He was pleased to see it deserted, nobody paid any mind to the site anymore. All that remained of the previous day's activities was a small grassless dip where the Firestone had once stood. The hole had been refilled, grass would eventually grow over the dip, and the episode would pass into Firestone's arcane history. He stood by the remains of the scene and took his instrument from his case, stalking about as he had a few days earlier. The dial did not shift, the energy had dissipated. He noted the results in his little notebook, then took his camera from his bag and began taking pictures. When he was quite satisfied he walked along the road that headed to the parade of shops that the residents called their town. He almost immediately bumped into Bill, who was in the company of a middle-aged couple pushing a pram.

'Inspector!' Bill called excitedly.

'Ahh good afternoon Bill how are things?' They stood and shook hands, exchanging smiles.

'Fine Inspector, yes very good. This is my, err, what are you again my dear?' Bill asked the young lady that accompanied him.

'I'm your cousin's niece... though I'm not sure what that actually makes us,' she replied with a laugh.

'Well anyway, this is Gloria and Humphry. I wrote to my cousin, just like you suggested, but it turns out she died a while back. Gloria and Humphry here live in her house now, so they got the letter, and came up to see me.'

'Well that is good news,' the Inspector replied. 'Though I am sorry to hear about your aunt.' He turned politely to Gloria.

'Oh thank you Inspector,' Gloria replied, gratefully.

'And have you been to Bill's house?' the Inspector asked leadingly, if a little guardedly, looking to Bill to try and gauge how much his newly found relatives knew of the house hidden in the trees.

'Yes, well Humphry thinks we should try and open it up, don't you mate?' Bill turned to his newly discovered relative.

'Well, what with the discovery of the stones, I think there's going to be a great demand for accommodation in Firestone.' Humphry spoke enthusiastically and confidently. 'It will take some work but I think we owe to it the old place to get it fixed up, see if we can open it as a hotel.'

'Oh that would be wonderful, such a beautiful old place. So full of history,' the Inspector enthused, genuinely pleased to see Bill so happy and to hear of the plans.

'Yes, we might even make a few quid out of it if we're lucky!' he laughed. 'We're just going to The Green Man for lunch if you'd like to join us?' Humphry asked. 'I believe it's partly down to you that we are here, would be nice to thank you properly.'

'Oh well that is very kind, but I have a prior engagement I must attend to,' the Inspector thanked them with a smile. 'You may want to pay a visit to the Vicar next week, we discovered a relic of your family history in the graveyard.'

'My, really?' Bill enquired interested. 'There has been so much excitement in the town over the last few days I'm not sure if I'm coming or going,' he admitted.

'Well there's an old tomb there that was hidden in the copse, it's quite remarkable.'

'My goodness,' Bill cried, surprised. 'Well we'll get up there and see him,' he told him, intrigued.

'Well, I'll tell him to expect you,' the Inspector replied, pleased to have seen them. 'I'm afraid I must be off, enjoy your meals, the lamb is very good,' he suggested. They went their separate ways and the Inspector continued on through town. The streets busied as he approached the shops. News of the stones had spread, so the townspeople had come out to investigate them. Visitors from neighbouring towns had also descended upon Firestone, and a few of the shops had opened to make the most of the opportunity. The Inspector continued on up the road, nodding respectfully at Ivy Cole who was in deep conversation with a gaggle of her pensioner friends. Ivy nodded curtly back before they continued with their discussion. He walked in the sunshine through the busy streets, up the hill out of town past the Vicarage, and to the site of the stones. The two policemen were stood on the entrance as usual, and the crowd of people around them had grown significantly.

'Good afternoon gentlemen,' he said as he approached.

'Ahh good afternoon Inspector,' they replied and the men all exchanged respectful handshakes.

'All well here I hope?' the Inspector asked.

'Yes, good work on finding Atkins and the others last night,' the older Constable congratulated him. 'Good to have them all back sir, thank you.'

'Well, not quite all, Banks managed to evade us once again,' the Inspector told them.

'Well, he'll turn up eventually,' the Constable replied. The Inspector wondered just how prophetic his words would be.

'Well let's hope so. I'm just going up for a look around, is that alright?'

'Yes of course, up you go,' they stood to one side and he continued on his way up the path. As he walked he surreptitiously removed his device and began casually taking readings. The needle hovered over zero, steadfast and unmoving. He continued around the stones but the needle didn't move. Pleased with his result he replaced the machine in his bag. He made a few notes in his notebook, before mingling around the soldiers and the stones. He took pictures and studied the space between the monoliths that had been his and Drew's focus of attention a few hours earlier. He noticed a few of Samson's colleagues moving about between the trees and made his way over to them.

'Ahh Inspector!' Simon called to him as he approached.

'Good morning Doctor, how goes it?' the Inspector asked as they shook hands. The trees had lost their feeling of foreboding, the shapes in the shadows had disappeared.

'Very well yes, the more of the copse we cut back the more stones we find,' he replied merrily.

'Charles predicted you might find more, I wonder if he expected such an expansive site,' the Inspector pondered.

'Come in here and have a look,' Samson suggested, and the Inspector followed him into the trees to the object of his excitement. A huge stone lay on its side, surrounded by digging men.

'We think it's one of the monoliths, knocked over out of its position, but we don't know from whereabouts exactly, to find that out will require a lot more of digging,' he told the Inspector excitedly. 'We're going taking a leaf out of your book and try and restore it to its original position. We'll have to clear some of this back obviously to make it easier to get to.' He motioned to the trees. 'Any chance of borrowing your army men for a while longer?' Samson asked the Inspector hopefully.

'No, I'm afraid not,' he answered, simply but friendlily. 'This will be their last day at the site, so use them wisely.' Simon smiled off his disappointment as he wondered at how long it would take without the Inspector's help.

'When can you open up to the public?' the Inspector asked.

'We need to get the area certified as safe, I've got a man coming over in the morning to have a look. Usually takes ages to get someone out but he bloody jumped at the chance as you might imagine! As soon as we get the all clear we can let them up, but we won't be able to open it all at first,' he explained.

'No, of course, but the sooner the better I think, don't you?' the Inspector asked.

'Rather!' his excited friend agreed.

'I also have this for you.' The Inspector reached into his case and removed a folder. Doctor Samson opened it.

'Oh, my photographs.' He began studying them, fascinated. 'Thank you.'

'I have also added some of the pictures I took, to help record the moment.' A few carefully selected photographs had been added to the file and the Doctor admired them appreciatively.

'Well that is kind,' he enthused.

'No problem. Sterling work here, well done,' the Inspector congratulated him with a pat on the shoulder. 'After I've gone I want to be kept up to date with any and all new discoveries, whether they are stone or otherwise,' he advised him. 'And of course, with how the reconstruction plans go.'

'Of course, how do I get hold of you?' Samson asked him.

'Go to Firestone police station and inform Constable Gates, he'll be able to let me know,' the Inspector told him.

'Right you are Inspector,' Simon nodded. The Inspector took one last look about the trees. The space between them felt lighter now. It wasn't just because of the sun that shone through the branches, alighting on the fallen leaves and brushing the woods with a rusty hue of red and brown. The space was airier, the trees no longer felt close. The sun's warmth brought with it the scent of drying wood and warming foliage, which lilted ruefully across the air.

'Wonderful,' the Inspector sighed, turning back to Doctor Samson. 'Best of luck with it all.' He bid him good day and made his way back out of the trees to the stones, where he found the Major.

'Inspector,' he nodded respectfully in welcome.

'Good afternoon Major, how are you and the men?' he asked politely.

'All well thank you. A bit of sunshine always helps lift the spirits a little. We have most of the earth shifted now, a few more loads and I think we'll have it all cleared,' he told him efficiently.

'Marvellous. I must thank you and the men for all your hard work this week,' the Inspector informed him gratefully. 'Not the sort of thing you would usually find yourselves doing I imagine.'

'That is true but the men have enjoyed themselves, it's been good to use their skills for something rewarding.' The Major looked about him at the men, and at all they had achieved.

'Well as the mound is practically cleared, and that was what I asked you to help me with, we can safely call today your last day on the job,' the Inspector informed him.

'Understood,' the Major told him.

'Good to work with you Inspector.' He offered his hand and the Inspector shook it.

'And you Major. You run a tight ship.'

'Thank you sir,' the Major nodded appreciatively. The Inspector took in the impressive sight of the stones for the last time before leaving the Major and stomping back down the path to the road, then along to the Vicarage.

98.

Aldous paced around his cottage nervously. He was already dressed in his black shirt, black trousers, and white collar from the morning service. He checked his telephone every few minutes to ensure it was still working, in case anyone was trying to call and couldn't get through. He paced, he glanced out of windows, and generally found himself completely incapable or relaxing. For all the years he had lived quietly in Firestone the last week had been the most eventful he and the town had seen. He paced to the back door and looked out, still barely able to perceive the massive changes that had taken place. Thanks to his own efforts and the efforts of the army men the trees at the end of the graveyard were now fully cut back, revealing a space three times what had previously been accessible. The earth had been dug, the trees had been chopped, and gradually the space had been rescued from the copse. As per the Inspector's instructions the soldiers had dug a grave at the bottom of the graveyard where Aldous had instructed them, and it was this hole that caused Aldous to pace many miles from room to room in anticipation. He was waiting for the arrival of the man that had caused such upheaval in his life and in the village of Firestone Copse. He checked his watch for the hundredth time that day; half past two. Finally came the sound he had been anticipating; three short sharp knocks on his front door. He rushed to open it.

'Afternoon Aldous,' the Inspector greeted him with a tip of his hat and reached out a hand for him to shake.

'Good afternoon Inspector, so good to see you,' Aldous shook his hand warmly. 'I'll put my coat on and show you round the graveyard shall I?' he suggested eagerly.

'If you like yes, it would be good to see it.' The Inspector indulged the Vicar and allowed him to give him the full tour. Aldous led the way around the side of the Vicarage to the graveyard, where all the hard work was displayed in its full glory.

'My word,' the Inspector exclaimed. 'There's so much more of it than I had pictured.'

'Yes, it's rather impressive isn't it?' the Vicar replied without a hint of modesty and wearing a proud smile.

'Can we take a look at the tomb? the Inspector asked.

'Yes of course, it's certainly quite a feature isn't it?' Aldous hobbled over to it, and the Inspector politely followed.

'I spent most of this morning clearing moss off of it, and it's quite a sight now.' Piles of fallen moss lay about the dark walled building.

'Yes.' The Inspector approached the door and peered as best he could inside but the dark room was not giving away any secrets. He tried the stone door with a tough shoulder budge but it was immoveable. 'Shame,' he muttered then stalked around it.

'I saw Bill in town, told him about it, so he may be up to see you soon.'

'Oh really?' Haven't seen Bill for a while,' Aldous told him.

'Nice chap,' the Inspector told him. 'I am sure the two of you will get on famously. Could we look at the stone wall?' he asked, nodding towards the back of the graveyard.

'Yes of course,' the Vicar replied, and they made their way through the crooked stones over askew ground.

'I've been out here every moment I could, studying the gravestones, trying to clear the moss off them a bit.'

'I can see you have been working hard,' the Inspector replied, impressed. They reached the wall and the Inspector removed his instrument from his bag, but once again there was no reading. He looked about the trees, the space was more open, it was as though the trees were breathing a sigh of relief and retreating. Aldous eyed the contraption suspiciously but politely didn't ask about it.

'Good afternoon gentlemen,' came Drew's voice from behind them. They turned and saw Drew and Casey standing at the roadside public entrance to the graveyard. Both were dressed smartly in black. Drew wore his best suit, Casey had managed to find a modest black dress and a pair of high heels. Her arm was interlinked with his casually, as if it somehow belonged there.

'Ahh, good afternoon,' the Inspector called in reply, and Drew and Casey made their way through the graveyard to them, Casey made traversing the ground look easy in her heels.

'Aldous this is a colleague of mine Doctor Ward, the finest pathologist I have ever worked with,' the Inspector introduced them on their arrival.

'Oh I bet you say that to all the girls,' Casey replied with a smile. 'You can call me Casey, Father.'

'Nice to meet you Casey,' Aldous said, and they shook hands.

'And you Aldous,' she replied. The Inspector made a few notes in his book and turned to face them properly.

'What do you think then Drew?' he asked.

'Well it's certainly changed a bit since I was last here,' he admitted.

'What was it like the last time you were here?' Casey asked, intrigued.

'Well, a few days ago when I was last here the trees extended right down, almost to the path,' Drew told her, pointing toward the Vicarage.

'Yes, well the lads from the barracks have done a wonderful job,' Aldous replied. 'I'm starting to clear some of these old stones off, thought I'd try and restore the place a bit now the trees have gone.' He looked into the copse, the winter sun was breaking through the branches and illuminating the interior.

'I have to say, it's nice to have a change in the weather at last,' Aldous spoke for them all.

'Indeed it is,' Drew agreed.

'We should have Andy and Jim with us shortly,' the Inspector told them. 'They will be bringing the bodies along, then we can get started.' As he spoke they heard the familiar sound of the ambulance engine coming to a halt outside, and they made their way to the front of the Vicarage.

'Afternoon Inspector,' Andy called as he jumped down from the ambulance. He hurried up to them and they took turns to shake his hand. 'Shame we must always see each other in such circumstances.'

'Yes, such is our lot I suppose,' the Inspector replied. 'I presume our friends are in the ambulance?' the Inspector asked.

'Yes, they're in the back,' Andy told him, and they made their way round to the doors at the back of the ambulance. Jim threw them open and inside were a pile of cardboard boxes of various sizes.

'Would you mind helping us move them to the grave?' the Inspector asked Andy.

'Course not, we don't mind do we Jim?' Jim gave a quick shake of the head and they all picked up a few boxes each. When they reached the grave Drew climbed down, and they passed their boxes down to him. He put them down carefully and respectfully on to the wet slippery mud in a neat pile. When all the boxes had been successfully moved Jim and Andy helped Drew out of the grave again, they then bid them farewell, and made their way back to the ambulance. Casey, Drew, the Inspector and Aldous then stood over the hole looking solemnly down at the boxes. The sun still hung gloriously over their heads, giving warmth to the chilly air. The breeze swayed the trees in unison, the branches waved freely around them. The Vicar gave a cough.

'Though we have no connection to the individuals we are burying here today I have a feeling, like I do at any funeral, that I am in some way experiencing something.' He paused, trying to find the words to express what he was feeling. For once his words at a graveside were unrehearsed.

'We are witness to the passing of someone from this place to another, whether you believe that place to be the Christian idea of heaven, or the Valhalla of the Vikings, or whatever you might believe, there is still a passing. A change has occurred, and the world is different because of it. When these poor souls passed, they were mourned but they could not be put to rest. Their relatives can't be here to see this day to experience the passing, so we must witness it for them. The responsibility has passed to us, and so it is that we have all been brought here together today to complete their passing, and so we inter them once more to the soil.' He paused, thoughtful. Pensive. 'And so whatever we may believe, we hope and pray that these poor souls can find peace, as we return them to the soil from whence they came, and return ashes to ashes, dust to dust.' He picked up a handful of soil from the pile and threw it over the boxes, and the others all followed in turn, each throwing a handful of soil over those that had passed, so aiding their passing. After a few moment's contemplation the Inspector picked up one of the spades and began to fill the grave with dirt. Drew then took a spade and helped. Casey moved round to stand with the Vicar, linking her arm inside his. As the grave filled the sun slowly set, and by the time the mound of earth had gone and the hole had been filled the sky had faded to twilight, and the men were worn out from their efforts. They retired inside and the kettle was quickly boiled and they all enjoyed a hot tea that helped banish the cold. As they warmed up the Inspector noticed the time.

'Shall we relocate to The Green Man?' he suggested. I believe Her Majesty owes you all a hearty meal in reflection of the effort you have all put into this case.' They all agreed, and so took a slow walk down into the town and to The Green Man. They arrived to find main bar alive with townspeople excitedly contemplating the stones, all exchanging tales and wonder. The Inspector approached the bar, nodding to those that noticed him.

'I believe there's a table booked for my guests and I?' the Inspector asked Lionel.

'Of course.' He stood from his stool and began rubbing his hands together in glee.

'Go on through to the Lounge Bar, there's a table set up for you in there,' he told them. They made their way through and found Sergeant Frank Gates and Chief Constable Fairclough were sitting together at a large table.

'Ahh gentlemen, I am so glad you could make it.' The Inspector shook hands with them and took a seat.

'Thank you for the invite Inspector, and well done for finding our missing men.' Fairclough shook his hand determinedly, impressed. There were other parties in the Lounge bar enjoying a quiet drink and a few turned to watch the Inspector's party arrive. The Inspector nodded respectfully to them, conscious that he was disturbing their peace again. Mavis appeared and served them drinks and took more orders, and while they waited for their food they enjoyed a relaxed chat.

'What are your plans now then Inspector?' Aldous asked him when he could get a word in. 'How long will you be staying in Firestone?' The Inspector checked his watch.

'Approximately fourteen hours,' the Inspector replied humorously. A low chuckle echoed around the table. 'My train departs at seven thirty tomorrow morning.'

'Leaving so soon?' Aldous asked, failing to hide his disappointment when he realised he was serious. 'Does this mean the discovery of the man in the copse has been solved?' Drew had also been slightly taken aback by the announcement of the sudden exit but did well to hide it.

'Well the case has not been solved, however I have extinguished all leads that Firestone afforded,' the Inspector informed the captivated table. 'Tomorrow I will be moving onwards with the case, following up a lead on our missing Sergeant Banks,' he informed them. Drew raised an eyebrow in surprise.

'What are your plans Casey?' the Inspector asked. 'When are you heading back to London?

'Well, I thought it best I work from here and send my results back,' Casey told him, a little shyly. Drew shifted uncomfortably in his seat, and the Inspector deduced the situation with a wry smile.

'I see, a wise move. Good decision,' the Inspector informed her, and took it no further. Their meals soon arrived, and they all tucked in fitfully.

'I am sorry to be enjoying this lamb for the last time,' the Inspector informed them, as he tucked in heartedly. With their meals thoroughly devoured members of the party began to drift between the table and the bar as they relaxed. Drew left Casey chatting to the Inspector and made his way over to an empty seat next to his uncle.

'Evening Drew,' he looked up from the remains of his pipe and welcomed Drew over with a smile.

'Evening Frank, shame to see him go don't you think?' Drew asked.

'Yes, well, he's got a job to do you know,' Frank reminded him. Drew nodded.

'Casey looks like a bit of alright,' he nodded toward her. 'Well done mate.' Drew laughed.

'Yes, she's a surprise out of all of this. She's staying on, but she doesn't have to,' Drew informed Frank.

'I see,' Frank nodded. 'You think it's serious then?' he asked.

'It could be, but we'll see how it goes. She's still got her room at The Swan and Dove. It's not as if she's moving in just yet,' Drew smiled.

'No she's probably waiting for you to tidy up first!' Frank joked. He took a swig from his beer. 'Look there's something else I need to talk to you about,' Frank told him quietly. He glanced over to the Inspector and Casey to make sure he was distracted.

'The Inspector's been speaking to Fairclough, and there's talk of making you Sergeant over at Firestone.' Drew gawped.

'Really?' Drew cried. 'How do you know?'

'Fairclough told me. Asked me if I thought you were up for it.' Drew smiled.

'What did you say?' he asked knowingly. Frank shook his head.

'What do you think I said?' he laughed. 'Not that the Inspector needs telling,' he pointed out. A bell suddenly sounded out from the bar area.

'Last orders please,' Lionel yelled regrettably over the ruckus. It had been a lucrative Sunday evening.

'Keep it quiet though alright?' he asked. 'Look surprised when he tells you.' Drew shook his head with a laugh.

'Alright,' he agreed, wondering if he could lie to the Inspector. 'Do you want another one?' Frank asked, standing with his empty glass to make for the bar. Drew was watching Casey stretch her arms high with a charmingly small yawn. The Inspector was standing and saying goodnight to the Vicar.

'No I think we're going to head off,' Drew replied. 'I've got an early start in the morning.'

'Right you are,' Frank said, and headed to the bar before it got too crowded. The Inspector and Casey appeared and Drew stood.

'Can we head off Drew?' Casey asked. 'I'm knackered.'

'Yes, me too.' Drew put his coat on. 'Are you off to bed Inspector?'

'Yes, we've an early start tomorrow, first train to Swindon,' the Inspector reminded him.

'Swindon?' Drew thought for a moment. 'The lead on Banks?' he asked, a little confused.

'Yes, Mr Berrow's home town of all places,' the Inspector nodded.

'I'll come through to the bar with you and say goodbye to Frank and Stuart,' the Inspector told him to change the subject. Drew led the way, and at the bar they found Fairclough at the end of an anecdote of his policing career, charming a few locals with his storytelling. Frank listened to him retell a story he'd heard at least a dozen times while he waited for his pint.

'So I sneak in, and see the bed,' Fairclough was saying, whiskey in hand. 'And I know it's just sheets under the covers to make it look like a person, but I can't let on that I know, I have to get into bed, and cuddle up to it, and let the bugger escape!' they all laughed raucously, even Frank who still found it funny.

'They caught him in reception red handed!' This caused more merriment, and for a moment the bar was alive with laughter.

'Ah Inspector!' Fairclough welcomed him when he had his breath back. 'Can I get you a drink?'

'A kind offer, but I have an early start so I'll be turning in now,' he declined politely.

'Well I bid you good evening then.' Fairclough shook his hand warmly. 'Thank you again for returning the men, it was impressive to see someone from the Yard at work.'

'My pleasure, Chief Constable,' the Inspector replied modestly. 'It'll be goodbye to you as well then Sergeant.' The Inspector reached a hand out to Sergeant Frank Gates.

'Aye, goodbye Inspector.' Frank nodded and shook his hand, passing on an unspoken respect to the Inspector. The all said their goodnights and went their separate ways. The Inspector then returned to his room, quickly writing up the last of his reports before turning in for the night.

Monday 10th November 1969

99.

Drew arrived at The Green Man at six forty five promptly the next day to collect the Inspector. He had declined Casey's offer of cooking him breakfast, letting her have longer in bed. He found the Inspector sat alone in the bar area at his usual table, enjoying his breakfast. A second breakfast had been laid out for Drew, and so he took this opportunity to share one last meal with the Inspector.

'Morning Drew,' the Inspector welcomed him when he had finished his mouthful.

'Morning Inspector, what activities do you have planned for us today?' he asked smiling.

'Oh, I've an easy day for you today,' the Inspector smiled back. 'One last trip as my personal chauffeur and your life can return to some kind of normality.'

'Almost seems a shame,' Drew admitted. 'I think I'm actually going to miss working with you.'

'Well, the case is by no means closed,' the Inspector reminded him. 'We still have the case of the missing Banks, and I do not doubt for a second that more remains will be found in the trees. I am glad Casey decided to stay, it will be good to have her on hand as the archaeologists' exposure of the copse continues,' he explained. 'I have some other news.' the Inspector told him proudly.

'Oh yes, what's that?' Drew asked.

'Well, there is of course the matter of your promotion.' The Inspector took a swig of tea. Drew let a smile spread across his face.

'Actually I spoke to Frank last night, and he said he had been talking to the Chief Constable. He told me about the Sergeant's post at Firestone and seemed to think I was assured the position.'

'Did he? Good, I do so like it when people don't keep secrets. Makes our jobs easier, don't you think?' he was serious but smiling, as if he had predicted that was what would happen, as if he wanted the uncle to tell the nephew the good news.

'Well, he didn't quite get the whole story, so perhaps I should fill you in,' the Inspector suggested.

'You want me to come and work for you,' Drew guessed. The Inspector opened his mouth to speak, but stopped to smile at Drew's intuition.

'Good guess, and the answer is yes, and no. Her Majesty's Government, at my recommendation, are offering you a job.'

'The job of Sergeant in Firestone?' Drew guessed again.

'Well, yes and no,' the Inspector replied again.

'How so?' Drew asked.

'Well, I think you'll agree that over the last week we have revealed a lot about the sleepy little town of Firestone, and I feel we have really only scratched the surface. There is a lot more to discover. What we need is a watcher, someone we can trust to keep a look out for more bodies, more odd occurrences, and help us deal with them properly and quietly. We need someone to monitor the stones, to see if the gateway opens again, and see if anything, or anyone, comes through it,' he told him seriously. 'So initially, yes you will be Sergeant. Superficially, you will be Sergeant.' He took another swig of tea. The pub was empty and deadly quiet at this time of day, he thought to how busy it had been the night before. 'However, you are now working for the Department of External Affairs. Your first post is here, in Firestone, to monitor activity. You'll still need to apply for the Sergeant's post, and take the necessary exams, but you are already well qualified for the position. We are not cheating anyone by giving you the job.' He held up his cup in a toast. 'Welcome to the team.' They knocked their cups carefully together to toast Drew's new position and took the last swigs of their tea, their final breakfast together finished.

'What should I do?' Drew asked. The Inspector could not help but laugh. It was a good question.

'The right thing, Drew,' he smiled. 'Always do the right thing and you will be fine.' Drew guessed this would have to do for now, so decided to follow the advice carefully.

'Well, now you're part of the team, perhaps you'd do me one last service and deliver me back to the train station?' the Inspector asked.

'Of course,' Drew agreed, and pulled on his coat. The Inspector's cases were ready by the table, and the two men left the empty bar quietly, the bill already settled. Drew lifted the case heavily into his car boot, his hot breath puffing clouds into the air. The roads were deserted this early, and the trip went quicker than Drew wanted it to. The sun broke over the bleak grey moors as they drove, slowly banishing the dark of the night and bringing the land to life with a pallet of browns, greens, and yellows.

They arrived at the station with plenty of time, and the day slowly ground into motion as people arrived for their train. Drew carried the heavy case up to the platform, and they stood and waiting together with the other commuters in the cold bleak morning.

'Well Drew, it would appear this is goodbye.' The Inspector held out his hand and Drew gratefully shook it. There were no words he could give to convey how much the Inspector had changed his life over the last seven days, nor what a difference he had brought to the lives of the residents of Firestone Copse.

'Will I ever see you again?' he asked, trying not to sound too dramatic.

'That depends on how well you handle things here, Sergeant. I will read all your reports, contact will always be available if you feel you need it, though it may not be with me. You will receive more guidance as time goes on.' A whistle down the line announced the train's imminent arrival.

'For now, certainly, this is farewell.' They stood well back from the edge of the platform as the train steamed past them. The carriages clattered by, gradually shunting to an impressive halt. No doors opened, no one was stopping at Nettlewood that morning, but those awaiting its arrival began pulling wooden doors open and climbing on. The Inspector opened the nearest door to him and went to pick his case up.

'Help you with your luggage sir?' a passing guard offered.

'Oh, yes please my good man,' the Inspector agreed and the guard hauled the case on to the train. He followed him on, and then turned to Drew with an outstretched hand.

'Well Drew, goodbye.'

'Yes goodbye Inspector, safe trip.' They shook hands again, and then the Inspector made his way in to the carriage and found a seat. He made himself comfortable and in a few moments the whistle blew, and in a great puff of smoke the train began to chuff slowly away from the station.

Drew watched it chug down the line until it was completely out of view and he found himself alone, looking down an empty track. He cast one last look about him at the cold leaf strewn platforms before returning to his car, and driving home to Firestone Copse.

Printed in Great Britain
by Amazon